2324 Hours
Fish Hook 703

The sensor operator tore at his helmet, trying to discard his earphones. His video screen flared bright yellow.

Commander Tran could not see or hear anything. His connection to the world 2,600 feet below had just self-destructed, taking 135 men and a billion-dollar warship with it. He had been told that however they died—there were differing opinions as to what was likely to happen inside a ruptured pressure hull at that depth—it was mercifully fast.

Although the half-moon still hung low in the overcast night sky, Tran could see little out his window.

He called to Rocky Petrocelli: "To our next stop, James. And step on it."

"THE SIXTH BATTLE, as a novel, draws me into the high-tech world so completely that I wonder how I was a part of that world in earlier years. The author shows his knowledge of varied weapons inventories of today, and commands some breath-taking battles."

—Capt. Walter M. "Wally" Schirra
U.S. Navy, retired

Bantam Books by Barrett Tillman
Ask your bookseller for the books you have missed

ON YANKEE STATION: The Naval War Over Vietnam
   by Barrett Tillman and Cdr. John Nichols, USN
THE SIXTH BATTLE
WARRIORS

THE SIXTH BATTLE

A Novel of the Next War

Barrett Tillman

BANTAM BOOKS
NEW YORK · TORONTO · LONDON · SYDNEY · AUCKLAND

THE SIXTH BATTLE
A Bantam Book / March 1992

All rights reserved.
Copyright © 1992 by Barrett Tillman and John Tillman.
Cover art copyright © 1992 by Alan Ayers.
Insert art copyright © 1992 by Roger Loveless.
Maps designed by GDS / Jeffrey L. Ward.
No part of this book may be reproduced or transmitted in any form
or by any means, electronic or mechanical, including photocopying,
recording, or by any information storage and retrieval system,
without permission in writing from the publisher.
For information address: Bantam Books.

ISBN 0-553-29462-8

Published simultaneously in the United States and Canada

Bantam Books are published by Bantam Books, a division of
Bantam Doubleday Dell Publishing Group, Inc. Its trademark,
consisting of the words "Bantam Books" and the portrayal of a
rooster, is Registered in U.S. Patent and Trademark Office and in
other countries. Marca Registrada. Bantam Books, 666 Fifth Avenue,
New York, New York 10103.

PRINTED IN THE UNITED STATES OF AMERICA

OPM   0 9 8 7 6 5 4 3 2 1

Dedicated to Rush Limbaugh:
"The Most Dangerous Man in America."

Acknowledgments

Much of this book results from three years of living with the U.S. naval aviation community—occasionally afloat and too rarely aloft. But thanks are due USS *Ranger* (CV-61) and *Independence* (CV-62), plus exposure to Antisubmarine Squadron 41 at NAS North Island, California, and "Strike University" at NAS Fallon, Nevada. My tour as managing editor of *The Hook*, the quarterly journal of carrier aviation, put me in everyday contact with the people who make navy air work. From the guys in the Miramar parachute loft to battle group commanders, the education was comprehensive. Aside from the tactics and hardware, I learned something of what motivates men to leave their homes and families for half a year at a time, as well as how they think and express themselves. The dedicated folks in the operational forces are among the finest this country has to offer. May their military and civilian leaders ever be worthy of them.

A handful of technical items depicted herein are fabricated, the most notable being nuclear–armed antisubmarine torpedoes. Most of the ships mentioned on both sides are genuine, but USS *Langley* is a mythical *Forrestal*–class carrier, a throwback to the sensible days when the U.S. Navy named its premier warships for historic vessels and battles rather than politicians.

Times are given for Pretoria unless otherwise noted.

Contact was made with almost every naval aviation community in an attempt to ensure the highest degree of accuracy yet achieved in a "technothriller." In some cases the authors' questions drew responses like, "We could tell you, but then we'd have to kill you." Nevertheless, heartfelt

thanks goes to the following individuals and organizations—
our "committee of experts"—by whatever name they choose
to be known:

Bob, Bomar and everyone at "Irish Mist," The Real
Brillo, Captain Hook, Clint, "Grigori," Hey Joe, Jake, Jeff,
Pete, Pirate, Rat, Rick and Robbie.

There are two kinds of history offices in the aerospace
industry: Grumman's, and everybody else's. Lois Lavisolo at
Bethpage runs the former, providing the most esoteric information with typical ease.

Topographical and meterological data proved surprisingly difficult to find, but Sally Dewey of the Arlington
County (Virginia) Public Library became a one-stop shop-
ping center.

John Gresham provided computer support and Becky
McClure hosted the "First Techno-Nerd Convention," while
Robert F. Dorr provided some of his Korean fluency plus a
lift to Dulles.

Joining the struggle from beginning to end has been my
friend and editor, Greg Tobin. Together we rode out the
vagaries of geopolitics, revising the scenario in light of
changes in Europe and Africa.

My coauthor and I feel indebted to every learned writer
and speaker in the labyrinths of Washington, D.C., the Soviet
Union and South Africa whom we have ever read or heard.
We also acknowledge the standard references by Dr. Nor-
man Friedman and David Isby; Norman Polmar; Vladimir
Solovyov and Elena Klepikova; and "Viktor Suvorov."

Finally, an explanation about authorship. The publishing
business insists upon one name on the cover, but few books
in this genre are single-author volumes. Therefore, it is necessary to acknowledge my brother John Tillman's immense
contribution. While I was completing *Warriors,* working up
another proposal and holding a more-than-full-time job, he
prepared the proposal for this project. His world view and
technical knowledge greatly expanded the boundaries of this
novel. But I'm still keeping half the royalties.

BARRETT TILLMAN
ATHENA, OREGON
JUNE 1991

MORAL OF THE WORK

"Where are the carriers?"
- —Franklin D. Roosevelt, 7 December 1941
- —Harry S Truman, 25 June 1950
- —Dwight D. Eisenhower, 14 July 1958
- —John F. Kennedy, 22 October 1962
- —Lyndon B. Johnson, 2 August 1964
- —Richard M. Nixon, 6 October 1973
- —Gerald R. Ford, 12 May 1975
- —J.E. "Jimmy" Carter, 3 November 1979
- —Ronald W. Reagan, 14 April 1986
- —George H.W. Bush, 2 August 1990

"Where are *their* carriers?"
- —Franklin D. Roosevelt, 7 December 1941
- —George H.W. Bush, 19 June 1944

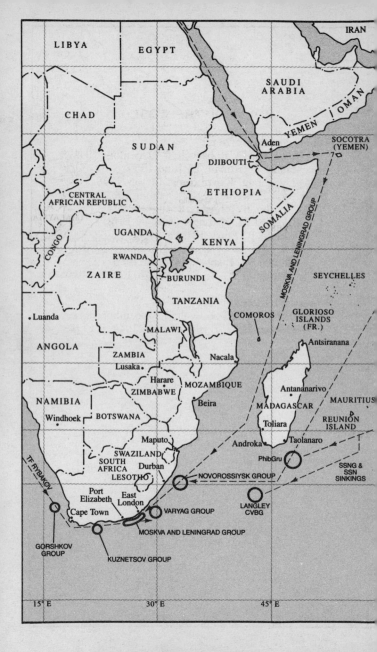

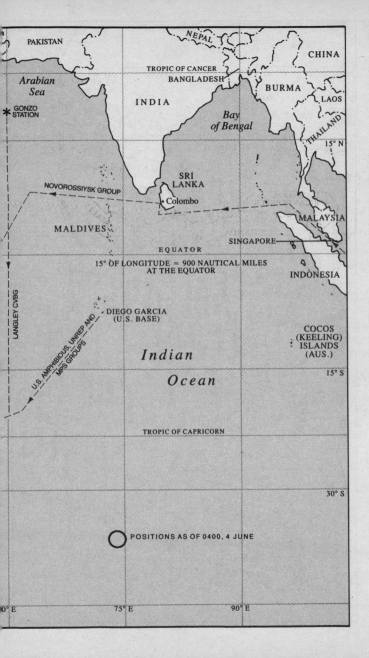

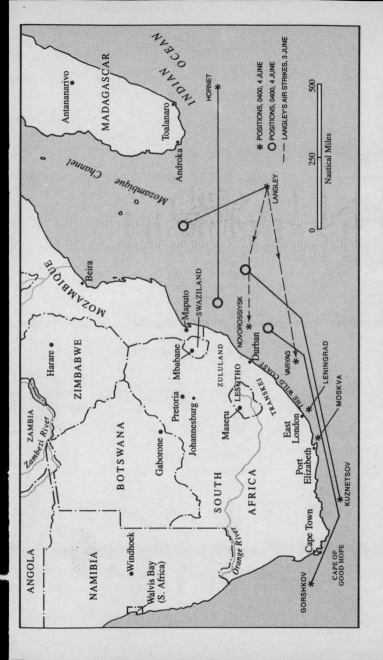

ANGOLA

NAMIBIA

Windhoek

Walvis Bay (S. Africa)

BOTSWANA

Gaborone

ZAMBIA

Zambezi River

ZIMBABWE

Harare

MOZAMBIQUE

Beira

Pretoria
Johannesburg

SOUTH

AFRICA

Orange River

Cape Town

CAPE OF GOOD HOPE

GORSHKOV ✳

KUZNETSOV ✳

Maseru

LESOTHO

Maputo

SWAZILAND

Mbabane

ZULULAND

TRANSKEI

East London

Port Elizabeth

THE WILD COAST

MOSKVA ✳

LENINGRAD

VARYAG ✳

Durban

NOVOROSSIYSK ✳

LANGLEY

HORNET ✳

MADAGASCAR

Antananarivo

Toalanaro

Androka

INDIAN OCEAN

Mozambique Channel

✳ POSITIONS, 0400, 4 JUNE

◯ POSITIONS, 0400, 4 JUNE

– – – LANGLEY'S AIR STRIKES, 3 JUNE

Nautical Miles

0   250   500

PART ONE

Grigori Meets the Ramp Monster

1

5 November to 29 December

1058, Thursday, 5 November
Cape Town, Republic of South Africa

Dirk Vorster gripped the transmitter more tightly. His gloved palms sweated, his heart beat faster, yet he remained calm. The Orange Free State Afrikaner was usually not a patient man, but when he had a job to do, the mission absorbed his concentration fully. Then he heard the first shot.

The guard was not killed instantly. He dropped his missile and tumbled off the roof of St. George's Cathedral, landing near the yellow and blue Casspir armored police carrier blocking access to Government Avenue. A second constable atop the library went down in a clump, still holding his Blowpipe surface-to-air missile. Two other guards ducked; the snipers fired again to warn the cops to keep their heads down. Police and soldiers in the Botanical Gardens frantically searched for targets but saw nothing.

Vorster heard the radio-controlled Cessna 172 approaching from the north. Loaded with 400 kilograms of mining explosives, it dived through dense but ineffective small-arms fire over the Anglican cathedral, toward the Houses of Parliament. Inside, security personnel hustled officials outside and onto the lower floors. The lightplane crashed into the roof. A shattering blast showered the street with flying glass, masonry and burning debris.

Across Wale and Adderley streets from Parliament, the police-uniformed snipers on the roof of the Good Hope Savings Bank and the Old Supreme Court Building started toward staircase doors. They left their scoped rifles next to the bodies of the guards they had shot with silenced pistols minutes earlier, and put their gloves on the victims' hands. The marksmen's own hands had been shaved clean to avoid leaving a traceable hair inside the glove.

Overhead, another Cessna followed the first. Facing little antiaircraft fire, it smashed through two floors before Vorster twisted the dial on his transmitter to command-detonate its charge. The walls of the unlovely nineteenth-century structure bulged from the blast wave, retracted again as if breathing, then fell apart. Dust obscured the streets, which were now filled with racing fire engines, rescue vehicles and ambulances.

But inside, African National Congress President Nelson Mandela, *Inkatha* Freedom Party leader Mangosuthu Buthelezi and State President F. W. de Klerk were dead, along with most other constitutional negotiators. Their dark and light pigments were spread paper-thin across the remaining walls of the collapsed building. For them, apartheid had finally ended.

Happy Guy Fawkes Day, Kaffir lovers, Vorster thought.

0400, Saturday, 28 November
Southern Maputo Province, Mozambique

Siphageni could smell the border. The wind had shifted in his favor, blowing from the southwest. The gentle but steady breeze carried the sickly-sweet odor of death. Its cloying stench overpowered the late spring scents—the chlorophyllous fragrance of new Highveld grass underlain by the mustiness of sedately decaying old growth.

He did not fully trust his partner, Hamilton "Not Out" Mangope. Though an experienced ANC operative, the former St. Peter's College cricket star was not a Transkei or township Xhosa like most *Umkhonto we Sizwe* fighters, but a Tswana from the western Transvaal. Worse yet in Joseph S. Siphageni's eyes, Mangope remained a politically incorrect bourgeois intellectual rather than a disciplined Party member.

Their crossing guide was an eleven-year-old Mozambican who tracked the movements of South African border patrols. Siphageni assumed the boy also logged changes in the routines of the Mozambican guards, who were conveniently absent from this stretch of the frontier tonight. He knew the lad would rather have been guiding starving countrymen seeking work in South Africa than saboteurs, but the ANC paid better.

They stopped at a rise and slumped against a solitary baobab tree that thrust defiantly up from the savanna. Mangope rested his pack against the tree, trying to relieve the pain in his shoulders. He knew twenty kilos of Semtex high explosive was too heavy a load, along with the rest of their equipment and supplies. But with an athletic reputation to uphold, he hadn't objected.

The moon was down, but the night was clear. Through his StarLite scope, bought with funds donated by Western celebrities, church groups and sympathetic ordinary citizens, Siphageni could make out the frontier barriers. Just as the boy had said, there were no South African patrols in evidence across the cleared zone and wire. Shielding his red-filtered flashlight with his free hand, the guerrilla switched it on and examined a map. They could not afford to get lost if they were to meet their contacts waiting across the border before first light. Nor could Siphageni allow himself to be captured alive; he knew every target of the planned, month-long terror offensive in Zululand.

A colonel in *Umkhonto we Sizwe*—"Spear of the Nation"—the military arm of the African National Congress, Siphageni also held the rank of major in the *Tsentral'noye Razvedivatel'noye Byuro* (TsRB), formerly the KGB. His father, who had been "shot while trying to escape" from police custody during the 1961 Pondoland uprising, would have been proud of both commissions. Though Siphageni had long ago dropped the middle initial "S.," Joseph had in fact been named for his father's hero, Stalin. Now the field-grade officer looked to the boy for advice; the lad nodded his head. Siphageni folded the map and signaled for Mangope to keep a safe interval in the rear. Silently they hefted their loads and moved out.

Captain Mangope didn't like his communist Xhosa superior, but respected his fieldcraft and was glad to let him carry the detonators. Mangope had never operated on this front before; his specialty was Botswana border crossings, but the apartheid regime had stepped up Commando and South African Police (SAP) patrols along most of its length. That frontier was closed tight, so he'd been transferred to Siphageni's command. High, light clouds drifted across the stars. Mangope stumbled downhill through the darkness. At the bottom of the rise, the boy held up his hand. Siphageni halted and crouched; Mangope bumped into him. Both men cursed in hushed voices. In Portuguese the boy said, "Mines. Follow close." Maputo provided the ANC with mine-field maps, which were seldom current. As they advanced, Mangope could feel more than see the change from dew-damp grass to cleared dirt.

The stench engulfed them now. The clouds drifted on and the stars returned. By their light and the first hint of a glow in the east, Mangope could see the remains of refugees from the former workers' and peasants' paradise. He remembered that, even after its Bulgarian agricultural advisers had produced mass famine and with Pretoria-backed guerrillas controlling its countryside, Mozambique's government billed itself as the most politically advanced in the world.

He knew all about the woes of this land, but still found himself unprepared for the sights at his feet. Jackals, vultures and other medium-sized scavengers would not set off the mines, so there were few complete skeletons in the bare, pockmarked earth. Even bones were rare, as the wild dogs carried them off. But the wire zone was littered with ghostly, sun-bleached mementos to human desperation. The recent remains were even more hideous than the collections of sinew and bone. The border guards saved money by letting their dogs feed on the fresher corpses.

Mangope prided himself on attacking only installations, not people. *For which Siphageni considers me a rank sentimentalist,* he realized.

The boy worked rapidly and quietly. He preferred wherever possible to crawl under the wire and lift it for the men. The less cutting, the better their chances of entering South Africa unnoticed. The North Natal Commando and Zululand Police looked for gaps. They were only too glad to cooperate with the ex-Marxist frontier troops. On the South African side, there were no mine fields or wired zones, just a cleared-and-plowed strip. They would emerge in the Ndumu Game Reserve. Mangope hoped there were no Great White Hunters about, stalking prey in the foothills of the Lebombo Mountains.

In a roll of rusty concertina at the base of the last high wall of wire, Mangope could just make out an assemblage that appeared to be the bones of a pregnant woman and her seven- or eight-month fetus. He did not stray from his guide's path to verify the ghastly Madonna scene. He thought of a Mozambican girl he had met in Soweto, who worked illegally in the house of a Portuguese businessman. She had made it through the deadly obstacles to the strange Promised Land and her baby had been born there. *At least if we win, we'll probably let immigrants be citizens and her kid will be eligible.* The thought provided him little comfort.

He watched Siphageni. *Does he understand?* Mangope wondered, recalling their argument earlier that night in Catuane over the relative merits of command and market economies. He felt the tragedy of failed ideology represented by the border was too great for him to say I told you so, unless the Xhosa pressed him again. Siphageni was too serious, too dangerous to cross lightly, simply for the sake of discussion. *Yes, he sees the gruesome border, but through the filter of his faith,* Mangope concluded.

Siphageni decided that, if Mangope made some reactionary, antisocialist comment, he would have to admit that not all of Mozambique's troubles were due to the colonial legacy or South African destabilization efforts. The Marxist government had made some mistakes as well. They had tried to rush straight from feudalism to communism, a most un-Marxist thing to do. To Siphageni, the lesson of recent world history was that socialists had not heeded Marx's emphasis on the need for a bourgeois stage prior to transition to the dictatorship of the proletariat, then to true communism. The ANC, under the guidance of its vanguard, the South African Communist Party (SACP), would not repeat the errors of national liberation movements in other Third World countries. Perhaps alone among African nations, South Africa had already experienced its capitalist phase and was now ripe, he believed, for socialism. And for the reckoning. The whites were no longer useful. They and their Zulu running dogs would feel his vengeance. He would repay their capitalist, colonialist exploitation, with interest.

Mangope, the fool, thought the whites would still be needed in the new South Africa, his Azania. They and the bloodsucking, monopoly-capitalist, neocolonialist, multinational corporations that sustained their parasitic existence. Those who thought like Mangope had better watch out, too. For now, it was an unpleasant necessity to make common cause with them. But, like bourgeois society itself, the expendables would have to be sluffed off when the time for proletarian revolution arrived.

They were through the wire half an hour before dawn.

1630, Monday, 14 December
Kwazulu Police Station, Ulundi, Zululand, Natal Province

Police Colonel Nigel Mkize needed to make up his mind. In the first place, he still hadn't gotten Julia anything for Christmas. Secondly, he had promised to answer his friend Celani's hard question this evening.

Last night the ANC terrorists had blown up more power stations—at least Mkize thought it was the ANC. *Too professional for the Pan-Africanist Congress,* he considered. To set a good example during the brownout, he had ordered both air conditioners in the station office shut down. Mkize was tired, hot, sweaty and not looking forward to fighting the crowds after work, but he told himself he couldn't complain. If not for Julia, he would have to buy gifts for all his numerous relatives himself.

It would have been cooler downstairs with Constable Ndhlovu and Sergeant Gumede, but Mkize didn't want either subordinate to see him spending government time poring over the kitchenware brochures collected by his sister and the crockery advertisements he'd clipped himself. Besides, Nandi Ndhlovu was distracting, even to a happily married man.

Despite her steadfastly unencouraging attitude, Nandi had minutes ago received flowers from some poor soul of a "secret admirer." The delivery mini-van was still outside, and over the intercom Mkize had ordered Derek Gumede to check it out. You just couldn't be too careful these days, and Nigel Mkize was nothing if not careful.

The sergeant had gone outside and inspected the van, but without an explosives-sniffing dog there wasn't much he could do to check a locked vehicle. He had yelled for the delivery boy to come back, but from down the street the teenager had held up another bouquet and pointed it around the corner. In Zulu, Derek had yelled for him to make it quick.

Even out of sight of her, Mkize's thoughts dwelt on Nandi. She may have drawn his station as her first assignment because the chief of personnel was Derek's uncle, but Mkize attributed the choice to Personnel's concern for the girl's virtue rather than his nephew's amusement. Mkize knew that Personnel considered him straitlaced and excessively devoted to his wife.

In fact, Mkize knew he could not have come nearly so far without Julia, and now Celani was trying very skillfully to shame him into risking his family's future. As a trained interrogator, Mkize appreciated the deft touch Celani had brought to his dangerous advocacy. The lawyer knew just which buttons to push. Mkize smiled and shook his head in admiration of Celani's artistry and in disgust at his own susceptibility, then decided to concentrate on gift selection. When he finally braved the mob of last-minute shoppers at the central market, Mkize intended the operation to be a quick in-and-out, with primary and alternate targets already selected. He took a last look at the handout on a damnably dear hammered copper mixing bowl he knew Julia wanted, then turned to drop the folder into the dustbin.

Mkize was dazed by an intense white flash at the half-open window. In the next instant, a ferocious blast of acrid, hot air knocked the breath from his lungs and blew him backward in his chair. On the way down, high-velocity window glass grazed the top of his head, the back of which hit the floor hard, splitting the skin. While he lay stunned, a vacuum followed the initial moving wall of compressed air across his body. Secondary shock waves reflecting off the ceiling, floor and walls rippled over his unconscious form.

As ceiling plaster powder settled, Mkize recovered. He felt a warm, sticky ooze on the top and back of his scalp. His head ached where it hit the floor. He managed to bring his right hand to the side of his face and found a trickle of blood from the ear; Mkize knew the drum was broken. *Not so bad,* he thought. If the bottom half of the window had been closed, shards would have punctured his upper body and might have cut the jugular.

The colonel slowly, painfully picked himself up and, finding he could move his limbs, awkwardly dusted off. His ears roared but his vision focused as he steadied himself against the heavy desk. The picture of Julia and the girls had blown off the desk and shattered. Blood from his scalp wounds had splattered across it. As the fluid in his inner ears stabilized, the roaring sensation stopped and Mkize started to regain his balance. He yelled hoarsely for Nandi and Derek, but got no answer. Carefully, still clinging to the desk, he knelt to lift the phone off the floor. He put the receiver to his left ear—no dial tone.

Mkize hobbled toward the window. With his back braced against the wall, he peered over his shoulder out into the street. He could see no civilian victims, but large pieces of the van had ricocheted off buildings on both sides of the street. Nearly every window had been broken by the blast or flying debris. Toward downtown, he noticed dust clouds and smoke rising. He couldn't worry about that now.

He realized he had heard not a peep from the downstairs office. Keeping one hand against the wall, Mkize tottered to the landing and weakly descended, a step at a time.

Nandi could not be seen or heard. Mkize called her name, but got not even a groan in response. Speaking induced a coughing spell. He spit up blood and felt lightheaded. *What have we here,* he thought, *a little lung hemorrhage, perhaps?* Then he dismissed the concern. *It's only to be expected from a blast that powerful.*

Against the far wall, opposite the double doors, Derek lay limply on one side, bent at the waist. Mkize hobbled past the counter, under which he hoped to find Nandi alive. Gumede showed few cuts or bruises, but he bled from the mouth, nose and ears.

The wobbly colonel knelt and held two fingers to Derek's neck. Nothing. Mkize had learned that human beings are highly resistant to blast; as he recalled, it took a peak overpressure of three to six atmospheres—up to ninety psi— to kill a man outright by air shock alone, while a frame house was flattened by one-third of an atmosphere, or merely five psi. Mkize had seen shock waves produce surprising, unpredictable effects. With the army in Angola, his "troopies" had overrun a Cuban position in which one man against the forward wall of a shelled trench was dead and his comrade at the rear was unconscious but alive, though neither was scratched. Mkize figured that Derek had not been killed by the blast, but from impact against the wall. Internal bleeding, he thought—probably brain hemorrhage. On standing up, Mkize felt faint. He leaned against the wall to recover.

Where is Nandi? He prayed she had been in the loo at the time of the explosion, but knew she would have answered him in that case.

He found her at her station behind the counter. She had been knocked out, but was breathing. A stool had broken her fall. She'd been standing, so her head had been at the level of the flying window glass. *Damn! I should have taped the windows this morning,* he reproached himself. Several projectiles had lacerated her upper body and some had penetrated, but it seemed no major blood vessels were severed, and no wound looked fatal. Perhaps the second, raised window had reduced the force of the shards. Her face was shredded, and her dark peasant skin had suffered second- and third-degree flash burns. "The only natural advantage of the white man in combat," he remembered telling his Bushman, coloured and black troopers who insisted on rolling up their sleeves, "is greater resistance to flash burn."

Mkize knew there wasn't much he could do for Nandi. *Thank God she's unconscious,* he thought. He squatted beside her and made sure she wasn't choking on her tongue. He was trained never to move the wounded until a medic arrived, but under fire from small arms, automatic grenade launchers, mortars or rockets he'd dragged or humped casualties through the bush more times than he cared to remember. Fearing Nandi's lungs were filling with blood, Mkize bent over and struggled to prop up the girl to keep her from drowning before help arrived.

1311, Tuesday, 15 December
National Command Center, Voortrekkerhoogte, Transvaal

General Christiaan Jacobus de Villiers had not been home for over two weeks. Since late November, when the Front Line States had begun massing troops at South Africa's frontiers, home had been a reinforced concrete bunker under Outlook Hill. The command center lay beneath the foothills of the Magaliesberg Range, five miles southwest of Pretoria and barely a mile from South African Defense Force headquarters in Voortrekkerhoogte—"Pioneer Heights" in Afrikaans. From this ridge in 1837 the Trek Boers fleeing British rule at the Cape first beheld the site of their future capital; a de Villiers had driven two span of oxen in that wagon train.

Directly above the general's bunker was the Old Military Cemetery, overlooking the suburb of Valhalla. *Not only are we already buried*, went the joke, *but halfway to heaven as well.* Right now, Christie de Villiers's idea of warrior's heaven was Clubview, the subdivision adjoining Zwartkop Country Club, just beyond Valhalla. Were he at the cemetery instead of under it, so to speak, he could easily see his new house on Mashie Street opposite the 18th hole, but he knew it might be a long while before he could even come up for air long enough to look at it.

It's just as well I'm here, the general thought. *The new place is lonely without Helena.* He was glad he had a lot of work to do. It had been nine months since the bone cancer had carried her away.

The noon briefing had ended; each session for a week had brought new reports of attempted clandestine crossings from every border command. On the Namibia, Botswana, Zimbabwe and Mozambique frontiers, infiltrators had been killed or captured. During the night, both naval commands had also detected close coastal approaches by submarines, presumably to insert agents or pick up those whose murderous tasks had been completed. But no subs were ever found, and he estimated that fewer than half the infiltrators were caught. They seemed endless and, regrettably, most had been born in the republic or its Bantustans, the nominally independent tribal homelands.

A staffer, Major Sluys, hung up the phone and approached the general. "I'm sorry, sir," Sluys said in Afrikaans, "but the state president wants an unscheduled meeting of the State Security Council. It seems the government has been pressed in the assembly over mobilization plans. He and the others have offered to come here."

"Considerate of him," the general grunted. Sometimes

he thought the man was too decent to lead a nation about to fight for its life. *Would have been good to have an excuse to disentomb myself,* de Villiers considered. *Still, better this way—avoids any possible security compromises.*

Sluys returned to the signals module to arrange the SSC meeting. Staff officers bustled quietly in the large, stale room. The ventilation system worked surprisingly well, but the air was inevitably stale. He took in the bare concrete walls, decorated only with maps and corkboard. Sluys reappeared and said in Afrikans, "It's all set, sir."

It gratified de Villiers to hear his mother tongue around Voortrekkerhoogte. During his first tour at headquarters thirty years ago, the standard language was still English. Most of the brass were of British descent in those days, too. Not anymore. Nine of the top twelve officers in the South African Defence Force (SADF) were now Boers, like him. Only his chief of staff and the navy and air force chiefs were Irish or British. Yet, unless you counted Angola, the Boers as a group had not won a war in 112 years. Plenty of Afrikaners had fought in the world wars and Korea, but most, including his own father, had been anti-British and sat out the 1939–45 conflict. Now the world was against them. He never let his doubts show. It was a cliche, but literally true that the prospect of defeat was too horrible to contemplate.

The general called for the mobilization schedule files, then inhaled the impure air deeply, exhaled and sat down heavily at his desk.

0016, Monday, 21 December
Ulundi, Zululand

Mkize didn't know where he was. It was dark in the unfamiliar room, but someone else was there, under a dim lamp. "Julia?" he asked hoarsely.

There was a slight pause before a response came, and the rustle of a magazine. "No, Colonel," spoke an alto voice in Zulu. "I'm a sister and you're in hospital. I will ring up your family and the commissioner."

"Ring them up? Why aren't they here?"

"I'll fetch the commissioner." She left, returning shortly with a doctor.

"Happy Christmas," the doctor said in English, looking

at his chart. He asked Mkize the usual questions to determine organic brain damage, but of course the patient didn't know what day it was. "It's Monday morning; you've been out for a week," the doctor said. He proceeded to check the colonel's vital signs, then silently indicated for the nurse to inject Valium into his IV solution. "Looks as if you've pulled through with flying colors, Colonel," the physician concluded.

"Where is my wife?" Mkize asked again.

"The commissioner is coming," the doctor replied.

"That's not what I asked." Mkize's growing anger gave him strength.

"Your family are here. Now, please just relax for the moment."

"Why can't I see them?"

The doctor was scribbling on a clipboard, aided by a penlight. "It's too soon. We have to discuss your condition with the commissioner first."

"In bloody hell, why?" Though groggy, Mkize tried to sound assertive.

"We want to make sure you're able to receive visitors."

"The commissioner knows nothing about medicine," Mkize protested.

"We promised to consult." Another nurse entered and whispered to the doctor. "Ah, here he is now." The doctor sounded very relieved. He stepped into the hall, from which voices could be heard murmuring.

The doctor escorted the commissioner of the KwaZulu Police into the dark room. Sounding like a politician standing for election, the top cop greeted him warmly. "Well, Mkize old boy, I'm glad to see it takes more than a hundred kilos of HE to do for you." The big, rotund commissioner—called "Josh" behind his back for his uncanny resemblance to Joshua Nkomo, the Zimbabwean Matabele leader—took the colonel's hand. "But then we knew that already, didn't we?" His tone changed. "You're the only station colonel left, you know."

"No, I didn't. How'd they miss you, sir?"

"Pure luck. They drove a Nissan pickup lorry loaded with a ton of C-4 into Government House. Killed just about everybody, but the lord mayor and I were with the chief in Durban. Very much a short-notice thing, thank God. Putting final touches on security planning meeting for the holidays, actually."

"Well, good on you all the same, sir. Before I passed out, Nandi, Derek . . ."

"Yes, quite. Ummm, Sergeant Gumede, unfortunately, is dead. But you'll be glad to know that Constable Ndhlovu will live. Bit botched about the face, but they do marvelous things these days, y'know. We suffered similar casualties at the other stations."

"They hit all of them, then?"

" 'Fraid so, Nigel. Yes. You really are the only colonel I have left."

The faces of his friends and rivals on the force rose before him singly and in groups. Then he asked, "When can I see my family?" There was urgency in the question. The commissioner looked at the doctor, whose affirmative nod was just visible in the dim light from the hall.

"I must tell you that Julia is dead, Nigel. Car bomb in the market. The girls are here. 'Dwina will live. Doctor says Celia is critical. Over a hundred people were killed there. Four other casualties are here in this room, heavily sedated." He stopped momentarily to gain control of his voice. "We took some to Durban, but they were hit, too. And 'Maritzburg, of course. ANC deny responsibility. I've resigned, effective tomorrow. The job is yours if you want it. I'll stay on until you're up and about."

Mkize was stunned as if by a second bomb. He couldn't breathe. The roaring returned with a rush, drowning out the commissioner's last sentences. He tried to speak; his body bucked, loosening IV and oxygen tubes. The doctor motioned for the commissioner to help; the men and nurses kept him from hurting himself. The doctor shot him full of quick-acting barbiturate. Nigel Mkize, widower, lost consciousness before he could scream his wife's name.

1003, Tuesday, 22 December
SADF National Command Center

State President van der Merwe convened the third emergency meeting of the State Security Council in a week. The new president was from the liberal wing of the National Party, but de Villiers liked him anyway. The general doubted, however, whether the personable politico would make an effective war leader. Van der Merwe had, after all, been chosen to continue de Klerk's policy of cooperation with the nonwhite majority. Though de Villiers had supported de Klerk in 1990, he believed that the time for conciliation and compromise had passed.

As at the two previous meetings, the most pressing issue was whether to call up the republic's reservists, and, if so, how many of the 500,000 to mobilize. But the chief of staff did not consider invasion imminent or anything but a very limited mobilization justified. Oddly, de Villiers thought, its civilian members were the hotheaded, scared rabbits on the SSC.

One civilian—Davie Steyn, the sharp young head of the National Intelligence Service—agreed with the general. But the presence of all those heavily armed blacks on the borders made some of the other civilians unduly nervous, perhaps because, as military novices, they were overly impressed by numbers. Even Defense Minister Wentzel, who should have known better, was urging mobilization. De Villiers figured Wentzel had bureaucratic reasons for wanting to call up Citizen Force reservists.

The foreign minister also sided with de Villiers and Steyn. "General mobilization will make us look bad, especially when the attack doesn't come," he objected.

"Better look bad than get surprised," the law-and-order minister huffed.

"The whole point of the exercise is probably to provoke us into overreacting," the foreign minister maintained.

"Yes," agreed Steyn, "that and to desensitize us for next time."

"What makes you think there will be a next time?" van der Merwe asked.

"Well, in the first place, because they're not really ready yet, for the reasons that General de Villiers has repeatedly stated. They have all these armored vehicles and planes, but they haven't had the time to develop effective command and control of the new equipment, or even to operate the hardware effectively. They probably never will. And, while the Front Line States' formations may have sharp teeth, they still lack the logistic tail to sustain a conventional attack. Too many tanks; not enough trucks. Not enough rail capacity, too few advanced airfields.

"Additionally, there really aren't enough of them. Even without mobilizing, we're only outnumbered about two to one—their 500,000 to our 255,000, counting Citizen Force reserves in camp for normal active-duty stints, Commandos and police. True, we have under a tenth as many tanks and aircraft as the FLS, but over half as many light-armored vehicles, and our interior lines, mobility and training multiply our force at least twofold. Even if you throw in some terrorist activity by the Azanian People's Liberation Army or *Umkhonto*, we're not in bad shape. Judicious call-ups of selected Citizen Force personnel, plus Commandos and police in border areas and to guard key installations, should suffice.

"Despite their recent conscription drives, Angola and Mozambique can't afford to commit more than half their ground forces to an invasion, given the possibility of renewed insurgencies at home. That cuts available expeditionary strength by 100,000 men.

"In the second place, now isn't the best time to invade; not this month, not this year. The summer storms in Natal and the Lowveld will make unpaved roads impassable. That's most of them and they're bad enough in the dry season. General de Villiers will bear me out on this.

"Autumn is more likely, after the roads dry out in the east but before winter storms hit the Cape—March, April, May. Since Russian doctrine is to attack on Friday night or, if possible, shortly before a major holiday, around Easter is the most probable time. Possibly Independence Day, but that's cutting it close to the onset of bad weather. Also, if the past is any guide, the invasion will come just when peace talks have been renewed or seem to be making rapid progress.

"Thirdly, I don't think the Front Line States would have gone to all this trouble and expense just to intimidate us back to the bargaining table with the ANC. This must be a prelude to something else. I think the Russians are behind it. They've already gained a lot from their arms shipments and stand to gain more. That's why I said this time was just to desensitize us. Our agents in the FLS capitals and the ANC don't exactly know what's up—perhaps no more than contingency plans—but something is definitely in the works. There may have been no final decision, but whoever's calling the shots wants the option of direct military intervention in our affairs.

"Right now, the buildup serves a useful purpose, but it's just a bluff, a blackmail tool and a provocation."

The law-and-order minister, justice minister and police commissioner remained unconvinced. "Better safe than sorry," is all the law-and-order minister said after listening to Steyn's reasoning.

"Consider the economic consequences of mobilization," the NIS head pleaded. "We're on shaky enough ground right now, with the global recession lingering, commodity prices down and the renewed sanctions. What will taking 500,000 people out of the civilian economy do? Not to mention the direct costs of moving all those people around, caring for them and exercising them."

"That's not really your worry, is it, Davie?" van der Merwe asked in his best kindly-uncle tone. "That's a cross we politicians have to bear. Jack, care to comment on that?"

J. W. Burton, the Anglo-South African minister of industries—an ex-officio member of the SSC—answered, "Actually, with the holiday season upon us, no one is doing much work, is one? A call-up would definitely hurt retail trade. Have to hire blacks to run the shops, wouldn't we? Not such a bad show, that. Call-up would put a scare into people. Probably help some businesses—jewelry, that sort of thing. People are already buying negotiable things legal to take out of the country, aren't they?"

De Villiers was tired of all the aimless discussion. "Gentlemen," he broke in, "two days ago the general staff presented a schedule for limited mobilization of essential personnel. I believe such a program would position us well to meet any change in FLS readiness without greatly interfering in the normal life of the nation. I believe that restricted mobilization is the proper response to current and immediately foreseeable threats. Such restraint would show self-confidence and send a stronger message to potential adversaries than full mobilization, which I consider ostentatious overreaction. My staff concur in this view.

"We firmly believe that the forces on our frontiers can mount no major hostile action against us without tipping their hand three days in advance. This is plenty of time for us to respond. Full mobilization from a cold start would take a week, but our plan provides us all the head start we need. It envisions holding actions at the borders by active units for four days, enabling reserve formations to be brought up to strength.

"Finally, we should send a clear message to all hostile capitals in our region by increasing the air defenses and ground security around the National Nuclear Research Center reactors at Pelindaba, the Valindaba uranium enrichment plant and the Koeberg nuclear power station. We should also test-fire both battlefield missiles—short-range Sjambok and medium-range Majuba—on azimuths toward the capitals closest to our borders. We should use the intermediate-range Crux to launch a surveillance satellite, whether we need another one right now or not. The Israelis can't afford not to sell us extras.

"If we show strength, we may yet be able to spend Christmas with our families." For de Villiers, this was wishful thinking. His son Piet, a fighter-bomber pilot, was on alert at Hoedspruit Air Force Base near the Mozambique border and his daughter Elize was married to a liberal journalist whom the general could not tolerate.

Though in overall agreement with de Villiers, the foreign minister asked, "How can we rattle our nuclear sabers when the enemy has his own missiles, loaded with tons of poison gas, and, for all we know, germs? The Israelis don't have enough Patriot and Arrow antimissile missiles to defend their own cities."

"Oh, that's easy," de Villiers replied. "We know where all their mobile missile batteries within range of us are. All of them, all the time. Don't we, Davie? It takes an hour to prepare them for launch. My own boy is ready to take off at fifteen minutes' notice to destroy them. The defense against weapons of mass destruction is preemption." He wanted to add, *Anybody knows that.*

"I hope to hell you do know where they all are, gentlemen," the president said. "The nation is relying on you as never before." Were a British-South African not present, he would have said *die Volk*—the Afrikaner people—rather than "the nation." Van der Merwe concentrated silently for a moment. "If there is no further discussion, I propose that we begin relying on our professional defenders by accepting the program of the general staff."

The vote was unanimous. "Thank you, gentlemen," the president concluded. "The danger to our nation has never been greater. I am proud to see that we have met it without flinching."

1154, Wednesday, 23 December
Ulundi

Mkize's visitor brought no flowers, but under his arm he carried a long, flat present, professionally gift-wrapped. "Happy Christmas, Colonel. How are *we* this sunny day?" the obnoxiously chipper intruder asked in English.

"Do you really care, Celani?" Mkize coughed in Zulu. Celani, looking around the room to see who else was there, seemed not to hear the response. Finding the room empty, he locked the door, turned a fan on full, moved lamps and tables away from Mkize's bed toward the fan, closed the windows and pulled the curtains. Then the short, barrel-chested, fortyish man pulled a chair close to the bed, sat down and leaned forward. "Of course I do," he answered at last, whispering in Mkize's left ear. "You are more important to the movement now than ever." He leaned back and laughed, showing gold-capped teeth. "But it is most indiscreet of you to say my name out loud."

"Why not? The nurses have by some coincidence taken all my roommates out for air this morning, or to lunch."

"Remarkable luck, isn't it? Still, the room could be bugged. It hasn't been swept. Well, enough idle chitchat. Let me get straight to the point."

"You, barrister? Never. These are truly disordered times."

Again drawing near, Celani said under his breath, "Be that as it may, my brother, I've come for the answer to my question of last week. Nothing that has happened changes the need for a prompt answer, except that a week has been lost due to the attempt on your life. I should have thought that the events of Monday last would have helped you make up your mind. We can't wait any longer."

"You know that the commissioner has offered me his job."

"The old fool fears for his life, that's all. Better to keep him in a highly visible position like that. He's expendable.

Men like you, real leaders with military experience, you're precious."

"Flattery won't work on me, Celani. It repulses me, so shut up."

"Not flattery. Precise truth."

Mkize knew he was right. "Well, I think the commissioner is right to offer to resign. He must bear some responsibility for the success of the attacks. I can't believe we caught only a half dozen of the terrorists."

"Look here, you know perfectly well that this is no longer a job for the police," Celani said, *sotto voce.* "We're going to be invaded. I can understand why you didn't want to get involved in the fighting in the Valley of One Thousand Hills or the townships. Ugly, brutal, but necessary. But this is different. This is foreign invasion, not just Xhosas with *pangas* and necklaces, but communist mercenary armies coming with attack jets, ballistic missiles and tanks to steal our land and enslave our women and children. You can't turn us down."

Mkize wondered why Celani didn't mention Julia. His wife was dead and his daughters were in relative safety with relations in Durban, their needs met by the Zulu tribal political movement, *Inkatha.* So Mkize had only his own safety to worry about now. That mattered less than the safety of his nation, Zululand.

And what of my state, South Africa? he asked himself. *Do I owe it any loyalty, the regime that wouldn't let me, a college-educated, volunteer staff sergeant with three years' combat experience, battlefield decorations and a spotless record, be an officer in command of white draftees—raw farmboys or soft cityboys? No, my family first; second, my people, and my state a distant third. When Pretoria respects me, I shall consider respecting her, fighting for her. Not before.*

Celani had grown tired of waiting for Mkize to respond. "You helped the white professionals train, equip and organize 121 Battalion," his friend went on, referring to KwaZulu's legal "regional unit," as Pretoria called the defense forces of its semi-independent, black homelands to distinguish them from the infantry battalions of the nominally independent Bantustans. "And before that, 21 Battalion," Celani continued, reminding Mkize of his status as one of the original sixteen volunteers for the first black unit in the regular South African Army, raised in 1974. "How can you back away from leading 121 and our irregular *impis*?" The lawyer used the Zulu word for regiment.

"Assuming I resigned from the police and went to work for you full-time, what good would it do? A hundred irregulars have to take turns using a single war-weary AK in so-called 'marksmanship' training. The rifles are so worn out they don't shoot straight and are downright dangerous. We have virtually no machine guns, let alone mortars, artillery, antitank or antiaircraft weapons. Worse yet, fewer than a third of the irregulars have received even a week's worth of real military training."

"Don't be such a defeatist," Celani said, feeling he was going to win. He hadn't known how best to get at Mkize, but was now glad he hadn't appealed to lust for revenge. "Aren't you the one who said that what matters most in war is the will to do what it takes to win? Most of our boys have that. They had it to begin with, and you've helped their confidence against conventional forces, as well as against *panga*-wielding Xhosa murderers."

"Yes, but desire substitutes for arms and training only so far."

"Well, we're working on the equipment problem. While you've been chasing purse-snatchers and lying here taking it easy, I've been hard at work. We now have 10,000 automatic rifles—mostly AKs, but some South African R-types—plus 1,000 light, medium and heavy machine guns, a few hundred mortars and antitank weapons, even some 107mm multiple rocket launchers. We haul in more every week. By the end of the month, we'll be able to equip 20,000 men with military firearms or launchers, plus 30,000 more with useful civilian firearms—pistols, shotguns, hunting rifles, .303 Enfields and the like."

Mkize remained skeptical. "That still leaves over 50,000 men with nothing but edged weapons—*pangas, assegais*—or clubs and fists, unless you have some bows and arrows. And what about the women auxiliaries? You've nothing at all for them, except maybe kitchen knives, scythes or hoes."

"Nothing except the will to fight and risk death. As I've heard you say, where there's a will, there's a way to steal or capture the enemy's weapons. As the men get more firearms, we can arm the women better. Besides, *pangas* are quite lethal," Celani concluded, referring to heavy machetes used to chop sugarcane.

"When I said all those high-flown things, I didn't expect we'd have to fight mechanized brigades anytime soon."

"Then you'll do it?"

"Celani, the doctor tells me my lungs are pulp. The capillaries burst like sprung pipes and the alveoli popped like balloons. He says I need at least a month's bed rest to recover."

"Would I ask you to do anything that might endanger your health?"

"You already have, repeatedly. And my family's security."

"Oh, don't be such a hypochondriac. You've already had over a week to recuperate. You're a fast healer and you have big lungs. Lots of excess capacity. I know; I've heard you, the human public-address system. Just don't climb any mountains for the first couple of weeks." His jovial tone grew more serious. "That may be all the time we have left to get ready, and you have to get better. I don't think they'll invade this year, but it's possible."

Then Celani reverted to his cheery mode. "You haven't opened your present yet. Go ahead."

Mkize tore the wrapping off the package slowly, yet still made a mess of the paper. He studied the long, narrow box, then lifted the lid.

It was a finely made *assegai*, a short stabbing spear. Mkize paused a moment before picking up this beautiful example of his people's traditional weapon, worth a small fortune. The steel blade was burnished to a mirror finish. The handle was ebony, hard as only African wood can be. "I thought of you when I saw it," Celani explained, immensely pleased with himself, "and had to have it. The antique dealer said it drew British blood at Isandlwana. They all say that, of course, but I took it to the university, and a chemist, an anthropologist and two historians all said the blade was new but the shaft was authentic and old enough, so I guess it's possible. It was probably an *induna*'s; pity the family had to part with it at some point. Ha! 'Point,' get it?"

"You might get it, with this," Mkize said, stabbing at his friend and smiling at last. "Thank you," he forced himself to say, replacing the spear in its box and the box under his pillow. Both men knew that, in the traditional culture, Mkize's acceptance of such a wonderful gift required a comparable or greater sacrifice in return.

"Well, I have things to do, people to see. Can't spend all my time cheering up the sickly. Deal?" He stuck out his hand. Mkize looked at the hand as if at a strange fungal florescence protruding from a tree, then grasped it in slow motion. He stared hard at Celani, who was startled by the ferocity of the look. "Good," the *Inkatha* operative managed. "No time to lose. Meet me in Government House, ten A.M. Monday." He shook Mkize's arm decisively. "Right, then, I'll be off. Already told you too much for a man on medication." He let go, but Mkize gripped even harder.

"I choose my own staff and *impi* commanders." He squeezed tighter.

"Done. Wouldn't have it any other way," Celani said, the pain telling in his voice. "Unless high command wants them someplace else."

"I'll give you the names on Monday," the soon to be ex-police colonel said, relaxing his hold a little. "I'm going to do this my way."

"We want you for your experience and initiative, you know," Celani answered warily. "But we also need a unified defense. If you aren't prepared to carry out the high command's orders, then better stay a copper. If I don't misunderstand you."

"No, I don't think you do," Mkize said, releasing Celani.

"Capital! Now I must run along." He rose, replaced the chair and turned to leave. "Oh, one other thing. I'm authorized to say you'll be commissioned major general in the KwaZulu Defense Force. We're giving you a division, just as I promised. This appointment carries the added bonus of making you officially an enemy of the state, like the rest of us criminals. By the way, my code name is Dloko."

"*Mamba*," Mkize snorted. "In honor of your third leg, no doubt."

"Naturally. I'm willing it to the Durban snake museum. Largest specimen known to science. I got to choose my own *nom de guerre*, but we'll assign you one." Holding the doorknob, Celani said, "See you Monday morning in Government House. Or what's left of it."

1206, Thursday, 24 December
SADF Command Center

Major Sluys projected another reconnaissance photo. "This one was shot by a Mirage at 0814 hours south of Gabarone, near Ramotsa," the briefer said. "It clearly shows a Botswanan infantry battalion pulling out of the forward defenses they've occupied for nearly a month. One battalion in three has been left behind. We assume that units now will take turns manning forward positions in rotation. The other six recce planes have recorded similar activity all along our borders." He displayed shots of Mozambicans entraining for Beira and riding in trucks toward Maputo, the country's major coastal cities. Zimbabwean and Namibian troops were also pulling back, in some cases hundreds of kilometers. More significantly, the Angolan, Zambian and Tanzanian units that had joined the forces of countries bordering South Africa appeared to be returning home.

"It is important to note, however," Sluys concluded, "that these troop movements involve mainly personnel, no heavy equipment. The only vehicles being withdrawn are lorries. The men are leaving, but the tanks and other armored vehicles are staying behind, for the most part in hardened shelters." He clicked on pictures of shelters taken in each of the four large countries with which South Africa shares a border. "Furthermore, construction continues on improved frontier fortifications, road and rail links to the border and military-style airfields in the interior of each country. As usual, the airfields are said to be for tourist use, but are capable of operating fully-loaded medium bombers. Concrete is still being poured for hardened depots within twenty kilometers of the frontier. This very morning Russian roll-on/roll-off cargo ships unloaded a hundred armored vehicles plus supplies at Benguela, Angola, and Beira, Mozambique. As you know, the World Bank has financed major upgrades to the container-handling facilities at these two magnificent harbors, which fell into disrepair in the first fifteen years after independence."

De Villiers was relieved, not so much that the massed forces were being withdrawn as that he had been proven correct. They'd be back, he believed, probably better prepared and in greater strength.

The Union of Eurasian Republics, as the USSR was now calling itself, had offered to mediate the crisis in the second week of December. The Russian foreign minister—actually an Azeri—had made a great show of shuttling between Pretoria and the capitals of Front Line States, where he met with local leaders and ANC central committee members. De Villiers believed this diplomatic road show was a sham, but it had "worked." The FLS troops had pulled back; Pretoria had agreed to lift martial law at home, and the UER got the credit for bringing peace to the troubled region. State President van der Merwe had played along. Constitutional negotiations would resume in the first week of January. A joyous Christmas and New Year's would be celebrated in churches and homes throughout southern Africa and the world.

But de Villiers was sure the rejoicing would not outlast the southern summer. His nation was as alone as he himself would be this Christmas.

1233, Monday, 28 December
Northern Zululand

The driver of the Toyota Land Cruiser did not speak during the circuitous 200-kilometer trip from Ulundi to the headquarters of the KwaZulu Defense Force Northern Command. It seemed Celani never stopped chattering the whole way. "Talk about indiscreet," Mkize had finally said in an effort to shut up the KZDF chief of staff.

"Oh, you can trust Dumisani," Celani replied. "He's my nephew."

"Yes, but can I trust you?" Mkize said. The silent Dumisani smiled. Celani was unusually quiet for the last twenty minutes of their journey on the N2, the national route along the coast.

Northern Command HQ was a widely dispersed collection of abandoned sugar shacks a few kilometers from the Hluhluwe railroad station. Cane fields protected approaches on three sides; the swamps to the east ran clear to the renowned St. Lucia Lake Game Reserve, access to which was forbidden without special permission.

Celani had explained that the regional commander, Lieutenant General Madide, was inspecting troops on the upper Black Umfolozi River, the southern and western boundary of his command, largest of Zululand's three defense zones. Therefore, Celani would show Mkize around HQ.

Celani truly had not lied about being busy. New telephone lines were stretched across the marshes and fields; well-sited, unobtrusive defenses had been built. In the communications center, Mkize found modern South African radios, capable of frequency agility and burst transmission. "Where'd you get these?" Mkize asked.

"Friends in high places," Celani said, and shrugged.

In the fields surrounding the camouflaged hovels were arms caches, each with company-scale equipment—a hundred automatic rifles, some bolt-action scoped sniper rifles, a dozen light and medium machine guns, several antitank rocket launchers, a few recoilless rifles, three 60mm mortars, a pair of automatic grenade launchers, boxes of hand grenades and crates of ammunition. It was an almost unimaginable treasure trove. Celani enjoyed watching the new general's delight.

"Where'd you get all *this*?" Mkize gasped after catching his breath.

"Money talks." With a self-satisfied air, Celani added, "There's more where this came from. We have several stashes like this at each HQ and one-third as many at each divisional depot. They'll be dispersed more if . . . ah, *when* we mobilize."

Mkize picked up a rifle at random. It was old but in good condition, without obvious rust or pitting in the barrel. "I'm impressed," he said, not even trying to hide his pleasure. He felt like a kid who had found everything on his list under the Christmas tree. "You have done well, my brother." He tossed the Kalashnikov at his stocky friend. Next he reached for a PK, the superb Russian general-purpose machine gun. It was the original version with a fluted barrel, but still in excellent shape. Most of the other equipment Mkize examined was also well-maintained, although he wouldn't want to fire the Russian AGS-17 automatic grenade launchers himself. Celani dragged him away from his new toys. "I have work to do back in Ulundi tonight," he reminded his subordinate. "I can't play tour guide all day."

They went to the map room—or rather, map shed. Celani left his nephew outside with the guard, then showed

Mkize the area of responsibility of his new command—the northernmost division guarding the borders with Mozambique and Swaziland. The maps, stamped "Most Secret" in English, showed the current dispositions of Zulu forces and their depots. If an attack came, the main invasion routes would pass through Mkize's territory. He was thoroughly familiar with the lay of the land there.

"This is all fine," Mkize said at last, "but when do I meet my troops?"

"Next stop on the tour," Celani said. "The men are up north, such of them as there are. Most of your staff are nearby, but not here. They don't need to know about this place." After collecting Dumisani they drove back to the railroad station by a different route. Then they continued west on a secondary road, crossed the N2 and entered the Hluhluwe Game Reserve. In a battered, long-wheelbase Land Rover and a Ford pickup near the visitors' information center, Mkize found his division staff. They were the men he had requested; again Celani had come through.

First out of the Rover was Conco, his chief of staff. They embraced. Mlongo received the same greeting. Then came Dhlomo; they wrestled until Mkize started wheezing and gasping for air. His friends hadn't realized how ill their leader was. Mtetwa waited for Mkize to recover, then got out of the pickup and shook hands, clasping his boss's forearm. Mtetwa was a prince of one of the main Zulu clans; among his other leadership qualifications was snob appeal. These last three were his *impi* commanders. His intelligence, operations and logistics staffers piled out of the back of the pickup. The other man in the Toyota was unfamiliar; Celani introduced him as Mxenge, a reliable *Inkatha* operative who would serve as Mkize's political officer.

Mkize looked askance at the stranger, but shook hands formally. "I hope your job isn't making speeches," Mkize said. "We don't have time for that."

Mxenge started to respond, but Celani interrupted, saying, "No, it's more a liaison role, to keep GHQ apprised of your activities."

"A spy?" Mkize inquired incredulously.

"No, not your activities personally, but the division operations, in case we can provide assistance."

Mkize studied the man as an entomologist might examine a new, potentially dangerous insect species. He could not bring himself to say welcome aboard, so he said nothing. Instead, he punched Conco. "We really had to scrape the bottom of the barrel to assemble this lot, you know," he said, "but we'll make do." In fact, he and they were all aware that there could not be a stronger staff among the whole Zulu Army's ten divisions.

Celani bid the crew farewell; his nephew peeled out, showering the distinguished men with gravel and the mud of their homeland.

The staff of the Ninth Light Infantry Division—the Zulu Army had no other kind—promptly held its first meeting under a large acacia tree. They knew the country of northern Zululand was ideal defensive territory—swampy or marshy on the coastal lowland; the inland plateau cut by deep ravines and covered with virtually impassable brush; the east mountainous, heavily forested by South African standards and bisected by precipitous gorges. Invaders were limited to a few obvious corridors, but the largely roadless terrain also presented defenders with difficulties in moving men and materiel to meet enemy thrusts.

They ate lunch and planned for the defense of their homeland against the most powerful foe it had yet faced—or at least the most heavily armed. Zulus had been defeated by superior firepower before, notably by the Boers in 1838 and the British in 1879. Now they were outgunned again, but not hopelessly so. Conco had a plan to raid Mozambican depots, but his colleagues doubted *Inkatha* GHQ would approve it. Even if successful, it might force Pretoria to clamp down on Zulu military activity.

Impressive as the arms caches were, Mkize's division, 10,000 men at full strength, was still badly underequipped. Essentially, his units were issued materiel on a scale appropriate for one level lower—that is, his 500-plus-strong battalions were armed at company level and his *impis* at battalion level. The *impis*, with 2,500 to 3,000 men if the troops all showed up when called, were equivalent to large regiments or small brigades. Yet they had less equipment than a Mozambican infantry regiment, let alone the mechanized and armored brigades they might face. The Zulu formations were especially deficient in fire support, antitank and anti-aircraft weapons—they had no artillery heavier than man-portable mortars, and no missiles at all. Mkize's division had far less firepower than a Russian-style motor rifle regiment, let alone a brigade or division.

Still, the amount of good military hardware Mkize's men did have was more than he could have dared hope for even two weeks previously. And they could buy, steal and capture more, both before and after the onset of hostilities. The problem was how to make effective use of the equipment, given that his men had little or no training. GHQ provided each division a platoon from 121 Battalion. Training paramilitary forces was not in violation of South African law; up to a point it was encouraged. So these thirty-odd soldiers would become the battalion commanders and *impi* staff personnel, specialists in combat support roles like communications, combat engineering, reconnaissance, defense against chemical and biological weapons and instructors in more complicated weapons like mortars. In the coming months, the men would receive only practical training in small-unit tactics and weapons use and maintenance. No parades, poetry, sports, music, singing or dancing for now. If God smiled on the Zulus and South Africa, those activities would have their season. But the arts of war must precede the arts of peace.

0524, Tuesday, 29 December
St. Lucia, Natal

The stench of the fish hold reminded Siphageni of the border. He tried every trick he knew to resist retching, but the rank odor of dead fish, the bucking of the ancient trawler in the surf, the diesel fumes of its struggling engine and the unspeakably foul vapors emanating from its sloshing bilges conspired to defeat Dramamine and his willpower. He worked his way out from under the tackle that hid him, lifted the tarp covering the fishing gear and added his own effluent to the bilge scuppers. Siphageni wiped his mouth, then crept back under cover.

Realistically, there was little to fear. Even with all the bombings, the odds of their being stopped by a South African Navy coastal patrol craft were slim. He figured the poor, exploited draftees were probably all too hung over from celebrating the holidays and peace for the boats to put to sea. In the unlikely event the trawler was boarded, what lackadaisical swabbie or crisp-uniformed ensign would notice vomit on the fish-hold grating, or become suspicious if he did? Anyway, a crewman would be in eventually to clean it off. No, Siphageni's being sick hadn't given away his hiding place, but he prided himself on his self-discipline, strong stomach and stable inner ear. Once, lecturing at the Soviet terrorism school on the Caspian Sea, he had advised new recruits to learn how to combat nausea, both from motion sickness and vile smells. Most means of insertion into hostile territory involve one or both, plus claustrophobia or acrophobia. Siphageni especially hated submarines.

No sub this time, he reflected. *But twelve hours in this stinking hold, probably with fish on top of me. Then, once in Mozambican waters, transfer to a patrol boat for the trip into Maputo. Just a nice, relaxing sea voyage.* He hoped for calm weather, and that Mangope's suffering on the egress route through Swaziland was as great as his own. *Next time I will come not with a bourgeois and a boy, but with hundreds of men, and stay for good, not skulk back into exile after a month.*

Joseph Siphageni curled himself into a less painful position. The promise of the future eased the discomfort of the present.

2

29 April to 12 May

2130 Local, Thursday, 29 April
Russian Aircraft Carrier Varyag, *Black Sea*

Lieutenant of Aviation Grigori Dmitrichev recognized the physiological signs: the heaviness in the arms, the increased pulse rate, the raspy dryness in the throat. As he rolled out on final approach for his third attempt to land aboard the new ship, he was almost glad *Varyag* was experimenting with no-radio procedures this dark night. The moon was obscured by windswept clouds much of the time, compounding the difficulty of getting aboard. Though Dmitrichev had fumbled his previous two tries, at least the landing signal officer wasn't screaming insults into the pilot's earphones.

Beneath his oxygen mask the twenty-five-year-old aviator coached himself down the invisible glideslope. On his first try he had done reasonably well, planting his Sukhoi 25 attack plane squarely on the angled deck, but his tailhook had skipped over the last arresting wire. He had botched the second pass, lining up too high and failing to note that the illuminated lens with its reflected datum lights alongside the deck was invisible under his nose until too late. This time he resolved to get aboard, regardless of what it took. Dmitrichev realized his very survival was at stake, but so was something equally important—his pride.

The Sukhoi pilot consciously relaxed his grip on the control stick. He flexed his fingers briefly, squirmed in his seat and flicked his head to ward off the tiny sweat beads threatening his vision. Watching the interval of the aircraft ahead of him, he extended his downwind leg slightly and noted that the running lights of another plane indicated a smooth left turn onto base leg at 270 meters altitude. Dmitrichev wasn't sure, but he thought it probably was Senior Lieutenant Antonov, the unbearably competent Muscovite who seemed the best carrier pilot in the entire air wing. Dmitrichev reflected that Antonov's scheduled time overhead the ship was forty minutes before, and that would be enough time for this to be the third and last required night landing. "He's three for three," Dmitrichev thought bitterly, "while I'm still trying for number one."

Judging himself far enough astern to begin his own approach, Dmitrichev eased into a standard-rate turn, neutralized the controls and waited until he was perpendicular to the ship's wake, visible on the dark sea. Then he turned port again, aligned with the carrier's heading for final approach. He inhaled deeply, held his breath, then slowly released it. He felt better. With nearly a hundred arrested landings, he was a reasonably experienced carrier pilot. But those evolutions had been in daylight, usually under radio guidance of the landing signal officer with cross-cues from the ship's electronic suite showing centerline and glideslope. Operating without such aids in daytime was somewhat more difficult, but doing it on a windy night in medium-high seas during the dead of winter was like learning to fly all over again. The lieutenant concentrated on his approach, watching his airspeed and altitude indicators.

Driving up the churning wake, Dmitrichev was satisfied with his lineup. The vertical row of lights on the stern—what the Americans called "drop lights"—matched the centerline. But he did not catch the almost imperceptible loss of altitude so far from the carrier's stern. At a mile and a half he glimpsed the tiny mote of light he knew to be the landing-aid lens, but it was yet too far for useful reference. Out there he had twenty-five meters leeway up or down for eyeing the "meatball." But he did not recognize that the mirror's position in his windscreen was too high.

In his six previous night carrier landings Dmitrichev had

had the benefit of radio instructions and navigation aids. Getting low at the start of his descent had been noted early enough by the LSO to correct in most instances, but not tonight. Operating under combat conditions, without any kind of electronic emitters, called for a degree of skill and judgment an order of magnitude higher. Now those complications were piling up. By the time he was close enough to see the lens clearly—under one and a quarter miles—Dmitrichev recognized that the orange ball was a diameter below the horizontal datum lights. He knew his mistake immediately—he had instinctively nursed back on the stick, attempting to gain height without a simultaneous increase in power.

With his heart racing again, Dmitrichev pushed his two throttles. The Tumansky R-13 turbojets responded and the Sukhoi climbed to intersect the glideslope. He saw the ball rising to meet the datums, then pass slightly above them. Chopping the throttles, he leveled off to kill the ascent while trying to stabilize his attitude. *No good,* he thought. Close to the ramp, too high, he lowered his nose and viciously shoved the throttles to full power just as the LSO activated the blinking red lights ordering a waveoff. Grigori Dmitrichev cursed to himself as he turned port. He would have to try again.

"This time," he said. "This time I plant this bitch on the deck or else."

2133

On *Varyag*'s landing signal platform Captain-Lieutenant Anatoli Altukin turned to his assistant. "He's only getting worse with each attempt," the senior LSO shouted above the wind and jet noise. "We should send him back to base before he kills himself."

The junior lieutenant checked his watch. "Dmitrichev has enough fuel for two more passes with a safe reserve. Perhaps we should let him try again before sending him home." Another Su-25 and two Su-27 fighters already had been ordered to land at their home base this night for similar inability to get aboard. It was not only a disgrace, it cast serious doubt upon the professional future of each flier.

Altukin glanced astern into the blackness, noting the landing lights of the next aircraft. It looked well lined up.

"We'll give Dmitrichev one more try at the deck. If he doesn't make it, send him back to Sevastopol."

2138

Turning final for the fourth time, Grigori Dmitrichev had a death grip on the stick and throttles. He was conscious of the onset of a serious headache and he yearned for a drink of water. But he managed to shrug off his body's unwelcome warning signs and to concentrate on the task at hand. He was aware that he no longer shared the pattern with other planes; the rest of the pilots had either safely made their third landings or had been sent to base in ignominious silence.

Dmitrichev recalled his error from the previous pass and closely monitored airspeed and altitude in his illuminated head-up display. Gear, flaps and hook still down, he drove parallel up the wake, nose-high and steady in the attitude optimized for smacking onto the angled deck and engaging his hook on one of the four arresting wires. At one and one-quarter miles the ball was reasonably centered and the tired aviator relaxed. He almost had it made. All he needed was to maintain his attitude and rate of descent and he would snag the second or third cable.

Half a mile from the ramp Dmitrichev riveted his gaze on the ball. He desperately wanted the two more landings that would qualify him in this frightful endeavor without having to refuel aboard ship. That would only prolong the agony. Staring at the ball, he gained the eerie sensation that the deck was hurtling backward at him. He capitulated to the powerful tendency to look at the deck instead of the lens. Then he realized his error.

"Damn!" The cursed ball was well above the datums, slipping from its previous well-behaved position in the few seconds he allowed his attention to wander. In that moment Grigori Dmitrichev learned a valuable lesson: no landing is completed until the airplane is stopped and tied down.

In close and high, above the two-meter-high limits of the lens, the frightened pilot pushed forward on his control stick, pulled off a fistful of power and forced his unwilling aircraft toward the deck. On the LSO platform Captain-Lieutenant Altukin recognized the panic reaction and thumbed the button that activated the waveoff lights while

shouting "Waveoff!" into his radio handset. He choked down
the urge to jump off the platform even as his assistant was
scrambling for the port safety net.

The Su-25 momentarily reached a level flight attitude as
Dmitrichev abruptly neutralized his controls and crammed
on more power. But the laws of gravity and Newtonian mechanics screamed their outrage at the pilot's transgression
and refused to accommodate the inertia of 25,000 pounds of
aircraft and fuel. The blinking waveoff lights and the unnatural attitude of the flight deck as seen through the windscreen
were Grigori Dmitrichev's last conscious impressions of the
outside world. Inside, the initial rush of adrenaline had
barely peaked when his universe strobed from black to brilliant orange to sudden nothingness.

2139

From the flag bridge, looking aft, Admiral Pyotr F.
Rybakov sensed the impending explosion and pressed forward against the thick glass for a better look. He had seen
ramp strikes-before, but seldom at night. His flag lieutenant
was far less experienced and reflexively raised an arm to
cover his face as the aircraft's midsection struck the rearmost
portion of the flight deck, left wing low.

There was a dull *ka-whoom* as the Sukhoi's airframe was
wrenched apart, spewing jet fuel onto hot engine exhausts,
which immediately ignited into a brilliant fireball. Flames
and debris spewed everywhere, enveloping the LSO platform while flinging shards of metal and aircraft parts far up
the deck. Seconds later the crash siren blared into life, accompanied by the crackling roar of flames.

Rybakov was tempted to lend some advice to Captain
First Rank Yuri Gulaev, but thought better of it. *Varyag's*
skipper was an experienced naval officer, and his well-drilled
crash crew was fighting the fire less than one minute after
Dmitrichev died. The flames were smothered under a deluge
of foam, and though flight operations necessarily ceased that
night, they could have been resumed in a couple of hours.
However, two new landing signal officers would have been
required; Captain-Lieutenant Altukin was incinerated at his
console and his assistant suffered serious burns despite the
protection of the catwalk.

0003 Local, Friday, 30 April

Rybakov presided over the midnight postmortem. Senior officers of the ship and air wing met in the wardroom to watch Grigori Dmitrichev's ultimate disgrace on videotape, repeated in stop-frame and slow motion. The admiral ordered the machine shut off. Turning to face the roomful of grim-faced officers, he chose his words carefully. "Gentlemen, this incident contains no new lessons." Previously he would have said "comrades" when addressing other professionals. But under the new constitution of the Union of Eurasian Republics, many of the old ways had changed. *And many have not,* Rybakov thought bitterly. "We have seen this sequence too many times before. This pilot should have been ordered back to base after three previous attempts to land aboard. Why was he not?" The gunmetal blue-gray eyes rested on the air wing commander, Colonel of Aviation Nikolai Glinka.

Glinka fidgeted in his chair, then caught himself. *Never show fear to Rybakov,* he thought. *It's a sure way to trouble.* "Admiral, the choice was that of the senior landing signal officer. It is standard procedure."

"Yes, of course you are right." A tight-lipped smile told Glinka the admiral was playing with him. "The question is, should we revise our standard procedures? Should the wing commander or the carrier captain make such decisions?"

Glinka glanced around, unintentionally locking eyes with Captain First Rank Gulaev. Nobody offered an opinion.

"No, I think we'll not change things yet," Rybakov stated. "The landing signal officers are intimately involved in these operations. As we've seen tonight, they can pay the price for misjudgment as much as a pilot." If that sounded hard-hearted, so be it. This command had a lot of maturing to do in a very short time.

Glinka sat up straight in his chair, and Rybakov sensed the man wanted to speak. He nodded at the wing commander.

"Sir, I think we need to speak frankly. At risk of . . . drawing criticism on myself, I wonder if we are not proceeding too rapidly." He paused to test Rybakov's reaction. The response was imperceptible. "We sent three other pilots back to base tonight because they did no better than Dmitrichev.

All our pilots are new at this business of night carrier operations with minimal landing aids. Perhaps the answer lies in more practice before attempting such difficult maneuvers."

Rybakov said, "Under other circumstances I might agree with you, Nikolai Alexeyvitch. But take it on good faith that I would not stress these operations without good reason." He glanced around the room. "And I have good reason, gentlemen."

A shuffling, uncomfortable tension ruffled through the room. Apparently *Varyag* and her escorts were being groomed for a higher purpose than mere proficiency. But every man present knew better than to ask details.

Glinka spoke again. "Admiral, we know that the Americans regularly fly from their carriers at night. But they have decades of institutional experience. The French take a more cautious approach to night flying. Can we meet our operational responsibilities with a level somewhere between the U.S. and French navies? That might expedite our training."

"As I said, there is ample reason for the schedule I have laid out." Rybakov regretted the clipped tone of voice; his response sounded more like a condemnation than an answer. "Glinka, your squadrons have come along well. You've done a good job getting them whipped into shape in these few weeks. But if we're going to match the Americans or the French in carrier aviation we have to be every bit as good as they are, in all phases.

"Now, I know that nothing on this earth is more difficult than landing a jet aircraft on a carrier at night. Nothing. No sane man enjoys it. But we're going to do it regardless of what it takes. And if that means blood on the flight deck, then we'll just have to make that sacrifice. There's a reason for it." Rybakov paused to gather his thoughts.

"You all know the May Day celebration is approaching." That was one constant that the demise of the old Soviet regime had not changed. "I propose to give as many men as possible part of the weekend off—from a half to a full day. Because, my friends, it will be the last rest period for a long time."

The admiral turned to a world map behind him. "We will give the men a day to sober up. Then, on Tuesday, the fourth of May, we sail to join the Pacific Fleet." There were mutters of surprise in the wardroom and Rybakov held up a hand. "I know, it's earlier than expected. But en route we will conduct antisubmarine exercises with the Fifth *Eskadra* in concert with *Leningrad* and *Moskva*." He indicated the Mediterranean, haunt of the two older helicopter carriers. Tracing a curve along the North African littoral, he continued, "Then we will join the *Kuznetsov* group in the mid-Atlantic for aviation exercises. It will be a great moment for all of us—the first time two Russian conventional aircraft carriers have steamed together." Every man in the room knew that was the goal toward which Pyotr Rybakov had devoted his adult life. Only four other nations had ever developed indigenous, conventional carriers—Britain, America, Japan and France. Now only America and France remained.

"Next we round the Cape of Good Hope to join the *Novorossiysk* group in the Indian Ocean, where further exercises will be conducted." Most of the officers present had served in *"Novo"* or one of her three sisters of the *Kiev* class. Commissioned between 1975 and 1988, they were the second generation of Soviet carriers, one step up from the pure helicopter ships. The *Kievs* operated both helos and V/STOL "jump jets," not as capable as big-deck carriers like *Varyag* or the American *Nimitz* class, but part of the evolutionary process.

"Finally, after Indian Ocean exercises, we will proceed to our new home port." Rybakov tapped the coast of the Sea of Japan. "Vladivostok." The anticipation of such a journey— nearly 18,000 nautical miles—stirred the men's excitement and imagination. *And they don't know the half of it,* Pyotr Rybakov thought to himself. *But as yet, they don't need to.*

1440 Local, Thursday, 6 May
USS Langley, *Northern Indian Ocean*

Rear Admiral Charles Gideon stepped aside in the combat decision center and stopped for a moment. The commander of Battle Group Charlie had been called from the aircraft carrier's flag bridge, and it took his eyes a moment to adjust from the bright afternoon sunlight to CDC's subdued tones of blue, red and green.

Commander Brad Thaxter glanced up when Gideon entered the cool, air-conditioned spaces. As CDC watch officer, Thaxter coordinated the efforts of radar, communications and threat-warning personnel in the nerve center of the battle group. From his seat at the primary console, Thaxter rose to attention as Gideon entered. The admiral waved him down with a motion of one hand. "As you were, guys."

Charles Gideon was like that, Thaxter mused; easygoing by nature, whereas some flag officers were impressed with their own importance. Because of the admiral's informality, Thaxter had heard sailors refer to Battle Group Charlie as "Battle Group Chuck."

"What've we got, Brad? Sounds like everything's happening at once."

"Uh, yes, sir. That's why I called you." Gideon took his place in the commander's chair beside Thaxter. "We've got two primary items of interest, Admiral. The Hawkeye has contact with what we think is an Indian Bear almost due north; Captain Ballantine's division is investigating. And Fish Hook 702 has a possible submarine contact to the northeast."

Thaxter identif d each item on the large tactical display screen opposite the admiral. To the uninitiated, the electronic images and esoteric symbology looked almost incomprehensible, but Gideon read them like a second language. He took in the eleven-ship battle group, steaming southwards 300 miles off the Indian coast, but it was only part of the overall picture: friendly, neutral, potentially hostile and unidentified ships and aircraft.

"Clean it up for me, Brad." Thaxter deftly flicked his controls to show only the ships and aircraft of Battle Group Charlie, and the two elements with which Gideon's forces were in contact. In seconds the cluttered screen was cleared of all distractions. "Thanks," Gideon said. "Now, what about the sub?"

Thaxter nodded at the duty antisubmarine warfare officer. The full lieutenant swiveled in his chair to address the admiral. "Sir, this is almost certainly the Victor III that was reported down here day before yesterday. We think it's probably number nineteen. Soon as Fish Hook gains contact we'll have a better ID. At any rate, we do not classify the contact as overtly hostile."

Gideon knew what the young officer meant. The U.S. Navy had been taping the acoustical signatures of foreign submarines for decades. Since each had an individual "thumbprint" it could be identified by computer comparison with existing data banks stored for that purpose. This particular submarine was the nineteenth of the Victor III class positively identified, though its official Russian name was unknown. Fish Hook 702 was a Lockheed S-3B Viking from *Langley's* Air Antisubmarine Squadron 23, which would stay on top of the contact until relieved or ordered back.

"Okay," Gideon said, "now what's this about my air wing commander playing footsie with the Indians?"

Gunshot 100

The haze was ever present, varying with altitude depending on the time of year. But once on top, the weather was CAVU—ceiling and visibility unlimited. That was what Captain Rob Roy Ballantine wanted for this milestone flight, his 1,000th from a carrier. He had just launched in a VF-181 Tomcat—his "personal" F-14B with the callsign Gunshot 100 signifying the air wing commander's aircraft. Actually, every squadron but the helicopter outfit had a "CAG bird." Originally CAG meant "commander of air group," but in 1963 the navy adopted the term "air wing." However, the old title stuck: nobody wanted to be led by a CAW. Knowing the occasion, the Fightin' Felines' maintenance crew had added a digit to the nose number. Now the Tomcat's identity was "Gunshot 1000," and that was Ballantine's radio callsign for this mission.

"One Thousand, this is Frisbee 605. Airborne contact, bearing 020 distance eighty-five. Single aircraft heading 180 at 425 knots. Your signal is buster."

Ballantine acknowledged the E-2C controller's call with a quick "Rog," aviator shorthand for "roger." He looked over at his wingman, Commander Frank "Buzzard" McBride in Gunshot 101. The CAG and Fightin' Felines skipper had begun their professional relationship as leader and wingman sixteen years before, so it only seemed natural on this historic occasion. Ballantine led Buzzard and the second section into a hard right turn, accelerating to maximum cruise speed to intercept the unannounced visitor from the Indian subcontinent. Like all carrier fliers, he was suspicious of shore-based aircraft. But four Tomcats could handle a lot of suspicion.

1445
Langley

"Tell me about the Bear," Gideon said.

The Tupolev 142 in its many guises is a familiar sight to American carrier airmen. Battle Group Charlie had seen them once or twice a week ever since entering the "Bear Box" passing Midway westbound from San Diego. But what made this one so interesting was its configuration. "It's a Bear Foxtrot, Admiral. Mod Two." Brad Thaxter consulted his notes from the radio transmissions monitored in CDC a few minutes before. "Bubba's division is escorting it inbound."

Gideon was mildly surprised. The Tu-142M, the second-oldest variant of the Russian turboprop antisub and patrol plane, was increasingly rare in the world. He turned to Thaxter. "I figured the Indians would have replaced their old Foxtrots by now."

"Uh, no, sir. Their navy still flies one squadron for maritime reconnaissance."

"Anything unusual happening?"

"Well, sir, the usual procedure. We photograph them, they photograph us. Neither side makes any threatening moves."

"Okay, Brad, keep me informed."

Gunshot 103

"Hey, Ozzie," chirped Lieutenant Fred "Fido" Colley, "get me upsun of the Bear for some pictures."

Lieutenant Commander Michael Ostrewski inhaled deeply, ingesting the molded-rubber scent of his oxygen mask. Observing proper escort etiquette, he kept his distance from the big, silver Tupolev. He noted the tail guns were elevated in a nonthreatening manner, but he remained out of their cone of fire. As leader of the second two-plane section in Ballantine's division, he had more to think about than posing aerial photographs. Ozzie squirmed in his F-14's ejection seat and replied over the intercom, "Take it easy, Fred. It's only a Bear."

Fido was unconvinced. The radar intercept officer was a keen photographer, and this was an opportunity not to be missed. "I'll make points with CAG this time," Colley insisted. "Him in formation with the bogey. Just in time for fitreps, too."

Ozzie chuckled over the intercom system or ICS. "Man, it'll take more than a brown-nose picture to improve your fitness report." Colley's episode with the Olongapo shore patrol had required Captain Ballantine's personal attention during the port period in the Philippines. Not even Ozzie knew the full details—something about two "waitresses" at a "social club" and an angry male "cousin" with a wickedly sharp *balisong*.

Fido appeared not to hear. "Maybe if I make an enlargement. You know, a really big one for CAG's I-love-me wall. And I could frame it, like, for his birthday or somethin'. . . ."

"One-Oh-Three from One Thousand," Ballantine called. "I'm forming on the Bear's port wing. Fido, how 'bout some pictures?"

Colley switched his radio to the guard frequency. "Sure thing, CAG. Wish I'd thought of it myself." Ozzie groaned aloud from the front cockpit.

1450
Langley

Brad Thaxter took in the multiple sources of information available to him, both electronic and audio. "Admiral Gideon, it looks like Captain Ballantine is breaking off escort. The Bear has turned back following radio warning at the hundred-mile mark."

The battle group commander straightened in his chair. "Okay. Anything noteworthy about the transmissions?"

Thaxter could not suppress a chuckle. "Lieutenant Colley in Gunshot 103 asked them to smile and said he'd send them a postcard from Sydney."

Gideon wasn't surprised. Even the admiral had heard of Fido's exciting evening in 'Po City. But he knew Ozzie Ostrewski as one of the best pilots in Air Wing 18, regarded by many as the leading light of the Fightin' Felines. And while it was common knowledge that the battle group planned a port call in Australia, communicating that information to friends of the Russians was not an approved procedure. "Get 'em on the horn," Gideon said, "and tell them to can the chatter. Keep us informed, but no fraternizing with the enemy."

"Aye, aye, sir."

Gideon glanced at the map. "You can bet those Indians are telling naval headquarters in Bombay our general location. And that means the Russian Embassy in Calcutta will have it before noon. Make sure the CAP is reinforced. Even with just one snooper out there now, I want to keep our strength up as long as we're this close to land. Who's available?"

"Uh, Circus 200 and 202, sir." Gideon visualized the pair of F-14s from VF-182, *Langley*'s second Tomcat squadron. Anticipating the group commander's next question, Thaxter hastened to add, "We have two Hornets on deck in condition one alert, Admiral, with two more on alert five." He ran a finger down the chart at his console. "Rampart 302 and 305 with Bronco 403 and 406."

"That's fine, Brad. I'm going to play a hunch. Launch the Ramparts and bring the Broncos to condition one."

The CDC officer picked up his phone and issued the orders. Gideon anticipated that in sixty seconds or less the two F/A-18Cs of Strike Fighter Squadron 183 would be airborne, en route to a prebriefed orbit point. The pair of VFA-184 aircraft would be ready to reinforce the combat air patrol on a minute's notice. Meanwhile, orbiting S-3B Viking tankers were ready to refuel any thirsty fighters in flight.

"Good thing the Fish Hooks are up there." Gideon grinned. "If I know Bubba, he'll want to hassle with Ozzie on the way back."

1540
Gunshot 100

In thirty minutes Bubba Ballantine would make his 1,000th carrier-arrested landing, qualifying him for the Tailhook Association's elite "Grand Club." But following a two-on-two dogfight with Ozzie's section, the CAG needed to top off with JP-5 fuel from the airborne tanker. In his Georgia drawl he called the S-3B Viking orbiting on the tanker track, though refueling normally was accomplished zip-lip. "Fish Hook 703 from Gunshot 1000. I have a visual on you, about four miles back at your seven o'clock."

The reply shot back. "Ah, roger, CAG. We're extending the drogue. Over."

Ballantine chuckled aloud over the intercom. "Hey, Slats, this is getting to be a top-heavy evolution. Did you know Rocky was up here?"

"Oops. Must've skipped my mind." Commander Patrick Slattery snickered over the intercom system, indicating he was in on the conspiracy. In fact, he had coordinated the daily flight plan with Commander Antonin "Rocky" Petrocelli, CO of VS-23. Ordinarily an A-6E Intruder bombardier/navigator, Slattery was Ballantine's deputy air wing commander, responsible for planning and leading strike missions in wartime. But he also had a stake in the upcoming event. Today would be his own 900th career "trap."

About a mile astern of the Viking, Bubba eased back his throttles and adjusted to a barely perceptible overtake on the tanker at 275 knots. He saw the underwing "buddy store" trailing a basketlike device at the end of a long, snaking hose. Ballantine knew from long experience that a slow approach was preferable because once he got in close, the rate of closure would become more apparent. The trick to making quick contact with the refueling drogue was a slow, smooth approach with minute adjustments. "Fencing with the basket" inevitably resulted in a botched attempt.

The CAG extended his refueling probe, and a faint electronic grinding sound hummed in the cockpit. The probe arced out of its stowage on the right side of the Tomcat's nose and locked into place as Bubba continued his approach. Slowly the Lockheed grew larger in his windscreen, and he concentrated on flying formation on the S-3B. Slats, in the backseat, had a better view, and coached the pilot into the basket. "Steady closure, Bubba. Up and right a bit—good!"

With tiny control corrections Ballantine finessed the Tomcat into alignment with the gently weaving basket and felt the soft touch of contact. His left hand advanced the throttles slightly as he drove the probe into the pocket. "One Thousand's plugged in," he called, noting the green contact light on the S-3's underwing package and a visible ripple the length of the refueling hose.

"Rog, plug-in complete," the Viking replied. Electric pumps began forcing kerosene into the Tomcat's fuel system. The two jets flew intimately linked for a few minutes as Slattery watched the fuel totalizer on his own panel. Then, satisfied with the load, Ballantine backed off the power and disengaged from the drogue. A white mist appeared around the nozzle as excess fuel was vented, and then the probe retracted into the fuselage.

Bubba and Slats slid out to let Buzzard and Lieutenant "Teeny" Feeney in Gunshot 101 line up for refueling. Then, with enough fuel for three tries at the deck, they broke away and began their descent into the carrier's marshal pattern.

Langley

The admiral leaned back in his comfortable chair and pondered the situation. Chuck Gideon occasionally said he almost felt better, dealing with the new Evil Empire instead of the unknown product of *perestroika*. Even with a revised government and constitution, the Union of Eurasian Republics seemed running to the old form. *They don't fly the hammer and sickle anymore,* he thought, *but they operate the same way.*

However, it was curious how he had so much in common with some ex-Soviet military leaders. In carefully chosen circumstances, a few of them had expressed attitudes toward their leaders—and politicians in general—that many American officers shared. *Wouldn't it be ironic,* Gideon thought, *if the soldiers of the world were the only ones who could govern in peace because they're the ones with most to lose in war.* He shook himself from his pondering. The Constitution delegated control of the military to the civilian side of government. His job, officially, was deterrence. But it came down to being ready to fight a war at sea. . . .

"Admiral?" It was Thaxter's voice, rousing him from his reverie.

"Oh, I'm sorry, Brad. I dropped off the scope there for a minute." Actually, it had been nearly fifteen minutes.

"I wanted to draw your attention to the submarine contact, sir." The CDC officer highlighted the symbols near the top of the electronic screen. "We now have positive ID on the nuke boat. It's Victor III number nineteen, all right. We have two helos and the same S-3 on the scene. The Russian has dropped back. We judge him no threat, sir."

"Keep me informed." Officially the Soviet Union no

longer existed, but Chuck Gideon remained skeptical. He had spent nearly a year of his youth dodging Russian flak and SAMs, and that was bound to make an impression on a young man.

Besides, he admitted, *in this business a little skepticism can be a healthy thing.*

1600
Gunshot 1000

Bubba Ballantine was three-quarters of a mile astern of *Langley,* twelve seconds from the deck. Riding an invisible three-and-one-half-degree glideslope, he let the landing signal officer know he saw the reflected "meatball" on the mirror landing system. "Gunshot 1000, Tomcat ball. State two-point-four." The LSO now knew the identity and type of aircraft and its fuel state—2,400 pounds. Ballantine was to be the last aboard before securing flight quarters for the day.

"Roger, CAG. Paddles contact," replied Lieutenant Commander Jack "Bumble" Bea. Like so much of naval aviation, tradition refused to give way to technology. "Paddles" was an ancient term for the landing signal officer, when LSOs waved planes aboard with hand-held paddles. It was similar to CAG—a linguistic link to the past.

At 130 knots the 45,000-pound Grumman continued its approach, lined up with the angled deck, eleven degrees off centerline. Bumble Bea caught an audible clue that other LSOs might have missed. He spoke into the phone in his right hand while holding aloft the "pickle switch" in his left, controlling the mirror lights. "Little power," was all he said.

At that instant Slats Slattery was about to tell Ballantine that a slight drop was visible in the meatball. *Damn, that LSO's good,* he thought admiringly. Bubba already was correcting, adding just a touch of throttle to keep on glideslope.

Four seconds later Gunshot 1000 slammed onto the deck at 130 knots, imposing a sink rate of eleven feet per second on the tires, landing gear and airframe. The extended tailhook snagged the third wire—actually a two-inch cable—as Bubba shoved on full power in case he had to go around. But both aviators were flung forward against their restraints and Ballantine retarded both throttles. The Tomcat rolled backwards slightly, crewmen gave the "raise hook" signal and the pilot flipped the switch on his left-hand console. Then he engaged his nosewheel steering.

Slats Slattery whistled softly. "Not too shabby, Bubba. If you keep at it, you might make a career of this."

Parking forward on the flight deck, the CAG and deputy CAG climbed down from the cockpit and immediately were swarmed by well-wishers. They posed for the ship's photographers, shaking hands under the "Gunshot 1000" logo, and a public-affairs officer announced that Ballantine was the 280th member of the Grand Club since 1962. Then the crash crew arrived. Decked out in white flame-resistant suits, the fire fighters gleefully turned a low-pressure hose on the aviators, dousing them to the skin: flight suits, G-suits, torso harnesses with survival gear, even their boots.

Bent on revenge, Bubba handed his nav bag to Slats and leapt upon the chief petty officer wielding the hose. At 210 pounds, the CAG took the CPO down with him and won the wrestling match for the hose. When he came up again, Bubba sprayed everybody in range—the guilty and the innocent alike. A maintenance man spat out a mouthful of water and gurgled, "CAG, isn't there something in regulations against this?"

Ballantine shut off the fog nozzle and wiped his wet face on a wet sleeve. "If there isn't, there sure as hell should be!" Then, one arm around Slattery's soggy shoulders, he sloshed off the flight deck, feeling as good as an aviator can feel.

0932 EDT, Wednesday, 12 May
White House Oval Office

President Vernon "Buddy" Callaway stretched out his tortilla-thin frame and tilted his chair ever farther backward. With growing alarm, National Security Adviser Dr. Arthur Epstein and Chief of Naval Operations Admiral Domingo "Hub" Fernandez watched their boss execute this precarious maneuver. Finally, the high-backed chair came safely to rest on the table standing between the flags—American and presidential—on either side of the middle window. The two officials relaxed.

To anchor himself in this elongated position, Callaway, a big raft of a man, stuck his bony legs and size twelve feet under the ornately carved oaken desk. They scarcely fit, but he seemed momentarily at ease, out of immediate danger. The President knit his skeletal fingers behind his long head and then, wagging his knobby elbows for balance, told the CNO, "You may fire when ready, Hub. We have an hour."

"Thank you, sir," the admiral responded, positioning himself in front of three easels, two holding maps and the other graphs. He then picked up a pointer and held it at port arms. Callaway knew that "Hub" was short for "Hubcaps," an unkind nickname assigned a big Puerto Rican kid by Naval Academy upperclassmen. But Fernandez took "Hub" as his tactical callsign in the "Hellrazors" of Fighter Squadron 174, and bore it as a *nom de guerre*. He hadn't gotten used to addressing his old Annapolis classmate as "sir," but neither had he yet neglected to do so. "Mr. President, as of yesterday, more Russian warships are loose on the high seas than at any time in world history."

Spare us the melodrama, please, Epstein thought. He considered the CNO unreliable at best and possibly downright dangerous—altogether too ideological, by which the adviser meant reactionary. Scuttlebutt had it that as commander of a carrier battle group off Lebanon in the mid-'80s, Fernandez had said to his chief of staff, "Damned if I'll bring ten billion dollars worth of military hardware and ten thousand men halfway around the world and not kill somebody." Whereupon he allegedly "went hunting" in Moslem West Beirut, armed with a Bennelli semiauto twelve-gauge, two smoke grenades and two frags.

After a pregnant pause the CNO continued, "The Soviet Navy currently has deployed forward some 426 naval units, to include by latest count sixty-five surface combatants, 105 subs, forty amphibious ships, nineteen mine-warfare vessels and 197 auxiliaries. To these totals could be added numerous ex-Russian warships transferred to client states and now operating in conjunction with Soviet units—"

"Please excuse me, Admiral, Mr. President," Epstein interjected, rubbing his bald head. "Forgive the interruption, but I really do feel that in order to avoid public embarrassment, our service chiefs should use the proper nomenclature for a major power.

"It is not mere pedantry to insist on 'Union of Eurasian Republics.' We would do well to habituate ourselves to use of the official style of the new government."

Callaway and Fernandez exchanged looks. Epstein read the meaning. *These two cowboys consider me a worm.*

"Go ahead, Hub," Callaway told Fernandez.

"Yes, sir. As I was saying"—a glare in Epstein's direction —"in addition to unprecedented numbers of Moscow's warships at sea and dozens of client-state naval vessels operating with the Russians, scores of merchantmen are carrying cargos on routes that suggest some connection with the naval combatant deployments. And we suspect that the 'tourists' on several of their cruise liners are in fact marines.

"Thanks to war-footing maintenance activity and spares production over the past year, naval equipment is currently at high availability; we estimate that seventy-five to eighty percent of all major ships and planes in their active inventory are good to go. The rest are undergoing repairs or routine maintenance.

"This level of readiness has been achieved through merciless exploitation of yard crews and naval factory workers.

"The frenetic pace of production, replacement and repair has paid off, as Graph One here shows." Fernandez pointed to the easel closest to the President's desk, which displayed a series of bar graphs.

"Right now, the Soviets—er, sorry, Doctor—Russians have forward-deployed over half of their active major surface combatants. This translates into all eight carriers, all four *Kirov*-class nuclear-powered battlecruisers and all four *Slava*-class missile cruisers, their newest. Totality of this order is unprecedented. Also, eighteen of their twenty-eight most advanced destroyers are forward-deployed, to include eight of the antisub *Udaloy* class and ten *Sovremenniy*-class antisurface and antiair escorts." Fernandez lowered the pointer.

"Similarly, all available units of their three newest amphibious ship classes are forward, to include thirty-six vessels, plus four minesweeping versions of the older *Polnocny* class of medium landing ships, of which thirty remain in Eurasian service." Epstein bit his lip and literally sat on his hands—a bit of body language the CNO relished. "Some forty-eight *Polnocnys* have been transferred to client-state navies, including all those currently conducting joint amphibious exercises with the UER: Angola, Cape Verde, the Congo, Madagascar, Mozambique, Namibia and Yemen, plus exercises recently completed with Vietnam and Cuba. Throw in North Korea's own 'phibs, and that's one hell of a lot of amphibious tonnage in the hands of clients.

"Among subs, more than half of their active nuclear-powered attack and cruise-missile boats are deployed forward. A smaller share of diesel-electric attack subs is deployed forward, but still nearly twice the usual fifteen percent of active inventory."

As a former naval officer and member of congressional intelligence and armed forces committees, the President was familiar with the CNO's acronyms: SSN for nuclear-powered torpedo attack submarine, SSGN for a nuke boat that "shoots" cruise missiles and SSBN for a ballistic-missile "boomer."

"Mr. President, may I comment on the ballistic-missile submarine deployments?" Epstein requested.

"Okay, but keep it short; we're on CNO's dime here," Callaway responded.

"Thank you, sir," Epstein said. "Surely it is not irrelevant that in order to comply with the START agreement, the UER must decommission all twelve of its obsolescent Yankee-class ballistic-missile subs now at sea.

"Is it not also true, Admiral, that the Eurasian Union announced earlier this year that it was transferring the twelve aged Yankees to India? And were we not given the routes they would follow, and have not the subs in fact adhered to these routes?" Epstein inquired pointedly.

"I agree that as a direct threat, they're remote, but I think we can show their danger as an indirect threat to U.S. interests. For starters," Fernandez said coldly, "there are SLBM resupply ships with the substantial surface forces now operating around the Cape Verdes in the mid-Atlantic and with the Russian Indian Ocean Squadron. Need I remind you that Yankee boomers can be reloaded at sea?" The President knew that SLBM meant sub-launched ballistic missile.

"To what end?" Epstein asked.

The admiral paused before replying. "Call it regional deterrence, and I don't mean India versus Pakistan. Let's leave it at that for now. May I continue my presentation, Mr. President?"

"By all means, Hub."

"Very well. I'd like to review recent Eurasian naval de-

ployments for a moment." Fernandez stepped to the middle
easel, holding a large world map. He flipped a sheet of trans-
parent plastic over the map. "Here's the situation as of 1
May, eleven days ago."

Warship silhouettes were scattered across the overlay,
marking the positions of groups of UER naval vessels. Numbers of each ship type in the group were taped beneath the
symbols and a dotted line indicated tracks taken by each
group. A separate box in each ocean and sea summarized
single ships on solo missions, mostly subs and spy trawlers
lurking around NATO bases and trailing Western ships.

"On 1 May, Russian naval infantry units were conducting or about to commence *five* distinct combined
amphibious exercises: here, with Cape Verde in the mid-
Atlantic; here, with Angola and Namibia in the South Atlantic; here, with Syria in the eastern Med; here, with Yemen on
Socotra Island in the Arabian Sea, and here, with Vietnam in
the South China Sea. Cuban marines were also involved in
both Atlantic maneuvers. The total of surface warships and
subs with each amphibious squadron was in the normal
range, but the numbers of support vessels were staggering,
amounting to two-thirds of all types. As you may recall, the
Russians still maintain a base on Socotra, despite the *An-
schluss* of North and South Yemen. And last year they signed
treaties of friendship and cooperation with the Cape Verdes
and Madagascar, like existing agreements with the Seychelles
and People's Republics of the Congo, Angola and Mozambique.

"At this time, forward-deployed submarines totaled
about forty—within normal limits—but numbers underway
in Russian rear waters were at an all-time high." With a flour-
ish, Fernandez flipped another overlay on top of the first.
"Now fast-forward to this morning. Since the first of the
month, some sixty-five additional subs have sortied into the
Atlantic and Pacific, while not one has headed home.

"On May fourth and fifth, all hell broke loose," the
CNO intoned. "Last Tuesday the three Northern Fleet carriers sortied from Severomorsk, near Murmansk on the Kola
Peninsula. Flagship *Kuznetsov,* the first Russian conven-
tional-takeoff-and-landing flattop, led V/STOL carriers
Gorshkov and *Kiev.* Also on 4 May, the second big-deck Russian carrier, *Varyag,* stood out into the Black Sea from Sevas-

topol. On Wednesday, a week ago, Pacific Fleet V/STOL carrier *Minsk* departed Vladivostok. All five carriers were accompanied by six to nine surface and sub escorts and support ships. They made only about fifteen knots, so their oilers could keep up," he continued.

"The three other Russian carriers were already forward-deployed for the amphibious exercises: Black Sea helicopter carriers *Moskva* and *Leningrad* off Syria in the eastern Med and Pacific Fleet V/STOL carrier *Novorossiysk* off Vietnam in the South China Sea. The number of forward-deployed surface ships increased from some 220 on May first to 321 now. At the same time, escort subs and independent submarine flotillas steamed forward, so the total of all types increased from about 260 to 426." Fernandez was pleased to hear the President's low whistle.

It was one thing to hear the numbers, but to see the planet's oceans swarming with Russian warship symbols took Callaway's breath away. He counted over a dozen major groupings of surface ships and submarines, plus the usual dozens of lone spy trawlers and subs on independent missions. To the President, the color-coded lines tracing the route of each fleet, flotilla or squadron looked like so many squid tentacles grasping the world. Callaway eased himself out of his semireclining posture and sat up. *If Hub wants my attention, he's got it.*

"Please note the two clusters of nuclear-powered submarines grouped in the mid-Atlantic and the Philippine Sea. They contain forty-eight nuke boats.

"Here's the situation this morning," Fernandez continued. The President followed his CNO's pointer around the globe, starting in the North Atlantic. "The big-deck carrier *Kuznetsov* and the V/STOL carrier *Gorshkov* are traveling in consort. After passing Iceland, they continued south, but the V/STOL *Kiev* group turned west toward Greenland," Fernandez indicated. As the CNO continued, working his way gradually southward and eastward, Callaway saw that the cream of every fleet was involved.

"They also have the V/STOL carrier *Minsk* in the North Pacific. The South China Sea Squadron, consisting of V/STOL carrier *Novorossiysk* and escorts, is passing the Malacca Strait between Sumatra and Malaya, perhaps to join the large Indian Ocean Squadron exercising off Socotra." As he heard Fernandez detail the composition of each group, the President was shocked by the enormous concentration of forces.

Fernandez moved to the third easel, displaying a map of the Mediterranean and Black seas. "*Varyag*, second carrier in the *Kuznetsov* class, transited the Turkish Straits from the Black Sea to the Med a week ago and passed Gibraltar early this morning." The CNO traced her course. "She's flying the flag of their premier carrier commander, Fleet Admiral Rybakov. On the sixth, the *Varyag* group conducted antisub practice in the eastern Med with the Russian Fifth *Eskadra*. This Mediterranean squadron, containing helo carriers *Moskva* and *Leningrad,* returned to its base at Tartus, Syria, on the seventh, while the *Varyag* group proceeded west. On the eighth, the helo carrier group headed south, transited the Suez Canal and proceeded through the Red Sea. We expect it to combine with the Indian Ocean Squadron." Fernandez paused momentarily to allow the President to assimilate the data. The admiral could tell his boss was impressed. "But there's more."

Shit, Callaway thought. *That's enough!*

"There's a huge pack of twenty-eight nuke subs in the North Atlantic, plus about half as many on apparently routine peacetime patrols. Two Victor SSNs and six Tango-class diesel boats are also with the amphibious groups farther south. It's the greatest concentration of underwater firepower ever assembled, and though some of the boats are 1970s vintage, they pack one hell of a lot of SLBMs, cruise missiles, torpedoes and mines.

"You look at what's now in the Indian Ocean, and what could be there tomorrow . . ." He shrugged his big shoulders. "If somehow shooting were to start in the IO, it could be more than we can handle with the force available—the *Langley* carrier battle group, an amphibious group, a replenishment group, and Maritime Prepositioning Squadron Two at Diego Garcia." In the Arabian Sea, Callaway saw the lone blue title, "*Langley* CVBG," some 600 nautical miles northeast of the red-labeled "UER IndRon" off Socotra, which he knew stood for Indian Ocean Squadron.

"Shooting? Over what?" Epstein blurted out. "Don't you consider that a rather remote possibility, Admiral?"

"I have to consider every possibility. Even if we aren't a

direct target, we lack the power to influence events in the region. There's no shortage of flashpoints—the Horn of Africa, the Persian Gulf, Afghanistan, India-Pakistan, India-China, Sri Lanka, Burma, South Africa, you name it.

"We've got other things to go on. Their special forces, parachute divisions, heli-borne assault brigades and military air transport arm are in a high state of readiness. Ditto land-based naval aviation. Their Backfire antiship bomber regiments are exercising at levels comparable to the surface and sub arms. We've even observed increased maintenance and decreased domestic use of Aeroflot's long-range airliners. And virtually their entire naval infantry force is on maneuvers around the globe or at home. The marines, airborne and commando-type forces of Russia's major client states are also on heightened alert.

"Then there's the Russians' record. They have historically launched invasions after or directly from exercises, while peace talks were underway, after desensitizing the opposition and/or just before holidays or weekends. All of those conditions exist at this moment.

"The State Defense Committee of the Executive Council and a small working group in the Ministry of Defense are clearly planning something, but they're holding their cards even closer to their chests than usual.

"I believe we know what they have up their sleeve, but to do our theory proper justice would require a separate presentation. Suffice it to say for now that we strongly urge increasing naval strength in the South Atlantic and Indian oceans. That means getting every available CVBG underway, ASAP." Fernandez lay down the pointer and sat on a gold brocade couch.

Callaway turned to Epstein. "Okay, Doctor. Fire away."

"Thank you, Mr. President. Certainly the developments bear watching, but we have adequate forces in the region to do so. Assembling countervailing concentrations of our own would unnecessarily heighten tensions and increase the risk of incidents, for little or no gain.

"I should like to emphasize certain points that Admiral Fernandez failed to stress. It is true that the Eurasian Navy is currently mounting its largest open-ocean exercises in eighteen years, yet we have no reason to believe that they are anything other than maneuvers. After such a long time without global exercises, it's only natural that they should want to stretch their sea legs, so to speak. The UER particularly needs to integrate its new carriers into operational structures. Their navy has never before had the chance to exercise two carriers at once. I for one regard it as only natural that they should want to do so.

"The Eurasian Union has properly notified us of every one of these deployments. The advance notification has been in a manner consistent with the Incidents at Sea and Conventional Force agreements and other international understandings to which it and its predecessors are party. As Admiral Fernandez knows, we have observers with the three amphibious exercises currently underway in the Cape Verdes, off Angola and on Socotra. The UER even went so far as to inform us of the routes their aircraft carriers would follow.

"Further, Moscow has conformed to a schedule announced well in advance and in some detail. The Defense Ministry said that in April and May joint amphibious exercises would be held with Cape Verde, Angola, Namibia, Yemen and Vietnam. These have in fact transpired. Naval aviation exercises were to occur during May and June, followed by antisubmarine exercises in June and July. The exercising units are to return to their home ports by August. That schedule is plausible and the Eurasian Navy has adhered to it.

"I see nothing particularly sinister or threatening in these naval concentrations. A strong, responsible Eurasian Navy could in fact cooperate with us in a variety of imaginable peacekeeping operations."

I can't believe it, the CNO thought. *This is the same guy who thinks our carriers act aggressively. But Russian ones contribute to world peace. Go figure.*

"The preponderance of intelligence estimates supports the CIA-NSC view," Epstein said, "rather than the alarmist DIA assessment.

"I feel we must show restraint. Treating the UER as an equal is the best way to encourage continued development of healthy institutions there.

"We have the *Eisenhower* group well-positioned to watch the Soviet exercises in the Atlantic, as well as maritime patrol aircraft and submarines, not to mention NATO forces. Why risk provoking an incident?"

"If it is just a larger than usual exercise, sir, then our other carriers won't get there in time to provoke anybody," Fernandez interjected. "If it's something more, then we'll be in a better position to respond. I stick by my recommendation, sir. Better safe than sorry."

"Respond? How? To what?" the adviser questioned.

"In whatever way the President wants to," replied Fernandez.

Callaway leaned forward. He looked at the maps, then at Fernandez. "Well, Hub, I've never known you to exaggerate," he said. "Overdramatize, yes. Exaggerate, no, except maybe in budget testimony before Congress. I'd like to hear from Russian and regional experts, but I just can't fit 'em in today. Do you feel it's urgent?"

"I think we should take some steps within forty-eight hours, Mr. President. Just to be on the safe side."

Callaway rose and rounded the desk. "Okay. I'm going to take some action, but I need to sleep on it. We'll meet here again day after tomorrow, same time. You bring your people. Same for you, Doctor. Three specialists each. Thank you, gentlemen. Hub, you mind if I hang on to the maps?"

Fernandez told the President he was welcome to them. Callaway thanked the CNO again and wished him and the NSC director good morning.

The President stood alone, studying the CNO's maps.

3

13 to 18 May

1858 Local Time, Thursday, 13 May
Langley, Gonzo Station, Arabian Sea

In a previous life, Lieutenant Ross "Ghost" Caspar had been an A-6 pilot. But now he felt like a glorified *maitre d'* as he lit candles and double-checked place settings. He had to admit, however, that as long as he had to endure a nonflying billet, there were worse things than being Chuck Gideon's flag lieutenant. The professional insights Caspar had gained over the past several months already were more than worth the effort.

The problem was, once a month Admiral Gideon liked a semiformal dinner in his flag quarters. Officially the occasion allowed for a relaxed assessment of battle group activities, but Caspar knew better. Chuck Gideon loved to discuss professional reading—*his* professional reading. Everyone on his staff was required to absorb Mahan's *The Influence of Sea Power on History,* Gorshkov's *The Sea Power of a State,* Heinlein's *Starship Troopers,* Lord's *Incredible Victory* and Nichols's *On Yankee Station.*

As the staffers filed into the candle-lit room, Caspar finished last-minute arrangements with the steward's mates. Then he took his place as Gideon said, "Gentlemen, please be seated."

Seating was always rotated to facilitate diversity in discussion. This evening Gideon's table included Commanders Slats Slattery, deputy CAG; Rick Hallion, staff intel officer; Lou Tran, the Vietnamese-born antisubmarine specialist; and Ghost Caspar. Some junior officers would have been intimidated in such company, but Ghost was inured to it by now.

While the spinach salad was being served—Ghost had learned early on how to feed his admiral—Gideon served up his own menu. "Rick, I'm rereading *Starship Troopers*. What do you make of it?"

Hallion nodded a quick thank-you across the table to Caspar, who had seen the science-fiction classic on the admiral's bunk two days before. The man was a space junkie—a Trekker, in fact. Ghost felt that if he had to sit through one more viewing of "The Trouble with Tribbles," he'd crawl up the bulkhead. "Well, Admiral, I'd say that the Earth civilization advanced by Heinlein is almost idealistic. Not only is the military organization purely professional, it's fully integrated into the society. Even down to the classroom, where students are asked to quantify the benefit of risking several men to save one."

Gideon nodded, suspecting that his aide may have passed the word. *Next time I'll leave* Cathouse Showdown *on my bunk*, he thought. "Ghost, I think Rick makes a point. Can we quantify the risk inherent in rescuing one or two people against the lives of others?"

Caspar knew where the admiral was leading. Or thought so, which made the aide even edgier. "I don't think so, sir. No. Admiral Gallery was quoted in Commander Nichols's *On Yankee Station*. He said something to the effect that there was no morale setting on Mr. McNamara's computers."

Gideon laid his fork down—a sure sign of a prolonged discussion. His required reading list for his staff was limited to five volumes, but each one would be thoroughly analyzed during the cruise. "Well, what about it? Can we plug in the morale factor and compare it to one life versus many?"

Caspar felt more secure. "Sir, I'm an attack pilot. If I were flying deep into Indian Country I'd feel a whole lot better knowing there were guys back here willing to come pluck me from deep serious. It's a matter of trust, like Nichols said. If you have to explain that to somebody like a McNamara, he's never going to understand."

Gideon smiled. "Well, as an aviator of the attack persua-

sion myself, I have to agree with you. In fact, I agree with the
marine weapon and tactics community. They regard *On Yankee Station* as one of the four or five best books written on
war. It's original in concept and perceptive in analysis. But,
as we all know, marines have only lately learned to read."
There was laughter around the table, but Gideon felt the
navy would benefit from a required reading program similar
to the leathernecks'.

Lou Tran, the professional sub hunter, spoke up. "Admiral, I've been asked why Gorshkov still is on your list.
Some people wonder if a 1979 Soviet document is as perti-
nent today as when it was published."

"Fair question," Gideon replied. "But first, what do you
think?" Gideon already knew what the Vietnamese-born
Tran thought about Soviets.

"Well, sir, I think Gorshkov still is worth reading," he
said precisely. "If for no other reason than to see where the
UER navy is coming from. But beyond that, Russian naval
doctrine hasn't changed a great deal."

"That's right," interjected Hallion, the staff spook.
"They still read *The Sea Power of a State,* though they don't
quote it as often as before."

"Okay," Gideon replied. "Now you gentlemen tell me,
where do we fill in the blanks with the advent of Russian big-
deck carriers?"

Slats Slattery usually wasn't much of a literary commen-
tator, but he was feeling left out. "Admiral, as far as reading
goes, I'd say that leads us to *Incredible Victory.*" Before Gideon could ask the inevitable question, the D-CAG pressed
on. "It deals with a subject very close to us, and not only
because it's U.S. carrier aviation winning at Midway. . . ."

"Right," interjected Hallion. "Aside from being a triumph for naval intelligence—a community in which I take
special pride—the Midway story proves again that a small,
outgunned force still can win over a larger one. And that's
the kind of battle we can expect to fight. Gorshkov's 'war of
the first salvo' is a lot like Japanese strategy in 1941."

"Which might have worked, if our carriers had been at
Pearl," Slattery assayed. He felt a little intimidated intellectually—history was not his forte—but his usual response to
his fears was to charge straight into them and bowl them
over.

"That's right," Tran piped up, "and the Russian blue-water fleet was designed for one purpose—to sink the U.S. Navy. After which their subs and bombers could send our merchant convoys to the bottom with impunity. As a land power, it didn't matter to the Russians if they lost all their major surface combatants while wiping us out. A lot of their main classes don't even carry antiship missile reloads, but the ones in their launchers are big, fast and real destructive. First-strike, sneak-attack weapons."

"Except now their carriers give them fleet air defense and power-projection capabilities they never had before," Hallion added. "They can go out and control sea-lanes or coastal littorals, not just deny that kind of control to us." He decided to play the citation game. Reaching deep into his memory of classes at Annapolis, he made sure he had the terms right in his mind, then asked, "Isn't that Mahan's distinction—sea control versus sea denial?" *What a showoff,* Hallion thought, almost repulsed by his own knowledge.

Gideon moved his salad bowl aside, no longer hungry. *My brain trust,* he thought, *my guild of warriors. God love 'em.* "You're all hitting close to the X-ring tonight," he said, then steered them back to the topic he wanted discussed. "But there are lots of good books on Midway. Why did I choose Lord's?"

There were puzzled expressions around the table. "Okay, time's up," the admiral said. "I like Walter Lord's treatment because he sets the stage so well. He lived through that period, remember. He knew something of how those men felt. And he had just enough of a feel for the hardware to pull it all together. Others like Prange were more thorough, perhaps, but nowhere as salty. And that makes the difference."

"Like a couple dozen attack pilots made a difference," Slattery added. Though a bombardier/navigator himself, he shared the community's pride.

Ghost Caspar added, "Yes, sir! Like the bumper sticker said at Oceana: 'Fighter pilots make movies; Attack pilots make history!' "

Gideon hailed the next table. "Hey, Bubba. You hear that?"

Ballantine leaned back in his chair. "Well, sir, I may not be the Mozart of navy fighter pilots, but I reckon I'm the closest thing to an Elvis. And I quote the late Admiral Jimmy Thach, who, after Midway, said, 'Only fighter aircraft can keep our carriers afloat.' " He grinned under his mustache and returned to his salad.

Lou Tran forked a leaf in his bowl. He did not remind anyone that America's only two ship losses at Midway had been to a lone submarine.

"If we tangle with Rybakov's force, it'll only be the sixth carrier battle in history," Hallion added.

"How's that?" asked Gideon.

"Well, sir, there were five in World War Two; Coral Sea and Midway, followed by Eastern Solomons and Santa Cruz during the Guadalcanal campaign. Two years later was the biggest CV engagement of all, in the Philippine Sea."

Gideon nodded. "Right, the Great Marianas Turkey Shoot in June '44. But what about the Second Battle of the Philippine Sea that October?"

"Leyte Gulf?" asked Tran.

"Same battle, different name," explained Gideon. "But we sank four enemy carriers there, when Halsey got suckered north and left the 'phibs exposed off Samar. I'd say that was the sixth carrier battle."

Hallion felt defensive but sure of his ground. "Well, Admiral, the naval historians seem at odds on that point. Sure, we put four flattops on the bottom, but it was all one-sided. Most of those ships were empty, acting as decoys. They only had about thirty planes all told, and they never launched against us. I'd say it was more an execution than a battle."

Gideon suppressed a smile. "So you're saying that a fleet engagement must have a mutual exchange of air strikes to qualify."

"Ah, yes, sir. After all, there's never been a name to the action off Ceylon when the Jap . . . anese sank HMS *Hermes*. She didn't have any planes aboard at all, but that happened a month or so before Coral Sea. So does that mean there have been seven carrier battles so far? I don't think so."

The admiral raised his hands in surrender. "Okay, you win. The next go-round will be the sixth battle."

0116, Friday, 14 May
Varyag, *North of La Palma, Canary Islands, Atlantic Ocean*

Signal lamps blinked in the foggy night as carrier *Varyag* greeted her older sister *Kuznetsov* and smaller cousin *Gorshkov.* The groups of Russian warships stood just east of the main sea-lane along the northwest coast of Africa. Combining the fleet without transmitting or interfering with commercial shipping called for constant attention on the bridges of the three dozen ships and surfaced subs. But merchant shipping in these busy waters could help cover the Russians' movements when NATO satellites passed overhead, much as the darkness protected them from the eyes of their Portuguese, Spanish, British and Moroccan watchers.

Rybakov had known few thrills as great as *Varyag*'s acceleration when, safely past the Pillars of Hercules and with his fuel bunkers filled up, he had ordered all ahead three-quarters. The carrier and her escorts, new missile cruiser *Lobov* and anti-submarine (ASW) cruiser *Azov,* had soon left their oilers and other support vessels far behind. After tanking off Tangier, the warships averaged twenty knots over the 635 nautical miles to arrive at their rendezvous west of the Salvage Islands within minutes of the appointed time. He logged his position as precisely thirty degrees north, fourteen degrees west, recording calm seas and no problems en route.

All hands on *Varyag*'s flag bridge were pleased and proud to witness the first merging of two big-deck aircraft carriers in Russian naval history, but it was the admiral's joy to direct the operation. Task Force Rybakov also included V/STOL carrier *Gorshkov,* most advanced of her class, three of the four *Kirov*-class nuclear battlecruisers, numerous other surface warships and subs, plus support vessels. The task force would only grow in size and power as the fleet steamed southward, collecting additional ships, especially resupply types and oilers.

Most of Rybakov's staff realized that the fleet would refuel south of the Cape Verdes and again off Angola from tankers accompanying the amphibious squadrons recently exercising there. But only a few knew that, given the signal by Moscow, the task force would stay off the coast of South Africa longer than it took to sail past it.

The sycophantic young staff lieutenant who brought him

the logbook was definitely not in the know. He took the book back from Rybakov, came to attention and said, "Congratulations, sir, on commanding the largest Russian high-seas fleet in nine decades!"

"I certainly hope we don't meet the same fate as the Baltic Fleet," the admiral replied, not bothering to hide his disdain. Chief of Staff Smirnov winced at his CO's mention of the Baltic Fleet of 1905, which ineptly steamed 14,000 nautical miles to destruction by the Imperial Japanese Navy at Tsushima Strait. In this context, the reference constituted a potential breach of security. But Rybakov compounded the situation, adding, "Nor do I intend to emulate Admiral Rozhdestvensky." Smirnov hoped that meant he didn't mean to lose, not that he wouldn't go down with his ship if he did.

The lieutenant flushed beet red at his own clumsy *faux pas.* Trying to recover, he only made matters worse. "But, sir," the boy objected, "the Imperial Russian Baltic Fleet was composed of antique ships that should never have been committed to battle on the other side of the world, while our . . . uh, your warships are among the most modern and capable in the world." In typical ass-kissing fashion, he went on, "And how can Rozhdestvensky's blundering compare to your brilliance as the father of Russian seaborne, fixed-wing aviation?"

To rid himself of the pest and partially redeem his mistake, Rybakov allowed, "Yes, I suppose we might be able to avoid complete catastrophe if for some reason we should get in a fight." In his heart of hearts, Pyotr Rybakov wrestled with himself. *I know a fight is coming,* he admitted. *Warships, after all, are for war.*

0931 EDT
White House

To accommodate the half dozen regional experts he'd requested on Wednesday, President Callaway had the CNO's maps set up in the Cabinet Room. Admiral Fernandez brought fresh overlays for them.

The admiral stood in front of the fireplace, facing the long table with one easel to his right and two to his left. Behind him on the mantel sat JFK's model of frigate *Constitution,* "Old Ironsides," and on the wall hung Gilbert Stuart's

Washington. The CNO admired Callaway's decoration of the Oval Office and Cabinet Room. The basic theme was nautical, with some not discordant East Texas touches.

Fernandez seized the pointer and took a stance before the Atlantic Ocean. "Good morning, Mr. President, ladies and gentlemen. The latest Russian carrier, *Varyag,* and her escorts transited Gibraltar Wednesday morning, then refueled from accompanying fleet oilers. No longer encumbered by their underway replenishment ships and minesweepers, the warships steamed southwest at twenty knots. About midnight last night, the *Varyag* group combined with the Northern Fleet surface action group centered on carriers *Kuznetsov* and *Gorshkov* here, north of La Palma in the Canaries." He slapped a map of the North Atlantic, gouging the overlay. "They mixed and matched for a couple of hours, forming new groupings within a united task force, then headed west into the regular shipping lanes running south past the Canaries toward the Cape Verdes." He dragged the pointer down a line following the curve of the northwest African coast.

"The fact that *Kuznetsov* and *Gorshkov* have continued south rather than coming about indicates beyond any doubt that this is not a normal exercise.

"Clearly, this task force intends to refuel from the numerous tankers accompanying the Russian amphibious groups off the Cape Verdes and Angola before uniting with the *Novorossiysk* group now heading southwest across the I.O." He switched to the central easel's map of the Indian Ocean. "The *Novo* group is also beating cheeks, so my bet is the third amphibious group, here, off Socotra, will head south to refuel both the groups converging from the Atlantic and Pacific. This juncture could be effected anywhere in the southwestern I.O. Precisely where depends on how fast the surface action groups go and how much fuel they burn.

"It's clear that the three amphibious groups were positioned in advance to support the fast carrier groups as they pass. The Russian carrier groups not returning home to simulate U.S. CVBGs as in the past is worrisome enough. What bothers me even more is that the amphibious ships haven't come about, either.

"The *Kiev* SAG is still skulking around in the ice floes, and has steamed into the Labrador Sea, about halfway between Canada and Greenland. It is unusual for major Russian surface combatants to exercise this close to North America. In the North Pacific, pretty much the same deal. V/STOL carrier *Minsk* and her escorts have turned north toward the Aleutians rather than west toward the Kuriles. The best explanation for these moves is that they're intended to draw us away from whatever the SAGs headed for the South Atlantic and Southwest I.O. are up to.

"This global exercise—if in fact that's what it is—is unlike anything that's happened before, unless you count the Russo-Japanese War of 1905. It's about the size of the two *Okean* global exercises of the '70s combined.

"We queried them through regular channels—naval attaches and the standing committees overseeing treaties and agreements. They said it was all part of a global exercise and pointed out that we'd been properly notified. We said, like hell—this is way out of the ordinary. It was like the bad old days, when, if they observed agreements, it was only by the letter of the law at best.

"Yesterday I dialed Admiral Sorokin myself and asked what gives. After clearing my questions with his bosses, he got back to me this morning. I just got off the horn with him. I think the SOB liked getting me while I was still groggy." Fernandez smiled, then referred to his notes. "He claims the exercise is so big to make up for not having held major exercises over the last eight years. On top of that, their normal five-year training cycle had gone to hell under Gorbachev and they needed to make up lost time. He added that they had to practice with their new carriers, learn how to integrate them into their operational structures, plus they have new equipment and yadda-yadda."

Fernandez took a breath but tried not to show his uneasiness. "Mr. President, I believe the UER is going to support an invasion of South Africa by the Front Line States, with Cuban, Vietnamese, North Korean and maybe some Arab help."

The reaction in the room was stunned silence. Fernandez played his ace. He introduced Dr. Stanley Horowitz, the Defense Intelligence Agency's top Russian capabilities analyst and a published authority on Africa and the Middle East.

Epstein had to admit that the CNO's star briefer would be hard to shoot down. A twenty-year veteran of the DIA,

Horowitz's ability to forecast international developments was spooky. His record had earned him comparisons to Jeane Dixon and Edgar Cayce.

Horowitz's DIA team had always come much closer to estimating actual Soviet defense expenditure than the CIA. He had always maintained—correctly, it turned out—that the Kremlin devoted at least a quarter of its national product to its military, back when the CIA guessed six percent. He had predicted the 1979 Russian invasion of Afghanistan and the 1990 Iraqi invasion of Kuwait, which he viewed as a conspiracy among Iraq, Jordan and Yemen to carve up Saudi Arabia, with Kremlin connivance. In between, he had decried Soviet control of the international drug trade, foreseen the rise of *perestroika* and the collapse of the Warsaw Pact and assessed the risks, as well as the opportunities, these historical developments posed for the West. Unfortunately, even after years of his being right, political leaders rarely heeded his warnings.

Horowitz was not alone in predicting that, unless President Yeltsin could magically make bread, sausages and soap appear on Russian shelves, the failed 1991 coup would be followed within eighteen months by a new putsch attempt and civil war. The analyst claimed that the second coup would succeed because it would be led by the military—the only respected, competent Union-wide institution. Even though leaders of the armed forces were appointed by the liberal Yeltsin and their units ostensibly were controlled by separate republics, they would act to maintain order in the former Soviet empire.

The prophecy had come to pass. Democracy and free enterprise had not ended the people's misery rapidly enough. Russian nationalists bemoaned the loss to neighboring secessionist republics of territory they considered theirs. Ethnic Russians in the Ukraine, like Serbs in Croatia, rose up, demanding restoration of the Union. "Russians will accept food without empire or empire without food, but must have one or the other," Horowitz had opined before large-scale fighting broke out.

To end the chaos and prevent a new "time of troubles," the armed forces seized power in a smoothly executed coup supported by the majority of Russians and many in the subjugated regions. All the rebellious republics except the Baltic states and Moldavia were forced back into the Union.

Though espousing "democratic socialism," the UER was in effect, much like China, a fascist empire. Union president Rodinkov, the ostensible civilian head of state and government, was a puppet of the military dictatorship, embodied in the State Defense Committee. The reincarnated empire couldn't last, Horowitz was sure, but would cause vast suffering before falling—as had its communist predecessor.

Dressed in clothes as ill-fitting and unstylish as when new in 1973, Horowitz began by pointing out that the chief legacy of the USSR to the UER was a tremendous amount of military hardware and expertise. "This legacy is practically the only accumulated capital available to finance future economic growth. Besides God-given natural resources so vast not even a lifetime of Marxism could squander them all, weapons systems are the regime's only real leverage in the world. But maximizing the yield on its resources requires hard currency to buy Western technology and help. A backward, bottlenecked oil industry and lack of agricultural infrastructure are but two examples."

Horowitz continued in a monotone, "Overall Soviet military capabilities increased substantially during the Gorbachev years. The navy, for instance, merely cut back on operations. The value of procurements actually grew. Until recently, the Russian empire lacked the capacity to project power long distances. Though the USSR had great air- and sealift for its airborne and amphibious intervention forces, its transport aircraft and ships were primarily intratheater systems, designed for use relatively close to the Sacred Borders of the Socialist Motherland."

The gaunt, gawky analyst observed that the UER now had equipment for influencing distant events: improved armored airborne and amphibious vehicles, oceangoing escort and amphibious ships, enhanced at-sea replenishment capabilities and, most importantly, very-long-range, heavy-lift transport aircraft and big-deck aircraft carriers. The acquisition of *Kuznetsov*-class carriers and *Ruslan* transport planes allowed the Operations and Strategic Deception Directorates of the General Staff to refine plans previously developed for intervention on behalf of "progressive" elements in South Africa.

"The present State Executive Council members and the interests they represent," he added, "know that foreign adventures can divert dissatisfied people's attention. They also remember the lessons of 1905 and 1917, when military disasters sparked revolutions."

The DIA bureaucrat argued, "As with past interventions in the Third World, the ostensible goal of the operation would be national liberation, but this time the politico-economic system to replace the present so-called imperialist, exploitative regime will no longer be scientific socialism. Instead, it will be to extend to Africa the benefits of New Thinking—reinvigorated democratic socialism.

"But in stark geopolitical and economic terms, the real purpose of the project will be to maintain the Eurasian Union—that is, the Russian empire—into the next century and to sustain its essentially unreformed command economy. It is Russian socialism," Horowitz threw in, as he did every chance he got, "not Western capitalism that needs exploitable colonies to prop up its rotten, tottering structure against its own internal contradictions."

His basic contention was that the UER government was old, vinegary wine in new bottles.

"Although the adventure will enhance its prestige among certain Western and Third World publics, the benefits to Moscow are chiefly economic. Africa offers the Kremlin a last chance to capitalize on socialist ideology and its best hope for turning its huge investment in military preparedness into economic advantage. Capturing wealth by force of arms is the most attractive option for financing its continued industrial modernization program and for making it work through a halfhearted incentive system. And, I scarcely need to add, for keeping the disparate subject peoples of the UER content with its leadership.

"Although few if any leaders of the Kremlin's coconspirators in this adventure know the operational details of the scheme, you have to ask what's in it for the ANC, the Front Line States and Russian client states. The radical leadership of the ANC want to control South Africa before the forces of moderation and constitutional reform can produce a democratic, pro-Western government there. Despite the end of their civil wars, the Front Line States hope to benefit from ANC control of the riches of South Africa and from ideologi-

cal compatibility. Their troops have been promised farms in
the RSA. The hard-line regimes in Cuba, North Korea and
Vietnam benefit economically and by justifying their continued revolutionary character. Finding work for large armies
helps Cuba and Vietnam out of their unemployment problems."

Based on HumInt and SigInt sources, military exercises
and his own guesswork, Horowitz summarized the Kremlin's
reasons for embarking on such a risky venture. "One: ideo-
logical-political," the frizzy-haired genius said, holding up
one finger. "In the eyes of Third World peoples, the fight for
liberation of people of color in South Africa is one of the two
most important struggles against neocolonialism and multinational, capitalistic imperialism in the world. Successfully
aiding the ANC in this battle will improve the image and
influence of the UER in the Third World and among self-
styled progressive peoples everywhere."

Horowitz extended another crooked finger. "Two: geopolitical. South Africa is, almost literally, the economic and
geographical keystone of the whole sub-Saharan continent.
Acquiring control of it will unlock the great natural resource
storehouse of southern Africa, place Russian armed forces
athwart one of the West's vital commercial trade routes and
guard the UER's own sea lines of communication. Recall
Brezhnev's reference to the leverage provided by controlling
the world's two treasure troves—Mideastern oil and southern African minerals.

"Three: economic. Helping South Africa join the social
democratic camp will greatly expand the market for Moscow's only internationally competitive manufactured goods,
military equipment. This applies both to the pre- and post-
invasion phases. As noted, the UER has already profited
directly from exporting to southern Africa much of the hardware that the conventional arms treaties with the U.S. and
NATO required it to dispose of at some expense. Tanks and
chemical warfare agents are especially costly to destroy.
Much better to exchange these surplus products for hard
currencies.

"The standard Russian alternatives to economic trade
are to eliminate the competition and, at the same time, to
capture new markets by force. Revolution in South Africa
will achieve these ends. Russia's main—often its only—inter-

national competitor for many precious, strategic or industrial ores, minerals and gems is South Africa. The trade in gold, platinum, diamonds, chromium, antimony, manganese, tin, uranium and vanadium is worth about ten billion U.S. dollars annually. Moscow has already realized substantial profit from subverting South Africa—unrest there and renewed international sanctions have increased the market share and the price of competing commodities, chiefly gold and other minerals.

"Bear in mind that for many South African strategic mineral exports, the only other source is the UER. For a list, with relative global market shares, I refer you to the chart behind me." He turned and pointed. "Pretoria has refused to renew the secret price-fixing agreement it had with the USSR or to comply with Moscow's requests for commodity price hikes. I believe the Kremlin has cut a deal with the ANC to form a cartel that not only grants Moscow's demands but extends to all resources the sort of arrangement the old regime had with apartheid South Africa regarding diamonds, gold and platinum. In fact, the deal is even sweeter, since the ANC leaders will cut back mineral output and sales, thanks to their plan to nationalize the mines and other productive property and to redistribute income.

"Extraction of the remainder of the West's own once-ample reserves of uranium is rapidly becoming uneconomical. This makes African supplies critical for generating nuclear power, if not for producing atomic weapons, advanced tank armor and armor-piercing ammunition. And finally, after fifty years, Russia will at last have reliable access to unlimited quantities of uranium. This has always been the only concrete limitation on the size of its nuclear arsenal and power-generating capacity. Despite controlling one-sixth of the earth's land surface and superabundant supplies of every other mineral, the Russian empire is deficient in uranium."

Horowitz saw the Kremlin's South African plan unfolding in four phases. "Phase One lasted from 1 May of last year to 26 December," he maintained. "On the military front, it involved a number of preparatory activities and exercises, including the sealift of 100,000 tons of war materiel per month to southern Africa. Most of this combat technology was equipment that the 1990 conventional forces reduction treaty obliged Moscow to dispose of.

"The African arms deliveries earned Moscow billions in hard currency and saved the not-inconsiderable costs of otherwise having to destroy the transferred hardware," the sceptical analyst noted. "And the UER got excellent propaganda mileage out of giving impoverished people useful equipment like transport helicopters, trucks, engineering vehicles and communications systems to aid in famine relief and economic development.

"Phase Two started after the stand-down on December 27 and ran until Easter Sunday, April 11 of this year. In January the constitutional talks, suspended after the murders in November, resumed. But they were broken off again in March over the issues of voting age and special representation for tribal homelands and white-majority districts. Intertribal warfare flared up again.

"At the Ides of March, FLS troops again massed at the borders of South Africa, hoping to provoke Pretoria to attack them. This time, the Front Line States were supported by direct foreign military participation, not just the black Cubans secretly left behind in Angola. The return of the Cubans violated the 1989 Namibia accords and the number of North Korean advisers in southern Africa tripled. Materiel stockpiles greatly increased, including assault bridging equipment for the first time. All this hardware was left in place when the troops stood down again in April.

"Phase Three is now under way. Phase Four will be invasion. A million African, Eurasian and client-state troops are being assembled for the onslaught on South Africa. They will be equipped with hundreds of thousands of trucks, tens of thousands of armored vehicles and heavy weapons and thousands of combat aircraft. South Africa is overwhelmingly outnumbered and faces guerrilla action on the home front. Russian intervention cancels Pretoria's nuclear deterrent. The attacker has the advantage of picking his time and place; American forces are dispersed. Even if only contingently, we must plan now. Thank you, Mr. President."

Horowitz shuffled back to his seat. Epstein was ready to refute each of the DIA analyst's points, but not as eagerly as usual. He felt tired.

1143, Saturday, 15 May
Gwelo, Zimbabwe

Comrade Colonel Li Sung Hwa swung his MiG-29 smartly to the left off the taxiway and applied the toe brakes in response to the ground crewman's signal. Retarding the throttles, Li waited a moment as his wheels were chocked, then activated the canopy mechanism. Almost immediately the boarding ladder was in place and the forty-six-year-old fighter ace unstrapped from the cockpit, removed his helmet and descended with studied casualness.

Li donned his uniform hat and regarded the reception party, standing respectfully at attention. Many eyes were drawn to the twenty-four victory stars painted on his fighter's nose—testament to his skill and experience in almost a dozen wars over twenty-five years. They were generic red stars, though he would have preferred the insignia of America, Pakistan, Israel, Iran and a few others. He returned the salute, then strode forward to receive a bouquet from a small girl escorted by the base commander. A red and yellow ribbon proclaimed, "Zimbabwe welcomes the Democratic People's Republic of Korea Air Force." It was almost impossible to talk above the jet noise, which suited Li. He caught the sideways glance of General Edward Mweru and knew the meaning. *This African finds my disfigurement at once fascinating and abhorrent,* Li thought. *It's the same everywhere.*

Embarrassed, the Zimbabwean instantly returned his gaze to the other MiGs taxiing into line. The Korean's reputation was well-known in socialist states, as were the scars on his face. Reportedly the four-year-old Li Sung Hwa had suffered terrible burns in an American bombing raid on his hometown of Chongjin in the early '50s.

The Fulcrum regiment arrived by squadrons, ten minutes apart, and Li stood riveted in place until each fighter landed. With the reception committee, he watched the taxiing line of twin-engine, twin-tailed MiGs, their engine inlet doors closed to prevent ingestion of foreign objects. It was a matter of pride to Li and his handpicked pilots that each MiG-29 represented as much investment of time and materials as the Americans' vaunted F-14 Tomcat.

Li reflected on the effort that had gone into forming his unit. It had been an uphill battle, taking years of political and professional cajoling, bullying and sometimes threatening. *But we did it,* he thought, *and here is the proof.* The sense of pride and accomplishment he felt were almost visible as the fortieth and last fighter was guided to its spot and shut down.

Ironically, Li thought, his common language with his hosts was English. The language of imperialism and fascism, the language of The Main Enemy. He turned to the Zimbabwe commander and said, "General"—he did not try to pronounce the strange name—"my regiment and Democratic People's Republic of Korea, we thank you for welcome. I am proud presenting you finest fighters of my nation for victory over fascism." With that, Li gestured toward the ordered rows of his pilots, who saluted in unison as if they had rehearsed the move. Which was exactly the case.

Returning the salute, Edward Mweru strode toward the first squadron, beaming his welcome. He saw no warmth or appreciation in the stolid Mongoloid faces beneath the white helmets. But he'd expected none. The general recalled the dossier on this unit; how Li had formed it against high-level opposition to its elite nature, anathema in a communist society. How Li had ruthlessly cut away all but the absolute minimum of political "education" and influence. These men were finely trained, highly motivated and completely devoted to their commander. In short, they were as close to apolitical professionals as one would find in their nation, where ideological ardor and allegiance to the despotic Kims counted for more than competence. But Mweru expected great things of his Korean guests. Judging by what little he had seen thus far, he would not be disappointed.

1317
SADF National Command Center

During the second massing of Front Line forces at the borders in March, Christiaan de Villiers had reentombed himself under Outlook Hill. The enemy had stood down at Christmas and again just before Easter. In April, he had felt resurrected. Now here he was, buried alive for the third time since late November. He had not seen daylight since Monday. When he was condemned to his subterranean prison this month, the general had expected no prompt reprieve.

Still wearing most of his uniform, the chief of the South

African Defence Force stretched out on a cot in the small antechamber off his stuffy office. De Villiers figured that he had not slept for thirty-one hours, yet he could not drift off. *I'm becoming like one of those researchers that go down in caves and lose track of time,* he thought.

His mind couldn't let go of its worries, nor would his body relax. He tried to unwind, using stress-reduction techniques suggested by his staff medical officer, practices he must have learned from a Hindu fakir. It was damned ridiculous, but de Villiers followed prescribed procedure. He was still concentrating on his toes when the office phone just beyond the door rang rudely. Within seconds Major Sluys knocked. "Yes," the grumpy chief of general staff answered wearily.

"It's President van der Merwe, sir," the aide reported, "calling to schedule the Security Council meeting. Wants to know if half an hour is too soon."

"Tell him 'fine.' Give me a minute and I'll be out." He sagged deeper in the cot for a moment, then dragged himself into a slumped sitting position. The general hoisted himself up, lurched forward and caught the edge of a small washbasin. After steadying himself, he splashed water on his face, dried off and combed his hair and mustache. De Villiers was proud of his full head of hair. He fastened his top button, adjusted his tie, pulled on his tunic, straightened his posture and opened the door.

1406

Once again, the chief of staff allowed the youthful National Intelligence Service head to make his case for him. Davie Steyn detailed the latest developments on the border. Not only had the Front Line State troops returned in even greater numbers and with more and better equipment, but foreign "advisers" had multiplied as well. He explained that these had totaled in the thousands during the November–December buildup, in the tens of thousands in March and April, but now approached 100,000. About half were Eurasian; the rest included Koreans, Vietnamese and Arabs, but Cubans—many of whom had been in Africa over ten years—still dominated among the non-Russian "allies." The new forward airfields, roads and rail links made it possible to increase these numbers virtually overnight.

"Significantly, their deployments for the first time suggest offensive patterns," Steyn continued. "As before, the half-million-plus FLS troops are spread all along the frontier behind field fortifications in essentially defensive postures. They are clustered around key points, of course, but the whole border is manned at some density. The average is three or four meters per man—enough to blunt an attack but far too low to mount one.

"But the foreign 'volunteer' units are obviously concentrating around road crossings and other favorable positions from which to launch assaults. Of course, the FLSes have told the UN that this is merely to bolster their own defenses against our encroachments." His listeners made derisive noises. "During the previous two buildups, the non-African troops were primarily specialists and aviators. They generally were deployed well behind the front lines, unless leading cross-border recces or engineer or signal units working on the fortifications. Now they include combat forces—mechanized infantry, tank, self-propelled artillery, air defense and antitank units. Equipment scales indicate full battalions, but so far they're manned only at caretaker level. Clearly, regiments or brigades are being assembled. We expect that these will be concentrated into division- or corps-sized formations.

"The conclusion is inescapable, gentlemen. Our enemies are preparing to attack. The first two holiday buildups and stand-downs were plainly meant to desensitize us. The final decision to go ahead may not have been made yet in Moscow, Luanda and Maputo, but all the necessary steps are being taken to permit that option. The likeliest date is during or shortly before the Independence Day weekend. That gives us two weeks at best.

"Clearly, the plan is for the better-equipped and trained non-African formations to smash through our border defenses deep into our heartland, while the FLS infantry holds the frontier against any counterattacks we may mount. After the initial penetrations, the lower-quality African formations may advance along broad fronts to mop up resistance, consolidate the gains of the armored formations and occupy our homeland.

"We urge full and rapid mobilization. Our preparedness

may help deter the final onslaught. Despite the great disruption and economic costs to the nation this move will entail, not to mention the political cost to our party, we cannot afford to be caught unprepared. The danger justifies the risks."

Silence greeted Steyn's remarks. State President van der Merwe quietly asked for de Villiers's assessment.

"Your general staff concur with NIS, sir," the SADF chief said. "It's essential at this time. You know I resisted mobilization previously just so that the people would be more accepting when and if the need arose. It now has. Our limited call-ups in December and March helped us get the bugs out of the system, so we expect that mass mobilization will run fairly smoothly. We've also updated our lists of addresses and phone numbers and tested our procedure over the past month."

The general paused and Steyn rushed in. "I move we vote," he said. The defense minister seconded the motion. Van der Merwe called for the vote. It passed unanimously.

0227 Local, Sunday, 16 May
Varyag, North Atlantic

"We are 162 nautical due east of Sal Island, Admiral." The flagship's navigator indicated their position on the track chart of the dimly lit flag bridge. "If we average fifteen knots during the refueling period, we will clear the Cape Verdes completely in nine hours. Right on schedule."

Rybakov nodded absentmindedly and turned away from the chart table. He walked to the port wing of the bridge and stared eastward, as if seeking sight of Mauritania 222 miles into the blackness. He turned back to the navigator. "Are you beginning to understand why I chose this route?"

The captain third rank was caught off guard. He knew the fleet commander liked to toss unexpected questions at staffers, but this took him by surprise. The navigation officer on a Russian warship is nominally its exec or first assistant commander, designated BCh-1 for first combat department head. Nevertheless, navigators usually steered where ordered, regardless of the reason behind those orders. He opened his mouth to speak, wondering what he was going to say.

"Sir, we needed to refuel from the tankers left behind by the amphibious group," *Varyag's* BCh-1 suggested at last. He wondered why the amphibious ships had continued south after the exercises ended, preceding the carriers rather than turning for home, but knew better than to ask.

"Certainly," the admiral responded, "but we could just as easily have met the oilers to the west of the Cape Verdes, out of the main shipping lanes."

"But this route is shorter," the navigator assayed. Since he didn't know their destination, he couldn't be sure of that, so added, "Unless we're headed for Brazil."

"True, we save time and fuel on this course," Rybakov allowed. "But I'll tell you something else," he said, sparing the man further agony. "By sailing between the mainland and the Cape Verdes, we put some breathing space between ourselves and the American battle groups northwest of us. They cannot track us here from their position farther north without diverting to avoid Verdean airspace." Rybakov waved a deprecating hand. "Oh, I know. They can follow us by satellite anyway. But the North Atlantic is a huge body of water and this is one of the world's busiest trade routes. It's hard to distinguish large warships from big freighters by satellite, and we're remaining under electronic silence." He looked into the night again, where signal lights blinkered messages from ship to ship.

"And if they persist in trailing us, their shortest course will take them through Verdean waters," Rybakov added. "Where they will necessarily have to slow down," he concluded. *A bit more than usual, if the Verdeans keep their bargain,* he thought.

Turning his attention to the chart again, Rybakov motioned the navigator close. "You know, Brukov, naval combat is much like chess. The contest is played out upon a vast board, divided into squares by degrees of latitude and longitude. The many classes of warships available to each contestant equate to the types of chess pieces; each according to its combination of mobility, range and power. Yes, I am a chess master. But I am striving to become a master of naval combat."

"Yes, Admiral," the navigator replied noncommittally.

Capable enough, Rybakov assessed the man, not for the first time. *But no spark of innovation, not a thinker. He sees his duty as a means to itself instead of a means to a larger end.* Still, he decided to prod Brukov once more. "You know, the trick to winning at chess or naval warfare is to learn all the rules so you can break them at the right time."

"Yes, sir. I see what you mean." Brukov's eyes were dark ovals beneath his visored hat.

Oh, no you don't, Rybakov decided. *But I do.*

0654, Monday, 17 May
Welkom, Orange Free State

Dirk Vorster peacefully dreamed violent dreams. One moment he was happily butchering an endless row of steer carcasses, and the next he was rudely poked awake. He opened his eyes, ready to lash out at his tormentor, but the first thing he saw was the barrel of a twelve-gauge fifteen centimeters from his face. Behind it was an out-of-focus shape in two shades of blue, and behind that, another. Then he remembered where he was. He smiled.

"Good morning," he said in Afrikaans, sitting up slowly with his hands open. Without making a fist, Vorster rubbed the sleep from his eyes.

"Good morning, *Meneer,*" the young jailer replied. "The colonel wants to see you."

Early-morning interrogation, Vorster thought. *Good technique.* But he said, "Fine, just let me make water first."

The junior copper kept his shotgun in Vorster's back while the Boer used the loo. He knew he could take the gun-toting youth, who was standing far too close, but there was no point. He would never make it out of the jail. So he shook off, zipped up and extended his hands behind his back to be cuffed.

0703

The South African Police colonel was a tired-looking bureaucratic sort. He yawned, ordered Vorster recuffed with his hands in front of him and offered the prisoner some coffee.

"As you know, *Meneer,*" the station chief began, "under the martial-law rules, we can hold you without charge for another day. If you haven't cooperated and we can convince a judge of your probable guilt, we can hold you three more days. In your case, we could probably get detention extensions almost indefinitely."

"Fine with me," Vorster replied, yawning in turn. "Your food's not bad, your beds are just right. The rooms are on the chilly side, though."

"Your family must miss you and your income."

"We have a lot of friends." Vorster emphasized *a lot*.

"Yes, well, it's about those friends that we'd like to question you."

"So I gathered. What they do outside my house is none of my business."

"Look," the colonel sneered, raising a finger. "You know we can hold you for questioning until the next century or the lifting of the state of emergency, whichever comes first. Is that really what you want?"

"I already told you, I don't know anything," Vorster replied evenly. *And I don't know what you want, either.*

"Come off it, Vorster. We have witnesses who identified your mobile slaughter lorry near the scene of both armories on the nights of the break-ins. Cosmoline and explosives residues were found in your van. At the least, we could try you as an accomplice in theft of government property."

"Residues? *You* come off it, Colonel. I use firearms in my work, and explosives fumes could be almost any chemical. You have the weakest kind of circumstantial evidence, and you know it. Look at your witnesses—a couple of Kaffir farmhands. No jury of my peers is going to put me away on what you've got. *My* witnesses will say that I was slaughtering at their farms."

"Your bravado may be admirable, Vorster, but I should tell you that the federal authorities seem to think they can link you to some very serious crimes. My superiors tell me that they have suspects who are willing to talk about some of your previous activities, acts that make theft of government property and blowing up union meeting places look like crossing against a traffic light."

"So there's some crooks someplace who'll say whatever the state wants to lighten their sentences. That'll make a big impression on a jury." He kept up an unconcerned front. But beneath his tan he blanched at the news and hoped the copper couldn't see the blood draining from his skin.

The colonel eyed him for several seconds, then looked at some papers. "Well, here's something else for you to think about, Vorster. Last night the government ordered certain categories of Citizen Force reservists mobilized. Now, I see by your file that you are a platoon sergeant, so you fit. I also see that your record is exemplary. My guess is that if there's going to be a war to save our people, you want to be in it. Not as some thief in the night, but as a soldier fighting for your way of life." The colonel paused; Vorster said nothing.

"Now look here," the colonel continued. "I vote Conservative, just like you. If I were a younger man and not on government service, I might be a bit of a White Wolf myself. I daresay some of the younger fellows around here might do more than just sympathize with you. But you got nicked. And, in a time of crisis like this, we can't have our armories pillaged to equip private armies." He raised a hand to cut off Vorster's reply. "Don't bother denying it. At the very least, you're guilty of extreme indiscipline. Your record shows you know better. Whatever you may think of the government's kowtowing to the blacks, you're a soldier. Legally, of course, we all are. But I suspect *you'd* have volunteered for the border fifteen years ago if there had been no draft. Yet you endangered your comrades by stealing those automatic weapons and plastique. Perhaps you even endangered your own unit.

"Now, I'm prepared to offer you a deal. Return the stolen material and I promise no questions will be asked. You don't have to give us any names. In exchange, I'll release you with a clean record, so you can join your company. It's up to me; the state's attorney will accept my estimate of the evidence. If we charge you, not only will you stay here, but you are out of the army for good. If this deal isn't what you want, then you're not the man, nor the patriot, I think you are."

Vorster was quiet a moment, then replied, "If by rumor I happen to know where a cache might be, how do I know you'll keep your word to release me free and clear?"

"I give you my oath as a fellow *Broederbonder*," he said, having noted the prisoner's membership in the men's association of the Dutch Reformed Church. "What more can I do?"

"I've learned not to trust high-sounding idealists," Vorster sneered. "But I want in this fight, if it comes. So I guess

I have to trust you. I'll call you this afternoon, saying where to find the goods. Don't follow me, or the deal's off. I'll rot in jail before I'll betray my . . . anything or anybody that stands by me." He extended his hands.

"Uncuff him," the colonel ordered.

Vorster rubbed his wrists and smiled. The colonel reached across the desk. The two men shook hands.

"Don't make me regret this decision, Vorster," the policeman said, still grasping the ex-prisoner's hand.

"I'll kill a bloody red Kaffir for you, Colonel," the butcher replied. "Give me your phone number."

Instead of a business card, the officer scribbled his private line on a scrap of paper and handed it over. "Here, destroy that when you're done. Now get out of here." Vorster acknowledged the command with a lupine smile. "And good luck, Vorster."

1145 Local
Ready Room One, Langley, *Gonzo Station*

Ozzie Ostrewski opened the refrigerator and withdrew a Classic Coke—he'd gone through eight months of withdrawal symptoms when the original formula was unavailable back in '85—and marked his tab on the sheet. For the 200th time he read the sign taped to the door: "Duty officers failing to keep this space clean will be ostracized." Beneath the legend, somebody had neatly penciled, "With a dull ostracizer."

On the bulkhead next to the fridge was a hand-painted sign bearing the conventional wisdom of the Fightin' Felines. It read:

VF-181 Lessons to Live By

1. You can only do what you can do.
2. You won't rise to the occasion—you'll default to your level of training.
3. There's no such thing as a free lunch.
4. A little subtle keying helps on radio calls.
5. At 90 degrees angle of bank, the lift slides off the wings.

6. Use the sun, but remember everyone else is there.

7. Be King Kong on the radar and have King Kong eyes.

8. When the BBs are flying, it's time for your Last Best Move.

9. Think big—think basics—and cheat like hell.

10. When planning a fight, see Rule No. 1.

Nobody applied the rules better than Ozzie. Now, with his Coke in one hand, he mussed his crew-cut hair with the other as the mission debrief wrapped up. He and Fido had just kicked some serious butt.

"Well, that's it," summarized the squadron CO, Buzzard McBride. "As usual, Ozzie won two out of three setups. The third was a standoff." The fact that the skipper had again been on the receiving end of a patented Ostrewski trimming seemed perfectly normal. The Felines usually saved some fuel for a few short hassles before landing back aboard *Langley,* and the Ostrewski/Colley team seemed camped at the top of the squadron's air-combat maneuvering ladder.

"Oz, you're slipping," intoned McBride's RIO, "Teeny." "Normally you're three for three." He was still pale, his skin clammy. Like most fleet RIOs, he puked at least once a year, and Buzzard had really been bending the airplane today.

"Well, even the world's greatest Polish fighter pilot can have an off day," Ozzie replied with a grin. He quickly interjected, "Even Fido's gotta cut me some slack now and then." Most F-14 pilots were careful to include their RIOs in such conversations—some people spoke as if the pilot were alone in a Tomcat.

Teeny snorted in mock derision. "Yeah, the world's greatest Polish fighter pilot is likely to hose his leader on the cat."

Ozzie set down his Coke and turned on his most earnest voice. "You may be interested to know, Lieutenant Feeney, that in World War Deuce there were over forty Polish aces. Skalski got twenty-one Germans and Urbanowicz bagged twenty total—including a Russian and two or three Japs. Gladych and Horbacewski were both triple aces and then some. Not to mention that great American, Gabby Gabreski

—twenty-eight Krauts and six and a half MiGs. But he was an air force puke."

The RIO's face betrayed his amazement. "Geez, where you'd hear all that? 'The World Book of Trivia'?"

"It's well-documented—for anybody who can read. Ask Fido; he's seen the record book." Colley rolled his eyes and shrugged eloquently. The RIO lived in dread that Ozzie would some day start playing polkas over the F-14's intercom.

McBride waved a deprecating hand. "Ancient history, Oz. Besides, none of us is likely to *see* twenty MiGs in a lifetime, let alone bag that many."

"CO, Polish people are very spiritual. Michael is the Patron Saint of Poland. I'm named for him and I pray to him regularly." The others couldn't tell if Ozzie were serious or not. Religion was seldom a ready-room topic.

"Pray for what?" asked Teeny.

Ozzie stood up. "I pray for MiGs. Lots and lots of MiGs." Fred Colley knew that Ozzie Ostrewski was as serious as a Sidewinder up the tailpipe.

4

19 to 22 May

0204 Local, Wednesday, 19 May
The Equator, Mid-Atlantic

The watch officer called out the reading, "One minute north latitude; twelve degrees, twenty-six minutes, nine seconds west longitude" on the GLONASS satellite navigation receiver—like the U.S. GPS, a system accurate to within meters. *A nautical mile north of the equator,* Rybakov realized. *Three minutes to go.* He walked out onto the port bridge wing. With more than a twenty-knot breeze on his face, he remembered the first time he crossed the Line. That was in the Indian Ocean during the global blue-water exercises of April 1970. Under the rigid class system of the Soviet military, he was spared the humiliation of the vile Line Crossing ceremony—for which he was grateful then but sorry now.

On that first crossing, he had been in the aircraft control station of helicopter carrier *Leningrad,* looking aft over the short flight deck. The forward three-fifths of the second *Moskva*-class carrier looked like a missile cruiser, heavily armed with antiaircraft and antisub weapons. For the Soviet Navy, operating 17,000-ton *Moskva* and *Leningrad,* though they were just barely carriers, was a learning experience, and no one had learned more about handling aircraft at sea than Pyotr Rybakov.

As a thirty-three-year-old captain third rank and *Lenin-*

grad's BCh-6, head of its air department, he commanded fourteen Ka-25 antisub helos. He knew that the 38,000-ton *Kiev* was to be laid down that year in the same Black Sea yard that had built *Leningrad* and *Moskva*. Yet the Russian Navy was a submarine force and would always remain so. He had seen real aircraft carriers, including USS *Enterprise*— the world's first CVN or nuclear-powered carrier. It seemed that few besides himself dreamed that Russia would ever build its own big-deck flattops. *We can't afford them,* he realized, *but we have them anyway, and now have found a use for them.*

Not even Rybakov, the young dreamer, expected in 1970 that he would one day command a task force centered on *two* real, 65,000-ton carriers, with over 300 fixed-wing aircraft and helos under his control, including forty-eight of the world's finest air-superiority fighters, sixty-four other conventional takeoff jets and forty-eight jumpjets.

The tropic sun was blazing that day in 1970; True Communism was expected within a decade. Since then, the bloodthirsty, false god of Marxism had claimed millions of more lives and squandered trillions of rubles, but the Russian navy had grown and prospered beyond the dreams of avarice, though not beyond those of the late Fleet Admiral of the Soviet Union, Sergei Gorshkov, or of Fleet Admiral Pyotr Rybakov, very much alive at fifty-six.

At the advanced age of thirty-seven, he had gone through jumpjet flight school. This departure from the usual path to command of a first-rank warship risked more than just his career. But completion—and survival—of the course made then-Captain First Rank Rybakov the obvious choice to command *Kiev*, the first Soviet carrier to operate fixed-wing aircraft. Now, from flagship *Varyag*, he was commanding a carrier battle group and the task force of which it was a part. No other officer had served in such responsible positions on all three classes of Russian carriers.

The navy remained a submarine force; Fleet Admiral of the Eurasian Union Sorokin was the second submariner in a row to serve as its C-in-C. Success off South Africa would assure Rybakov of exchanging the four smaller stars on his shoulder for a single large one, the naval equivalent of Marshal of the Eurasian Union. Despite being a surface and air officer, he would surely follow Sorokin—the only desk job Rybakov had ever wanted.

One of the powers that might deny him that job was still 2,000 miles behind him to the north. On the fifteenth, U.S. *Nimitz*-class CVNs *Eisenhower* and *Roosevelt* had both suddenly altered course. *Ike* had quit following the diversionary *Kiev* group ever deeper into sub-Arctic Canadian waters and *TR* had returned to Norfolk, presumably to prepare for forward deployment. After clearing the southern limit of sea ice, *Ike* had steamed south-southeast at high speed, trying to close the distance between herself and the Russian carriers then refueling underway past the Cape Verdes. *Eisenhower* had far outpaced its Russian spy trawlers, but from submarines, Tu-142 maritime patrol planes and RORSats—nuclear-powered, radar ocean surveillance satellites—Rybakov knew that the CVN would enter the 200-mile zone claimed by the Verdeans for their exclusive economic use.

He also knew that in the Indian Ocean, *Kiev*-class V/STOL carrier *Novorossiysk* had left Sri Lanka, steaming west. A direct course from Sumatra to South Africa would have taken her too close to the American base at Diego Garcia in the Chagos Archipelago in the middle of the Indian Ocean. It might also have tipped the Russians' hand. So the Pacific Fleet carrier group proceeded west across the northern Indian Ocean toward a rendezvous with Black Sea Fleet carriers *Moskva* and *Leningrad*. Rybakov's old ship was once again operating in the waters it had known when young. The twenty-five-year-old hybrid cruiser-carrier—designed to hunt U.S. ballistic missile subs armed in 1965 with Polaris missiles—was no longer the pride of the Russian surface fleet. But it could prove useful in supporting amphibious landings.

Although Rybakov approved when Leningrad voted to revert to St. Petersburg, he was glad that the carrier had not been renamed. The government said *Leningrad* now commemorated the siege of 1941–43, not the city. The admiral felt there had already been too many ship name changes. Carriers *Baku* to *Gorshkov*; *Brezhnev* to *Tbilisi* to *Kuznetsov*; *Riga* to *Varyag*; cruiser *Kuznetsov* to *Lobov*. It was to punish rebellious republics, but it made the navy look ridiculous. Wisely, the service had not renamed less-visible ships, many of which honored organs of the disbanded Communist Party.

After the Eurasian carrier groups combined, they would head south down the east coast of Africa and through the Mozambique channel to take up stations off Durban, Natal and the Eastern Cape cities of Port Elizabeth and East London.

Overhead, Rybakov admired the mix of familiar and strange constellations. He located the Southern Cross, its upright post pointing toward the South Pole, off to his right. He picked out the great trans-equatorial constellation of Orion. Working south from the Hunter's belt, he found the brightest star in the heavens—Sirius, the Dog Star—forming the chest of Canis Major. On cloudless nights over the Black Sea, he had watched Orion pursue Taurus, the bull, along the celestial equator from southeast in mid-winter to southwest in early spring. Now *Eisenhower* was the hunter, chasing Rybakov southeasterly across the terrestrial equator. Orion never caught Taurus, and the American would not catch Rybakov in time.

The admiral inhaled deep drafts of the tropical air. The shortest course from the bulge of West Africa to the Cape of Good Hope took his ships away from land. They would make excellent time through the lonely South Atlantic. This crossing of the Line came at night, but Rybakov's future had never appeared brighter. Looking past *Varyag*'s flight deck, he saw the lights of cruisers *Lobov* and *Azov*. In the wakes of these mighty warships, the sea phosphoresced.

1700 Local, Thursday, 20 May
USS Langley, *Gonzo Station*

"Why does it always have to be called the Fo'c'sle Follies?" Gremlin whined. "Every boat in the world uses that term."

Brillo leaned forward in his folding chair, his elbows on the wardroom table. "Because the awards are always given in the ship's fo'c'sle, that's why." Lieutenant Commander Peter Huggins mussed his wiry brown hair and shook his head at the new aviators. *Nuggets,* he thought. *Appoint 'em to a committee and suddenly they're king.*

Lieutenant (Junior Grade) Dennis Gresham, a blond electronic countermeasures officer in *Langley*'s Prowler squadron, felt defensive. He was aware that as a first-cruise aviator he had much to learn. But he also thought that he brought some badly needed original thinking to the Air Wing 18 "follies." At the end of the current line period, the traditional party would honor *Langley*'s top pilots—those at the apex of the landing-grade ladder. But squadron as well as individual honors would be determined, and Gremlin—so named for his uncanny ability at tracing electronic glitches— was VAQ-144's representative.

"Okay, I guess it doesn't matter what we call the . . . follies," Gresham replied. "But let's do something different. Like give the centurion awards near the mirror instead of on the fo'c'sle." He eyed Brillo's flight jacket, which bore patches for 200 landings on *Langley*—a "double centurion."

The A-6 pilot nodded. "Yeah, that's fine by me. Good photo opportunity, too. Maybe we'll get more pictures in *The Hook*." There were grins around the table. Each air wing seemed to vie with the rest of the navy for most ink and photos in the quasi-professional journal of carrier aviation. Junior officers' fitness reports had been known to be determined on how successful squadron public-affairs officers were at hyping their units.

"Hey, Gremlin, speaking of photos, I saw your brother's picture in the paper a while ago." Lieutenant Eric "Psycho" Thaler, a Hornet pilot, enjoyed verbal jousting with anybody, anytime. "You didn't admit he's an air force puke."

Gremlin waved a hand in dismissal. "Hey, man. I don't dig up your family skeletons." Despite his tone of voice, Dennis Gresham was extremely proud of his older brother John. "But, yeah. Hooter's an F-16 driver at Kunsan. He made ace in that Korean thing a while back." He gave Psycho an evil grin. "Uh, how many MiGs you got, babe?"

Thaler thumbed his nose palooka-style. "Hey," he mumbled, "I coulda been a contendah. My brudda shoulda looked out for me some, ya know?"

Huggins shook his head. He didn't know how these fads got started, but *Langley*'s current mania was movie dialogue. He tapped the table with his pencil. "Guys, can we keep this meeting on track? Now, somebody has to make the squadron badges . . ."

On cue, the six other fliers around the table rose to the occasion in lusty unison. "*BATCHES? WE DON' NEED NO STEENKIN' BATCHES!*"

Brillo threw his pencil into the air. With a pleading look upward he asked the immortal question, "Where do we get such men?"

0826 EDT, Friday, 21 May
White House

Callaway paced the Oval Office with giant strides, flapping his arms and hollering. "Just *whom* do they think they're dealing with here?" the President shouted. "You know it was the Russians!" he yelled toward the CNO. "I know it was the Russians! I'm gonna make 'em pay."

Callaway's first pass in front of his desk caught Fernandez unawares. The CNO narrowly dodged an uppercut to the jaw from his commander in chief's long right arm. Fernandez lay down his pointer, sidled away from the easel holding a map of the central Atlantic and kept a respectful distance. He had unpleasant memories of boxing with the beanpole at Annapolis—not much power but long reach and lots of desire to win.

"Did you catch Churkin on CNN?" Callaway asked, turning on Dr. Epstein.

"How can he dish out that crap? He must know better, but then maybe not. There's people in this country who sound just like him."

That kind of talk smacked of McCarthyism and made Epstein uneasy, but he kept quiet. He also steered clear of Callaway's warpath, a semicircle around the front of the desk, already well-worn only four months into the administration. Now, even before the CNO could provide the White House with an update on the *Eisenhower* incident, the President was already riled. "They're guilty as sin. More innocent blood on their hands."

Callaway took a breather and leaned against his desk, built from timbers of H.M.S. *Resolute*—once it had been rescued from Arctic ice by a Yankee whaler—and given to Rutherford B. Hayes's White House by Queen Victoria.

"What's the latest on the wounded sailors?" Callaway asked.

"Another one died about two hours ago—CPO Johnson; he wasn't expected to make it. Three of the others are still critical. The rest will probably pull through, but to see those boys they're still working on at Bethesda . . . well, it makes me want payback, I can tell you that."

"I'm gonna go see 'em," the President promised. "Okay, what's the latest on what happened?"

"Well, it now looks like *Prouse* will make port, assuming the weather holds. The blast pretty near tore her bow off; it's just held on by the deck plating. We may have to cut it off en route to Las Palmas. We'll patch 'er up there and then bring her home or send a floating dry dock out to her.

"She's the same kind of ship as *Roberts,* you know, the *Perry*-class frigate that struck a mine in the Gulf. *Stark*'s one, too. For low-end of the mix ships, they really take a beating."

"Any more on how it happened?"

"Well, she was out ahead of the carrier, looking for subs. We're still investigating, but right now it doesn't look like there was any negligence. In the dark, she never saw the mine. Those crude old things pack quite a wallop. We're lucky only six men—seven—were killed and sixteen wounded, as of this morning.

"We figure the Verdeans actually sowed the mines themselves, probably from barges, like the Iranians, or large fishing craft. Maybe less than an hour before *Prouse* ran into one. A vessel of the right size was detected in that area, but we can't ID it from radar tapes. Wooden boats can be mis-leading."

The President lurched forward off the desk edge and made two passes in silence. Epstein could see that Callaway was mulling something over in his swampy mind; the adviser felt sure he would shudder when he found out what it was. Suddenly the President stopped, straightened and addressed Fernandez. "So, where does that leave us?"

"Well, the Kremlin's denial of complicity is plausible on the face of it," the CNO responded. "Cape Verde could have gotten the mines direct from Iran, but more likely they got 'em from the Russians, with Libya as a cut-out. Making the rap stick, well, that's another matter."

"Yeah, but I want to bust 'em. How would you make the case?"

"In court or on TV?"

"Either. Both."

"Well, I'm the wrong guy to ask. I already believe the Russians are almost always up to no good, and you know what I think they're up to at the moment. But, for circumstantial evidence, this just does them too much good to be coincidental."

"Won't hold up in court."

"Well, it doesn't help anybody else, but it achieved what I think the Russians' goal was—to slow up the *Eisenhower* group. Bear in mind that *Kiev's* screen interfered with *Ike* and her escorts when they turned south on Saturday, as if dodging icebergs wasn't bad enough. They did everything but ram our ships."

"Don't think I've forgotten, Hub," the President reassured him. "We're still pursuing diplomatic protests, aren't we, Doctor?" Epstein nodded. "How'd you like to have a first-class bi—er, great American like Starla Parry hounding you?" Callaway asked, referring to the secretary of state.

"Well sir, I suspect she cares a lot more what happens in South Africa than to American sailors in the North Atlantic."

"You're way out of line, there, *Admiral*," Callaway said icily, much to Epstein's appreciation.

Damn my big mouth, Fernandez thought. *Even CNO has a boss.* "Yes, sir. You're right," he said with meaning. *But Buddy knows I'm right.*

"Just don't do it again," the President said. "Now, back to your area of responsibility. What else do we have on the Russians?"

"Well, last night, the group based on their helo carriers *Moskva* and *Leningrad,* operating as you recall south of the Yemeni island of Socotra, headed south by southwest. The oilers and amphibious ships in that group had already gone south two days ago. They're all on courses that would take them down the Mozambique Channel between Madagascar and Mozambique. Then this morning we spotted the *Novorossiysk* group. They've also veered southwest from their previous heading, on a course that'll take 'em past the east side of Madagascar, west of Reunion Island. I don't see how anybody can doubt that the Russian carrier groups will congregate off South Africa."

"Mr. President," Epstein spoke up. "As I've noted before, most of these movements were announced in advance, at least in broad terms."

"They didn't say anything about amphibious ships preceding the carriers," Fernandez replied. "Normally you'd expect them to return home after distant exercises, not proceed even farther away. But let me finish connecting these movements with the minings. As I said, I believe they were to slow down *Ike*'s CVBG, just like the *Kiev* group's interference and its approach to Canada in the first place. Same goes for *Lincoln* following *Minsk* toward the Aleutians." Callaway waved him on.

"First, the mining costs the *Eisenhower* group two escorts, the mined frigate and a destroyer to tow her to the Canaries. Second, the rest of the force has to hold up waiting for us to send extra choppers capable of towing minesweeping sleds. Then the group has to go slow while the choppers sweep and so its lookouts can spot floating mines. Third, the Kremlin probably figured we'd retaliate against military targets in the Cape Verdes, such as they are. Launching a strike might slow us down some more. The Verdeans have some ex-Soviet Osa-class fast attack craft armed with antiship cruise missiles and some shore-based missile launchers. Their SS-N-2 Styx missiles are old and slow and don't pose much threat, but a lucky hit would slow us down just that much more. Fourth, assuming we do retaliate, that draws attention away from the Sov . . . uh, Russian surface action groups, which are now in the South Atlantic. Focusing attention on our supposedly aggressive acts serves their interests at this point."

"Great," Callaway said with a sigh. "I have to convince the world that the Russians are about to attack South Africa so I can persuade everybody that the Kremlin was behind this incident. Fat chance. Hell, you haven't completely sold *me* on the deal yet, although this mining sure as hell reduces sales resistance. Their interference with the *Eisenhower* group on Saturday should've tipped me off. But I bought their excuse." The President thought for a moment. "Do you think we should retaliate, Hub?"

"Hell, yes," the CNO responded. "If for no other reason than to uphold the right of innocent passage. The Styx launchers and Osa bases are made-to-order targets. We can hit 'em in passing. Won't slow us down any more than we already are. No sweat."

"Doctor Epstein?"

"I see no point in attacking the Cape Verdes just now. Particularly if Admiral Fernandez's view of Eurasian intentions is correct. If we are to bring our full moral force to bear on peacefully resolving the crisis in South Africa, we can't fritter it away on knee-jerk retaliations against tiny countries."

Talk about knee jerks, Fernandez thought. But he said, "We gotta hit 'em like we hit Ghaddafi after the disco bombing. We can't allow tinhorn dictators to kill American servicemen with impunity."

Callaway resumed marching, audibly grinding his teeth as he strode. On the third cycle he looped behind the dark, oaken desk. With his fingertips pressed against its top, he asked, "Hub, you got anything else for me?" The CNO shook his head.

"Okay, I'm going with the good doctor on this one," the President announced. Fernandez wound up to interject, but Callaway cut him off with a raised hand as dry and long as the Llano Estacado. "I know, I know, it'll make me look like a lily-livered pushover, but so be it. How it'll play politically is my lookout. Overnight polling shows public opinion about evenly divided, so it shouldn't hurt us too much if I don't exact immediate vengeance. That makes it my call."

"Yes, sir," Fernandez replied, clearly disappointed in his old classmate.

"Tell you what I will do. That's what you wanted me to do Friday and I should oughta done, which is move *Kennedy* and *Langley* south. I should've ridden to the sound of the guns, no matter how distant. You warned me the guns were firing. My mistake; I admit it. Brief the other joint chiefs for me, will you?" The CNO assented. "Thanks, Hub. Keep me posted."

Placated, Fernandez said, "Thank *you,* sir. I'll be in the Pentagon Naval Ops Room for the rest of the day." He gathered up his papers and left without wishing Epstein goodbye.

1904 Local
Langley, *Gonzo Station*

Lieutenant Caspar approached the admiral, bent over and whispered in his ear, "Flash for you, sir. Eyes only. Gold Channel."

The battle group commander replied, "Very well," then

pushed back his chair and stood up. His staff did the same. "As you were, gentlemen. I've been called away. I don't know how long this will take. Please carry on."

He followed the flag lieutenant out the room. *Probably the signal Hub gave me the heads up on . . . when was it? Almost a week ago.* Gideon felt excited as he walked the familiar passageways. It was not just anticipation of something new, less routine and more interesting than hot, boring Gonzo Station. He hoped that the message marked the beginning of the time for which he had trained all his life; somehow he sensed that was the case. *Wishful thinking?*

At fifty-one, Gideon felt he would never be better able to handle whatever the mission might be. His physical powers were still impressive, his mental powers agile as ever, formed by the experience of an eventful life during which other people's lives had often depended on his judgment and performance. This was the moment. Gideon was sure of it now. He felt transported. *No more command theory. Action!* The admiral pounded his fist on the bulkhead. *Kid must think I'm nuts,* he thought and, as if to prove it, chuckled to himself and shook his head. "Private joke," he explained.

"Ah, yes, sir. Right, sir," came the response. The young man turned his head only furtively as he spoke to his admiral, who trailed him up the ladder.

1947

Boilerman Third Class Harry Repogle felt like a gladiator preparing to enter the arena. Elbow-length asbestos gloves protected his hands and forearms, while a plastic mask and goggles covered his face. His "weapon" was a lengthy iron rod with which he would do battle with fire. Harry Repogle was a "snipe," one of thousands of below-deck sailors who made things happen in *Langley*. He had never met an aviator.

Walking down the alley between a series of brick fireboxes, Repogle stopped before the designated boiler. He turned and lowered the ladle end of his rod, brimming with fuel oil. His partner, another twenty-year-old named Hector Gonzales, produced a cigarette lighter and ignited a length of oil-soaked rag attached to the ladle. In an instant Repogle's ladle was burning, casting an eerie yellow light in the engineering room.

Repogle inserted his flaming rod into an aperture in the boiler called Alpha One, where rows of water pipes lined the twelve-foot-square cavern. "The torch is still lit," Repogle called. Above and behind him on a grilled platform the chief boilertender gave a thumbs-up and replied, "Do it!"

Standing a few feet to Repogle's right, Gonzales turned a valve counterclockwise. His action induced raw fuel oil, under pressure of compressed air, into the boiler. Gonzales heard the blowers kick in and began his count. "One thousand one." Nothing happened. "One thousand two!" Still nothing. *Come on, come on* . . . If ignition didn't occur in three seconds they would have to shut down to avoid an explosion. "One thou . . ."

Hector Gonzales saw the reflection on Repogle's mask as the torch sparked the fuel-air mixture into a pure, white flame. "Fire's lit, chief!" Repogle withdrew his rod and the two snipes turned away from boiler Alpha One, their watch completed. In three other 1,200-psi boilers fires also were burning, starting to superheat water in the pipes that would evaporate into high-pressure steam to drive turbines. Eventually the four twenty-one-foot-diameter screws at *Langley's* stern would begin to turn, getting the aged carrier underway on an uncertain mission.

0809 EDT, Sunday, 23 May
White House

Buddy Callaway had heard enough. The President launched himself out of his chair, sending it swirling past the American flag toward the drapes. Bent slightly, his shoulders hunched, he charged around his desk and yet again commenced pacing and flailing his arms.

"I tell you, Art, I'm fed up to here with Rodinkov's excuses!" Callaway declared, indicating his prominent Adam's Apple. "No, up to here!" He raised his hand to the level of his nose. "Who do they think I am? Jimmy Carter?"

Epstein gingerly ventured, "As with the Cape Verde minings, sir, we can't actually prove that the Eurasian Union instigated the Suez Canal closing."

"Is that true, Hub? What do we have on the bastards?" Callaway asked.

"Well, sir, Dr. Epstein may be right. The fact that the Libyan tanker turned sideways before sinking is a dead give-away, but without somebody's testimony, some commo intercepts or a paper trail, we can't prove it was intentional. Even if we could, how do you connect the Russians to it? The Mozambican freighter is ostensibly responsible for the so-called accident, which is plausible, given the crew's inexperience."

"You mean to tell me that with all the ferret satellites we have up there, we didn't pick up a single communication in any way connected with this thing? It had to be coordinated. How'd they know right when the JFK group was gonna enter the canal? How'd they slip two ships in ahead of us and another behind us?" Callaway asked.

"Well, sir, the ahead part wasn't too hard, given the length of the canal. And behind, well, it wasn't that hard to coordinate. The freighter evidently went into a holding pattern outside Port Said as soon as it got word that the *Kennedy* group was headed that way. Where the signal for them to move came from, we don't know. The Mozambican that rammed the Libyan had been waiting in the Great Bitter Lake; engine trouble again. It got going just in time to hit the tanker.

"The other thing is, a whole slew of Eurasian merchantmen stuffed to the gunwales with armaments went through the canal just ahead of us," CNO explained. "Big bulk cargo freighters and container ships, plus more militarily-useful types—roll-on/roll-off, etc.—that can unload real quick or at undeveloped ports. Some of the ro/ros even have variable-gauge rails for railroad cars. A real slick operation."

"Damn!" Callaway exclaimed. "Guess I should've listened to you, Hub. Too late now. How long will *Kennedy* be stuck there?"

"Depends. It's a big priority for the Egyptians, but the lack of cooperation from the ships involved slows things up. They've got to pump out the tanker, then raise her from the sandy mud. The oil spill doesn't help. The freighter has been cut free, but of course her boiler's damaged so she has to be towed. Best estimate—ten days to two weeks.

"But *Kennedy's* not stranded permanently. What's

worse is what the Russians are doing in the Mid-Atlantic, across the equator between West Africa and Brazil, and in Indonesia. Remember all those subs I told you about last week?"

"Boy, howdy!" the President exploded.

"Well, sir, some of them are crossing the mid-Atlantic and passing the straits through the Indonesian islands connecting the Pacific and Indian oceans, then adopting defensive postures. We're not sure how many will ultimately be involved, but certainly three dozen; maybe more than forty." Epstein looked down at the sea-green rug.

Callaway's mouth went agape; he sprang forward toward the maps, eyes blazing. "Damn their souls to eternal hell!" he was finally able to enunciate. "Show me," he ordered in a low growl.

The CNO lowered his pointer. "Mr. President, the Russians have sealed off one-quarter of the globe. The quarter containing southern Africa."

At least he hasn't said I told you so, reflected Epstein. *Not yet.*

Callaway glared from one map to the next. The Atlantic —isolated by an apparently impenetrable sub barrier; his closest carrier battle group slowed by mines and the next available one still in port. The Suez Canal—another CVBG bottled up. The Indian Ocean—also isolated, with his nearest carrier weeks away in the North Pacific. The President's fists opened and closed, his fingers grabbing at invisible, out-of-reach throats. The most powerful man in the world appeared the most frustrated. *Damn!* he thought. *I've got me to blame for this; nobody else. Hub warned me.*

The president sat down, stuck his legs under Hayes' desk and pressed his skeletal fingertips to his temples. "About the Cape Verdes. The doctor's right, there. Hub, don't attack any land targets in the Verdes, but go ahead with planning. And *Eisenhower* is authorized to fire on any boat, plane or shore battery that shoots at her or her escorts. Just make sure we have proof of the attack."

"Aye, aye, sir," he replied, none too cheerily.

"Art, I'm going with CNO on getting the 'phibs and maritime prepositioning ships underway from Dee Gar. And on the submarine deal. Hub, give me everything we've got and can spare from other essential ops. When and if it comes time to force these sub barriers they're putting up, I want maximum force. And make all necessary arrangements with Egypt to fly JFK's planes from at anchor and to support 'em at Egyptian bases. You'll have to coordinate with State, distasteful though that may be to you. 'Flanchor' whatever portion of the wing you deem advisable."

"Aye, aye, *sir*," came the more eager response.

"Okay, Hub, you've got your marching orders. I know where to get a hold of you." The President stood. "Thanks a lot. Again."

Fernandez didn't like leaving the President alone with his staff, but the White House was not CNO's realm. "Thank *you,* sir," he said on the way out.

Callaway slumped deeper into the chair, ran his fingers through his hair and took self-appreciative note of Epstein's silence.

After a moment, the adviser regained his composure and said, soothingly, "Mr. President, it's all the more remarkable that you have responded with such restraint and wisdom to what some, even in our own party, have called provocative behavior by our Eurasian friends."

"Yeah, and I hate myself for it. I just hope I don't have more reason to regret not blowing the bastards out of the water before they could assemble so much force around Africa. I hope to hell more American boys don't die because of my laudable restraint." Epstein knew that Callaway's father had died on the carrier *Yorktown* at Midway in 1942.

The President twisted twice more in his seat, then said, "Thanks, Doctor. Your advice has been good. I'm glad you're on board. Any mistakes we make are mine. The whole shooting match is my call."

Epstein asked if there were anything else. The President shook his head; the adviser left without another word. As Epstein closed the door behind him, the restless man sat with his angular elbows perched on the desk, his hands again tucked prayerlike under his chin, motionless for once.

5

24 to 28 May

1839 Local, Monday, 24 May
Varyag, *South Atlantic*

Pyotr Rybakov held out his hands, fists clenched. Sitting across the table in the admiral's flag quarters, Anatoly V. Smirnov tapped Rybakov's left hand. The fist uncurled, palm up, exposing a white pawn. "You always choose the left hand," Rybakov said.

"And you always put white in that hand." The chief of staff smiled.

"We're both predictable, Anatoly Vladimirovich." Rybakov placed the two pawns on their respective sides of the board and sat back, awaiting his friend's first move. "Well, surprise me this time, Smirnov. Do something different!"

The chief of staff laughed. "You mean, like win a game?"

Both men savored these private moments, which were increasingly rare. The situation was only compounded with the merging of the *Varyag* and *Kuznetsov* groups. Smirnov liked to say that when force size doubled, staff work quadrupled.

The elegant dinner recently completed in the flagship's wardroom, with captains of all major vessels in attendance, had been pleasant enough. However, Rybakov was concerned with the air of overconfidence evident during the reception. It smelled faintly of smugness. True, the task force was capable of operating sophisticated fixed-wing jets far from home. But he devoutly wished for more tactical training in his air wings. Pyotr Rybakov had never been accused of complacency.

With his shirtsleeves rolled up and tie loosened, Rybakov concentrated on game strategy. His full-dress blouse was casually draped over a chair, the gold-embroidered lapel emblem of a full admiral gleaming in the light. On the table, his Czech wife Ivana's photo peered over his shoulder. Smirnov moved his first pawn to White King Four.

Rybakov said, "Well, if you won't be different, I will." He countered with Black to Queen's Bishop Four, leaving one square offset between the combatant pawns.

Smirnov's eyebrows arched. "I've not seen the Sicilian Defense in quite some time now." He looked across the board at the former junior master of the Soviet Union. "But I might have suspected it. Spassky says the Sicilian does not lend itself to a draw." The meaning was implicit. Pyotr Rybakov had never entered any endeavor seeking a draw.

"It's as good as it ever was," Rybakov replied. "Ever since Polerio described it in the sixteenth century." Smirnov sensed another philosophy-of-chess lecture. "The Sicilian sets up a large number of pawn configurations," Rybakov explained. "And the endgame favors Black because the early White advantages can be depleted."

"Much like naval warfare, Admiral?"

"No more lectures tonight, Anatoly. Go ahead, play."

Rybakov tried to concentrate fully on the game; he knew he needed the relaxing diversion it provided. Odd moments during the six-day voyage from the equator to the Cape of Good Hope would be the last he had for any recreational pursuit. Every hour that he cruised at twenty knots and *Eisenhower* at fifteen put the American carrier five miles farther behind—120 miles per day, 840 in a week.

The stressful news was that the Americans had turned *Roosevelt* around more rapidly than he thought possible. Apparently the carrier had put to sea from Norfolk without a full complement of escorts or a fast unrep ship. But then nuclear-powered carriers and cruisers had less need of underway replenishment than oil-fired ships. And *Roosevelt*'s deficient group could hook up with *Eisenhower*'s, which, even after the mining, still had five escorts and an oiler. It would take time for the Americans to form this potent task force, however, and time counted even more in warfare than in chess. Besides, *Roosevelt* was still 6,500 nautical miles from the Cape, and the American hounds faced still other obstacles to overcome as the Russian hares bounded away.

"Your move, Pyotr Fyodorovich," Smirnov said, drawing the admiral's attention back to the game at hand.

0902 Local, Tuesday, 25 May
Hospital Ship Ob', *Northeast of Madagascar*

Senior Lieutenant Viktor Koshkin saw the landing craft approaching and immediately knew he had a problem. Turning to the petty officer with the plan of the day, he asked, "Aren't the Vietnamese supposed to arrive this evening?"

The wind on the quarterdeck rustled the sheets as the seaman flipped through the schedule. "Yes, sir. According to this, we are to receive them at 1900 hours."

Koshkin looked at his watch, which read 0902. "Damn it," he cursed. Some idiot clerk on the amphibious ship *Ivan Rogov* obviously had made a typo, moving forward the Viet naval infantry's "visit" by ten hours. The officer of the deck walked to a hatch and picked up the phone. "Executive officer," Koshkin said. After a wait he began. "Comrade . . . excuse me. I mean, sir." Old habits died hard. "We have the Vietnamese alongside now. They're several hours early. Shall we take them aboard?"

The sailor heard the lieutenant say, "Yes, sir. I will try to be diplomatic." Koshkin hung up the receiver and strode back to his post. "We're to delay them at least ten minutes," he explained. "The executive officer says we're under orders to treat our socialist comrades with courtesy. They may take offense if we send them back, and the task group commander places great importance on allied cooperation."

The petty officer grunted a noncommittal comment. *Those girls belowdecks will never get ready in time,* he thought. Even with the medical staff pitching in to help change sheets and put up additional partitions, the two wards couldn't possibly be cleared of the Russian marines now enjoying their own scheduled time with the "nurse's aides." He shared his superior's unease. *This could turn ugly.*

"Alert the SS duty platoon," Koshkin ordered. As the noncom reached for the phone, the lieutenant reflected that *"Sekretnaya Sluzhba"*—Secret Service—was a poor choice for the new name of former KGB security troops and battle police. He knew that the "reformed" State Security Committee had chosen to apply the titles of American agencies to its supposedly separate branches, but nobody much liked the sound of "SS."

As the medium landing craft pulled alongside, a cargo net was draped over the ship's hull. Almost immediately the Vietnamese began scrambling up the net with astonishing speed.

First over the rail was a trim-looking officer who saluted Koshkin and, in fair Russian, announced himself and his intentions. Koshkin returned the salute and granted permission to come aboard. He regarded the Viet carefully: a small but well-built man in his late twenties, muscular and obviously fit. "Please form up your men aft, Lieutenant," Koshkin said pleasantly. "When you're ready we'll escort you below."

The Vietnamese turned and barked an order, sending his men into perfectly arrayed ranks. It took about thirty seconds. The officer then turned back to Koshkin, pointedly looked at his watch and said, "Ready."

Viktor Koshkin swallowed hard. He had never anticipated the role of unwilling pimp on an international floating bordello. But as the group commander noted, until hostilities began, *Ob'* had no other purpose. The French, he knew, understood such things.

Not knowing what else to do, Koshkin led his guests through the hatchway at a stately pace. He decided to take the long way around, hoping the Viets wouldn't realize they were being detoured. It was a good plan, fully in keeping with his orders, and might have worked.

Koshkin had just turned a corner, feeling the pulsing expectation crowding behind him, when a swarm of Eurasian marines emerged from the companionway below. Swearing and tugging on uniform items, their displeasure at being interrupted was obvious. Two of their noncoms took one look at the Vietnamese and deduced the cause-and-effect relationship.

With growing dread, Koshkin realized that most of the Russian marines were not only angry—they were drunk as well. And like marines everywhere, they were belligerent drunks. They resentfully allowed the Viets to pass, but followed Koshkin's band belowdecks, bellowing insults. "Ass-faced monkeys, outta my way!" the last Russian naval infantryman slurred.

Emerging into the hundred-bed hospital ward, Koshkin made directly for a phone. The Vietnamese lieutenant still had a grip on his men, but only barely. Koshkin called for security, then turned around and bumped into a plump prostitute. Other girls emerged from behind their partitions. Some gestured beckoningly to the new arrivals, some betrayed unsocialist and unprofessional racial intolerance, and some obviously were frightened.

Koshkin still might have retrieved the situation if the intoxicated noncom hadn't started elbowing Vietnamese out of his way. Jostling turned to shoving, which sparked a full-fledged brawl. Vietnamese and Russian marines lit into each other. A few girls were mauled in the process, adding high-pitched shrieks to the din. Gurneys were kicked aside, medical cabinets were smashed, footing became precarious as the deck was littered with spilled fluids and pummeled bodies.

The security team—SS marine battle police—arrived with bayonets fixed. One of the guards made a menacing move toward a Vietnamese. Another Viet swung a roundhouse right that connected with the Russian's left ear. The Russian went down in a heap and the tough little soldier picked up the guard's AK-74. Another Russian saw the threat, chambered a round, pushed his selector to full-auto and fired a short burst. The Viet and a woman were struck and fell together.

The Vietnamese lieutenant, panic in his eyes, tried to intervene. He got a bayonet in his shoulder. Two of his men jumped the offender, knocked the wind from him with kick-boxing strokes and scooped up the rifle. Other Viets also armed themselves. The close-range firefight lasted perhaps ten seconds. The noise in that confined space was unbearable. Muzzle blast and concussion overwhelmed everybody. Later, Koshkin figured that ear damage alone had stopped the shooting.

When it was over, the ward was littered with eight corpses and eleven wounded.

1200 Local, Wednesday, 26 May
Amphibious Ship Ivan Rogov, *Indian Ocean*

Half of the helipad and much of the aft superstructure were lined with off-duty sailors and marines. Many others had been ordered to attend the spectacle about to occur, for an object lesson was being played out.

Six men emerged from the hangar bay, closely guarded by SS personnel. Single-file, with hands bound behind them, the condemned were prodded toward the stern, where they were lined up, facing aft. Three Soviets and three Vietnamese had been selected for execution following the violence aboard the hospital ship. Stripped to their underwear, most of them stoically awaited their fate. But one wept aloud and another trembled visibly. Somehow, nationality did not matter now.

Rogov's captain read a brief statement of charges and cited the regulation authorizing capital punishment. With that, he ordered the SS riflemen—two per prisoner—to form ten meters from the prisoners. The skipper reflected that the scene he was about to watch was appropriate, since his ship was named for a notorious political officer in Stalin's navy.

Private Yuri Sverdlov was thankful that the condemned men's backs were turned. Blindfolds were for executioners more than victims.

The major in charge wasted no time. He shouted in a clear, even voice, "Load your weapons!" Bolts snapped forward in the AK-74s, stripping single rounds from the magazines into twelve chambers.

"Aim!" The killers shouldered their rifles, centering their sights between the shoulder blades of their designated targets.

"Fire!" A ragged volley snapped out across the helipad. Ten rounds found their marks, including two that went high and mercifully smashed the skulls of two Russians. Five victims toppled overboard. But one, only struck in the right side, slumped to the deck and writhed in agony.

The firing squad commander was livid with rage. To botch this simple task in front of all these witnesses! He barked a command to secure weapons, then paced briskly to the wounded man. With one fluid movement, the officer kicked the Vietnamese overboard, then turned on his own men. Face-to-face he berated the two troopers who had failed to make a clean kill. One had missed completely and one had flinched, gaining only a marginal hit—at ten meters.

The major screamed at the pair, saving his bitterest invective for the younger man. Nineteen-year-old Yuri Sverdlov was red-faced with fear and embarrassment. He did not know that he had been chosen for this duty as a means of seasoning him. "What do you have to say for yourself, Sverdlov?"

The soldier made an attempt to swallow but dared not open his mouth. The silence, however, only incensed the officer more. He shoved Sverdlov. "I asked you a question, private! You will answer me! What's your excuse?"

"Sir . . . I . . ." His next word was lost in a thick liquid gurgle as the contents of his stomach spewed over the officer's tunic, pants and polished boots.

Moments later sailors hosed disgusting substances off the helipad.

1558 Local
Langley, *Arabian Sea*

A duck-walking boatswain mate waddled under the nose of the E-2C as the nosewheel was positioned at the catapult shuttle. The greenshirt secured the Hawkeye's tow bar, running from the nosewheel to the shuttle, and checked that it was locked into place, as was the holdback running aft of the nose gear. On his signal, tension was taken up on the catapult and Frisbee 601 was now ready for launch. Catapult crews are professionals at nonverbal communication—the flight deck is far too noisy for anything but hand signals and body english.

Looking to his left, the hookup man saw the catapult operator hold up one finger in the "ready" signal. Still beneath the aircraft, the hookup man rotated his right forefinger above his head, then pointed toward the bow. The petty officer plane director took in this ritual and uncrossed his arms from over his head, and in the cockpit a pilot named Mitch released tension on his toe brakes and shoved up the throttles to full power. The twin Allison T-56 turboprops screamed out a combined total of over 8,000 horsepower.

Standing well forward of the aircraft, the officer in charge of the two bow catapults repeated the rotating hand signal with two fingers extended. Ailerons and elevators moved through their control arcs as the pilot tested freedom of movement. Three more sailors ran the length of the fuselage, checking for last-minute leaks or malfunctions. Finding none, they flashed thumbs-up. The cat officer pointedly leaned toward the hookup man, who gave a final check of the shuttle connection, then sprinted away.

Mitch saw the cat officer's head rise toward him and, knowing the meaning, saluted smartly, then braced his helmet against his seat. In the fuselage compartment, three radar controllers sat facing forward, equally braced. Finally the cat officer pointed at the deck-edge sailor, knelt low and touched the deck. Then his hand came up, and he stretched himself forward into an exaggerated pushup. Every cat officer has his own set of "deck-edge turns," competing for style points with all the other "shooters."

The sailor lowered his hands to the console. Checking fore and aft, and finding no safety obstructions, he jabbed the button. One deck below, a light flashed on a panel and the cat controller fired. Propelled by immense steam pressure equal to two million horsepower, the six-foot catapult piston slammed forward in its well. Two seconds later it smashed into its water brake at 160 mph and came to an abrupt stop.

On the flight deck, the shuttle attached to the cat overcame inertia and shot a twenty-five-ton airplane into the air. The Hawkeye had gone from zero to 130 knots in 300 feet. But not a word had been spoken.

1601
Over the Arabian Sea

In Frisbee 601's pressurized tactical data system compartment, the combat information center officer, Lieutenant Anthony Chimola, let out a whoop. A cat shot was always exhilarating. The CICO nudged his radar operator and grinned. "Beats commuting all to hell, don't it?" The RO merely smiled. Tony Chimola always said that, so nobody would realize he was thinking of his girlfriend Michelle back in La Jolla at these moments. He unlocked his seat, rotated left and began checking his equipment.

On climbout the Hawkeye droned noisily upward, the vibration and noise from the big turboprop engines penetrating the Tactical Data System compartment. Still, the AWACS mission was ever challenging. Though aged and in need of replacement, the E-2 remained one of the four best airborne warning and control system aircraft, or AWACS, in the world; probably third in capability behind the Air Force E-3 and Russian Mainstay, but still ahead of Russian types in computer software, radar power, range and field of view.

Chimola regarded the Hawkeye as a miracle of packaging and, to help radar see, of design. The original '50s technology had been constantly updated. For carrier operation the twenty-four-foot rotodome folded, but E-2s usually were stored on the flight deck. They were the only U.S. carrier prop plane left in the inventory—a link with naval aviation's historic past.

Climbing steadily toward 25,000 feet, Frisbee 601 would take station 175 miles ahead of the battle group. From there, Tony Chimola, his RO and air-control officer could monitor three million cubic miles of airspace with their powerful APS-125 radar. *All for only sixty-five million dollars,* Chimola thought. *A bargain at twice the price.* He welcomed the diversion of his job to concentrate upon. At least he wouldn't dwell upon the voluptuous Michelle for the next four hours.

1603 Local
Varyag, *Southeastern Atlantic Ocean*

Rybakov leaned against his chart table. He picked up a three-centimeter-long plastic silhouette of a *Kiev*-class carrier. Working the model through the fingers of one hand, he stroked his chin with the other. At last the admiral placed the ship outline on a chart of the waters off the Western Cape of South Africa. He moved it to a position a hundred miles due west of Saldanha Bay, a new cargo facility. *Like a boy with bathtub toys,* he thought. *Horrifyingly deadly toys.*

He had to decide on the attack dispositions of his forces tonight, before the eastern contingents—the groups centered on helo carriers *Moskva* and *Leningrad* and V/STOL carrier *Novorossiysk*—approached Natal. Radio signals had to be kept to a minimum, but the precise positioning of his task force was left to Rybakov's discretion. The final details depended on weather conditions, moves by the South African Navy and coastal defense units—however negligible they might be—and the reactions of French, British and American forces in the region. Thankfully, the NATO navies were not in evidence, not even subs.

His captains would have to pull off some tricky maneuvers to shuffle the ships in Task Force Rybakov on the 27th and 28th, mostly under cover of darkness. His own Baltic Fleet flag group, for instance, needed to exchange cruisers and destroyers with the Pacific Fleet *Novo* group to achieve the proper balance of capabilities.

Rybakov plopped *Kuznetsov* down on the chart and scooted the big-deck carrier 250 miles southeast from *Gorshkov,* just past Cape Agulhas, the southern tip of Africa. *Vasco da Gama couldn't imagine what he started almost 500 years ago,* the Russian sailor considered, full of admiration for his Portuguese predecessor.

With his brass compass, a gift from Navy C-in-C Sorokin, Rybakov measured 550 nautical miles from *Kuznetsov*—an hour's flight time for a Sukhoi 27 at full military power or a day's steaming at twenty-three knots. He dropped *Varyag* onto the spot, a hundred miles off the Transkei's Wild Coast. With a smile, he stuck a red flag into a hole in the piece.

More rapidly now, he positioned *Moskva* off Port Elizabeth in the Eastern Cape and *Leningrad* to her east-north-east off East London. Both helo carriers were well beyond the range of South African shore batteries but within the admiral's protective barrier of subs, surface escorts and aircraft from the conventional carriers.

Finally, he pushed *Novorossiysk* southwest from Madagascar, then flicked the V/STOL carrier into place a hundred miles due east of Durban, Natal. His head cocked to one side, the admiral silently admired his handiwork from different angles, one arm folded across his chest and the other at his jaw.

"Smirnov," Rybakov called, and his chief of staff hustled to the table. "What do you think?"

After studying the deployments for a moment, Smirnov suggested, "What about moving *Gorshkov* a little farther south and *Kuznetsov* east? In case we have to combine rapidly?"

"I don't see that as a possibility. We'll have plenty of warning if any of the American carriers approaches within attack range. Get the staff to work setting up patrol zones, squadron operational schedules and shore bombardment assignments based on this disposition."

"Aye, aye, Pyotr Fyodorovich." Smirnov wrote down the ships' coordinates. This work completed, he said, "Oh, I have to report our first sighting of a South African maritime patrol plane, a C-130."

"What did you do with it?"

"A pair of *Gorshkov*'s Yaks forced it back well outside the hundred-mile zone."

"Very well. It would have been satisfying to shoot it down, but we mustn't tip our hand." *About all a Yak is good for,* Rybakov reminded himself, *is killing unarmed, prop-driven patrol planes.* Pilots of the supersonic Yak-141's predecessor, Yak-38, hung signs on their subsonic jumpjets reading, "Unfit for Human Use." The new V/STOL aircraft was better both as a fighter and attack plane, but its development had suffered years of delay because of bureaucratic infighting. The air force was responsible for developing it, but since the navy would also use it, the "sister service" starved the orphan program nearly to death.

"Yes, sir. Too bad. But there will be plenty of opportunity later, and against worthier game," Smirnov consoled his CO.

Even Cheetahs are barely worthy, the admiral thought, *though the SADF pilots are good.* He knew that only Tomcats or Hornets could truly test his Knight squadrons' Sukhoi 27s. *I'd just as soon not learn about the outcome of that game.*

Rybakov's navalized Su-27s were even more capable than the superb air force models, perhaps the premier fighter-interceptors on earth. Highly maneuverable with the addition of canards, Flanker-Ns also boasted the 190-mile "Flashdance" fire-control radar for the long-range AA-9 missile, both developed for the MiG-31 Foxhound of the National Air Defence Force. Still, American pilots were better trained and their Phoenix air-to-air missiles outranged even the Russians' AA-9 Amoses. Rybakov looked over the table, his grand chessboard, one more time. "I adjust," he announced in French to his chess opponent Smirnov, smiled and slid *Kuznetsov* a few miles closer to *Varyag*. "Note the position, Anatoly Vladimirovich, then you're excused." Opening moves completed, the admiral felt like hitting a timer.

0429, Thursday, 27 May
Hoedspruit South African Air Force Base,
Eastern Transvaal

Captain Piet de Villiers loved the Lowveld, particularly its animals. Perhaps it was the drama of his introduction to it that had won him over so completely. He was ten when his father had been posted to command the Seventh South African Infantry Battalion at Phalaborwa; Mozambique had just gone communist and the army was beefing up the border defenses. The pilot of the wonderful old Dakota had invited him up to the cabin. Minutes later they'd crossed the crest of the Drakensberg escarpment and the land had dropped away beneath them.

Suddenly, a mile below, a vast savanna stretched to the Lebombo Mountains, marking the border with "enemy" Mozambique. It was breathtakingly beautiful: tens of thousands of square miles of open, parklike grassland, broken by hillocks—*kopjes*—and mixed with dense bush—mopane, acacia, marula—and baobab trees. Most exciting of all, herds of elephants, zebra, impala, wildebeest and other large, wild herbivores stampeded as the C-47 descended to the Phalaborwa airfield, right on the border of the magnificent Kruger National Park. The boy he was then had thrilled to watch the plane's shadow race over the herds, to see great flocks of birds take flight en masse at the drone of the transport's engines. And so too the man he had become, now with eight tons of thrust at his command and the whole Lowveld his to patrol and defend.

De Villiers jostled in an air force lorry through a pre-dawn morning lit pink by the alpenglow on the 7,000-foot peaks of the Drakensberg. He had been delighted when the air force transferred his squadron to the Transvaal from the Orange Free State.

Hoedspruit AFB was one of the best-designed and

-engineered military airfields in the world, modeled on Israeli installations, with a few defensive wrinkles of the SAAF's own. It was the most important in all South Africa, housing as it did two of the three squadrons operating the Cheetah Mark I, the SAAF's premier interceptor and ground-attack fighter, plus some reconnaissance variants of the Dassault-Breguet Mirage III, from which Cheetah was developed. Like their base, plans for Cheetah were derived from an Israeli upgrade of the French jet.

De Villiers was proud of the base, built about the time his father had served near here. The whole facility was camouflaged and each plane had its own hardened shelter. When circling for a landing, even the fliers based at Hoedspruit had trouble spotting structures until just a few miles out. The first feature a pilot could pick out would be the main runway, then the long taxiway that doubled as a runway. On final approach, he could see the ready-alert shelters at both ends of the main taxiway, and at last some of the sunken taxiways leading to squadron areas. With hostile ballistic missile launchers just eighty-five miles distant, every plane was moved within minutes of landing to its shelter. The final touch was situating the living areas nine miles away to minimize risk to the aviators' families in case of attack. Not even old Russian Scud short-range ballistic missiles were that inaccurate.

Piet's six-year-old twin son and daughter loved the bush as much as he did, but his wife Suzaan hated it as much as she loathed the air force. Life thirty-five kilometers from Kruger Park, surrounded by public wildlife reserves and private game parks, held few charms for the cultured city girl. She wished Piet would get a real job and give up this boyish infatuation with jets, especially now that war loomed just beyond the eastern horizon, a hundred kilometers away, over the Mozambican border.

This morning Suzaan would pack up the kids. Tonight they would leave to stay with her parents in Jo'burg's eastern suburbs. On Monday, the government had agreed to return to the bargaining table with the ANC, but Piet knew war was coming. His father couldn't tell him much, but he didn't have to. The recce flight at Hoedspruit brought back daily pictures from the border. The traffic was in one direction—

toward the frontier. There would be no stand-down this month, as in April and December.

The sun loomed up behind the Lebombos; from out of enemy territory its rays probed the dewy Lowveld and painted the great escarpment pink. Piet de Villiers knew that this might well be his last routine dawn patrol and his family's last day of normal life, of peace.

0802 Local
Langley, *Western Indian Ocean*

"Gentlemen, I want to know why we haven't been able to shake our Russian friends," Gideon declared. "We've tried just about every trick in the book short of ramming but haven't been able to shake 'em permanently. We outran the spy trawler and the diesel sub that dogged us off Gonzo Station. A burst of speed left them behind, but before we crossed the equator we picked up another AGI trawler. We gave him the slip during the night after refueling from the unrep group. We haven't been spotted by so much as a fishing boat. We've been in strict EmCon—haven't emitted so much as an electronic peep since coming off station, not even to facilitate our rendezvous with the UnRepGru." He looked around the wardroom.

"Commander Hallion tells me we haven't been busted by any of their satellites. Yet, now we have this new boy on us like a roach in the projects. They must have had trawlers positioned every few hundred miles along our probable routes of advance. Besides which, our ASW screen reports two top-of-the-line Russian subs on an intercept course toward us. This is most perplexing, gentlemen. I expect some answers." Gideon surveyed his staff, then said, "Hallion, this is your bailiwick. Explain yourself."

"Well, sir, I'd say it was a RORSat, but we haven't been painted by one for days," intel officer Rick Hallion said. "They launched a new one just to keep an eye on us when we came off Gonzo Station, but it hasn't illuminated us. Maybe its nuclear power source failed. They haven't sent up another one. Those they have watching our other three carriers at sea may have diminished their supply.

"It could be an IRSat. Ours can detect and classify large warships from their thermal characteristics, and we believe theirs are just about as good. But our path hasn't crossed the field of view of any of theirs since Saturday, when we still had an intel trawler on us.

"That leaves an optical photo recon satellite. Again, ours can ID ships just from their wakes, even without computer imaging. Theirs aren't that good and their imaging techniques are more primitive. Our EmCon also rules out ferret ElIntSats—so I gotta ask, what's that leave us with?"

"I hope to hell you're going to tell us," Gideon interrupted.

"Well, I have some suggestions, sir."

"Let's hear 'em."

"You're gonna laugh, but one possibility is the *Mir* space station."

"You've got to be shitting me," chief of staff Captain Nathan Gottlieb blurted.

"I'm not laughing, Rick; I like it," Gideon interjected. "It's out there, literally. I hope you're not saying that just because I made you read *Starship Troopers.* How's it work?"

"From low earth orbit, it's within the resolving capability of a good Mark I human eyeball to distinguish larger from smaller ships. With minimal optical aids to reduce pixel size, the same eye can discriminate between supertankers and carriers. Using folded optics, either a normal camera telescopic lens or video camera, you can ID the type of carrier. It's theoretically possible to track a carrier visually across a largely cloudless body of water like the I.O."

"What's folded optics? I'm not too proud to ask," Gottlieb admitted.

"Well, to get a longer focal length and better resolution in a package that isn't too long to handle easily, you put mirrors inside the instrument that lengthen the path the incoming light has to travel. So, say in an 800mm telescope, you get a 1200mm focal length."

"Oh, so there are Russian spacemen up there looking for us with folded telescopes. Candid-camera cosmonauts?" Gottlieb asked.

"Yeah. It's possible. More likely CCD cameras, though. You know, video cameras. Digitalized helps if you're going to image the data."

"Is *Mir* even manned right now?" Gideon asked.

"Yes, sir, it is. And with naval cosmonauts."

"If NASA could launch a shuttle in less than thirty days, maybe we could form up on *Mir* and block their view," Gottlieb joked.

"I want to hear the rest of what Hallion has to say." Gideon was slightly perturbed.

"I was about to say, sir, that the other possibility is a lot closer to home than outer space."

"You mean a spy?" Gottlieb asked, suddenly more serious.

"Why not?" Hallion responded. "I don't want to sound like a conspiracy kook, but look at the Walkers. How many more rings like that are out there? *Glasnost* and *perestroika* haven't changed the Russian hunger for secrets. Quite the opposite. The KGB has changed its name, not its spots, and the GRU hasn't even changed its name." Many officers in the room had been approached by agents of Soviet military intelligence.

"Wouldn't they risk exposing him by following us so blatantly?" Gottlieb inquired.

"If not now, when? The operation they have in the works now, with all these exercises, may justify the risk. Moving *Mir* around could just be a cover. Or a double check on the rat's info."

Hallion continued: "After they get those nuclear subs on our tail, they won't need him anymore."

"Is that all, Rick?" Gideon asked. Hallion said it was and the admiral asked if anyone else had any suggestions. No one had anything to add.

Gideon then wanted to know what course of action his staff recommended to lose the AGI currently shadowing them before the subs got close enough to track the CVBG on their own. The admiral had already permitted his escorts to do anything short of ramming the trawler to block its access to the heart of the battle group—*Langley* herself and a "goal-keeping" cruiser. So far there'd been no bumping and no warship had needed to place itself athwart the AGI's bow.

"Okay, I'm going to get radical," Hallion announced. "Counting the four frigates with the unrep group, we have ten ships with tails," he pointed out, referring to the towed sonar arrays carried by *Knox*- and *Perry*-class frigates, *Spruance*- and *Burke*-class destroyers, *Ticonderoga*-class cruisers and *Los Angeles*-class subs. "We could use one of the frigates' towed arrays to foul the AGI's screws. Just drag it right in there and make it look like an accident."

"You've got to be shitting me," Gottlieb exclaimed again, with more feeling. "And you an intel weenie. With the emphasis on weenie. No shit they'd think it was an accident. Give them an SQR-18, free for nothin'? What a cockamamie idea."

"Not exactly free for nothing, sir. We get away," Hallion replied defensively.

"If you want an accident," Nate Gottlieb insisted, "let's 'accidentally' ram the sucker tonight."

"I'll take your suggestion under advisement, Commander," Gideon told Hallion. "But it won't do us much good, will it, if the eyes of cosmonauts are upon us or if we have a traitor aboard one of our ships. Just in case, I'd like you to prepare a plan to smoke the rat out."

"Counterintel isn't exactly my strong suit, Admiral, but I'll give it my best shot."

"I'd like to shoot him," Gottlieb said, "and be done with it."

"Could be a she, sir," Hallion pointed out. "The *McClure* has women on board," he said, referring to the newer, *Kaiser*-class fleet oiler in the unrep group or URG. "Both among its ninety-eight civilians and twenty-one naval personnel. In fact, her sole navy officer is female."

"Please, we just ate," the intel officer's own roomie said.

"Okay, if none of you chauvinist, sexist pigs has any other constructive suggestions, then you're all excused, *gentlemen*," the admiral ordered wryly. "We begin sensitivity training sessions at 0600 tomorrow." The joke still contained a hint of threat. "Hallion and Nate, stick around."

When the room had cleared, Gideon told his intel officer and chief of staff, "I was thinking, if we can't shake our shadow, can we use it to our benefit? Keep thinking about ways to lose the trawlers and subs, but maybe we don't want to, not just yet. We'll definitely want to give them the slip after we rendezvous with the PhibGru, but maybe not before."

The two staffers agreed.

"If you can't beat 'em, trick 'em?" Hallion asked rhetorically. "Sounds good to me."

" 'Nuff said for now," the admiral responded. "Another

thing, Nate," he said to Gottlieb, "With those subs bearing down on us, I want to beef up my inner zone defenses. Borrow an FFG-7 from the unrep group. Make it *Meyring;* she's been the most aggressive—encountered that Ka-27 helo with the new Swingdome surveillance radar and detected the SSN and SSGN first. Detach her for the duration; the unrep people will squawk, but 'the needs of the many outweigh the needs of the few.' Not to mention the needs of the more expensive and offensive. I want her to cover my ass, literally."

"Aye, aye, sir," Gottlieb replied.

"That is all, gentlemen. Thanks for your input."

1034
SADF National Command Center

Christie de Villiers believed that one of a general's greatest skills was timing; the best commanders knew intuitively when to attack and when to withdraw. He had awakened this morning certain that the time to strike was within twenty-four hours. He could give good reasons for this decision, but it was gut instinct that had made up his mind.

All the data pouring in today reinforced the feeling. Now, at what would probably be the last peacetime meeting of the State Security Council, he had to convince his political leaders that the time to strike was tomorrow, before the enemy's blows fell.

"It's now clear that the Russian armada off our coasts is not there just to put pressure on us," de Villiers told his colleagues on the SSC. "They mean to attack us. They make all the difference. Their presence negates our nuclear and chemical option. Even with the enemy's tremendous numerical advantages in equipment and adequate superiority in troop numbers, the invaders could not be assured of defeating us. Clearly, the primary mission of the Russian fleet is air superiority. This they will in all likelihood achieve. The Russians' naval fixed-wing combat aircraft alone outnumber our entire air force; the average quality of their aircraft is superior to ours and many of their pilots are probably the equal of ours. When you add in the so-called allied fighter squadrons, especially the Koreans and Vietnamese, we are hopelessly outnumbered in the air and technologically overmatched.

"Nor, of course, is air power the only threat. The enemy's ballistic missile launchers are capable of knocking out a substantial portion of our fixed command and control centers, key transport and communication facilities and the like," the general summarized.

"Signals analysis and other intelligence suggest that the onslaught will begin between midnight and 0400 hours day after tomorrow, the Saturday of Independence Day weekend. Tomorrow morning is also possible, but I think not. Aeroflot and the national airlines of Libya, North Korea and Vietnam have begun concentrating their long-distance passenger and cargo planes, sufficient to lift tens of thousands of additional troops into southern Africa. For all intents and purposes, the invasion has already started."

Just try and convince the world of that, he told himself, *and see if they care in any case.*

"For this reason, I strongly urge that, beginning tomorrow morning, we mount a massive preemptive strike against every important target within range of our tactical aircraft, missiles and artillery. Our stroke will not only neutralize or destroy critical targets, but interfere with the enemy's assault preparations.

"The plan calls for a three-hour assault, starting with artillery, rocket and missile strikes from 0735 hours, followed by the first wave of air strikes at 0745, with subsequent waves every ten minutes. More than that I can't divulge in regular session.

"We have prepared prioritized target lists and a constantly updated attack schedule. These remain highly classified, but I'm prepared to provide you with such details as may be appropriate at the level of your decision-making. The same applies to loss estimates and predicted effectiveness. I can say, indeed already have stated, that enemy ballistic missile launchers are the highest-priority targets, along with command and control centers. Other obvious targets include air-defense systems, transport nodes and high-value depots. Unfortunately, we can't hit all the targets on the list in one salvo or sortie. I'll gladly answer your questions, but I urge a rapid decision. Thank you."

State President van der Merwe spoke first. "I'm sure we all agree that invasion is imminent. Davie, here, assured me last week that the Russians' offer to mediate the crisis was a sure sign of impending onslaught. As you are aware, we accepted the ANC's bid to reopen negotiations on Monday in the full knowledge that it was a ploy. The absence of so many government ministers no doubt hampered our efforts, but failure to accept would have telegraphed our suspicions."

Your absence was not such a great obstacle, de Villiers thought. "Our emergency command arrangements functioned well enough while you were out of the country, Mr. State President. I'm just glad they didn't kill you."

"That would have telegraphed *their* intentions, I suppose," the president said. "In any case, we need foreign support, gentlemen. General de Villiers has told us so, and I for one agree with him. Recall that our ancestors counted on French, Dutch and German aid in 1899, but were disappointed. Without it, they stood little chance. I suggest that we need American and European assistance today more than the Orange and Transvaal Republics did then. That's why we can't afford to be branded the aggressors in the coming conflict. I'm not saying that we shouldn't hit first, just that we should consider carefully before doing so."

Intelligence chief Davie Steyn spoke up. "The military advantages of a successful first strike outweigh the diplomatic cost. I emphasize *successful.* Given the enemy's defenses—not only against aircraft but also tactical missiles—there's a finite chance our preemptive strike will do little real damage. But we can't afford to risk using nuclear weapons, so we have no alternative. It's possible that a first strike will do enough damage to the enemy that we can get by without foreign backing. A slim chance, but real. Conversely, without preemption, we may not be able to resist the enemy long enough for Europe and America to make up their minds about our chances. Their governments won't risk such a politically unpopular move unless they think we stand a chance of success.

"That's my professional assessment," Steyn concluded. "I could be wrong, but I don't think I am. Callaway will back us if we put up a good enough fight and enough blacks side with us or stay neutral. His problem will be with the blacks and liberals in his own party. We'll have to get our story out, since the Western media won't, but his inclination would be to fight the communists."

"You seem overly optimistic to me, Davie," the defense

minister said, "but I concur that we have little alternative to a first strike."

President van der Merwe called for a decision on the motion to launch air, missile and artillery strikes on selected enemy positions and targets within twenty-one hours. The vote carried unanimously.

My boy may not live to see the sun rise again, de Villiers thought. *But then, better he should die in the air, fighting, than on the ground, waiting. Whatever happens to him, die Volk will survive.*

1213 Local
Langley, *Indian Ocean*

Chief Petty Officer Ira Odum sat down on his bunk after coming off watch. He was known among his fellow communications specialists as "one smart son of a bitch." A few commo people may have rankled at the adjective, but none would have balked at the compound noun. His very first division officer—a lieutenant aboard the command ship *Blue Ridge*—had lost enough bridge games to the portly, abrasive Southerner to recognize the man's intellect. "But mark my words," the officer had said, "someday that SOB is going to outsmart himself."

Because Odum could make people trust him, he had learned of that assessment from another sailor who became his partner in an after-hours liquor scam. Ever since, he reminded himself that the lieutenant had eventually left the navy to sell insurance. But Ira Odum had stayed the course. He had put up with the Mickey Mouse regs and sucked up to the thick-headed officers; waited for some opportunities and created others. Now, after twenty-six years of honorable service, he was about to retire comfortably. *And not,* he often thought, *because of the frigging chicken feed the U.S. Navy calls retirement benefits.*

Sitting alone in CPO country, Odum secured the top of an ordinary-looking humidor bearing the logo of a brand-name coffee. He had consulted the satellite schedule secreted in his well-thumbed copy of *Hoyle's Bridge* and already had entered the required data on the humidor's hidden digital keyboard. He checked his gold-plated Rolex. *Twenty-eight minutes. Plenty of time.* He sat back with his hands behind his bald head, and thought about his career as a traitor.

Even after eighteen years, Odum still didn't know exactly how the arrangement had come about. He had always suspected that his success at bridge had drawn the Soviet "cultural attaché" to him, as the initial contact had been made at a tournament. Only months later, after he had accepted his first three payments—and they had been lucrative—did he realize that he had been manipulated exactly the way he handled his own superiors. Alexander, his control, had appealed to Odum's pride and arrogance. For a day or two Odum had considered backing out, but had decided against it for two reasons. One, the Russians would blackmail him into accepting less money for his information. And two, they might kill him.

But his biggest windfall had come in the last few years. When the Berlin Wall crumbled and Eastern Europe went its own way, Odum philosophically decided that the end had come. He was money ahead—way ahead—and couldn't be too disappointed. But Alexander surprised him. Calling a rare face-to-face meeting, he had told Odum that Russian Military Intelligence would increase payments by fifty percent, if specific information were forthcoming. Odum readily agreed.

"But after all, Alex," he had purred, "I'm about to retire." The GRU had known that all along, and insisted that Odum recruit fresh blood. That had an unpleasant vampiric connotation, and Odum had refused. *That's how that stupid bastard Walker got himself bagged,* Odum thought. *Serves him right. The dumb shit.*

The new information was not even very difficult to obtain. Contrary to the code ciphers and high-level message traffic that Odum had expected his masters to request, he was tasked with obtaining technical information—nuts-and-bolts data about aircraft carrier construction and systems. That was beyond Odum's expertise, but he knew people who knew people. He had laughed aloud, telling Alexander, "It's not *what* you know, it's *who* you know that counts." More recently he'd been asked for position reports of the *Langley* battle group on this, his last cruise. It was child's play for an experienced, efficient operator like Ira Odum. Besides, what harm could it do? The Cold War was over. Everybody knew that.

0735, Friday, 28 May
Hoedspruit Air Base

Captain Piet de Villiers accelerated through 250 knots, tucking his wheels in the well as he climbed away from the beautiful base. He glanced in his rear-view mirror to make sure his wingman's Cheetah was there. Against the towering, dawn-lit escarpment of the Drakensbergs to the west, he saw van Damm's green and brown fighter—a familiar delta-wing silhouette with canards behind the intakes. Satisfied, he turned northeast toward the Mozambique border sixty miles away.

De Villiers gently pushed on his control stick, leveling off at 150 feet, and continued accelerating. At 550 knots indicated, he felt secure and familiar in the snug confines of the remanufactured Mirage IIICZ. He had flown this profile dozens of times, and the landmarks ticked off in his mental computer. He had an aeronautical chart tucked under one leg—the human thigh still was a wonderful map-holder—but he hardly needed it. He knew the topography, trees, power lines and buildings by heart.

If anything, Piet de Villiers felt an eerie sense of *deja vu*. He was no novice at combat—few South African pilots were. But this mission was unlike the familiar cross-border ops into Angola from Namibia. Flying a preemptive strike before a new war against a still-unidentified enemy massed on South Africa's borders was like starting over again, despite the familiar terrain. He had experienced the same anxious uneasiness on his first combat flight eight years before.

Still, de Villiers took comfort in his skill and pride in his unit. Number Two Squadron, SAAF, was heir to a fighting tradition dating from Tunisia, Italy, Korea and beyond. *If only the bloody aircraft weren't so bloody obsolete*, he thought. But he was more fortunate than most SAAF pilots. South Africa's first French-made Mirages had been built in the early 1960s. The Cheetah upgrade, with features nearly identical to the Israeli Kfir TC7, dated from only 1986. That was a matter of pride in the SAAF, whose U.S.-built AT-6 trainers and C-47 transports were 1930s designs of 1940s construction. An American aviation magazine described their condition as "exceptional," the best-maintained examples of their types in the world. *Small consolation,* he mused. *The rest of the frigging world hates our guts. Dad's right enough about that. Thank God for the mercenary French and the self-serving Israelis.*

De Villiers forced himself to concentrate on the mission. He raised a leg, withdrew his map and double-checked his route. Five minutes to initial point. He checked his armament switches: 30mm cannon, low-drag bombs and rocket pods. Ten minutes from target, suddenly he felt much better.

0741
Socialist Republic of Vietnam Antiaircraft Artillery Site,
Gaza Province, Southern Mozambique

"Take positions!" Comrade Captain Nguyen Ma Bac's shouted order sent his 57mm battery to full alert. Three of his six S60 guns were manned full-time, but reports of inbound fascist aircraft required one hundred percent readiness. Nguyen confirmed his unit's status with battalion HQ on the command radio net, then set out to double-check the supply of ready ammunition.

Trotting across the battery's circular disposition, Nguyen saw the radar dish atop the trailer stop rotating. It was wavering back and forth, generally southeasterly. He sensed an electric charge between his shoulder blades. *This is the hour,* he exulted. His six guns and most of his seventy-two men had traveled 7,000 miles for this moment. The knowledge that all his training and experience would be put to use filled him with a weighty expectancy.

Slaved to the tracking radar, previously warned by the battalion's Flap Wheel early-warning set, Nguyen's guns would fire patterned barrages against designated targets. His well-drilled crews had only to service the S60 artillery pieces to maintain a lethal volume of fire. Sited on a hill overlooking Massingir Dam, Nguyen's battery prepared for its first major combat since 1972. Not even the 1979 defeat of Chinese aggression compared to the victory over American imperialism won in part by the air defense forces.

0744
Approaching Massingir, Mozambique

Piet de Villiers had flown northeast to Shamiriri, a peak above the gorge of the Olifants River through the Lebombos. At this landmark, he had popped the stick back, rocketed to 8,000 feet and dived toward the border on the same heading. In enemy territory, he struck the Shingwedzi River, turned hard right and followed it to its junction with the Olifants, below Massingir Dam. Now, dead ahead on the paved road ten miles southeast of the town, he found what he was seeking. No longer concerned with radio silence, he keyed his microphone button. "Springbok Two from Leader. Attacking now. Follow me in, Joni."

A half-mile astern, First Lieutenant Joni van Damm turned to the attack heading. He saw Piet's rockets flash from beneath the Cheetah's wings, leaving smoky tendrils in the air. Then he concentrated on his own sight picture, off-setting to starboard for a slightly different aspect. Armored security and thin-skinned transport vehicles cluttered the road; bridging equipment stood immobile in a turnout.

Their transport scheme has broken down, de Villiers realized. *No truly professional army would allow its vehicles to bunch up like that. But then, they weren't expecting us.*

It was delicious. The Cheetahs had caught the Scud surface-to-surface missile brigade just preparing to move out of its daytime hide. De Villiers knew that the eight-wheel launchers would reposition during the night to presurveyed sites over twenty-five miles from the border—out of G-5 howitzer range. From these positions, the SRBM unit would have struck targets up to 155 miles inside his country. Even at his velocity, the pilot could tell where the twelve launchers were camouflaged—the netting was not ideal for savanna vegetation.

Medium-caliber flak instantly cluttered the sky. Because Piet was first to roll in, he achieved a measure of surprise. He gave no thought to the second section, scheduled to attack from the south simultaneously. It was a matter of selecting the most lucrative target, emptying the rocket pods and, if time allowed, punching off his cluster bombs. He was rewarded with multiple bright flashes sparking upward from the ground—a small fireworks display—then rippling secondary explosions as the pyrotechnic bomblets ignited lorry petrol tanks. A spectacular eruption told de Villiers he'd torched the liquid fuel in one of the seven-ton missiles. The blast wave rocked his Cheetah. *Cut that a little close,* he reprimanded himself. *Amazing, the energy in ballistic missile fuel.*

Recovering at 3,000 feet, above effective small-arms range, de Villiers felt the compressive force of gravity. His vision went gray as blood drained from his head toward his belly. But he was astute enough to jink erratically, avoiding a predictable flight path. He felt the shudders and, in his rear-view mirror, saw the satisfying flashes of more Scud launchers going up. Behind him, smoke already rose from the burning savanna. Wildly joyful, he banked for the prebriefed rendezvous and called Joni.

"Springbok Two, rejoin as briefed." There was no reply so he called again. And still no reply.

0753
Vietnamese AAA Site

Everybody claimed the kill. But Captain Nguyen Ma Bac was seething mad. He shoved jumping, cheering gunners back to their mounts. The more enthusiastic were pummeled with kicks and fists. Nguyen screamed at the top of his voice, reciting the litany of commands. "Take your positions! Correct your aim!" Hardly anyone paid any attention.

In a way, Nguyen could understand it. The fascist jet—he guessed it had been a Mirage—had taken what appeared to be a direct hit. He further estimated that one of his battery's 57mm shells had detonated the bomber's ordnance. How else to explain the tremendous explosion? Some wind-blown smoke and debris still lingered in midair.

Nguyen calmed himself. He realized with a start that his behavior had hardly been better than his men's. In his own way, he had lost control of a combat situation, allowing an enemy aircraft to escape. How much damage the fascists had done was hard to tell, but flames and roiling smoke from the river junction boded ill. Nguyen made a mental note to point out his own failings at the evening self-criticism meeting.

0801
Hoedspruit Air Base

Piet de Villiers could tell something was wrong. At first he couldn't identify the problem, even from a couple of miles away at 1,500 feet. Then it hit him. The lack of observable activity reinforced de Villiers's sickening suspicion. Instead of approaching for a normal landing, he circled the base once. A radio call from the living area confirmed the supposition. His insides turned over.

He knew the routine—the base and its two Cheetah squadrons had practiced often enough—but it was hard to turn away to the alternate landing site.

Gas! he thought as he banked away to the northwest. *Probably hit us with nerve agent first, to kill any exposed people. Then probably mustard or some other persistent agent—to force surviving ground crew into suits, keep us away and maybe mess up the equipment.*

His two wingmen dutifully followed the turn, and Piet felt certain they shared his sense of remorse and outrage at the loss of the base and their friends among the ground crew. Their aircraft's weapons stations were empty after the strike mission, but foresight had allowed for this contingency. The three Cheetahs added power, pulled up as they crossed Fort Colpieba and followed the R40 through the Tshukudu Game Reserve.

Then, swinging down into a long final approach, evenly spaced, the jets dropped gear and flaps. The pilots glanced down at traffic blocked on the highway—all they needed to know. Feeling for the ground, they dropped onto the mac-adam and popped their drogue chutes. Braking to a halt, they were met by a weapons carrier with a waving mechanic in the back. Thirty minutes later, sitting under a large cam-ouflage net, Springbok Flight was rearmed, refueled and ready to take off. Piet de Villiers noted that his loadout in-cluded napalm and cluster bombs. *Good,* he thought. *Incin-erate the bastards, then blast them to little pieces.*

He was now a man with a mission.

6

29 to 31 May

0230, Saturday, 29 May
Varyag, Off The Wild Coast

Admiral Pyotr Rybakov stood on the wing of the flag bridge, watching history unfold below him. Ten Sukhoi 25Ms lined the flight deck aft, laden with bombs, rocket pods and napalm canisters. In the lead aircraft, Black Rook 50, Colonel of Aviation Nikolai Glinka taxied into position at the base of the island, 200 meters from the bow, and braked to a halt.

"Nikolai has the honor of the first combat launch," Rybakov said to his chief of staff, Captain First Rank Smirnov.

"It's only right—he worked hard to get this air wing into shape."

Rybakov said nothing. It was true that Glinka had prepared his squadrons for routine daylight carrier ops, but the time investment had been immense. Tactical training had suffered accordingly, both for the attack planes and the Su-27 fighters.

The onlookers watched as the holdbacks rose out of the flight deck and the Rook's main-gear tires rolled against them. Astern of the attack plane, the jet-blast deflector elevated and Glinka ran up the power to his engines. Smirnov took in the procedure—he'd seen it dozens of times—and shouted above the jet noise, "Maybe we really don't need catapults after all."

Rybakov had pushed for steam-powered cats like the Americans and French used, but the naval constructors had resisted. Too complex, too expensive and maintenance-intensive, they said. Well, maybe they were right.

As the Sukhoi's engines reached full military power, the launch officer leaned forward against the relative wind and pointed his finger, and the holdbacks snapped forward. The Rook accelerated toward the bow, up the ramp and was flying. Glinka banked into his clearing turn as the next pilot followed him. Behind him jet exhaust and running lights flared on the deck.

The first carrier-launched combat mission in Russian history was under way.

0257
SADF National Command Center

Every hourly update since sundown had brought de Villiers more bad news. The general had imagined that, after months of waiting for the blow to fall, he would feel some relief when the invasion actually began. But he had not realized how soon and close to home the stroke would hit. Even before the first eighteen-year-old private died under the enemy's artillery preparation of the frontier defenses, several of his middle-aged friends were killed in their cities, including State President van der Merwe.

During the Thursday meeting of the State Security Council, the chief of staff had warned his colleagues to join him in the SADF HQ complex or to take cover in one of the alternate command bunkers scattered around the country. All but Davie Steyn had stayed visibly above ground; most went to Cape Town to answer questions in Parliament. He admired leadership by example, but their courage had proved foolhardy. Dead leaders can inspire but they can't lead.

Security had been too tight around Parliament, still under reconstruction, for ANC and PAC guerrillas or Russian SpetsNaz special forces commandos to get close. So no one had died before or during the angry session that debated the government's decision to preempt the invasion, but several members of the government were killed afterward. The law-and-order minister was gunned down en route to Malan International last night; the foreign, defense and industries ministers and State President van der Merwe had each died in a different manner back in Pretoria between midnight and two A.M. this morning.

It wasn't just his own colleagues who had perished. All across the country on Friday, attempts were made on the lives of tens of thousands of political figures, public officials, police officers and businesspeople; hundreds were killed and thousands wounded. Guerrilla bands ranging in size from three to thirty attacked hundreds of "key installations"—telephone and telegraph exchanges; government offices; radio, power and police stations; major industrial plants like the Sasol coal-to-oil conversion facility; bridges, harbors and airports.

Nearly all these assaults were defeated by police or paramilitary forces. From a professional perspective, de Villiers considered the attacks premature. He supposed that, with the SADF already mobilized and war already assured, the attempts hardly compromised the enemy's element of surprise. Still, the ANC terrorists' attacks would have been more effective if mounted in concert with regular troops once the invasion had begun in earnest.

Intel estimated over 100,000 armed, semitrained guerrillas, terrorists and other irregulars would control the Transkei and Ciskei homelands, most of Eastern Cape Province and southern Natal. In conjunction with tens of thousands of unarmed Young Comrades and plain, old-fashioned thugs and looters, they might well dominate the Rand townships as well.

The ANC had not yet attempted to break out of the townships, largely because it had its hands full fighting the Zulus, whom de Villiers had been forced to provide firearms. The bloody tribal warfare had resumed Friday morning after a few days' letup following the phony final peace initiative. If the Xhosas defeated *Inkatha* in Soweto, it might require 10,000 paramilitaries and police to contain them.

Luckily, Smuts International was thirty-two kilometers on an air line from the nearest parts of Soweto—Diepkloof and Orlando East. ANC-dominated Soweto—short for Southwestern Township—and the international airport were at opposite ends of the Johannesburg metro area. Luckier still, Smuts was bordered on the west by Kempton Park, a mostly Zulu township effectively ruled by *Inkatha* since 1990, when Buthelezi's organization won the fierce battles with ANC activists for control of the workers' hostels there. The general knew he would never get back the rifles and grenades handed out in Kempton Park, but he for one preferred Zulu gunmen to Russian paras.

The State Security Council had ordered all three international airports closed from 1800 hours Thursday to keep SpetsNaz troops posing as businessmen or tourists from flying in to seize the facilities with arms supplied by ANC agents. But the move hadn't helped. Attacks by SpetsNaz-led guerrilla teams preceded the airdrop by half an hour. The 1,200 Russian paratroopers in the initial drop—three battalions and a regimental HQ—landed on Smuts International virtually unopposed. Only four of the thirty An-12 Cub intratheater transports approaching the objective from three directions were shot down. Pockets of resistance on the ground not subdued by the guerrillas were quickly overcome by the paras.

The second wave of three more battalions jumped from their An-12s, but the third and final wave was able to march out of Cubs safely landed on the now-secure runways. Over the past year, six Front Line States had each received thirty Cubs—the equivalent of C-130 Hercules—recently replaced in Aeroflot or Russian Military Transport Aviation service by Ilyushin 76 Candids—comparable to the U.S. C-141 Starlifter.

Within an hour intercontinental transports arrived from the UER. Rather than having to drop palletized loads of up to ten tons by parachute from medium height, the transports were able to deliver them out their rear cargo ramps by low-altitude parachute extraction. The arrival of regimental and division-level equipment was followed almost immediately by more Cubs carrying heavy weapons and specialist and support troops.

The chief of staff marveled at the combat power of Russian paratroop forces; these lightest of UER divisions were in fact mechanized, combined-arms formations with as much firepower and more armored mobility than most of the world's normal infantry divisions, let alone Western airborne formations. They lacked only tanks and manpower.

The intel officer's estimate of the final total of Russian and allied airborne troops that might eventually drop on or land in the republic was 60,000. This awesome number of elite, well-equipped troops included reserves and assumed—as seemed likely—that few transports would be shot down. It did not include the heliborne air assault brigades and separate battalions that seemed to be attached to the invader's five army groups—called fronts by the Russians—and twenty-five corps. He said the air assault troops might number 30,000. Special forces plus airborne, amphibious and air assault forces thus might come to 140,000—a staggering one-seventh of all regular ground troops arrayed against the republic. The effects of these first-rate soldiers' attacks behind the SADF's front lines were amplified by the depredations of ANC and PAC guerrilla gangs.

All major airports not seized were hit by persistent nerve agents delivered by land-based and sea-launched ballistic missiles.

The assassinations and paradrops had in the past half hour forced de Villiers to reconsider his decision to remain at the Voortrekkerhoogte command center. The bunker complex was proof against all conventional artillery, missiles and aircraft ordnance. And the center was safe from airborne or special forces assault as long as Witwatersrand Command controlled the 81st Armoured and 72nd Motorised Brigades, the Rand Light Infantry, and the de la Rey and Witwatersrand Regiments. Voortrekkerhoogte, however, was only 250 kilometers from the border—under four days at the rate of advance the Russians expected tank formations to achieve. *But they won't*, he promised. Still, de Villiers knew he would eventually have to counterattack with those well-equipped, active-duty brigades and regiments. That would leave the national command center guarded only by its own defense battalion and local Commando militiamen.

Yet he determined that remaining close to the action was the right move. Even with the political leadership removed, the military chain of command would continue to function if Voortrekkerhoogte were wiped out. The place was mined so that no useful information or equipment could be captured from it by a successful assault. The location of the main alternate command post was the blackest of SADF secrets. The complex under Witkoppies Mountain, a 7,662-foot-high Drakensberg peak in desolate eastern Orange Free State, normally controlled Crux intermediate-range nuclear missiles, but could also command all conventional forces. If for some reason Witkoppies couldn't carry on, the third national center, under Kompasberg, an 8,213-foot mountain in the Eastern Cape's Sneeuberg, would take over. The general knew he was far from indispensable.

The security troops atop the Voortrekkerhoogte bunker complex told de Villiers that they could hear the monstrous Antonov 124 Condor transports fly overhead through the dark. Condor—named *Ruslan* by its makers, after Pushkin's giant—carried heavier loads farther than the American C-5 Galaxy. To the general now surveying the main situation map, the airlift seemed no more than the thunder before a storm. He knew that it was along the land borders that the tempest would break in full fury.

0300
North of Mafeking, Bophuthatswana Bantustan

The detonations lifted Dirk Vorster off the ground. *Must be 122mm,* he thought. The furious storm of solid-fueled rockets came from at least a six-truck battery of BM-21 launchers: salvo-fired in seconds. Fired from twenty-kilometer range, 240 of the ten-foot rockets shrieked across the border from Botswana. A Grad-P rocket barrage was bewilderingly violent, but blessedly inaccurate. The experienced noncom knew that *grad* meant "hail" in Russian; the ex-farmboy fervently hoped the inclement weather of warfare would soon change.

Launched from near-maximum range, the rockets had overshot the company's two forward platoons but landed amidst Vorster's reserve platoon. He was with one of the two eleven-man sections deployed forward in the platoon position. Nine troopies had dismounted from their six-wheel-drive *Ratel* infantry fighting vehicle; two others—the driver and the 20mm cannon gunner—stayed with the IFV. The 122s hit behind the section, close enough for their impact-fused warheads to shower the prostrate men with alkaline clods of Highveld turf. But the grass roots, sandy soil and loam substrate absorbed most of the fragments.

Vorster shook his head to clear his senses—no sign of concussion. The stench of high explosive and excavated earth was enough to gag a hyena, but he heard no cries from his troopies. He switched on his red-light torch and looked around. The boys were splattered with yellowish-gray earth, but no blood. He yelled for a count-off and status report.

"It'll take 'em ten minutes to reload," Vorster shouted. Few of the troops had served in Namibia or Angola, but neither had the platoon's shavetail lieutenant. "Have the boys check themselves for wounds," Vorster told the section leader, Sergeant Coetsee, a neighbor from the rural Welkom District. "I'm going to see du Plessis; I'll check on the *Ratel* on the way. The Kaffirs may not shoot the second volley at us, but I'm not taking chances."

Coetsee nodded, uncertain what his friend meant.

Platoon sergeant Vorster found the IFV crew rattled but unhurt. The same could not be said of the vehicle. All three right tires had been punctured and were settling down onto their foam fillings, which allowed the *Ratel* to run on flats, albeit roughly. The vision blocks for the firing ports on that side were also shattered, but the 8mm-thick side armor had not been penetrated. In the red light, Vorster could see that the nearest of dozens of visible impact craters were about a meter away. A close call. He hurried off in search of his lieutenant.

As he trotted briskly south, he thought, *This is it. War at last. No more politics; no more compromise. It's us or them now.* He was exhilarated.

Vorster discovered his platoon leader, *Tweede Luitenant* J. J. du Plessis, just where expected. That is, just where the lad shouldn't be—in his command *Ratel*, a variant of the IFV without an autocannon but with extra electronics. The driver's forward vision blocks of the coffin-shaped steel monster were broken, but the *Ratel* was otherwise unwounded. Du Plessis was studying a map; Vorster closed his eyes to protect his night vision and knocked on the vehicle's right rear door.

"Put out the bloody light," he shouted, then diplomatically added, "sir." The .50-caliber machine gunner looked at the officer, who nodded. The crewman switched off the light.

Vorster opened his eyes and climbed inside the cramped IFV.

"Nobody was hurt in Coetsee's section, Lieutenant," he reported in Afrikaans. "How about the other two sections?"

"No section leaders have checked in yet." The boy looked white and clammy, clearly shaken by the ferocity of the bombardment.

Vorster contained his anger. "Don't you think it would be a good idea to see how the men are doing? Sir?"

"Yes, I'll do that," du Plessis said, looking for someplace to lay his map.

"Before you go, sir, I have a . . . request." That sounded better than "suggestion."

"Yes," the officer mumbled, still fumbling with the map folder.

"In case they unload on us again, I suggest we move forward. They probably don't have any spotters, so they're not likely to shorten their range. They'll probably lengthen it. I assume they were trying to hit our two forward platoons."

"Do you think so, Staff Sergeant?" It seemed the lieutenant was coming around. "That's not by the book, is it?"

"I don't know what our bloody book says," Vorster snapped, "but I know what Russians, Cubans and Angolans usually do. I figure Botswanans, Arabs, Koreans—or whoever we're up against—they'll go by the same Russian book. They're near maximum range now; if they hit us by accident, I doubt they took air density into account on the first volley. So I think we should move up 200 meters."

J. J. du Plessis realized with a start, *This field slaughterer really is a soldier.* "We're supposed to protect the mortars and company support units, but I don't see how 200 meters can matter much. All right, Sergeant. I'll give the order. Then I'll visit the sections."

"Good. Thank you, sir." Vorster gave the hint of a salute and backed out into the chill night of the subtropical 5,000-foot Highveld. During the Boer War his great-grandfather had scourged the British across this plateau, riding with de Wet's Commando after the siege of Mafeking was lifted in May 1900. Dirk Vorster had never heard the French saying *plus ça change,* but he did recognize that precious little had changed in ninety-three years.

Vorster's company was to back up the battalion's two

forward or "up" companies, just as his platoon backed up the company's other two platoons. It was a good place to be—rearmost of the mechanized battalion's nine rifle platoons. If there were a breakthrough, his company and platoon would fight the mobile, counterattacking battle.

No sooner had the IFVs driven past the foxholes than another horrendous salvo exploded behind the moving platoon. Inside the *Ratels,* alarms sounded. "Gas!" Vorster yelled. "Button up, quick!" Coetsee's section, with whom the platoon sergeant preferred to ride, closed all the hatches rapidly. Unlike more recent SADF armored vehicles, *Ratels* lacked a collective protection system, which produced a slight overpressure that kept contaminated particles out of air filters. Nor was there room in the cramped interior for twelve men to put on cumbersome protective gear or "noddy suits." Masks, gloves and long sleeves would have to suffice.

As he scrambled to pull on his mask, Vorster strained to remember which way the wind was blowing outside; he had to be sure. "Driver," he ordered, "turn right. Radioman, tell the lieutenant what we're doing. It'll limit our exposure to the stuff."

Good Russian tactic, Vorster thought. *First high explosives to tear open our noddy suits, in case we have 'em on, then hit us with gas.*

The scared troopies, stifling in their old-fashioned rubber masks, listened to the obnoxious alarm. Through his foggy eyepieces, Vorster saw that the chemical attack sensor indicated semipersistent nerve agent. *Means they might come this way. Otherwise they'd hit us with a persistent agent.*

The alarm faded, but Vorster was unwilling to rely on a warning device. He dug out his atropine syringe, looked around for the least-effective member of the section, found him and gestured for the overweight reservist to remove his mask. The man turned away. Vorster lunged forward and ripped the mask off his head before the soldier could get to his rifle.

"Now breathe!" he shouted, sounding like Darth Vader. Vorster knew this probably wasn't necessary, since a droplet of GB or GD nerve agent on exposed skin would kill in under a minute, but he took no chances.

The reservist waited as long as he could, then gulped in

short, tentative gasps. Sullenly, he breathed more deeply. Finally, he smiled and savored the relatively fresh air. He showed none of the disgusting signs of nerve poisoning, so Vorster lowered the injection he had poised over his victim's femoral artery.

Have to watch this man from now on, he told himself. *If I were he, I'd kill me first chance I got.*

The other infantrymen removed their masks. To Vorster, the swampy, stale air, reeking of diesel fumes, lubricants and fear-scented sweat, smelled as sweet and cool as the Highveld in the full flower of November.

Coetsee grinned at his neighbor. "Maybe you should be running this platoon, Dirk."

Vorster snorted derisively. "Hadn't you noticed yet, chum? I *am* running this platoon." The two friends laughed aloud. Vorster admitted, "That was close." He didn't add, *I was only fifty-five percent sure we turned right.*

"Where the hell was our counterbattery fire after the first salvo?" Coetsee wondered.

"Just not enough 155mm howitzers and multiple rocket launchers to go around," Vorster suggested.

Coetsee was unconvinced. "What good is it to have the longest-range artillery in the world if it isn't there when you need it?"

"I'd say most of it's with the other new equipment, defending the Rand."

"Just like the politicians, ain't it?" Coetsee opined. "Cover their own worthless asses and let us real Boers suck hind tit. Who needs the fuckin' Rand? Let the commies and Kaffirs have Jo'burg. The limeys took it in the last war and a fat lot of good it did 'em." Vorster found it not the least strange that to Coetsee the "last war" that mattered was the Boer War. He pointed out that the Rand's gold was what paid for a lot of their wonderful military hardware, from Mauser rifles in 1896 to Mirage jets in 1966.

Before Coetsee could reply, the radio operator announced that he could not raise the lieutenant. He'd tried every usual freq and was able to talk to the other two *Ratels*. The two sergeants looked at each other. Vorster wondered if all the implications occurred to his friend. It was unlikely that every antenna on the command IFV had been torn off or knocked out by the first Grad volley, but he couldn't be sure.

Vorster cursed himself for not having checked the vehicle more closely. *If du Plessis didn't get the message to avoid the gas, he and the command section probably didn't make it.* "Try to raise Company," Vorster snapped.

"I think maybe it's your platoon now officially," Coetsee said with mixed feelings. He tried not to think about the eight other men in the command vehicle with young du Plessis.

0556

Already there were more calls for air support than Task Force Rybakov could satisfy, and the Eastern Cape Province landings were supposed to be the easiest show. Luckily, *Kuznetsov* was well-placed to support both the Western Cape and Eastern Cape landings, though less easily than *Gorshkov* was able to "service" the Cape Town area and *Varyag* the Port Elizabeth and East London operations. It was *Novorossiysk,* supporting the Natal landings, that was hardest to reinforce. She was hanging out there pretty much on her own and, of course, she and *Gorshkov* lacked conventional takeoff attack planes and fighters, and had no specialized electronic countermeasures (ECM) or AWACS aircraft. The amphibious operations around Cape Town and Durban relied on land-based planes from Namibia and Mozambique and, given the distances involved, the naval infantry and airborne troops there would have to do without air support much of the time.

From his brief conversation over the secure net with Lieutenant General Ouspensky, the naval infantry commander aboard the amphibious ship *Moskalenko,* Rybakov had concluded that the Eastern Cape landings were going much as planned. But local opposition was better organized and resistance stiffer than anticipated. The intelligence appreciation of South African territorial troops, organized in so-called regional "Commandos," had apparently underrated their military utility. The Eastern Cape Commandos were indeed overstretched, but were performing better than expected both in their primary mission as counterinsurgency adjuncts to the police and as combat troops.

"Where exactly is Glinka going?" Rybakov asked.

Smirnov checked his ever-present clipboard. "An enemy strong point east of Grahamstown. It's barely inland, almost midway between East London and Durban. One of our main axes of advance."

Rybakov recalled the area on the map. "Why don't our forces simply bypass it? That's usual doctrine."

"That's true, sir. But General Ouspensky's headquarters specifically requested this target. It was passed to us from front headquarters."

Rybakov rested his forehead on his folded arms. *Damn marines*, he thought. He knew Ouspensky slightly—a capable enough officer, but headstrong. A fighter more than a thinker. Rybakov looked out to sea again. He fervently hoped that the historic mission was not being launched merely to satisfy the ego of the commander of naval infantry.

0734 EDT, Saturday, 29 May
White House

"This tears it!" Callaway screamed into the speaker phone. "I want everything you've got on it before we take it public, got that?" After thirty seconds of silence, the president said, "No, you stay there, Hub. Send somebody else over to brief me and the NSC staff. Thanks. I'm gonna rip their hearts out and ram 'em down their lying commie throats!"

Callaway slammed both fists down on the desk. He resumed pacing, strode back and forth three times, then asked Mrs. Thornburgh to send up Dr. Epstein. "And please have one of the young ladies bring me an easel." The President felt he was becoming addicted to maps and tables lately.

The girl from the outer office had just set up the easel when Epstein arrived. Even before the adviser had closed the door to the Oval Office, Callaway yelled, "The slimy bastards rammed *Roosevelt*!"

"I just heard," Epstein said, shutting the door. "But the navy told me it was a collision with a sub surfacing underneath the carrier. You may recall the same thing happened about ten years ago in the Sea of Japan."

"Yeah, that's why they thought of using it this time. I tell you, it's an intentional ramming. *Roosevelt* turned around more quickly than they thought she could and made better time to the equator. Those wolfpacks of subs that closed in on her last night meant to do this. You think it's an accident this happened within an hour of the Russian invasion of South Africa? This was no accidental collision, by God! Hub agrees with me."

Surprise, surprise, thought the assistant for national security affairs. "That's certainly a possibility, Mr. President."

"Try 100-percent, gold-plated certainty. No way that sub didn't know exactly where it was. It was a Yankee conversion. Hit *TR* right in the screws with its concrete-filled launch tubes. You call that an accident? Beautiful. Right in the sweet spot." Still striding, the President clasped his arms behind his back; his pose and gait reminded Epstein of Groucho Marx. "She could be outa combat for the duration, however long that might be," he huffed.

Combat? the adviser thought. He feared Callaway had not used the word figuratively.

"Of course it was an old Yankee," the President bellowed, sounding personally wounded. "Perfect."

A Yankee had caught fire and been scuttled east of Bermuda in 1986, but Epstein assumed Callaway was hinting at an intelligence coup rumored to have happened in the '80s. In San Diego, American experts were said to have examined a Yankee-class boomer rescued from sinking by the U.S. navy off the coast of Baja California. Not quite a real-life *Red October,* but close.

Since he had no need to know, Epstein had never tried to confirm the report, but he'd heard the SSBN called *Dresnavia* or some such improbable name. As far as he knew, the navy hadn't bothered to try to visit the Bermuda Yankee's grave. By contrast, the CIA, using Howard Hughes's *Glomar Explorer,* had gone to great trouble in 1974 to recover the primitive *Golf*-class boomer that sank in mid-Pacific in 1968—a bad year for submariners around the world.

"They've been ahead of us every step of the way," the President said bitterly. "We've been sold out again, I just know it. I wanna get the FBI and naval counterintel on it." Epstein became uneasy when Callaway started seeing Reds under beds, as he often did. Now he was on another jag.

"I was on the Senate Select Intelligence Committee for

six years, you know," the President went on. "When the secret history of this century is written, it'll make your hair
stand on end. It's incredible the treason that went on in high
places in every Western country. The Russian agents that we
know about are bad enough—a prime minister of Canada,
the best friend of a British prime and maybe the P.M. himself, the head of one of Britain's main intelligence agencies,
the chief of staff of a West German chancellor and all those
other low-life, upper-level moles and spies. And the murders;
they bumped off a leader of the British Labour Party to get
their man the job and tried to rub out the Pope. But it's
what's in the Russians' files we don't know about that'll knock
our socks off some day. It's a tribute to the vitality of democracy and free enterprise that we were still able to come out
ahead. That's why we've gotta nip this African ploy in the
bud."

1400
SADF National Command Center

Now that the nightmare of his people's collective consciousness had come to life, the monster held a certain mor-
bid fascination for de Villiers. The ten-foot-tall situation map
looming behind Major Sluys was like an enlarged, mutant
page out of the Afrikaner propaganda playbook. Here it was,
in giant handwriting on the wall, in all-too-vivid reality, the
Boer bogeyman: Total Onslaught.

Eleven hours into the invasion, the actual enemy territorial gains were as yet limited—nowhere deeper than twenty
kilometers—but concentrated at vital places. On the map,
red splotches had grown like warts at eight main road or rail
crossings of the frontier—wherever assaulting mechanized
troops had managed to break through the thin crust of border defenses. More than three dozen smaller spots sprouted
like cancers within the country, at bridges, around the main
ports and airports—wherever heliborne, airborne, amphibious, guerrilla and special ops forces had seized a key facility.
General de Villiers realized that it was his job to direct his
nation's immune system to surround and devour the internal
cancers and to scrape or burn the warts off its surface.

De Villiers admired the invaders' organization as much
as he envied their wealth of hardware. The brigade-corps-

front structure was suitable to the enemy's resources, needs and shortage of competent field-grade and general officers. *Just how I'd have done it*, he reflected approvingly.

Long stretches of the border were held on the defensive by comparatively immobile, 4,000-man infantry brigades, each composed at full strength of four 625-foot soldier battalions and an armored battalion with thirty-one old T-55 and T-54 tanks or even older T-34s. Each 27,000-strong infantry corps included a mechanized brigade and antitank battalion to stop or slow down any SADF formations counterattacking across the frontier—plus lots of artillery to discourage such an attempt in the first place. De Villiers saw that, on average, each of the seventeen infantry corps covered a hundred kilometers—far too thin a garrison by textbook standards, but then the SADF's force-to-space ratio was even worse.

Economy of force, the general realized. *Beginners' Clausewitz.*

As Davie Steyn had predicted, the enemy had concentrated his mobile, mechanized corps in the eight to ten sectors intended for breakthroughs. Though about the same size as the infantry corps, these motor rifle corps were much better armed; their equipment was all armored and self-propelled rather than towed. They were organized for independent operations deep in enemy territory, with fewer infantry but more tanks, helicopters, fire support systems and specialized units like long-range reconnaissance, electronic warfare, pontoon bridging and assault river-crossing troops.

But even the mechanized corps still had to be resupplied by thin-skinned lorries. It would be the job of the SAAF and the SADF's long-range artillery, minelaying engineers and mobile raiding columns to cut these supply lines. There were also paramilitary forces—the white Commando units and, de Villiers hoped, maybe some of the Bantustan forces as well.

Like a squall line running ahead of a massive, violent storm front, heliborne battalions had descended on airports, bridges and rail yards forty to seventy kilometers beyond the breakthrough sectors. This told de Villiers what the first day's objectives of the motor rifle formations were, but those in most cases were obvious anyway.

From the West Front in Namibia, Cuban mechanized corps were poised to strike south down the Atlantic coast on the N7 and east up the Orange River on the R32. From the West Central Front in Botswana, a Libyan and Angolan corps would drive across the Kalahari toward Vryburg, a key road junction. The Central Front posed perhaps the greatest immediate danger. Its two North Korean mechanized corps clearly would thrust east on two axes—one aimed north of Pretoria and the other south of Jo'burg, encircling the Witwatersrand industrial heartland in a great pincers movement. On the East Central Front, a corps made up of Zimbabwean, Zambian and Tanzanian mechanized brigades with Korean and Vietnamese tank battalions would charge south down the N1 through the northern Transvaal toward Pietersburg, another vital hub.

Finally, out of Mozambique would storm the two Vietnamese corps of the East Front. One would advance west along the N4 into the eastern Transvaal, threatening the Rand from the opposite direction as the Koreans. The other corps was advancing south into Natal, both directly from Mozambique and by violating Swazi neutrality.

It would be very hard to save Natal, under attack from three directions. Xhosa guerrillas from the Transkei controlled the southern districts of the province and today or tomorrow would reach the naval infantry perimeter at Louis Botha International. The Russian and Viet marines had surrounded Durban. Undoubtedly, they would now march up the N3 toward Ladysmith. From there, they could either continue north into the Transvaal, endangering the Rand from yet another point of the compass, or turn northeast to effect a juncture with the Viet corps pouring down out of Swaziland and Zululand.

So, the SADF would need help from *Inkatha* to hold on to Natal, just as in the Rand townships. But de Villiers doubted the Zulus could stand up to armor, artillery and air power. *If we are to get any help from France or the U.S.,* he reminded himself, *it will have to come through our airports or Natal first. Must keep Natal, somehow. Too bad we didn't equip* Inkatha *better,* he regretted. *But even with invasion armies on the frontiers, arming South African blacks still made a lot of Afrikaners nervous. Even Zulus. Especially Zulus.*

But at the moment his biggest headache remained the 60,000 Korean and African mobile troops warming up their engines less than 250 kilometers from where he stood. He could visualize streams of aircraft flying above their armored columns; ahead of them he knew stupefying artillery and rocket barrages would crash, reducing fortifications, paralyzing command networks, surrounding pockets of resistance and weakening his soldiers' and people's will to fight. Units cut off by the mobile forces would be subdued by siege artillery and foot soldiers brought up at the enemy's leisure, or pounded into surrender or smithereens by fighter-bombers.

As the general shook his head, the map faded and Sluys came into focus. The major was presenting another smashup lecture. *Must pay attention to these things,* de Villiers chided himself. Take care of the details, he had learned in Angola, and the war will win itself. But this was different. He was now responsible for strategy, not merely tactics and logistics. He had to think big.

0800 Local, Sunday, 30 May
Langley, *Indian Ocean*

Commander Rick Hallion opened a folder labeled "UER Naval Forces, South Atlantic and Indian oceans, Current as of 28 May" and laid it on the steel table. Gathered around the air wing intelligence officer were other prime players in the strike-planning process: deputy CAG Slats Slattery; his operations officer, Commander Blake Sawyer-Lange; the wing weapons officer; and two lieutenant commanders of the tactics section.

Slats adjusted the document to read its preface, which was updated periodically. He was already intimately familiar with its contents, but the rules of engagement and composition of enemy forces—make that *potential* enemy forces—were subject to change. "Okay, here we go. Admiral Gideon anticipates possible war-at-sea strikes against one or more Eurasian task forces within the next two weeks." Slats paused for the audible reaction he knew would follow. There were arched eyebrows, some low whistles, but nothing else, so he pressed on. "Evidently the admiral thinks President Callaway won't let South Africa go under without a fight. Now, there's not much we can do to help them ashore right now, but the invasion support depends on continuous sealift. If we can negate Russian sea control, the whole thing might bog down

into a stalemate." He shrugged. "Maybe that's what the dip-
lomats are waiting for.

"Anyway, Bubba wants us to tweak up our contingency
plans for strikes against the *Varyag* and *Novorossiysk* forces."

Hallion interjected. "Slats, does that mean independent
or simultaneous strikes? Obviously, we'll be stretched awfully
thin if we have to take down two task forces at once."

Slattery unzipped a wry grin. "That's right. So you and
your staffs will have to work overtime, and then overtime
some more, keeping the specifics current. We're going to
start uploading ordnance on mini-strike packages to save
time later on. But CAG wants to show Gideon at least two
variations on each plan in about forty-eight hours."

Hallion inhaled, let out a breath and stood up. "Okay.
But I'd feel a whole lot better if we had some help." His blue
eyes locked onto Slattery's, and the message was implicit: *If
we tackle two or more Russian groups with one aging carrier
and its escorts, we'll be swimming pretty soon.*

"Can't be helped," Slats replied evenly. "With *Kennedy*
bottled up in the canal and *Ike* and TR crippled or sweeping
mines, surrounded by packs of subs, I don't see we have
much choice. Any help from other carriers is at least a week
off. *Lincoln* is even farther away and has to run the sub
barriers in Indonesia." He shrugged fatalistically. "Looks like
we're on our own until further notice."

"Then we better get busy," Sawyer-Lange said. He
walked over to a computer console and sat down. Taped to
the bulkhead above the work station was a yellowed, wrin-
kled poster with a faded photo of a famous actress sighting
an antiaircraft gun. Below the picture was printed, "Jane: call
home. 1-800-HANOI."

Though proficient with the Integrated Strike and Mission Planning system, Sawyer-Lange had never used it in
earnest. Typing in the entry codes, he booted up the main
menu and skipped to Item Five. The first four were already
completed: initialization of planning files, editing data bases,
prioritizing targets and weaponeering targets—assigning
numbers and types of ordnance necessary to kill certain
classes of hostile ships in the *Varyag* group.

With a separate list of *Langley's* onboard ordnance,
Sawyer-Lange began narrowing his options, working on Item
Five: allocation of weapon systems to specific targets. Shortly

he would integrate strike aircraft and Tomahawk cruise missile engagement sequences. Then he and the rest of the staff would "deconflict" the plan, resolving interference of any one aspect with others. Finally, the staff would assess the overall plan, war-game it, poke holes in it and play devil's advocate. When they were satisfied, they would devise another approach.

Next they would repeat the process for an air wing strike on the *Novorossiysk* group, with an alternate. Then they would repeat the process: a maximum-effort, high-tech plan for simultaneous strikes against both of the nearest Russian SAGs, with a less-complex alternative.

As Slattery turned to report his staff's progress to Ballantine, he noted that the two junior members already were double-checking ordnance tables for "PK"—probability of kill—against *Kuznetsov*-class carriers. Despite the computers and the silver bullets, it still came down to the basics: aviators flying in harm's way to destroy something valued by the enemy. Once again the D-CAG read the poster on the bulkhead.

THE MISSION: ATTACK

1. The mission of the aircraft carrier is to put ordnance on target. Everything else—including anything that starts with "F"—is simply support for the mission.

2. You win the war by killing the bastards by the thousands, not one at a time at 20,000 feet.

3. "Defensive combat maneuvering" is something the attack pilot uses to turn and shoot some asshole in the face who's trying to stop him, before going on to destroy the target.

4. Concerning the tally of Medal of Honor winners in Southeast Asia, the score tells it all: Attack, 5. Fighter, 0.

5. In wartime, our POWs were not released because the enemy sent representatives to sit smugly at "peace talks." They were not released because domestic antiwar groups unwittingly played into the hands of the enemy and tied the hands of their countrymen at arms. They were released because

brave men took their bombers downtown and
spoke personally to the captors in the only language
the enemy understands: iron bombs raining down
upon his head.

6. These lessons have been forged in blood and
steel by all those attack pilots and bombardiers who
have gone before; back when happiness was flying a
"Whale"; back when "Spad" roamed the valleys
and spit death at those who would try to stop the
Skyhawks. And the enemy hid every 1 + 45 because
he knew the next cycle of the attack carrier was
headed his way. Times change, technology changes,
but the men in the cockpit must be the same brave
warriors every age has counted upon in time of
peril.

7. Finally—and this is the bottom line—real men
fly attack because they understand the most funda-
mental law of wartime negotiations: you "negoti-
ate" with the enemy by placing your knee on his
chest and your knife at his throat.

Slats Slattery pounded the palm of his left hand with his
right fist. Then he walked purposefully through the door.

0502, Monday, 31 May
Southeastern Swaziland

"Poor bloody, stupid bastards," Mkize said, handing the
binoculars to Colonel Mtetwa. The lean Zulu prince agreed
with his general; the headlights looked like the transport
company of an entire Vietnamese mechanized brigade—perhaps five dozen African-manned lorries and pickups. It was
too easy. The Mozambican company commander's security
arrangements were so abysmal that Mkize wondered if it
were a trick.

In the dawn light, the *Inkatha* officers could see that the
column had fairly good air defenses—four lorry-mounted,
twin-14.5mm KPV heavy machine guns, plus eight tall
soldiers standing in four other trucks with SA-7 Grail SAMs
on their shoulders. But only four BRDM armored cars
guarded the trucks against land attack; each car carried a
single-barreled KPV heavy and a 7.62mm medium machine

gun in its turret. The transport company commander had put out no flank or rear security patrols; his armored cars were interspersed throughout the column, apparently between lorry platoons. Nor, thank God, was there any sign of helicopter gunships covering the convoy.

In case the slack security were a ruse, Mtetwa deployed only one company forward, within 200 meters of the road, and two back, along the military crest of the hill. But he gave the "up" company all six RPG-7 antitank rocket launchers, holding only his two cumbersome B-10 recoilless rifles as an antiarmor reserve. Mtetwa shook the general's hand and walked down the hillside toward his forward company's positions.

Though Mkize had 600 men, a reinforced battalion of Mtetwa's *impi*, neutralizing the security vehicles would tax his meager weapons to the maximum. If his troops did not knock out the KPV trucks and BRDMs in the first blow, then the Zulus would take heavy casualties. He didn't know how his soldiers might react to the violent deaths of their friends. This ambush would be the hottest firefight Mtetwa's men had ever experienced. For most, it would be the first.

Clearly, the Vietnamese expected no ground attacks so far behind the line. Two days into the war, this would be the first Zulu raid on Swazi soil; Mkize was glad it would be lucrative. One battalion in each of his other *impis* was also setting up ambushes on the Natal side of the Lebombos, but there the Viets had beefed up their route security. It would become harder to pull off coups like this, but in fifty hours of operations, he had already nearly doubled the equipment holdings of his division, courtesy of the People's Republic of Mozambique, the Socialist Republic of Vietnam and the Union of Eurasian Republics. Soon the three battalions in each *impi* would no longer have to take turns attacking; there would be enough mortars and antitank weapons to go around.

This morning Mkize would have to attack from one side only; there hadn't been time to infiltrate men across the road before daybreak. But he had 82mm mortars that would discourage the enemy from taking up defensive positions to keep his men away from their booty. It was just as well he hadn't got one of his companies over to the west. When fighting the Mozambicans, he decided, it's best to leave them an avenue of escape. *They do half our work for us by running away.* If the drivers merely wanted to flee in the opposite direction, Mkize wouldn't stop them.

He remembered Sun Tzu's advice always to give your opponent a way out. *Unless annihilation is your objective,* the Zulu thought, *which mine isn't. At least not of Mozambicans. I just want them out of the war.*

Both the head and rear of the column were now within range of two of his 12.7mm DShK heavy machine guns, sited 1,500 meters apart within 800 meters of the road. As the lead BRDM mounted a double hillock between the mounds of which the road passed, Mkize told the mortarman to fire an illumination round.

The 7.5-pound shell burst into phosphorescence above the little valley in which men had just lived the last seconds of their lives. The white light was followed by green and red tracer rounds from the *Dashika* machine guns, heavier than the American Browning .50-caliber but only marginally more effective. The gunners walked their fire into the lead and rear trucks, which promptly torched in violent gasoline explosions. Simultaneously, the Zulus' other 12.7s opened up on two of the air-defense trucks. Light and medium machine guns and automatic rifles sought out the other two 14.5mm-armed lorries. These returned fire at the *Dashika* gunners, but the Zulu 12.7 teams were protected by *sangars.* These hastily built rock fortifications were quickly pulverized by the high rate of fire of the twin-KPVs and their heavy bullets. One Zulu DShK was silenced, but within a minute all four thin-skinned antiaircraft trucks were set ablaze.

The Zulus' three surviving heavy machine gunners shifted fire to the enemy 12.7mm- and 30mm-carrying lorries. Other trucks tried to get off the road, but the *Dashika* gunners picked them off in the light of the flaming battlefield. The Zulus' fire detonated lorry-loads of ordnance, blowing trucks to sheet-metal shards and spare parts. More cargo vehicles were abandoned by their crews; these trucks, of course, were spared.

A few lorries shot back, but the *Dashikas* were beyond effective range of the 7.62mm machine guns and 30mm grenade launchers, and the Mozambicans' own 12.7-gunners were less well-protected than the Zulus. It was an uneven duel, and not many Mozambicans felt they had enough at stake to continue fighting. The first illume round faded; to help keep his forward troops hidden, Mkize ordered no replacement. The rising sun and burning vehicles provided enough light for his men to pick out targets.

Mkize was surprised to see the four BRDMs turn left to charge up the slope toward his position. A brave RPG gunner rose up from behind a rock about 150 meters ahead of the leading armored car and fired. The BRDM's turret slewed toward him and remaining machine gunners in the trucks unloaded in his direction, but the RPGist's first round struck the vehicle's sloped nose—and bounced off.

"Shit!" Mkize exclaimed, sure that the teenaged RPGist shared his sentiment. To date, about forty percent of the Zulu's RPG rounds had been duds. The boy's even younger loader was nearly cut in two by 14.5mm hits, but the blood-stained gunner crawled to a new spot.

The persistent RPGist screwed a rocket motor onto another warhead and tried again. He got a second hit on the vehicle; this time a horrifying sheet of flame sliced clear through the BRDM, igniting its fuel. Mkize felt sorry for the men—whether Vietnamese or Mozambican—inside. *Probably draftees. At least my men are volunteers fighting for their homes. They have something worthwhile to die for.*

Two other BRDMs concentrated their fire on the little hummock sheltering the brave boy. Mkize saw him torn to pieces; his rockets ignited, starting yet another grass fire. Then four shaped-charge rockets flamed toward the armored cars; two hit and one detonated. The turret popped off and landed on the other BRDM, from which both crewmen piled out. The fourth armored vehicle was also abandoned by driver and gunner. The company captain or security platoon leader fired his AK at the fleeing men, but a Zulu sniper shot the officer. Mkize hoped the communist was only wounded. Captive officers were almost as valuable as captured mortars and antitank rockets.

In moments the firing died out.

Mkize could see the haul would be tremendous. It looked as if over a dozen trucks, at least a half dozen pickups and two BRDMs—one badly dented—would be captured in working order. He ordered machine guns and radios salvaged from damaged vehicles. Two Portuguese-speaking Zulus were assigned to monitor the radios and communicate with any enemy units inquiring about the column's fate. In case enemy troops riding to the rescue might not be fooled, Mkize sent a drivable antiaircraft lorry back north to ambush any approaching helicopters and the two BRDMs to hold off road-bound relievers.

Mkize found Mtetwa. Their long shadows knifed across the road as they pounded down the slope. The sniper was standing over his victim, the captain of the transport company. "Sorry, general," the sniper apologized. "Looks like I killed him."

"Don't feel too bad," Mkize comforted the marksman. "He's only a captain. Good practice for a shot at a field-grade officer or a general." The young man drifted away, still dejected. *He's learned an important lesson,* Mkize thought. *The difference between target-shooting and man-shooting.*

A private hustled over to the officers, saluted and reported, "We've found some suitcases in a pickup. My sergeant was very happy when he saw them, but wants your advice before opening them."

Mkize and Mtetwa looked at each other, smiled broadly and said, "Show us, quickly, lad!"

The sergeant lifted a tarp and revealed the treasure: a ground-mount AT-3 antitank missile launcher and a number of reloads packed between boxes of RPG warheads and sustainer rockets. The Zulu Army had just acquired its first antitank guided missiles.

The sergeant's rifle squad had found seven other similarly loaded, cargo-intact pickups, four of which were operable. Sadly, nine had burnt or blown up. But three of the undamaged Nissans each contained a 73mm SPG-9 recoilless rifle as well as a 120mm AT-3 missile launcher, called "suitcase sagger" by NATO. Also found were crated rounds for the two crew-served antitank weapons and for RPGs, the warhead of which also fit SPG-9s.

Several SA-7 launchers were found intact, but every reload missile—known as *Strela* to the Russians—was damaged or destroyed. There was no way of knowing if the launchers were operable. Since tactical aircraft were the Zulus' greatest danger, SAMs were always the first loot Mkize's officers sought in the wrecked trucks.

Mtetwa's company captains and the battalion major reported that ammunition and weapons were taken in abundance, but little food or medicine. Classic Russian-style supply arrangements: lorries take forward nothing but fuel and ammo and bring back the wounded. The troops are expected to live off their rations, the land, or do without for five days of continuous combat, after which they are reckoned to be dead or used up.

Mkize estimated that the seventy-odd trucks and overloaded pickups had carried around 200 tons of supplies—mostly artillery, rocket, tank gun and mortar rounds. Mkize guessed that, before so many of the trucks blew up, there must have been close to 2,000 122mm howitzer rounds—over a unit of fire for a twenty-four-gun battalion. About forty tons in nine old, Russian ZIL heavy trucks. There was a similar load of 122mm rocket rounds, 120mm mortar shells and 100mm ammo for T-55 tanks.

Reports proved that, as Mkize expected, the cargo was all ammo; no food, clothing, medicine, nor any petrol, oil or lubricants. Apparently the POL supply column was on a different road, or the Viet mechanized brigade was relying on capturing fuel. *Maybe they're using helicopter-delivered bladders.* He had found no pipeline.

"Hurry it up," Mkize ordered. "The enemy won't let us stay here forever." As one company packed up the Zulus' old weapons and prepared the wounded for travel, another fanned out as a security screen north of the ambush site and the third crawled all over the battalion's booty.

With the captured weapons to shoot the dozens of tons of ammunition, the antitank guided missile, recoilless gun and RPG rounds, the ambush had yielded enough ordnance to keep Mkize's division in the field for weeks of intensive raiding. He was well-pleased but anxious to get off the road and back into the hills.

Then the general heard Mtetwa shout: "We're rich! We're rich!" He cupped his mouth and yelled to Mkize, "Gre-e-mlins!"

Mkize thought, *All right!* but wondered what his English-speaking soldiers must think of their highest-ranking officers. He jogged toward Mtetwa as fast as dignity allowed.

"It was practically the last lorry we examined," the *impi* commander said breathlessly. "Its tires were shot out and it skidded off the road."

"I can see that," Mkize replied impatiently. "Are there launchers?"

"Oh, didn't I tell you?" the colonel asked slyly. "Just look." Mtetwa threw back the canvas cover. Wedged between long crates of missiles were the even longer, wider carrying cases of two surface-to-air missile launchers. Open on the crates was a third case; the launcher was clearly not for a Grail. It had to be for an SA-14 Gremlin—*Strela-3*. The two officers looked at each other, wide-eyed. Gremlin was far more advanced than the twenty-year-old, easily decoyed Grail. In fact, SA-14 compared favorably to the U.S. Stinger.

When they settled down, Mkize said, "Well done. Now let's move out."

The men hastily loaded everything they could onto the remaining vehicles. The lighter booty they lugged themselves. Everything else was detonated from a safe distance. As Mtetwa's engineer platoon lined the road with newly acquired mines, the Zulus trudged north and east up the escarpment of the Lebombos—lower but no less steep than the Drakensbergs. Soon the smells of phosphorus and burnt grass, trucks, ordnance and bodies were replaced by clean mountain air.

The sappers heard helicopters in the distance; the Portuguese-speaking radiomen told the enemy pilots everything was under control, but asked for ambulances. The choppers did not turn back.

The trucks and pickups driving triumphantly north added as many RPMs as their overburdened Russian and Japanese engines could stand. Their goal was Cecil Mack's Pass, where Mozambican guards had been overcome by a Zulu platoon at the same moment the white phosphorus mortar round had arched through the dawn. The *Inkatha* supply column turned east toward the pass, at the entrance to which three tall Zulus shouldered Gremlins.

The sun illuminated the port sides of the Hinds; where it glinted on their bullet-proof canopies, the Gremlins' "all-aspect" infrared seekers found what they were looking for. The Zulu gunners heard the tone they'd been told to listen for. They held their breath against the toxic rocket exhausts and fired.

The missile plumes and dust back-blast alerted the Viet pilots to their danger. They popped flares and banked to

evade the streaking SAMs. But they were too low and their
helos too unresponsive. The missiles liked the hot engine
metal they now saw even more than the reflected sunlight.
Two Gremlins hit the same armored Mi-24 amidships. Now a
kerosene fireball, it autorotated to the Swazi earth, then exploded violently. The third SAM missed the second helo,
whose pilot had already turned tail.

A Zulu *impi* had victoriously entered the missile age.

1200
SADF National Command Center

The changed map covering the wall behind Sluys required new metaphors. De Villiers now saw Saturday's warts
and cancers as structural defects in his nation's architecture,
brought on by a continuing earthquake. The border crossings
had enlarged and grown together. They were the entering
wedges for the armored wrecking crews. The general knew
that, when the holes torn in his forward defenses had been
sufficiently widened, the enemy corps commanders would
release their armored brigades through the openings into the
SADF rear.

Last night and early this morning, five 2,600-man air-
assault brigades, complete with light-armored vehicles, had
been transported by Mi-26 Halo and Mi-8 Hip helicopters
onto objectives two or three days' march ahead of the most
advanced enemy mechanized corps. The landings had been
covered by Mi-8 and -24 Hind gunships. Giant Mi-26 Halos
—the world's heaviest-lifting helo—had carried the brigades'
eighty-one armored fighting vehicles and recon or antitank
armored cars.

De Villiers would try to wipe out these airheads and
shoot down the helos resupplying them. Whether they held
on or not, the heliborne units accelerated the enemy's pace
of advance. The most exposed air-assault brigade had occupied Prieska, Cape Province, after a fierce fight with local
commando militias. Prieska was at least three days' drive
down the R32 from the current position of the Cuban mechanized corps advancing along the Orange River from Up-
ington. Ryneveld Airport there had been captured in the first
hours of the war by a Russian battalion and a Cuban company of heliborne infantry; these 550 men had held out until

relieved by the Cubans charging out of Namibia. The general had decided it was worth diverting active-duty troops to retake Prieska, two-thirds of the way from the Namibian border to the critical road and rail junction of De Aar.

The existing air-assault brigades were not de Villiers's main worry. He expected the avalanche of armored brigades tomorrow or Wednesday. The tank formations would penetrate deeply, spring on South African command posts, overrun artillery batteries, seize vital junctions and render his remaining border positions untenable. He would have to order a general withdrawal to avoid encirclement. There was nothing else for it. Work had already begun on interior defense lines.

Yesterday de Villiers had considered counterattacking into Botswana to get behind the Korean corps's supply lines. Most of the enemy's side of the frontier was very weakly held by third-rate foot soldiers. But they were in strong defensive works, backed by corps- and front-level fire support and counterattack forces. Yet de Villiers gave up the idea less because of potential enemy opposition than because his own units were too heavily engaged defending themselves to be pulled out of line, shaped into a counterattack and provided with coordinated air and artillery support.

Although two more airborne divisions had landed at Smuts International, these elite forces had not yet tried to punch through the meager defenses surrounding them. A few transports had been shot down, including one of the giant *Ruslans*. But now there was an airborne corps in the northern suburbs of Jo'burg, including heavy artillery, long-range multiple rocket launchers and surface-to-surface missiles. The counterbattery fire of these weapons outranged even the SADF's six-inch gun-howitzers—superb but limited in number—so shelling the airport garrison into surrender was no longer possible.

The general did not regret holding back the regiments with which he might have swept the airport clear of the first three battalions of paratroopers. The Russians were well-equipped with antiarmor weapons and he could ill afford to have lost *Bufels*, *Ratels*, *Elands* and *Rooikats* this early in the game. Now he would have full-strength formations with which to counterattack the Korean mechanized corps, forty and fifty kilometers closer to Jo'burg and Pretoria today than yesterday. This was a slower rate of advance than called for in Russian textbooks, but the armored columns were still approaching steadily. Besides, if they hadn't been able to capture it, they'd have gassed and bombed Smuts. So far, it had proved wiser to seal off the airborne divisions like an encysted infection. They were doing less damage there than they might have on other fronts.

Nevertheless, de Villiers half expected at least one of the parachute divisions, although not designed for the role, to take the offensive tomorrow. He surmised it would try to secure a corridor around Jo'burg to Soweto, but it might head north instead, toward Voortrekkerhoogte. His staff had already made plans for abandoning the Outlook Hill Center and moving to the Witkoppies Center in—under—the Orange Free State Drakensbergs.

When the British forced us out of Pretoria and Jo'burg in 1900, de Villiers reflected, *the war dragged on for two more years. Turning guerrilla didn't work then; it's not even a serious option this time. Partisan warfare against an ANC regime would mean annihilation. No, we have to hold onto the Rand now. Which means putting pressure on somewhere else. But where?*

His gaze was drawn southeast toward Natal, toward the sea.

7

1 and 2 June

1530 Local, Tuesday, 1 June
Langley, 350 Miles Southwest of Reunion Island

Chuck Gideon needed some air. Stepping onto the wing of the bridge, he walked aft along the island superstructure. Then he climbed a short set of stairs, taking steps two at a time, and arrived at the radar platform overlooking the stern. They had crossed the Tropic of Capricorn that morning, but metal surfaces exposed to the afternoon sun were still almost too hot to touch.

The admiral relished the cloud-streaked sky, the sight of the ship's wake, the oiler steaming in formation alongside. The faint odor of stack gas was tolerable, carried away to starboard.

Gideon leaned over the rail for a moment, inhaling the refueling that was underway. Support lines and fuel-oil hoses linked *Langley* and the *Sacramento*-class AOE, USS *Roseburg,* like umbilicals. Which, in a very real sense, they were. Navies had progressed through four eras of propulsion—oar, sail, coal and oil—and now were well into the fifth. He knew a lot of Imperial Britain's colonies had been established as Royal Navy coaling stations. *Come to think of it,* he realized, *Cape Town got started as a stopover for Dutch East Indiamen. This whole South African mess ultimately springs from some people's need to control the commercial and naval seaways. Then and now; 1652 and over 340 years later.*

Though oil-fired ships would be plentiful into the foreseeable future, Gideon felt that nukes eventually would displace them. Wars had been fought over the quest for naval oil, World War II being the biggest. Gideon had read that, at war's end, Premier Tojo identified America's ability to keep task forces at sea for prolonged periods as instrumental in Japan's defeat. So in their own way the plodding, ungainly supply ships were just as important as submarines and long-range bombers.

As *Roseburg* plowed alongside the carrier, Gideon noted that Captain Jerry Cooley was keeping station splendidly. Command of the oiler would qualify Cooley for a more prestigious ship next time out. *He's a real good man,* Gideon reflected. *Deserves a carrier of his own.*

The admiral looked aft and found two lookouts manning the platform, one with hand-held binoculars, the other with a swivel-mounted set. The senior rating, a third-class petty officer, saw the khaki shape and nudged his partner. Both sailors came to attention and Gideon returned their salutes. "As you were," he said, stretching his arms wide. "I'm just enjoying the scenery." He eyed the third-class, a good-looking black kid. "I know you, don't I?"

"Uh, yes, sir. Petty Officer Elias."

"Oh, sure. We were both in the liberty boat back at Dee Gar."

Elias smiled. "That's right, Admiral. We didn't expect you to ride in with us."

Gideon recalled the incident—an impromptu decision to go ashore at Diego Garcia. Rather than call his own launch or crank up a helo, he had joined a scheduled liberty boat shuttling between *Langley* and shore. Gideon still wondered what sailors found to do on that forlorn island, but maybe it was enough just to get off the ship for a few hours.

The lookout turned away and purposefully scanned the horizon with his 7 × 50s. Gideon sensed an uneasiness in the sailor. Nothing definite—but it had not been present at Diego. The admiral decided on a direct approach.

"What is it, Elias? Something on your mind?"

The twenty-year-old from Detroit hesitated a moment. He was unsure of his ground, but realized he would not soon have another chance to talk with the battle group commander. Elias looked down, then plunged ahead.

"Admiral Gideon, I was just thinkin' about us bein' involved in this war on South Africa's side. I mean . . . well, a lot of the fellas they say it isn't right . . ." His voice trailed off and his gaze drifted away from the admiral.

Gideon shifted in his seat. *Here goes. This was bound to happen.* "You mean the United States shouldn't be supporting a racist government."

"No, sir. I mean, yes. That's what they're sayin'."

"Well, what do you think?"

The lookout's eyes widened. He was unaccustomed to people asking his opinion on anything—especially admirals. "I gots to wonder if we're doin' the right thing, sir."

So do some people in Washington, Gideon thought. "Elias, I could say that we've been ordered by the commander in chief to follow this course of action. And I'd be right. Officially, that's all the reason we need.

"There are good reasons for supporting Pretoria—I mean reasons for us, right here on this ship." He paused a moment, then said, "One of the reasons is right down there." The admiral pointed at two Tomcats parked aft. "You see those F-14s? A fourth of the material in them is titanium and some of the rest is made of other strategic metals. No major power can last long without strategic minerals."

Elias nodded, uncertain where all this was leading. "Well, Admiral, what's that got to do with us backing South Africa?"

"You got one guess as to where exotic metals like titanium, chromium, manganese and vanadium come from. Not to mention a lot of the world's uranium, gold, platinum and diamonds. What's worse, in a lot of cases, the only other major supplier of some of these things is the UER."

Seeing he'd made a point, Gideon changed tack. "But also consider this: a large part of the South African Army is composed of blacks. They could turn on the whites overnight, but they haven't. And thousands of black people have died trying to get *into* South Africa, from Mozambique and elsewhere. Just think about that." Gideon knew he had made a telling point. "Elias, as bad as things are in South Africa, do you suppose those people know something that your friends don't know?"

The Detroit street kid nodded slowly. "Nobody ever said nothin' about that, sir. I mean, not to me." He thought a moment. "Things must be really bad in those other places, if black people want to get *into* South Africa, huh? Sir," he hastily added.

"Elias, you know about street gangs, right? Well, a thousand years of tribal warfare makes Washington or LA look like a Sunday school argument. None of us can imagine it; nothing comes close." He winked conspiratorially. "Next time your bros lip off about South Africa, you tell them what I said. If they still want to argue, tell them to come see me."

"You mean it, Admiral?"

"I sure do, Elias."

1600
SADF National Command Center

The war was assuming shape. Clear-cut forms had precipitated out of its fluid early phase. One pleasant surprise for de Villiers was the performance of his territorial militias in main battle conditions.

The younger Commando reservists—aged thirty-two to forty-five—were proving remarkably effective in containing the amphibious landings. Conventional combat was not in their job description, but on the defensive in the Western Cape, Eastern Cape and Natal, they had given good accounts of themselves when recruited to beef up the regulars' lines.

Most Commandos were white men who had completed nine months to two years of active-duty national service between 1968 and 1981, followed by twelve years of thirty- to ninety-day call-ups as Citizen Force reservists. Militia with less military experience or older—white males forty-six to fifty-five, plus some white women and nonwhite volunteers— were nevertheless proving useful in their intended "home guard" role as police auxiliaries, protecting key points from guerrillas. The inconveniences endured by the white populace in militarizing to maintain apartheid was paying some useful dividends.

And the 20,000 male and female Air Commandos were invaluable as artillery spotters and scouts; unfortunately, they were suffering heavy losses and morale was declining in their thirteen squadrons.

The Russian, Cuban, Korean and Vietnamese naval infantry had secured and widened their bridgeheads in Western and Eastern Cape Province and Natal. The invading marines controlled the Eastern Cape coast from the Gamtoos River west of Port Elizabeth to the Great Kei River beyond East London. All major Eastern Cape towns had been seized on the first day of the war by ANC urban guerrillas and partisans from the Xhosa Bantustans of Ciskei and Transkei. From the Great Kei all the way to Durban, the shore and everything inland to the Lesotho border was also secure, since the ANC dominated the Transkei and southern Natal.

The division-sized force of mechanized Russian and Korean marines working its way up the R32 from Algoa Bay, through the gorges of the Great Fish River, now threatened Cradock. This mountain town was the last cork bottling the attacking force in the river valley. The Cradock Commando was fighting well, helped by good defensive terrain. Last night, the Russians had outflanked their positions in the natural fortress of the upper Great Fish Valley by helicopter descents on passes northeast of the town. De Villiers expected Cradock to fall or be bypassed tonight. Then the marines would roll across the interior plateau toward De Aar, where a second Russian airborne division had landed early this morning.

Reports of naval air strikes showed that the offensive was concentrating on Cradock. On the previous three days, *Kuznetsov* had helped *Gorshkov*'s jumpjets support the Russian and Cuban marines in the Western Cape. Now it appeared that *Kuznetsov*'s air wing had been dedicated to objectives in the Eastern Cape mountains as well as *Varyag*'s.

De Villiers knew that one reason the enemy advance in the Eastern Cape was more successful than in Natal was the pro-ANC orientation of the local Xhosas. Quite the opposite was true in Natal, where the majority Zulus were raiding the supply lines of the invading naval infantry stalled before Pietermaritzburg. Enemy hopes of a general rising by oppressed blacks had proven illusory. Despite the Young Comrades' most persuasive efforts—necklacing with burning tires and hacking to death with *pangas* suspected government or *Inkatha* collaborators—the majority of blacks remained neutral. Still, over 100,000 South African blacks, and some whites, Coloureds and Asians, had sided with the enemy. A similar number were actively resisting the invasion, if not in fact actually supporting Pretoria. *Even if we win,* de Villiers realized, *the bloodshed will go on unless there is a new regime in power, neither ANC nor National Party. No time to think about that now.*

He surveyed the coastline. Before the war, de Villiers had fought to keep the navy's budget down, and the entire service had been swept away on Day One. South Africa could never have built a navy able to resist the Russian invasion armada, but now he regretted his opposition to indigenous construction of two more subs to augment the three upgraded ex-French SSKs. With five subs, one might have survived, silently to keep an eye on the Russians. It greatly chagrined him not to be able to provide the sort of information that Jackson, the cheeky black American naval attaché, kept demanding.

On the bright side, the strategic withdrawals de Villiers had ordered yesterday were going better than he had expected—a tribute to the SADF's training, discipline and officer corps. Nowhere had the orderly retreat turned into a confused rout. By sacrificing small units fighting rear-guard actions, Northwest Command had pulled back to a temporary defense line along Harts River with acceptably light losses. The command maintained its cohesion; if, as expected, the enemy let loose its tank brigades tomorrow, there would be no forward positions to encircle.

The next stage of the phased withdrawal would be to the prepared fortifications along the Vaal River, the boundary of the Orange Free State. De Villiers knew he could not trade space for time indefinitely. Having a strong, continuous defense line would enable him to hold the enemy with fewer troops. Behind the Vaal, he would build a counterattack force to be transferred from the stabilized front to wherever it would do the most good. The central location of the OFS made it the logical place to assemble a counterattack formation.

De Villiers saw three options for counterattack out of the OFS. Relieving De Aar would be the easiest, but also the least productive. The most promising stroke was the least likely of success—hitting the right flank of the southern tong of the Korean pincer trying to surround the Rand. The third option—Natal—required moving units the greatest distance, but had a good chance of success once they attacked. And the possible result—knocking Mozambique out of the war—might justify the risk of transferring troops so far without adequate air cover.

Which brought him back to his mission to contact Mkize, the Zulu divisional commander who had been an SADF sergeant. When Sluys had scoffed, de Villiers had reminded the major that the winningest general of World War II, Marshal Zhukov, had begun as a czarist cavalry sergeant.

Sluys came through with just the men for the liaison job. The team consisted of, as the major had put it, "a Pom poof egghead Kaffir lover, a local boy and one of us, a real man." The unmarried, Anglo-South African academic was Aubrey Wilkes, a thirty-year-old Citizen Force captain who in civilian life was a politically liberal anthropologist studying cultural change in the remote, cockroach-infested *kraals* of northern Zululand. The "boy" was Staff Sergeant Dennis Khanye, a burly, twenty-eight-year-old Zulu in the regular army, a former regimental boxing champion with a good service record in Angola and Namibia. Both were jump-trained and familiar with radio equipment and procedure. The "man" was Warrant Officer Louis Mulders, an Afrikaner Recce Commando medic and veteran of two long-distance raids in Angola. Sluys pointed out that competent medics were always welcome in guerrilla camps, regardless of creed or color. "And," the major added, "Mulders ensures the loyalty of the other two. He's completely reliable. He'll follow valid commands, but is under orders to shoot the other two if either shows signs of going native."

De Villiers had accepted the men and Sluys's operational planning for the mission without reservations. The staff officer was an anti-Bantu racialist and anti-British bigot, but could rise above his prejudices when the job required it.

Just in case, however, the general had chosen a different staffer to coordinate with the *Inkatha* leadership in Ulundi. Since the murder of Chief Buthelezi, the Zulu chain of command was as murky to Pretoria as the ANC's had been in exile. De Villiers suspected that it might be almost as unclear to the *Inkatha* leaders themselves. With or without Ulundi's approval, the liaison team was scheduled to drop into the Lebombos tomorrow night. The location of Mkize's HQ was unknown, but Sluys assumed the Zulus would find the SADF team no matter where it landed. The general would have preferred more time for the men to get to know each other, but, considering their differences, perhaps it was just as well.

1404 Pretoria; 0804 EDT, Wednesday, 2 June
White House

"Well, then, we're agreed." Buddy Callaway lazed in his chair, stocking feet propped informally on the Oval Office desk. His gaze rested on the face of General Garrett Blivens, chairman of the Joint Chiefs of Staff.

"Uh, yes, sir," Blivens muttered. He glanced at the other three men in the room—Secretary of Defense Mario D'Abruzzi, Chief of Naval Operations Domingo Fernandez and National Security Adviser Arthur Epstein. "Sir, under Goldwater-Nichols—"

"Yes, General, I know about the JCS reform act. I co-sponsored the damn thing that gave you so much authority."

Callaway swung his oversized feet onto the floor and leaned his bony elbows on the polished desk. "I want to repeat for clarity and for the record, gentlemen." He meant the tape recorder that preserved every word of the meeting. "I'm going to allow our field commander, Admiral Gideon, as much latitude as possible. That's the reason I'm basically circumventing JCS and DOD. You know and I know and every pundit in town knows why. American military failures traditionally owe their origins to a top-heavy command structure. Successes, like Desert Storm, happen when field commanders are allowed to command."

Each man's face was expressionless, except for Hub Fernandez, whose demeanor spoke immense appreciation.

"I don't want to short-circuit the unified command structure. CentCom will still have a role to play, especially if it comes to land combat." A marine lieutenant general had succeeded Norman Schwarzkopf as honcho of Central Command; as long as no senior air force personnel were slighted, Callaway knew Blivens wouldn't care too much whether that joint regional structure were bypassed or not. "Since the relevant carrier battle groups and other naval units are in the areas of responsibility of both Atlantic Command and CentCom, I want Hub to control them directly. The unified commands will coordinate any joint operations. Admiral Fernandez isn't too proud to ask for Harpoon-equipped B-52s to pull his boys' chestnuts out of the fire if it gets too hot for his carriers. Are you, Hub?"

"No, sir," Fernandez replied. "But you know I can't recommend using our carrier groups in uncoordinated attacks against numerically superior forces."

"I hope it won't come to that. The Russians have done everything they can to keep our carriers apart, but it looks as if the South Africans will be able to hold out long enough for us to gather a task force. Or at least hit 'em from two directions at once."

Yeah, but what if Pretoria can't? Hub wondered. *Are you willing to sacrifice that many American boys to try to save South Africa?*

Blivens put in, "Mr. President, just what is our role?"

"Consultation, General. I want the JCS and DOD to remain on top of things. Keep yourselves and your staffs available 'round the clock—no out-of-town trips, that sort of thing. But I'm reducing our command and control structure to the absolute minimum throughout this episode in the I.O. I'll work directly with Admiral Fernandez, since his people are going to do the shooting. I'll have to consult with SAC and with General Delaney's marines as the need arises. At this point I hope I don't need them, but if the Contingency Force gets involved I'll work with the army, too. But I repeat: if we lose this tussle, it won't be because of multitiered C-cubed. I'm giving the shooters as much elbow room as possible, and if anybody has to take the political heat it'll be me." He punched his chest with a long finger.

"Yes, sir." Blivens's voice seemed small and hollow in the room. The resentment was tangible.

1500 Local
Langley, *Southwest Indian Ocean*

On the bridge, Gideon leaned over a chart, his arms spread widely, hands resting on the table. After refueling yesterday, Battle Group Charlie had finally changed course from south to southwest. The group steamed for twelve hours at just under twenty knots on this heading, then turned due west. Maintaining this course would take the group within 110 miles of Cape Sainte Marie, the southernmost tip of Madagascar—which is just where Gideon wanted the Russians to think he was going.

In fact, PhibGru Three—the PhibRon, its support ships and meager escorts—would pass almost that close to the Russian-allied island, well within the coverage of Madcap AWACS planes based in southeastern Madagascar. The amphibious group had taken a more direct route toward southern Africa than the CVBG. The admiral planned to use the greater speed of his warships to make up for their deceptive maneuvering. He intended to let the trailing Russian subs report on his present westerly heading and moderate speed, then shake the subs, change course back to the southwest and make turns for thirty knots. This would put him within striking distance of the Russian big-deck carriers off the Eastern Cape before the enemy expected him even to arrive within range of V/STOL carrier *Novorossiysk*, off Natal.

The problem was how to get rid of the shadowing subs at the right moment and with the least suspicion. The admiral had decided to leave frigate *Meyring* behind to drop active sonobuoys all around the subs, in hopes the pinging would drive them deep and slow them down. *Langley*'s Vikings would also release noisemakers imitating the carrier's propulsion plant along what would have been her path had she stayed on her current course. These ploys were far from satisfactory, but would at least make it harder for the Russians' inferior signal-analyzing software to keep track of the CVBG. In addition to the acoustic tricks, Gideon had ordered the PhibGru to break electronic emcon at irregular intervals—but only to radiate with systems shared by the CVBG. He prayed the ruses would work. If it came to shooting, his best hope was to confuse the enemy. *Enemy—there's that word again. What's old is new again,* he reflected. *Story of the world.*

Gideon was thankful that the Space Shuttle had gotten back on track in the past few years. The new generation of ferret satellites and SurSats kept him well-informed on the positions of Russian surface ships. Their radio navigation and communication signals were picked up by the ElInt ferrets and downlinked to *Langley*'s satellite receivers, making it easy to distinguish ships operating aircraft. Much to his relief, Gideon's group had yet to be illuminated by a Russian

RORSat. He assumed that, with the subs following him, Fleet Admiral of the Eurasian Union Sorokin hadn't felt the need to launch a radar surveillance satellite just to track *Langley*. Gideon pushed himself upright and off the table.

The admiral was headed for the ladder when the top-secret Gold Channel printer began spewing out an unexpected, highest-priority message. The staff commo officer said, "Sir, you'd better look at this. It's for you, from Washington. Your eyes only."

Gideon glanced at the sheet, which bore a few lines of printed gobbledygook. From his breast pocket he took a well-used pen with faded blue letters proclaiming, "Survivor, Tailhook '85, Las Vegas Hilton," and initialed the receipt. He told the commo officer, "Have Captain Gottlieb meet me in my quarters in fifteen minutes." Then he folded the message into his pocket and headed out, marine lance corporal in tow.

1526 Local

Gideon unlocked the secure cabinet in his quarters, replaced the decoding book, then withdrew the subcom schedule and locked the cabinet again. After studying this material, he set it aside.

What a break! the admiral thought. *Literally the answer to a prayer. Scratch the old evasive plan,* Gideon decided. *I've got a better one.* He hauled a giant oceanographic atlas off his bookshelf and turned to seafloor maps of the southwest I.O. When he found what he was looking for, Gideon couldn't believe his luck. Some 430 miles southeast of Madagascar—about an hour dead ahead of *Langley* and five to eight hours for the trailing Russian subs—was a 17,600-foot-deep hole. He measured it with his fingertip, and, sure enough, it was just wide and long enough. Not the deepest nor biggest hole around, but, *'Twill suffice, 'twill serve . . .* He couldn't remember the whole quotation.

Nathan Gottlieb knocked and was invited in. The marine orderly opened the door; Gottlieb entered. Gideon marked the page, closed the book and motioned for the captain to be seated. His CSO pulled the chair close and Gideon handed him the signal.

"Nate, read this. It's from the President."

The CSO read Gideon's decoded message twice, especially the portion underlined in ink: "Prepare to strike UER fleet units your op area but do not yet attack Russian ships or aircraft except in self-defense. On-scene commander has full backing of National Command Authority." There was also a contingency code word for broadcast to Washington: "Tequila."

Gottlieb's expression told Gideon the CSO knew the message was genuine, but the admiral followed procedure anyway. "Here's the key to the cabinet for your authentication. You know which one's the codebook."

Moments later Gottlieb had verified the message. He stared at his friend and superior. "What's your call? You just got a license to kill."

Gideon said, "We're authorized to take whatever action is necessary to defend this battle group. Now, our most immediate threats come from the subs trailing us. The next greatest threats are from air and space surveillance, don't you agree?"

"Affirmative. But there's not much we can do about any of them, at least not until they shoot at us, as I understand our orders."

"You're one-third right. Par for the course." Gideon smiled. "You're dead right about the satellites; until Congress gives us ASats, there's nothing we can do there except jam or decoy 'em. But I can damn well do something about subs and planes. On my own responsibility, I'm going to splash any enemy aircraft within detection range of us."

Gottlieb said evenly, "You're the boss. But just what counts as 'enemy'?"

"I've thought about that, and I mean any combatant nation fighting inside South Africa. That includes every Front Line State, plus Russia, Cuba, North Korea, Vietnam and any others that may be identified. Officially it has to include South Africa, but shooting at them isn't why we're here."

The CSO leaned back in his chair, clasping his hands behind his head. He was not as relaxed as he appeared. "Boss, let me ask you one unofficial question." He didn't wait for permission. "How do you feel about this . . . personally? Intervening for South Africa, I mean."

Gideon raised his hands, palms upturned. "I take orders, Nate. I like to think I'm a pro." He brought his hands together, and Gottlieb noted the tension in those strong fingers. "I could resign anytime. But I won't."

"That's what I thought." Gottlieb turned the conversation back on track. "So where do we stand now? Do we keep in touch with the President?"

"Hub tells me Buddy Callaway believes in letting his tactical commanders run the show, unlike Johnson and Carter; he doesn't want to appear in the same historical footnote with those two. Besides, we're in emcon. I acknowledged Callaway's message, knowing my interpretation of his orders will be questioned. So, on my head be it."

"Okay. Now, what about the subs?"

Gideon leaned forward. "Nate, I'm going to sink them."

Gottlieb's eyes grew wide. "Judas Priest! Come on, you know there's a difference between splashing an airplane and sinking a warship. Anybody can claim a shoot-down was an accident, and airplanes just drop off the scope all the time, never to be heard 'rom again. But sinking a billion-dollar ship with a hundred men aboard! It's—"

"It's an act of war," Gideon interjected. "And it's necessary."

Nate Gottlieb regarded the admiral and thought, *Great big brass ones.* "Chuck, that's awful damned dicey. We'd have to sink both trailers simultaneously to avoid a tip-off and retaliation. A damage or mission-kill's no good. How do we do that?"

Gideon rested his chin in one hand, studying his friend's face. "SKINCs."

The size of prop shaft bearings, Gottlieb amended his assessment of the admiral's testicles.

SKINC—the CSO had always considered the ugly acronym funny, but the thought of subkiloton insertable nuclear components was no longer amusing.

Gideon presented a sheet of paper he had personally typed and already signed. "You know I don't need National Command Authority authorization for subkiloton ordnance, but I can't issue a nuclear release order for even low-yield stuff without your cosignature. I'm accepting complete responsibility for this, Nate, and I'd rather not put you on the spot. But with those subs trailing us, we don't stand much chance against the Russian task groups. We have to stay hidden as long as possible. I'm gonna sink 'em, then change course and speed up."

"If I refuse?"

"Regs require a countersignature. If not you, then the next senior officer. But I'll order an attack with conventional ordnance if I have to. That's even riskier, because our conventional air-launched ASW torpedoes will hardly dent an Akula, let alone an Oscar. But it's not as risky as letting them follow us."

After a long moment, Gottlieb leaned over and pulled the cheap souvenir pen from Gideon's pocket.

He signed his name under Charles Gideon's.

"One other thing, Nate. How many people do we let in on the SKINCs? Preempting the Russians is bad enough, but nuking them? Some crewmen may have trouble with that, not to mention the eventual political repercussions. If a crew can drop SKINCed torpedoes using normal procedures without endangering themselves, as I imagine the case to be, then my feeling is that we should hold this knowledge as close as possible. What do you think?"

"I don't like sending operational people out in ignorance of key factors in their mission profile, either. But in this case I think security concerns override remote safety considerations."

"I concur, but first I'd like to confirm that the mission can be safely flown following normal procedures. That means bringing someone else in on the deal. But we'll have to do that anyway—somebody has to insert the SKINCs and safe and arm the torpedoes. Unless you know how."

"Negats. Let's run it by Lou Tran," Gottlieb concluded.

1611 Local

"I am Commander Tran, here to see Admiral Gideon," the officer announced, returning the marine orderly's salute. For an instant the Vietnamese-born ASW specialist thought he saw something in the sergeant's brown eyes—bewilderment or resentment. Then Tran shrugged it off. Resentment was something Dhat van Tran had learned to cope with early, growing up in the fiercely competitive world of Gulf Coast shrimpers. Even changing his given name hadn't helped. But he had found a home in the U.S. Navy, where he was after far bigger game.

The leatherneck opened the door to Gideon's flag quarters and Tran stepped in. The admiral beamed. "Hello, Lou." Everybody on Gideon's staff knew it was short for "Louisiana." Nate Gottlieb motioned Tran to a seat at the table. "You got up here in record time."

"Well, sir, I figured if you wanted to talk to me on such short notice it must be important."

"I can't emphasize how important," Gottlieb replied.

Satisfied that Gottlieb had impressed Tran with the seriousness of the situation, Gideon said, "We need your advice on a very sensitive matter."

He glanced at Gottlieb, who said, "Now hear this. Every single word spoken here must *never* leave this room. Ever. You already signed the usual forms when you began your Pentagon tour, but before we continue, I want you to read and sign another one. You can't know in advance what this is all about. If you decline to participate, that decision will not be reflected in your record in any way. It's entirely voluntary."

"Gentlemen, may I know whether you want anything more than a discussion, or am I going to do something?"

"A discussion, definitely," Gideon said. "Perhaps an operation, depending on your advice."

"Advice is my business, sir. Where do I sign?" Tran carefully read the typed document and signed his full name.

Gideon smiled at Tran. "Welcome aboard, Lou." He reached over and shook hands. "Nate says you're our expert on unconventional ASW weapons."

So that's it. I should have guessed. "I worked on the SKINC program during my Washington tour, sir. If that makes me an expert."

Gideon leaned back and said to Gottlieb, "Go ahead, Nate."

The CSO began. "We're going to actively support South Africa, and probably tangle with the Front Line States' Vietnamese friends before it's over." He allowed that to sink in.

Tran's expression never changed. "Captain, that would be just fine with me."

"Now," Gottlieb continued, "you know all about the Akula and the Oscar that have been trailing us. Right now we think the Oscar may be within range for a shot at us without mid-course guidance. We don't know just what they're up to, but we'd rather not learn firsthand. Our orders from Washington, as we understand them"—a significant look at Gideon—"give us considerable latitude. What we need is a hard kill on both those boats."

Tran was shocked that the admiral and his CSO were planning an apparently unprovoked attack on two Russian subs. Before responding, he considered questioning the legality of the order, if it was an order. He decided instead to treat his superiors' request for information merely as contingency planning.

Finally he said, "Yes, sir. A direct hit from a Mark 48 AdCap might kill an Akula, but probably not an Oscar. A lightweight torpedo will only make him mad. Oscar's just too big and tough, maybe 17,000 tons submerged, with double hulls of HY-140 steel—not as hard as titanium but less brittle. Her steel is tougher than our subs' even without being double. And her anechoic tiles give extra blast protection, as well as lowering her acoustic signature."

"Okay," Gottlieb replied. "We're on the same track. Even if the 48 were effective, we only have one sub of our own, and as you know, she's not in position to fight the Russians anytime soon. The UER trailers will have to be hit with air- or ASRoc-delivered Mark 46 or 50 lightweights."

"And that means you need SKINCs," Tran said. He looked at both officers. "No more Mr. Nice Guy, huh?"

"Just not taking any chances, Lou," Gideon replied matter-of-factly. "Hell, I've heard horror stories about Oscars. They take a silver bullet. Now, we've looked at the SKINC damage-radius charts, but they're too generalized. That's why we need you."

The chief of staff checked his notes. "As I understand it, a half-kiloton insert has a high kill probability against even an Oscar. Is that right?"

"Yes, sir, at least the way we ran the computer simulations. May I refer to the manual?" Gottlieb plopped the thick document on the table. Tran quickly found the data he wanted. "Yes, sir. Half a KT should do."

"Now, here's the crunch," Gottlieb said. "We may consider SKINCs conventional weapons, but the Russkies probably won't. At least not ours. We don't want to give them any excuse for using highly super-kiloton nukes on us, do we?"

Tran looked up from the manual. He didn't know if the CSO's question were rhetorical or not. *Jesus, Captain. One 350-kiloton antiship missile can ruin your whole day. And they've got 'em up to a megaton.* "Uh, no sir!"

Gottlieb picked up the manual and examined a graph. "This indicates that a hit or real close miss with a one-hundredth kiloton insertable component would probably sink an Akula but might not kill an Oscar. I mean sink, not mission-kill," he clarified. "Do you concur?"

"As well as we can simulate underwater shock-wave formation, and as much as we know about the construction of those two classes, yes. Unfortunately, we don't know much about double-hull subs, except that they're a lot more battleworthy than ours. The Brits tested an advanced heavyweight torpedo—comparable to Mark 48 AdCap—against one of their old double-hulled subs. It worked, but the Russian boats are a lot bigger and made out of higher-test steel or titanium. Plus, they're highly compartmentalized to contain damage effects." He grinned at the advertising saying. "Built to take a lickin' and keep on tickin'."

Gideon asked, "What empirical tests were conducted with ASW nukes?"

"Well, none with SKINCs, Admiral. There've only been five U.S. underwater nuclear tests, and they were all at a lot higher yield—on the order of ten kilotons to test nuke depth charges and ASRoc. But that was over thirty years ago, and none was real deep."

"Okay," Gideon said. "Could the Russian signal-processing station on Madagascar distinguish a one-hundredth kiloton detonation—that is, ten tons of TNT—from a conventional explosion at our distance?"

"Well, sir, without knowing their software and hardware capabilities, the water conditions, explosion depth and so on, it's hard to say."

"Let me put it this way. Could we detect it, using SoSuS?"

"Probably, given knowledge of the water conditions between there and the det point." Tran knew about the underwater ocean surveillance system.

"Would a ten-ton detonation at, say, 800 meters clear

the surface? I'd rather not have any Vikings steam-cleaned by high-speed, hot, radioactive seawater."

"That's a tough one, since we never tested. I'd say a bulge would form, but not a spout or a base surge. That's pretty deep even for a big bubble."

"Then what about the other SKINC yields?"

"At 400-plus fathoms? I'd have to estimate from fireball and bubble dimensions, rising and cooling rates. But I'd say one-hundredth KT, no noticeable plume. Five-hundredths, probably not. One-tenth, hard to say; it depends. One-half, probably yes, even at that depth."

Gottlieb drew on his own ordnance knowledge and said, "Allowing for the superiority of RDX over TNT, for the large nonblast share of the total energy of a nuclear explosion and for the nonlinear scaling of weapons effects, ten tons is about equal in blast effectiveness to the four- or five-ton high explosive bomb load of an A-6. I can see why SKINCs are regarded as conventional weapons. But those ten-ton equivalents are in a single fifty- or sixty-pound package instead of four or five 2,000-pound HE bombs."

Tran was impressed with the CSO's knowledge, but pondered the concern over visible effects of an underwater explosion. Then it occurred to him. *It's not just S-3 aircrew safety. They don't want a Russian plane or satellite to see the bubble.*

"What about blue-out?" Gottlieb asked.

"If an SSN shoots from farther than five miles, no problem. Our sonar performance shouldn't be degraded for long by a low-yield detonation. For that matter, it wouldn't blue out their SSN's sonar, either. But our sub's not in position, is she?"

Gideon turned to his CSO. "No, we'll have to use air-dropped lightweight torpedoes. What's your recommendation, Nate?"

"Looks to me like the intermediate SKINCs are the way to go—five-hundredths for the Akula and one-tenth KT for the Oscar."

Gideon looked at Tran. "Lou, what do you say? Don't be slow to argue."

"No, sir. I concur. How about coordination, though? We have to take down both boats almost simultaneously. The best bet for that is one S-3 armed with four SKINCs. Two

Vikings would be better, but then more people would have to know."

Gideon absorbed that thought. "Concur. We don't have an ASRoc-capable ship in range, so the torpedoes have to be air-dropped anyway. *Meyring*'s helos will have to finish 'em off with conventional lightweights if the Viking blows it. Plus, we'll load a ready Viking on deck with SKINC torpedoes in case the primary bird can't proceed. The backup crew won't know they have SKINCs unless we have to launch them. I'll coordinate the S-3s from here, and I'll have our electronic suppression people standing by to jam any transmissions from the subs."

"Yes, sir." Tran thought a moment. "Admiral, may I make a suggestion?" Gideon nodded. "I'm on good terms with Rocky—Commander Petrocelli. I'd like to fly the mission."

Gideon was aware that Tran and the VS-23 skipper were Annapolis classmates. He studied his antisubmarine expert for a moment, seeking a motive. But only one thing mattered —he was qualified. "You still up to speed as a TacCo, Lou?" Not all staff aviators had time to practice their mission specialties. But Tran was still a qualified tactical coordinator.

"Yes, sir, Admiral. Rocky will vouch for me." *He better. The turkey still owes me big-time for getting him through calculus and differential equations.*

Looking at Gottlieb, Gideon said, "Well, it would be a good idea to have somebody on board who knows what's going on. Okay, Lou. Good luck."

"Thank you, sir!" Tran said as he hastened through the door.

Gideon opened the book and pointed to the hole in the bottom of the sea. Gottlieb looked and nodded. He could see that the deep spot would accommodate two subs operating fifty miles apart. "Drop them into that hole and no one'll see 'em again until after there's no longer such a thing as a Union of Eurasian Republics," the admiral said hopefully.

The CSO agreed with the optimistic assessment. "The Russians will never find 'em."

2237
Lebombo Mountains, Northern Zululand

A thin blanket draped over his wasted shoulders, the old man leaned on his stick, lifting one foot, then the other. The boy hopped up and down to stay warm. Both sentries were miserable but alert. One thing you could say for late autumn nights in the mountains—they helped keep you awake. The lookouts knew they could be shot for falling asleep, but there was a positive reason for attending to their duties tonight.

When the boy heard the engines, the man—fifty years a tracker—began scanning the overcast sky. His weaker but practiced eyes detected movement against the clouds. He raised the stick and pointed.

Three gray parachutes blossomed. The man threw a little petrol on a smoldering fire. More like diving birds than drifting flower petals, the rectangular chutes swooped toward the light.

The strangers landed not a hundred meters from the fire, which the old man quickly doused. The boy ran toward the interlopers; in Zulu, the man ordered him to stop. In the same language, one of the white men said there was nothing to fear.

"We come as friends," Wilkes continued. In English, he ordered his two companions to raise their hands. "You may disarm us," he then said in Zulu. The man told the boy to do so. "Take me to your leader," the SADF officer asked, wondering if his rural compatriots would get the joke.

The old Zulu didn't laugh. Instead he blindfolded the men and marched them aimlessly around mountain trails for half an hour. The medic grumbled the whole time in Afrikaans. At last they came to a cave occupied by five *Inkatha* riflemen. When he removed the Boer's blindfold, the old man spoke to him in Dutch. "Hope you like our guest worker hostel."

Then two of the Zulu soldiers picked up the team's radio and left with the two sentries. The other three tied the SADF men's hands behind their backs.

"Dive!" Captain Second Rank Yevgeny Grechko ordered. The *podvodnaya lodka atomnaya raketnaya krylataya* promptly nosed downward at a steep angle. "Diving officer, level off at 600 meters."

"Six hundred, Comrade Captain. Aye, aye."

Grechko grabbed a handhold and braced for the descent. Over the control room speaker system he and his staff heard the amplified pinging of two active sonobuoys, one above and one below his cruise missile-shooting PLARK, a type designated SSGN by NATO. The computer on board *Young Communist League of Komsomolsk* analyzed the transmitters as SSQ-75s at twenty and 450 meters depth and about 1,500 meters range, bearing west.

"Switch that cursed loudspeaker off," Grechko told the sonarman. "But keep us informed." To his assistant commanders—BCh-1 navigator and exec, BCh-2 missileer, BCh-7 command and control officer—he said, "I don't know whether this provocation is the prelude to an attack or not, but we must be prepared and treat it as such. Sound battle stations."

The BCh-1 went on the address system to sound the alarm and issue orders. Over the wailing of the siren and scurrying of crewmen, Grechko told his missile control officer, Captain Lieutenant Boris Shcherbitsky, to prepare to fire all nonnuclear antiship cruise missiles as soon as the American attack ended—if it was an attack. "They are trying to drive us down, but why?"

"What does it matter? They've succeeded. Let's get the bastards, now!" the eager BCh-2 replied. "An air-delivered torpedo could damage four or even six of our missiles. One of them might even hit our fin or props. Who knows? We're close enough to at least one of the Ami antisub ships for our missiles' own search radars and designation systems to find targets without mid-course guidance. We can't attack the carrier, and we probably couldn't put it out of action on our own, anyway. But we can easily take out the frigate and clear a path into the inner defense zone for *Seventy Years of Kom-*

somol Patronage now or improve the odds for another torpedo attack sub later. Let's do it!"

"No. In the first place, we don't know if we're at war yet. I'll wait until we are actually attacked or until we can come to comm depth to receive battle orders. In the second place, opening the missile-launch tube doors would slow our descent too much. If we keep diving, no lightweight torpedo can hurt us. When they realize their error or run out of torpedoes and give up, then we can launch a proper retaliatory attack. Assuming we determine our orders permit it."

"But Yevgeny Filipovich, what if they don't stop? What if their damned Seahawks and Vikings keep after us like Siberian mosquitoes after a calf elk? What's to keep them from siccing their attack sub on us? If this sonobuoy location exercise isn't some dreadful accident, the SSN may be stalking us right now.

"I believe that this attack is no accident. It is better to launch a less effective attack now than a textbook attack later. Should an American torpedo hit our fin, it may knock out our communication or missile fire-control systems. We might not be able to signal CinC Ninth Squadron or anybody else, at least not without trailing a commobuoy. Our missile attack will send the right message. Even if it is ineffective, our comrades off South Africa will be forced to help us."

"I'm surprised at you, Boris Glebovich. Attack imperialist ships without orders? I'm amazed." *He's just scared shitless*, the captain decided.

"Six hundred meters," the diving officer sang out. "Ballast out. Leveling off."

"Very well," Grechko replied. *I wish I really knew what the depth capability of American torpedoes was.* "Stand by to take us deeper," he ordered.

"Aye," the diving officer said. Though the man looked straight ahead, Grechko could feel his doubts. At this depth, a crash dive was out of the question; if they overshot their mark, the descent would become a crush dive.

2319 Local
Fish Hook 703, Over The Southwest Indian Ocean

Tran hoped it would be over quickly. He concentrated on the mechanics of the job at hand—do what was necessary to sink this sub, then get the other one before it could report a suspicious explosion. The ASW staffer fed the latest targeting data from the sonobuoys into the first Mark 50's AKY-14 programmable digital computer. He hoped the new torpedoes worked as advertised; if not, he relied on the airborne Prowler to jam any transmissions by the Akula while SH-60B Seahawks from *Meyring* worried the enormous Oscar to death with barrages of lightweight torpedoes. Tran wondered if keeping the operation secret were worth the risk.

Commander Antonin "Rocky" Petrocelli's flight profile followed Tran's attack plan as the Viking approached out of the west at 400 feet. Rocky opened the weapon bay doors and the S-3 slowed to 180 knots. At 1,500 yards from the Oscar's estimated position, Tran released one of the Mark 50 Barracudas.

The pilot banked sharply and climbed; the torpedo's retarding chute deployed and the fish slid safely into the water. Its data-relay antenna bobbed to the surface and began broadcasting; within seconds, information from the torpedo's sensors and self-audit systems appeared on Tran's console. The Mark 50 had successfully started its downward-spiraling, helical search pattern, but Rocky circled at 500 feet in case another pass was needed.

The Viking had to stay within range of the rather weak signal from the floating transmitter-receiver attached by twin fiber-optic cables to the fast-running fish. Tran could control the torpedo's "flight" until it acquired the Oscar on its own small sonar, which suffered from limited range and view angle. But he let it conduct its programmed search. Tran wanted desperately to proceed and kill the next sub, but dared not depart until the first one was definitely dead. He found it strange that he was more nervous about not screwing up than in learning if the SKINCed Mark 50 would work.

2322 Local
Komsomolskiy Komsomolets

"Comrade Captain!" the *michman* at the sonar set fairly screamed. "Torpedo in the water!"

"Patch us in!" Grechko ordered. The skipper did not want to believe his ears, but there, amplified in the control room officers' headphones, was the steadily increasing, low hum of an American lightweight antisub torpedo diving in passive mode. Though still too distant to be heard directly through the hull, the Doppler shift in the sound of its turbine-driven pump jet indicated the torpedo was running at high speed. Its operator was making no attempt at stealth. Grechko knew it would hit soon—perhaps within a minute— or destroy itself trying.

The captain flipped the switch connecting the control room with the torpedo compartment. "Fire forward noise-makers," he ordered. "Thirty knots, present depth and heading." Then Grechko called the engineering spaces. "Battery power! Scram the reactors." Even with the reactors disengaged, their pumps shut down and piles cooled by natural convective circulation, the huge sub would take a long time to decelerate without reversing propellers—too noisy against an acoustic-homing torpedo.

Without warning, Grechko called "Dive! Take us to 800 meters." The control room crew scrambled to find hand-holds; all were quiet until their grips were secure and feet in stable positions. The thirty-degree dive angle was exhilarating, but no stowage came loose. As a stickler who ran a tight ship, Grechko was gratified to find things properly secured.

The officers looked at each other and the captain. They knew 800 meters was crush depth—safe as long as there was no sudden downward change in trim, such as a large detonation close aboard might cause. Or as long as the hull welders back in Severodvinsk had not been too drunk or cold, nor the weld inspector neither drunk nor bribed. Nobody wanted to show fear, but Grechko could easily read their feelings.

"We should have launched while we had the chance," Shcherbitsky blurted out. The captain ignored the insubordinate remark, chalking it up to nerves.

"Why are the Americans doing this?" BCh-1 asked in a detached tone.

"How can we be sure it is the Americans?" the communications officer wanted to know.

The captain decided not to tell the commo officer to shut up. "The sonobuoys were U.S. type, and only the Americans have the Mark 50," Grechko explained. "Its power plant and, consequently, its acoustic signature is noticeably different from their older types. Besides, this one is too fast for a Mark 46. If it keeps coming after us we'll know for sure.

No old American lightweight has ever been detected below 600 meters."

Grechko, a former torpedo officer, did not need the computer analysis displayed on his console to identify the sound, nor to tell him the Mark 50 was diving straight toward his PLARK at over fifty knots. There was no mistaking it for a Mark 46; despite its greater weight and length, its fuel-cell-powered, closed-cycle steam turbine moved the Mark 50 faster, more quietly and deeper than the old solid-fueled, cam-engine-driven model with twin, counterrotating props. He had read the Mark 46 manual, but military intelligence had not yet acquired a Mark 50 handbook. In about thirty seconds they would all learn the depth and other capabilities of the new antisub torpedo. The odds favored their survival; they could share their hard-won information with the GRU.

Even as one of its products bore down on him, aiming to damage his ship, the captain had to admire American technology. But Grechko felt U.S. military doctrine left much to be desired. *In spite of its advanced guidance and propulsion, the Mark 50 probably can't reach our maximum safe depth, let alone crush depth,* he thought. *Even if the Mark 50 catches us, its 45.5-kilogram warhead can't do us much harm, despite being a shaped charge. The Americans' technology may be brilliant, but shooting at us with such puny weapons is foolish.*

The diving officer sang out depth readings at fifty-meter intervals; no one else spoke for long seconds. Then, in a cracked, high voice that betrayed the emotional Doppler shift of nerves, the *zampolit* said, "Well, the warmongers will get what they deserve." In a lower register, he concluded, "They've played right into our hands. Now we don't have to trail them. We can sink them."

"Maybe we've already started shooting at them, and just haven't gotten the word. We're too far south for ELF signals to reach us and we haven't trailed a VLF antenna for four hours," the commo officer chimed in.

"Well, it doesn't matter now," commented Shcherbitsky. "Aren't we authorized to shoot back?"

Before Grechko could respond, the sonarman announced, "The torpedo is gaining on us, still descending, Comrade Captain."

2323 Local
Fish Hook 703

There it was on Tran's screen—an ultrasonic image in green of the giant Oscar, displayed as his son had been in his wife's womb. With a light pen, the ob-gyn had traced the unborn boy's penis for the expectant parents.

In his torpedo's-eye view on the video display, the sub's image was blurred around the edges, but its basic shape and gross features were visible. From its girth, Tran could have ID'd it by class without other data.

Tran concentrated on the picture transmitted via the fiber-optic cables from the torpedo to its floating antenna, thence via data link to the S-3's receiver, and through the image generator onto his console. The Oscar loomed ever larger as the torpedo dived on it from the starboard bow. Tran adjusted the fish's course slightly to gain a topside, midships angle on the SSGN for a good approach. The hull was double there, but the inner pressure hull was not further protected by the side-mounted SS-N-19 launchers.

The Mark 50 was reaching the end of its tether. Swimming at about eighty feet per second, its thin glass guidance cables would break in a few seconds and Tran's baby would be on its own. Armed with a light pencil similar to the obstetrician's, he designated a spot at the base of the fin, right in front of the acoustic window. Tran believed the torpedo's active homing sonar would get a good return from that area. And sure enough, the Mark 50 obediently locked onto the prominent, sensitive feature. Given its performance thus far, Tran elected to set the fish free. He selected fuse setting, ordered a high-speed terminal, active-homing phase, transmitted the final instructions and sat back to watch, with his fingers crossed.

Like a father sending his kid out into the cold, cruel world, he thought.

Komsomolskiy Komsomolsk

"It has gone active!" the *michman* at the sonar console exclaimed.

Grechko went to the operator's station. The oscilloscope showed a frequency in the inaudible range—thirty-five kilohertz. He turned to the commo officer. "Signal the torpedo room to fire both decoys." The officer's mouth went dry; he fumbled with the switch as he obeyed.

All hands in the control room realized their peril. They were within the somewhat restricted view of the torpedo's on-board active sonar. Silently, Grechko cursed Russian naval intelligence for underestimating the depth capability of the Mark 50. This deep, the sub didn't dare maneuver rapidly. It was all relative speed and geometry now.

"Patch in the Doppler audio," Grechko ordered. A high tone transposing the torpedo's ultrasonic signal into audible sound filled the officers' earphones. Its pitch changed continuously as the Mark 50 approached—the undersea equivalent of the lonely, midnight wail of the engine's whistle as a freight train passes an isolated steppe *kolkhoz*. Grechko—the South Ukrainian *kolkhoznik* farm boy—had never felt more isolated or lonely.

As the Mark 50 accelerated to sixty knots for its final run-in, the homing tone rose to an almost unbearable pitch. All the officers except Grechko ripped off their headphones. The sonar operator switched the simulator to a lower register while constricting his sphincter muscle.

It all happened in less than a second—just enough time for Grechko to be surprised by the magnitude of the shock and inrush of cold, dense seawater. In the next instant he died, not by drowning or crushing, but by fire—incinerated by the spontaneous combustion of the sub's oxygen under the pressure of 150,000 psi of saltwater and imploding steel.

2324 Local
Fish Hook 703

The sensor operator tore at his helmet, trying to discard his earphones. His video screen flared bright yellow.

Tran could not see or hear anything. His connection to the world 2,600 feet below had just self-destructed, taking 135 men and a billion-dollar warship with it. He had been told that however they died—there were differing opinions as to what was likely to happen inside a ruptured pressure hull at that depth—it was mercifully fast. Nearly instantaneous. Yet doubts nagged at the edge of his consciousness. What if the elaborate compartmentalization of Russian subs postponed death for men in some spaces? He was consoled by the fact that, unlike most UER personnel, submariners largely are volunteers—professionals like himself who accept the risks. Still, he was glad to have other things to think about.

He called to Rocky: "To our next stop, James. And step on it."

Although the half-moon still hung low in the overcast night sky, Tran could see little out his window. Emcon rules and the nature of their mission required that they use their inverse synthetic aperture radar only on low power settings, but even so the system could easily detect any bulge big enough to be still visible after the sun rose. As they banked to head west toward their next target, the ISAR painted the ocean surface with the highest resolution of any airborne radar.

The computer-generated radar image in Tran's scope showed the water bulge upward just slightly, forming a shallow dome that rapidly fell back upon itself. A shock wave rippled away from the bulge, but only weakly. He determined that its expanding circle would probably dissipate by sunup.

If the Akula is higher, the blast wave may break the surface, he calculated, so was glad that a smaller nuke was up next. Tran also hoped that the frigate's helos had driven the Russian SSN down. The S-3B's magnetic anomaly gear would be of little use in pinning down the titanium-hulled attack sub, so he ordered the detection boom retracted.

As the Viking "sped" back toward the Akula at 440 knots, Tran expected that when the boat heard the explosion it would dive rather than immediately come to comm depth or take time to deploy a commobuoy or antenna. It was a safe bet, but he wished again that Gideon were less concerned with security and had authorized another Viking. You just couldn't be sure what a submarine under attack would do.

He called up the sonobuoy data while still within range. Most signals were "blued out" by reverberating blast waves, but one active transmitter showed two strong returns. *No decoy could produce those data,* Tran told himself, trying not to let his hopefulness blue out his analytical judgment. It appeared the immense beast actually had broken in two.

He made a fist and exclaimed aloud, "All right!"

The enlisted SensO stared at him. Tran smiled and cocked his head. He was not embarrassed; he hoped that, later, he would feel some sadness or remorse over his opponents' deaths. But he had to admit that for now he was relieved—overjoyed, in fact—to learn that "his" torpedo and SKINCs had worked on a tough target.

8

0008 to 1612, Thursday, 3 June

0008
Railroad Siding, Kroonstad, Orange Free State

The humping freight wagons knocked Dirk Vorster out of the sleep of the dead. He felt just as tired as he had at sundown, when his company loaded its remaining *Ratels* onto flatcars for the trip south from the Vaal. And now, lying next to the six-wheeled armored personnel carriers, he was also colder and more uncomfortable.

The brevet captain didn't know where the train was taking his men; he tried to recall where he had been each previous day of the war. On Saturday, his battalion had pulled back from the border to avoid being surrounded when units on both sides were overrun by Korean motor rifle brigades. His company CO was gassed; that much he remembered. The battalion regrouped for a stand at Harts River below Lichtenburg on Sunday . . . or was it Monday? No, Sunday.

Then Vorster's expendable Citizen Force company was accorded the honor of covering its regiment's "fighting withdrawal" toward Klerksdorp on the Vaal. Much to everyone's astonishment, including his own, the company successfully held up the enemy and somehow managed to extricate itself relatively intact. He knew that the CO, XO and all three platoon lieutenants were killed or wounded, because it was he, the ex-slaughterer, who had led the company safely to Klerksdorp. Vorster was sure that was Monday night to Tuesday morning. Pulled out of line on the Vaal early yesterday morning without a chance to sleep, they'd been herded toward the rear during the day. It looked like he'd saved the asses of his few remaining troopies just so the imbeciles in Voortrekkerhoogte could waste them somewhere else.

He recognized the railyard as Kroonstad's. At least he was back in his own country, the provisional *Boerstaat* that he and other radical Afrikaners dreamt of. He thought of looking for a phone to call his wife and kids, just sixty kilometers away in Welkom. But he figured the lines would be overloaded with military traffic, so Vorster tried to get some more sleep.

0616 Pretoria; 0016 EDT
White House

"You can tell Rodinkov he's damn lucky I haven't low-yield nuked his ass!" Buddy Callaway yelled. He'd just received a hot-line message from the President of the UER. He felt caged in the cramped Situation Room. "But couch it diplomatically. Like, 'We look forward to a frank discussion of our differences, et cetera.'"

The President resumed his pacing. "If this don't beat all. What a cheap goddamn trick! If there *were* any subs out there—which I doubt—he prob'bly nuked 'em his own self. The lying, low-down polecat. Typical. Just typical. They never change. Well, we all'll show him out. I want the tapes of every U.S. ship with a sonar for 1,000 miles in every direction from those supposed blast sites. I dare him to take this to the UN or The Hague. Not that half the Third World wouldn't claim to believe the lying son of a bitch anyway." Callaway had to come up for air.

Epstein grabbed the opportunity. "What if they're right? It's a possibility we haven't considered."

The chief of naval operations stood up. "Are you nuts? Or worse?"

The security adviser arose, too. "Look, Admiral, I know

I'm not supposed to know, but I think we have SKINCs . . ."

"That better be guesswork on your part, bud, or I'm launching an investigation." Fernandez's calm voice veiled his ire.

"Well, it's my guess that we do," Epstein retorted. "And we have given Gideon a free hand. Over my objection, I might add." He felt Callaway's anger flare, but did not regret indulging an I-told-you-so urge. "Admiral, given the toughness of Russian subs, wouldn't you have used them?"

"If I had 'em, maybe," Fernandez admitted. "Depending on the rules of engagement. The Russians may have provoked him. We don't even know if there *was* a nuclear release. If we had SKINCs, they'd be considered effectively nonnuclear. We've already developed doctrine on that."

"But we have to admit that there were detonations of some kind, by whomever. British and French assets probably picked up the same signals."

Callaway intervened. "See what you can find out from our British cousins and our glorious French allies, Arthur. If I have to phone Prime Minister Hughes and President Dionne, I will. The immediate job is answering Rodinkov." He turned to Epstein. "What's the blackmailing bastard want again?"

The adviser checked his notes, then said, "Yes, umm. Two comparable U.S. subs sunk with all hands and one billion dollars indemnity for the loss of Eurasian lives. That's a million per man for a claimed 250 wrongful deaths, quadrupled for felonious intent or negligence." The President snorted. His assistant continued, "In lieu of the two subs, they'll accept two billion dollars, plus quadruple damages, for a total of nine billion."

"Blackmail," Callaway replied. "I've always said they're nothing but the Mafia writ large, as Dr. Horowitz would say. Running rackets—protection, drugs, extortion, murder, you name it. They prostituted nations and whole peoples. Marxism's why this planet is armed to the gills and can't feed itself. I wish I had me some of them Pershing IIs my brain-dead predecessor traded away for spit. I'd be doing the human race its biggest favor by dropping a nuke on the Kremlin during a State Council meeting, or whatever they're calling the Politburo these days."

"But it would be wrong?" Epstein asked wryly and nervously.

"Hell, no, it wouldn't be wrong. But it might set a bad precedent."

Fernandez shifted uneasily. "May I return to the hotline message, sir?"

"Yeah, by all means, Admiral. Shoot."

"There's a big problem. We can't get the sonar records without breaking emcon, and Rodinkov will just claim we doctored the tapes anyway."

Callaway rubbed his bushy hair. "Yeah, I hadn't thought of that. All right, I'll deny the charges and play for time. By the time this thing reaches the UN maybe the war'll be over or Gideon won't need emcon." He looked at Epstein. "Doctor, you got anything else?"

"No, Mr. President."

"Okay, I'll resort to the unexpected—I'll tell the bastards the truth. I don't know anything about it. I'd like to see their proof. That'll put 'em on the spot. Emphasize that I don't want a war or acts of war, that I'll do my damnedest to find out what's going on. But among us, I won't ask Gideon to break emcon. Doctor, kindly have your staff draft a reply along those lines. Thanks." Epstein walked briskly through the door.

"Now, Hub, tell me what you think."

"I know Chuck Gideon, sir. He'll do whatever he honestly believes necessary to protect his command. He's about the most people-oriented officer I've ever known."

"Would he nuke Russian subs without being fired on first?"

"Possibly. Under certain circumstances. Hell, so would I."

"Should we radio him to explain himself?"

"I'd say not yet, sir. The Russians may have trumped up this whole thing just to force Gideon to reveal his whereabouts by signaling us. Besides, either we trust our field commanders or we don't."

Callaway pondered the implications of his policy of hands-off leadership. "Good enough for me. Stick close, Hub. But get some sleep. It could be a long day. Long couple of days."

"Aye, aye, sir."

The President and Fernandez both knew that precedent existed for nations' exchanging subs after "accidental" sinkings—the naval equivalent of Secretary Kissinger's city-swapping concept to avert wholesale nuclear war. Although he didn't cite the instance, Callaway assumed that Epstein had heard of the rumored French and Israeli exchange in '68. He may have conjectured about other instances, but there were some things you didn't talk about, even in the Oval Office.

0703
Lebombo Mountains, Northern Zululand

Wilkes was rudely awakened by a rifle barrel in the ribs. The roughest-looking of the Zulu guards motioned for him to stand up. As the SADF captain complied, the *Inkatha* fighter got behind him and jammed the barrel into his spine. "I do speak your language, you know, Sergeant," Wilkes said in Zulu, guessing the uniformless soldier's rank. The guard only grunted.

Two more guerrillas entered the cave, wearing what passed for a uniform in the Zulu Army—a red headband, with feathered arm and leg bands to indicate rank and unit. Wilkes had not yet figured out the system. They were followed by a stately middle-aged man dressed in a khaki uniform and black beret, carrying a zebra-hide shield and an *assegai*. This officer, backlit in the cave opening, created an impressive figure.

Wilkes came to attention and nodded for Khanye and Mulders to do the same. Like a good soldier, the Boer did so with no outward sign of disgust.

"Sir," the team leader said in Zulu, "I am Captain Wilkes of the South African Army. These men are Warrant Officer Mulders and Staff Sergeant Khanye. We are here on orders from the chief of staff, General de Villiers. We request an audience with Major General Mkize of the KwaZulu Defense Forces." Khanye and Mulders had both assumed that the Zulu officer was Mkize. Khanye had thought he knew what the former Ulundi cop looked like, but now realized he didn't.

The officer examined the men silently for a long while. "I am Colonel Mtetwa," he said at last. "Welcome to Zululand. Follow me."

About three kilometers from the cave, the team encountered another group of Zulus coming up the trail. Wilkes gathered from snatches of conversation that the newcomers had been raiding last night. He also determined that the leg band with one white and two black feathers worn by all uniformed Zulus must be a unit insignia. Rank designators must then be worn on the arm, he deduced.

One stocky, balding man, armed only with a Browning pistol, wore no arm band but joked with the splendidly accoutered Mtetwa. *Ah, an adherent of the antiheroic school of military leadership,* Wilkes thought, then decided to yell, "General Mkize, I presume?"

His impolite outburst earned him a hand clamped on his shoulder and a gun barrel raised to the base of his skull. The unromantically attired man scarcely seemed to notice. He finished his discussion with Mtetwa, then sauntered over to the SADF men. "You presume correctly, Captain," the Zulu answered in English. "But then it wasn't a presumption, was it? You have my photo on file."

"Yes, sir," Wilkes replied. "Dated 1979. You look much the same."

"Well, a policeman needs to stay in shape."

"Mmm, quite. I hear you've arrested quite a few trespassers in this vicinity."

"Yes. It's been quite shocking, really," Mkize played along. "Most of the poor misguided youths we find run away. Those who resist arrest I fear we've been forced to deal with most harshly."

"Law enforcement is not a garden party, is it?"

"No, indeed." The general ordered the guards to untie the visitors' hands.

Wilkes promptly saluted. Mkize returned the salute, then shook hands with all three interlopers. The captain immediately said, "General, I need my radio."

"It's safe and near," Mkize replied, then started walking rapidly downhill. "I'm tired," he told Wilkes. "I've gone nocturnal; sleep days, like a male lion. We'll talk later."

"Very good, sir," the SADF officer responded, "but I was to give you a verbal message at the first opportunity."

"Then do so," Mkize said without breaking stride.

"It's most secret, sir. I can't whisper while walking."

"Oh, very well," the perturbed leader said and, waving

off his bodyguards, pulled the captain off the track and behind some acacia scrub. "Make it quick, Captain."

"Thank you, sir. In a nutshell, it's that GHQ want to cooperate directly with you. Not to beat around the bush, so to speak, General de Villiers offers you an SADF colonelcy if you'll put your men under his orders. We undertake to provide you with air-droppable weapons and ammo, but can't really promise too much in that regard. I'll provide you more details at your convenience." Wilkes felt a little ill at ease, uncertain as to how Mkize would react.

"Let me get this straight," the general replied. "Your army wouldn't let me be a lieutenant, but now I can be a colonel?" Wilkes, embarrassed, gulped and lamely said, "Times have changed, General."

"And after the war?" Mkize asked.

"I suppose the commission would be a brevet, sir. I'm not up on military bureaucracy, but my guess is, you'd revert to a reserve captain after hostilities."

"Just so; me, a major general commanding ten thousand men more effectively than all those stuffed shirts of yours. And for the other half of your bribe, you promise me arms?"

"I would suppose infantry weapons up to and including 120mm mortars."

Mkize laughed coldly. "In the past two days, we've captured more of those than we can use. We should probably give you our extra ammo. I can't tell you all the systems we have, but I suspect we're better-armed than most white Commando units. Unless you can offer me howitzers and armor, your attempt to buy my loyalty is not only odious, it's insulting."

"What on earth made you think I'd abandon *Inkatha*?" Mkize wrapped up, shouting loud enough for all to hear. "I ought to have you shot as a saboteur. My political officer, Mxenge, would be happy to oblige me."

"Shoot me if you want, sir," Wilkes replied. "But that wasn't our intent. I don't see why you can't remain an *Inkatha* officer and work with us. We merely want coordinated action. We'd rather not have it on an ad hoc basis. That's why we wanted you officially on the team."

"*Inkatha* wouldn't see it that way," Mkize said, settling down. "In fact, there is equipment we need. Not weapons

but medicine, communications and other specialist gear.
We've already drawn up a list."

Now Wilkes didn't know if Mkize had feigned outrage
or not. The general lifted the automatic from his belt, pulled
back the slide and checked the chamber. He said *sotto voce,*
"Make it major general, and I'll think about it." Mkize released the slide and tucked the pistol back into place. "Anything less is an insult to me, my men and *Inkatha.*"

"I believe that would require an act of Parliament, sir,"
Wilkes replied.

"Just the same, you have my demand." Mkize stalked
around the shrub. "Mxenge," he ordered sharply, "take
charge of our guests." Without another word, the general
bounded down the trail.

0821 Pretoria; 0921 Local
Whale Watch 007, over the Southwestern Indian Ocean

Lieutenant Barton "Barf" Ponderette stifled a yawn and
adjusted the steering bug on the ES-3's instrument panel.
The orange-colored autopilot indicator brought the electronic surveillance aircraft onto the next leg of its racetrack
orbit for another quarter hour. For the umpteenth time that
morning, Barf missed the happy era when he was an antisubmarine pilot and there was potential, however remote, for
some action. Now, shanghaied into the new ES-3 electronic
intelligence community because of his experience with the
Viking "platform," he regarded himself as a chauffeur for
the spooks in the back end of his airplane. Barf glanced at
the electronic warfare officer to his right. The kid was every
bit as bored as Ponderette.

At that moment a coded transmission was uplinked from
Langley to the circling Viking. One of the two electronics
specialists riding behind Barf noted the instructions and prepared to pass the message to the addressee, the U.S. naval
attaché in Pretoria. The aircrewman depressed a transmit
key and the microburst message was on its way, far too fast to
be jammed and with minimal chance of being intercepted by
the wrong people.

Langley

Rear Admiral Charles Gideon stood behind the flagship's radio watch and awaited confirmation that the message he had just sent via the ES-3 was on its way. He mused that if the crew of Whale Watch 007 knew the contents of that message, they might prematurely follow it over the horizon to Pretoria, continuing on to Norfolk. He reread it once more:

"Urgently recommend draft contingency plan for seizure of airfields in Natal with troops to hold primary and dispersal strips in event *Langley* air wing must fly ashore next 24 to 48 hours. Coordinate with South African Defense Force for aircraft servicing and ordnance. Report result this command soonest. Commander Battle Group Charlie sends."

0906
SADF National Command Center

General de Villiers stared at the 1:250,000-scale map of Natal on the wall of his bunker. Vryheid was about at the tall general's eye level. "There's only one choice," he said to the U.S. navy officer. "Vryheid is the only other fully developed airport in Natal besides Durban. It's farther inland, but it's near territory we still hold, across the Pongola in the Transvaal. It was captured by a battalion of air-assault troops, as opposed to the North Korean marine regiment at Botha International. Some local militia or national guard troops—we call them Commandos; confusing, I know—and a company of regulars managed to push them off last night. Your planes can fly over Zululand to reach it, avoiding most of the Russian ships off Durban and Mozambican SAMs. But that's obvious to the enemy as well."

"Yes, sir. I'm afraid so," agreed Commander Dexter Jackson, naval attaché from the American Embassy. "But there's a real limit on what our boys can do from bush airstrips. The marines can get by with their jumpjets, but to make the most of the Hornets and Intruders, we'll need concrete to avoid foreign-object damage to engines. And the navy planes will need plenty of ordnance. They'll have to be supplied by airdrop."

De Villiers hadn't thought about FOD to jet engines. *This boy knows something of his business,* the Boer conceded. "Well, then there's nothing for it but to seize and hold Vryheid. I think we can take it back and keep the enemy ground troops out, but damned if I know how to defend it from air and missile attack. You wouldn't happen to have any Patriot SAMs about the embassy, would you, Commander?"

"Sorry, sir. No."

"Too bad. Well, we can't afford to let those priceless aeroplanes of yours languish on strips hacked out of the bush, can we?"

"If I were in your shoes, sir, I wouldn't want to."

De Villiers stared into Jackson's impassive dark face and wondered if the American were rubbing salt in the wound of Pretoria's reliance on the U.S. The general decided there wasn't time to defend wounded pride. "Commander, let me ask you something that's not contained in writing."

"Certainly, sir."

"I agree it's a fine idea to have Harriers in the enemy's rear, but why not keep the *Langley's* air wing at sea? Your people have tremendous mobility out there and still can support us ashore." A staff major turned to listen.

"General, I've thought about that, too." Jackson felt better now that the conversation had taken a professional tone. "I think there's only one reason Admiral Gideon would even contemplate a plan like this." Jackson looked de Villiers straight in the eye. "Carriers usually would operate in pairs during wartime. This plan is a hedge against the time he may lose *Langley*—maybe his whole battle group. And General, that means one hell of an investment in the future of your country."

As a military professional, de Villiers knew exactly what that meant. It also portended huge American political influence in a postwar South Africa.

"Yes, that's just what *you people* want, isn't it?" De Villiers and Jackson turned toward the major standing behind them. The American felt his cheeks flush and his fists clench as he fought for control. The Boer continued. "Telling us how to live our lives, printing lies and—"

"MAJOR SLUYS, THAT IS ENOUGH!" De Villiers took two paces toward the officer and, half a head taller, glowered at him from a distance of four inches. That de

Villiers shared Sluys's opinion mattered little now. There simply was no time for old arguments. The general dismissed his aide with a frosty glare and turned back toward the American.

"My profound apologies, Commander Jackson. That was totally uncalled for," he said in a trembling voice. "All I can say is, emotions are running very high. We're in dire risk of losing our nation."

Jackson knew it was not easy for the proud Boer to apologize to a black man, even under these circumstances. "Yes, sir," Jackson replied noncommittally. "Now, what about holding the fields and coordinating with *Langley*? She'll need to know when the fields are available sometime before . . . before they're needed."

"Our man with the Zulu guerrillas in northern Natal will try to persuade them to join in the effort. If we have to drop in Commandos, we will scrape them together somehow. Colonel ten Eyck has a list of possible landing sites to discuss with you. Rest assured I shall keep you closely informed of this scheme." He paused a moment. "We shall need God's blessing to succeed this day and those ahead. Thank you, Commander."

"On behalf of the United States of America, you're welcome, General. I hope you can pull it off. Saving our aviators, I mean."

"I didn't suppose, young man, that you meant saving our government."

"Good, sir. Then we understand each other. I have my orders and I have friends in the *Langley* battle group. So we're in this together."

1002
Lebombo Mountains, Northern Zululand

Mxenge awakened Mkize from his morning nap, an interruption that in no way improved his demeanor. "General, the white man wants to talk to you. He insisted."

Wilkes, cap under arm beneath the canvas tent, came more stiffly to attention. "Signal from GHQ, sir. Most secret." This with a pointed nod toward Mxenge.

Still groggy, Mkize splashed water on his face from a

basin. "Captain Mxenge has my confidence, Captain. Proceed. Please."

"It's rather a long message, but briefly it requests the North Natal Light Infantry Division (Irregular)—that's you —to seize and hold certain objectives. I'm to provide you a list to be sent, mixed with false signals, over the next hour."

"Am I to know the objectives?"

Wilkes glanced at Mxenge again. The SADF officer regarded him as an *Inkatha* spy at worst, a political hack at best. But orders were orders. "They are selected airfields and landing strips, sir."

Mkize looked up from his towel. "I did not know the SADF had any aircraft left, let alone for Zululand."

Wilkes stiffened again, resentful of the veiled criticism. "I don't know the particulars. All I know is that the request was rated urgent. General de Villiers considers our compliance of the highest possible importance."

"More important than what we're doing now—strangling the Viet mechanized corps's supply line?" The war chief held out his hand. "I'd best read the message, if you please."

Wilkes reached into his shirt pocket. "Certainly, sir. But I must insist on privacy. It's marked for your eyes only, and I'm to destroy it after you've read it." He pointedly turned his back on Mxenge.

Mkize motioned for his subordinate to leave, and Mxenge sulked out of the tent. Wilkes then did up the flap.

"Sit down, Captain, while I examine this." Caught off guard by the unexpected courtesy, Wilkes obeyed. Mkize joined him at the small camp table. The white officer considered whether the fate of a nation and perhaps the continent lay at this moment in the hands and mind of this black warrior at his rickety table in the wilds of Zululand.

When Mkize finished reading, he smiled. "U.S. marines, is it?"

"That's what GHQ say."

"Apparently with armor, artillery and aircraft?"

"As I read it, yes. Not to mention antitank guided missiles, SAMs and a great deal of specialized support. Under your operational command." Wilkes was not certain that Mkize was hooked, and did not wish to push too hard. But what leader could resist such an offer?

Mkize pondered for a moment. *This is it,* thought Wilkes.

"I'll need to see the list of sites. I won't spread us too thin."

Thank the good Lord! "You have the final say, General. I feel I've made GHQ well aware of your strength and capacities." Pretoria had accepted Mkize's demand for an SADF major generalcy, while retaining his KwaZulu rank.

Mkize paced briefly. "GHQ are one thing. You know what Mxenge will say."

"Yes. It's a plot to wipe out the Zulus while helping Pretoria win the war and remain in power. That the government wants to sacrifice you the way Hanoi did the Vietcong during the Tet Offensive. That either way, the apartheid regime wins, just as did the North Vietnamese."

The gleaming smile returned. "Full marks. And what do you say?"

Wilkes rose. "Sir, I say that if no Americans land in Zululand, Captain Mxenge may have the great pleasure of personally shooting me."

Mkize's bass laughter filled the tent. "Then we'll have to make sure the U.S. marines get ashore, won't we? Come, we have plenty to do. I intend to keep after the Viets *and* give you these airfields. Keep your radio operators on alert and prepare for the briefing I'm going to order."

The general held up a cautionary finger. "This doesn't mean I've decided to accept de Villiers's offer." Wilkes nodded. "And, Captain, please don't speak unless I ask you a question. Some of my men share Mxenge's attitude, but they will follow my orders. You understand?"

"Yes, sir. You mean they'll resent the hell out of me."

1331
Near Machadodorp, Eastern Transvaal Province

It looked good. Springbok Lead had the target in sight —lorries and tracked vehicles idling on both sides of the N4 —and was seconds from weapons release.

Then Piet de Villiers's radar homing and warning panel went crazy.

Damn it! Air-to-air band, probably Fulcrums. There was no warning from the two-plane section escorting his three strikers, but that wasn't unusual. Back-to-back sorties, constant losses, diminishing numbers of planes and degraded systems. It amounted to a descending spiral of capabilities. With mere seconds to spare, Piet made a decision. Without wasting time on proper procedure, he called, "Frans, try to head them off. We're attacking!"

The first pass was worthwhile. Piet forced himself to concentrate on the sight picture in his head-up display, snaking in low and fast to put high-drag bombs on target. Only ineffective automatic weapons fire and SA-7 missiles contested the three Cheetahs. But pulling off-target, Piet de Villiers sensed something dreadful. High-pitched, muffled radio calls, missile plumes in midair, a fireball in his periphery. He glanced around. *Where's Brian?*

Snow Tiger Lead

Comrade Colonel Li Sung Hwa could hardly believe his good fortune. His eight MiG-29s had barely arrived on their patrol station when the radar controller gave them a vector. Fascist jets heading toward a Viet column stalled on the main east-west highway had to be intercepted, quickly. At first Li was inclined to detach his second flight, led by a promising young captain of Snow Lynx Squadron. But the regimental commander had not yet drawn blood in this war, so he led his Snow Tiger pilots outbound. The radar data was good, and he instructed his flight to lock on and fire AA-10 long-range radar missiles. He knew the chances of one or two kills were poor, since the targets were hugging the *veld*. But the missiles might distract the fascists long enough for the North Koreans to engage.

It didn't quite work. Li noticed flashes on the ground and churning black smoke. Apparently a fuel stash had exploded. But then he glimpsed a dart-shaped shadow on the ground. His experienced eyes, still rated at 20/8 despite his forty-six years, instantly latched on.

The South African saw the MiG at that same moment. Pulling hard into the threat, the Cheetah temporarily spoiled Li's tracking. But the Korean was not concerned. Jamming his two throttles through the afterburner detent, he pulled up, cutting a diminishing-radius turn across the Cheetah's flight path. Li knew that most delta-wing jets were "bleeders," losing energy after one or two tight turns. He bided his time.

Springbok Lead

Piet de Villiers immediately recognized the setup. Low to the ground, with the MiG high in his rear hemisphere, was nowhere to be. Muted radio calls told him that his wingman was down, hit by a standoff missile. Something about a parachute in the trees and Fulcrums everywhere. In 'burner himself, Piet had energy for one desperation move. He reversed his turn, hoping the MiG would commit to following him. With his head turned, straining against the force of five times normal gravity, he watched the Fulcrum slide out of view behind his tail. Timing was crucial now.

Piet sensed more than knew where the Fulcrum must be. About 2,500 feet back, its pilot surely would be turning right, bringing his nose into line for a short-range missile shot when the Cheetah rolled out of its reversal. But Piet did not complete the turn. Instead, he continued his roll underneath and stopped in knife-edge flight after 270 degrees. Then he pulled hard left. He looked over his right shoulder, expecting to see the Fulcrum's belly sliding away from him.

What he saw turned his guts to ice.

Snow Tiger Lead

Colonel Li admired the South African's nerve and skill. Against another pilot, the move might have worked. But Li had seen it before, even used it himself years ago against a well-flown Israeli Mirage. So now the Cheetah belonged to him. Low and slow, energy depleted, directly ahead at 500 meters range, it was his. Li centered the camouflaged jet in his head-up display and pressed the trigger on his stick. His 23mm Gatling spooled up, shredding the Cheetah's airframe.

Piet de Villiers hardly felt a thing.

1550 Local
Langley, *Southwestern Indian Ocean*

At midnight, after sinking the subs, Gideon had ordered most of his CVBG to head southwest at thirty knots. This course had skirted radar range of Russian Madcap AWACS planes operating out of Madagascar. Now, 475 miles later, his ships were safely south of the detection arc of An-74 Madcaps flying racetrack orbits 200 miles from their bases at Androka and Taolanaro, formerly Fort Dauphin. The admiral signaled his group to steer course 270 degrees true—due west.

Twelve more hours at thirty knots on this heading would bring Gideon's group to within extreme striking range of his primary target, *Varyag*. He'd be even closer to his secondary, diversionary target, *Novorossiysk*. Preliminary planning indicated it might be possible to mount effective attacks on both Russian carriers. The final decision would await current positional data—and the go-ahead from Washington.

Gideon tried to maintain as normal a facade as possible while leading warships at high speed toward probable combat at sea against a superior foe. Having taken every precaution, he was justified in behaving normally. After refueling but before attacking the Russian subs, he had detached his destroyers and sub on a direct path toward *Novorossiysk*, still operating a hundred miles off Durban. To keep their appointment, these Tomahawk Antiship Missile-armed ships would have to average twenty-five knots.

Frigate *Meyring* could not sustain thirty knots, so had also been detached toward the position that Gideon intended to take up after launching his strikes. In order to cover an amphibious landing, this was off the northern Natal coast. The guided missile frigate (FFG) would stake out the area against subs.

SSN *Eureka* was running loudly and deaf to reach her station, but the antisub escorts with the PhibGru screened the first part of her high-speed run. Similarly, in order to make twenty-five knots, guided missile destroyer (DDG) *Carl* and antisub destroyers (DDs) *Davenport* and *Wheatley* had to retract their "tails"—towed sonar arrays. Their other passive sonars also lost effectiveness at that speed, due to high levels of self-noise. But their helos could still monitor the ocean ahead of them for echoes of lurking subs.

These four ships should arrive within TASM range of the Russian V/STOL carrier an hour before *Langley* reached her launch point. The destroyers' course took them within detection range of the Madcaps, but that wasn't necessarily bad. Gideon figured it might even promote his deception effort. He wanted the Russians to think that *Langley* was farther north and west than her true position.

There was still a good chance that a maritime patrol Bear or sub on picket duty would identify his CVBG. Or that Moscow might send up another RORSat. The admiral had to hope all these recon assets—and Hallion's spaceman spies in low Earth orbit—would look in the wrong place.

But so far had been so good. He knew about where the enemy was and would receive constant updates from American satellites; as far as he knew, the enemy did not know where he was—Situational Awareness State Numero Uno. Gideon felt as confident as a man can who faces odds of four to one, with 10,000 lives weighing in the balance of his performance.

1612
Near Bethlehem, Southeastern Orange Free State

Vorster was still tired and sore from his overnight train ride. Under prodding from a new battalion CO, he was pushing his men's repair work on their armored personnel carriers harder than he felt was wise. Now this.

The filthy brevet captain glowered at the staff major, then lowered his head to reread his orders. The major in the sharply creased, clean uniform cleared his throat and shifted uncomfortably, pretending to study the refueling of his helicopter. The other company commanders and battalion staff —all regulars—apparently liked their orders no better than the reservist did.

Vorster read a moment longer. At last he spat, "Bloody stupid nonsense."

The staff officer, Major Clive Edward St. John Snodgrass-Reeves, pivoted to face the group again but ignored the insubordinate Boer, whom he knew had been a reserve sergeant only four days before.

"What is this abortion all about?" Vorster guessed that he was supposed to be impressed by the staff officer's descent into the dusty realm of mere mortals.

"Not even GHQ could be this detached from reality," chimed in Lieutenant van Hoek, another new company commander. "It's madness."

Vorster knew none of the other officers, either. The "battalion" was still being stitched together from the disparate cloth of OFS subunits that had survived the enemy's initial combined-arms onslaughts. The units' sister companies and troops had been dispersed or effectively destroyed, forcing the battalion to start from scratch. Given a few days of shakedown, Vorster felt the new organization might fight cohesively on the defensive, perhaps even mount limited counterattacks. But what GHQ wanted was plainly beyond achieving. Vorster knew that every officer present agreed with him. Probably so did Major Snodgrass, if he had half a brain and an hour's combat experience, which was by no means certain.

"You must be aware, Major, that this is a battalion in name only. Further, many of the men under my command are reservists," explained the CO, Lieutenant Colonel Lubbers. Vorster appreciated the man's grasp of the situation. "This is their home. I don't know if you've ever commanded Citizen Force reserves, but they fight well when given good reason. Could you tell us why we're to be pulled out of the Orange Free State? Without reserves, the OFS could be lost."

"I may tell you alone, sir. Strictly a need-to-know basis, don't you know? After that, I'm afraid it's up to you to convince your troops of the urgency of their assignment without providing further details."

"Very well, but I want my ranking territorial officer, Captain Vorster, to hear your reasoning. The reservist troopies will come along if he does."

"Quite irregular, against my instructions. In fact—"

"I fear I must insist," Lubbers interjected. "Success of the mission depends on it, don't you know?"

Major Snodgrass ignored the sarcasm. He sighed and, without a word, strode to his helo and withdrew a map case. Lubbers followed, motioning Vorster to accompany him. The Boer thought he might have to reconsider his opinion of active-serving officers.

The three officers arranged themselves around the map. "Now this is all *dreadfully* hush-hush," the major began in his best briefing voice. "Your ultimate objective is here, gentlemen." His finger indicated Vryheid, 200 kilometers east-southeast across the Drakensberg Range in northern Natal.

"Bloody hell!" Vorster exclaimed.

"Go on," said Lubbers.

Snodgrass continued, "Colonel, your battalion is to help defend the airport against the Vietnamese mechanized drive on Vryheid. This and the Russian and Viet naval infantry advance north from Durban are the most dangerous enemy thrusts at the moment. If the communist marines and tanks link up, Zululand will be separated from the rest of Natal."

"Let the Kaffirs have Zululand," Vorster responded. "I'll keep the OFS."

"It's not just Zululand, old boy," replied the staffer. "Without Zululand, Natal will be lost, don't you see? The province is under intense pressure from the west by ANC terrorists out of the Transkei, from the south by the foreign marines and from the east by the Viet motor rifle brigades. Loss of Ladysmith and Vryheid will finish her off." Vorster had to admit that the white parts of central Natal and the port of Durban were important to the republic, but it seemed to him that they were strategically less so than the OFS, which connected Cape Province and Transvaal.

The battalion CO asked, "Can you tell us why the loss of Natal would be more catastrophic than loss of the middle of the country, which would cut us in two?"

Lubbers must be reading my mind, Vorster thought.

"GHQ did not elaborate for me," Snodgrass said defensively, "but I assume they believe OFS may hold out longer than Natal. But Natal will surely fall without reinforcements. I shall add, for your ears only, that the enemy will probably bisect the country in central-eastern Cape regardless. Round about De Aar, which is currently home to three Russian para divisions, with another en route from the UER. We've precious little left there to stop these two prongs from meeting." On another map, he dragged his index fingers simultaneously across Cape Province southeasterly from Namibia and northwesterly from East London.

Lubbers pinned the major with a frosty glare. "And I presume my *battalion*"—the spite poisoned his voice—"is the only reserve available."

Snodgrass dropped his gaze to the ground. "Yes, sir. That's it."

"Bloody hell," repeated Vorster.

"It's a case of either you go in or we lose Vryheid,"

explained Snodgrass. "Just among us, the situation in Natal is the worst we face on any front. The terrain there has been our most effective general. Bit of a botched job, actually. Not that the lot defending the Rand are winning any prizes, mind you." He returned his focus to the map. "Now, this is where we need you by tomorrow mid-morning or, frankly, we shall have to chuck it all in.

"If the Korean drives on the Rand turned south, they could cut the Transvaal and Natal off from the OFS. How long we can keep corridors open between the provinces is uncertain, but long enough for you and the other reserves to get through tonight. That's where you come in, Captain."

Vorster still had trouble recalling he was an acting captain. The staff officer plainly resented having to explain orders to a "citizen soldier." That Snodgrass bothered at all meant Vorster's understrength reserve company might actually be as vital as the major claimed.

"Frankly," Snodgrass added, "I was on to your regimental people this morning. They told me you've proven rather adept at this sort of thing—moving smartly under pressure. So we've tabbed you to lead the whole parade, with a tank platoon, some engineers and an NBC recce detachment." The major emphasized the NBC—nuclear, biological and chemical recon unit.

Vorster made a scoffing sound, recalling the night march south from the border battles. *March, hell—more like a headlong retreat.* But he was glad to learn the brass realized his company had managed to pull back in more orderly fashion than anyone else.

Snodgrass turned to Lubbers. "Sir, your battalion will not be going in alone, but I cannot say in what strength this move is being made."

"How will I liaise with whoever's behind me if I'm the lead battalion?"

Snodgrass raised a finger. "It's all to be done under strictest radio silence. Regiment will provide you with guides, runners and signalers to keep in touch with units around you."

Neither Lubbers nor Vorster spoke. The implications of the major's information, if accurate, were horrendous. If GHQ had to pull reserves out of Orange Free State, it meant things really were desperate everywhere else. For the first time in his life, Vorster felt that he actually could lose his country.

"There is a bit of good news," the staffer threw in. "We scraped together a supply of light antitank weapons for your men. They'll be waiting for you on the objective."

I'll believe that when I see it, Vorster thought.

"I do suppose your chaps are familiar with the American and British LAWs as well as both RPG series?"

"Yes, quite, old chap," the Boer replied in remarkably good mimicry.

"That's quite enough, Vorster," Lubbers jabbed.

The unflappable staffer didn't seem to take offense. He straightened in his seat and closed his notebook. "I've already told you too much, but there's one last thing. The operation is code-named Gethsemane; we thought Nativity a bit too obvious. Should we have to contact you, your callsigns are in your orders. Burn them after reading. Maintain listening silence." The major looked at each man. Relieved to hear no questions or comments, he wrapped up. "Well, there you have it, gentlemen. I'll leave it to you what to tell your men. They need to be impressed with the importance of this mission, but mustn't know just how desperate things are, or what the objective is."

Lubbers ordered Vorster to return to his unit and to say nothing to the other company commanders. "Let me talk to them."

Vorster replied, "Yes, sir," saluted and walked away.

From a distance, he watched Snodgrass and Lubbers talk. Van Hoek pulled up in his jeep and joined him. In Afrikaans, the lieutenant asked if things were really as bad as they appeared.

"Don't ask," Vorster responded.

PART TWO
Splash One Mudhen

9

0107 to 0534, Friday, 4 June

0107 Pretoria; 0207 Local
Madcap AWACS Aircraft, over the Southwest Indian
Ocean

Strapped into the darkened interior of the An-74, Warrant Officer Kemal Abdukhmaev checked the switches on his console for the upcoming four-hour mission. As the twenty-five-year-old Azeri performed these preliminaries, the Russian AWACS, called Madcap by NATO, droned through the night sky, leveling off barely twenty minutes after leaving Taolanaro, Madagascar. Abdukhmaev and his six crewmates nervously anticipated the hunt for a major American naval force.

The Madcap had barely reached the initial point of its first search leg when Sasha, the surface-search radar operator, was startled. There, in the glowing phosphors of his scope, was the unmistakable layout of a carrier battle group. He gulped, allowing one more sweep of the radome atop the tail until he engaged his microphone switch. . . .

Before Sasha could speak, Matvei, the electronic warfare support measures (ESM) operator, sang out, "American shipborne air-search radars! Bearing one-one-zero. They've found us!" Matvei checked his console. The computer told him the signals probably emanated from an SPS-48 radar—a type used aboard American aircraft carriers. Suddenly Matvei's mouth was very dry. His voice possessed little of the modulation taught in aircrew training.

The pilot abruptly banked the ungainly jet, with its twin overwing turbofans, into a turn away from the threat. Then he ordered the radioman to send a contact report and a call for help from the MiGs ashore. Sasha, through a constricted throat, managed to report his surface contacts.

Then in his earphones Kemal heard, *"Praporshchik,* two airborne contacts, bearing zero-eight-five." Boris, the air-to-air radar operator, at least had control of his octaves. "Evaluate them as large twin-engine types. Probably Tomcats." His heart raced at that dreaded word. "Altitude 2,000 meters and climbing out of surface clutter, intercept bearing for us!"

Rawhide Flight

At that moment the thermal blur on Major Grady "Mule" Halloran's forward-looking infrared screen sharpened into the image of a Madcap. Launched from USS *Hornet,* the AV-8B Harriers of Halloran and his wingman had been vectored toward the snooper by a radar controller aboard the 40,000-ton amphibious landing ship. Now within three miles of the lumbering Antonov, the Harriers were well positioned at dead six o'clock. With his FLIR set penetrating the dark, Mule got a missile tone and knew his Sidewinders were tracking the twin heat sources of the AN-74's turbofans.

Halloran thumbed his mike button. "Alpha Bravo from Gunshot Lead," he called, using a VF-181 callsign and *Langley's* current designator. "Positive ID, one Madcap."

"Roger, Gunshot. Cleared to fire," *Hornet's* controller replied. Mule fired both his Sidewinders. They ate up the distance between the hunter and hunted. Both AIM-9Ls connected, knocking out one engine and severing fuel lines. Burning jet fuel torched the modified STOL transport, which fell flaming into the black void below. Halloran looked down and thought it wasn't much of a victory. *Well, what the hell. A kill is a kill.* Then he thought of the tapes from KAL 007. *The target is destroyed.*

Returning to the amphibious group, both marines

double-checked their electronics panels to ensure that the radar enhancers remained on. The aviators wondered if they had in fact appeared to Russian radar as larger, twin-engine interceptors. They fervently hoped so, but only time would tell.

0130
Varyag

The heart of the message strobed at Rybakov from the communication form. *Disposition typical of American battle group 250 miles southeast Madagascar . . . AWACS believed destroyed by carrier-based interceptors 175 miles southeast . . .*

Rybakov crumpled the flimsy in an angry reflex. Catching himself, he smoothed out the paper, initialed it and shoved it at the communicator, who hastily withdrew. AWACS Control at Maputo was maddeningly ambiguous about the details of the An-74 message and the fate of the patrol plane. But the communications staff on Madagascar was familiar with Admiral Rybakov's preferences. If more were known, it would have been included in the data-linked message.

Rybakov tried to envision the Antonov's last moments. The excitement of the carrier group contact, the stark dread of hanging in the breeze, unescorted in that remote stretch of sea and sky. The Tomcats or Hornets—it must have been one or the other—would have enjoyed an easy time.

But why would the Americans allow themselves to be seen like that? Why not evade detection rather than draw attention by splashing the Antonov? Rybakov bit a thumbnail, concentrating hard. The amphibious squadron remained undetected so far—at least to all appearances. Maybe the Antonov had been allowed to see something resembling a carrier group.

He asked his chief of staff, Captain First Rank Smirnov, "Anatoly Vladimirovich, what do you make of this?"

"We presume it was aircraft from *Langley* that sank our two trailing submarines late Wednesday or early yesterday," Smirnov replied. "Apparently that was here, about 430 miles southeast of Madagascar. Since then, at seventeen knots the U.S. carrier group should have moved 400 miles rather than only the 180 miles to the contact reported by the An-74 before it was shot down. Perhaps the Americans do not want to provoke us by approaching Madagascar."

"Most unlike the U.S. navy," Rybakov commented. "Is it true that only carriers use the SPS-48 radar?"

"Various versions of it are also fitted to nuclear-powered and older oil-fired cruisers and *Kidd*-class destroyers. The versions are indistinguishable from their operating and pulse-repetition frequencies alone. One of the older cruisers is with the carrier group and a *Kidd* is with the amphibious squadron, so . . ."

"So it may or may not have been *Langley*."

"I'm afraid so, Admiral. If the only reason for suspecting the reports are not the *Langley* group is that the contacts were made at all, then I'd say that's not enough. We should assume the carrier has been located."

"Yes, that is reasonable. We should both be delighted. I may be overcomplicating the situation . . ." The admiral's voice trailed off. *Well, no matter*, Rybakov decided, shaking off some of his doubts. *With four surface-action groups, I can handle the* Langley *force and whatever else is out there*, he thought. *I'll decide where to commit my strength later*.

Rybakov said, more decisively than he felt, "Anatoly Vladimirovich! If you please, instruct our aviation department to arm the Su-25s for predawn ground-attack missions, as briefed. But have the ordnance staff keep antiship weapons ready for quick loading. We may find ourselves striking in two directions simultaneously."

"At once, sir."

0132 Pretoria; 0232 Local
Langley

"Jeezus, Bubba. Doesn't anybody sleep on this ship anymore?" Commander Michael Slattery, deputy commander of Air Wing 18, tried to keep the complaining tone from his voice.

"Not lately," Captain Rob Roy Ballantine responded to his deputy. "And not tonight for sure." Both aviators acknowledged the marine sentry and stepped into the battle group commander's staff office.

Chuck Gideon looked up from the map table. "Hey,

guys. You're just in time for the war." Neither his face nor his voice indicated he was joking.

Ballantine took a deep breath. *This is the real thing. My God.* "When do we go, sir?"

"Sometime this morning. To some extent, the timing's up to you guys. Come take a look." Gideon stood aside so the two senior aviators could see the tactical layout. "I've directed the 'gators to spark up their emitters and make sure the Russian patrol planes see them on radar." He tapped the map with the position of the amphibious squadron—the " 'gators"—which would shortly begin radiating to simulate a carrier battle group. "They're southeast of Madagascar, to our northeast. Their Harriers are maintaining a CAP and already splashed a snooper. SigInt indicates it spotted the PhibRon, but apparently didn't VID the 'phibs—just what the deception doctor ordered. That's the first part of the plan."

Ballantine said, "Okay, sir. Where do we fit in?"

"I want you guys to activate your plan for coordinated strikes against the UER carrier groups." Gideon paused to gauge the airmen's responses, which he found satisfyingly predictable.

The two fliers looked at one another, wide-eyed. A short-notice, come-as-you-are war, just like the worst-case scenarios drafted by Strike Warfare Center at Fallon, Nevada.

"Here's how I see it. I like your idea for the diversionary strike on *Novo*, tanking permitting, with the main blow falling on *Varyag* about half an hour later," Gideon began. Both men nodded agreement.

The admiral returned to the map table. "As you know, according to OTCIXS," he began, citing the Officer in Tactical Command Information Exchange System, the secure data links which keep U.S. warships at sea informed of the movements of all maritime traffic in their areas, "*Novorossiysk* is still here." Gideon indicated a position fifty miles off the central Natal coast. "The Outlaw Hunter out of Dee Gar and our own surveillance also agree she's still accompanied by eight escorts, two or three of which are detached on shore bombardment."

Ballantine grasped only the essentials of OTCIXS and its even higher-tech spin-off, the Copernicus command and control architecture. He knew, however, that the sea-surveillance system had already proved itself in the Gulf War. Since Tomahawk cruise missile's range is greater than that of any navy fire-control system of the late-'70s, the service had to develop means of targeting enemy ships beyond the radar horizon of U.S. vessels. The USN not only wanted to know the positions of Russian ships at all times, but to avoid hitting friendly and neutral ships. The aviator recalled that, instead of developing new over-the-horizon (OTH) sensors, the navy had decided to rely on processing and distributing data from existing American shiptracking resources—underwater, surface, air and space. For the Outlaw Hawk-Outlaw Shark program, Tiburon Systems designed a software package that could fuse information from all sources.

Tomahawk Antiship Missile (TASM) targeting platforms came to include some not originally intended for surface warfare, like land-based P-3C Orion antisub patrol planes. A few Orions, dubbed Outlaw Hunters, were equipped with a Viking-like ISAR, a Global Positioning System (GPS) receiver and a track-keeping computer. Ballantine knew that the French had allowed P-3Cs from Diego Garcia to refuel at Reunion Island on an "emergency" basis.

Amazingly, the "track-correlation" computer program and OTCIXS worked first crack out of the chute. In the fall of 1990, two hundred Joint Operational Tactical System (JOTS) terminals—commercial desktop work stations—were shipped to the Gulf and installed on coalition vessels enforcing the embargo against Iraq.

Gideon's tone turned ominous. "Now it appears the battlecruiser *Frunze* has been moved from her previous fire-support position east past *Novo*, presumably to provide an air defense screen against us."

Outstanding, thought Slattery. *A Navy Cross waiting to happen.*

"This may indicate that they expect us to attack the *Novo* group, their most northerly unit. I hope my deception plan—using the 'gators to imitate us—will contribute to this belief. I'm betting they don't know we're also in range of *Varyag*—or will be within two and a half hours, I hope. I want *Varyag* as the primary, not just because she's much more of a threat, but because they probably expect it less. She's here, about 200 miles south-southwest of *Novo*, with six or seven escorts." He indicated some hundred miles off the Transkei coast.

"Besides the electronic support and ForceCAP assets I agreed to release for the strikes in the preliminary plan, we've managed to get three TASM-shooting destroyers in range of *Novo*. I take it the *Varyag* attack will be supported by S-3s with Harpoons?"

"Yes, sir," Ballantine replied, proud that his innovation was accepted.

Manned strike aircraft had never cooperated with Tomahawk Antiship Missiles before. Besides helping the following planes penetrate the *Novo* group's defenses, dozens of TASMs might help convince the Russians that the diversionary attack was in fact the main one. The Harpoons would also grease the skids for the main strike against *Varyag*.

"My SWO staff will fill you in, but *Eureka, Carl, Davenport* and *Wheatley* will be in range to shoot at *Novorossiysk* by 0500 or sooner. They've really had to bust their turbines to get there, but it looks like they'll make it with a little time to spare. By borrowing *Meyring* from the PhibRon to cover our ass from the subs until sinking them, I freed up both *Spruances* to follow an independent course to their TASM launch points. As you know, I've pulled all their nuke land-attack Tomahawks and replaced them with every TASM *Roseburg* had in her hold.

"Only four of *Eureka*'s twenty Tomahawks are antiship and we're stuck with that; it's not easy to reload a sub. But we pulled seven TLAM-Ns from each *Spruance* and replaced them with antiship Tomahawks, so they each have thirteen TASMs now," Gideon continued. "All told, we're gonna shoot thirty at *Novo*. I've assigned six S-3s to the *Varyag* strike, loaded out with two Harpoons each. I also want the main strike to include six Hornets with twelve SLAMs. That's a total of fifty-four antiship cruise missiles. *Novo* gets more, since she'll receive fewer manned aircraft. The destroyers are too far away to shoot at *Varyag*, anyway."

Slattery emitted a low whistle. "That's a lot of cruise missiles, Admiral. I hope we don't get in their way." He envisioned the airspace over the target area, crowded with his own aircraft, TASMs, Standoff Land Attack Missiles (SLAMs) and Harpoons, plus shorter-ranged, air-to-surface ordnance like Mavericks, antiradar missiles and bombs. Not to mention an incredible array of Russian missiles and gun ammo as well.

"It's a lot, but not enough—just about three per major surface combatant in both groups. I've decided not to release any land-attack Tomahawks for use against the ships as decoys. We may need all our TLAM-Cs against air bases on Madagascar and in Mozambique or South Africa. Have to save 'em and try to take out any Badgers that land within range. The Antsiranana base is too far, of course, but if they come at us from Angola, they'll have to recover in Madagascar or Mozambique, so we'll have a shot at 'em there. Unless they refuel in flight, which isn't likely."

We should only live long enough to use that many TLAMs, the admiral thought.

"As for your concern about timing over the target, my staff's working on that right now," Gideon resumed. "They will coordinate the engagement schedule, but there isn't much time. Quicker is better." There was a short pause while the two aviators absorbed the magnitude of their task.

"I've given you resources, targets and a general strategy. The rest is up to you. Now, how do you want to do it?" Gideon asked at last.

Ballantine and Slattery exchanged glances. They shared the same thought. *Chuck's still giving us a free rein. Outstanding.*

As the senior aviator, Ballantine spoke first. "Sir, I think we'll show the Russians a tacpro they'll expect, something they've seen us do in exercises." That wouldn't be hard, he thought. After almost fifty years of observation, the Russians knew standard U.S. navy tactical profiles as well as the pilots of Air Wing 18. "We'll jab 'em with a couple of lefts, then hammer 'em with a hard right cross. And we'll try to be in and out by 0700. Depends on when we can launch and the tanking numbers crunch."

Gideon sat back while Ballantine and Slattery briefly discussed the problem. The two CAGs already had the basics on paper—they had done little else for the past two days but refine the myriad aspects of contingency plans for war at sea against the Russian invasion fleet. Now they had narrowed their options, seeking to balance the multiple factors: the time/range tradeoff, fuel, numbers of aircraft, weapon selection and more. Slattery produced a computer printout, upon which he and Ballantine added notes.

Finally Slats Slattery spoke, as he would lead the mission. He handed Gideon the outline, with newly penned addenda.

Gideon scanned the paper. "Just thirteen strike birds against the *Novo* group—that's gutsy."

Ballantine said, "Admiral, the *Novorossiysk* attack is a diversion, but we need to do as much damage as possible. The odds are real slim that so few manned aircraft can get through that group's defenses. *Frunze* alone has 264 SAMs; if she's escorted by *Stoikiy* that's 308 right there. That's why we expect to even up the odds with your thirty Tomahawks.

"The deception strike will fly an initial north-northwest heading to avoid the *Novo* group's radar, then turn due west to appear we're well north of our true position."

"Hmmm. Are you sure it's worth giving up twenty-four Mavs or eight AIM-120s for twenty-four decoys?" Gideon queried.

"We agreed so, sir," Ballantine answered. "It's an essential part of our deception plan. Plus, it cuts down on fuel consumption."

"I see why you were concerned about that. I just hope I don't regret this," Gideon pronounced, gloom dripping from his words like icicles.

"Admiral, when you see the TARPS photos of a flaming battlecruiser, I've got to believe you won't." Ballantine remained an optimist.

Gideon said gruffly, "Don't you gentlemen have something more constructive to do than make promises?"

"*De*structive, sir," Slattery added.

Ballantine smiled. "Since our main target is *Varyag*, we weighted the attack heavily against her," the CAG explained. "We assigned only enough resources to *Novo* to convince the opposition that she's the only objective. That's where the decoys come in. We've given up a lot of strike or ForceCAP potential to help the deception work."

"I'll say! The *Novo* strike has essentially no CAP," Gideon observed.

"It doesn't show on the outline, Admiral, but we're gonna hang 'Winders on the Intruders," Slats noted.

"Look," Gideon went on, "if you pull off the deception

and Rybakov does detach fighters, the Hornets are gonna be in a world of hurt—short on missiles and fuel. And without them, the Flankers will shoot our A-6s outside Sidewinder range."

"We were thinking more of Yaks, sir. Without more F-18s or some F-14s, the bombers'll get wasted by Flankers no matter what. A deception can't be strong." Ballantine shrugged. "Just in the nature of the beast."

Gideon knew he was right. A commander sometimes had to risk some lives to accomplish the mission.

"Very well," Gideon said. "I'll review your calculations. Thank you, gentlemen. Slats, I believe you have better things to do right now than make excuses to a superannuated sailor. You're dismissed."

"Thank you, sir. I'll get right on it. I still need to prep the squadron COs for their briefings ASAP to meet the 0430 deadline." Ballantine gave his deputy a go-get-'em slap on the shoulder and Slattery strode purposefully from the room, cataloging the hundred details of his first combat mission.

0230
Varyag

Pyotr Rybakov stood on the flag bridge, leaning against the portside windows overlooking the darkened flight deck. Below and aft, Rook Two-One's tailhook snagged the third arresting wire and both engines spooled up to full power in event of an overshoot. But the cable brought the Sukhoi attack plane to a halt in just a few meters. Watching the deckhands rush to direct it forward, the admiral was satisfied.

"Recovery is complete, Admiral." Rybakov turned to his chief of staff, Captain Second Rank Anatoly Smirnov, who checked his Japanese watch. "Just a few minutes over fifty hours of near-continuous strike operations. The air wing has performed well."

Rybakov punched the air with a clenched fist. "I think you are right, Anatoly Vladimirovich. Our workers have definitely fulfilled the plan." The admiral smiled broadly. "We may have to increase their quota." He looked down at the flight deck again. "That last Rook made a perfect landing, and the pilot must have flown three missions today. Pass my compliments to Nikolai Ivanovich and his whole wing." He thought a moment, then picked up his command phone. "Get me the landing signal officer."

Seconds later a respectful voice answered. "Laveikin here."

"This is Rybakov. Who is the pilot of that last Sukhoi?"

"Harshenko, sir."

Rybakov thanked the LSO and hung up. "Leonid Harshenko," the admiral said to Smirnov. "I know him. He showed me a picture of his wife and baby boy in Saki." Smirnov neither knew Harshenko nor cared about children, but accepted his superior's paternalistic attitude toward subordinates—especially aviators.

"If we're going to do as well tomorrow, I suppose we had better begin the staff conference on time," Rybakov said.

"The staff *is* waiting, Admiral. They are anxious to begin the third day of carrier strike operations in Russian history."

0238

Standing before a map of southern Africa and the adjacent Atlantic and Indian oceans, Rybakov faced a roomful of staff officers. All in attendance looked as tired as the airmen now gratefully slumping into their bunks, but the officers knew they would get little rest before dawn.

The admiral used a pointer to illustrate Task Force Rybakov's next moves. "I propose to leave *Novorossiysk* here, a hundred kilometers off Durban, to continue supporting our ground forces. The South Africans are still pressing attacks in these areas. But *Novorossiysk*'s surveillance aircraft also will look for the U.S. surface-action group and amphibious squadron. And the Americans will have a replenishment group somewhere in the area." He turned to his chief of staff. "Any word on that unit?"

Smirnov shook his head. "Not yet, sir. We expect reports from the An-74s on Madagascar and the submarines after daybreak."

Rybakov tapped the Atlantic off Angola. "Last intelligence places the *Eisenhower* battle group out here, at least three days from Capetown. That means two days' range from *Gorshkov*." He indicated his westernmost group. "If the Americans attack us, then *Eisenhower* will have to contend with the division of nuclear attack submarines and the pair of cruise missile shooters following its group. Further, I intend to operate under the principle of mutual support. We'll keep *Gorshkov* as far east as possible while remaining in air-support range of the amphibious landings around Capetown."

Rybakov cracked a wry grin. "Yak-141—while supersonic and a triumph of aviation technology—unfortunately lacks the range of Harrier II, especially with useful ordnance loads. Therefore, we cannot keep our V/STOL carrier groups as close together as we might prefer. Nevertheless, *Kuznetsov* will proceed northeasterly toward us, while remaining within fighter range of *Gorshkov* off the Western Cape and, of course, the *Moskva* and *Leningrad* groups supporting landings in the Eastern Cape." He indicated the areas around Port Elizabeth and East London.

"Surveillance aircraft will conduct extensive searches for all elements of the U.S. forces. It's going to be a big job, gentlemen. That's a huge, open ocean area, and we cannot count on satellites doing our work for us." His pointer described a wide loop on the map south and east of Madagascar.

Varyag's skipper, Captain Yuri Gulaev, raised a hand. "Admiral, what is our mission priority? Maintaining support of the landings or hunting down the Americans?" Rybakov recognized it as a textbook question, in keeping with the leftover tenets of pseudoscientific Marxist-Leninist military thought. Rybakov sighed inwardly. *Full marks, Captain. But a more original thinker already would have grasped the possibilities.*

"We will seize both opportunities, my friends. If attacked by the Americans, or if ordered to strike them first, I propose to destroy *Langley* and then turn to engage *Eisenhower* before the enemy surface-action groups can combine against us. Thus, we apply the principle of mass against the separate enemy formations. By the time our work at sea is finished, the land war should have been won by our progressive allies." He punctuated his remark with another clenched fist. "As scheduled, our air wings will launch another strike with all available aircraft, at 0500." Everyone looked at his wristwatch—there was still plenty of time.

After Rybakov's address, a staffer presented a folder to him. "The file you requested, Admiral."

Rybakov dismissed the intelligence officer and opened

the folder labelled "Gideon, Charles, USN." The most recent picture of the American admiral—a large, high-resolution headshot in color with the year but no source information—immediately arrested his attention.

The eyes, Rybakov thought, *the color of a coastal sea.* He had never seen eyes that shade of green, nor guessed it was even possible.

After reading Gideon's record for a moment, he called Smirnov over. "Look here, Anatoly Vladimirovich," the admiral said. "This is the man who sank our subs."

After scanning the document, the CSO arched his eyebrows, then met the gaze of his boss.

"You have the conn," Rybakov told Smirnov. "I'm going to try to catch a little sleep. But first, I plan to study this man for a while. If it comes to a fight, I want to know my opponent."

0243 Pretoria; 0343 Local
Langley

Chief Ira Odum strolled with studied casualness from his desk in the communications spaces, clutching a batch of papers to his bulging belly. He had undergone a conversion. Twenty minutes before he had been a well-placed spy in the pay of Moscow, with years of success behind him. Now he was a devoutly committed ex-spy on a personal mission—to purge all evidence.

The means of his conversion still echoed in his mind. If he had not stopped by the head after finishing his watch, he never would have heard the air wing staffers talking. *Possible launch against the Russian task force before dawn!* Ira Odum knew his colleagues—he didn't have any friends—considered him arrogant and abrasive, but not stupid. Nor was he. One does not continue dropping commobuoys from one of the most prestigious targets afloat when one paints a bull's-eye on his own bald head.

Odum stopped by his bunk and stuffed the rest of his espionage equipment into a large handbag. He looked around for something to weight it, but feared asking anyone for a piece of metal lest he arouse suspicions. So he crammed everything into the bag: Russian satellite schedules hidden in

Hoyle's Guide to Bridge, radio codes, miniature burst transmitters—the works.

It was not quite dawn when Odum stepped onto the starboard catwalk and worked his way aft toward the fantail. The first faint gray light was tinting the eastern horizon. *Good. Nobody'll notice an object this size in the darkness, and it should sink before long.*

Odum heard the round-the-clock clatter reverberating behind him in the cavernous aft hangar bay but, as expected, found nobody on the fantail. He set down the bag by the stern rail, strapping it shut when he heard voices above the pounding screw noises. His adrenaline surged and he abruptly turned back toward the shadows—and smashed into a stanchion. The pain in his forearm caused the bag to drop from his hand.

"I'll be right there, bro." A Hispanic voice, coming from starboard—and close. Odum now heard footsteps. He glanced down at the bag, decided there was no time to retrieve it and desperately kicked at it. His foot only nudged it against a cable. Odum ducked into the shadows.

Petty Officer Third Class Emiliano Cruz really needed a break. The twenty-year-old aviation metalsmith had worked back-to-back shifts and wanted a few moments away from the noise and heat of the hangar deck. The coolest, quietest place nearby was the fantail. He rounded the corner and tripped over something bulky.

"Damn," he exclaimed aloud. He bent down to examine the item. *Man, who left this thing here? Loose stowage, man. Bad news.* He glanced around, then stood up. Ira Odum lurked six feet away.

Cruz opened his mouth to speak when Odum leapt at him. In the paunchy CPO's mind was a single impulse— knock the boy overboard into the drink, where he would drown in the churning wake or, with luck, be sucked into the propellers and shredded to shark bait. Though startled, the young Chicano managed to sidestep Odum's lunge and lock the pudgy older man in a half nelson. They went down in a tangle of arms, legs and fists.

The traitor had more than forty pounds on the sailor, and the desperation that comes of being cornered. Emiliano Cruz had almost two decades on the mean streets of east LA.

He knocked off Odum's glasses and jabbed a thumb in one eye. The fight ended eight seconds after it began.

0258
SADF National Command Center

Commander Dexter Jackson was glad the South African GHQ staffers showed him right in to de Villiers's bunker, but was not surprised. Even without access to dispatches, it was obvious to him that the invading forces had made potentially disastrous penetrations.

"Good to see you again so soon, Commander," de Villiers said with a cheerfulness that did not seem forced. "Hope you weren't kept waiting."

"Not at all, sir. Thanks for seeing me. You must have pressing business."

"Not really. Being stuck down here is quite frustrating. It's good to see a new face. But please do proceed."

Jackson appreciated the general's stiff-upper-lip routine. "What I need, sir, as current as possible, is a summary of attacks against South African land targets by enemy carrier aircraft."

Without a further word to the American officer, de Villiers repeated the request into his intercom. Then he turned to Jackson. "Staff should be right along with that. What else can we do for you, Commander?"

"Nothing at this point, sir, besides what we discussed earlier."

"Very well, then. Please go through into the briefing room and Major Sluys will, I trust, see to your needs. It's been a pleasure," the general concluded, extending his hand. The black American still felt odd in these moments of contact with the top South African soldier, but had to admit he respected de Villiers, even if he could not feel entirely at ease with him.

"Good-bye, General," he said. "Thanks."

"I shall look forward to seeing you next time." Jackson came to attention, then turned toward the briefing room.

Sluys soon appeared. Without speaking, he handed the American a folder and stood back. The attaché studied the three pages of information, then asked Sluys to show him the sites in Natal and the Eastern Cape bombed, strafed or rocketed within the past half hour by Russian naval aircraft. Still silently, Sluys indicated the attacked positions on situation maps. Jackson stretched his hand out along the map key scale, then measured distances to points offshore.

"How reliable are these reports?" he asked sharply.

"Highest reliability—all visual ID, excepting the stand-off missile attacks. Based on missile type and range considerations, these could only have been mounted by Russian naval aircraft. Radar data and ESM confirm this assessment."

"I guess I'll have to take your word for it." Sluys did not respond. "Please ask General de Villiers to press hard in these sectors wherever possible to encourage the Russians to rearm their attack planes for more land strikes." On a carbon pad, he wrote out a formal request to the same effect, handed it to Sluys and added, "Make sure the general sees this, understand?" After a moment, the major accepted the note gingerly by a corner and nodded slightly. Jackson tore off the copy and pocketed it. "Good. See to it immediately." Neither man moved. "Well," inquired the U.S. attaché, "what are you waiting for?"

Sluys knocked on de Villiers's door and handed the message to an orderly.

"Thank you," Jackson said. "Now please show me out. I'm in a hurry." Then he smiled broadly and, hip-hopping to the exit, said in his best South Chicago intonation, "I gots to go win dis here war for you all, suckah."

0315 Pretoria; 1115 Local
Andersen AFB, Guam

Colonel Gary Tate stood at the nosewheel ladder of the lead B-1B. Seeing him off was a former Air Force Academy classmate, Colonel Tom Milkus, who obviously envied the wing commander. "Y'all come back and see us, Gary. Y'hear?"

"I sure aim to, Stretch. But don't wait up for us." Tate hadn't used Milkus's nickname in years. It caused a brief pang to the five-foot-seven Tate, who had roomed with the six-four basketball star. Milkus sensed the wingco's uneasiness and decided to change the subject. Pointing to the fierce knight painted on the B-1's nose, he laughed aloud. "Hey, it beats the artwork back at Carswell all to hell."

Tate glanced up at the cartoon and its legend, *Lancer Lead.* "It sure does." When they'd finally gotten their own crews, the two B-52 pilots had been anxious to paint warlike images on their "Buffs." But the wing nose-art committee— the wing commander, his wife, the base chaplain and the maintenance chief—had insisted upon motifs like the Lone Star flag, the Alamo, or a snorting Texas longhorn. The one exception was the name of the "wing king's" wife. Well, RHIP. However, the existence of any nose art at all was considered racy in SAC at that time.

As Tate's three-man crew climbed aboard, yellow tow tractors pulled away from the B-1 with empty missile trailers. There had been almost no margin for delay in loading the AMRAAMs—Advanced Medium-Range Air-Air Missiles— on the Lancers' rotary launchers. *And none for talk with an old friend,* Tate thought. He hefted his helmet bag and put a foot on the ladder. "I have to run, Stretch." They warmly shook hands. "See you on campus."

Tom Milkus watched his classmate's polished boots disappear into the nosewheel well.

0316
Zululand

By lanternlight, Mkize read Celani's response to his message:

Remove your command from under SADF orders, resign SADF commission, and cease cooperation with U.S. forces, pending decision of Inkatha *Defence Council. Send representative Ulundi to explain actions to date.*

He crumpled and threw the paper to the ground. Even for a Zulu marathon runner, it would take two days to cross enemy lines and reach Ulundi, 160 kilometers away, unless he got a ride at some point. Another day might well pass before the council came to a decision. Mkize knew he was in effective command of all *Inkatha* forces in northern Zululand, cut off as they were by the invaders' mechanized and naval infantry advances. Celani must realize as much, and that the vast majority of Mkize's men were personally loyal to him rather than to the remote *Inkatha* political central committee or military high command. In fact, three whole *impis,* various battalions and numerous subunits and individuals had rallied to Mkize in the past two days, defecting from his two neighboring, less aggressive division commanders.

Even if Celani were willing to promote a mutiny in Mkize's division—now swollen nearly to corps size—the rest of the political leadership might not condone such a ruinous, fratricidal course. Mkize wished Chief Buthelezi had not been murdered; he was pro-American and would probably not have objected to cooperating with the USMC expeditionary unit. Mkize considered going over his nominal boss's head by radioing the new chief's bunker directly. Instead, he decided to signal Celani that he would dispatch a representative, but that until the chief decided otherwise, his *impi* would continue to cooperate with the Americans.

Mkize wondered how Celani could be so blind. Giving a politician supreme military command was a bad decision by the chief. The Zulus could not by themselves defeat the forces invading their homeland. Even were they able to, their isolated victory would do little good if the communists controlled the rest of southern Africa. The war could be over by the time a military *indaba* or council made up its collective mind. Mkize smiled. *Well,* he thought, *at least Celani had the good sense to recruit me.*

He drafted a response to Celani's signal and took it to the communications shack. For the PR job, he selected the most loyal and intelligent lieutenant among his long-distance runners and told him to pick three resourceful enlisted men to accompany him through enemy lines to Ulundi. He gave the lieutenant a communications schedule so Mkize would know whether to send a replacement team or not. After the mission briefing, he walked with the cousin of Derek Gumede and his team to the edge of the camp, wished them Godspeed and sent them on their dangerous way.

0348 Pretoria; 0448 Local
Langley

Bubba Ballantine popped two aspirin. After the previous two hours, he felt the onset of Excedrin Headache Number Eighteen. The CAG thought he had seen frantic activity in his previous seven deployments over the past twenty-two years. He thought of his first F-14 cruise and the recalled strike against Idi Amin's Uganda in '75. But nothing—absolutely nothing—compared with what CAG-18 was witnessing this dark morning.

Langley's flight and hangar decks still seethed with activity. "Grapes" and "ordies"—sailors in purple or red jerseys —swarmed over aircraft, fueling and arming Tomcats, Hornets, Intruders and Vikings or servicing Prowlers and Hawkeyes. Yellow gear buzzed everywhere as tractors pulled aircraft into position on the flight deck while plane handlers and directors coordinated with the overseers in hangar and flight deck control. The greenshirts on the catapults stood by, knowing their turn was coming soon.

The strike plan lay before the CAG, carrying notations from Slats, the mission leader. Appended tactical notes reflected the contributions of the air wing operations officer, the intelligence spooks and the battle group staff. The fundamentals were laid out in Admiral Gideon's "Clausewitz for Beginners" formula: MMMOUSSSE. This acronym, condensing the Prussian's classic tenets of war into a simple innocuous word, contained a wealth of wisdom: Mission, Mass, Maneuver, Offensive, Unity of Command, Security, Simplicity, Surprise and Economy of Force. A commander ignored any one of those at his peril, and Chuck Gideon had ignored none. He even added another "S"—for Speed. As the admiral had said two hours before, "Speed is life; more is better."

The senior CAG was pleased with another display of speed—the quick finalization of the plan. It would not have been possible without the staff's exacting contingency planning over the previous days and the amount of apparently good intelligence available to them. The planners had to some extent compromised simplicity for the sake of deception, but, considering the numbers of aircraft involved, it was still an easily grasped operation.

Air Wing 18's two-phase, fifty-plane strike was depicted on the map: a diversionary attack against the *Novorossiysk* group first, followed by primary air strikes and missile attacks against the *Varyag* SAG. Though simple in concept, the plan was enormously complex. Timing and coordination alone posed major problems, not to mention weapons delivery, defense suppression and standoff jamming.

Four Vikings and six Intruders—all airworthy but most with one or more avionics systems degraded—had been fitted with wing-mounted "buddy stores" to be used in refueling both prongs of the large strike force. Ten were barely adequate, but the operation would last long enough for the tankers to top off the outbound strikes, return to the carrier, refuel and fly back out to meet the homeward-bound jets. If the two spare Intruders were not needed to replace A-6s malfunctioning at launch, they could also help refuel returning strike planes. Most of the remaining thirty aircraft would provide battle group defense until the strikers came home.

However many make it home, Bubba admitted. It was inconceivable that he would get everybody back from so ambitious a mission against so strong an enemy. But CVW-18 was ready. He and Gideon had seen to that with the most rigorous training cycle of any air wing in recent history.

"CAG, Slats is wrapping up." Ballantine felt a hand on his shoulder and turned to see his ops officer, Commander Joe "Cool" Hool, standing at his side. The video briefing was televised in each squadron ready room.

Ballantine headed for the ship's TV studio, entering in time to hear his deputy say, "That's the plan, guys. I think it's a good one. We'll know just how good in a couple of hours." Slattery rolled his shoulders under his flight suit. He had considered a rousing finish but decided that was too melodramatic. *These guys are pros. They'll do all right.* "Let's man up."

Slattery turned to go, picking up his helmet bag and gear. His gaze met Ballantine's and their eyes assessed one another for a moment, suspended in time. Slats thumped his friend's chest. "Gotta go, Bubba. Gonna sink me a carrier." He raised a hand, palm outward.

"Best of luck, Slats." They gave each other a high five. Then Slattery was gone through the hatch. *"Best of luck,"* Ballantine sneered to himself. *Christ, is that all you can say to a guy who may be dead before breakfast?*

0401
Northern Zululand

Mkize went to the ops shack to check on progress in improving bush airfields for the Americans. Mxenge reported that their agents in all six selected villages had been able to muster labor units, apparently without yet being detected by enemy recce troops and without having to fight for any of the sites. Mxenge would have preferred to be attacking the enemy, but Mkize wanted him where his staff skills could be used to best advantage and where he could keep an eye on him. Mkize had chosen not to tell the *Inkatha* loyalist of Celani's disapproval of the *impi's* cooperation with the SADF and the Americans.

Captain Wilkes reported that SAAF cargo planes had already taken off from rough fields in the Transvaal to paradrop steel mats to cover the grass strips and to repair damage to asphalt fields.

"The freighters will fly low, but we'll be very lucky indeed if they're not picked up on enemy radars," Wilkes added. "Don't know how long we can keep the bush fields secret. GHQ have assured me that any and all concrete slabs not used in the border defenses will be made available to us as aircraft blast shelters. They're going to drop us an engineer team to supervise the construction."

"This camp is going to be crawling with bloody Boers," Mxenge said, only partly in a jocular vein.

"Let them do the digging," Mkize said to placate his radical subordinate. "We'll do the fighting."

0402
Off South Africa

Predawn launches must be the same in every navy, thought Captain Second Rank Nikolai Glinka. *Varyag's* air wing commander banked his Su-25 to port immediately after clearing the ship's upturned ski-slope bow, raising his wheels while carefully monitoring attitude and airspeed in his HUD. The only thing worse than a night launch was a night carrier landing, and thank the war gods the latter would not be necessary on this mission.

With minimal radio calls, Glinka formed up his own planes—eight Su-25s and four escorting Su-27s—and set course westerly. En route he passed the picket ships of Task Force Rybakov, double-checking his Identification Friend or Foe (IFF) transponder for the daily identification code. Then, twenty-five miles from the coast, he received a radio call.

"White Rook Leader from Black Rook Leader. I see your navigation lights and am joining on your starboard beam."

Glinka looked over his right shoulder. There, strobing in the darkness, were the running lights of several more aircraft. *Arkady Yestigneev, right on time,* thought Glinka. He knew that *Kuznetsov*'s contribution to the strike against unexpectedly heavy fascist opposition ashore was six more Su-25s, and grinned inside his oxygen mask. Glinka recalled that when Rybakov had passed out chess-related radio call signs, "Rook" had been a natural because *Varyag*'s senior pilot usually flew the Su-25, nicknamed in Russian for the migratory bird, which in English is an alternate name for the castle in chess. The CAG wondered about an admiral who enjoys bilingual puns. Then, rousing himself from his reverie, he checked his kneepad for the frequency of the paratroop unit he was supporting today.

Glinka looked around him once more, satisfying himself that the fighters were properly positioned. Yes, there they were, above and ahead of the bombers. He knew they probably would not be needed, but a little caution paid dividends. Smirnov's briefing had been careful on that point. South Africa's air force was nearly gone, but apparently a surveillance aircraft had reported the American carrier group well to the north, near Madagascar. It would bear watching.

Nikolai Glinka came three degrees port. *On course, on time. Good.*

0416 Pretoria; 0516 Local
Langley

"Captain, we're there."

Philip Ray, skipper of the carrier, swiveled his elevated captain's chair on the darkened bridge. "Thanks, Ben," he said, acknowledging the information from his navigator and spinning back forward. Then he picked up one of several phones arrayed alongside his seat and waited for the response. "Nate, this is Phil. We're at the spot the admiral requested, 560 nautical east-southeast of Durban. We'll hold this course until you say different."

In flag country, Nate Gottlieb picked up another phone and uttered a few brief phrases, awaited acknowledgment and hung up. Then he walked around the corner, parted the two-starred curtain and nudged his boss, dozing in an overstuffed chair. Gideon instantly came awake.

"Admiral, we're in position. *Davenport, Wheatley* and *Carl* will all reach their launch points within the hour. *Eureka* is already on station."

Gideon envisioned the three destroyers pounding westward through the early-morning darkness to reach their Tomahawk firing position. The SSN *Eureka*, had a head start on them. "Okay, Nate." He rubbed his eyes and checked his watch. "And not a moment too soon. Wasn't sure we'd make it on time." The admiral thumped Gottlieb's arm with a friendly fist. "Send the word to Washington." Then he leaned back and closed his eyes, trying to look calm for his staff.

Ninety seconds later the uplink was on its way 23,000 miles overhead to the geosynchronous comsat, which relayed the one-word message to Buddy Callaway.

0418 Pretoria; 2218 EDT
White House

It was 10:18 P.M. local when the President received The Word. The White House chief of staff rapped on the door of the President's sitting room, entered and handed the paper to Buddy Callaway, who had been listening to the Sons of the Pioneers. Unfolding the message slip, the lanky Texan saw The Word: TEQUILA.

"What's it mean, sir?"

"It means *mucho trabajo* for all of us," Callaway replied. He glanced up. "Call the JCS and NSC staffs to the Situation Room *muy pronto*. There's about to be some excitement in the Indian Ocean."

0419 Pretoria; 0519 Local
Langley

Phil Ray picked up the phone by his high chair. "Captain speaking."

"Phil, this is Chuck," said Gideon from his flag quarters. "The first birds are on the cats. Let's turn into the wind for launch."

"Aye, aye, sir." *Langley*'s skipper replaced the phone in

its cradle. It was unusual for a flag officer "riding" a carrier to direct such a mundane maneuver—good admirals let captains drive their own boats. But Ray also knew that Chuck Gideon's sense of history—colored with a bit of pride—was behind the personal order to launch the first fleet engagement in nearly fifty years.

0423 Pretoria; 0523 Local

Chuck Gideon entered the flag bridge, waved everyone to be at ease and headed straight for the port wing. He stepped through the access and pointedly closed the door behind him, leaving his marine orderly inside. Gideon wanted to be alone for a few minutes—just enough to watch the launch commence. *I'm committing this force to the first carrier battle since WWII,* he thought. *I'm entitled to reflect on it.*

Looking down from his perch, staring hard into the dark, Gideon sensed more than saw what was happening with the thirty planes on deck. Occasionally plane directors' wands slashed through their ritual arcs, putting aircraft into position on deck. First off would be four Viking tankers, followed by four buddy-store Intruders, then the Harpoon-shooting Vikings bound for *Varyag,* then the *Novorossiysk* Prowlers and their deception strikers—four Intruders and six Hornets. Then, after the first thirty minutes, the airborne CAP would be recovered and replaced, and the launch against *Varyag* would continue.

Gideon reflected that the two-phase launch was a tremendously complicated process requiring only slightly less planning than the attack itself. Peering into the halogen lights' ghostly illumination, he shivered involuntarily—and not from the bracing, twenty-six-knot wind. Gideon felt an eerie affinity with other carrier admirals. *I wonder if Admiral Spruance felt this way at Midway.* With a start, Gideon realized that "his" battle came on the same date as Spruance's—the fourth of June. And, like Midway, this carrier duel would be fought across time zones. Then he roused himself as the four catapults fired, flinging the first tankers into the dark. The jet exhausts were quickly lost in the inky blackness. Gideon watched them disappear, then turned back toward the flag bridge.

0430
Northern Zululand

In the ops shack, Mkize received his requested update on progress in airfield development. He regretted not being able personally to lead any raids on supply columns during the night, but the airfield operations had to take priority. All his men, at least those who weren't cowardly, enjoyed these attacks—the modern equivalent of their ancestors' cattle raiding.

"We will have to divert far too many men from attacking the enemy to guard the bush airstrips," Mxenge complained in Zulu.

"I couldn't agree more," Mkize answered in English. "I'm not using men."

"Auxiliaries?" Mxenge asked, betraying shock. His colonel nodded. "But, but . . . they're not adequately trained."

"Guarding is what they are trained to do. Only instead of protecting their villages while their men are with us, they'll be garrisoning airfields. Either way, it's defensive combat, of which I believe them capable."

"But they'll be much more exposed to attack, once the strips are discovered. The communists might not bomb villages with no strategic value, but the airfields will be prime targets. They'll throw everything at them—HE, gas, incendiary, ground attack."

"You'd rather they survive to exist under communism, under a Xhosa-dominated Natal, than die fighting for freedom? You want them used as whores for the invaders?"

"No, but . . ."

"But we have no choice. You said it yourself. I figure a Zulu woman is at least as effective as a Mozambican or Xhosa man. Besides, they're already there in the coastal flatlands; we don't have to infiltrate any troops across enemy lines. I've made up my mind. I'm assigning the auxiliaries from each of the six nearest villages and from as many others as we need to guard the dispersal fields. We can't spare any more trained fighters, and the untrained construction battalions can't be relied upon to defend the strips against even saboteurs. Old people, nursing mothers and children from the defenseless villages will walk or be moved to the nearest protected places. Please work out the details and issue the necessary orders immediately."

Wilkes piped up. "With a bit of luck, the marines and any refugees from the American carrier group won't need all six fields. In any case, they may be too rudimentary for the naval aircraft. But we can't take any chances."

"Have the steel mats been delivered?" Mkize asked.

"Yes, sir. And GHQ assure me that antiaircraft and anti-tank weapons will be dropped next, along with camouflage netting. They won't deliver ordnance for the U.S. planes until it's clear which fields will see use."

"Very well, gentlemen, carry on," Mkize said, and swept from the shack.

0457 Pretoria; 0557 Local
Langley

Slats Slattery settled himself in the bombardier/naviga-tor's seat of the lead A-6E, Talent 500. He leaned down to snap his leg restraints to the ejection seat, then secured his torso harness fittings, oxygen, radio and G-suit leads. He was now part of the airplane.

Behind him the carrier's darkened flight deck was filled with the howling, whining roar of high-performance jet and turboprop engines. Wings came down and locked into place, planes were taxied onto the four catapults—two on the bow, two at the "waist"—and the main launch commenced.

Slats and his pilot, Jim "Crunch" Neslie, were spotted on Cat Two. They felt the nose-tow catapult fitting take up tension, compressing the A-6's nosewheel oleo. Responding to the tacit query from the launch officer, Crunch turned on his nav lights to indicate he was ready, then he and Slats braced themselves. Seconds later a green-clad sailor at the catwalk console depressed a button. The catapult fired and a six-foot-long cylinder slammed forward in its groove.

Looking ahead into the black void, the A-6 crew felt gravity's elephant step on their chests. Then the pressure was gone. Crunch grasped his controls and began a wing-level instrument climb to join the jets already overhead. Behind them, each of the aircraft bound for *Varyag* was off in the allotted thirty minutes. All but one.

The pilot of Talent 507, equally well-trained but less

motivated than his fellows, found his radio "inoperable" and had to abort. His B/N could hear the carrier wave but was too disgusted for words—those would come later. Meanwhile, deckhands directed the spare Intruder into position. Talent 510, flown by Happy and Sleepy, was affixed to the cat and flung off the deck. Incredibly, that was the only delay; there were no serious mechanical failures. The only malfunction was of a single human heart.

In two groups Air Wing 18 climbed into the slowly lightening sky, aviators searching for the strobing green lights of their airborne tankers before proceeding on the mission assigned.

0515
Suez Canal

Captain James Fanin Kinney paced the bridge of USS *John F. Kennedy,* rereading the message traffic "Big John" had received from Washington in the past hour. He was a tall man in his late forties, a onetime Notre Dame miler who still could wear out most of the teenagers who followed his morning laps around the supercarrier's flight deck. JFK's sailors widely believed their skipper had obtained his prestigious command because he had been the only O-6 with the same initials as the ship's namesake. Kinney didn't know if the men were right; only the gnomes of Naval Personnel in Washington could say for sure.

Kinney felt something else, for certain. "The goddamn Russians are behind this! I knew it." He waved the message flimsies to the bridge watch. "It was too much a coincidence that Cuban- and Libyan-registered ships blocked the canal. SigInt from ComSixthFleet confirms it's intentional. The bastards boxed us in here to keep us from getting to the IO." He scanned the latest presidential flash message for a moment. "Well, this opera ain't over until the fat lady sings. Mister Bellows, ring the CAG and tell him I'm on my way to see him. You have the conn."

"Aye, aye, sir. I have the conn," responded the watch officer.

Moments later Kinney met the commander of Carrier Air Wing Three, Captain Clarence "Red" Hesselyn, in CAG ops. Though an accomplished fighter pilot, Hesselyn was revered for his skill at red dog poker. He would not have a chance for ship command, but his air wing tour counted almost as much toward flag rank.

"CAG, I don't think Admiral Grace will be back from his diplomatic errand to Cairo before we can execute the president's plan. You know that practically every air force tanker in the region has been released to support us if necessary?"

"Rog, I saw the message traffic earlier this morning." Red Dog's mind raced, and immediately grasped Kinney's intent. "You and the president still thinking what I'm thinking?"

"Yup, flanchoring. Callaway's one shrewd cookie. Flying at anchor has never been done in the Canal, but I don't see any reason we shouldn't."

Hesselyn's blue eyes sparkled. "Neither do I. Technically we're in international waters. We don't need anybody's permission. And I bet the Egyptians will let us operate from Aswan."

Kinney leaned close, a conspiratorial grin on his face. "Let's huddle with your staff. We have secure comm with Sixth Fleet and I think we can help ol' Chuck's *Langley* troops."

0522 Pretoria; 0622 Local
Brillo Flight, Southwest Indian Ocean

In the cockpit of the A-6E called Killer 530, Lieutenant Commander Peter "Brillo" Huggins of VA-187 felt an electric jolt through his nervous system. For an instant he had the impression that he was wired to the Intruder's avionics package, as the ALR-50 radar warning receiver evoked a physiological response.

Sitting beside Huggins, his bombardier/navigator experienced a similar sensation. Lieutenant (Junior Grade) Justin Olsen was a straight-arrow kid from Park City, Utah. Though his name tag bore the title "Jet Mormon," he was sardonically called "Sleaze" by less devout squadronmates. But Sleaze was all business. His left hand shot out to the RWR scope. "Lobe to the northwest," he intoned. "We've been picked up by their Madcap."

Brillo checked his clock. Only six minutes had elapsed

since he had led his ten-plane deception group onto the westerly heading. He told himself that because the RWR could detect the Madcap's signal did not mean that his plane's echo was strong enough to show up on Russian scopes yet. But a pro never took anything for granted. His pulse felt more under control. "Okay," the pilot replied. "Call the Hornets and Prowlers and confirm with them. It's showtime."

0523 Pretoria; 2323 EDT; 0723 Moscow Daylight Time
White House and Kremlin

From her station in the West Wing, White House watch officer Mary Margaret Kelly spoke into the red phone. *"Da, Nikolai Panfilovich,"* she said, as three Situation Room colleagues—two note takers and another interpreter—listened in. *"Ya znayu, chto rano tam. Zdes pozdno noch'yu."* After a pause, Kelly responded, *"Khorosho,"* then switched to English. "Mr. President, the line is open."

Callaway knew the regular hot-line computer system might serve more efficiently to conduct negotiations in this crisis, but he wanted as direct a contact as possible with his opponent. He felt you could learn a lot from hearing a man's voice, even if you couldn't understand his language.

Though they had met only once, in Geneva, Callaway and Rodinkov had spoken by phone three times. But no previous call had left the President feeling like Henry Fonda in *Fail-Safe* or, worse, Peter Sellers in *Dr. Strangelove.*

Seated in the Oval Office, Callaway thanked Kelly, then said into his white desk phone, "Mr. President, this is the President of the United States. Good morning to you, sir."

Rodinkov understood most of those words and replied, in heavily accented English, "Good evening, Mr. President." Then he promptly got down to business, saying in Russian, "It seems we have a situation of mutual concern in the Indian Ocean." The phrase was rapidly translated in the Kremlin and the translation accepted in the West Wing.

The sumbitch sounds like he's holding four aces and knows I know it, Callaway thought. *Guess I won't be able to stall him.* "We can resolve the situation peacefully if all foreign forces in the region agree to withdraw immediately," the President replied. The male translator waited for him to finish before translating the brief statement.

"That is most unlikely, Mr. President," Rodinkov responded moments later. "Aside from our unalterable commitment to our progressive, democratic allies, the objective reality is that we can absorb considerable losses and still gain our just goals." He paused to let the interpreters catch up, then resumed. "You, on the other hand, can only lose invaluable men, materiel and prestige. You are already outmaneuvered, with a lone battle group isolated from any timely help. Dear sir, to avoid pointless loss of life and resources, you are advised to withdraw while time allows." He paused again for emphasis. "There will not be a second chance."

Patronizing bastard, Callaway thought, but exclaimed aloud, "Boy, howdy!" Wishing his boss were less colloquial, the White House translator rendered this as, "Indeed not!"

The U.S. President continued, "Since you're spoiling for a showdown, you can have it." Feeling his own heart beat faster and watching the reactions of his aides, Callaway said, "The only thing for us to decide is how to contain the battle. I'm sure neither of us wants, should I say, the most serious consequences." *Chew on that thought, Ivan.*

The delay told Callaway he had taken Rodinkov by surprise. "Are you actually suggesting that we continue hostilities? Even after your forces provoked us by sinking two submarines without cause?"

"As I already said, we don't know what happened to your subs." *Not for sure, anyway. Fingers crossed, little white lie.* "And I think you know that." Callaway was glad for the moment's respite in translation. "But our forces remain in place and they will fight. So let's define the rules of engagement and get on with it."

"You are mad, Callavaiy!" Rodinkov shouted in English. From his tone, the reaction did not sound like play-acting. *Gotcha,* the Texan thought.

"Sane or otherwise, you're stuck with me, Rodinkov. Just be glad I'm giving you warning. Now, what do you say?"

"One moment," Rodinkov said icily, and went off the line.

"He's not just talking it over, Mr. President," CNO commented. "He's probably launching his antiship bombers and certainly notifying the invasion fleet."

"I reckon you're right, Hub," Callaway responded.

"Their Badgers in Africa and Backfires in the UER have all been on generated-alert status since yesterday afternoon. They've already transferred two Backfire regiments from the Black Sea Fleet to advanced staging bases on the Iranian border and moved the Badger regiment on Socotra down to Madagascar. The first bomber attacks on *Langley* can be expected in three or four hours and to go on for up to twenty hours."

"I hope to God they don't know where ol' Chuck is," the President prayed. "But God helps those who help themselves."

Twenty seconds later Rodinkov was back on the line. "We accept your invitation to battle. Do you intend to follow historic precedent in such matters?"

"Sure thing. The 1962 Cuban missile crisis is a case in point. Kennedy and Khrushchev decided on areas and operating procedures, as you well know. I propose a similar agreement, to include the following main points, which I'll send you over the cable."

Callaway pulled a previously prepared contingency sheet from his main desk drawer. Then, over the same phone, with the Russians listening, he told a hot-line watch officer, "Go ahead, Sugar." In the Situation Room, Kelly, a tweedy FBI brat, sent a translated copy of the sheet over her fax terminal.

Shortly, members of the UER State Defense Committee read:

"1) No nuclear, chemical or biological weapons. 2) No attacks on our respective homelands or upon any of their overseas territories. 3) No attacks on any installations located outside the theater of hostilities, defined as all land and sea areas within 1,500 nautical miles of the recognized borders of South Africa, excluding islands and the enclave of Walvis Bay. 4) Noncombatants include all states without combat personnel involved in South African hostilities."

0532
Varyag

In the command and control module of CDC, the secure channel decoder-unscrambler-printer clattered. A cy-

pher clerk tore the printout from the machine and passed
the message to the commo *michman,* who in turn handed it
to *Varyag's* BCh-7. After examining its heading but not its
content, the BCh-7 carried the signal to Rybakov.

The admiral read the communique from the State Defense Committee and felt as though his whole life had been
distilled into an elongated instant. He had been born with
good sea legs, but for a moment his knees went weak.

"Very well," he said. "Circulate it to our department
heads, and send copies to all SAG commanders. Then have
the department heads meet me here immediately." The officer abruptly turned to comply when Rybakov called him
back. "Also, inform all ships' captains to explain the immediate situation to their crews." Rybakov stared into space for a
moment. Finally he added, "I'll address our crew personally,
and the captains may read their men my comments if they
wish." His voice trailed off, and the BCh-7 realized the admiral was finished.

Battle Group Charlie

On the bridges of three destroyers 175 or more miles
west-northwest of *Langley,* sailors covered their eyes as solid
rocket motors boosted Tomahawk cruise missiles—twenty-
one-foot-long, twenty-one-inch-wide cylinders—from their
vertical launch cells below the ships' deckhouses. The boosters trailed roiling white exhaust like billowing, fan-shaped
bridal trains. The TASMs flew toward the northeast in a
nose-high attitude.

USS *Carl* Commander Theodore Mahar, skipper of the
Burke-class antiair destroyer reflected that the blinding brilliance of the rocket exhausts in the predawn semidarkness
would leave any UER satellites overhead in no doubt as to
the location of his and the other two Tomahawk-launching
ships. Mahar told his helmsman to come about 180 degrees
as soon as the last of *Carl's* four TASMs was fired. He was
grateful his ship had to expose herself for only a third as long
as the two *Spruance*-class antisub destroyers, each now firing
thirteen TASMs from positions over the horizon to *Carl's*
southwest and northeast. And, thank God and OP-03, the
Burke class was less detectable on radars than the older
Spruances, and better able to defend herself against air at-

tack. In fact, air defense of the other two destroyers and the western approach to *Langley* was now his main mission.

After burning out, the solid-fuel boosters fell away from the 2,645-pound missiles, and their Teledyne turbojet engines kicked in. The TASMs' tail fins snapped into place and their on-board flight control computers directed fin actuators to dive the missiles to one hundred feet above the nearly waveless sea, at which level radar altimeters maintained them. The ring-laser gyroscopes and accelerometers of their inertial guidance systems adjusted the sea-launched cruise missiles' courses toward the target areas, where their active radar homing heads could search for and lock onto ships ID'd by the Tomahawks' on-board ESM systems.

Mahar hoped the OTH-targeting system worked as advertised on this, its first combat use. The JOTS terminals of the Tactical Warfare Control Systems on board *Carl* and all other Tomahawk-shooting surface ships displayed track-correlating data transmitted via OTCIXS. This information was precise enough for programming TASMs to fly within recognition range of enemy battle groups. Once in the ball park, the missiles' own electromagnetic signal receivers and processors could identify individual targeted ships by their characteristic electronic emissions.

In case this technique failed, the skipper took comfort from the knowledge that, as a backup measure, Seahawk helos from the two *Spruances* would attempt to designate battlecruiser *Frunze* for the Tomahawks. *Even if they don't hit anything*, Mahar thought, *at least they'll soak up SAMs*.

0533 Pretoria; 0633 Local
Langley

E-2C data links showed Gideon that twenty-seven of the thirty TASMs fired by *Carl*, *Wheatley* and *Davenport* had successfully arched downrange. *Langley* soon learned that twenty-four of the SLCMs had properly initiated cruise phase. The missiles were flying into a light wind, but their guidance systems were compensating correctly. Gideon viewed the screen with relief. He knew the headwind would not be a problem, except that there would be less fuel on each missile to start fires on any Russian ship they might be lucky enough to hit. Though launched from about 240 nautical miles—near maximum range for early versions—the Tomahawks were all of the recent Block III variety with extended range and, thanks to (supposedly) good intelligence, would (presumably) not have to waste JP-8 in a prolonged target search routine.

Following Ballantine's plan, the EA-6B Prowler crew of Pine Tree 621 prepared to help *Langley*'s escorts get their cruise missiles to the Russian warships, already located by Hawkeyes and surveillance satellites.

The naval might of a nation—manned and unmanned aircraft—sped westward through the dawning. The world's first supercarrier battle was under way.

10

0540 to 0618, Friday, 4 June

0540
Varyag, *off South Africa*

Pyotr Rybakov envisioned the American strike plan unfolding at over 400 nautical miles per hour—about seven miles every minute. Sitting in the command spaces, his attention was forced to the *Novorossiysk* group as his electronics and communications staffers kept up a running commentary. But he only half listened, absorbing key phrases: "Radar contacts with standoff jamming to the east-northeast . . . presumed cruise missiles inbound in three streams from southeast . . ."

Rybakov was more concerned with what might be headed his way than with the fate of the *Novorossiysk* SAG. *Varyag* and *Kuznetsov* were clearly the key targets. He turned to his chief of staff. "Anatoly Vladimirovich, quickly. What do you make of this situation?"

Smirnov again looked at the tactical display. "It is much as we predicted, knowing their doctrine. A deception group composed of decoys, here"—he tapped a spot on the screen east southeast of *Frunze*—"or possibly genuine antiship missiles. A fire-suppression group"—he indicated the position of the more northerly contacts—"and probably an attack group hidden behind the suppression force." He moved his finger farther east.

"Yes, but as yet we do not know what waits just below the radar horizon. Even within this apparent strike on *Novo,* which group of contacts is a real threat and which, if any, the deception? These so-called cruise missiles approaching *Novorossiysk's* screen—they could be air-launched decoys or, as you suggest, Tomahawks. The jamming up here"—he pointed to the northeast of *Novorossiysk*—"could be a feint. But there's another question about this presumed attack on Admiral Kostolev: Where did it come from?"

"Smirnov," Rybakov said, "your analysis is no doubt valid as far as it goes, but you've commented only on what the Americans have shown us so far. It's possible that both groups approaching Kostolev are a diversion and that the real attack will fall on us."

"Could *Langley* be far enough south to attack us?" the aide asked.

"*You're* supposed to answer *my* questions, you know," the admiral said testily. "But he wouldn't need to be. With midair refueling, the American carrier could be a thousand miles away. However, I doubt Gideon would launch from that distance—he hasn't enough tankers to mount a decent strike."

The chief of staff took a shot. "Well, if we assume the surface contacts reported by the AWACS before it was shot down to have been *Langley,* that puts him here, southeast of Madagascar, over four hours ago. Not yet within striking range of *Novorossiysk.* But if he has sped up since then, he could be close enough by now. Say 120 miles . . ." Smirnov tapped the map and traced a line toward the V/STOL carrier. "About 800 miles from *Novorossiysk*—marginal, but feasible for an air-refueled strike."

"If I were Gideon," Rybakov said, "I wouldn't want to be that close to Madagascar. Worse yet, if he has steamed at top speed since early yesterday, he could be even farther west. And south, if he changed heading after he sank the subs. In fact, he's conceivably within range of us, assuming heavy tanking support. Unlikely, I'll admit, especially against us. *Novorossiysk* could be attacked with fewer aircraft, so is more probable."

Smirnov exhaled and commented, "It's all we have to go

on, Admiral." The staffer brought the pointer to port arms.
"The previous position report was from one of the lost subs
—several hours before the incident. No direct satellite, airborne or surface observation for days. They've jammed our
RORSats, shot down our planes and disabled our surveillance trawler. And if *Langley* is farther west and south, then
what did the AWACS spot and who shot it down?"

"Damn it. I need more information." Rybakov studied
the map. "What if *Langley* sped up right after sinking the
subs—perhaps twenty-four hours ago? He might have
steamed 700 miles, although we have no solid evidence to
suggest that. He could be anywhere."

The admiral clenched his fist. "Have any of our escorts
been able to acquire the alleged hostiles headed toward Kostolev's group?"

"They're trying, sir," the BCh-6 answered. "But either
we're out of range or the American jamming aircraft is still
operating there." He moved the cursor on his electronic display thirty miles east of *Frunze,* where he assumed a lone
Prowler orbited with its powerful magnetrons activated. Radar performance was badly degraded in that sector, which
may or may not have been the actual threat axis.

"All the RORSats and SpySats, most of the maritime
patrol planes and spy ships and half the subs in the world,
and what good are they?" Rybakov steamed, his frustration
boiling over. The admiral intended to make a decision, so he
forced himself to cool off.

"If the contacts Kostolev reported are in fact real aircraft, he will need more and better interceptors," the admiral
told Smirnov. "His Yaks won't be able to handle a deckload
strike of Hornets and Intruders." Rybakov quickly calculated
Kostolev's needs. If *Novorossiysk* didn't request fighter support, Rybakov might release some himself once more was
known about the radar contacts. *What is that fool Kostolev
doing?*

Grunt Flight, Novorossiysk Strike Group

Lieutenant Commander Grant "Grunt" Grundmeyer in
Rampart 302 checked his watch. As the sweep hand ticked
through the mark, he rocked his Hornet's wings to signal his
wingman. Then Grunt turned seventy degrees starboard and

accelerated to the north-northwest. In eight minutes he and Rampart 305 had an appointment for an assassination.

0541
Varyag

"Kostolev requests interceptors, Admiral," Smirnov reported.

"Well, that's a relief," Rybakov responded. "Did he say why now?"

"No, sir. The AWACS found no new contacts before being jammed, nor have his Yaks spotted anything. Kostolev still suspects a diversion, but cannot rule out a genuine strike force. So far he has authorized no defensive action by surface ships other than distraction-mode chaff."

Rybakov did not respond. A commander had to know his subordinates, if only to gauge how much to discount them. He had chosen the other two SAG commanders himself. Kostolev was a relatively unknown quantity, having served most of his career in the Pacific Fleet. Whatever his general ability, his judgment was almost certainly faulty now. The Madagascar-based Antonov had been shot down by fighters last night. The contacts picked up this morning southwest of Madagascar by the *Novorossiysk* group and the AWACS out of Mozambique had to be either *Langley*'s main strike force or a diversionary group. In the latter case, the main attack could be aimed at *Varyag*, and he would need all his fighters here.

Rybakov promptly stirred himself. He had read enough history to realize his mind-set could prove fatal. *My God, I could become the Russian Nagumo—dithering over options while the enemy approaches unchecked, just like Midway.* The admiral forced himself to concentrate more on action and less on possibilities.

Turning to Smirnov, the fleet commander snapped out his decision. "Order fighter control to release immediately the eight Su-27s in our combat air patrol to reinforce *Novorossiysk*'s Yak-141s, then launch our ready interceptors to replace those detached. The *Novorossiysk* group's peril is greater than ours. Then signal *Kuznetsov* to ready a squadron of Su-27s to replenish our CAP. After recovering the ground-attack planes, rearm half the Su-25s with air-to-air missiles and half with 1,200-liter fuel tanks and refueling pods."

As Smirnov hastened to comply, Rybakov glanced at the theater map. He felt better having made his decision, but he recognized the risk. *Novorossiysk* was only 250 miles to the northeast; *Kuznetsov* was more than twice that distance southwest. It was a race between the Su-27s and whatever the Americans may have descending on the two northern groups. *Well,* Rybakov acknowledged, *admirals are in the business of taking risks.*

Pyotr Rybakov sat back in his cushioned seat, biting the end of his pen. Action made him feel better, but he could not shake the feeling that he was being played like a balalaika.

0542

Smirnov told his admiral that a direct signal from the nuclear cruiser *Frunze* had come in, bypassing *Novorossiysk.* "Captain First Rank Bulba reports popping distraction-mode chaff four minutes ago. He says the American cruise missiles —if they are missiles—appear not to have taken the bait. He blames the failure on Admiral Kostolev and complains about getting no timely instructions. This is insubordination, Admiral. Bulba should be brought up on charges."

"He will be, I assure you. If he survives," Rybakov responded. "But for the moment he seems to be doing quite well."

Rybakov wondered if the problem really was Kostolev's command indecision, or if enemy jamming was to blame. With no sign of the latter, he assumed the worst; that is, the usual. *The problem is not Kostolev himself. Kostolevs exist in every navy. It is whoever promoted him. It is the system.*

0548
Grunt Flight

At the end of their seventy-five-mile sprint, Grunt and his wingman, Lieutenant "Psycho" Thaler, were in position. Thirty miles south of the Russian AWACS plane, they had the Antonov on their radars. Grunt did not know for sure, but had to assume that his presence was undetected, since the EA-6B was to have begun jamming a few minutes before.

Grunt's own radar picture was clear as he designated the orbiting Madcap and gained a radar lock. With his entire focus on his glowing green scope, he was barely conscious of the predawn darkness around him. He rechecked his switch-ology, engaged Master Arm and pressed the trigger.

The night was rent by ignition of two missiles below Rampart 302. The high-impulse rocket motors lit off with a white-orange flame, shooting the medium-range AIM-120s on their way. Grunt kept his F/A-18's nose pointed at the Madcap, which must now have been aware of its peril. But he knew—and probably the Russian crew knew—there was no escape.

0549

Grunt and Psycho saw a garish explosion strobing out of the lightening sky. Burning fuel traced a descending fiery finger toward the Indian Ocean. Then, satisfied that half their mission was fulfilled, the two VFA-183 pilots turned southwesterly and bent their throttles. They had another ren-dezvous in twenty minutes.

Varyag *Strike Group*

In Frisbee 601 Lieutenant Tony Chimola was about to spring an ambush. The E-2 controller watched with rapt fas-cination as the APS-125 radar, rotating through a complete turn every ten seconds, painted him a deeply gratifying pic-ture. He had Grayhound Flight on his scope—two VF-182 Tomcats assigned to destroy *Varyag*'s Mudhen AWACS be-fore the Russian early-warning bird could detect *Langley*'s main strike group. In keeping with the overall deception plan, the two F-14s had flown northwest from *Langley* out-side the Mudhen's detection range, then turned sharply to enter the Antonov's search radius on a southwesterly heading from the northeast.

Chimola also painted two Flankers on their advanced CAP position east of the Mudhen; Grayhound would have to deal with them, too. The controller engaged his mike.

"Grayhound Lead, Frisbee 601. Your bandits bearing 240 for eighty-five." He watched the Flanker blips reverse course, apparently now warned of their peril by their airborne controller. "Confirm Link Four, over." He made sure that the Hawkeye's data-link connection with the F-14s was operable, then passed the electronic information to the fighters. *Git some.*

Courtesy of the data-link relay, the two Tomcats had a God's-eye view of the Russian disposition without radiating themselves. Farkle, Grayhound's redheaded RIO in Circus 201, acknowledged the message. He checked with their wingman in 203 to confirm targeting data.

On signal, two fingers pushed two firing buttons and the big AIM-54Cs dropped off their racks. The motors ignited, sending the Phoenixes into soaring climbs. Tony Chimola watched the drama unfolding with a curious sense of detachment. He momentarily tried to envision the reaction in the Flanker cockpits—pilots alerted by their radar warning gear, maneuvering to counter the unknown threat. Then he returned to his job.

And business was good. The Su-27's one shortcoming was lack of a very-long-range missile. Consequently, the volley of AIM-54Cs was unopposed and one Phoenix found its target. Though a direct hit was not likely against so agile a target as a Flanker, a hit was not necessary. Thanks to its 135-pound warhead, close counted with AIM-54C. A third Phoenix launch at slightly lesser range tore apart the second Sukhoi.

Another missile trace flashed westward; the Mudhen exploded into chunks large enough to show on the Hawkeye's radar. The kinetic effect alone of a Mach-5 Phoenix impacting a target was catastrophic; the detonation resulted in windblown shards of metal and burning jet fuel.

Chimola checked the Tomcats departing northeasterly, retracing their approach. Grayhound Flight had just gouged the first chink in the armor of the formidable *Varyag* group. He knew the strike birds trailing Frisbee 601 would exploit the opening within forty minutes, by which time survivors from the diversion group would already be headed home.

0550
Varyag

Captain First Rank Smirnov took the proffered message form from the communicator. The sailor's expression told the chief of staff that it contained no good news. Smirnov read the terse note and strode toward Rybakov's position.

"Admiral, we are faced with more problems. The Mozambique AWACS and our own have both disappeared within minutes, as well as the two Su-27s controlled by our Antonov."

Rybakov took the paper, scanned it and initialed the form. "This is no coincidence," he began, lowering a hand from his chin. "We must assume the Americans shot down both AWACS. Order the Antonov orbiting in our southeastern sector to move northeast to replace the one we just lost." He paused to study the perspex board, then continued. "Release all four of our inner CAP fighters to take over air search of the western sector until the replacement Antonov arrives. Then launch another flight to replace the inner CAP."

He waited for Smirnov to comply with the order, then asked, "Now, why were our outer CAP aircraft attacked along with the land-based AWACS? Why didn't jamming it suffice?"

The CSO referred to the status board. "Well, the Americans may have more urgent ECM targets now that they're nearing the *Novorossiysk* group. And the presumed cruise missile tracks are within our AWACS' search radius from the northern end of its orbit. They might want to keep the missiles' course hidden," Smirnov said.

"Yes, but the missiles' targets are obvious. Since the presumed strike planes are outside our AWACS' search arc, secrecy alone doesn't explain the attack," Rybakov observed.

Smirnov offered the school solution. "Then are we to assume the shoot-down was to draw our attention away from the major attack against the *Novorossiysk* group?"

"Perhaps, but that also is what the Americans may want us to think. There's an equal chance they mean to attack this task group as well. If so, there's a southern strike aimed at us, escorted by Tomcats that destroyed our AWACS."

The staff officer shrugged. "We're operating in the dark, then."

"Correct. But is it just Clausewitz's normal fog of war or an intentional smoke screen?" *An electronic and information fog compounded by darkness. But what does it mean? What does it mean?*

"We'll have to cut through the clouds either way,"

Rybakov said. "The northeast sector is the more likely zone of approach for any enemy attack on this group. Have the ready AWACS take off to replace the southeast one. Detach all four Su-27s in the CAP flight to cover the northeast quadrant until the An-74 can arrive. Have them conduct sweeps with their air-intercept radars of the whole ninety-degree sector. If our fighters can find and destroy the Tomcats that shot down the AWACS, so much the better, but the F-14s already may be gone."

"Aye, aye," Smirnov responded, admiring his superior's decisiveness.

0553
Bambi Flight approaching Novorossiysk *Group*

Lieutenant Commander Brian "Bambi" Deere double-checked his Hornet's inertial navigation readout. Satisfied, he shifted in the seat of Bronco 404 and looked around. He could not see the trailing A-6Es, but angled astern of him were three other F/A-18Cs. Rocking his wings, Bambi signaled the VFA-184 division and pushed his two throttles around their detents. In afterburner, he led his pilots in a steep climb toward 25,000 feet.

Leveling off and coming out of burner, he turned to his specified westerly heading. Then he engaged the secure UHF, waited for the synchronization tone and keyed his mike. "Bambi Flight, arm 'em up and launch in sequence."

According to the prebriefed plan, each pilot selected his Hornet's two outboard, underwing ordnance stations and counted off the seconds. First Deere's external stores dropped off their triple-ejector racks, then his wingman's, then the section lead's and finally number four's. In less than a minute, twenty-four bomb-sized, lozenge-shaped decoys were gliding downward toward the *Novorossiysk* group.

After releasing the decoys, Deere's division selected afterburner and streaked toward the enemy SAG. Bambi Flight wanted to fight; its four strike-fighter pilots searched eagerly on their Hornets' APG-65 radars for *Novorossiysk's* airborne Yaks. Eight V/STOL fighters were spotted, and Deere detached his second section to hook around for a radar missile shot. The VFA-184 "Jousters" were outnumbered two to one, but as the jets closed one another at over 1,000 miles per hour Bambi Flight knew who held the advantage.

0555
Brillo Flight

Lieutenant Commander "Brillo" Huggins in Killer 530 led his other three Intruders into the teeth of the *Novorossiysk* group's outer defenses. Killer 531 and he were each armed with four Skipper II laser-guided, 1,000-pound bombs and four Shrike antiradiation missiles. Killer 532 and 533 were the suppressors, assigned to knock out the Russian air defenses, allowing the others to get within Skipper range of *Novorossiysk.*

The two suppressor crews' fire-distribution plans were similar. Killer 532, going against *Frunze,* faced the greater risk. But thanks to the nuclear battlecruiser's position at the eastern edge of the SAG screen, 532 could head for home sooner. Antisub cruiser *Tallinn,* maintaining a "goalkeeper" station close to *Novorossiysk,* posed a slightly lesser direct threat to Killer 533, but attacking her required flying into the heart of the SAG and staying longer. If Flankers appeared while the strike force was still inbound—well, the imagination wandered.

Brillo knew that, according to plan, Pine Tree 623 had waited for the Russian air-search radars to get a good look at the strike group before commencing jamming. Thanks to the destruction of the Madcap by Grunt and Psycho, an EA-6B had enough power to white out even *Frunze*'s mighty electronic suite at this range.

The job of the two suppressor A-6Es was made a little easier by the Prowlers escorting the TASMs and Brillo Flight. Each of the two EA-6Bs carried a pair of jamming pods and two HARMs—big, high-speed antiradar missiles mounted one under each wing. The combination of HARM and jamming gave Prowlers a capability for both "hard" and "soft" kills on enemy radars—a choice savored by electronic warriors.

Hanging HARMs on the outer wing pylons rather than two more ALQ-99 jamming pods gave Prowlers a "hard-kill" capability, but at the cost of four "soft-kill" channels. The ECMOs—electronic countermeasures operators in Pine

Tree 621—had told Brillo they weren't sure the trade was worthwhile. If the EA-6Bs had in fact knocked out the most threatening SAM fire-control system—*Frunze* and *Chervona*'s Top Dome radars providing mid-course guidance for the SA-N-6s—then the HARMs may have been worth it.

Against so many enemy surveillance and guidance systems, and with the Prowlers' need to carry HARM as well as ECM pods, there simply were not enough EA-6Bs to go around. The success of the mission and the odds of survival of the two "strikers"—Killer 530 and 531—depended on the skill of the two suppressors. To neutralize the enemy's air defenses and allow the attackers a good shot at their target, 532 and 533 each packed four HARMs and twelve imaging, infrared-guided Mavericks.

When Pine Tree 623 began jamming the powerful air-search radars on cruisers *Chervona Ukraina, Frunze* and destroyer *Stoikiy*, Huggins detached one of his two suppressors against the huge battlecruiser. He watched Killer 532, flown by Lieutenant Rob "Fortune" Kent, veer port off base course toward *Frunze*, a floating SAM magazine forested with radars. Unless the ship's vast, nuclear-fueled power supply allowed its air-search radars to burn through the jamming, 532 should be able to approach its target undetected.

Brillo felt his CAG's plan made good use of the limited resources available for the diversionary attack. Pine Tree 621 was approaching the SAG's most potent escort, battlecruiser *Frunze*, from the southeast, flying above the three converging streams of Tomahawk Antiship Missiles. As soon as *Frunze* beamed its Top Dome long-range SAM guidance radars at the oncoming TASMs, the Prowler would launch its two HARMs tuned to the Top Dome frequency. The HARMs were programmed to home on those radars no matter what. If the Russians shut down to avoid getting hit, the HARMs' on-board computers would estimate the radars' position changes and continue guiding the missiles toward the targets' last known position. The Russian operators could not keep their MFC radars turned off indefinitely without severely reducing the SA-N-6s' ability to find incoming TASMs.

Meanwhile, Killer 532 would close the battlecruiser from the northeast. The main function of the Intruder's two HARMs was to back up Pine Tree 621's in case they misfired, were shot down or missed. But 532's antiradar missiles

were programmed to home on secondary targets if the Top
Domes shut down or were destroyed by the Prowler's
HARMs. *Frunze*'s Top Sail and Top Steer air-search radars
were the highest-priority secondary targets. However, if the
A-6E got safely through the SA-N-6 zone, the missiles could
be reprogrammed to home on two of the battlecruiser's six
short-range SAM guidance radars or five AAA fire-control
systems. The multiplicity of these radars made them better
candidates for jamming than "HARMing," though not all
these guidance systems could be brought to bear on the
TASMs simultaneously. That was the theory; now it would be
subjected to the acid test of combat.

Bambi Flight

Brian Deere in Bronco 404 caught the flash of a distant
midair explosion. *Cuddles's AMRAAMS are doing the job,* he
thought. His second section's end run had at least partially
succeeded, taking out the lead element of the Yak formation
with radar missiles. He depressed his mike button. "Bambi
here. Cuddles, go high. I'm taking 'em from starboard." He
got a quick "Rog" in reply.

The VFA-184 pilots had outranged the enemy and were
having things entirely their own way. Keeping their airspeed
up, they used "blowthrough" tactics to deny the nimble Yaks
any advantage. With a good angle, Bambi made a quick Sidewinder kill, then hosed an elusive jumpjet with twenty mike-
mike. The twin-boom Yak lurched crazily out of control and
dropped toward the ocean. *Damn, I'm good!* Deere looked
around and noted that his other pilots had splashed two
more, reluctantly letting two survivors scoot off. He checked
his gauges; it was time to head for the rendezvous.

0556
Starburst 41

The sweep second hand of the pilot's wristwatch ticked
off the last five seconds. ". . . three, two, one. Now! Take
her up, Marty." The copilot increased power while pulling on
the collective. The LAMPS III SH-60B rose vertically from
its wavetop hover, and in the crewman's compartment the
sensor operator fine-tuned his equipment. "Holy shit," he

gasped. "Thar she blows!" The target-designating radar revealed the Russian battlecruiser almost exactly where it had been predicted. ESM analysis verified the vessel as *Frunze*.

"Well, what did you expect?" replied the pilot. "Light 'er up." He looked at his watch again and wondered if it were really possible that so little time had passed since the frantic scramble from the *Spruance*-class destroyer *Davenport*. With a mixture of pride and apprehension, he realized that the lowly helo might not have fired the first shots in this battle, but it would guide the Tomahawks to their target.

Tomahawk Antiship Missile Flights

The TASMs' brains resembled those of their smaller cousins, the Harpoons, but contained an extra lobe capable of receiving and using inputs from over-the-horizon targeting systems. The eleven antiship missiles responded to the information beamed into their brains from the target-designating helicopters, acting as remote eyes. With the locations of their targets stored in memory, the TASMs could dispense with the "expanding box" search phase of the attack routine, cutting flight time and saving fuel, which on impact could produce a bigger fire on the enemy ship. Just as important, external designation meant the Tomahawks could leave their terminal-homing radars off longer, decreasing the odds of early detection.

The flying bombs hugged the wavetops, staying below the lobes of *Frunze* and *Stoikiy*'s searching radars. They moved eight miles closer to the battlecruiser each minute.

0557
Varyag

Smirnov soon returned with another message. Rybakov was getting no time to think. "Admiral, *Novorossiysk* reports that his escorts have been illuminated by radiation classified as a target-designation signal for Tomahawk Antiship Missiles," Smirnov said.

"Well, then this looks less and less like a deception with every passing minute," the admiral opined calmly. "At least the cruise missiles are likely to be real. And our replacement Madcap hasn't seen anything yet?"

"Negative."

"Hornets?" Rybakov wondered. "Why not Tomcats?"

"They could be to the south, guarding against any fighter reinforcement we may send," Smirnov suggested. "That would explain the shoot-down of our Madcap at the same time as theirs. With our Madagascar Tu-16s coming, the Americans could not afford to release many F-14s from ForceCAP to escort their strike."

Rybakov replied, "Well, either way, it shows that there actually are strike aircraft headed toward *Novorossiysk*. The Sukhois I released won't be wasted. We still don't know what might be headed our way."

0657 Local
Langley

Nate Gottlieb blanched as he scanned the report coming off the Link Eleven printer. Relayed through a cruiser's SH-60B from the detached, air-defense destroyers, the signal brought the worst possible news: *Carl* and both *Spruances* were under cruise missile attack! As soon as the machine stopped clattering, the CSO tore off the message and hustled to Gideon.

The admiral's eyes widened as he read the communique. "How did they find them?" he managed, gulping.

"Must have backtracked the TASMs, but that would only get them in the ballpark," Gottlieb surmised. "Without precise designation by overhead targeting assets or midcourse guidance from a ship or helo, I don't see how the Russian SLCMs could possibly have pinpointed our destroyers, unless their missiles can conduct a broad area search."

"Maybe they can do more than we give them credit for," Gideon responded, still shocked from the rude surprise. "Just 'cuz our missiles can't doesn't mean theirs can't. Ours don't need as much on-board smarts, given our carrier airpower. Plus, their SLCMs are a lot bigger and faster than ours."

"Possible, sir, but more speed just makes it harder for any search-and-self-designate software and hardware."

Gideon referred back to the message; some of the shock was wearing off. "Well, thank God no hits."

"Not yet, sir. But they say more have been detected inbound."

"Why don't they shut down until the missiles are in range? The second wave could be homing on our tracking or jamming signals."

"Could be, Admiral. SSN-19 shipwreck is credited with home-on-jam, but not self-designation. *Carl* has to track to provide area defense for the *Spruances*. Their own Sea Sparrows couldn't handle a mass attack." Gottlieb shook his head. "Hell of an expensive way to buy intelligence."

0558
Brillo Flight

Forty miles from the screen the Intruders approached the limit of the fast, maneuverable SA-N-6s on *Frunze* and, to her northwest, *Slava*-class cruiser *Chervona Ukraina*. If the plan worked, HARMs should knock out these most threatening systems, but suppressing the wealth of other defenses would require a combination of jamming and "weaponeering" timed to Brillo Flight's penetration—a precarious balancing act.

Minutes before, the EA-6Bs had begun their tightrope walk by jamming the ships' early-warning and air-search radars when still eighty miles from the SAG's eastern escorts. Pine Tree 623 operated against *Chervona Ukraina*'s, *Frunze*'s and *Stoikiy*'s Top Pair, Top Steer and Top Plate radars. This occupied all four of the bands on its two ECM pods. The jamming directed at *Novorossiysk*'s outer escorts also partially degraded the carrier's own Top Sail and Top Steer 3-D search radars, but did not completely white them out. Pine Tree 621 used one of its four channels to jam the Head Net-C air-surveillance radar on the "goalkeeping" cruiser *Tallinn*, leaving only three Prowler bands open.

The Prowler used its remaining three bands to jam five medium- and short-range SAM and gun fire-control frequencies as the TASMs approached *Frunze* and *Stoikiy*. When the missiles came within range of the battlecruiser's overlapping, short-range air-defense systems and the destroyer's medium- and short-range systems, three would not suffice. If either Prowler switched from jamming just one air-search radar to a

SAM or gun fire-control system, the strike planes would be exposed to tracking.

0600

The abrupt, high-pitched tone in his headset told Brillo Huggins that his Intruders had been painted by fire-control radars of the highly capable SA-N-6. Nothing else in the tactical aviation world elicited such a response, for *Frunze's* two Top Domes controlled ninety-six of the long-range SAMs and *Chervona Ukraina's* single Top Dome controlled sixty-four more. Despite his personal concern, the division leader was aware that the missile fire-control (MFC) radars also might be tracking the inbound TASMs fifty miles to the south.

Seconds later Huggins heard a more welcome sound— the two-tone synchronization of his VHF scrambler radio. "Brillo Lead from Pine Tree," came the familiar voice. "Shotgun, repeat, shotgun."

Brillo gave a brief acknowledgment and turned to his B/N, Sleaze Olsen. "Man, I don't know 'bout you, but I spell relief H-A-R-M." The terse message told him that Pine Tree 621 had just fired two high-speed antiradar missiles, stalking the Russian electronic sentries.

Thirty seconds later, the Top Dome alarm signal abruptly quit blaring. Brillo and Sleaze looked at each other. They wanted to be jubilant, but knew the HARMs had not yet struck the radars. The Russians had stopped radiating to avoid having their eyes shot out. This allowed the TASMs to get closer, but unless the HARMs' memory guidance fortuitously flew them within their warheads' blast radius of the Top Dome radars, the deadly system would be able to engage the strike planes as they approached *Novorossiysk*.

Even though both Top Domes were shut down, the Russians continued firing SA-N-6s at the TASMs. Sleaze knew that an SA-N-6 could home semiactively into the general area—the "basket"—of a target aircraft on radio waves reflected off the jet from the battlecruiser's air-search radars, although not as precisely as from the Top Domes. Once in the basket, the SAM's own small radar would provide active terminal homing. So jamming the air-search radars remained critical; the enemy ships were boosting power, trying to "burn through" the Prowlers' ECM. In the last resort, the EA-6Bs could jam the SAMs' terminal-homing radars. When the strike force came within range, its planes would make even better targets than the cruise missiles.

Sleaze watched Killer 531 close up on Pine Tree 623. He had to smile; most of his fellow aviators lacked his knowledge of electronic combat. Their avionic understanding tended to be minimal, based nearly as much on sci-fi as hard knowledge. That certainly applied to the pasty-faced Trekker called "Data," flying 531. Try as he might, Sleaze just couldn't convince Data that Prowlers had no Klingon "cloaking device."

Killer 532

Fortune and his bombardier-navigator realized that "hard-killing" *Frunze* was up to them. Their two HARMs were programmed to home on Top Dome frequencies as the primary threat. But now it appeared that Pine Tree 621's HARMs would probably not be able to kill the Top Domes, barring a luckout. Therefore, the A-6E crew programmed the missiles to home on *Frunze*'s Top Pair and Top Steer air-search radars, knowing their HARMs' on-board logic would revert to the higher-priority threat if Top Dome should come back "up" during the missiles' ninety-second flight.

Fortune raised his jet's nose above the horizon and, on cue from his B/N, pressed the trigger. Lofted in a high arc, two HARMs rocketed from the Intruder, headed nearly forty miles away toward *Frunze*, sniffing the ship's electronic scents. The B/N—a short gnome of a flier nicknamed "Smurf"—monitored the complex game.

The crew of Killer 532 followed their missiles toward *Frunze*, exposing themselves to the barrage of SA-N-6s. Even though the big SAMs were being fired at a slow rate and with degraded accuracy, due to the Prowlers' jamming and shutting down the Top Domes, they still posed a serious threat. The Intruder's Mavericks were the last boost the strike force and TASMs would get up and over *Frunze*'s defenses. To reduce their exposure time, Fortune accelerated to maximum speed, but it would still be three minutes before he got close enough for low-level Maverick release.

Meanwhile, north of the battlecruiser, in Killer 533,

Fortune's wingman—a pilot called "Runner" and a B/N known as "Chevy"—continued west with the main body of Hornets and Intruders.

0601
Varyag

"*Novorossiysk*'s escorts are under attack by air-to-surface missiles, Admiral!" Smirnov announced excitedly. "Initial classification, Maverick and HARM. TASMs still presumed inbound."

"Very well," Rybakov responded. "Time is answering some of our questions, at least." He forced himself to think in professional terms, as a gamesman, really. Later he might consider the human cost of his moves on the broad board of the sea—or he might not. He didn't know what he would think or feel at another time. Now he wondered if his immediate group would be next and desperately wanted information that would help answer that question. The admiral decided that his defensive dispositions were the best he could make.

After another moment's reflection, he made a tough decision. "Rearm all returning fighter-bombers for antiship attack."

0602
Killer 530

As the strikers passed through the SA-N-6 zones of *Frunze* and *Chervona Ukraina*, Sleaze was as deeply relieved as any human could be that the big SAMs were not guiding properly. The combination ECM and HARMs seemed to be working. Though "Jet Mormon's" faith assured him of an afterlife, he was in no hurry to experience eternal bliss. The earthly joys that his religion did permit—indeed, encouraged —still held much appeal.

The B/N also was delighted that his radar receivers showed that, far to the south, Pine Tree 621 was fritzing out *Stoikiy*'s SA-N-7 fire-control radar. This enabled the TASMs to get within fifteen miles of *Frunze,* which, to reinforce its own short-range air defenses and to compensate for its denigrated long-range SA-N-6s, was staying within the destroyer's medium-range SAM zone.

Grunt Flight

After splashing the Madcap, the two Hornets barely made their rendezvous with the deception strike. Grunt had known it would be close, and what he saw below convinced him that he and Psycho were none too early. His radar homing and warning panel indicated that *Chervona Ukraina* was active, its Top Dome radars emitting their SAM-guidance signals. The cruiser became Grunt Flight's primary target.

Grunt called his wingman in the clear and made sure that Psycho understood the plan. The section leader moved his stick slightly, refining his heading toward *Chervona Ukraina*, and kept his F/A-18 pointed southwesterly. With his outboard pylons selected, Grunt nosed up slightly for a maximum-range shot and pressed the trigger twice.

Within moments four AGM-88As streaked away from Rampart 302 and 305, bent on the single-minded mission for which they existed. Satisfied that he could do no more, Grunt led Psycho in a descending left-hand turn toward the egress point east of the Russian SAG. Looking back at the smoke trails and flak bursts, the section leader wondered if there would be any Intruders to escort clear of the area.

0603
Killer 532

After shooting HARMs at *Frunze*, Fortune and Smurf continued closing on the battlecruiser at top speed and medium altitude, grateful that the combination of HARMs and jamming had neutralized the potent SA-N-6 system. From ten miles—still outside the battlecruiser's short-range SA-N-4 and SA-N-9 SAMs and 130mm AAA system—they launched their six Mavericks.

Though the sun was up, Smurf viewed the rapidly enlargening *Frunze* through his forward-looking infrared screen. He wanted to see a picture similar to that provided his Mavericks by their computer-enhanced imaging infrared trackers. Both FLIR and IIR units operated in the eight- to twelve-micron region, a wavelength "window" whose radiation penetrated haze and smoke better than visible light and many other IR bands. Cooler areas of the target appeared dark green or black on the screen; hot spots glowed lighter shades of green. Each AGM-65F's thermal imager produced pictures sharp enough to discern ship types, and to provide rough aimpoints as well.

In his FLIR scope, the B/N designated areas on the battlecruiser that he wanted his IIR Mavericks to home on. He handed off these instructions to the guidance systems of the six missiles mounted on 532's inboard pylons.

Smurf chose aimpoints along *Frunze*'s 740-foot water-line, where the thermal contrast between warm hull and cooler ocean was greatest—although in the warm Agulhas Current the contrast was not vast. Should a Maverick break lock on its aimpoint, Smurf relied on its default program to guide the missile toward the target's center of mass. With ships this big, IIR Maverick should not miss if it worked at all.

The missiles kept the heat-viewing gaze of their seeker heads fixed on Smurf's designated spots. The Mavs' charge-coupled devices—essentially the same as in hand-held, visible-light video cameras—picked up the IR radiation emanating from the selected points. The seekers tracked the ships as unswervingly as cobras' eyes follow the motions of their prey.

Air-to-surface missiles usually "let air in at the top rather than water at the bottom," but with Maverick, the bombardier had both options. While Smurf shot for the hull primarily because of its thermal contrast, he also felt that the 300-pound blast-fragmentation warheads detonating there probably would penetrate the ship's innards. No matter how many Mavericks made it through the dense thicket of *Frunze*'s and *Stoikiy*'s air defenses, just forcing the Russians to counter them improved the chances that some TASMs could reach the battlecruiser or destroyer. But Smurf knew that on a ship bristling with so much equipment, even "misses" could hit something valuable.

The 637-pound AGM-65Fs came off their underwing triple-ejector racks and accelerated to their supersonic maximum velocity. Fortune and Smurf had a lot of firepower at their disposal, but they were not sanguine—they would take all the help they could get. All four Intruders also relied on both Prowlers jamming *Frunze*'s and *Chervona Ukraina*'s short-range SAMs and heavy AAA fire-control systems.

It would take over a minute to lock all six missiles onto their aimpoints but less than a minute for each to reach the ship, over ten miles distant. Then Fortune would hightail it for home.

0703 Local
Langley

A somber Nate Gottlieb approached his admiral. "The preliminary damage estimates are in from the destroyers, sir," the CSO told Gideon. "It's bad."

If the man hadn't been wearing such a hangdog expression, Gideon would have asked, "How bad is it, Johnny?" But not now. Matching Gottlieb's mood, he said grimly, "Let's have it."

"Well, E-2 data indicate nearly forty Sunburns and Shipwrecks were fired successfully—about two-thirds from surface ships and one-third sub-launched," the CSO reported. The admiral whistled; Gottlieb continued. "Yeah. They unloaded on us. The last missiles hit at 0601. Frisbee 605 hasn't picked up any others, so we assume the attack is over."

"Okay. That's enough buildup. Gimme it straight," the admiral said, bracing himself emotionally.

Gottlieb straightened. "Yes, sir. The short of it is, *Davenport* and *Wheatley* are dead in the water, and will probably have to be abandoned. *Carl* survived a near miss. Sprung leaks, but otherwise okay."

"Jesus," Gideon exclaimed. "Casualties?"

"Preliminary estimates are hundreds—over fifty percent on both ships."

Images of hideous death tried to muscle into Gideon's mind, but he forced them out. "What are we doing to rescue the wounded?"

"We can't spare any ships. Both *Spruances*' helos have already flown off a few cases, but of course the SH-60s can't carry more than a couple at a time. They're taking them to *Carl* for now, but they'll have to be transferred here, to our escorts or to *Hornet*. The destroyers have requested UH-46s to fly off the worst cases. I need your approval to order *Rose-burg* and the PhibRon's choppers to the rescue."

"Okay. Give them as many as we can spare, but we'll need them back to fly SAM reloads to our cruisers after the bombers hit us. Have 'em carry reloads out to *Carl,* too, and back-haul the wounded." Gideon thought for a moment. "Anything else, Nate?"

"That's about all we know right now. *Carl* isn't sticking around. She's heading for our rendezvous. That facilitates transferring wounded from *Davenport,* but makes it tougher for *Wheatley.*"

"Thanks, Nate." Gideon wondered if the price paid to Tomahawk *Frunze* had been worth it, but decided there wasn't time for second guesses now. His calculations had assumed the Russians wouldn't be able to retaliate against the TASM-shooters. "How'd they find us?" he asked. "That self-designation system you suggested?"

"Looks that way. Apparently no aircraft, subs or satellites made the destroyers. As you know, the missiles leave their launch ship with general course data and flight-profile commands stored in their inertial guidance systems. We estimate they can receive corrections from *Frunze*'s electronics suite out to 200 miles, or about sixty percent of their maximum range. Less for the other platforms. Their SSGN, if in radar range of our ships, could have designated targets for the whole flight of missiles, regardless of which ships launched them. But there's no indication it was within range and, as I said, no paint. Obviously, its radars aren't mounted very high, so their horizon is low. Incidentally, the only good news is that the sub's launch of Shipwrecks gives us a fix on it."

"Great. Now we can close the barn door after the horses are out."

"Well, it can still shoot torpedoes and probably still has six nuclear SLCMs," the CSO rejoined, sounding a little hurt. "Assuming the standard loadout of three-quarters conventional and one-fourth nuke."

Gideon's mind cycled to the unanswered question. "How'd they find us?"

"Only thing we can figure is that some of the missiles could designate targets automatically for themselves and for accompanying or following SLCMs. In effect, the leading missiles, presumably Shipwrecks, could act like designating drones. They'd still suffer from limited field of view, but they could fly expanding-box search patterns. At Mach Two-plus and high altitude, they could sweep thousands of square miles per minute. In fact, *Carl* reported that some of the first wave of missiles—Shipwrecks—did fly both high and low. They also got indications of data-link transmissions that might have been a targeting handoff from the high-fliers to the deck-huggers."

Gideon whistled again and shook his head.

"What's more, any SAMs we fired at this first wave would also help them locate our ships with on-board ESM. Maybe even pinpoint us for the next wave, mostly Sunburns." Gottlieb paused to let the surmise sink in. "It's theoretically possible," he went on. "We've never seen them practice anything like this, but if it worked, it would give blind-fired SLCMs a chance of finding and hitting their targets without mid-course guidance or designation by other ships or aircraft." He stopped again to give the admiral a chance to end the dissertation.

"That it?" Gideon asked.

"Yeah. Just guesswork at this point. If Shipwrecks can in fact act like recce drones, it's a neat trick—and the best-kept secret in Russian naval warfare." He instantly regretted applying the adjective "neat" to a capability that may have just killed 200 American boys, maimed or burned an equal number and placed others in risk of drowning.

"All right," Gideon said tiredly. "Keep me posted. For now, carry on with that rescue program. Just hope the choppers don't lead 'em to us."

"Aye, aye, sir," Gottlieb replied. "We'll be careful."

0604
Killer 530

Sleaze punched Brillo's right arm and pointed to the radar warning panel. "Lookit! Top Dome to the west-northwest's down," Sleaze's voice came through the pilot's earphones.

Brillo nodded slightly, reluctant to turn his gaze from the bright, frightening world outside. He wanted to see everything that could kill him. But he stole a glance in the cockpit. Sure enough, the electronic lobe from about the ten o'clock position on the three-ring scope was gone. "HARMs must've clobbered the cruiser," he offered.

The same notation was made in two other A-6 cockpits, where four other aviators shared those feelings.

Killer 532

Wow. Intense, man, Smurf thought in 532 as he watched the frantic ECM, SAM and AAA defensive measures being conducted by *Frunze* against the Maverick and TASM onslaught. *Thank God for standoff weapons.* Smurf did not want to try to visualize flying through such defenses—a vicious eruption of SA-N-4 and -9 SAMs trailing white plumes in booster stage, followed by muzzle flashes from 30- and 130mm guns. Yet he knew other Killer aircrews would do just that against *Varyag* in about half an hour.

Both aircrewmen saw the bright flashes that indicated good hits. At least one sent up a waterspout as well—a hit low on the hull. Smurf earnestly wished for his Nikon with the 200mm lens. *I'd make the cover of the* Naval Institute Proceedings *fersure!* He gaped at the scene, trying to burn the impression onto his retina like an acid etching. It was the moment to which he and Fortune had devoted their adult lives. It was beautifully lethal, professionally rewarding and personally thrilling. And it was time to leave.

With Killer 532's last AGM-65F locked onto its target, Fortune banked the Intruder safely outside SAM range and headed for home. It comforted him to know that two Hornets were to cover the A-6s' getaway. He regretted that the hi-lo-lo-hi mission profile required him to egress on the deck, where he would burn more fuel. *Survival first—fuel later.*

The crew would not be able to see the results of the CVBG's combined punch of air- and sea-launched missiles. The pilot and B/N might never know how many TASMs made it through the enemy air defenses. Fortune only knew that, by HARMing radars and possibly slowing the big warship with hits on the waterline or boiler exhaust stacks, he had done his best to help the Tomahawks—still inbound a few miles to the south—to get through. A job well done. Now Job One was getting home.

Brillo Flight

The little strike force pressed on toward the heart of the SAG—*Tallinn* and *Novorossiysk* herself. The escorts' area-defense SAMs were still suppressed, but the Intruders were approaching the goalkeeper's and carrier's SA-N-3 arc. Soon after that they would come within range of enemy point-defense SAMs. Brillo shoved the throttles to the stops; Data in 531 followed suit.

Black Knight 40

Flight Lieutenant Igor Gnido knew he was too late. Oily black smoke coiled up in the distance like a beacon. His two Su-27 flights would have no trouble finding the scene of the American crimes. Wanting to ride to the rescue, not merely to avenge, he ordered afterburner.

Since leaving the coverage of surface-based radars and the replacement AWACS, Gnido had kept only one radar in each flight radiating to search for bandits; the others were in standby mode. Every five minutes, the radiating pilot switched to standby and the next man lit up. Without a friendly AWACS in the vicinity, the Flanker pilots would have to find enemy aircraft on their own, with help from their ships.

0607
Brillo Flight

Forty miles from the carrier, the strike group of three Intruders, four Hornets and one Prowler approached the points at which they would bank off their westerly course, turning south-southwest for their final run-ins toward *Tallinn* and *Novorossiysk*. Thanks to the suppression of *Chervona Ukraina*'s and *Frunze*'s air defenses, the attackers remained unscathed. The surviving enemy radars still could burn through the jamming, and fighters were probably en route from *Varyag*. Reducing exposure to air defenses was essential; the attackers would shoot and scoot.

Right on cue, Pine Tree 623 briefly suspended jamming air-search freqs to give the Russians a chance to paint the strikers. The ECM operators hoped the defenders would switch on their Head Light long-range SAM fire-control radars so the emitters could be HARMed.

Bambi Flight

The Hornets peeled off first. They pushed past 500 knots to take up a CAP station south of the SAG, between *Tallinn* and *Stoikiy*. They drew ineffective SA-N-3 fire, making it safely past the two targeted warships. Despite morning mist, Bambi and the other three F/A-18 jocks picked up the missile launches and evaded the hurtling SAMs with some drastic jinking. Bambi was mindful of the McDonnell Douglas ad quoting a naval aviator who said, "I don't want to fly anything else." Thankful for the Hornet's high-G airframe and outstanding agility, he shared the sentiment. The missiles self-destructed in huge brown spheres. The distant blast waves jostled the Hornets like mild turbulence in an airliner.

Killer 533

After coming to the new course, Runner and Chevy waited for their RHAW to announce a SAM fire-control radar paint. While still thirty miles out, they got it. Killer 533 promptly launched its two HARMs toward *Tallinn*. The cruiser was moving at flank speed to stay between the oncoming strike planes and *Novorossiysk*. Even so, each of the missiles locked onto one of *Tallinn*'s two Head Light radars, which guided her long-range SA-N-3s. The fast missiles would be very hard for the Russians to shoot down, especially with their short-range SAMs subject to intense jamming.

Bambi Flight

"All units, be advised, high-speed multiple bogies bearing 230 for fifty from Point November. Assume they are hostile. Frisbee, out."

The E-2's powerful transmitter cut through the ambient electronic clutter, telling Brian Deere—and everyone else in radio range—that unidentified aircraft were approaching *Novorossiysk* from the southwest. Bambi quickly calculated the geometry. He anticipated a missile exchange in the next few minutes. He quickly calculated that, unless the bogies went to burner, they would arrive only after the attack planes had struck. *Thank God the Hawkeye moved closer after we splashed the Yaks,* he thought. *Or we might not have picked them up in time.*

Bambi led his flight on a heading to intercept the bigger, better-armed, more advanced fighters. In order to save fuel, they avoided reheat.

0609
Killer 530

The RHAW still shrilled the tune of the SAM fire-control radar, but only from one direction—*Tallinn*'s. Brillo had seen bursts of light and wisps of smoke on the distant *Novorossiysk,* so it seemed his luck was holding. Though pleased that the SA-N-3 radars on the carrier had apparently been blasted, he was distressed that *Tallinn* was still operational. The cruiser was staying within SAM range of *Novorossiysk,* still covering the carrier. Since the strikers remained vulnerable to SA-N-3s, Pine Tree 623 had to continue jamming Head Light freqs, tying up one of its four precious bands, which would soon be in demand for use against short-range air-defense systems and, possibly, air-to-air radars and missiles.

Brillo bore down on the carrier, accelerating to 520 knots, with Data on his wing and Runner ten miles to the east on the same heading. Meanwhile, the Prowler orbited out of SA-N-3 range. Standoff jamming required more power, but EA-6Bs were too valuable to risk over a well-defended target.

Killer 533

Chevy peered at the enlargening cruiser through the FLIR. He prepared to select Maverick targets on *Tallinn* similar to Smurf's on *Frunze,* but this time it would be 533's squadron that benefited from their efforts, instead of cruise missiles. The cruiser was maneuvering wildly, so landing six missiles on selected aimpoints would be difficult. But Russian warships were so jam-packed with high-energy ordnance, you just had to hit something juicy—likely to produce spectacular secondary explosions.

0610

Proceeding southwest from twenty miles out, Chevy locked his first volley of two Mavericks onto *Tallinn*'s hot exhaust funnel just abaft midship—his best long-range target area. With damaged uptakes for its four 30,000-hp gas-turbine engines, the cruiser would at least be slowed, making life easier for Killer 530 and 531 en route to the carrier. Also, a hit there might knock out nearby radar dishes or electronic-surveillance antennas. Every little bit helped.

Chevy targeted his remaining four Mavericks along *Tallinn*'s waterline, wishing all the time that he could aim for SAM or ASW missile launchers, the better to ignite secondaries. Twelve miles from the cruiser, Runner put 533 in a dive and Chevy began shooting.

0611

As he fired the last Maverick, Chevy took a moment to glance up. "Jesus, look at that!" The ASW cruiser, momentarily obscured by flak bursts and missile plumes, seemed to jump at him. It stretched almost clear across his FLIR display. Concentrating on his aimpoints, he had not realized how rapidly they were closing on the 9,700-ton ship.

"Look quick, bud. We're outta here!" Ordnance expended, Runner wrapped the Intruder into an eighty-degree bank, "getting out of Dodge." He had a fleeting impression of Maverick strikes on the ship, then was on his way out. *Egress aggressively,* he thought, recalling Strike U. doctrine. Running as low and as fast as he dared, Runner cleared the screen southeasterly, drawing petulant SA-N-9 fire from *Novorossiysk.*

Brillo Flight

Peter Huggins led his two Intruders out of the northeast, through the gap in Russian air defenses carved by HARMs. Ten miles to the east, Killer 533 advanced on the same heading, shooting Mavericks at the *Kara*-class cruiser

Tallinn. Brillo and Data made straight for the flattop, packing a Sunday punch—four Skipper II laser-guided bombs each. Brillo knew where to direct them. *Novorossiysk's* Head Light SA-N-3 guidance systems weren't radiating, so Brillo assumed Pine Tree 623's HARMs were responsible. With this advantage in mind, the two A-6s maneuvered for a better aspect on the carrier.

Looking forward, past their refueling probe, Brillo and Sleaze watched in fascination as *Novo* turned crosswind. "She's trying to keep her stern to us," the pilot observed with a calm that surprised him. But no thirty-knot ship could long evade a 500-knot aircraft. Moments later Brillo and his wingmen—Data and Shaft in 531—had the angle they wanted on the carrier. They turned in to attack.

Killer 530

Sleaze Olsen chose his aimpoint carefully, designating the SA-N-3 launcher aft of the carrier's superstructure, or "island." The engagement sequence made sense: shoot out the air defenses, then penetrate the flight deck to the vulnerable hangar below. Killer 531 would engage with similar priority from starboard.

Sleaze's first target was the forward Cross Sword MFC set mounted just aft of the island's forward bridge. The Head Light SA-N-3 radars had been HARMed and the Cross Sword's SA-N-9 radars were being jammed, but something could always happen to the Prowler, and *Novo's* SAMs were thought to have optical backups.

As Brillo held the Intruder steady, nose-low after the pop-up and roll-in, the B/N confirmed his laser designator paint on the twin-arm SAM launcher. The data from the A-6E's chin-mounted target recognition attack multisensor (TRAM) turret—incorporating a FLIR, radar link and combined laser range finder/target-designator—told Sleaze he was nearing the heart of the Skipper envelope. Since the TRAM's spot tracker operated on a slightly longer wavelength than the laser range finder, the B/N was able to use both systems at once without confusing any airborne Skippers. He lased once more for range, saw it was nine miles and pressed the trigger. A circuit closed, solenoids activated and the first Skipper came off the port outboard pylon. The solid-fuel rocket motor ignited and powered the 1,200-pound weapon to transonic velocity.

The gimballed seeker head on the guided bomb angled down to keep its laser-receptive nose in the coherent beam of reflected light. The seeker's movement actuated the control surfaces, flying the explosive-filled, high-tensile steel shape toward its destination.

Soon the booster burnt out and the Skipper began to lose flight stability and speed. Sleaze was not alarmed when the ungainly bomb flittered like a wounded goose, pitching and yawing awkwardly. He recognized normal Skipper behavior and knew the weapon was still homing on the laser beam, headed downrange under his control. During its nearly minute-long flight, the laser-guided bomb (LGB) passed safely through the barrage of 30mm fire from the carrier's AK-630 close-in weapon systems (CIWS). *Maybe its erratic flying makes it a hard target,* Sleaze considered.

Seconds from impact, the subsonic Skipper's flight path evened out and it dove straight as Greg Louganis toward the sweet spot in the center of the invisible beam. *They do that every time. Man, I love reliable, off-the-shelf components. They work and they're cheap enough to practice with.*

Abruptly, a bright white flash burst on *Novorossiysk*'s island, below the aft bridge. Then flame, smoke and debris erupted from the SA-N-3 launcher. SAMs and parts of SAMs shot out like firecrackers. A viciously expanding cloud engulfed nearby radars, the aft 76mm mount and the bridge. *So far, so good,* Sleaze thought as he gawked at the spectacle for an instant that became imprinted in his memory. Then he thought, *Men have died. Boys. Eighteen-year-old conscripts. I killed them. Blew them away and burned them alive. Oh, well. It's what I do.*

Killer 531

Shaft fired his first two Skippers at the forward deckhouse, designating the starboard Cross Sword installation as his aimpoint. The first missile was tracked by the island-mounted point-defense systems. Shaft's screen flared as one of the 30mm, radar-guided Gatling guns found its mark, exploding a Skipper in flight. He quickly switched to a natural light display and reacquired the target. The second

Skipper homed on the designation beam and punched into the island, destroying its forward AK-630 and Cross Sword installations. The explosion occurred well inside the ship, but her plates bulged and smoke erupted from the entry hole.

As Data held their Intruder steady for the run-in, Shaft checked to see that Killer 533 was in position, above and behind 531. In 533, Chevy would guide Shaft's first two bombs toward the carrier's island from maximum range. Freed from this chore, 531 fired its third and fourth Skippers at the fo'c'sle. Data followed the missiles toward their target as Shaft lased *Novorossiysk*'s forward 76mm gun turret. In under a minute, six guided bombs were streaking toward the flattop.

0612
Killer 530

Eight miles out, Killer 530 was inside SA-N-9 range, but Pine Tree 623 was, according to plan, still jamming the Cross Sword radars from afar, and two of the four MFC systems were knocked out. With diminished range and medium-caliber flak bursting uncomfortably close, Brillo pressed his run, still hardly believing his luck. From the corner of his eye, he saw Sleaze quickly shift targets. The B/N designated the carrier's midships elevator. Carriers are thin-skinned ships crammed with volatile materials. One good hit could pay long-term dividends. The last two Skippers rocketed away, eating up the distance to *Novorossiysk*.

Before 530's Skippers left their hardpoints, a midair explosion told Brillo that flak from the carrier's forward 76mm gun turret must have connected with Killer 531's third Skipper. But the next big missile dived into the fo'c'sle near the AAA mount, producing a shattering secondary that jostled Killer 530, some five miles distant. Out of the lurid flame and smoke blew the remains of the gun turret.

Brillo watched Data bank 531 for home, followed by 533. He could almost hear Runner saying, "Miller time, dudes."

Envious of his flightmates, Brillo would join them as soon as he could, but he still had two more missiles to deliver. Killer 530's second Skipper slammed into the middle of the carrier's flight deck. Moments later, as Sleaze fired his third flying bomb, the midship elevator exploded at an upward angle, its framework twisted. Evil-looking smoke poured out of the shaft and through sprung deck plates.

Sleaze directed his LGB through the thickening smoke toward the V/STOL landing circle 300 feet aft of the ruined elevator. The asbestos-coated circle, labeled "M," made a convenient aimpoint. The ship's maneuvering conveniently allowed the wind to carry the smoke away from the spot.

Approaching two miles, the pilot banked to keep Killer 530 out of 30mm range. The Intruder's TRAM mount was stabilized; within limits Brillo could maneuver while still keeping the guidance unit on target.

Fired this close, the Skipper's flight time would be brief. For that, Sleaze thanked God—no mere turn of phrase to the devout B/N. The two six-barreled Gatling guns on the aft port CIWS sponson elevated and began firing a hundred 30mm rounds per second at the LGB.

Brillo was unhappy that the previous hits hadn't been enough to scramble the aft close-in defense radars. He thumbed his arming switch and fired 530's single Shrike radar-homing missile. Tuned to the Bass Tilt radar frequency that controlled the AK-630 CIWS, the ARM arced downward. Its warhead shattered the drum-shaped radar on the sponson, but the gunfire continued, although less accurately. *I hate optical backups,* Brillo thought.

Somehow, the ship's helmsman knew to angle her hard astarboard to bring the other aft CIWS to bear. *With both bridges out, they must be steering from CDC,* the pilot reflected. *Must still have good comm. We'll see about that.*

The last Skipper was already on its way. Sleaze was designating *Novo's* stern, hoping to immobilize her with hits on the rudder or engineering plant. *With these damn Gatling guns, we should have bombed our way forward rather than aft,* Brillo decided in retrospect.

Seconds later the Skipper impacted smack in the middle of the stern, just below the round emblem. The LGB punched out the third Cyrillic *O* and first *C* in the ship's name. Sleaze thought of his first elk, of his father's hand patting his back. He exclaimed, "Yahoo! Bull's-eye."

"Nah," Brillo countered. "A little low."

"No way, Jose. Good shot, no meat wasted." *Will I ever hunt elk again?*

The carrier began trailing ugly black smoke, slowed and circled. Oil darkened her wake like blood from a shark-bitten swimmer. The fliers knew they'd made a good hit—something bad had happened to the prop shafts, gears or rudders, or maybe all three.

"Let's blow this pop stand," Sleaze added. Brillo thought, *We're outta here,* laid his stick hard over and shoved up the power.

At once frightened and elated, the aircrew glimpsed the bright flashes of weapon impacts on their target, leaving smoke and flames as testament to their accuracy. Jinking away from the carrier—his "Navy Cross"—Peter Huggins could see that the forward fire was raging toward the bow missile launchers. Antlike damage-control crews were trying to hose down the plates, but had obviously lost pressure in their hoses. *Novo*'s SS-N-12 antiship missiles began exploding singly and in groups, ripping huge holes in the topside fo'c'sle and spreading flaming jet fuel across the flight deck and forward to the twin 76mm mount and SA-N-9 launch silos. These secondary explosions caused the deck plates to ripple, lofting men into the air as in a giant blanket toss; some were thrown overboard.

Sleaze knew that "weaponeers" reckoned five Harpoons would take a *Kirov* battlecruiser or *Kiev* carrier out of action. *Novo* had sustained six hits from bombs packing twice the HE of a Harpoon warhead. He also knew that doubling a weapon's energy increased its blast effectiveness by twenty-five to thirty percent, so he calculated that the carrier had endured the equivalent of seven or eight Harpoon hits. If the weaponeers were anywhere near right, she was a goner.

0613
Killer 532

Outbound well to the east of the action, Smurf suddenly nudged his pilot. "Yak, two o'clock, slightly high!" Thinking his B/N even sounded like the cartoon character, Fortune leaned slightly forward, looking past Smurf. *Thank God he's more alert than I am,* Fortune thought. About three miles away, crossing above them, was the silhouette of a Yak-141. "He hasn't seen us, yet," said the pilot. "Look for a wingman."

Doing his best Linda Blair imitation, Smurf screwed his neck around almost 180 degrees. "We're clear."

Without further thought, Fortune thumbed his weapons selector to bring his single Sidewinder on line. He turned thirty degrees starboard, nosed up slightly, heard the tracking tone in his earphones and pressed the trigger. The AIM-9L smoked off the rail, corkscrewed slightly, then streaked for the unsuspecting Yak.

The V/STOL pilot, without a place to land but blissfully thankful to escape the Hornets' mini-massacre, noticed his peril too late. He began slewing his nose to port, into the threat, when the 'Winder connected. There was no time to cry out, no time to eject, no time to do anything but die. The Yak's carcass dropped into the sea like a wing-shot duck.

Smurf was wide-eyed beneath his visor. "Damn, that was neat. We're gonna be heroes when we get back."

Fortune kept a rein on his emotions. "Yeah, *if* we get back. Keep a sharp lookout. There may be more." The pilot was not one to gloat, but this was shaping up as a very good day.

Killer 531

Data quickly pondered the chances for another damage-assessment pass on the crippled carrier. Flames and explosions burst from the streaming black smoke. Then the pilot remembered the Buzzards' unofficial motto: "Over the target you're on government time." He banked away from *Novo,* looking for a good egress route.

As 531 pulled off-target, Shaft the B/N saw the slightly damaged cruiser *Tallinn* to starboard. In his excitement, he forgot to engage the ICS switch with his foot and punched the pilot's arm. "Lookit. Let's shoot our Shrikes at that." Data pondered the tradeoff—firing two ARMs at the big, handsome cruiser. *Well, why bring ordnance home?* He nodded his assent and rolled into a steep bank.

Killer 530

Two miles away Brillo saw 531 explode. In that sharp turn his wingman unwittingly had rendezvoused with an optically aimed SA-N-4 that a less eager crew might have spotted and dodged. The SAM detonated 531's nearly empty center-line tank, peppering the ocean with shards of metal.

Once eight miles from the carrier and out of danger, the pilot and B/N exchanged friendly punches. Then Sleaze twisted in his seat, looking for 533. "Where's Runner and Chevy?" The question infected the cockpit of Killer 530 like a gnawing cancer.

Frisbee 605

Strapped into one of three sideways-facing seats in the Hawkeye's data system compartment, Lieutenant Commander Allan "Candy" Caine monitored the developing air battle. His radar operator already had "interrogated" the eight unidentified blips at the periphery of his electronic vision and, getting no response, labeled them as hostile. He was sure they were Su-27s and updated his previous call. "Bambi Flight, Frisbee. Be advised bogies are probable Flankers closing your posit."

Seconds later came a breathless response. "Ah, Rog, Frisbee. We got radar warning signs from the southwest." There was no signoff. *Those Hornet guys are gonna be awful busy,* Caine thought.

Moments later the phosphors on his scope showed the bandits—no longer mere bogies—break up. Two of the second flight spread line-abreast, streaking toward the locale of the Prowler, the high-priority target. Despite its peril, Pine Tree 623 was still jamming Russian radars from the north. The other six Sukhois pressed on—two hunting the egressing Intruders while four tried to track Bambi Flight on its TarCAP station south of the A-6s. Caine engaged his mike again. "All units, all units, this is Frisbee. Bandits have split. Two headed for Pine Tree; remainder heading Bambi. Will keep you advised."

Brian Deere's strained voice shot back. "Ah, Frisbee, Bambi. No calls for a couple minutes. We're kinda busy. Out."

Caine took no offense at the request. He knew the E-2's radio could jam the common frequency, preventing crucial calls from getting through. Still following the electronic drama displayed before him, the controller watched the lead Flankers and Bambi Flight face one another across miles of sky. He heard the missile shots called by Hornet pilots as the last AMRAAMs crossed paths with AA-9s—the long-range "Phoenixskis." Several calls were unintelligible, the result of violent evasive maneuvers.

The range continued to close, and Caine feared the Hornets would be out of radar missiles while the Flankers could still shoot Alamo As and Bs in pairs—Soviet doctrine called for simultaneous heat-seeking and radar-homing engagement. But the Prowler, God bless him, was still jamming, even with a pair of Flankers hunting him. Caine saw the Sukhois nearing the EA-6B and decided it was time for another call. "Pine Tree, Frisbee here. You got two bandits now two-zero miles southwest, closing steadily. Possible Amos launch parameters. Out."

There was a garbled reply and Caine knew the Prowler crew must be clipping the wavetops, shutting down its ALQ-99 system. The AA-9 "Amos" was known to have home-on-jam capability. Moments later Pine Tree 623 dropped off the scope without a word.

Caine's misted eyes returned to the main event. Two of the Flankers now were bearing down on Brillo Flight, trying to evade eastward. The Hornets closed from the south, the other Flankers from the west.

He watched the blips merge.

0614
East of Novorossiysk

With the Prowler dead, Igor Gnido suddenly regained use of his Flanker's helmet-mounted radar sight. He calmly selected one heat-seeking and one semi-active radar homing AA-10 against the nearest Intruder. At ten miles he pressed the trigger and felt the "Alamos" shoot off the rail.

Craning his neck, Runner jinked Killer 533. He frantically popped chaff and flares while relying on his ASPJ system, which provided limited active jamming. The first two missiles were decoyed, and the Russian fired another volley. The second IR-guided Alamo B also was spoofed, but the second SARH missile connected. Its advanced, blast-fragmentation warhead detonated against the A-6E. Runner and Chevy died instantly.

Gnido lined up the other Intruder and selected the maneuverable heat-seeking missile NATO calls "Archer." As Brillo and Sleaze gaped incredulously at the big Sukhoi, a missile plume erupted beneath its wing and the AA-11 ate up the distance. Brillo popped flares and wracked into an evasive turn. Then he felt the explosion.

Black Knight Flight

A warning snapped in Gnido's earphones. *Hornets, six o'clock high!* For Russian pilots, it had to be the number one bone-chiller call of all time. Gnido shivered involuntarily as he lost tracking on 530 and pulled a break turn into the Hornets.

Twelve thousand feet over the task group, Brian Deere and Igor Gnido led Bambi and Black Knight flights at each other, and momentarily both sides were satisfied. The Hornets were enabling the surviving A-6s to escape, while the Flankers locked the F/A-18s into combat, knowing the Hornets probably had insufficient fuel to spare and carried few missiles.

0616
Bronco 411

Lieutenant Raymond "Humpy" Dunphy was terrified. Not scared, not frightened—genuinely terrified. "Cuddles," Dunphy's element leader in 407, had bagged a Flanker with his last Sidewinder, then took two direct hits and exploded. The Hornets had been sandwiched between two Sukhoi formations. Bambi had called on guard freq, saying something about turning eastward with battle damage. Then there had come the piercing noise of an emergency beacon; presumably the division leader had ejected. Dunphy had no idea what had happened to Bambi's wingman, "Sweathog" Travolta in 410. And at this moment in his twenty-six-year-old life, Ray Dunphy simply did not care.

Streaking from the combat area, Dunphy finally remembered to check his tail. He jinked left and right, straining to see if any of the thrusting, aggressive Flankers were pursuing him. None were in sight, and his RWR was silent for the first time in an eternity—three minutes at least.

Dunphy's mind flashed back to the recent violent events

now receding in his jetwash at ten miles per minute: the first pass at the Flankers, their wall of missiles, Cuddles exploding, the mind-numbing evasive turn. With his heart in his arid mouth, his forearms feeling like lead blocks, Dunphy dimly sensed the trickle of recrimination that would surge into a flood of remorse. But for now he was blessedly, wondrously *alive*.

0617
Varyag

"*Novorossiysk* is badly hit, unable to continue operations!"

Pyotr Rybakov spun in his chair, surprised at the effect of the communicator's words. Even in war, somehow the news of battle damage carries unexpected force. *That beautiful ship* was his first thought. Then his professional instincts shoved aside the emotional ones. "Damage report?"

"Several guided-bomb hits, Admiral." The *michman*'s eyes were saucer-wide, but his voice was controlled. "Serious fires, loss of steerageway. *Tallinn* is alongside, and the enemy air attack seems completed." The boy's hands were pressed to his earphones, eyes narrowed in concentration.

"Status of our aircraft?" Rybakov asked.

"Most of *Novorossiysk*'s CAP Yaks are believed destroyed. The twelve assigned to ground-attack missions are diverting to *Leningrad* or bases ashore." The sailor listened again. "Apparently two of our Sukhoi interceptors were lost as well . . . heavy losses among American aircraft." Another pause. "That is all, sir."

Rybakov nodded. *That's all? That's enough!*

0618
Starburst 33, Southwest Indian Ocean

On their way home after designating targets for the TASMs, the pilot and copilot of Starburst 33 had seen the exhaust plumes and contrails of over a dozen supersonic missiles streaking the sky above their SH-60B. Ominously, the Russian SLCMs were headed southeast. Nine minutes later, the fliers had got the word that their destroyer, *Wheatley*, had suffered severe damage from antiship missiles and that they were to divert to *Carl*. The DDG lacked a hangar, but they could land on the destroyer's helipad or refuel while hovering. Though 33 was orphaned by the SLCM storm, its aircrew could still help rescue surviving shipmates.

After eight more minutes on the new heading, the co-pilot, Lieutenant (junior grade) Robert Caldwell, pointed to his left front and asked over the intercom, "What's that, out there at eleven o'clock?" The pilot of the Seahawk followed the finger.

"Looks like another helo," replied Lieutenant James Waddy. "I don't think it's one of ours. There aren't supposed to be any other friendlies between us and the Russians." He checked his kneepad. "Unless maybe it's Spin and Marty diverting to *Carl* like us. If so, it's a major bummer."

"Fer sure, dude," Caldwell replied, wondering how the Russkies could have knocked out both ASW destroyers.

"Whatever they are, keep an eye on 'em," the right-seater ordered.

"Rog." Caldwell increased speed while climbing slightly in case maneuvering became necessary. Then he saw the unidentified aircraft pivot, momentarily viewed in profile. "Jim, it's a Helix! Look at that!"

The Ka-27 pulled up vertically from its wavetop hover two miles from the Seahawk, rolling onto its side before straightening out. "Pilot has control," said Waddy. "Call in the sighting. It's probably a targeting bird."

Caldwell had just engaged the scrambler when both pilots saw the plume of an AA-8 missile erupt from the Helix. "Jesus, he's shooting at us," Waddy exclaimed. He pulled the Sikorsky into a tight evasive spiral, but his timing was off. The Russian heat-seeking missile easily corrected in midcourse and smashed into the Seahawk near the jet exhaust. The warhead detonated, igniting JP-5 fuel that erupted into a fireball. The wreckage of Starburst 33 dropped 350 feet into the ocean, where burning fuel and debris spread across the waves.

Gold Pawn 68

Captain of Aviation Vasily Yegorov turned casually to his copilot. "You see, Alexei? They never suspected we were armed." He checked his watch, then noted the time of the encounter on his kneepad. "Not a totally wasted morning," he said in a toneless voice. "We found no American ships, but I'd say we filled our quota."

The copilot kept the Kamov helo on course to return to *Novorossiysk*, which might, for all they knew, be a flaming hulk. The brief recall signal carried no additional information. Yegorov clapped shut the metal cover of his kneepad. "Not a completely dull morning, either," he said, clipping the pen onto the pocket of the cutoff trousers he wore instead of a flight suit.

Yegorov banked the Helix targeting helicopter northwestward toward ARKR *Frunze*, wondering whether his cruiser remained afloat.

11

0620 to 0634, Friday,
4 June

0602 Pretoria; 0702 Local
Above UER Naval Aviation Base, Antsiranana, Madagascar

Captain Yuri Bulgakov had the dawn sun in his eyes. He lowered his nuclear flash visor as the noisy Tupolev 16 anti-shipping bomber lumbered higher into the moist air. His was the last of eighteen Badgers to take off; he maneuvered to join the other two Tu-16s in his flight. The tropical sun glinted on their canopies and bare metal skins.

As he swung the creaking bomber to the south-south-west, Bulgakov wondered how much longer the navy would keep these antiques flying. They were no older than the Americans' B-52s, but he doubted that Russian maintenance was anywhere as good. It was as if the government had pensioned off the old bombers to a retirement settlement in the sunny south. Well, he thought, a Tomcat may save the navy the trouble of scrapping this one.

Frisbee 601, Varyag Strike Force

Tony Chimola was setting up another bushwhack. This time he had Critter Flight on his screen—four VF-181 Tom-

283

cats five minutes ahead of Slattery—assigned to clear enemy interceptors out of the way.

For about half an hour, Chimola had tracked the four Flankers sent to replace the Mudhen and two Sukhois shot down by Grayhound Flight. The Russians had just arrived at their advanced CAP position east of the *Varyag* force. *Too late, comrades,* Chimola thought. *But some guys are waiting there to reach out and touch someone.* Again, he engaged his mike.

"Gunshot Lead, Frisbee 601. Four bandits bearing 260 for seventy-five." *Git some more,* he thought as he data-linked the situation to the Tomcats.

Lieutenant Commander "Gopher" Grundy, the RIO in Commander "Critter" Hawthorne's Gunshot 105, confirmed the link. Then the aircrew checked with their wingmen—Meatball and Bullwinkle in 107—and queried the second section's status. Stretch and Groceries in 106 with Smoke and Kiwi in 111 all acknowledged.

On Critter's signal, his flight's initial Phoenixes dropped off their racks and all four Rocketdyne motors ignited. First one, then two hostile blips disappeared from the 601's scope. A second missile volley followed; soon a third bandit dropped off the screen. Chimola tracked the surviving Sukhoi back toward the Russian carrier group while Critter Flight swept ahead, clearing a path for Slattery's strike force. In the Tomcats' wake, Frisbee 601 gingerly extended its orbit a few minutes westward as well.

Off to the southwest Chimola's radar displayed another Mudhen approaching the Americans' line of advance, while a second orbited almost directly overhead *Varyag*. Both AWACS now held position, beyond Phoenix range but still radiating. Chimola assumed that the four Tomcats providing close escort for the Intruders and Hornets would take out these two Antonovs. *Not much future in the ol' Mudhen biz.*

Varyag

"Admiral!" Smirnov yelled to attract the attention of his busy erstwhile chess partner. "The Anotonov in the southwestern zone has been painted by radiation consistent with Tomcat search-mode illumination. He requests additional interceptor escort or radioelectronic combat support."

Rybakov rapidly reviewed in his mind the locations and missions of his Sukhois. Stress clogged his thought processes. He could divert *Kuznetsov*'s fighters toward the threatened An-74M, but they probably wouldn't arrive in time, and launching missiles from beyond visual range risked hitting the AWACS with friendly fire. He just might be able to get an ECM Flanker within range in time, but then he risked losing that—a type almost as precious as an AWACS itself. He was reluctant to detach any more of his own Su-27s until the Su-25 attack planes being rearmed with heat-seeking missiles were airborne to reinforce *Varyag*'s inner defense zone. Finally, the admiral decided that, valuable as it was, he could not afford to reinforce the AWACS' fighter escort or risk ECM support.

"No," he said. "They'll have to make do."

Frisbee 601

This is getting monotonous, Tony Chimola thought. Seldom in all his training had he been exposed to the possibility of directing successive intercepts on three or four enemy AWACS. But there was yet another one, approaching from the southwest. *Must be from the* Kuznetsov *group,* he surmised. *Well, welcome to the party, dude.*

The airborne controller checked his inventory of remaining assets—that's how he thought of the escort Tomcats, with their expendable credits of fuel and ordnance—and selected one. Gunshot 107 had two Phoenixes left and Chimola gave it a heads up. "Your vector is 240 for eight-zero. Confirm target ID and lock on."

Chimola received a confirmation, and within moments the priority target was under attack from beyond human vision. Chimola counted down the AIM-54's estimated time of flight, fully expecting the blip to strobe and die like the others. *Four, three, two, one* . . . Nothing. *What th' hell?*

The controller engaged his mike, ordering a follow-up shot when he caught the turn. He cross-checked with Whale Watch's electronic eavesdroppers, who informed him, "Ah, Frisbee, the Mudhen stopped radiating abruptly. He must have shut down when he got a radar warning."

No, Chimola thought, *the timing doesn't work.* He checked his scope again. The Mudhen definitely was turning away. Whale Watch came back on the discrete freq. "Frisbee, we got real-time voice intercept on the AWACS. He's hollering like mad, in the clear. Took battle damage and is returning to base. Whale Watch 007, out."

Fuse malfunction, Chimola exulted. Apparently the Phoenix's powerful warhead had detonated a shade too soon. But diving on the ungainly target from overhead, its blast must have destroyed or damaged the radome. *Shot their eyes out,* the controller thought. Not as satisfying as a splash, but a mission kill was good enough.

The Tomcat was wasting no time, either. Chimola saw it turn back north to rejoin the Intruders. *So far, so good.*

Then Chimola's scope whited out. He realized that an Su-27E jamming bird must be out there somewhere, essentially doing to him what the Tomcats had done to the Mudhens. Until Critter Flight could kill the electronic warfare Flanker, Frisbee 601 also was blind. The combat fighter would proceed without the Argus-eyed sentries on either side.

0621
Varyag

"Admiral! An emergency call from the replacement AWACS aircraft." The communications officer hesitated, absorbing the information through his earphones. Moments later he looked back at Rybakov and the horror was visible in the man's eyes. "They went off the air in mid-sentence. They reported Tomcats, then nothing. . . ."

Rybakov envisioned the Mudhen ripped apart by Phoenix missiles from the F-14s that surely would precede a heavy strike. He lanced Smirnov with a decisive look.

"Could that be the same Tomcats that shot down the original AWACS, what, forty minutes ago?" the admiral asked.

"Possibly," the CSO replied. "If they continued toward us. The Antonov wasn't even on station yet."

"That settles it," Rybakov said sternly. "The *Langley* force is farther south than we thought. Order our ground-attack aircraft recovered immediately and have them armed for naval combat. Meanwhile, have *Kuznetsov* launch every available search aircraft toward us at top speed." He looked again at the tactical display panel, which only showed part of the American forces. "We aren't getting much satellite assistance, Anatoly Vladimirovich. We'll have to conduct our own reconnaissance, it appears."

"It was to be expected, I suppose. . . ."

"Air defense alert!" The commo officer's interruption sent a chill down Smirnov's spine. *Bad news comes in threes,* he thought. *What next?*

"Ship-based radars report inbound missiles and twin-jet aircraft . . . powerful jamming also." The radioman's litany of lament seemed endless.

Rybakov bolted from his chair, standing before the display panel. "This is the main attack," he said to no one in particular. "I can feel it."

0623 Pretoria; 2223 EDT
White House

Before leaving the West Wing, Admiral Fernandez checked with the navy operations room in the Pentagon. After hanging up he intoned, "I have some bad news, Mr. President."

"Shoot," Callaway responded.

"We just got a real-time satellite shot of Badgers taking off from Luanda, Angola, in regimental strength. A regiment equals what we call a wing, normally three squadrons. There's also SigInt of a similar number from Antsiranana, Madagascar."

"Damnation!" the President exclaimed. "My fault. No excuse to leave those bomber bases standing. I knew I should've Pearl Harbored their Red asses from the start." Epstein rolled his eyes.

When Callaway showed signs of cooling off, Fernandez interjected, "You couldn't have done much more, sir. The only in-theater asset we have in range of Antsiranana is *Grouper,* a *Sturgeon*-class boat with just eight Tomahawks. Only four are conventional land-attack missiles. We couldn't have destroyed all their bombers even if we had sneak-attacked them."

Epstein was delighted the CNO sounded reasonable for once. "I have to agree, Mr. President. The results wouldn't have justified attacking without warning, which is a serious breach of international law."

"I already told you-all, my job is to protect national security, not to uphold 'international law,' whatever the hell that may be," the Texan declaimed. When he settled down he asked, "Hub, can Gideon handle 'em?"

"The Badgers, yes. We shouldn't lose any ships to them. There will probably be sixteen to twenty Badgers in each force. Dunno whether the three forces will try to attack simultaneously to overload our defenses or just fire their missiles as soon as possible.

"But even if they do hit us at the same time, and even if the bombers are escorted by fighters, we should be able to survive. I doubt they know where Gideon is for sure. They might attack the PhibGru instead."

"Thanks, Hub. Is that it?"

"No, sir. That was just the bad news."

"You mean there's some good news?" Callaway's spirit rose.

Fernandez shook his head. "No, sir. Some really bad news. Additional PhotInt and SigInt indicate that eight Backfire regiments are headed south. That leaves them with just five Badger and two Blinder regiments at home. No reason not to use 'em all, with our other battle groups out of position. The bombers en route appear to be headed for staging bases on the Iranian border. Apparently Teheran has approved overflights."

"Figures—birds of a feather," Callaway sneered. "How many in a regiment?"

"Twenty-seven to thirty at full strength, though the Blinder units are smaller. The Russians historically have one regiment for each of our carriers—more now that we're down to thirteen CVs, including the one in overhaul. So this is a huge concentration against a single carrier, or two if they go after *Eisenhower* as well. My guess is they'll concentrate on *Langley*. Chuck Gideon's group will be able to handle two, maybe three, regiments. But eight is overwhelming odds." The CNO thought for a moment. "With the Badgers already in theater, call it 220 to 240 bombers."

Callaway sat down, his mind instantly set. "Hub, have every carrier that can float steam at flank speed toward Russia, except those now headed for Africa. How soon can they be under way?"

"Sir, we're stretched to the max right now—six of our twelve available CVs are deployed. Three were on station when the crisis started, though *JFK*'s stuck in the Canal. Three more have moved forward in the past two weeks. We can surge two more from each coast in about forty-eight hours but the other two, it might take a week."

Callaway nodded. "So we're stuck with what we've got in place."

CNO replied, "For the next two days, that's about the size of it, sir. By then we can have four more besides *Indy* headed for the Kola and Kamchatka peninsulas. Even if we wanted to threaten the UER directly, we can't for a week or more."

Damn, I should have known," Callaway whined. "Carriers are like antifreeze. You can't have 'em too soon, you can only have 'em too late."

0624
Aswan Airfield, Egypt

In Gypsy 205, Commander Dave "Hey Joe" Pearson and Lieutenant Jim "Dog" Cohen swiveled their necks, keeping track of the skyful of Tomcats. Both of *Kennedy*'s fighter squadrons were airborne on time, each F-14 armed with four Phoenixes, two Sparrows and two Sidewinders, plus two external fuel tanks. There was no radio chatter, but the intercoms were abuzz.

"Dave, what do you think of this plan? Really." Dog wanted convincing.

Hey Joe feigned confidence. "I gotta believe the spooks from the briefing. They seem convinced that the intel is solid."

"But how can we have real-time information that accurate?"

Pearson knew his pilot's doubts. No sources were revealed—for obvious reasons. "My guess: radio intercepts and maybe a guy or two on the ground."

Cohen made no reply. Finally he said, "Well, if it all comes together, I just hope there's enough of us to handle the job."

Pearson knew what he meant. One of the Tophatters' jets had gone down on deck and a Swordsmen crew was left with a hydraulic hemorrhage on the ground. But CAG Hesselyn formed up the other eighteen and, at 490 knots, set course for his rendezvous with U.S. Air Force KC-10s on the briefed tanker track. Fighter Squadrons 14 and 32 had a date over the Arabian Sea.

0625
USS Carl, *Southwest Indian Ocean*

Captain Theo Mahar had never seen anything like it. The skipper of the Aegis-equipped antiaircraft destroyer had practiced "defending" a carrier battle group against simulated cruise-missile attack by supersonic drones, but no exercise had prepared him for an onslaught by dozens of giant SLCMs. The reality was a more sudden, bewildering and violent experience than he could have imagined.

He didn't even know how the missiles had found his *Burke*-class destroyer and the two *Spruances*. Smoke rose from beyond the southwestern and northeastern horizons, marking the position of the burning antisub destroyers. Blood-curdling damage reports relayed hysterically over Link Eleven from the stricken DDs' helos indicated *Wheatley* had been hit twice, was aflame virtually from stem to stern and was sinking fast. The Seahawk pilots said that where not covered with burning diesel oil, the water around her was churned white with swimmers and flecked yellow with rafts. One of *Davenport*'s SH-60Bs radioed that she took just a single hit, but was dead in the water and afire amidships.

Though *Carl*'s area-defense SAMs had functioned reliably, her SM-2 Standard SAMs had saved only herself, not her two TLAM-launching partners. The barrage of big, fast Russian SLCMs had clearly overwhelmed the *Spruances*' defenses—electronic countermeasure systems, six Sea Sparrow SAMs, ten point-defense Rolling Airframe Missiles, a single five-inch gun and two 20mm CIWSes. Mahar's air warfare officer was trying to sort out what had happened, starting with how the SS-N-19s and SS-N-12s had located the U.S. ships.

Carl had emerged from the ordeal almost unscathed; a near miss had sprung some hull plating, but the leakage was under control. Apparently the passive-homing, antiradar versions of Shipwreck that had locked onto the Aegis destroyer's fire-control signals had all been shot down by the new Block IV SM-2s loaded in ten of her vertical launch cells. *Too bad those Block IV babies are too big to be reloaded at sea,* Mahar recalled ruefully. The follow-on SLCMs with active seeker heads had all been decoyed, jammed, dodged or knocked out by missiles or gunfire.

The SLCM attack had nearly depleted Mahar's SAMs, leaving a few land-attack Tomahawks and twenty ASRoc antisub missiles in his ninety vertical-launch cells. Reloading was a painfully slow process even in port, let alone under way at sea. He would not be able to help defend the CVBG from the attack by backfire-launched cruise missiles he knew must follow.

Since somehow the enemy had pinpointed the U.S. destroyers, Mahar could not afford to linger in this vicinity. In any case, his orders required him to move swiftly to take up a new position. He desperately wanted to pick up survivors from *Wheatley* and *Davenport,* but without transport helos, rescue operations would necessitate slowing down. Mahar realized he might soon have four Seahawks under his command, as the choppers from *Spruance*-class destroyers would try to find *Carl* now that their own ships were out of action. His *Burke*-class destroyer had no helos of its own and no hangars, but could operate them from its landing pad. Unfortunately, an electronics-laden SH-60B could carry few wounded and his next job required that he head north by northeast immediately. The best he could hope for was to rescue some of *Davenport*'s wounded in passing.

His orders were to steam toward a rendezvous with *Langley* 350 miles off the northern Natal coast, from which position her group could cover an amphibious landing. Since he was closer to the rendezvous point than *Langley* and since she had to recover her aircraft before heading north by northwest to the new position, his ship would arrive on station long before the carrier. But his mission was now to stake out the new position, listening for enemy subs in the vicinity and watching for Badger or Backfire antiship bombers. He had too few SAMs left to shoot down the strike planes or their missiles, but he could act as a radar picket—or the world's most expensive decoy.

His air warfare officer handed him a preliminary report. Mahar scanned it, then looked at the staffer in grim disbelief.

"That's the best we could come up with, sir," the officer said. "It's pretty much *all* we could come up with."

"If you say so, Chip," Mahar said. "It's hard to swallow. I knew Shipwreck was a capable system, but this! Self-designating cruise missiles? Hunter-killer SLCMs? You say they're big robotic drones *and* antiship missiles?"

"Looks that way, sir. As best we can tell, most of the ARM variants homed on us, but there were still too many of the regular old active-seeker types for *Davenport* and *Wheatley* to handle. 'Specially since we had to concentrate on the antiradar versions headed our way instead of covering the *Spruances.*"

Mahar leafed to the next page. "What's this? The Shipwrecks communicate with each other and SS-N-12s? The high-fliers search ahead, then designate targets for the low ones?" he asked, dripping incredulity. "How do you figure?"

"The electronic data clearly indicate a search frequency and pattern distinct from the active terminal-homing signal, plus there's this transmission." The commander tapped a hastily printed table. "It's directional, but's gotta be a data-link of some sort. And it's linked down from the divers to the trailing skimmers. After three decades, looks like they've found a way around the mid-course guidance update and OTH designation problems. And until the searchers run out of fuel, they keep looking. Like the Terminator, they don't give up."

A sailor handed the skipper another report just up from CDC. The signal was from one of *Wheatley*'s choppers, inbound. Mahar read it and blanched: ". . . explosion lifted rafts and men several yards through air, dozens of yards downrange. More survivors sucked under by whirlpool of sinking vessel. Blast appeared to kill other men in water. Estimate virtually one hundred percent casualties; fifty percent fatalities . . ."

At least 170 men dead, he realized. *So far, on one ship.*

0627
Southwest of Vryheid, Natal Province

They were late. They had run late all night, and now would pay the cost. *Still,* Vorster considered, *bloody marvelous all six old French choppers made it over the Drakensbergs in near daylight. No nice, new South African-made Oryx helos for us sacrificial lambs.*

Since there was now enough light for the enemy in the mountains east of town to bring accurate artillery fire down on the airport, they would have to land across the railroad tracks west of town, out of 120mm mortar range. As long as the helicopters flew low, they would be safe from the Viets' antiaircraft weapons, but Vorster knew that while unloading their cargo of tired, airsick Boer reservists the Puma helicopters would be pitifully vulnerable to 122mm howitzers and Stalin Organs.

Captain Vorster saw that it was worse than he had feared. Not only were the bloody wogs shelling the landing zone as his heliborne company descended, but he spotted Major Snodgrass on the ground to meet him. The unwelcome major's uniform had lost its crispness.

Vorster rode with his radioman, a medic and seventeen men from Ian Macdonald's platoon. No helicopter carried more than a single officer. Machine gun rounds zinged through the troop compartment. Time-fused howitzer rounds burst around them, peppering the chopper with fragments. The men had been sitting on their helmets, but as the bird descended, they put them to their intended use.

Vorster stood in the door and jumped, twisting his ankle. Troopies followed, piling out of the chopper before it touched down. They hit the ground running, headed toward the poor shelter of railroad siding structures. Many toppled, either under the weight of their kit or from enemy fire. Vorster moved at a relative saunter, hobbled less by the pain in his ankle than by his leadership training, in the British tradition of which an officer never runs but shows contempt for the enemy's fire.

"Good morning, Captain," Snodgrass puffed upon intercepting the limping Boer. They moved in a crouch under the rotor downdraft and airburst fragmentation fire. "Glad to see you were able to accept our invitation to this little party."

"Bugger off," Vorster responded.

"Mmm, quite. But fear not just yet, old boy," Snodgrass said with emphasized upper-class tones. Out of breath, both officers flopped down behind the cinder-block wall of a freight shed. Vorster peeked around the corner to see how his men were doing. His own chopper lifted off, was hit and exploded, spewing its remaining fuel over the LZ. Flame, hurtling debris and spiraling rotor blades destroyed half a dozen lives and sent wounded men sprawling. A burly machine gunner was scythed in two. In the back of his consciousness Vorster heard the major say, "No, I'm afraid you'll have to bear with me a bit longer."

The Boer, inflamed by his own helplessness, turned on the Brit, grabbed him by his red-tabbed collars and slammed him against the wall. "Stay out of my way, old boy," he said, jerking his quarry forward and slamming him back again. Vorster brandished his trophy 5.45mm Kalashnikov an inch from the major's surprisingly calm face. "See this?"

"Couldn't help but, old man. AK-74, isn't it? Very fine specimen. Still rather more rare than the AKM or AK-47."

"One of those wogs just might drill you from behind if you hang around my company any longer," Vorster spat out. "Get it?"

The major ignored the threat. "We're on the same side, don't you know?"

"More's the pity. Isn't that what you people say?" Vorster looked around again, then shoved his runner off to collect the platoon leaders. He poked Snodgrass with the AK's barrel and asked, "You still here?"

"Yes, old man, and after once more like that, you won't be." The major jammed an ancestral .455 Webley revolver into the Boer's crotch and Vorster went pale. "Now do be a good captain and give a listen. I'm not in this scenic spot entirely to enjoy the mountain air."

A series of impact-fused howitzer explosions preceded the arrival of platoon leader Ian Macdonald. Though Macdonald was the only non-Afrikaner officer in his largely Orange Free Stater company, Vorster liked him anyway. The big lieutenant had played rugger for the University of the Witwatersrand in Jo'burg; he hadn't completed officer candidate training there before being posted to Vorster's command, but had performed well on the Vaal. Vorster waited for the last dirt clods to splatter down. "Report" was all he said.

Still out of breath, Macdonald answered, "Eight or nine dead altogether, including section leader Coetsee. . . ." The boy paused, but Vorster nodded him on. "Twenty effectives, sir, including four or five walking wounded."

"Christ! Two-thirds strength and not even in line yet."

Snodgrass wanted to say, *Welcome to Vryheid,* but thought better of it. Vorster seemed close to his men.

"All right, Macdonald. Stay close for a bit," the captain ordered.

In the next moment, Snodgrass was glad he had kept silent. "Coetsee was my neighbor," Vorster confided. "It's not like the actives."

Snodgrass showed Vorster and his lieutenants the best route toward the airfield—four kilometers east by southeast —and then the platoon leaders returned to their subunits. The company formed up as best it could under the maelstrom of artillery fire sweeping the LZ. The ninety-odd men rushed across the railroad tracks in ten-man sections, then dodged from cover to cover between the few buildings on the southeast outskirts of town. From safe positions in the eastern hills, enemy gunners hounded them every step of the way.

0628
Varyag

"I don't like this, Anatoly Vladimirovich," Rybakov said to his chief of staff. "The American attack on Kostolev's force appears too weak to be the main thrust. What do you think?"

Smirnov looked up from the damage reports of *Novorossiysk*'s group. He shook his head in despair. "I simply do not know, Admiral. If it were a diversion, it inflicted far more damage than would be expected. And it was well-coordinated with cruise missiles and electronic warfare." He brandished the papers in his hand. "Both *Frunze* and *Novorossiysk* sustained severe damage and *Tallinn* and *Ukraina* were moderately damaged. To me, it seems too heavy a strike for a deception." Smirnov did not fear to disagree with his CO; Rybakov encouraged differing opinions.

"But how many planes were involved?" the admiral asked.

"We can't get a reliable estimate. Over twenty-four strike, ECM and fighter aircraft is possible, but men under attack are likely to exaggerate, and the same planes might have been counted repeatedly. The possibility of decoys exists. We'll have to analyze the electronic data. If in fact some two dozen manned aircraft were involved, the attack was easily large enough to be a main-effort strike, especially if launched from long range."

Rybakov said nothing, but it was clear he found this "information" next to useless. "And cruise missiles?"

"We have a better fix on that. Probably around thirty."

Rybakov absentmindedly spun in his chair, deep in thought. At length he said, "So, apparently far more missiles than aircraft, especially since you can probably halve the estimate of planes. For this reason I believe that we are the primary target, which is proper doctrine."

"The Americans often do not follow proper doctrine, Admiral. Look at their tactics in Vietnam," Smirnov observed.

"True, they have in the past subordinated war-fighting to politics in illogical ways, but they have learned much since Vietnam. And this admiral has already showed himself clear-thinking and cunning, less childlike than most Americans. We will know soon enough. If Gideon gives us time to retrieve our detached Su-27s and rearm our Su-25s for antiship strike, then for him, the war is over."

"But could he be within range of us?" Smirnov asked yet again.

"I would arrange to be so, in his position," Rybakov answered.

"The Su-27s sent to investigate the An-74 shoot-down have found nothing headed our way," Smirnov reminded the admiral.

"That doesn't mean much, does it, given the limited field of view of their radars," Rybakov replied tendentiously. "An American strike force could well come in on a course north or even south of the traverse of the fighters' air-intercept radars. The other Madcap is still out of position."

Rybakov thought for a moment. He had only two flyable and two nonoperational Flankers left on board. Four were escorting his morning ground-support strike of sixteen Su-25s and an ECM Flanker variant. He had detached eight other Su-27s to help *Novorossiysk*. Only three of these had survived, and were now limping home. Of his remaining ten interceptors, four were returning from their wild-goose chase after the Antonov-killing Tomcats, four were on combat air patrol and two were ready on deck.

Rybakov decided to reinforce his air defenses immediately and accept the risk of his fighters running low on fuel if the American attack were delayed an hour longer. "Launch the last two fighters. Then how soon will the air-defense Rooks be ready?"

"The first flight could launch in fifteen minutes, but you know the pilots aren't well trained in air combat."

"Every bit helps," the admiral said. Then he ordered, "Keep them close to *Varyag*, but out of the zones of *Andropov* and our short-range SAMs—about eight to ten miles from both of us. Even with short-range, heat-seeking missiles, the Rooks can provide the last-ditch edge we may need. Deploy the Flankers on two axes farther out, beyond *Ustinov*'s long-range SAM zone and *Otlichniy*'s medium-range SAMs. Dispatch the CAP eighty miles northeast right now at maximum cruise. Send the ready pair the same distance east as soon as possible. If I were Gideon, that's how I would come at us. When the inbound flight gets close, refuel them from the Su-25s. We'll reinforce whichever flight makes contact first."

Rybakov hoped that the air-to-air missiles NATO called Aphid and Archer were in fact as superior to Western heat-seekers as operations analysis suggested. If not, his pilots were in for more than mere disappointment.

0630
Slats Flight

In Talent 500, Commander Patrick Slattery had plenty to think about as his strike package approached ship-based detection range of the *Varyag* group. But in the last few minutes before the Russians tried to kill him, he weighed his chances against eight of the world's most advanced warships and up to two dozen of its most capable fighter-interceptors.

Langley's eight Intruders, eight Hornets, six Vikings,

three Prowlers and eight Tomcats tickled the lobes of Russian air-search radars as little as possible. The humidity was not such that serious electromagnetic ducting occurred. To the north, safely out of surface radar range, orbited the ES-3A and a Hawkeye. Slats realized that, with luck, the Russians still might not know what was headed their way, as the Mudhen shoot-down had been integrated into the timing of the *Novorossiysk* strike. Even the Flanker kills fourteen minutes ago might be meant to cover the egress of the northern deception group. Only if the AWACS coming up from the southwest had detected Slats's force would Rybakov be sure that the main attack was about to fall on him.

The strike group's thirty-six Harpoons, SLAMs and Mavericks—plus thirty-two HARM and Shrike antiradar missiles—would help clear the path for Elvis Flight's eight Skippers and Slats Flight's twelve "iron" bombs. The twenty Skippers and bombs were earmarked for *Varyag,* as were eight SLAMs. All twelve Harpoons and twelve Mavericks, plus four SLAMs, were intended for the secondary target, the highly capable battlecruiser *Andropov.*

According to damage-estimate tables, the weapon loadouts would suffice to suppress escorting vessels' air defenses and sink the primary and secondary targets, but only if a minimum number of aircraft got through and if enough of their ordnance hit home. At his discretion, Slats could divert some of the bombs to *Andropov* or SLAMs and Mavericks to *Varyag,* but to minimize radio chatter and the risk of screwups, he would stick to the original game plan if at all possible.

Slattery personally led the southern pincer of his two-pronged attack, although Elvis Flight's four A-6Es preceded Slats Flight, as did the six Harpoon-armed Vikings. Commander Duncan "Brandy" Alexander of VFA-183 controlled both F/A-18 flights, inbound some fifty miles north of the Intruders and Vikings. Both prongs were escorted by a Prowler and two Tomcats. The E-2C and ES-3A orbited at safe standoff distances, while Critter Flight's four Tomcats conducted a sweep between the attack planes' axes of advance. The third EA-6B, Pine Tree 624, followed Critter, concentrating on air-to-air jamming. The defense-suppression mission was a complex assortment of "soft" and "hard" kills against air and surface threats. Slattery especially wished he had fourteen more HARMs, but the suppression phase of the plan solved most difficulties to his satisfaction.

There remained the problem of *Varyag*'s chief weapons —Flankers. Armed with ten superb air-to-air missiles, equipped with Tomcat-style avionics and the world's most advanced sighting system, the highly maneuverable Sukhoi 27 fighter-interceptors posed the gravest threat to the strikers. The whole mission depended on how well the TarCAP did against the Flankers, but the only advantages the outnumbered, outgunned F-14Bs and F/A-18Cs had were in aircrew training and in the range of Phoenix missiles.

If the deception had worked and Rybakov diverted even two Flanker flights to *Novorossiysk*, Slattery's crews had a fighting chance. The prospect of failure was, he knew, very real. Real but unthinkable. Slats felt it was a good plan. Now everything depended on execution.

Once again he checked the disposition of his Intruders. All were in order. The Hornets, Tomcats, Prowlers, Hawkeye and ES-3A were invisible to him, but it did not matter. He knew they would be where they were needed.

0632
Varyag

"Outer air defense zone interceptors report medium-altitude radar contacts, Admiral!" the task force BCh-6 sang out as soon as he received the information from his commo *michman*. "Initial classification, twin-engine fighter aircraft. Negative IFF response. Interceptor flight leader requests permission to engage."

Pyotr Rybakov spun in his padded chair and launched himself toward the air defense console. Still rising, he said, "Permission granted." In eight steps and four heartbeats he was standing at the tactical display, trying to make sense of the cluttered, confusing symbology. "Disposition of forces?" the admiral asked his air warfare department commander, who had already relayed the go signal.

"Two Su-27s orbiting us, here, ready to be deployed as needed," the BCh-6 said, indicating their positions on the perspex board between *Varyag* and *Andropov*, "and four out here to the east, beyond *Otlichniy* and *Ustinov*'s SAM zone.

The two Antonovs are here, over us, and here, approaching the outer CAP aircraft from the southwest.

"Also, Admiral, there is much electronic warfare activity in this quadrant now," the BCh-6 stated, moving his cursor northeasterly.

Rybakov ordered, "Display engaged aircraft." The BCh-6 nodded and a *michman* tapped the keyboard, deleting all but the directly threatened fighters. Rybakov absorbed the situation in a glance: beyond the missile engagement zone were three hostile blips that he took to be Tomcats opposed by five Flankers—his duty CAP and the survivor of the previous combat. They were supported by an Su-27R electronic-warfare variant. "Black Queen Five is jamming the American fire-control radars, Admiral," explained the BCh-6. Rybakov nodded. "Good, our interceptors will need help against those odds."

Then the fighter controller called, "Missile launch warning! Presumed American long-range AAM." An AWACS downlink appeared.

Rybakov and the controller watched anxiously as three Phoenixes, launched beyond AA-9 range, streaked toward the ECM aircraft. The Grumman fighters had longer reach. Rybakov's fists tightened. "The American missiles are programmed to home on jamming," he muttered. The men watched as violent death bore down at Mach Five on their precious fighters. The Sukhoi pilots could turn and burn, but were almost as helpless as the frustrated staff. Not for the first time, Rybakov asked himself, *Why have we not developed such a missile?*

In the midst of this torment, the command and control officer announced a flash signal from *Ustinov*. The BCh-7 reported that two presumed HARMs had knocked out the cruiser's long-range SAM fire-control system. "The radar had been lit up for scarcely two minutes," the staffer explained. "Even our Antonov detected no obvious launch maneuver by the hostiles."

The BCh-6 studied his perspex board, then said, "It must have been a lofted launch for maximum range. Our search radars are jammed, so we don't know if the antiradar missiles came from strike planes or an EA-6. The AWACS can't discriminate at this range. ESM indicates the antiradiation missiles could have been fired by an EA-6."

"We have to assume that a Prowler would escort real attack aircraft," Rybakov commented. "Dispatch the last two Su-27s to cover the northeastern axis of approach." *How many Americans can there be out there?* he wondered. *It's all happening so fast, from so many quarters.*

"At once, Admiral," the BCh-6 answered, but Rybakov didn't hear him. He was again mesmerized by the electronic imagery of doom, now only half a minute distant for his fighters. The symbols became real aircraft, struggling like snagged fish to free themselves from the hook.

0633

As Rybakov watched, the blip of Black Queen Five strobed and died. Moments later, two more Phoenix barrages destroyed a pair of Flankers. *Three kills from eight missiles,* Rybakov fumed. He knew Tomcats could control up to six missiles at once; professionalism now dominated his thinking. *Better than we expected of Phoenix C in an electronic environment.* He made a mental note to check on improved AIM-54 electronic counter-countermeasures.

The local fighter odds now stood at three to three. Rybakov realized that, with Phoenix depleted, the F-14s' AMRAAMS and Sparrows were slightly outranged by the Flankers' AA-9s. All three Sukhois announced medium-range, active-radar missile launch. Six arrow symbols flashed on the screen, accelerating to Mach 3.5 toward their targets over forty miles away. The admiral jubilantly shook a clenched fist.

He also noted with pleasure that the enemy ECM aircraft were either too far away or too occupied to jam the AWACS immediately overhead. Since ESM suggested there were up to three Prowlers and perhaps a distant Viking, it must be the range or power differential, Rybakov figured. An-74s were almost too big to operate from *Kuznetsov*-class carriers—they took off with minimal fuel, then topped off en route to station—but the Russian AWACS' power output was higher even than Hawkeye's.

0634

Rybakov saw a Tomcat symbol disappear from the scope. Over the VHF link, the staff heard the flight leader's voice say, "The target is destroyed."

The remaining aircraft symbols converged at over 1,000 miles an hour. Six Alamo Cs and six AMRAAMs passed one another; when the blips merged one F-14 was left to face two Su-27s.

The admiral was excited, but didn't let it show. He wanted to see the short-range dogfight played out, or better yet, to be in it. He knew how it should end—*we must have six times as many missiles left as the Americans, and longer-ranged guns, if it comes to that.*

The fighter controller reported, "Both interceptors have launched R-29T and R-29R missiles!"

Rybakov saw the AAM symbols streak toward the Tomcat, but the F-14 also fired two Sidewinders head-on against its opponents. *AIM-9L series,* the admiral thought, full of respect for the world's first all-aspect heat-seeker, and its AIM-9R development. The Grumman disappeared first, followed in seconds by the Sukhoi it had targeted.

The fighter director pointed out the lone survivor. "Black Knight 21 is retiring, Admiral."

Rybakov checked his watch. In a matter of minutes nine aircraft contesting half a million cubic miles of airspace had been reduced to one. The admiral shifted his gaze easterly, where two more hostile blips appeared. "Let him go," Rybakov said wearily. "He cannot fight more Tomcats." *Hundreds of millions in hardware and perhaps a dozen highly trained men, gone just like that,* he thought. *It will get worse.*

"Black Knight 18 and 19 request authority for radar-guided missile release," the fighter director stated.

"Very well," Rybakov responded, hoping for a better success ratio in the exchange against the hostiles in the northeastern sector. *If the northern Tomcats had Phoenix, they'd have used them by now,* he reasoned. *Those god-damned Prowlers are our biggest headache.* "Order them to target the radio-electronic combat aircraft first," he quickly added.

What a fool to send Novorossiysk *those eight Sukhois!* the admiral berated himself. Now all he could do was hope that the two interceptor flights from *Kuznetsov* arrived in time to kill the enemy after they attacked his ships. He weighed carefully in his mind the need for speed against the need for fuel. "Order the two White Knight flights to go to afterburner," Rybakov told the fighter controller.

12

0637 to 0648, Friday, 4 June

0637
Talent 500

Slats Slattery wished he had a tape recorder. *"Ride of the Valkyries" should be playing right now,* he mused as he led his eight Intruders out of the early-morning sun toward the enemy screen. *Langley's* deputy CAG would have preferred to attack from the west, egressing into the rising sun to help mask his tailpipes from heat-seeking missiles. But the fuel considerations were prohibitive. *Too far the long way around,* he mused.

Slattery twisted in the B/N seat of the lead A-6E, making almost 500 knots at 200 feet. Glancing back, he checked the disposition of his jets one more time. *Yep, everybody right where he belongs.* He hoped that Brandy's Hornets were deployed as well to launch SLAMs and Shrikes, then provide target CAP for the Intruders. For one last time, he thanked God for delivering his force from the evil of Flankers. *God, Grumman and Hughes.*

A gloved hand ticked off each item of the combat checklist on Slattery's kneeboard. The strike leader already had confirmation that the game had begun; with enormous relief he had heard over the guard channel that Critter Flight had evened the air-to-air odds.

Satisfied that there was no immediate air-to-air threat, Slats flexed his fingers over his attack system's typewriter keyboard, much like Victor Borge preparing for a piano concert. "Okay, Jim," he said to his pilot. "Let's go to work."

Fish Hook 703

"Approaching launch position," called the tactical coordinator, Lieutenant Lester "Mauler" Maul to his CO, Commander Rocky Petrocelli.

Eighty miles due east of *Andropov* and about fifty east-northeast of *Otlichniy*, six Vikings prepared to release their Harpoons. In the lead S-3B, Mauler entered the range and bearing of the battlecruiser, entered in data banks before launch and updated by the E-2C circling behind the Vikings. He knew that, in shipping lanes as busy as those around southern Africa, firing Harpoons in the bearing-only launch mode was just too dicey. A freighter or fishing smack could wander across the missile's flight path.

Trusting in the reliability of U.S. detection systems, Maul programmed the Harpoons' cruise phases to end at the last of three possible points, producing the smallest of three available "target-acquisition windows." At this point, the AGM-84As' active-search, terminal-homing radars would switch on. Setting the acquisition window on "small" rather than "medium" or "large" would limit the enemy's reaction time, but required precise knowledge of target ships' locations. To avoid locking onto *Otlichniy*, Rocky Flight's Harpoons were programmed to go active only thirty-five miles from *Andropov*'s presumed position. The drawback was that this delay gave the battlecruiser time to launch chaff and other decoys.

Mauler tapped at his keyboard, checking the memories of the two Harpoons' guidance systems. Symbols on his display flashed green. "RBL mode selected, sir," he reported over the intercom. "Range and bearing launch data entered. Systems all up."

With that assurance, the CO keyed his mike and heard the two-second high-low tone as the scrambler synchronized with the other four S-3Bs. "Rocky Flight, we're launching . . . now!" The six Vikings nosed ten degrees upward. In the back of 700, the TacCo flipped the release switches and the crew saw the two Harpoons drop off the leader's hardpoints. Their Teledyne CAE J402 turbojets kicked in 600 pounds of thrust, closely followed by ignition of the other missiles.

Rocky watched the Harpoons, each weighing nearly 1,200 pounds, accelerate past and under him to around 500 miles per hour. But he saw one missile drop like a rock into the Indian Ocean. *A million-dollar bird in the drink, probably 'cause some ordie forgot to plug it into the socket on the pylon,* he guessed. *Still, not so bad.* He had been told the McDonnell Douglas birds were ninety-three percent reliable, and, sure enough, he counted ten of the twelve flying. Only one had failed on its own. Rocky led his flight in a low-level turn amid the comforting radar clutter of the sea.

0638
Varyag

The antiair officer stood at attention before Rybakov. *"Andropov* and *Otlichniy*'s early-warning and air-search radars report multiple low-level contacts, inbound for *Andropov,* eighty miles from him," the BCh-6 said in a soft, breathless voice. "Initial classification, twin-engined aircraft." The staffer paused, then added, "Presumably strike planes tickling the lobes preparatory to launching Harpoon cruise missiles."

Rybakov stood up. "Do we have a Doppler from the Antonov?" he asked, knowing full well that his remaining AWACS was badly out of position and could not move east without risking attack by Phoenix missiles.

"Nothing, Admiral. He probably can't discriminate the targets against sea clutter at this range."

"Could they be decoys?"

"Always possible, but less probable than genuine aircraft. At least some of the returns must be real threats."

"Very well. If there's nothing else, you may return to your station."

It appeared to Rybakov that the battle to defend his flag group against American air attack had begun in earnest. The task force commander wanted to get closer to the action; the electronic world of CDC now seemed too removed from the life-and-death struggle his ships were about to commence. He decided to take the elevator to *Varyag*'s vulnerable bridge rather than remain in the carrier's "citadel"— spaces deep inside the ship armored and protected against nuclear, chemical and biological contamination. *In any case, my CDC is not as integrated as Gideon's,* he reminded himself. *I can fight practically as well from the bridge.*

"You have the conn, Anatoly Vladimirovich," the admiral told Smirnov, and strode away before his CSO could object.

Harpoon Antiship Missile Flight

One lobe of the leading Harpoon's electronic mind— the gyros and accelerometers in the inertial reference unit— knew exactly where it was. This part of its brain referred back to the bearing coordinates stored in its memory to keep the missile on course, just a few degrees south of west.

Another lobe—the Honeywell radar altimeter of its Northrop altitude reference system—told the missile how high it was. The AGM-84 could see that the sea was fairly smooth—no whitecaps big enough to swamp it. So, through its electromechanical nervous system, its guidance package directed the rear-mounted cruciform fins to fly the missile at one hundred feet unless the waves got higher. The other nine Harpoons followed suit.

0639
Rampart 301

Commander Duncan "Brandy" Alexander looked at his watch, then checked his inertial navigation readout. He tried to concentrate on the job at hand, but couldn't help thinking about his shipmates in Pine Tree 622, killed three minutes ago by a home-on-jam AA-9. It wasn't just friendship. The Prowler was more important to the mission than he himself, any of his eight Hornets or the two VF-182 Tomcats. But 622's jamming and absorption of the Amoses let the F-14s kill the Flankers. And now was the time to put the loss behind him.

Alexander signaled with a slight movement of his stick.

Noting his waggling wings, his flight followed him onto south-southwesterly run-in headings. He personally would lead two F/A-18s, each armed with six Mavericks, and two other strike fighters, each with two SLAMs, toward *Andropov*. Puppy Flight, with eight SLAMs, continued westward; in two minutes, the VFA-184 Hornets would also turn southwest toward *Varyag*.

The only "hard penetration aids" carried by the eight Hornets were ten Shrike antiradar missiles. Although SA-N-6 was the most dangerous SAM on both *Ustinov* and *Andropov*, the cruisers' three Top Dome radars had to be engaged by HARM, since Shrike's range was less than the Russian missile's. The late Prowler's apparently successful HARM attack on *Ustinov*'s fire-control system allowed the Hornets to pass safely through the *Slava*-class cruiser's long-range SAM zone.

So far, so good, Brandy thought. But the depressing fact was that the F/A-18s would be in the heart of *Andropov*'s SA-N-6 envelope long before they reached Shrike range of the battlecruiser. He had to hope that Pine Tree 620 and 624 or Killer 535 and 537 would kill *Andropov*'s Top Domes.

Once on the new heading, about seventy miles from their target, Brandy's second section—Zorro and Doppler in Rampart 306 and 310—popped up to see if the air was clear enough for good IR visuals on the battlecruiser. Although the Harpoon-derived SLAM could fly over eighty miles, its imaging infrared guidance system—identical to Maverick's—was useful against large warships at only a fraction of that range. The operating wavelengths of Standoff Land Attack Missile's seeker penetrated atmospheric vapor and dust better than visible light, but not as well as radar.

To save precious fuel for the trip home, the Hornets were to fire as far away as IR conditions and *Andropov*'s maneuvering allowed. This reduced the missiles' lethality, but preserved forty-million-dollar aircraft.

Initially, the mighty battlecruiser would appear to the missiles' imaging infrared seekers as nothing more than a distant, fuzzy warm spot. But SLAM could talk back to its parent aircraft over a data-link system originally developed for the old Walleye glide bomb. As the Harpoon-derived missile approached its target, the pilot could lock up a particular feature of the ship, as seen through the SLAM's own IR vision.

Looking ahead, Brandy saw the big missiles fall off 306 and 310's outer wing pylons. All four turbojet engines kicked in. *Outstanding!* he thought. Zorro and Doppler then dropped back below the ships' radar horizons, but would have to pop up again, about the time Brandy and Lieutenant Paul "Colonel" Tomb began firing their twelve Mavericks.

Thankful that Pine Tree 622 got its HARMs off before dying, Brandy uttered his Prowler prayer while continuing south through *Ustinov*'s SAM zone. *Hope to God 620 and 624 do the same job on* Andropov. *Or, if not them, then Elvis Flight.* But he still hoped some of the Intruders' HARMs would be available for use against the battlecruiser's thirteen other SAM and AAA fire-control systems.

Brandy checked his watch again—about eight minutes to Maverick launch. Despite the climate-controlled cockpit, nothing diminished the amount of sweat drenching the thirty-eight-year-old squadron commander.

0640
Varyag

"*Andropov* requests permission to engage cruise missiles with distraction-mode chaff and radio-electronic combat systems," the BCh-7 said, summarizing the flurry of signals from the screen over the past half minute. "*Otlichniy* requests permission to engage with medium-range SAM fire. *Ustinov* reports long-range SAMs nonfunctional due to destruction of fire-control system."

"Permission granted for all active and passive defensive measures to both effective combatants," Rybakov promptly replied.

0641
Frisbee 601

Whale Watch was right, Tony Chimola thought as the computer-enhanced blips ghosted across the edge of his scope, west-southwest of the *Varyag* group. *The IFF signals had to be these guys.* Multiple contacts—undoubtedly Flankers rushing to *Varyag*'s aid from *Kuznetsov* some 500 miles to the southwest. The controller engaged his mike switch and broadcast on his powerful radio:

"All units, be advised. Eight bandits bearing 250 from Point Romeo, distance fifty-five. Airspeed 500 knots, altitude uncertain. Frisbee, out."

White Knight 20

Lieutenant Colonel Ivan Vorozheikin double-checked his heading: 072 degrees, the same track he had pursued for almost fifty minutes. His two flights had made excellent time at high cruise and now he deployed his *Kuznetsov* Su-27s in repelling the American strike. With eight Flankers, the Russian knew he stood a good chance of inflicting heavy losses on *Langley's* air wing. He hoped they were not too late. Avenging an attack would be sweet, but preventing it would be better yet.

Vorozheikin thumbed his armament switch and double-checked his look-down, shoot-down radar. He grinned beneath his oxygen mask.

Bronco 400

When the two SLAMs fell off his Hornet's wing pylons, Lieutenant Puppy Perez felt more than the release of 2,400 pounds of air-launched antiship missiles. As if reborn, his jet sprang into new life as a fighter. But beyond the physical unburdening of his plane's wings, he experienced emotional relief. With his air-launched cruise missiles locked onto their aimpoints before the Flankers shot their way through the escorting Tomcats, Puppy had accomplished his main mission. All but one of his flight's SLAMs were headed toward the carrier. A gracious God had answered the aviators' perennial prayer; they had not fucked up. Not yet.

The four F/A-18s followed their ALCMs south, Shrikes armed and tuned to the Cross Sword fire-control frequency. Puppy hoped that, in the spirit of his popular country-western parody, "Stand by Your SLAM," his flight would do everything possible to help the antiship missiles penetrate. *Now*, he thought, *if only the Flankers will cooperate.*

0642
Varyag

"*Otlichniy* reports his long-range chaff has not distracted the radar targets," the talker announced, without knowing what all the words meant. He had been trained to repeat precisely the standard formulas he heard over the secure voice channel. "He is engaging with medium-range SAMs."

The number of radar targets had doubled, indicating that the twin-engine aircraft had launched cruise missiles or decoys, then retired. Contrary to standard Russian practice, Rybakov had freed his outer escorts to fire at will. Even the supposedly secure comlinks were under electronic attack by the American ES-3. The picture he received of the air defense battle was therefore fragmentary.

0643
Harpoon Flight

After cruising for five and a half minutes downrange from the S-3s, the air-launched cruise missiles neared their turn-on points. All four remembered that their first big move was due . . . now!

The missiles zoomed upward at a steep angle, leveled off, nosed down slightly and opened their radar eyes. The active-seeker heads gimballed back and forth along the horizon through a ninety-degree arc, looking for likely targets. Seeing nothing, the missiles began the first leg of a programmed, "expanding-box" search, conducted by turning starboard for a few miles, then, if no targets were sighted, port for a slightly longer distance, then port again for a longer leg yet, then starboard, which brought them back to their original heading. They would repeat this widening pattern until receiving a radar echo.

Each missile knew to home on the first, not the largest or most radar-reflective target, it saw. After surveying the horizon and finding nothing, the Harpoons dived back to one hundred feet above the waves. If they encountered no suitable target, they would self-destruct in another six minutes.

The electronic eyes—a solid-state radar—in the head of the lead Harpoon continued to sweep back and forth along the horizon, relentlessly searching for a target. The missile ended the third leg of its search, came ninety degrees starboard and popped up for a new look. There, within its ninety-degree gaze, was a strong radar return.

Guided by inertial systems programmed with valid positional data on the enemy vessels, the lucky missiles had found targets early in their search pattern—within half a minute—saving precious time and fuel. But the missile's suspicious brains asked themselves, *Is the target valid?*

Varyag

Rybakov was called to the bridge's CDC intercom. It was Smirnov with an update. His good news was that *Otlichniy*'s medium-range SAMs had bagged at least one target. The CSO's bad news was that the presumed cruise missiles's radars had gone active, but had not been deluded by *Andropov*'s passive and active decoys. Also, the destroyer and battlecruiser were under intense airborne jamming from two sources.

"If any further proof were needed," the admiral responded, "that confirms that this is the main strike. They've committed three of their five Prowlers to it, counting the one shot down." Smirnov concurred. "Damn," Rybakov continued, "with our forward AWACS splashed, we need *Andropov*'s electronics suite. Not to mention his 312 SAMs. Direct the fighters to concentrate on the EA-6Bs."

0644
Varyag

"*Andropov* is engaging incoming cruise missiles with long-range SAMs, Admiral," Rybakov's antiair officer reported from CDC.

"Understood," the task force commander replied. "Keep me informed." It would be several minutes before *Varyag* came under direct attack.

"Update from *Andropov,* Admiral," the staffer said. "One long-range SAM illuminator has been destroyed by an antiradiation missile."

Rybakov looked put out and nodded. *Why aren't the Americans jamming this channel?* he wondered. *I'll think*

about that later. Too much else more important right now.
"Wait. Where are the strike aircraft?"

"About forty miles out, Admiral—right behind the missiles. Although there is always the possibility that some are penetrating on the deck with the missiles. *Andropov* has been attacked by antiradiation missiles. Both he and *Otlichniy* have been engaged by radio-electronic combat systems. Also *Ustinov*, but from a different heading."

"So there are at least two attack axes?" Rybakov asked.

"It would appear so, Admiral," the BCh-6 agreed.

Even though his battle group was still under attack, Rybakov was already planning his retaliation. "I want to trail the American strike planes home to find out where *Langley* is," he said. "Get tankers airborne. Whatever we have left that can fly should follow their egress. They're probably flying deceptive headings, so triangulate every known American ingress route. It may help us locate the carrier. They also probably have Tomcats or Hornets waiting to jump us in case we do trail them, so order *Kuznetsov* to send us eight more Su-27s.

"Signal *Andropov*. I want her antiship missiles saved for our counterattack. The destroyers' are too short-ranged, and they haven't enough in any case. I know Captain Vershinin is busy, but order him to maneuver to reduce the odds of a fo'c'sle hit, if he isn't already." Rybakov hoped that, since the nuclear battlecruiser's air defenses are thickest forward, the fo'c'sle-mounted SLCMs would probably survive the attack, although perhaps not their fire-control system. Even if *Andropov*'s antiship missile fire-control system were destroyed, the *Varyag* group's PLARK could guide the ARKR's SS-N-19s as well as its own. Rybakov could hardly wait for his chance to strike back.

Harpoon Flight

To lessen the chance of hitting a friendly or noncombatant ship, each Block II-model AGM-84A carried an electronic support measures system. Before permitting a missile to lock on to the first radar return it encountered, the ESM system monitored the target's electronic emissions. If the ship produced electromagnetic radiation in any of three wavelength bands common to Russian naval air-search radars, the missile's own internal, computerized "conscience" allowed it to lock on.

The Harpoons detected the telltale C- to F-band frequencies of the mechanically steered Top Pair and electronically steered Top Plate air-search radars. The missiles' software logic determined that this combination meant *Andropov* or her sister ARKR *Kalinin,* so they decided to attack the apparently authorized target and dived back to a hundred feet for run-in on terminal homing. The missiles' unblinking radar eyes followed their victim's every move, stalking their prey like huge, white, flying sharks.

Frisbee 601

Tony Chimola no longer monitored missile guidance frequencies, but had resumed participating in the E-2C's main mission—radar surveillance of vast oceanic areas. There was a lot to see.

His attention was focused on the missile exchange in progress. Chimola felt curiously involved yet detached, watching HARMs inbound to the Russian ships from forty miles out—beyond SA-N-6 range—as the rotating radome gave a splendid view of the action. That was hardly surprising, as the Hawkeye was optimized for overwater operations. However, Chimola also noted that only four Harpoons had disappeared from his scope so far—victims of SA-N-7 or SA-N-6. *Not bad,* he thought. *But not good enough, since* Andropov *is the toughest nut in the world to crack.*

0645
Varyag

On the bridge, the CDC intercom buzzed. Rybakov answered it himself. Smirnov told him that *Andropov*'s SA-N-6s had apparently killed their first Harpoon. "Which is good," the CSO added, "since *Otlichniy* reports his SAM magazines depleted. And *Andropov* has initiated jamming."

"Very well," the admiral replied. He checked his watch, then ordered, "We're probably out of Harpoon range, but fire distraction-mode chaff, anyway. Range 5,000 meters. Burst height, 150 meters." Rybakov noted with pleasure that wind conditions were perfect. In the still morning air, the chaff pattern might stay aloft for hours, slowly thinning out as the fibers settled to the surface or drifted away.

From his lookout station on the starboard bridge wing, *Matros* First Rank Andrei Rudenko was startled to see canisters arc up from the chaff mortars below him. About five kilometers downrange, they bloomed above the waves. The sailor knew little about electronic countermeasures, but had been told that chaff was very fine, aluminum-coated glass filaments sized strongly to reflect the millimetric operating wavelengths of American aircraft radars and cruise missile seeker heads. The decoy material dispersed into a large, silvery cloud. To the young lookout, metallic confetti seemed a flimsy shield against antiship missiles.

Frisbee 601

Even to the average avionics expert who might have hunched behind him in the Hawkeye's cramped fuselage, the glowing traces on Tony Chimola's scope would have been indecipherable. But the esoteric symbology was merely a second language to the controller. Orbiting some 200 miles from *Andropov,* the E-2 took in most of what happened 22,000 feet below.

After the antiship missiles reached their turn-on points, the combat information officer had started monitoring their active-homing frequencies. He assumed that his colleagues in the Prowler ECM aircraft did the same. Shortly after the Harpoons went active, a supernova seemed to explode on the screen, displaying their operating frequency. "Shit!" he yelled over the intercom. "They're jamming the Harpoons!"

"Wha'd'ya expect?" asked the radar operator.

Chimola couldn't do much but stare at the whited-out scope. Nor would the escorting EA-6Bs be able to help; the missiles lacked the power to burn through jamming. It was all up to the limited electronic counter-countermeasures (ECCM) equipment on-board the AGM-84s. "Goddamn! Wish we could link targeting data to the missiles, like the Russkies do with theirs," he exclaimed.

Harpoon Flight

The receiver components of the missiles' active radar registered not a single return—the echo of the target onto which they had locked—but around-the-clock snow. The wavelength of the electromagnetic blizzard matched the missiles' homing radar's own frequency. The Harpoons were snow-blind.

0646
Varyag

Smirnov was back on the line. "*Andropov* says that the Harpoons went frequency-agile at 3,000 meters."

Rybakov replied, "I didn't know they could do that." Smirnov admitted that neither did he.

"*Andropov* has launched his short-range chaff in seduction mode," the CSO added.

Rybakov rang off and walked to the starboard windows to witness the spectacle. *Andropov* steamed just within visual range from the bridge. The massive battlecruiser accelerated and came hard to port, trying to get out from behind the chaff cloud without any seduced missiles' reestablishing lock-on.

Harpoon Flight

The lead AGM-84 "saw" the new, large radar target, but was not seduced by its pleasing, voluptuous form. Instead, the oncoming missile remained locked on to its true love—the first return it had seen, electronically interrogated, found suitable and faithfully homed on ephemerally ever after. The six following Harpoons also continued tracking the course of their original target.

Frisbee 601

As airborne control officer, Tony Chimola was enjoying his electronic ringside seat at history. It was exciting, certainly, and so far he wasn't terribly nervous. But in seconds his optimism melted. He recognized the changing disposition of the enemy formation and knew what it meant.

"All units, all units. Frisbee advises Point Romeo bandits launching long-range missiles at this time. Heads up. Frisbee 601 out."

Watching the strike escorts, Chimola noted the Tomcats turning to face the threat. A standoff missile exchange was developing.

White Knight 20

With curt orders, Colonel Vorozheikin tried to direct his pilots' radar search patterns. Doctrine required launch authority from an airborne or surface controller. The American jamming made voice contact difficult, and Vorozheikin feared there would be duplicate targeting, leading to inefficient missile employment or, worse yet, the shooting of friendlies. *Well, it cannot be helped,* he thought as the big, angular Flankers illuminated their targets—a damnably troublesome Prowler and its low-flying strike aircraft. Sixteen AA-9s came off their fuselage mounts. Two continued into the Indian Ocean, but twelve began guiding. With his missiles' fifty-mile reach, the Sukhoi leader felt confident that they would break up the presumed A-6s now approaching the inner screen of Task Force Rybakov.

0647
Harpoon Flight

The Harpoon saw the radar image of its target change shape—elongating in two directions and apparently reaching out from its center toward the missile. The position of the augmented central part of the return also moved relative to the rest of the image—a radio-frequency kaleidoscope. All this motion was enough to make the Harpoon electronically nauseous, but it managed to keep its eye on the prize. Thanks to recent "brain surgery," its software ordered the missile to follow the moving left-hand edge of the image rather than stay locked on to the center of the return.

The radar return split in two, then three. As the images separated, the Harpoon's ESM interrogated them again. Both proved valid. Unable to decide, it chose a point between the two return peaks.

With precise radar pictures of the battlecruiser stored in

their memories, the Harpoons did not fall for this electronic shell game.

Talent 500

Slats got on the scrambler to Elvis. "Killer Lead from Talent Lead. How do you read? Over." A tonal message-receipt signal vibrated in his headphones. "Program four HARMs for Cross Sword. Repeat, Cross Sword. Acknowledge." Again the tone came through. *Outstanding!* Slats thought. *They're not jamming our VHF.*

Another advantage of targeting the more advanced radars was that *Andropov*'s four Tin Man optronic devices were located near the SAM fire-control sets, so a HARM hit on a Cross Sword might also knock out a Tin Man. Intel didn't know if SA-N-9's electro-optical fire control—a low-light infrared TV camera backup system—was located on the missile's Cross Sword complex or if it used the four Tin Man optronic and laser devices halfway up both sides of *Andropov*'s island. By contrast, the two Pop Group SA-N-4 fire-control radars definitely did not combine both EO and radio-frequency guidance units, and in any case they controlled only forty missiles instead of 128.

Varyag

Rybakov spoke into the intercom. "Yes, I know," he said, craning to look out the bridge windows while talking to Smirnov in CDC. "I can see *Andropov* has been HARMed. Wait, now he's firing his short-range SAMs. There go the Wasps," the admiral reported, sounding like an excited kid. Both officers knew that the older Wasp system—called SA-N-4 Gecko by NATO and fired relatively slowly from a twin-arm launcher—would soon be followed into action by the newer SA-N-9.

As the admiral watched, the sixteen vertical launchers for the advanced SAM, each holding eight rounds, started emptying furiously. Both ends of the distant ship were obscured by exhaust. It was a great relief to see that the troublesome, complex missile worked. Years after its introduction, not all ships designed to carry the SA-N-9 system were equipped with its Cross Sword fire-control system.

Those ships that did have operational systems carried civilian technicians to keep them functional.

Frisbee 601

Tony Chimola could see that at least half of the Flankers' missile tracks converged on the southern EA-6B. He called in the clear, "Pine Tree 620 from Frisbee. Many missiles headed your way. Get outta there!"

Seconds dragged by. Chimola was about to repeat the call when he heard the carrier wave—no time for the scrambler. "Frisbee, ah, Rog. We copy Amos launch. We're . . . okay. Six-Twenty, out."

The E-2 controller recognized the voice of Seadog, the squadron skipper, and was astonished at his nonchalance. Guiding straight toward the Prowler, he counted seven of the meanest AAMs in the world, excepting Phoenix. Six others were headed in the general direction of the Intruders and Tomcats—probably simply guiding on inertial reference. They would do no harm unless an unlucky American plane fell within the scope of an Amos's on-board radar when it went active. By continuing to jam, drawing the AA-9s toward itself, the Prowler was protecting the Intruders. But the strike force couldn't afford to lose another EA-6B. The machines weren't literally worth their weight in gold—only about a third that much—but when protecting over a billion dollars' worth of other aircraft and dozens of lives, their value far exceeded gold's. *Come to think of it, their canopies are coated with it,* Chimola reflected.

The missile tracks closed the distance to the Prowler at over Mach 2.5.

White Knight 20

As Ivan Vorozheikin neared his controlling AWACS plane, the Antonov's signal grew stronger and began to burn through the American jamming of commo and data links. No longer denied contact with the An-74M, Black King Three, the Flanker pilot finally saw that his airborne missiles were functioning. Moments later they went active and he received a still clearer picture—with mixed reactions. "White Knight Leader from Black King Three," came the staticky AWACS call. "Your arrows are tracking the electronic combat target. Prepare to reengage primary targets. White Knight Twenty, your heading for intercept is zero-four-zero. End of message."

Vorozheikin cursed to himself. *The goddamned Prowler soaked up our first missiles*, he thought bitterly. The *Kuznetsov* leader put the disappointment behind him to focus on the future. *We're close enough to engage the U.S. fighters with medium-range missiles.*

To comply with the AWACS' vector, Vorozheikin ordered his two flights split. The trailing flight, led by White Knight Seventeen, would break starboard to engage the nearest American attack planes now showing on his lookdown radar. Vorozheikin himself would lead the first flight farther east to merge with the other U.S. strike force approaching from the north-northeast. With his own long-range missiles and the Americans' Phoenixes presumably expended, it shaped up as a dogfight.

As he sped east-northeast, Vorozheikin heard White Knight Seventeen call, "Medium-range missile launch." He craned his neck for a look, but his bulky, helmet-mounted sight limited the arc through which he could rapidly turn his head without risking spinal injury. The air wing commander envisioned eight big, fast, maneuverable AA-10Cs diving on the low-flying Intruders, blasting them to aluminum-steel-titanium chaff and carbon-fiberglass powder. But he frowned beneath his visor, thinking, *Too late, too late.* Vorozheikin gripped the stick tensely, as if trying to energize the Sukhoi with the urgency of his own emotion.

Frisbee 601

With his colleagues monitoring the air-to-air melee, Chimola focused on the surface action. He noticed that another Harpoon had dropped off the scope, presumably a victim of SA-N-4 or SA-N-9. It appeared that the battlecruiser was out of Geckos. So he estimated that *Otlichniy* and *Andropov* could have fired as many as 140 SAMs so far, but had bagged only five Harpoons. *With launch failures, make it about 110 to 120 firings,* he allowed generously. *One kill per twenty-plus radar-guided SAMs—better than historical par.* As his Irish grandma said, *More's the pity.*

Talent 500

Slats absorbed the cacophony of information flooding his senses—from the physiological to the tactical. Though Air Wing 18 had practiced "zip-lip" war-at-sea strikes, many of his aircrews were more vocal than he wished. The deputy CAG fought to sort out the wheat from the chaff, to order his priorities while inbound to the enemy's most prestigious target at 500 knots airspeed and 200 feet altitude.

One useful bit of information flashed like neon through Clausewitz's fog of war, courtesy of Frisbee 601. *The Russians have another AWACS up!* Slattery knew the remedy to that. He called Lieutenant Commander Bert "Kidder" Kidd, leading the VF-182 escort section. "Circus 207, Talent Lead. Snuff the Mudhen over the carrier."

The response shot back, crisp and immediate. "Roger, CAG. Hang tight."

Turning in his seat, Slats waited expectantly while the lead F-14 locked on to its target. Moments later he saw two AMRAAMs streak away from the Tomcat two miles to starboard. *Looks just like a Cubi Point missile exercise,* Slattery thought. Somehow the familiarity of the procedure comforted him.

Rampart 301

Commander Brandy Alexander and his wingman, Lieutenant Paul "Colonel" Tomb in Rampart 303, anticipated a frantic few minutes. Running into the Maverick launch points against *Andropov,* they checked their switchology and selected "hotspots" on the cruiser's waterline and funnel. Then, in sequence, they designated the aimpoints and pressed their triggers, sending the infrared-imaging missiles on their way.

The Hornet pilots then armed up their Shrike antiradar missiles. With a previous tour at Naval Weapon Center China Lake, Alexander knew the thirty-year-old AGM-45 even better than his Porsche 911. The engagement sequence was equally well-briefed to the second section—Zorro and Doppler in 306 and 310. Pretuned against known frequencies of Russian fire-control radars, the Shrikes would help the SLAMs, Mavs and remaining Harpoons reach their targets.

Brandy wasn't sanguine about the chances of all six birds finding roosts, but, he figured, *If the gomers shut down some radars to break our homing, that's as good as a kill.* He refined his heading, pressed the trigger twice and felt the 200-pound missiles come off his jet.

0648
Fish Hook 703

Commander Petrocelli checked the time again. *Over nine minutes since launch.* Rocky wished he could see the results achieved by "his" ALCMs, but he and the Harpoons had already put about 150 miles between each other.

Behind him, Lieutenant Maul decided he liked Harpooning better than sub-hunting. Though surface targets could shoot back, the missions were over sooner. He knew that AGM-84As were great at doing the job they were designed for—taking out fast attack craft—but he wanted a bigger, faster, smarter antiship missile for use against major warships. *Harpoons are just too slow and dumb, and their warheads too small to do the job against 8,000-ton Russkie destroyers, let alone 28,000-ton battlecruisers and 65,000-ton carriers.*

Over the intercom, the TacCo heard Rocky say, "About a minute to go. The shit should start flying right about . . . now."

Talent 500

Slats Slattery had a good view forward, keeping visual contact on his leading Intruders two miles ahead. Elvis Flight from VA-187 was on course to its low-level Skipper launch point. But the most pressing concern was getting past the stricken *Andropov*'s surviving air defenses. Elvis Flight had used half its eight HARMs to help the Hornets put their SLAMs and Mavericks on the battlecruiser and the other four against *Azov*, so the Intruders had done all they could for now.

Apparently the HARMs with Prowler and Viking jamming were doing the job, since Slats's two flights had suffered no surface-to-air losses. The CAG risked an optimistic assessment to his pilot. "Crunch, this strike actually might work like we planned it."

Jim Neslie was about to reply when Slats saw him strain forward against the torso-harness fittings. "CAG, we got smoky SAMs or somethin' inbound to Elvis. You got it?"

Slattery's optimism melted in a warm rush of adrenaline. A wall of missiles screamed down on the four leading Intruders from a great height. Crunch already was hollering a break warning to Elvis as the Alamo Cs from the Flankers' second volley arrived. Two dirty orange-brown explosions rent the bright blue sky, spattering the cloud-shadowed sea with white geysers of wreckage. The other two A-6s jinked frantically, and Slats counted two or three large explosions on the water. *Missiles must've missed,* he thought. His anxious blue eyes scanned the heavens, but found no more of the lethal smoke trails.

Seconds later the CAG had a status report. "Talent Lead from Killer 535. Slats, we lost 537 and 541. Nobody saw any chutes. Elvis, out."

Slattery slumped back in his ejection seat. The two wingmen's Intruders—Kermit and Rowdy with Ratface and Ho—gone. Literally gone in a flash. *What did the grunts used to say? "Don't mean nothin'."* Slats did not share the sentiment, but he still had a job to do.

"Circus 207 from Talent Lead. You copy?"

"Ahh, Rog, Talent. We saw it." Slats knew that Kidder Kidd, leading his escort section, would move to deal with the Flankers. Circus 210, Kidder's wingman, had the TARPS reconnaissance pod and therefore couldn't afford a prolonged shootout, even though another missile exchange shaped up: two AMRAAMs against more AA-10s. *At least,* he thought, *if the Flankers carry their usual loadout, they're out of long-burn missiles. If it's a short-range missile fight, we might just make it.*

Six surviving Intruders pressed on toward their target.

Varyag

On the bridge wing, Rudenko saw the fire erupt on the battlecruiser. In the ninety minutes since *Andropov* had departed its goalkeeping station eight miles east of *Varyag,* the third-year man had intermittently followed the battlecruiser through his twenty-power binoculars. This was not his job; he was supposed to search for incoming missiles or aircraft, but the spectacle of the mighty warship's struggle with its insect-like tormentors was too powerful a distraction from his boring assignment.

For five minutes, he had tracked the flight of the American missiles by the brilliant SAM trails and explosions and puffs of 130mm flak visible above the horizon. Now that the huge ship was taking evasive maneuvers, the lookout could see the missiles streaking toward it, although they were too fast to keep the binoculars trained on for long.

Rudenko could see most of *Andropov*'s six last-ditch defense systems—hybrid radar, SAM and AAA mounts—swing into action, training and elevating to track the incoming antiship missiles. As the last SA-N-11 point-defense SAMs left their launch rails, each turret's twin 30mm Gatling guns opened up. Despite the masking daylight and obscuring missile exhaust, the sailor could pick out bright gun flashes decorating the fo'c'sle and superstructure of the handsome ship.

It seemed that missiles diving on the forward half of *Andropov* were being destroyed, but one must have hit the helipad aft without his noticing. Flames engulfed the rear of the nuclear cruiser, and Rudenko assumed that the missile had penetrated to the hangar deck and ignited the helicopters' kerosene.

As he watched, the forty-ton, 130mm gun turret popped off like a champagne cork, burst through the smoke and executed an ungainly swan dive dozens of meters toward *Varyag*. He was impressed. *Must have been some ammo left in the magazine.*

The fire turned sooty. *Looks like diesel,* he assessed with an objectivity he did not feel. *Must have spread to bunkerage.*

Rudenko briefly swept his binoculars along the burning ship, looking for the fire fighters. It scared him to consider how many tons of fuel *Varyag* carried; he immediately returned to scanning for inbound missiles. The young sailor knew that his ship could be next.

13

0649 to 0659, Friday,
4 June

0649
Talent 500

The smoke on the horizon told Slats Slattery where he was, without referring to his inertial navigation readout. Looking forward, past the A-6E's jutting refueling probe, he nudged his pilot. "The missile shooters did good. Look at that bastard burn." The aft third of *Andropov* was obscured by oily smoke. Slats couldn't measure the full extent of the damage, but decided to pass up the cruiser and concentrate on *Varyag*. If any ordnance remained after hitting the carrier, he'd dump it on the giant escort.

The strike leader was relieved that no more Flanker missiles tore at his formation. Now he could pay attention to business. He engaged his scrambler radio, waited for the tone and called the VA-187 crews. "Talent Lead to Elvis Flight. Go for the carrier. Proceed as briefed." Cryptic acknowledgments came from the forward division leader, Lieutenant Commander "Elvis" Presley. Instead of breaking off for a Skipper run on *Andropov*, Presley's two remaining Intruders pressed on toward *Varyag*. Elvis and Gonzo in Killer 535 with Zipper and Clint in 540 were assigned a more roundabout run-in than Slats Flight, but their Skippers could be fired from farther away, so the timing seemed fine.

Slattery inhaled deeply, savoring the pure oxygen. Unless they were intercepted as they looped around the carrier to hit her from the opposite side, Elvis's A-6s would begin pounding rocket-powered bombs into the enemy flagship in under four minutes. Then Slats's division would launch a standoff attack with laser-guided iron bombs—crude but, he hoped, effective. *It's like Midway,* he thought, *except the bad guys have missiles and radar-aimed guns.*

Considering all his Intruders had flown through, Slats was surprised that six remained. The Russians still had plenty of ordnance to throw at them, but there just might be enough A-6s left to do the job.

Frisbee 601

Tony Chimola's mouth was dry. He was thirstier than he had ever been in his life. The menacing blips of four Flankers bore down on the ingressing Intruders, easily within missile launch range. For a microsecond his mind disengaged from the present and defaulted far back to his youth. He recalled his junior year in high school, and his third place in the Maryland State Speech Contest with his interpretation of "Gunga Din."

. . . when it comes to slaughter, you'll do your work on water, and lick the bloomin' boots of them that's got it. The controller shook his head, wondering if Kipling ever anticipated that sentiment moved to the third dimension with electronic perception of combat.

Then the instant passed and Chimola keyed his mike to warn the Intruders of their peril. He opened his mouth . . . and gaped at what he saw.

Two Flankers were gone—vanished blips. Chimola's brown eyes scanned the bronze-tinted scope in search of an explanation. But there was none. Then he knew. *Red on Red —Azov's SAMs bagged their own fighters!* It was just as well Pine Tree 620's jamming hadn't worked—it gave the A-6s a chance after all. Chimola realized he still had the mike button depressed, and made his call. "Talent Lead from Frisbee. CAG, two bandits are a splash. Two still inbound. Six-Oh-One, out."

Now Gunshot 207 and 210 have a fighting chance, Chimola thought. His mood brightened, but his throat remained parched. He knew the TARPS bird, 210, had to avoid a dogfight if possible, so 207 still faced a two-on-one situation if it came to close-in combat. The Flankers had already unloaded their AA-9s and AA-10Cs on the Prowler and Intruders, affording the Tomcats a range advantage. *If they can take one of 'em out with a BVR shot, then it's one-on-one for 207.*

Then, within fifteen seconds, Circus 210 broadcast two "Fox One" calls over the guard frequency. Chimola figured that left the TARPS bird with only two Sidewinders and its gun. In 207, Kidd and his RIO, Stone, were on their own.

Varyag

Rybakov ordered CDC to put all defensive systems on automatic; then, ignoring his staff's protests, he stepped onto the port bridge wing to check his ship's preparedness. Lookout Rudenko came stiffly to attention, but the admiral told the *matros* to stand at ease and return to his job.

The sight of *Andropov*'s ordeal was sickening, but the admiral was glad to see that its fo'c'sle had escaped damage. *We'll definitely have need of those antiship missiles,* he promised himself. *If the cruiser survives.* He switched his gaze from the distant horizon to his flagship.

Below, at intervals around the deck edge, Rybakov saw, were tall, husky sailors balancing SA-16s on their shoulders. It was the most powerful SAM of its type in the world and its operators necessarily were exceptional—tall and strong with above-average intelligence. Reinforcing the close-in defenses with heat-seeking SA-16s was an idea borrowed from the Americans, who had armed sailors with Stingers off Lebanon.

The flight deck was cleared of fixed-wing aircraft, but around the island asbestos-clad damage-control crews were poised to go into action. He hoped all was equally well-prepared down on the hangar deck, where he had ordered steel blast curtains hung to divide the cavernous space into three damage-control bays.

Rybakov witnessed at close quarters the first damage to *Varyag*. As he watched, an antiradar missile scored a direct hit on the carrier's aft air-search radar, producing a sickening fireworks display. The loss was unfortunate, but he knew that electronically steered systems were able to keep working even after sustaining battle damage, albeit in much-degraded fashion. Also, *Varyag* was blessed with redundant systems. With three other Sky Watch arrays and judicious maneuvering, Rybakov felt sure he could track the inbound attackers. The enemy's hardware was working, but so was his own— and he had more.

0650
Talent 500

"Talent Lead from Rampart Lead," a recognizable voice crackled over the air-to-air VHF net. "We're engaging Flankers." Despite electronic interference and a matter-of-fact delivery, Slats caught the note of tension in Alexander's voice.

"Roger, Brandy." Slattery wondered what else to say to a man who was fighting for his life. Commander Brandy Alexander was leading eight Hornets of VFA-183 and -184, and judging by the garbled radio calls, the Ramparts and Broncos had their hands full after the Circus F-14s' missile exchange. Brandy's own flight had unloaded its air-to-surface ordnance on *Andropov*. Now the four Hornets were free to act like fighters, as long as their limited fuel and eight air-to-air missiles allowed. Armed with Sidewinders and guns, the Hornets would be of use only if the Flankers closed to visual range. Still, Slats was glad to have their added protection for his bombers' last minute of ingress; then the Hornets could help cover the egress of the whole strike force. *Whatever is left of it,* he thought.

Circus 204

Ever since receiving the E-2's warning that four bandits continued toward him, Lieutenant Commander D. J. Howell, escorting the eight Hornets, had stared intently at his scope. The Russians' ship-based jammers that were trying to blind him were powerful, but so were American computers and signal-processing software.

Now the RIO picked out the first blips from amid the snow on his screen. He notified Lieutenant Tyler "Sleeper" Bauman, who wore a custom name tag stamped "DJ's Pilot" on his flight suit. "Sleeper, heads up. Multiple bogies bearing two-four-zero for fifty-five." Howell knew that, lacking data-link radar info from the Hawkeye, he would not have been able to discern the contacts without telling the opposition where he was. He interrogated the blips electronically, but got no IFF response. "They're no friends of mine. Master Arm safe, AMRAAM selected?"

"Roger. You say the word," Sleeper replied. DJ was leading the VF-181 section and would order when to fire. Seconds ticked off as the range closed. Then DJ's radar warning receiver lit up. *Shit. They've painted us!*

"Circus Lead here," came Howell's voice on the secure channel. "Illuminate and fire according to plan."

Gripping the RIO's hand control, DJ designated the targets in his prebriefed sector, then pressed the red-and-white-striped launch button. Circus 204 trembled slightly as the missiles fired. The same sequence was repeated in 206 as the AIM-120s burned off their rails, sending the AMRAAMs toward invisible targets now over forty miles away. "Never thought I'd see ordnance fired for real," Sleeper commented.

"This is all the reality I can handle." DJ checked his radar again. The range was down to thirty-eight miles. With AMRAAM's "launch and leave" capability, the two Tomcats quickly shifted targets, directing four missiles southwest at Mach Four.

Once again the F-14 cockpit filled with the blaring of radar warning receivers. Within seconds the RIO heard on the UHF link with Frisbee 601, "Gunshot 204, seven missile tracks headed for you!"

White Knight 20

Vorozheikin held his nose on the invisible target, illuminating it with his missile fire-control radar. He and his wingman were after the two fighters that had apparently broken off from the American formation to merge with his interceptors, while the other two White Knights attacked the Hornets with medium-range, semiactive missiles. The distance between his aircraft and the Americans' disappeared at thirty-five kilometers per minute.

White Knight Twenty's RHAW receiver sounded shrilly. Since the shoot-down of their airborne controller, the

Kuznetsov Flankers had had to rely on radar warning receivers to alert them to missile launches from beyond visual range. The news that he had been locked up by an enemy fire-control radar did not jar Vorozheikin out of his well-rehearsed routine. He knew his training aimed to produce stereotyped, almost automatic, cockpit behavior, and was very glad that it did. *"Hard in practice; easy in battle,"* he thought, recalling the maxim of Great Catherine's ever-victorious General Suvorov.

0651
Frisbee 601

About fifty-five seconds after Kidd and Stone in Circus 207 had fired two AMRAAMs at the lone survivor of the southern Flankers, Chimola saw the Russian blip jink hard right, apparently in an evasive maneuver. Too late. The Su-27's own desperation shots were out of range, burning out even as the Flanker's remains plunged toward the ocean. Chimola made a fist, pumped the air with a crooked arm and exclaimed, "All right!" Then he called, "Talent Lead from Frisbee. CAG, you're clear into the target."

White Knight 20

Vorozheikin's blue eyes detected the reduced-smoke trails of the American medium-range missiles. His radar warning gear indicated that, nearing their targets, the AMRAAMs' guidance switched from semiactive to active homing—from pursuing echoes of the Tomcats' fire-control system to tracking the targets with their own small radar. White Knight 23 saved himself with well-judged maneuvering, and Vorozheikin—also bending into an evasive turn—was thankful the missiles weren't as agile as his Flanker.

Another AIM-120 malfunctioned or was deceived, and Vorozheikin saw it plunge into the sea. But looking to his left, off to the north, he glimpsed an ephemeral flash followed by a prominent fireball suspended in space. White Knight 25 had just died. The other Flankers were busy regaining their positions. *The missiles are meant to disrupt us,* Vorozheikin realized. He quickly toggled his switches and designated a target for his first combination of heat-seeking and radar-guided short-range missiles, then accelerated toward his victims. It would be just as the Su-27 pilot had wished—close combat.

Circus 204

Sleeper and DJ felt desperately alone. Their wingmen, Mongo and Hooch in 206, had disappeared from the abeam position after the second scissors with a pair of Flankers. By the time DJ regained visual, there was too much separation. Pulling himself around to check their tail, one hand gripped on the canopy "hassle handle," the RIO saw 206 at least forty degrees off the nose of a Flanker in a level turn. The F-14s had lost mutual support, but they'd certainly be all right for the next ten seconds.

DJ saw a smoke plume erupt under the Flanker's wing, a good three miles from the big Grumman. *What's that gomer doing?* he wondered. *His nose isn't anywhere near Mongo.* Watching incredulously, the RIO saw the Alamo-A short-burn radar missile dart ahead of the Sukhoi, alter course about sixty degrees and streak directly into the Tomcat. An explosion, smoke and debris, a tumbling F-14, a seat firing—then nothing. DJ had forgotten. *Goddamn Flankers have helmet-mounted sights!*

White Knight 20

Colonel Vorozheikin had forgotten no such thing. He tracked the wreckage of Circus 206 only briefly, then scanned the horizon, looking for another AA-10 shot. The radar dish in the nose of his Su-27 followed his head movement, for he saw the world not through a conventional head-up display on the instrument panel, but through a circular sight affixed to his helmet visor. Within certain parameters, Vorozheikin and his pilots knew they could kill anything they could see, merely by looking at it, locking on and pressing a trigger. He was controlling this fight nicely.

0652
Circus 204

Sleeper Bauman had padlocked the sky-blue Flanker with the white number twenty painted on the nose, thumbing his stick-mounted armament switch to the "SW" detent. He told DJ to "keep checking six" while he stalked the Sukhoi, intending to kill it with a Sidewinder. But as Sleeper was pulling his nose into line, Vorozheikin dived away to the east, and abruptly Bauman was staring at the big intakes of another Flanker turning toward him. *Where'd you come from?* He pressed the trigger and sent an AIM-9L into the Flanker's face. The all-aspect heat seeker homed on the hot metal of the Sukhoi's leading edges. Detonation occurred at minimum range, and Sleeper jinked violently to avoid the worst of the debris.

DJ Howell knew he could never comprehend what had happened in the last two minutes. Everywhere he looked he had seen airplanes—all with red stars on them. He was too pumped up to notice, but he had sprained a shoulder while pulling against a seven-G turn trying to keep a lookout behind their tail, and now sweat was running in his eyes. He shook his head to clear his vision. When he looked back again, a Flanker was beautifully positioned between the twin tails, a mile and a half back. Two missile plumes erupted from beneath the Sukhoi's wings. *We're dead.* . . .

DJ braced himself in his seat, hollered "Eject, eject!" into the ICS, then blew himself and Sleeper out of Gunshot 204.

White Knight 20

Under the weight of his helmet, Vorozheikin craned his neck carefully, systematically sweeping the sky. He had lost half his flight—more than necessary—and had heard nothing but faint missile launch signals from his other four Su-27s; far too few such signals. But, with the Tomcats dead, the Hornets were now his for the taking. He still had five AAMs left and White Knight 22 had four. The missile that NATO called AA-10A/B Alamo outranged the Hornets' Sidewinders, although the heat-seeking AA-11 Archer did not. The other Sukhoi formed up on his wing. Then the surviving *Varyag*

Flanker appeared in the southern distance, apparently vectored to the scene of the action by a ship-based controller or riding to the sound of the guns on guard freq. Either way, Vorozheikin admired the man's spirit.

Half a minute later, his search-mode radar display indicated four hostiles merging at 1,200 knots. *The fools,* Vorozheikin thought. *They're coming to meet me.*

Talent 500

"Talent Lead from Elvis Lead. Skippers away." Slattery looked at his watch, pleased at how quickly Elvis had reached his twelve-mile launch position. The deputy CAG had barely allowed himself to think the coordination might work this well—Elvis's Skippers with the Hornets' SLAMs. *I'd rather be lucky than good anytime.*

Slats thought it also helped to have good weapons. The greater accuracy of LGBs as opposed to unguided bombs enabled attackers to deliver ordnance outside the optimum range of *Varyag*'s close-in weapon systems.

Slattery could not see much of Elvis's run-in. But he saw the Skippers arc toward their target; then his view was obscured by a curtain of SAM exhausts as the carrier's starboard SA-N-9 launchers began unloading.

Varyag

I should really go back inside, if only for better communications, Rybakov thought. *In fact, I should leave Captain Gulaev on the bridge and go to CDC.* But he hungered for the direct sensory experience of combat. When the SAMs commenced firing, the admiral felt his heart jump into his throat. *Just a little longer,* he told himself.

Propelled by high-pressure air, SA-N-9s popped steadily from the carrier's six silo clusters, ignited and sped purposefully toward the inbound threats. Above and behind him on the island, the port forward Cross Sword MFC radar trained and elevated smoothly. It was splendid.

Talent 500

In the final moments before pop-up, Slats traded lita-
nies with Crunch. The familiar routine helped suppress fear.
As *Varyag*'s SA-N-9s passed their maximum effective range,
the SAMs self-destructed in gray-white clouds all around
Slats's bombers. He tried to ignore the flak.

Through the detonations and residual smoke, Slats
thought he could make out small cruise missile exhaust trails
crossing from right to left and top to bottom across his field
of view. He hoped it wasn't wishful thinking. Then he was
sure; a good-sized explosion blew large chunks of the carrier's island onto the flight deck and beyond. *Outstanding!
The first hit on a real aircraft carrier in forty-eight years,* he
exulted. He felt the joy settle, then mix with cool assessment
—he was surprised that a SLAM's 500-pound warhead could
have inflicted so much damage. *Must've had some fuel left.*

Varyag

Rybakov scanned the horizon with hand-held binoculars. There they were, the subsonic jet trails of incoming
antiship missiles. His heart missed a beat; looking at death,
he felt alive. *Probably Harpoons,* he judged, *but why no
chaff or jamming?* It wasn't incompetence; his CDC crew
was the best.

Rybakov counted six ALCMs—four diving and two hugging the waves. He was glad the Americans had never developed a heavyweight, supersonic antiship missile. *But then,
they had no need, before we got carriers.* Still, it was almost
insulting to attack *Varyag* with such puny weapons. As one
after another of the ALCMs was blown apart or tumbled out
of control into the sea, he wondered why it was necessary to
shoot down such an "incapable" missile, considering the
quantity and quality of the carrier's advanced electronic combat systems. *The Americans must have better ECCM than we
credited them.*

Now Shrikes arrived, preceding the ALCMs. The older
ARMs were noticeably slower and smokier than HARMs. As
Rybakov watched, a Shrike took out the port aft Cross Sword
MFC radar. He flinched instinctively. This was tedious, but

not disastrous. With three more Cross Swords, plus EO backups, the SAMs could still be guided.

Smirnov came outside and tried to drag his CO back into the deckhouse. At that moment, another missile hit near the Cross Sword platform just above the officers. The radar ceased turning, slumped over and threatened to crash on the wing. A high-velocity storm of hot, jagged metallic hail fell on the older men and the youthful lookout, followed by a gentle shower of sparks. They crossed their arms over their heads against the maiming, man-made weather. Pyotr Rybakov choked down the familiar, bilious taste of fear.

The lookout stared back out to sea while Rybakov and Smirnov gazed up at the wounded radar. "Duck!" the *matros* yelled, then threw himself to the plating. Rather than obeying the lad, his superiors turned to look in the direction he had been facing. In that instant, an ALCM penetrated the middle of the superstructure, through the louvers along the lower level of the uptakes. As the officers hit the deck, the missile exploded.

Large pieces of debris and a blast of hot air blew over Rybakov's head. He feared the wing might come loose, but the workmanship of the Nikolayev yard proved sound. In a few seconds the admiral felt his ship suffer another puncture and a deep, muffled detonation. *Goddamn it to hell!*

He found he could think as well as react; what he thought was, *Uptake. Waterline. Heat seekers—Standoff Land Attack Missile! That explains it.*

Talent 500

Despite his own cockpit chores, Slats saw two of Elvis Flight's four Skippers impact the ship. It looked as if Gonzo and Clint had hit their aimpoints; both elevators buckled upward.

The carrier had been well softened up; now it was up to the bombers to administer the *coup de grace.* The Skippers had powered into the starboard quarter; Slats's bombs were to dive through the flight deck. Slats remembered high school. *Like Coach Nibler taught: hit 'em high, hit 'em low.*

A storm of SAMs blew away from *Varyag* toward Talent Lead. Slats didn't flinch when exposed to the startling light and prospective horror of dozens of SAMs. Luckily, Pine

Tree 620 was still working, jamming like crazy. But he wished for some haze to hide in from the enemy's redundant optical guidance systems.

The A-6s were nearing the minimum effective range of the carrier's forest of SA-N-9s. Their Cross Sword fire-control systems also had been given the antiradar missile and ECM treatment, so posed a reduced threat. Still, Crunch found the exhaust trails streaking past him a little distracting. There was a slight chance that one would come within prox-fuse distance, assuming the missiles armed at this close range.

As Crunch watched, Dopey and Grumpy in Talent 505 were engulfed in a brilliant fireball. The blast wave rocked 500, but Crunch recovered smoothly, focusing on his job. Slats wasn't as sanguine, but talked himself through the crisis. *Save the grief for later.*

Suddenly the far edge of the carrier's flight deck erupted with flashes that could only be missile back-blasts; over a dozen smoky-white exhaust plumes snaked upward in Talent 500's general direction. There were too many trails to count. "Geeze!" Slats exclaimed over the hot mike. "The gomers got manpack SAMs. Break, break!" In response, deception flares blazed from the Intruders.

Two or three missiles headed for each A-6. The three guiding on Talent 500 took the bait and homed on the flares. Slats heard no damage reports; it looked as if they had lucked out again.

About four miles out, the A-6Es neared their pull-up points. Slats checked his armament panel, having set his ballistics computer for the proper interval and quantity of weapons release. From his file menu he selected the general loft attack, affording an accurate, survivable means of killing *Varyag.* Seconds later Crunch called, "Here we go!" and the CAG felt the onset of G-force as the Intruder pulled up at full power, looking for the maximum loft distance for its Mark 84s.

As the three survivors climbed, the 30mm Gatling guns opened up. It was clear that none of the carrier's fire-control radars was functional and that the Intruders were out of range, but the Russians might be able to track the A-6s optically when they nosed upward. Meanwhile, the gunners were resorting to good old reliable barrage fire.

Crunch concentrated on the intricacies of his attack profile, which, even with computer-assisted bombing, required precision. But he was not so intent on his job that he could ignore the muzzle flashes of all four starboard-side Gatlings blazing at him—twenty-four barrels each spewing nearly ten pounds of dense metal per second. He had been told that the effective radar-controlled range of the AK-630 system was 3,000 meters—about a mile and a half—so the Intruders, he figured, should be relatively safe. Since all *Varyag*'s gun-laying radars were being jammed, the CIWSes had to be optically aimed, further reducing accuracy. Still, every second, each six-barrelled gun threw fifty rounds toward him at 3,280 feet per second, so the chance of a hit was real.

Seemingly oblivious to the flak, Talent 510 managed to release all four Mark 83s while 502 lased the target. The bombs entered the "capture basket" of 502's laser beam; their gimballed seeker heads centered the bombs in the beam, controlling fins to adjust the Mark 83 LGBs' glide paths.

Despite the precision of the guidance system, two bombs fell short, detonating on impact with the Indian Ocean. They exploded simultaneously in a huge geyser that, combined with smoke and debris from other hits, might have interfered with 502's guidance. But the ship was making flank speed, and Slats expected the relative wind to disperse much of the smoke. He was right; the next two 1,000-pounders hit farther forward and more to port. Both punctured the flight deck and at least one went off inside the huge vessel. Smoke and flame shot from the holes like Roman candles on a lawn, visible evidence that the bombs had exploded on the hangar deck.

The flattop was wounded. Feeling like a hunter closing for the kill on a maddened lioness in tall grass, Slats Flight forged ahead.

With the big ship locked up on radar and FLIR, Crunch followed the steering commands in his sight until the yellow "in-range" lights began flashing. The pilot then pressed his "commit" trigger, and two seconds later the sight told him to pull up.

At thirty degrees nose high, the attack computer released the LGBs, which *thumped* off their racks microseconds apart.

Varyag

Rybakov knew more ordnance was headed his way, and decided to move inside—assuming he could move. He inhaled as deeply as possible while lying on his stomach; the smell of smoke, SAM fumes and burning electrical equipment singed his nasal membranes, eyes and throat. He had experienced enough. He looked at Smirnov and nodded toward the door. Steadying themselves on each other's shoulders, both men got stiffly to their knees. Two more hits aft and starboard in rapid succession flattened them again. Both bombs exploded powerfully. *Half-tonners,* Rybakov estimated, and glanced around. The lookout hadn't moved. His fingers were interlaced so tightly over his head that they had turned white; he was reciting prayers fluently. *Three-quarters of a century of socialism and a nineteen-year-old boy practices religion in front of his admiral on the Union's greatest warship,* Rybakov reflected. *Our system really is doomed. . . .*

Smirnov tugged on Rybakov's sleeve and started crawling toward the bridge. Two more impacts were each followed in a hundredth of a second by detonations. Rybakov felt his ship buck in agony; the plating warped beneath him. *Probably more half-tonners.* Then the admiral smelled burning jet fuel and knew the bombs had exploded on the hangar deck —a development too terrible to contemplate. "Shit!" he shouted, pounding the grating in rage.

Talent 500

From two miles away at 2,800 feet, *Varyag* looked ominous. Intellectually, Slats and Crunch knew that she was not quite as large as *Langley,* but emotionally—good Lord!— there was an enemy aircraft carrier, open to attack. The price of admission had been paid—three Intruders shot down. But now, bombs gone, *Langley*'s deputy CAG anticipated the payback.

Crunch never hesitated when the red breakaway lights began flashing in his sight. Smoothly coordinating the controls, he rolled into a 120-degree banked turn, dropping for the deck away from the rippling flak. For a moment he and Slats had an eerie, vulnerable feeling as they turned their

Intruder's exposed belly to *Varyag*'s guns. At that moment Talent 510 took over lasing duty from 502, which banked off to begin its own attack.

Meanwhile, 500's bombs found the basket and homed toward the 65,000-ton, burning target. Both weapons sliced diagonally across the smoky flight deck, from starboard quarter toward port bow. The one-ton Mark 84s were delay-fused, permitting them to penetrate the flight deck before detonating. They smashed through the overhead of the hangar and, hardly decelerating, pierced the next deck as well. Both erupted with incredible force within the confines of the carrier. Slats had only a vague impression of his LGBs' blast effects. *Nothing trivial, I hope.*

Ten seconds later Talent 502 released its ordnance. Either Bashful and Doc's aim had been spoiled by SA-16 and CIWS fire or the LGB's laser-seeking head was defective. Their first Mark 84 went straight into the ocean and exploded in the water twenty-five feet from the hull, where steel plates buckled under the concussion. But the second bomb glided smoothly along 510's laser beam, crashing through the angled deck, and . . . nothing. *Failure to detonate!* Slats choked down his fury. *Damn it to hell!*

Still turned in his seat, Slattery gawked at the geysering smoke and waterspouts from *Varyag*'s stern. The war whoop of elation died in his throat as 502 took an SA-16 hit and lurched visibly. "Bashful's hit," Slats told Crunch. "He's still behind us, but I don't know if he's gonna make it."

"Man, I don't know if *any* of us is gonna make it." The pilot jinked upward and starboard, slewing the Intruder erratically. He thought, *This must be how Luke Skywalker felt flyin' through the Death Star.* He shoved on the throttles again, but they were already against the stops.

Varyag

More long seconds passed. Then the boy unlaced his fingers and looked around. Rybakov saw him squirm as if he had wet his trousers. *Can't blame the lad,* the admiral allowed.

At least most of the air wing was aloft when this abortion happened. He tried to remember what planes were in the hangar, but couldn't. The admiral found himself thinking about the crewmen who already must have died. He envisioned men blown overboard by the first heavy hits aft—especially SA-16 missileers. But mostly he dwelt on his flagship. He feared the aft hits were on the elevators; that's where he would have aimed. *Air operations are still possible,* he thought, *if the hangar fires are contained to one bay.* Rybakov's mood swung again toward optimism. Anxious to hear damage reports, he tapped Smirnov and started to get up once more.

Then the 2,000-pounders struck.

0653
White Knight 20

Without a single friend or foe in sight, Vorozheikin felt he owned the sky. *My part of it, anyway,* he thought. The CAG knew that, to the west, four more Hornets continued south to cover the Intruders or attack *Varyag.* The F/A-18 flight that had been brash enough to attack his Flankers had been destroyed, but he was surprised at the cost—four Hornets armed only with Sidewinders for three Sukhois, armed with longer-ranged AAMs. But the aggressive F/A-18s had kept him away from the American strike planes. As far as he knew, only he was left now from *Kuznetsov*'s two flights. His calls to the second flight went unanswered, and he feared the worst.

With his few remaining weapons—one AA-11 missile on his port outer pylon and the 30mm gun in his starboard wingroot—he could not fight the surviving Intruders and Hornets, but he might be able to jump one of the Prowlers. If he could find them. He tried to raise any ship, but none responded. *All the radio-direction-finding equipment in the world down there, and I can't take advantage of it,* he thought, eaten by frustration. *I'd give my left foot for an An-74 right now.*

As he climbed to begin his lone Prowler hunt, Vorozheikin glimpsed ordnance impacts on *Varyag.* The sickening sight promptly doused his jubilation at destroying the enemy fighters. No matter how many Yankee pilots he killed, it was of little account if that fabulously expensive, brand-new capital ship were put out of action, taking hundreds or even thousands of Russian lives in the process.

*Kill the Prowlers and our remaining SAMs may be able
to kill the other Intruders and Hornets.* The urge for revenge
consumed him. Almost frantically, he tuned his scope and
radio-frequency signal analyzers, searching for any sign of
ECM aircraft.

Grim determination changed the chemistry of his brain
as Vorozheikin accelerated southeastward. He would not
have fuel left for the return to *Kuznetsov* but knew he could
recover in Africa—or eject over a Russian ship. Then
Varyag's fighter controller called him back. Fury reddened
his mind. Vorozheikin gritted his teeth, exhaled and obediently banked for home. He relaxed his muscles for the first
time in ten minutes.

Talent 500

Slats Slattery shook his head almost imperceptibly. On
his kneeboard were the call signs of the aircraft he had led
against the *Varyag* group. He knew that four of his A-6s and
a Prowler had splashed, and that five Tomcats and four Hornets—the whole of Brandy Flight—had failed to check in.
Fourteen of thirty-seven, Slats counted, including the two
F-14s that had safely shot down the first Mudhen and its two
escorts, but excluding the damaged or low-on-fuel that might
not make it home. He depressed the mike switch with his
foot. "Looks like I've lost about forty percent of the force."

Crunch nudged him with an elbow. "Slats, we sank a
cruiser and maybe a carrier. We did what we came to do."
He wondered whether to say what was on his mind. *You lose
people in a war. What did you expect?*

The deputy CAG leaned back, resting his helmet against
the seat for a moment. *I wonder how the other guys did up
north against* Novo?

Varyag

After the last impact, the bridge wing suddenly gave
way, half its bolts sheared by the violence of a secondary
explosion shuddering through the plating. The three terrified
occupants of the wing had slid forward, toward the edge. The
boy was screaming, but looked safe; Smirnov had also survived. Rybakov wasn't sure if the same could be said of his

ship. Even from his position, piled up against the bulkhead, he could tell that, below and aft, the flight deck was aflame. The smoke was suffocating.

Rybakov struggled crablike up the dangling wing toward the bridge, which appeared intact. Smirnov followed. People staggered carefully out to help them in. Rybakov was embarrassed to have lost his hat.

The admiral tried to use his still-fogged brain to count hits. He could recall four missile impacts on the superstructure and a similar number on the flight deck or hull. Despite the missile strikes on the island, he saw that the bridge remained functional. Windows were blown out; sailors struggled to lift a fallen overhead panel off their shipmates, but Captain Gulaev was talking to someone through a headset. A medic tried to get Rybakov's attention. "I'm all right," he told the aidman. "Attend someone who's hurt." The sailor looked at his superior dubiously, but obeyed.

When Rybakov had straightened up and regained his dignity, he asked for a report. *Varyag*'s skipper said that he had had communications with CDC, but did not yet know the fate of his tactical action officer or of any other staff officers there. The seaman in CDC he'd talked to was on oxygen; the *matros* told Gulaev the lights had gone out in CDC and torn cables had started a fire, the oily smoke of which seemed toxic. The captain had damage-control crews trying to get through. Rybakov wanted to follow them, but knew it wasn't safe. He asked Gulaev to go on.

"The report from the hangar deck's no better," the carrier skipper stated lugubriously. "Two half-ton or one-ton bombs detonated there. The second was more damaging; it blew up an Su-25 that hadn't been fully defueled. Burning jet fuel washed across the hangar bay. Pressure in the automatic fire-fighting systems was apparently halved or worse by the first bomb. Those two hits also must have fractured bulkheads and fuel lines and ignited some more fires and secondary explosions from ordnance and flammables. It's an inferno down there now. Damage-control says they don't know if they can put out the fuel-fed fires."

Though he had seen the flames with his own eyes, Rybakov felt as if he had been punched hard in the solar plexus. He couldn't speak; the wind had been knocked out of him. *This can't be happening.* He struggled to regain control of himself. *At least Gulaev is staying calm. I won't have to worry about hysteria on my flag bridge.* He swallowed hard before speaking, then asked, "Engineering?"

"Don't have a complete report yet," the captain first rank said, "but the missile hits on our uptakes blew out most of the boilers. Then a one-ton bomb penetrated to the propulsion spaces before detonating. Probably all four port boilers were destroyed and their two shafts and associated gears ruined. Maybe not. But right now we're coasting. We'll go dead in the water before we're able to relight the starboard boilers and see if their machinery works.

"Another one-tonner hit farther forward, near the angle. With the fires burning, it's hard to say what internal damage it added, but the hull and flight deck are torn apart out there. Even if we put out the fires, it'll probably take yard work to repair the damage enough to operate conventional aircraft," Gulaev concluded.

That must have been the one that nearly spilled Smirnov and me on the deck, Rybakov considered. "Very well, Captain," he said. "Sounds as if I may have to transfer my flag to *Kuznetsov.*"

"That may be advisable, sir," Gulaev agreed. "*Varyag* is not in danger of sinking, but neither are we an ideal platform from which to launch offensive operations, as I assume you wish to do."

"You assume correctly," the admiral replied in a steely tone. "Carry on."

Smirnov read from his notes. "First interceptors. Two *Varyag* Su-27s survived air combat over *Novorossiysk* and are returning. They'll have to land in the Transkei to refuel, then proceed to *Kuznetsov.* Same applies to the four *Varyag* fighters inbound from escorting the morning land-attack missions. All but one of the other *Varyag* interceptors were shot down by the Americans. It appears only one of the eight *Kuznetsov* Sukhois detached to reinforce our CAP remains. With the fourteen still on *Kuznetsov,* that gives us a total of twenty-two, if those airborne all make land safely. Some have battle damage or are low on fuel. *Kuznetsov* has tankers headed our way."

Less than half our original complement, Rybakov realized. *Most lost within an hour.* "Continue," the admiral ordered.

"The situation is much better for attack aircraft. I don't yet know *Novorossiysk*'s Yak losses, but some returning from air-support strikes in Natal diverted to *Leningrad*. Two ran low on fuel and landed in Transkei. The U.S. strike cost us the six Su-25s being replenished on *Varyag*. Our two carrier air divisions had previously lost five on air-support missions or to operational accidents—*Varyag* two and *Kuznetsov* three. So, assuming they all reach *Kuznetsov*, thirty-seven Rooks remain."

"Good," Rybakov said. "I intend to use them against *Langley*."

Smirnov weighed whether to comment, then asked, "What about our air-support obligations?"

"Anatoly Vladimirovich," Rybakov replied, "are you afraid to go after the Americans?"

"Certainly not, Admiral," the stunned captain responded, "but I believe our orders . . ."

"Have been changed. Since 0530 the American battle group has been our main enemy. I always considered it such. In any case, my orders are now clear. Our primary mission is to destroy *Langley*, then turn to meet *Eisenhower*, in cooperation with submarines and land-based air. Planning for the attack is to begin immediately."

"Yes, sir," the chastened chief of staff said, "but we don't even know where *Langley* is yet, or where it will move."

"The job of your intelligence department is to find out."

"From here, Admiral?"

"We may have to shift our flag."

I should have thought that was obvious, Smirnov considered. *I suppose it's hard for him to admit defeat, even if it's only tactical. After all,* Varyag *is the newest, biggest and most expensive ship in our navy.*

"Thanks, Anatoly Vladimirovich," Rybakov said, in a tone calculated to compensate for his earlier sternness. The admiral felt his self-confidence returning; he was overcoming the physical and moral shocks of the past hour and regaining control of himself and his forces. He knew his first decision must be whether to try to fight from *Varyag* or transfer his flag. To the carrier's skipper, he yelled, "Gulaev, you and Smirnov carry on here. I'm going to inspect the ship. I want complete reports when I return."

"As you wish, Admiral," Gulaev said, "but it's dangerous."

"Are we going to blow up any time soon?"

"No, sir," the captain replied. "I've flooded the magazines and the boilers are out."

"You have enough helicopters left to fly me and my staff off the ship, do you not? And the fo'c'sle is not on fire, is it?"

"Admiral, we have three operational helos fueled and ready, with more inbound from other ships, but the fire might spread or overheat the forward plating. The takeoff ramp limits our helo spaces forward."

"I'll be able to find out what I need to know promptly," he said, then grabbed a breathing apparatus and ventured down the ladder.

"He knows what his decision will be," Smirnov told Gulaev. "He just has to spend a few minutes to convince himself."

0659

At the bottom of the ladder, Rybakov decided Gulaev was right. Smoke was boiling up from the end of the passage. It was like an oven holding a giant burnt roast. The oxygen mask made matters worse. In anger and frustration, he pounded a fist on the hot bulkhead. *Don't let the rage overpower you,* he reminded himself. *Use it, control it, channel it.*

The deck was slippery with flame-retardant foam. Struggling to make himself understood through the mask, he ordered an asbestos-gloved damage-control officer to open the hatch letting out onto the catwalk. It wasn't working, so he pulled off his apparatus. "I know you don't want to let in the air, Lieutenant," he said, then took a breath. "You can close it behind me." The junior officer reluctantly obeyed. The hatch was warped, but opened widely enough for the admiral to squeeze through, holding the mask to his face.

The air was scarcely better outside. Rybakov saw that the fires burning up from the hangar deck hadn't subsided, but were smokier. He surveyed aft; the carrier he was accustomed to seeing in pristine condition was wrecked. Even having survived the American air strike, having seen and felt and smelled the results, he was appalled by *Varyag*'s condition. *It's like looking at another ship completely*, he thought. The twisted, blackened steel of missile impacts stood out, deforming the once-familiar silhouette of the brand-new vessel. *They've ruined my ship!* He had never hated Americans, only envied their naval air force. But now he resolved they would pay.

He banged on the hatch with a fire axe.

14

0700 to 1706, Friday, 4 June

0700 Pretoria; 2300 EDT
White House

"They've wiped out Diego Garcia and Ascension Island," Admiral Fernandez said. The CNO shakily replaced the phone in its cradle. "No word on casualties."

"How'd they do it?" Callaway asked. He bit off the words.

"Apparently with their new SS-N-24 cruise missiles, fired from Yankee Notch attack subs. That's an older SSBN converted from a boomer to a shooter—in violation of SALT."

"So what else is new?" Callaway sneered. "Anything else?"

"Well, just that the missiles are more versatile than we imagined. Before we lost communications, Dee Gar reported at least four types—runway-cratering munitions, radar-homing, an incendiary version . . ." Fernandez paused . . . "and chemicals."

"They gassed us?" Callaway screamed, rising from his chair.

"First reports are always wrong," Epstein interjected.

347

"The alleged gas could have come from ruptured storage tanks or . . ."

"No, Doctor," CNO replied. "The agent was liquid droplets, not gas. And we got a similar report from Ascension."

Callaway slumped back in his chair. "Okay. We'll play the diplomatic game with 'strenuous objections.' Art, that's your bag." He looked at Fernandez. "What do you recommend, Hub?"

"Well, sir, we can't hit back at Eurasian territory. How 'bout hitting their friends? Like the bomber bases in Angola and Madagascar?"

The President leaned back in his chair. "Do it."

0701 Pretoria; 0801 Local
Killer 530, Indian Ocean

"Sleaze, we're not gonna make it. Prepare to eject." Outbound from the *Novorossiysk* strike, Brillo Huggins was surprised the battered Intruder had lasted this long. He surmised that the Archer missile had detonated just beyond lethal range, but blast and fragments had punctured a fuel cell and badly damaged the tail. He and "Jet Mormon" Olsen had computed the time-distance equation twice now, and each time they'd come up short. If they didn't crash they would run out of fuel.

Brillo made the call on the guard frequency. "This is Killer 530. We have heavy damage and are ejecting four-zero miles west of Point Bravo. Killer 530, over." There was no reply, so he called once more.

"Uhh, roger, 530. This is Fortune. I have your posit. Am outbound with two Ramparts. A Pine Tree also is down near the target. Will relay SAR info immediately. Good luck, guy."

Brillo suddenly felt better, then wondered why. *Only two Hornets and just one A-6 clearing the target. Christ, the Russians even bagged a Prowler.* He briefly wondered if anybody else got away. Then he asked Sleaze, "You ready?"

The B/N finished cleaning up his side of the cockpit, then braced himself in the seat. "Ready to eject," he said in a voice that belied his emotions.

Brillo reached up, grasped the face curtain over his

head with both hands and forced his elbows together. "Will eject, eject, eject!" On the third count he pulled hard.

An instant later both seats punched through the glass canopy, Sleaze's slightly before Brillo's. The crushing onset of twelve rocket-boosted Gs brutally compressed both men. It was far worse than either had imagined. But then they separated from their seats, their parachutes snapped open and they were pulled up short, dangling 10,000 feet over the Indian Ocean. Killer 530 descended eastward to its fate.

Each flier checked his own chute and his companion's. Satisfied, they began the prelanding procedure. They disconnected their oxygen masks and let them drop. Brillo removed his gloves and stuffed them in his torso harness, while Sleaze kept his on. Both men pulled the beaded handles at their waists and were gratified when their flotation devices inflated.

Sleaze watched in fascination as the ocean came up to greet him. At the last moment he remembered to bring his legs together and to watch the horizon. Some aviators, concerned about chute entanglement, have been known to release their parachute risers before splashdown—several hundred feet before.

When Brillo hit the water, he was almost disappointed. It had been so peaceful, dangling quietly in midair. But immediately he was busy with more procedure. His canopy settled over him like a white tent spread on the water, and he began carefully backing out of it, reaching behind and passing the material hand over hand. But there was no end of it; he seemed draped in suffocating, waterlogged nylon. Brillo fought down the panic. He turned his head to look back and his chin struck a riser. He realized that one fitting had not separated on contact with saltwater, as intended. He unsnapped the Koch fitting and in seconds was free of the canopy.

Brillo and Sleaze had landed less than 300 yards apart. They sculled toward each other, inflated their individual rafts and, with some difficulty, crawled aboard. Then they lashed the rafts together and sat back, breathing deeply. Brillo had a weird thought: *I'll have to get another Tailhook card.* The organization's magazine had published a short account of his long-ago peacetime ejection, saying that a new, waterproof membership card would be issued with the warning, "Trashing of our attack assets is not approved." *What'll they say this time?* he wondered.

0714
Southwestern Outskirts of Vryheid, Natal

Major Snodgrass's jeep hurried south on Wes Street, which becomes the road to Babanango Aerodrome. Just out of town, he found Vorster's command section sheltering in a ditch along the road. He climbed out of his jeep, stood over Vorster and said, "Had a nice morning jog, I see."

About a kilometer off, a huge explosion shocked the air. Earth and flame geysered; smoke billowed. "Last of our petrol, I should suppose. Hope it doesn't spread to the diesel." Snodgrass squatted on the edge of the pavement and opened a map.

It annoyed Vorster that the staffer wouldn't get down in the ditch. *Probably more worried about keeping his uniform clean than getting shredded by mortar fragments.*

"Here's the situation," Snodgrass explained, still speaking English. "The aerodrome was seized by Viet and Russian heliborne companies early Saturday morning. The Vryheid Commando winkled the air-assault troops off the airfield on the 31st. Yesterday, the Viet motor rifle brigade kicked us off the heights east of town, but the territorial troopies stopped its ground assault on the airfield. At great cost, as you shall see.

"Your company is to rush across the tarmac to take up positions here, in the middle of the line." Snodgrass turned to indicate landmarks to guide Vorster toward the position. "We still hold Lancaster Hill, Height 1472, north of town." He twisted around again and pointed to the knob overlooking Vryheid. "Our defense line runs through the city and south-southeast along Route 34, past the aerodrome.

"It's a frontage of 8,000 meters, held by a reinforced battalion of 800 men, counting your lot. That's about one-tenth the textbook prescription for such a situation. Our saving grace may be the condition of the enemy. He's short on mortar and arty ammo."

Could have fooled me, Vorster thought.

"It appears we have the Zulus to thank for that,"

Snodgrass added. "Their raids on the Viet supply lines have hurt the invader badly."

Vorster snorted. "Just a different kind of cattle raid to the thieving Kaffirs."

"Most ungracious of you, old boy," Snodgrass said. "Regardless of supply problems, the Viets' mortar batteries alone have made the aerodrome nearly useless. They save most of their ammo for when aircraft arrive." He indicated each position. "The mortars are backed up by the brigade's three howitzer batteries and a BM-21 battery situated farther east, below the great mesa of Hlobane." He pointed north by northeast, into the valley holding the R69. "Hlobane's the central rise of a ridge that overlooks and controls Route 69.

"In case you're unfamiliar with local history," Snodgrass digressed in typical fashion, "I might add that Hlobane was the scene of the last Zulu victory in the 1879 war. In fact, Vryheid is surrounded by battle sites from the Zulu and Boer wars, but I fear you won't have much time for sight-seeing this trip. You're here to make history, not visit it, more's the pity."

"D-30s?" Vorster asked, ignoring the history lecture. He had learned to respect the highly mobile 122mm Russian howitzer, capable of accurately hurling forty-eight-pound HE rounds over fifteen kilometers.

"Mmm, yes. I fear counterbattery fire is quite out of the question, except against the mortars. Without our own G-5 or G-6s or *Valkiris*, they have us outranged. We've put in for air strikes, but there's quite a long queue for air support. Our situation resembles nothing so much as Dien Bien Phu," he commented with inappropriate cheerfulness. "But not to worry. This time the enemy's supply lines are not secure.

"The Viet is also running low on infantry. It's fortunate he split his mechanized corps, or we should have been quite run over, don't you know? Only two of his five maneuver brigades have come our way. It appears his other two motor rifle brigades and the tank brigade stayed north of the Pongola, swung west out of Swaziland and attacked toward Piet Retief. That's over a hundred road kilometers north of Vryheid on the R33. And it seems he's committed his corps-level support weapons to the Transvaal. It should take at least a day to turn them and advance within range of us.

"The rough bit is that his other motor rifle brigade operating in Natal is now headed our way along Road 618. It advanced south and crossed below the Pongolapoort Dam yesterday. It's mounted in tracked BTR-50s rather than eight-wheeled BTR-60 APCs and supported by the usual forty T-55s."

"I'm familiar with both BTRs," Vorster replied testily. He knew from direct experience that the old armored personnel carriers and 100mm-gunned T-55 tanks were still useful.

"Quite, well, yes, you would be, wouldn't you? Of course it also has a battalion of D-30s and a battery of BM-21s, but the Zulus have ravaged its supply lines as well as those through Swaziland. They work both sides of the Lebombos. I should like to shake their hands someday."

"Kaffirs are Kaffirs."

" 'Fraid I can't agree with you there, old boy." Snodgrass got back in the jeep. "Meet you at the freight hangars."

Vorster was glad to see the jeep go. He still didn't believe the enemy was low on ammo.

0725 Pretoria; 0825 Local
Langley

Phil Ray could stand it no longer. He eased out of the captain's chair and walked onto the port wing, scarcely hearing the watch officer call, "Captain is off the bridge." Without conscious effort, Ray turned his gaze to the point in the sky where the jets would appear. And there they were.

Singly and in pairs, the survivors of the *Novorossiysk* strike dropped into the landing pattern. *Good boys,* Ray thought. Despite the stress of recent combat 500 miles from their ship, the pilots kept the pattern tight—"lookin' good around the boat" counts for a lot for carrier aviators.

The Intruder and three Hornets passed by the ship at 800 feet on their downwind leg as Ray saw wheels, flaps and tailhooks lowered in the crosswind turn. The jets held their reciprocal heading from the carrier, darkly silhouetted against the white cumulus. Then, with proper spacing, each plane bent into a continuous left-hand turn to maintain sight of the flight deck and acquire the landing mirror. Killer 532 was first aboard, and Ray felt a pang as he realized the other three A-6s were missing. *Three F/A-18s out of six, one of two Prowlers and the Hawkeye still inbound.* Ray bit his lip as Bronco 411 boltered, added power and went around. *We've lost half the deception group. Christ, I hope it was worth it.*

0729
Babanango Aerodrome, South of Vryheid

Vorster waved his tired troops toward the company's position. He counted eighty men scurrying into trenches, earthworks and bunkers, where most promptly collapsed. Then Major Snodgrass drove up and offered a lift. Vorster declined; he preferred to inspect the defenses on foot.

"Jolly good," the irrepressible Brit said. "Mind if I come along?" Vorster knew it would do no good to resist. Leaving his exec in charge, he hustled off with his radioman and Snodgrass to survey the position.

The three men passed hideously distorted and bloated corpses stripped of weapons and ammo. The race of the grotesque bodies was often unclear. Here and there, pairs appeared to have died in each other's embrace. The stench of human effluvia and burnt and rotting flesh made Vorster gag. The radioman, straining under his heavy load, tripped and nearly fell over a string of entrails from a disembowled corpse.

They reached the cover of a burnt-out bunker. The device on Vorster's belt, resembling a beeper or TV channel-changer, sounded and flashed colored lights. "Gas!" he yelled, and began to pull on a mask, secretly glad to filter the air he had to breathe.

"Just residual," Snodgrass said reassuringly. "We believe they've shot their wad in that department."

The members of the section looked unconvinced. Vorster was embarrassed by his reaction to the alarm. *Long night,* he told himself.

"Don't bother with the masks," the major continued, trying not to gloat. "It was a nonpersistent blood agent. They wanted to break through here and did. We counterattacked immediately and cleared them out. You have to counterattack promptly. They crawl like reptiles to get in, then dig like badgers to stay."

Vorster looked around. Smoke obscured what would

have been a magnificent view of the Drakensbergs. Ahead, the eastern hills, partially shrouded and backlit by the rising sun, struck him as beautiful, yet he knew they sheltered enemy mortar batteries.

"They came at us last night in this sector with three reinforced mechanized battalions and at least a company of assault engineers," Snodgrass continued. "The Natal territorial boys stood but were overrun—middle-aged men, actually. We counterattacked with the first Citizen Force contingent to arrive. This morning it was hand-to-hand in the dark. Groping with sharpened entrenching tools. Terrible, but it was only one night. Offensive and defensive technologies tend to cancel out each other, don't you know?"

"Spare me the philosophy, staffer."

"The Natal Commandos did well, but they're completely shattered. We had to pull out those left—not many." The major's voice trailed off. Vorster could see that Snodgrass was not as boyishly chipper as before. "Yes, well, the sergeant here"—Snodgrass indicated a staff NCO standing outside a sandbagged ammo-storage bunker—"has some antitank weapons for you. Each section is to draw three LAWs and one RPG with three rounds from him."

I'll be damned! thought Vorster. *The little bugger came through.*

Snodgrass noted Vorster's reaction, but was too tired to rub in his logistical success. "Your frontage is 1,000 meters," he said matter-of-factly, "with a company on either side. We want you to hold this position with two platoons up and one back with your mortars. Form tank-hunting teams with a section of the reserve platoon and your antitank section."

Vorster took umbrage at this elementary instruction, but held his tongue. "Who's on my right and left?"

"What remains of van Hoek's company on the right— don't know who has it now—and Vlok on the left. Now, Colonel Lubbers is going to take a section from Vlok to form a last-ditch reserve . . . so you may have to reinforce them."

"Bloody hell! With what? Best wishes?"

"Mortar fire, if nothing else. My advice is to dig deep, patch up these fortifications. Intel don't know if they'll come through here again in the next round or hit us somewhere else, but be prepared, that's my motto."

A 120mm mortar bomb detonated nearby, showering the section with mud. The soldiers hugged the earth. Four more rounds bracketed them. "Spread out," Vorster told his command team.

Snodgrass whistled. "Good job they weren't airburst. Well, must be off."

"I'll say," Vorster threw in; too good an opportunity to pass up.

"Boer humor. Colonel Lubbers should be on to you in a bit, with sappers to help you emplace mines. The Viets cleared most of the first batch and went through the wire as if it weren't there. You'll find they're frightfully good combat engineers. Probably the best in the world, after the Russians."

"What do you think this is, some bloody kind of Olympic event?"

"Well, know your enemy, I always say. In the Viets' case, know and respect. They're not just good sappers; they're first-rate in all the arts of war. The most experienced soldiers on earth, don't you know? Fighting more or less continuously for three generations."

"Do you really think I have time to chat with the enemy? I'm only going to shoot out their slanted eyes."

"Suit yourself. You'll see I'm right."

"Don't let me keep you, Major," the insubordinate Boer captain replied.

Snodgrass said, "Well, good hunting."

As he continued his inspection, Vorster studied the eastern peaks. He imagined twenty-four mortars sited on ledges on four of those hills, with yellow and black men in machine-gun nests dug in below them. The Boer remembered the only mountain vacation he and his family had ever taken. That was in Dundee, southwest of Vryheid. Then the hills held only resort lodges. White women in flower-print dresses graced their balconies, while black men tended the gardens below.

The way it should be, Vorster thought. *The way it can be again.*

0800 Pretoria; 0900 Local
Langley

From the bridge, Captain Phil Ray surveyed the pande-
monium below and grunted his approval. The launch had
gone exactly on schedule, cycling four more fighters up to
the CAP stations. The daily air plan called for the relieved
CAP birds to recover with the returning strike force. Ray
double-checked the "spot" on the deck, noting that two
Tomcats each from VF-181 and -182 were parked in the "six-
pack" area on ready-alert status.

Ray turned to his air boss. "Bert, we should be recovering the *Varyag* strike group in about ten minutes. But I want
to keep the deck clear for emergencies. With only four Turkeys airborne on ForceCAP we may have to reinforce on
short notice. It isn't enough, but something's gotta give."

In Gideon's Tactical Flag Command Center, Nate Gottlieb looked again at the theater map, then turned to the
battle group commander. "Okay, boss. The strike should be
recovered in half an hour. Then where do we go?" Though it
was asked in a jocular tone, both men knew it was the most
important question Gideon would answer that day.

"Northwest," the admiral replied, his mind clearly already made up. "I want us up here, ASAP." He poked a
finger onto the map at a point southwest of Madagascar and
east of northern Natal.

The CSO was taken aback. Ordinarily the admiral would
ask for a variety of options—that was what staffs were for.
"So you mean to keep the rendezvous with *Carl.*" Gottlieb
had expected something more daring from an old seadog like
Gideon. "Sure you don't want to consider the other—"

"Unnecessary." Gideon patted Gottlieb's shoulder in a
gesture of understanding. "I know the alternatives, Nate. We
could head west to follow up the *Varyag* group and be in
position to intercept *Kuznetsov* if she moves north. But
that'd only put us well within range of land-based air and
expose us to more subs." He tapped the right edge of the
map. "Or we could do what Spruance did at Midway—disengage eastward and be satisfied with our handiwork.

"But as I understand things, our priority is to support a
landing on Africa. That means protecting the amphibs. Now,
I see two ways of doing that. One approach says the best

defense is a good offense. Instead of waiting for *Kuznetsov* to come north and break up the landing, maybe even wipe out the 'phibs, we turn south, head him off and hit first. Plus, we put more ocean between us and the Backfires. We bloody Rybakov's nose, slow him up and maybe get sunk ourselves.

"The other method is more a passive defense, which is what I've decided to do—head northwest to cover the Phib-Gru."

"That's kind of uncharacteristic, isn't it?"

"Uncharacteristic of what? Of my usual aggressiveness?" Before Gottlieb could reply, Gideon went on. "Earlier, my best judgment was to be offensive. Now I think we have a better chance of accomplishing our mission by pulling back, putting distance between us and *Kuznetsov*. It buys the 'gators the day they need to get close enough to land. If I could be sure of wiping out the Russian group south of here, I'd do it. But I can't be sure. Now, as my chief of staff, tell me if I've missed something."

"I'm not implying you've lost your nerve, Admiral. But doesn't moving closer to Madagascar make it easier for the enemy to find us?"

"Yeah, I thought about that, too," Gideon said. "If we move northwest, southern Madagascar comes within range of our land-attack Tomahawks. With luck, the BGM-109s could wipe out a lot of MiGs, Madcaps and Bears on the ground. At least we make the airfields unusable for a day."

Gottlieb quickly added up the TLAM-C loadouts of *Los Angeles*-class sub *Eureka* and the CVBG's two *Ticonderoga*-class cruisers. He knew these thirty-one cruise missiles would suffice to hit the seven fighter, AWACS and maritime patrol bases in the southern third of the island. Attacks on all these targets had already been plotted at Tomahawk Mission Planning Centers ashore. The Data Transfer Devices—hard disks holding mission data—had been flown out to *Langley* from Diego Garcia days ago and distributed to launching ships by helo.

"The aggressive move really tempted me," Gideon admitted, "but turning south to meet *Kuznetsov* means exposing our reduced force to combined-arms warfare—the Russians' specialty. Then we'd have to fight not only Backfires from the north but the *Kuznetsov* group's surface- and sub-launched missiles and aircraft, plus maybe land-based

Su-24s. It would increase the risk from torpedoes, too, given the greater density of subs in that direction."

"Okay, boss, you've sold me," Gottlieb said.

Bubba Ballantine, an observer to the conversation, spoke up. "I'm for it, too," said the CAG, hoping he didn't sound sycophantic. "We'll be positioned to launch ground-support missions or even to fly the air wing ashore if necessary. Incidentally, Admiral, we've had confirmation from the South Africans. Contingency plans are in effect to receive our birds at dispersed fields on the Natal coast."

"Good deal," Gideon said with feeling. "The cruisers should be in range early this afternoon," Gideon observed. "We can't risk running *Eureka* that fast, so she'll have to mop up later. Enemy defenses will be alerted by *Grouper*'s attack on the north end of the island this morning, so target as many antiaircraft sites as you can in the first wave."

"That's affirm," Gottlieb responded.

Ballantine eyed his watch and said, "Slats should be approaching marshal just about now, Admiral."

"Very well. After they're all aboard, we'll come to our new heading," Gideon concluded. "Now let's get to work."

0928 Local

"Well, it could have been worse," Gideon said. Instantly he hated himself for voicing the sentiment. *Thirty-nine men are dead or missing.* He looked at the officers seated around his table. Bubba Ballantine was expressionless; Slats Slattery, moments out of the cockpit, bit his lower lip as if stifling a reply.

The losses were in: seven Intruders, five Tomcats, seven Hornets and two Prowlers. The replacement cost of those twenty-one planes exceeded the production cost of a B-2 stealth bomber.

Gideon decided on a more upbeat approach. "Looks as if you guys might have sunk the battlecruiser, and Rybakov may lose his carrier, Slats. We'll know more when we see the TARPS pictures." Down in the photo lab the damage-assessment film was being processed from Circus 210's Tactical Aerial Reconnaissance Pod System.

Gottlieb interjected, "Admiral, we think there are ten or more bomber regiments headed our way. We'll need to keep the deck hot with recycling fighters, and we'll have to coordinate with the SAM shooters as well."

"That's affirm." Gideon consulted his notes. "Bubba, you know the plan for missile defense of the battle group, but let's not take anything for granted. I've ordered the Aegis ships to rendezvous with *Roseburg* and reload their launchers with Standard SAMs.

"Slats, your folks need to be ready for another launch ASAP. Have you had time to decide how to run it?"

Slattery perked up. "My tactics panel already has contingencies drafted. Don't worry, sir: we'll have a different wrinkle to show the Russians next time."

Gottlieb had been holding back but now decided he could wait no longer. "Ah, Admiral. Excuse me, but there's a growing personnel problem you need to be aware of."

Gideon turned, seemingly to ward off the blow. "Let's have it, Nate."

Gottlieb cleared his throat. "Well, sir, there have been some cases that technically constitute mutiny, and one of sabotage." The CSO hastened to finish the unpleasant task. "You know about the chief who's been giving the Russians satellite info. But additionally, one A-6 pilot downed his bird before launch when apparently nothing was wrong. An E-2 controller has discovered religion and now says he won't participate in the deaths of other humans. And a black plane handler was caught throwing ball bearings into an F/A-18's intakes. The plane captain, who is also black, beat the shit out of him." Gottlieb suppressed a smile. "The PC called the handler a 'professional nigger'; the division officer says he's a troublemaker."

Gideon rubbed his chin. "What's the disposition of these cases?"

"The exec is coordinating with the legal department and master-at-arms. Technically, the A-6 driver hasn't committed an offense until it's proven he knowingly downed a good bird. But his CO has grounded him and banned him from the ready room. And Commander Burch gave his E-2 controller a chance to reform, but he refused. So Burch assembled as many officers as possible and stripped the kid of his wings and squadron nameplate—everything but cutting off his buttons and breaking his sword. The controller broke down and was dragged out blubbering."

"What about the sailor with the ball bearings?"

"He's in the brig with Odum and the controller, awaiting disposition."

Gideon leaned forward, his neck veins pulsing. "Tell Hyers that I want these cases wrapped up airtight. No loopholes, no excuses. Clear?"

The air wing photo officer, Lieutenant Commander LeGarre, walked in with a handful of damp strike photos. He sensed the tension in the room and looked at Gideon. *The admiral's really steamed about something. Maybe these will cheer him up.* One of Gideon's fellow Trekkies, he grinned as he laid out the first shot. "Excuse me, Admiral, but look at this. A Romulan battlecruiser adrift in the Neutral Zone!"

Gideon turned the photo for a better look. It was *Andropov,* burning and listing. "You've got it wrong, Arch. Those people are the Klingons of Planet Earth." Gideon managed a tight smile.

The phone buzzed and Gottlieb picked it up. He listened for six seconds and responded, "Stand by one." The CSO looked over his shoulder. "It's CDC, Admiral. The northern E-2 reports Badgers inbound from Madagascar."

0834 Pretoria; 0934 Local
Over Mozambique Channel, southwest of Madagascar

Captain of Aviation Yuri Bulgakov squirmed in the left seat of his thirty-year-old Tupolev. Though he resented his second-class status as a Tu-16 pilot, Bulgakov harbored a grudging affection for the aging bomber the Americans called Badger. *Not a bad name,* he mused. *A ferocious carnivore.* Then he recalled that badgers also were prized for their pelts.

Bulgakov took little comfort in presumably being escorted by Vietnamese MiG-23s. He had flown from Cam Ranh Bay after the Americans left. Should have let the capitalists keep them, he told himself. Money-grubbing little yellow monkeys.

The Badgers had cleared the southwest coast of Madagascar 20,000 feet below without hearing from their ground controller. Nor in subsequent minutes did Bulgakov receive information over data link from any Tu-20 maritime patrol aircraft—big turboprops named Bear D by NATO. Three were supposed to be operating over the Southwest Indian Ocean, locating targets for his regiment and the Tu-16s out of Angola. The Tu-20s' I/J-band search and targeting radars were much more powerful than those in Bulgakov's Tu-16. The squadron leader was beginning to get nervous. As he considered breaking radio silence to make a query, he heard a strident call on his ICS.

"Electronics officer to pilot! We have radar-warning signals from two quadrants!" There was anxiety in Pushkin's voice.

"What quadrants, you idiot!" Bulgakov wanted information, not panic. There was a long pause.

"South and southwest. Consistent with F-14 fire-control radar."

That was better. "Are we targeted?"

"Uh, no. Not yet. I . . ."

Bulgakov cut off Pushkin. "Navigator, how far to expected launch position?"

The reply shot back immediately. "Sixty-five miles, Captain."

Damn, damn, damn. The Tomcats might have time to shoot the formation to pieces, and Bulgakov knew they would start with the jamming aircraft. He leaned forward, squinting against the sunlight in a futile effort to see something.

"Where are our goddamn escorts?"

0935 Local

In CDC, Gideon asked, "What do we have up, Brad?"

Commander Thaxter glanced at Bubba Ballantine, technically his superior charged with battle group air ops. But the four-striper nodded to Thaxter, who acknowledged. "Admiral, we have Buzzard's division up here in the northern quadrant"—he traced a halo around a symbol indicating the VF-181 CO's four Tomcats—"and a Circus section is outbound."

Gideon's green eyes flicked back and forth in the darkened room. "Why are the two Circus birds heading southwest?"

Ballantine jumped in. "My call, sir. I ordered the VF-182 birds to hook left for an end-around in case the Badgers split. Experience shows that Soviet Naval Aviation seldom goes for a single-axis attack. We may lose some initial contact time if they don't diverge, but in either case we'll have 'em in a Phoenix crossfire."

On the tactical display panel, Thaxter illuminated a high-speed contact outbound from southern Madagascar. "Admiral, we make this a squadron-sized force of Floggers, apparently meant to escort the Badgers. Radio intercepts indicate it's a Vietnamese MiG-23 unit."

Gideon showed extra interest. "Vietnamese—that's right, they've been there a while now. Just like old times, right, Bubba?" Everybody knew what the admiral meant. He and Ballantine were the only men in the room with combat experience dating from 1972.

"I sincerely hope not, Admiral."

"Hey, we were winning when I left. CAG Eggert and VA-147 kicked some serious butt." Gideon turned back to Thaxter. "Brad, it's clear to me the Floggers aren't going to intercept the Gunshot guys in time to prevent Phoenix launch. What do you make of this?"

Thaxter had a phone to one ear, raising a hand for silence. Moments later he turned to Gideon. "Admiral, real-time voice intercepts show the Russian Madcap controller is having a hard time with the Floggers. Apparently there are language difficulties." Thaxter chuckled aloud. "Whale Watch reports he called the MiG leader in patient Russian and said, 'Turn right. Turn right. No, you idiot, your *other* right!'"

Gideon pointed to the screen and said, "Okay, we're getting some Phoenix shots. There—two blips just dropped off the scope. But can we hold 'em?"

Ballantine eyeballed the geometry of the situation. "Admiral, we'll splash most of the Badgers, and the Floggers seem confused. I'd say so far, so good."

0936 Local
Bronco 401

Commander Jonathan "Lights" Leyden confirmed radar designation of his target and fired two Sparrows. Both AIM-7s fell free, the lanyards popped and the rocket motors ignited. One failed to guide but the other rode the beam as

Lights kept his Hornet pointed northwest, illuminating the targeting Bear. Lights watched the AIM-7 streak toward the snooping turboprop; he hoped it hadn't already found targets and alerted the Badgers.

As CO of VFA-184, Leyden agreed with Admiral Gideon. "I'd rather shoot Indians than their arrows" was the common philosophy of battle group defense. It was far more efficient to destroy enemy bombers before they fired their antiship missiles, which of course were much harder to destroy. *But you don't always get that chance,* Leyden realized. Almost as good as downing cruise-missile shooters was killing target-designating Bear-Ds.

A bright flash appeared in the atmosphere, ten miles or more ahead. Lights's heart leapt. *Got him!* He saw a flaming tumble of burning fuel and sunlit aluminum.

The controller confirmed the splash and ordered the section back toward the battle group. Lights knew what was coming. The Badgers, already being intercepted by Tomcats, would take heavy casualties. But some would get through. They always did. Even in war games.

0837
Gold Pawn 68, over the Southwest Indian Ocean

The casually clad Helix pilot leaned forward against his shoulder harness, compressing his beer-belly paunch. He turned to his copilot. "Do you see that smoke on the horizon?" The other flier squinted in the direction indicated—just north of east. A faint wisp traced the sky.

"Yes, I see it now." The copilot was amazed at Vasily Yegorov's vision. It seemed almost as acute as the helo's targeting radar, which had locked on to the American ship moments before.

"And another, there to the southeast?" Yegorov asked.

"Ah, oh, yes," the copilot lied. "Now I do."

"Obviously, two of the enemy destroyers have been hit by our cruise missiles," Yegorov said. He checked his fuel gauges. *Almost 175 miles from Frunze,* he thought. *We can't stay here any longer.* "I'd like to get closer for a good look, but we can't risk it. Our mission is complete." He put his ungloved hands and tennis-shoed feet on the controls, shaking the stick to resume command. "Notify the ship to send the contact report. We're returning to base."

0845
Badger squadron, over the Southern Mozambique Channel

Yuri Bulgakov could hardly believe he was still alive, though he doubted he would remain so much longer. Half his comrades shot out of the sky by the Americans' long-range missiles!

The first Phoenixes had homed on the jamming of his regiment's radio-electronic escorts, blowing all three Tu-16 ECM birds out of the sky. Unlike advanced Backfire strike aircraft, Bulgakov's old Badgers carried little electronic-warfare gear; their primary defensive system was merely a passive radar warning receiver. Consequently, Bulgakov's force had been slaughtered in three dimensions.

The Tu-16 pilot was enraged by the Madagascar MiG pilots, who obviously had been more concerned with their own miserable hides than with supporting the bombers. But approaching the launch point, he could not indulge in venting his spleen.

Bulgakov was the senior surviving officer. Unless the Madagascar ground controller suddenly spoke up, it was his decision. At that moment, the weapons control officer's voice shrilled in Bulgakov's headset.

"Targeting data uplink from ground control, sir!" the missileer shouted. "Valid targets confirmed, apparently by a helicopter, of all things. It must have followed the antiship missile tracks back to the American ships."

"I don't care if the information came from the moon," Bulgakov snapped.

Taken aback, the AS-6 missileer regained a professional tone. "Stand by for your heading to launch point."

0848

His checklist completed, Bulgakov compared readings on the Badger's inertial and satellite navigation systems. Over the intercom he called, "Pilot to weapons officer. Prepare for antiship missile launch. Confirm targeting data and firing co-ordinates . . ."

Moments later eight AS-6 missiles dropped free of the four Badgers, which lurched upward once rid of five and a half tons. Seven of the turbojet engines ignited, and while one Kingfish arced uselessly toward the ocean, the others soared upward from 20,000 feet. The mission profile added 100 or more miles to their 150-mile low-level flight path, but at three times the speed of sound their targets were still less than eight minutes way.

Langley

"Presumed AS-6s inbound toward the destroyers, Captain," the air-search radar console operator reported. Gottlieb walked from the antisub module to the antiair spaces in CDC. "Only seven tracks, sir," the seaman said. "They look too far west to be after *Carl*. I think they're headed for *Davenport* or *Wheatley*." The CSO knew that even as few as seven ALCMs might finish off the virtually defenseless *Spruance* DDs.

"Estimate eight minutes to impact on *Davenport*," the console operator announced. "About a minute longer for *Wheatley*."

God save 'em, Gottlieb thought. *Carl can't.* He knew that Mahar had only four Standard SAMs left. Though SM-2 was an area-defense SAM, *Carl*'s skipper would correctly retain them for point-defense of his own more valuable, intact destroyer.

0900 Pretoria; 1000 Local
Air Wing Three Tomcats, over the Southern Omani Coast

Dog Cohen and Hey Joe Pearson in Gypsy 205 backed off from the tanker with profound gratitude. With no indication of where the Air Force KC-10As had come from, the naval aviators only knew that, having overflown Egypt's Arabian Desert, the Red Sea, Saudi Arabia and Oman in two hours and forty minutes, they had needed fuel *bad.*

In a few more minutes all of Red Hesselyn's eighteen fighters were topped off by the five Extenders from March AFB, California. The *Kennedy*'s CAG was enough of a realist to imagine that this joint-service exercise conducted in foreign airspace had to involve an ungodly amount of back-channel communication between Washington, Riyadh and Muscat. But he would be astonished—if ever he learned—that Buddy Callaway had coordinated the whole evolution with four phone calls.

Unconcerned with the political niceties, Hesselyn regrouped his two squadrons and turned them southeasterly. With a short radio call he instructed his pilots to accelerate through the sonic barrier. Once past the Mach, they throttled back to sustain 1.1 times the speed of sound—"supercruise" the aviators called it. At that speed they would cover the next 400 miles in half an hour and start shooting Phoenixes at red-starred bombers.

Varyag

Between the island and the forward elevator, Rybakov waited for Helix helicopters. He felt the heat of the fires through the soles of his shoes. Damage-control crews struggled across the flight deck, trying to coax a flow of foam from their hoses. Noxious smoke swirled around the two dozen staff officers—department heads and their assistants—while sailors stood by to load boxes and communications gear onto the choppers. The admiral clutched his neatly folded command flag.

Fires still burned out of control; the carrier had coasted to a dead stop. Gulaev told Rybakov he believed he could save the year-old ship; but, lacking even a full suite of communications links, his hands were tied. Through gritted teeth, Rybakov had ordered his staff to arrange transport to *Kuznetsov*. *Varyag*'s own surviving Ka-27 antisub and missile-targeting versions of Helix carried too few people, so Smirnov had Ka-29 transports flown in from the amphibious ships operating off the Eastern Cape.

Four Ka-29s appeared from the west. When the first Helix settled onto the elevator—the only safe landing area left—Smirnov led a group of staffers forward. Against the twin-rotor downdraft, they ran toward the chopper, holding onto map cases with one hand and their hats with the other. The bird lifted off and banked west by southwest. The second and third groups loaded and departed.

As Rybakov watched the last knot of staffers rush up to the fourth Ka-29, the ship shook violently beneath him, nearly knocking him to his knees. *Forward secondary magazine,* he surmised. *Probably flooded due to broken waterline.* The admiral took a last look at his once-beautiful ship, faced astern, saluted and walked sadly toward the Kamov.

0927
Over the North Arabian Sea

The Backfire was handling like a garbage truck in winter mud. Colonel Rodion I. Berezhevoy thumbed the electric trim button again, trying to ease the heavy nose-down tendency. "We must have damage to the horizontal tail," he told his frightened copilot. Berezhevoy was not wholly composed himself, but a regimental commander had to inspire confidence. "Here," he snarled, "you take it." He raised his hands from the control yoke, glad to ease the tension in his arms from holding the crippled Tupolev straight and level. The copilot—a youngster with fewer than 200 operational flights —gripped the yoke and acknowledged that he had control.

Berezhevoy thought back just a few hours, to his takeoff from Iran. It had been grand, leading thirty-nine Tu-26s from two Black Sea regiments into battle. His main concern had been that, over such a distance, his planes could carry only a single AS-4 antiship missile semirecessed under the fuselage rather than one under each wing. The flight would be long but required no navigational genius. He'd considered this ambitious strike mission a truly suitable occasion for his 1,500th operational flight. Now the colonel wondered how much of a command he retained. *Those god-cursed Tomcats —the electronic signatures showed they had to be F-14s. Where in hell did they come from, this far north?*

Tuning to the command net again, Berezhevoy called each of his subordinates. "Order: squadron commander state remaining strength and composition of forces." Only two of the five answered. Reports of the other squadrons came from junior pilots. Still speeding south-southwesterly, Berezhevoy knew he would have to make a decision soon.

As he tallied each squadron's report, Berezhevoy realized the decision had been made for him. He pounded the instrument panel in frustration and rage. "Goddamn it!" He turned to the copilot, who had not been on the command net. "We've lost most of both regiments. Counting us, we're down to nine effective aircraft and seven damaged . . ." His voice trailed off.

Berezhevoy checked his watch and switched on the intercom. "Navigator: give me a course for Socotra."

While awaiting the new heading, Berezhevoy assessed his situation. The sixteen bombers could land at Socotra, some 400 miles southwest. There he knew the UER's Treaty of Friendship and Cooperation with the former South Yemeni regime would be honored by the current socialist government. Then, in about four hours, his survivors could join the three regiments from the Baltic Fleet, now taking off from Central Asia. The shock of landing might damage his missiles' circuitry, but he could do nothing else. Unless he regrouped, his small force would be chopped up piecemeal by *Langley*'s air defenses.

Gypsy 205

Hey Joe Pearson ignored the radar-warning signal and finished scribbling some tactical notes on his kneepad. Approaching the Arabian peninsula, his VF-32 flight soon would penetrate Omani airspace and land to enjoy hospitable "internment." He replaced the pen in his sleeve pocket and rechecked his armament panel. One Sparrow remaining. The ICS crackled as Dog Cohen inquired, "Well, XO, how'd we do?"

The Swordsmen's exec adjusted his oxygen mask. "We done good. I make it three splashes for us—two Phoenixes and a Sparrow. We'll sort it all out at the debrief, but we really riled 'em."

Up front, Dog squirmed in his ejection seat. "Uh, how we gonna debrief this hop? Where we're going . . ."

"Don't bother me, boy. You're not going to spoil the best day of my naval aviation career." Hey Joe was still pumped up from the intercept. God, that was great! Seventy-two Phoenixes and thirty-six Sparrows, more bandits than anybody ever saw—and no fighters to hassle with. The Tomcat's fire-control system could track twenty-four targets simultaneously, and only toward the end had Pearson's scope shown fewer bogies. *Must've been forty-plus altogether. Not as high a kill ratio as I'd like, but Backfire's got good ECM. Damn, wish we got a closer look at one of 'em.* Gypsy 205 hadn't been within ten miles of a Backfire, but the missile plumes, midair explosions and fireballs were a sight he already was working to remember in minute detail.

0929 Pretoria; 1029 Local
Langley

Chuck Gideon took the message slip from his staff communications officer. The full commander explained, "This was intercepted by an ElInt bird in the Persian Gulf. Looks like *Kennedy*'s trying to help us, sir."

Ignoring the date-time group and authenticators, Gideon read:

"American naval aircraft overflew part of the Arabian Peninsula this morning in flagrant violation of international navigation routes and procedures. The Royal Saudi Air Force intercepted the unannounced flight, which unlawfully carried armament, and escorted it out of Saudi airspace, southward into the Indian Ocean. No explanation has been offered by the American ambassador, but strong diplomatic protests are being lodged in Washington, D.C."

The admiral initialed the message and handed it back. "You can bet there's more to the story than it says there," Gideon opined. "The Saudis damn sure don't want to lose the South African market for their oil. For that reason alone, I'll bet a year's flight pay they gave back-channel approval for this overflight. Besides, they owe us for Desert Storm."

The commo officer thought for a moment. "So this amounts to a diplomatic smoke screen, sir? To square them with their Muslim brethren?"

"That's my guess." He shrugged. "If *JFK* is launching a long-range CAP to the Northern IO, Red's guys should shortstop some of the Backfires from Russia." He checked his watch. "Which reminds me."

Gideon picked up his command phone and waited a moment. "Phil, this is Chuck. Nate is still down in CDC, so I hope you don't mind me driving your boat by remote control. But let's launch the alert Tomcats a few minutes early. They may need the extra time to look for the Angolan Badgers."

Several minutes later Gideon heard four F-14s hurtled off Cats One and Two. He looked at the regional map and noted that the interception would occur uncomfortably close to hostile shores. But it couldn't be helped.

0930
Southwest End of the Mozambique Channel

Lieutenant Commander Ozzie Ostrewski realized that the ten-plane "package" under his control represented more versatility than some air forces could muster. The VF-181 ops officer had his own four-plane division plus a section from VF-182, controlled by a Hawkeye and a Prowler plus two Vikings—a tanker and an ElInt bird.

Nearing his lonely post off the South African-Mozambique border, Ostrewski split his six Tomcats to northern, central and southern CAP stations, with the support birds deployed at staggered altitudes and intervals well to sea. Looking inland, he wondered what was coming "out of Africa." His reverie was broken by his RIO's combat checklist.

"ALR-45 and -50," Fido Colley chirped from the backseat.

"Check," Ozzie replied, setting the volume of the radar receivers.

"Roll SAS."

"Off now." The pilot disengaged the stability augmentation system.

Fido called, "Phoenix coolant."

"On." Ozzie pushed the test button for each AIM-54 station and was gratified with green lights—four good birds.

Moments later Ozzie's RIO, Lieutenant Fido Colley, got blinking lights on his commo panel. The E-2 wanted to talk to him on the discrete freq. "Gunshot, this is Frisbee 603. We have Badgers climbing outbound." There was a pause. "Whale Watch advises Badgers are preceded by November Kilo Fulcrums. Will advise. Out."

Fido broke the silence over the ICS. "Oz, did you hear that?"

"Yeah, I heard. I'm contacting Cookie and Tuna on Button Eleven."

Colley blinked away the sweat in his eyes. North Korean MiG-29s! On a ten-point scale that news carried a pucker factor of nine-point-five.

Langley

Bubba Ballantine jogged down the passageway and turned hard right into CDC. He almost bumped into Chuck Gideon in the darkened space. "Oh, excuse me, Admiral."

"No problem, CAG. Our big concern right now is the Badgers coming out of Angola—and the Fulcrum regiment preceding them."

"Damn, a whole regiment?"

"Yeah—North Koreans, apparently."

Ballantine inhaled audibly. "That means big trouble, sir. We have to reinforce the CAP right now."

"Concur." Gideon nodded in the dark. "I've already released the four Turkeys on ForceCAP and we're launching eight Hornets ASAP, with tanker support. I need your advice, though. How should we play the intercept?"

Bubba looked at the disposition on the tactical board. "Ozzie's hanging out there with just three sections. No way he can handle thirty-plus. I'd say slow 'em down with Phoenix and pull back. The standby Hornets can add another wall of missiles. That far from the ship, we can trade territory for time."

"Do it." Gideon turned to the duty communicator. "Break emcon to alert the Aegises. Have one of the northerly S-3s drop a radio buoy for relay of further transmissions. It might buy us some more time."

0935
Southwest End of the Mozambique Channel

"Gunshot Lead, this is Frisbee. Confirm Link Four with new data, over."

Fido noted the additional symbols flicked onto the radar scope in Gunshot 102. The symbology data-linked from the E-2 told him more than he really wanted to know. Then the Tomcat's radar warning receiver went off. *Shit,* he thought, *when it rains it pours.* Fido confirmed the Hawkeye's data over the scrambler radio, then addressed his pilot.

"Oz, the Badgers are holding course and speed. We've just been ID'd by a Madcap, and Whale Watch thinks it's vectored the Fulcrums onto us."

"Rats. There goes the neighborhood." Ozzie thought for

a moment. He called Pine Tree 621, the EA-6B some thirty miles southeast, and told the Prowler to begin jamming enemy radar. *Maybe jamming from that sector will draw off some Fulcrums,* he thought. The inbound Badgers were the priority; everything depended on stopping them at the Tomcat picket line.

Almost two minutes later, his fire-distribution plan repeated to the other F-14s, Ozzie Ostrewski crossed himself and led his Tomcats in a fuel-guzzling climb.

0937

Comrade Colonel Li Sung Hwa shifted in the seat of Snow Tiger One, checking the formation of his MiG-29s. Noting the jamming from the southeast, Li took a chance and detached Snow Lynx Squadron to investigate the threat. He should still, he figured, have ample forces to gain local superiority, clearing the way for the Tupolevs. Then he turned his attention back to the east. Somewhere out there, within radar range—and soon within his own phenomenal vision—would be the F-14s.

Twelve AMRAAMs blazed away from Ozzie's six Tomcats, the solid-fuel rocket motors boosting the missiles to nearly Mach Five. Over the secure channel, the Fightin' Felines division leader learned that eleven were guiding properly—better than he expected. *At least we're getting the first shots,* he thought, beyond AA-10 range.

Eighty miles to the west, the Madcap operators noted the missile launch and called a warning to the lead MiG-29 squadron passing the AWACS patrol station. Yet another electronic battle was joined.

"Oz, they're jamming the freq," called Fido. "But it should be okay. The missiles are programmed to home on jamming." In the front cockpit of Gunshot 102, Ozzie grunted approval. The AIM-120's track-on-jam capability rendered initial countermeasures ineffective. Fido continued following the high-speed missiles to their destination. Additional ECM was brought to bear, but Pine Tree 621 was able to negate some of it with the Prowler's highly capable electronics suite.

Moments later, hostile blips began disappearing from U.S. radar scopes. The Tomcat RIOs saw four MiG-29s hacked out of the North Korean formation, lessening the odds against the badly outnumbered F-14s. But then the Fulcrums were through the U.S. missile picket, accelerating toward the two Tomcats delegated to tie up the bomber escorts.

Colonel Li's brown eyes picked the ephemeral canopy glint out of midair, estimated range fifty kilometers. He engaged his jam-proof radio, awaited the synchronizing tone and made the call. "Snow Tiger Squadron! Imperialist fighters at eleven-o'clock level. Attack disposition number three." After that it was warfare by rote. Li knew his well-drilled unit would follow procedure, leaving any innovation to him. The Korean ace kept Snow Leopard Squadron as close escort for the Tupolevs, reserving for his lead squadron—and himself —the honor of trapping the nearest F-14s. Li noticed that the jamming continued from that damnable Prowler somewhere to the east, denying effective AA-10 missile employment. *Never mind,* he thought. *We will overwhelm them by numbers.*

Moments later two Tomcats and eight Fulcrums met at the merge, hosing radar and all-aspect heat-seeking missiles at one another. The sky over the Mozambique Channel became crisscrossed with smoke trails, decoy flares, metallic chaff, aerial wreckage—and a few more parachutes.

Though aggressive by training and disposition, Li's pilots were mostly new to aerial combat. Some of them made small mistakes they seldom committed in practice, and a few of them died as a result.

Li's second flight leader had hooked left at the merge and now saw Circus 200 in a nose-low turn, evading another Fulcrum. The eager flight leader immediately loaded seven and a half Gs on his MiG, pulled hard right—and collided with his wingman.

In the backseat of 200, Chili Carney gawked at the fireball for two heartbeats, commented on the "cost-effective kills" and turned his attention elsewhere.

Three miles away, slightly lower, Cookie and Tuna in 211 had pulled a rolling vertical reverse and watched another Fulcrum overshoot them. The angle had been too acute for even a snapshot, so the MiG driver had wisely refrained from firing. But when the angry Tomcat threw a lag-displacement roll back to his six o'clock, the Snow Tiger pilot panicked. He jammed on full afterburners to his Tumansky engines, honked straight up, stopped the pitch movement and initiated the famous Fulcrum tailslide. With a one-to-one thrust-weight ratio, the MiG-29 appeared to stand motionless in midair. The pilot felt—erroneously—that no airplane in the capitalist world could follow that last-ditch maneuver.

For a moment suspended in time, Lieutenant (junior grade) "Cookie" Crisp admired the plan view of the two-tone blue Korean fighter. Though the Fulcrum was frantically popping flares to divert heat-seeking missiles, Cookie marveled that any gomer would use the maneuver intended to break a Doppler lock-on.

His RIO, "Tuna" Treble, called, "Tail's clear right now!"

Cookie shoved his stick full forward, popped his speed brake and initiated a low yo-yo as the range closed dramatically. Then Circus 211 pulled up as Cookie thumbed his selector to "Gun" and, in the instant available, placed his pipper on the MiG's tailpipes. He pressed the trigger and pulled.

With a windscreen full of Fulcrum, the M-61 cannon spooled up and a stream of 20mm slugs trashed the fighter from afterburners to radome. Inside 500-foot range, almost every round went home and the MiG exploded in Cookie's face. Instinctively he ducked his head as he flew through the fireball. Aluminum fragments were ingested into the Tomcat's big jet intakes, fodding both engines. Master caution and fire-warning lights lit up the cockpit like a cheap pinball machine. With two more MiGs diving in for the kill, Tuna braced himself, yelled "Will eject, eject, eject . . ." and pulled the handle between his knees. Both seats fired, flinging pilot and RIO into an eerie calm as their chutes snapped opened and they began descending toward the water.

Cookie looked around, estimated he was 8,000 feet over the channel and saw Tuna had a good chute. Then the pilot's heart leapt into his mouth. Another Fulcrum—they were everywhere—dived on Tuna and fired a long, vengeful burst. Cookie heard the cannon's loud, hollow moan as 23mm shells shredded the RIO's nylon canopy, and Lieutenant Commander Paul Treble fell to his death. The murderous MiG disappeared below, apparently without seeing Justin Crisp's chute.

0938

Ozzie Ostrewski was a broker of time. Fifty miles from the unequal dogfight, he had expended Circus 200 and 211 in exchange for time to engage the onrushing Badgers with his four remaining Tomcats. He knew it would be only moments until the remaining Fulcrums swarmed over his two sections, so his RIO already had prioritized targeting with the orbiting Hawkeye. He asked over the hot mike, "Fido, how we doing? We gotta shoot fast or get out of Dodge."

"Uhhh, just a sec . . . there! We're in business." The scope in the back of Gunshot 102 flicked with the tactical symbology data-linked from the E-2. Similar data was shown the RIOs in Gunshot 100 with 103 and 104. "The ECM birds are locked up," Fido explained. "Our first Phoenixes are directed for home-on-jam. We're cleared to fire."

Across miles of sky above cloud-shadowed sea, the long-range missile engagement began. Sixteen huge AIM-54s with 135-pound warheads dropped clear of the Tomcats. ECM aircraft escorting the bombers were accorded the dubious distinction of first priority, and in minutes the complex battle of the electrons began to resolve itself.

The E-2 and F-14 crews visualized the effect of the half-ton supersonic "silver bullets." Seven Tu-16s—all three ECM birds and four bombers—became vivid fireballs suspended in space, raining down burning jet fuel and airframe parts. Only an occasional dun-colored parachute gave ephemeral testament to the big bombers' presence as the widely dispersed survivors continued eastward at 700 kilometers per hour.

0943

"Gunshot from Frisbee." The call from the E-2 crackled in Ozzie's earphones. "Phoenix engagement has not, repeat not, turned back the Badgers. You have fourteen still headed your posit. Recommend you close to Sparrow range. Frisbee out."

Ozzie choked down a retort. *Easy for him to say. We'll be knee-deep in MiGs any second now.*

But the controller was right. Tomcats existed to defend the battle group, now some 350 miles away. At Mach One that was only a half hour's flying time. Ozzie told Fido to inform the Hawkeye and Prowler of his intention to press the intercept. The pilot felt the sweat on his palms beneath his gloves.

With moments to spare, the four Tomcats got off eight Sparrows at fifteen miles' range. They were then committed to keep their noses pointed at the Tupolevs until the AIM-7s impacted. And by then the Korean Fulcrums were upon them.

0946

The combat was not going entirely to Colonel Li's liking. His flight had skillfully boxed in Gunshot 103 and he had destroyed it, killing Buick and Jaws. But two more of his own fighters had gone down. Li grudgingly admitted to himself that these naval aviators were just as skillful as those who had depleted his comrades' ranks over Hai Duong in 1972. The problem was identification. With nearly twenty twin-tailed fighters engaged in close combat, it was difficult to tell friend from foe. Li himself had passed up a possible shot because the ID had been questionable.

The regimental commander again engaged his scrambler. "This is Snow Tiger Leader. All flights, regroup and engage remaining enemy by sections." Now, with a huge numerical advantage, Li could dispose of the remaining Tomcats and reorganize his bomber escort. He glanced around, spotted a lone F-14 dueling with two Fulcrums and called in another pair.

Almost four miles from Li, an excited Korean pilot also saw Gunshot 104, got a faint missile tone and ripple-fired four heat seekers.

Caught between the hammer and anvil, Lieutenant "Loco" Milton opted for one more kill before accepting destruction. He slewed the Tomcat's nose hard right, deliberately committing into the path of a MiG abeam. He got a quick Sidewinder tone, pressed the trigger and shot the Fulcrum in the face. The '29 staggered, lurched onto one wing and disgorged a blackish-orange flame as the pilot ejected. Then two AA-8 missiles speared Circus 200 amidships and the big Grumman exploded.

Fido Colley saw the flash in his peripheral vision. "They just nailed Loco and Chili!"

Ozzie Ostrewski did not reply just then. He was drawing a bead on a Fulcrum that had misjudged a barrel-roll evade and he pressed the trigger, sending his first Sidewinder off the rail. "Goddamn it to hell!" The pilot knew immediately that he had fired too soon, allowing the MiG to avoid the missile with a break turn. Low and alone, amid a swarm of unfriendly Orientals, was no place to be.

"Ozzie, another one rollin' in on us, seven o'clock high!"

From his perch above and behind the lone Tomcat, Colonel Li knew the time was right. He had democratically taken his turn in the aerial daisy chain over Gunshot 102 and now dived in, gaining an aural tone that told him his next heat-seeking missile was tracking the Tomcat's twin exhaust.

No matter which way the American turned, he would die. Li felt no particular elation—only a satisfaction at handing the vaunted carrier aviators a heavy defeat. He carefully aligned his nose to lead the Tomcat's turn slightly, easing the intercept geometry for his Aphid missile. His finger curled around the trigger. *Not yet, not yet . . .*

"Leader, break right, BREAK RIGHT!"

The call came from nowhere, yet everywhere. It made no sense. Li's mind processed the warning in microseconds, simultaneously wondering how the call possibly could be meant for him. There had only been four imperialist fighters, and he was about to destroy the last. Still, one ignored such warnings at one's own peril. Li's brain commanded his right arm to shove the stick to the right side of the cockpit.

Nearing the end of its four-mile flight, a stray AA-8 intended for Gunshot 104 sensed the presence of another heat source. Its laser-proximity fuse detonated the thirteen-pound warhead twenty feet from Snow Tiger Lead's empennage.

Li Sung Hwa's helmet cracked against the canopy and his hand was wrenched from the stick. He had never envisioned how violent a missile strike could be, but the Tiger of the North had never known defeat. His blurred mind registered a dizzying, spinning sensation as his Fulcrum, minus most of its tail, slewed crazily in midair.

"Colonel! Eject, eject, EJECT!"

His wingman's shrill voice pierced Li's dulled consciousness and brought him back to awareness. He braced himself upright in the K-series seat, fighting the lateral G, and pulled the handles.

Li Sung Hwa, the most experienced fighter pilot on earth, was rocketed out of his cockpit, out of the fight, and into a world he had never known.

1001
Vietnamese Command Post, Vryheid District, Northern Natal

Siphageni was grateful that the major general spoke good English—most Viet officers used French or Russian. Siphageni's Russian had rusted since his year in training on the shore of the Caspian Sea. He appreciated even more the fact that the brigade commander was leveling with him about the situation around Vryheid, the key to the enemy defenses.

"Resistance has been tough," the veteran Vietnamese said. "The fascists have brought in reserves from other fronts, which has aided our cause in those areas. But we're running out of infantry here. I want your men to participate in the next attack, which should be decisive."

Siphageni declined, saying, "My men are specialists, Comrade General. They are too valuable to waste in frontal assaults on fortified positions."

The general was astonished that the black was turning down the honor of liberating Vryheid, perhaps the Dien Bien Phu of South Africa. But he responded evenly. "This is a crisis, Comrade Major. In our military doctrine, which has repeatedly proved correct, we are trained to recognize the moment and point of decision. This is the time and place in which the battle and the war will be won. Now and here every last resource is to be concentrated and used. This is the only correct formula for victory."

The general paused to gauge the effect of his lecture on elementary Clausewitz, as amended by communist military doctrine. Siphageni was silently composing a response, so the general continued. "Were I a Russian motor rifle division commander, I would throw in my independent tank battalion at this point and lead it myself, to victory or death. I have no such high-powered reserve, but I will lead this attack just the same. I have already committed far more specialists than your unit—including my reconnaissance company, signalers and even electronic-warfare cadre. The cooks and truck drivers were used up before dawn. For the final assault, I've constituted my headquarters unit as an infantry company. The objective is worth the total destruction of my brigade. The last man left standing on that airport must be holding high the Red Banner!"

Siphageni, his thoughts interrupted, said, "Please, comrade. Save the romanticism for the Young Pioneers. I am a disciplined Marxist-Leninist and a professional revolutionary soldier. My objections are based on objective reality. My men will be needed in exploiting your certain victory here, as we advance to join our brothers now fighting on the Tugela."

The general countered, "Success here means there will be no opposition to such exploitation, hence no more need for specialist scouts. In any case, the marine and airborne formations are mechanized and coming to us. After they crush the fascists on the river line, they will meet only minor opposition to their advance from Ladysmith." He considered accusing Siphageni of cowardice, but the man's record proved otherwise. Yet, exasperated at casting pearls of wisdom before this obdurate black swine, the general noted, "Corps has attached your battalion to my command, comrade. If the precepts of military science do not convince you, then I shall *order* you to attack. It is the fate of *your* national liberation movement that will be decided. To your men should go the honor of winning the crucial victory."

"Then I shall obey, Comrade General, under protest."

"Very well, then. My chief of staff will issue your orders and, if you wish, brief you on our plan. He's with the rear CP."

Grimly, Siphageni said, "I do wish it. Thank you, Comrade General."

1005 Pretoria; 1105 Local
Langley

"Link 11 relay from *Carl,* Captain," the tactical action officer in CDC told Gottlieb. "She sustained a single Kingfish hit, right between her stacks." He paused for effect, then said, "A dud!" and smiled broadly. "Unexpended fuel fire reported under control. She still has one turbine operable."

"Luck of the Irish!" Gottlieb beamed. "That Mahar's a

hard SOB to kill." He wondered if the *Burke*-class ship's steel superstructure and "stealthy," slope-sided design helped save the 8,300-ton DDG. In contrast, the naval architects responsible for the slab-sided 3,700-ton *Perry*-class frigates had produced a radar cross-section larger than a 28,000-ton *Kirov*-class battlecruiser.

The CSO knew that *Carl* would be slow and noisy en route to her new station covering the CVBG and PhibGru— easy prey for enemy subs and attack planes. Without SAMs, the major function of the magnificent destroyer was now to soak up antiship missiles like a $700 million sponge.

Unless she can break all records reloading, Gottlieb reflected. On the perspex board plot, he saw that Gideon had positioned *Roseburg,* the CVBG's unrep ship, between *Carl* and the two cruisers northwest and north of *Langley.* But the big AOE was still seventy-five nautical miles from *Carl*— maximum radius for her two UH-46D Sea Knight helos with a slung load of six medium-range SM-2 SAMs.

Even with calm seas, reloading vertical launch cells while under way was slow and dangerous. Sailors had to manhandle each fifteen-foot, nearly one-ton packing crate onto a dolly, wheel it from the vertical replenishment spot or helo pad toward the fore or aft Mark 41 and attach it to the VLS crane. Then they had to lower the dangling, encased missile into a launch cell. In rough weather, forget it.

The Sea Knights would drop twelve missiles on *Carl*'s landing deck and vertrep spot. Gottlieb doubted the Russians would give Mahar's men the eighteen hours they would need to "strike down" and wire up the Block II SM-2s. Any crates left topside when the next wave of enemy bombers attacked would have to be heaved overboard—a million bucks in the drink each.

Gottlieb imagined the DDG trailing smoke like a beacon while steaming north to reunite with Battle Group Charlie. He feared the journey was a rendezvous with death.

1030 Pretoria; 1130 Local
USS Grouper, *Glorioso Isles*

Captain Darren Bates checked his watch and softly said, "Target time. Up mast."

The submarine's camouflaged electronic support measures mast emerged from the tropical waters of her haven west of the little archipelago. With his SSN sheltered from radar detection by the chain of islets and shielded from acoustic snoopers by the shallows, Bates felt briefly secure.

He knew the Tomahawks had by now crossed the isthmus west of Antsiranana or entered its bay from the east. Over the beach, the SLCMs would have switched from inertial navigation to TerCom guidance—terrain contour matching. Their onboard computers compared radar snapshots of the land ahead of and below them with digitalized imagery stored in their memory cards. Once their locations were confirmed, the computers would have ordered flight-control systems to make any adjustments necessary to keep the missiles on course.

Bates crossed his fingers and studied the ESM console for signs of enemy response to the attack.

1031 Pretoria; 1131 Local
UER Naval Aviation Base Antsiranana

Captain of Aviation Yuri Bulgakov had been too tired to reach his bunk. Feeling defeated, mourning dozens of comrades, he'd nibbled brunch, then slumped in a chair in the mess hall to catch some much-needed sleep. After less than half an hour, the bomber pilot heard sudden shouts. A clatter of tableware and cutlery, chairs screeching on wood floors, a babble of shouting, then a stampede of running feet. He stirred himself, wondering what was happening. Remote automatic-weapons fire rattled the walls and windows.

Bulgakov crowded into the doorway just in time to see cruise missiles sweep in from four directions: west, northeast, east, and southeast. *Tomahawks!* The shock, dread and thrill revived him. He scanned the sky for SAM plumes, but found none. The only missiles in view were American.

Two of the robot raiders went for the twin runways, spewing cluster munitions from their long, slim bodies. Bomblets burst along the painted centerlines of the pavement, gouging scores of craters as they went. Simultaneously the other pair popped up from their terrain-hugging flight profiles, selected their programmed targets, and dived into the ground.

One penetrated a major cell in the airfield's underground tank farm, igniting 250,000 liters of jet fuel. The volcanic eruption spread flame and shock throughout the facility. Fire-fighting crews could not even get close to the gigantic blaze, which sent gray-black clouds to 10,000 feet.

The fourth Tomahawk punched through the largest hangar on the field, where the 1,000-pound warhead detonated. Bulgakov ducked; other bodies piled on his. The hot blast wave roared over them; glass shattered all around. Uncovering his head, Bulgakov saw fire trucks careening ineffectively around the remains of two Badgers. And though most of the surviving Tupolevs were unharmed, the Tu-16 pilot knew they were trapped on the field with no hope of taking off for hours, perhaps days, to come.

The bleary-eyed, stunned squadron leader felt impotent rage race along his nerves like kerosene fire across the runways. *Where did the missiles come from? How had the Americans timed it to hit ten minutes after the remnants of the Angolan Badger regiment recovered here?*

The frustration burnt itself out, leaving the exhausted flier drained. Bulgakov felt like trying to sleep where he lay, but slowly picked himself up. He took in the rolling smoke and manic confusion, the widespread damage, and shook his head. He dragged back to his comfortable chair, propped his feet on a table and returned to sleep.

1100 Pretoria; 1200 Local
Langley

Ozzie and Fido sat in the Fighting Felines' ready room, rolling their eyes and gulping "medicinal" whiskey dispensed by the flight surgeon, Norm "Fighter Doc" Roberts. The Tomcat crew was scheduled for another launch in less than four hours, and technically should not have consumed alcohol for three times that long. But this was war, and they had just been through a hell of an experience. Six F-14s had launched; three had returned.

The RIO finally unzipped his G-suit and let it drop at his feet. "I tell you," Fido said to no one in particular, "we were dog meat. If the Hornet guys hadn't shown up, those Fulcrums would've had us for breakfast."

"But how'd you get away?" asked Lieutenant Commander "Foobar" Ruston, the squadron safety officer. "You said you were boxed in tight."

"We were," interjected Ozzie. "This one gomer had us dead to rights. We were out of airspeed, altitude and ideas all at once. Then BLAM! A missile came out of nowhere and blew his ass off."

"Had to be red-on-red," said Fido, slurping the last of his ration from the Styrofoam cup. "I think he just got hosed by one of his own guys."

"So you took advantage of the confusion and disengaged," said Foobar.

Ozzie looked at Ruston with tired eyes. The new ace's face still was creased from his oxygen mask. "That's one way of saying it. Fact is, we were scared shitless and bent the throttles in the direction the E-2 said. The F- and-A/18s started shooting AMRAAMs from BVR and fortunately didn't lock us up." He shrugged. "We were just goddamn lucky."

Fido looked around. "Any word on the other guys?"

The squadron intelligence officer walked up with a notepad. "Only Cookie. SAR helo's bringing him in, with one of the MiG drivers." The bespectacled AIO grinned. "The spooks definitely want to talk to that guy."

1323 Pretoria; 1423 Local
Black Sea and Baltic Fleet Backfires, over Socotra

For the second time this day, Colonel Rodion I. Berezhevoy led a formation of Backfires southward in search of the American carrier group. He had personally checked over the seven airworthy Tu-26s from his Black Sea regiments following the god-awful trap set by *Kennedy*'s Tomcats.

Berezhevoy gripped the control wheel so hard that he half-expected black juice to squeeze out between his fingers. He cursed long and fervently to himself about the delayed report on *Kennedy*'s launch of her two F-14 squadrons. Just before takeoff, Berezhevoy had learned from Naval Aviation Headquarters that the carrier trapped in the Suez Canal had in fact put her Tomcats ashore, and that they had been refueled over Arabia in time to intercept the Black Sea Backfires. *A lot of good that does us now!* the colonel thought bitterly. His subordinates never would have characterized him as a caring leader, but the thought of twenty-three of his magnificent bombers and their crews at the bottom of the ocean galled him. *An hour's delay would have thrown off their intercept . . . better not think of it.*

"Colonel, the command net is active," reported the radio operator. "All three Baltic Fleet regiments have reported in. Rendezvous will be made on schedule."

For the first time in hours, Rodion Berezhevoy breathed easier. He felt some of the tension slip from his hands. His own reduced force added to the more than sixty Backfires from the Baltic Fleet produced about seventy bombers—alone probably enough to overwhelm the U.S. battle group, already softened up by the sacrificial Tu-16 attacks. Yet he knew his Baltic–Black Sea strike would be followed by over 100 more Tu-26s—about forty from the Northern Fleet and sixty-odd from the Pacific. *It will be good,* he thought. *It will be very good.*

1502 Pretoria; 0902 EDT
White House

Hub Fernandez handed President Callaway a one-page, single-spaced document. Below the standard headings and security classification was the document's title. Callaway looked up at his CNO. "You gotta be kidding me! Who comes up with these names, anyway?"

The admiral smiled. "Like everything else, Mr. President, the code names are computer-generated."

Callaway's big hands waved in a what-the-hell gesture. "Okay, okay. But 'Operation Evil Hyphen' sure is gonna look weird in the history books."

"Actually, I kind of like it," Fernandez replied. "It rolls off the tongue."

"Well, I just hope it rolls off the 'phibs and over the beach." Callaway took time to read the briefing sheet, then looked back to his naval adviser.

Fernandez outlined for the President of the United States the details of only the second American amphibious landing on the African Continent in the twentieth century.

1620 Pretoria; 1720 Local
Below The Equator, Western Indian Ocean

Colonel Gary Tate was sensitive about callsigns. In his
first year at the Air Force Academy, upperclassmen dubbed
him "Junior" because of his five-foot-seven frame and cheru-
bic face. It was especially hard to take from the third- and
second-class female cadets. Twenty-three years later, with
eagles on his shoulders when he took command of the B-1B
wing, he adopted the supersonic bomber's name, "Lancer."

His air division commander still called him Junior.

For this mission Tate was given an innocuous radio
identification, "Golf Tango." *Well, at least it's my initials,* he
thought, although he would have much preferred to go into
the inevitable Air University study as "Lancer One." But
Golf Tango was so vague that electronic eavesdroppers could
derive nothing from it, even by inference.

So far things had gone uncommonly well. Tate regretted
the one abort, as it deprived him of sixteen missiles. But he
still had fifteen good birds orbiting at the expected interception point. *Any minute now,* he thought.

"Colonel, six minutes to estimated radar contact."

Tate engaged the mike switch. "Rog. Thanks, Bryce."
First Lieutenant Turno was smack on schedule, which was no
surprise. Tate felt that the finest navigator belonged in the
wing commander's aircraft, and though Bryce Turno was primarily a defensive systems operator, he definitely was the
best navigator. With just a few minutes more radio silence,
the Russians would finally learn the unpleasant identity of
Golf Tango.

1626 Pretoria; 1726 Local
Backfires

Colonel Rodion Berezhevoy was having a very bad day,
made worse by having had his hopes raised, only possibly to
be punctured again. First came the Tomcat ambush of his
Black Sea Backfires—the ensuing slaughter, the disrupted
flight plan and the divert into Yemen. Then the cobbled-
together strike force, vastly reduced from two regiments to
less than a squadron. The takeoff to join the following Baltic
Fleet regiments from the Motherland, while a hasty evolu-

tion, had elevated his spirits. And now this. His idiot of an electronic-warfare officer had just warned him of a physical impossibility. It had to be a screwup.

"Check again, Kasimirov," the colonel said in belabored tones. "You know damn well that can't be."

"Com . . . er, Colonel, I beg your pardon. But I have double-checked. The electronic signature is confirmed. F-16 band fire-control radar has locked on!" Kasimirov's voice carried a mixture of insult and fear over the intercom. "Bearing is almost due east, signal strength . . ."

"Goddamn it!" Berezhevoy cut off his EWO. "I'll check this myself." He turned to his command set to confirm the strange contact with one of his squadron commanders. *Somebody a lot more stable and competent than Kasimirov,* the regimental CO thought bitterly. *The young idiot. Even he should know there can't be any F-16s within 4,000 miles.*

"Black Sea Leader!" The panic in the voice was clear. Berezhevoy recognized the owner as the same squadron commander he was going to call. "We have warning of hostile fire-control radars bearing 095. Probable F-16s. Can you verify? Over!"

For a heartbeat, Rodion Berezhevoy was frozen in place. His hand lingered on the radio dial.

"Air-to-air missiles inbound! Many tracks!" The voice increased in pitch.

Berezhevoy's mind registered not just one word, but one overwhelming emotion. *No!*

Lancer One

Colonel Gary Tate was having the best day of his life. *Well,* he admitted, *Barb would understand.* He held the B-1B steady as the rotary launcher in the bomb bay unloaded its AMRAAMs at an unbelievable pace. In a way, it was vaguely unsatisfying to Tate. Like many bomber pilots, he secretly yearned to fly fighters. Now he was going to splash more bandits than any U.S. Air Force commander in forty years, but he would see nothing more than distant fireballs in the air.

In a matter of seconds the missiles in Lancer One had dropped off their spools, ignited and rocketed westward. The

B-1's APG-66 radar—identical to the F-16s—paved an electronic highway in the sky for the missiles.

Tate and his crew were confident of a good killing. For the umpteenth time, the wing commander did the mental arithmetic. *Let's see . . . fifteen B-1s each firing a dozen missiles, that's 180 AMRAAMs. Assume a valid launch ratio of point-eight, that's 154. Factor in a fifty-percent hit rate and the AMRAAM Pk against a big bird like that. We should splash twenty-plus.* He knew Backfires were packed with ECM and ECCM black boxes, plus speed sleds with, thanks to their "variable geometry" wings, surprising maneuverability. But as fast and as capable as their advanced Tupolev product was, the Russians couldn't overcome the sheer volume of the AMRAAM barrage in the limited time available. Though the ambush was a victory of intelligence and surprise, Tate realized with a start, *Hell, I could be Airman of the Year.* He chuckled aloud to his copilot. "Ted, I'd give a year's flight pay to see that Russian commander's face right about now."

Ted gave a big thumbs-up.

1730 Pretoria; 1830 Local
Baltic and Black Sea Fleet Backfires, over the Western Indian Ocean

Rodion Berezhevoy's face was clammy with sweat and red with anger. *The goddamned, blood-sucking, missile-shooting Americans are everywhere on earth today. First over the Arabian Sea, now down here below the equator. How is that possible?*

The regimental commander flexed his fingers, releasing his deathgrip on the controls. There was nothing to do but order the damaged Backfires to land on Madagascar. With the Russian base at Antsiranana closed, the swing-wing bombers would have to divert to the handful of civilian airfields on the island with runways long enough to handle heavy aircraft or to Mozambique.

At least his seven Black Sea Fleet Backfires had not been attacked by the AMRAAM-armed American "fighter-bombers." But the cackle of air-to-air communications revealed that forty-four of the sixty-three Baltic Fleet Tu-26s had been destroyed or forced to land with severe damage.

The twenty-six Tupelovs remaining battleworthy regrouped and continued south.

Berezhevoy knew that the Baltic and Black Sea Fleet Backfires left airborne were too few to mount an effective strike. He felt they should delay their progress to form up in flight with the two Northern Fleet regiments, about an hour back. He believed these included forty-odd Tu-26s, with a divisional commander. They also contained a high percentage of Backfire-Cs. This latest model featured better aerodynamic performance and, more important, improved ECM and ECCM avionics—vital to the success of the attack on the U.S. carrier battle group. The combined force of nearly seventy of the world's most powerful antiship strike aircraft would still be able to complete their mission.

1640
Route 69, East of Vryheid, Natal Province

Siphageni and a squad of his headquarters platoon rode on the outside of a BTR-50, an old Russian tracked, amphibious APC. The type was most renowned for its use by the Egyptians in the assault crossing of the Suez Canal in '73, but the guerrilla commander preferred to think this Viet vehicle might have helped liberate Ho Chi Minh City in '75.

The engine deck was uncomfortably hot and Siphageni was choking in noxious diesel fumes, but it beat walking. The brigade commander had requisitioned all the recce battalion's vehicles.

Siphageni was unimpressed by the understrength squad of Vietnamese motor riflemen standing up in the APC's cramped troop compartment. Though part of the world's most experienced army, these skinny, almost effeminate boys looked as if their previous experience of life extended no farther than the edge of the village rice paddy. He doubted they could read.

His intel officer, Mangope, said that to alleviate dire unemployment, Hanoi had promised land in South Africa to any survivors of the Viet Expeditionary Force, and to the brothers of those killed. Siphageni knew this promise had been made to Front Line State soldiers, but was surprised to hear the offer extended to Asians. It occurred to him that his people might be losing their land in the course of reclaiming it, but he quickly expunged the heretical thought from his mind. Under scientific socialism, there would be plenty for all.

As it crested the top of a low ridge, the BTR lurched to a stop; Siphageni barely managed to hang on. Some of his men fell ignominiously to earth. The Vietnamese laughed at them. The Africans reached for their rifles, but Siphageni ordered them to desist.

The rest of his battalion dismounted. The ridge ran south from the junction of the Hlobane and Zungwini prominences, connecting these heights with the north face of Besterkop. The men formed up six kilometers east of the Vryheid city limits. Their role was to support the Vietnamese sappers probing the enemy's defenses. Fascist reinforcements had been flown in during the day, but the brigade chief of staff estimated that the new troops scarcely compensated for the enemy's losses to Viet artillery fire during the past twelve hours.

The Viet mechanized troops would wait in reserve to launch a crushing attack through whichever portion of the airfield fortifications Siphageni's scouts and the Viet combat engineers found the most weakly defended. The combat engineers' assault vehicles would launch line charges to blast a path through portions of the mine field and heaviest wire, while the pioneers crawled into the wire elsewhere.

Siphageni still didn't understand why the Vietnamese couldn't wait for their other brigade to arrive from Zululand to reduce Vryheid. He resented the possible ruin of his command, but orders were to be obeyed. For some reason, time apparently was critical.

1643 Pretoria; 1743 Local
Bear D Targeting Aircraft, Southwest of Madagascar

Oleg Okun thought his pilot must be crazy. The surface-search radar operator hated officers who put the mission ahead of the lives of their men. For all the young draftee cared, the blacks could kill each other to their hearts' content, and slaughter the spoiled white capitalists in the bargain. Not that Okun had anything against making a profit. He fully intended to emigrate and get rich as soon as he escaped the navy's clutches. If the whites won in South Africa, he might even apply to move there. But everything about his present position worked against his future.

Now the suicidal-homicidal maniac piloting the Tu-20 had widened their search pattern unnecessarily. They hadn't spotted any American ships on their assigned orbit, which suited Okun just fine. He regarded selection for radar training as the greatest catastrophe ever to befall him. Previously officers or warrants held technical jobs, but the military manpower crisis had thrust him—a radio school graduate—into this unspeakable position. Surely American radar operators had seen the big turboprop by now; interceptors had probably already been vectored to blow them out of the air, as they already had done to three Bears in his squadron.

To Okun's great disgust, the imbecilic pilot flew even farther south. *The man is insane!* he thought. *Certifiable!* The whole squadron knew that the *Novo* group's SLCMs and the Tu-16's ALCMs had found targets to the southwest, but every other pilot had had the good sense not to venture too far in that direction—a course not even required in the search plan.

The operator was about to object to his pilot's foolhardiness when the outer edge of his scope suddenly lit up like a New Year's fir tree. It took a moment for the scene to glow in his consciousness as vividly as on the display terminal. Then he realized what the seven strong returns must be; the formation left no doubt. He had seen this phenomenon many times in training, but this had to be the real thing. Okun was looking at echoes of the most potent naval war machine on earth—a U.S. carrier battle group.

The shining phosphors awoke some sleeping part of his brain. The children's New Year's song *Malenkaya Yolichka* jingled in his mind. He hummed the first bar, *Little Fir Tree,* then discovered he couldn't remember all the words, only the music. Okun shook off the incongruous recollection and got on the intercom.

The excited pilot ordered the coordinates relayed to the Backfire regiments hurtling south down the Mozambique Channel and to Task Force Rybakov.

1706 Pretoria; 1806 Local
Langley

Gottlieb stared hard at the air-to-air console in CDC. "Make it over sixty Backfires, sir," the CSO reported. "Might be some more following still out of radar range. Looks like three or four regiments. They've rarely even practiced attacks with this many bombers all at once."

"Very well," Gideon replied. The long-delayed moment of truth had finally arrived after a day of anxious waiting. He wondered if steaming north toward the enemy had been the right move. *Not much choice if I were going to defend the PhibGru,* the admiral told himself.

Gideon reviewed Battle Group Charlie's air-defense network—a giant spider web traced in phosphors on tactical display screens throughout the force. Measured in fifty-mile concentric rings from Point Zulu—*Langley* herself—were twenty-degree wedges, with each arc designated alphabetically, beginning with Alfa. Inside arc Alfa was the fifty-mile missile engagement zone, which no interceptor was to penetrate lest it be considered hostile.

Air Wing 18 already had some aerial spiders waiting in the web. Operating in pairs, six Tomcats and six Hornets were controlled by two Hawkeyes circling at nearly 30,000 feet northwest and southwest of the carrier. Thus, the radar horizon was extended well beyond the ships steaming at the periphery of the battle group disposition. In his command center Chuck Gideon took in all the symbology and approved the setup for the outer zone of his air defenses. He knew it would be tested in the next several minutes.

Next, the CVBG commander surveyed the dispositions of his Aegis ships defending the group's middle antiaircraft zone—the lucky destroyer *Carl* and as yet unblooded cruisers *Bennington* and *Oriskany*. The destroyer was the only escort already on her assigned station; *Langley* and the cruisers would not reach positions to support the PhibGru for nearly an hour. Therefore, the three air-warfare vessels were currently deployed in an inverted V north of the carrier. The two CGs, steaming up to a hundred miles northeast and north-northwest of *Langley* and 150 miles apart, covered the likeliest Backfire approach routes. *Carl* was positioned between the two cruisers, roughly north of *Langley*. With her

SAMs virtually depleted, Gideon had condemned the destroyer to act as a radar picket that would provide early warning to the CVBG in case its Hawkeyes were knocked out.

The DDG also was the card up the admiral's sleeve in a new trick he intended to try on the Russians—cooperative engagement. Within limits, CE allowed the destroyer's three SPG-62 radars to illuminate incoming antiship missiles for SAMs fired from a distant cruiser. Software upgrades to the program run by the Aegis system's computers made CE theoretically possible, but the group had only practiced the procedure once, firing a single Standard.

Unfortunately, *Bennington* was one of the early *Ticonderoga*-class cruisers. Her two Mark 26 twin-arm missile launchers had been replaced by Mark 41 VLSes, but her computers—twelve UYK-7s and a single UYK-20—had not been updated. Unlike *Carl*'s five new UYK-43B and *Oriskany*'s powerful UYK-44 computers, the older hardware could not process the improved software rapidly enough to solve the fire-control problems involved in cooperative engagement.

Still, Gideon figured CE was worth a try. If it failed, *Oriskany*'s four SPG-62 SAM fire-control radars could light up. If it succeeded, every antiradiation missile on the Backfires' bellies would home on the toothless destroyer. Once the antiradar variants of Kitchen locked on to *Carl*'s signal, the cruiser could illuminate the Russian ASMs for her own Standards.

Gideon didn't like placing *Carl* in a sacrificial situation, but there was no doubt, as Mr. Spock used to say, that the good of the many—7,000 men on the carrier and the two *Ticonderoga*-class cruisers—outweighed the good of the destroyer's few hundred. Nate always reminded him that the English philosopher Jeremy Bentham had said that first, but Gideon felt the concept had probably occurred to some homo erectus before the first one ever migrated out of Africa.

The inner air defense zone was guarded by the goalkeeping *Belknap*-class cruiser *Arthur* and the *Perry*-class frigate *Meyring*. Both fired early versions of the Standard area-defense SAM, but from rotating rather than vertical launchers and controlled by mechanically steered search-and-track radars instead of the phased-array system of the

Aegis ships. The FFG and older cruiser consequently had less capacity for the multiple, rapid engagements needed to counter a saturation attack, but could handle any antiship missiles leaking through the middle zone.

Finally, for last-ditch self-protection, *Langley* and underway replenishment ship *Roseburg* were, like the *Spruance* destroyers, equipped with Sea Sparrow and Rolling Airframe Missile point-defense SAMs and Phalanx close-in weapon systems.

Gideon knew that, unless the Russians resorted to nuclear warheads, this multilayered defense system was a tough nut to crack. But the sixty-odd AS-4s now bearing down on his splendid battle group constituted the heaviest, swiftest air-to-surface hammer in the history of war at sea. The destruction of *Davenport* and *Wheatley* showed the havoc that giant, supersonic antiship cruise missiles could wreak.

The admiral felt he had done all he could do to help his force survive the coming onslaught. Gideon did not yet know how effective the sub- and cruiser-launched Tomahawk strikes had been on the air bases in southern Madagascar, nor the result of *Grouper*'s independent attack on Antsiranana in the north of the huge island. He appreciated that his force had been well supported by CentCom, Washington, the U.S. Air Force and other naval units. The inevitable had been staved off longer than he had considered possible. Now his leadership and the equipment and training of his own sailors would be fully tested.

15

1801 to 1831, Friday, 4 June

1801 Pretoria; 1901 Local
Langley, *Southwest Indian Ocean*

"Admiral! Frisbee 605 reports inbound tracks. Multiple contacts; range 400, bearing three-two-niner our posit. Presumed Backfires." The CDC communicator's report from the northern E-2 coincided with glowing red traces on the screen.

Gottlieb, hovering around the radar console, confirmed the ID. "Gotta be Tu-26s," he added. "The ones we've been waiting for."

"How bad?" Gideon's fingers gripped the arm of his seat.

The radar console operator tapped his keyboard, calling up another data display. "Uh, Hawkeye downlink shows sixty-six detected so far, sir," he answered.

"Divisional strength, Admiral," Gottlieb pointed out. "Unless they're decoys, this is the big one."

"Hawkeye has vectored outer CAP to intercept," the communicator called out. Gideon saw that the leading Backfires were about 200 miles north-northwest of the four Tomcats' patrol station; their heading to intercept the fast bombers was west-northwest. Within a few minutes, the

F-14s would reach maximum Phoenix range, but the admiral expected they would hold their fire until within sixty miles— about ten minutes, given current courses and speeds.

Gideon looked around at his staff. He knew that, following losses and battle damage in the *Varyag* strike and Badger intercepts, only nine of his remaining twelve Tomcats were fully mission-capable. Two battle-damaged survivors were not yet airworthy and avionic systems of the third were down. The latter's black boxes would soon be replaced, but the other two Tomcats might be out of action until tomorrow —too late.

Two F-14s were on outer CAP and two others were already airborne to relieve the pair on station. Two more were sitting on the bow cats; these might not be able to intercept the bombers before the Tupolevs fired their anti-ship missiles. The fourth pair were parked on the flight deck, their aircrew on standby. *Eight Tomcats against several dozen Backfires*, Gideon thought. *Thank God for the Aegis cruisers. We'll need every SAM in their magazines.*

Seven Hornets had been lost attacking *Novo* and *Varyag*, but none in the standoff combats against the Vietnamese and Korean MiGs escorting the Badgers. Air-to-air avionics were functional on all thirteen remaining F/A-18s, but three weren't airworthy. Currently, two were on CAP, operating in mixed sections with two Tomcats, while two others hunted targeting Bears or any other snoopers the enemy may have airborne. The last available pair was on alert status.

Fighting the oncoming Backfire regiments with at most twenty interceptors—half *Langley*'s full complement— would tax the air wing's management abilities to the limit, as well as the endurance of aviators and support crews. But Gideon had faith in his men and equipment. "Here we go," the battle group commander said. "You know what to do."

"Launch the ready-alert birds," Ballantine ordered the air boss over the intercom. "Replace them with F/A-18s and put two others on the waist cats."

If the alert F-14s failed to attack the Backfires before they launched their Kitchens, Gideon would order the Tomcats to shoot at the AS-4s. Phoenixes were fast enough to overtake Kitchens, but Sparrow and Sidewinder could only engage them head-on. Even in the thin stratospheric air, friction heated the Mach 3.5 antiship missiles' skin hot enough for all-aspect AIM-9Ls to home on the AS-4s' infrared signature from the front.

Baltic and Black Sea Fleet Backfires

In the crew cabin, lights flashed and buzzers sounded. "What is it?" Colonel of Aviation Rodion I. Berezhevoy asked.

"Still analyzing, Colonel," the systems manager responded, twisting dials on his vacuum-tubed, radar-threat console. He doubled as weapons officer, seated behind the copilot and next to the drafted radio operator/rear gun controller. "Signal consistent with APS-125," the systems manager answered at last. "E-2C paint," he said, delivering the bad news laconically.

At least it's not AIM-54C's active homing signal, Berezhevoy thought. *Not yet, anyway.* "Guess we're on the right track," he commented. *Where are those little yellow monkeys and big black woodblocks in MiGs? We've got friendly countries on both sides of us. When are the fighters going to get here?*

"Turn off the goddamn warning alarms, but keep a sharp eye and ear out for APG-71 transmissions," the colonel ordered. "I had my fill of Tomcat emissions this morning."

In a single day, the Black Sea Fleet Backfire force had been reduced from two regiments to one understrength, battered squadron. Berezhevoy urgently wanted to accomplish the mission that had ruined his naval aviation division. He was afraid that the longer it took to reach his launch point, the greater the chance his bombers would be intercepted. Yet, low on fuel, the Backfires could not afford to go supersonic. Therefore, he requested permission to speed toward the reported contacts.

The Northern Fleet divisional commander granted the Black Sea Fleet colonel's request. Although Berezhevoy's planes ran the risk of being intercepted before launch, the major general allowed him promptly to strike the radar returns relayed by the first Bear. The colonel would lead not only the seven planes surviving from his own regiment, but the nineteen aircraft in the two remaining Baltic Fleet squadrons as well. The twenty-six Backfires accelerated to maximum cruise.

Berezhevoy felt he had organized his makeshift regiment as well as possible under the circumstances. It included Backfires from five different regiments and two fleets, shuffled while airborne and under fire. That they could function as a unit at all was a tribute to their sound training, equipment and doctrine. All the suffering of those pain-in-the-ass, twelve-to-eighteen-hour practice missions was now paying off.

His force carried twenty-six antiship missiles and an equal number of antiradar *Buryas*. The latter were tuned to home on one of three different frequencies—the I-band target-illumination signals for the Standard and Sea Sparrow SAMs and the J-band gunfire-control of the Phalanx CIWS. In his trailing, ten-plane squadron, the colonel had placed all four Tu-26s armed with anti-Sparrow variants of *Burya*. Each squadron had one or two anti-Phalanx missiles; the other seventeen ARMs would lock onto transmissions of the SPG-60 or -62 Standard SAM fire-control radars. Berezhevoy did not expect his regiment to destroy many U.S. ships, but its missiles would deplete the Americans' magazines and, he hoped, soften up their defenses by knocking out some radars. After all, he knew that before midnight four other regiments would follow his into the attack.

Overhead, the strange stars shone brilliantly. Berezhevoy found the Southern Cross; it pointed the way to his heart's desire—revenge.

1805 Pretoria; 1905 Local
Langley

"The Backfires appear to be splitting into two or three streams," the radar console operator said nervously.

"Probably forming separate axes of attack, one per regiment," Nate Gottlieb assessed. It was not standard Russian strike doctrine, he realized, but was probably wise against an imprecisely located enemy and with another bomber division to follow. "These regiments'll probe us and soften us up, then the Pacific Fleet regiments'll press the attack home on whichever axis is weakened the most," he offered. Gideon merely murmured an acknowledgment.

The CAP birds had already responded. On the screen, Gottlieb watched them swing into action. He bit his thumbnail as four radar tracks broke off from the formation vectored west-northwest toward the Hawkeye. The two Tomcats and two Hornets took up a more westerly course to intercept about two dozen Backfires that had sped away from the main bomber stream. The fighters went to burner; if there was ever a time to guzzle gas, it was when Tupolevs started a launch run.

1910 Local
Backfires

"APG-71 up!" the systems manager called. Berezhevoy switched on his own RWR panel, and immediately lights blinked and alarms beeped. "Bearing oh-niner-one," the backseater added. The colonel turned his warning gear off.

"Here we go again," Berezhevoy said. "This is getting monotonous." He could tell the stiff-upper-lip bit wasn't playing well with his three crewmen. The radio operator/gunner was on the verge of cracking up. The colonel wished he had some means of fighting back more useful than a tail cannon. "Just let us launch," he growled to himself.

"Initiating radio-electronic countermeasures," the systems manager said. Berezhevoy had begun to suspect that, powerful though his bombers' jammers were, it didn't completely fritz out the Tomcats' new radar. It was inconceivable that, from a hundred miles away, the APG-71 could burn through the ECM. *Must be their computers,* he decided. *Signal processing, just like their ASW edge. It's their software engineers that will kill us all—Jews, Asiatics and awkward, degenerate weaklings in thick glasses.*

Once again, he cursed the Asian and African fighter pilots for leaving his magnificent bombers unprotected. He wondered if Russian fliers and ground controllers would have done any better.

Without a Madcap or Mainstay AWACS on station, Berezhevoy could not know how far away the Tomcats were, only their relative bearing. For all he could tell, they may already have fired their AIM-54Cs. In fact, he realized it was probable. Since the Hawkeye had told the F-14s where to find the Backfires, the interceptors wouldn't have to use their

APG-71s in the search mode, but only to acquire targets. For the third time that day, the colonel's big, slab-sided, non-stealthy aircraft was a target.

1911 Local
Langley

The symbols representing seven Phoenix missiles streaked toward their targets. It thrilled Gideon to witness his men at work in real time, over 300 miles away. "Seven out of eight," he observed aloud. "Not bad for missiles that have endured so many traps." The air wing had been forced to use its most abused AIM-54Cs. The controlled crashes that were carrier landings raised havoc with the intricate devices' electronics.

"Small miracle," Gottlieb agreed. "Hope their radars turn on." Fired in two volleys sixty miles from the bombers, the Phoenixes rapidly accelerated to their maximum speed of 3,200 miles per hour.

1912 Local
Backfires

"Five minutes to launch point at present course and speed," reported the systems manager, now functioning as weapons officer. Berezhevoy's regiment had traveled over a hundred miles since veering off from and running ahead of the other two bomber formations.

"Very well," the colonel replied with relief and gratification. "Prepare to begin weapons release run-in."

At that moment, the radar warning gear went off again. Quickly reverting to his former role, the backseat officer manipulated his defensive systems console. "Definitely active, terminal-homing signal of AIM-54C," came his unwelcome announcement. "Prepare for Phoenix engagement!"

"Radio operator, alert the squadrons," Berezhevoy glumly ordered, although most no doubt had functional RWRs. The four men tightened their harnesses and scanned the sky. All knew that the wounded, fully loaded bomber could scarcely jink to avoid the big Mach Five missiles, despite its low fuel state.

"Initiating radio-electronic combat," the systems manager said, upping the frequency of his jamming.

"Exhaust trails! At, uh, seven, no, eight o'clock," the young radioman yelled in a squeaky voice through a dry throat.

"Break!" Berezhevoy shouted over the plane-to-plane guard channel, then banked right. Each of the trailing, three-aircraft flights executed the well-practiced maneuver as well as sluggish, unresponsive Tupolev beasts could be expected to. The port planes banked left and down, the starboard bombers climbed right and the central planes dived right. The Backfire formation flew apart like a starburst.

Among the bombers, proximity fuses detonated, filling the sky with white clouds, each containing 132 pounds of continuous-rod high-explosive and metal fragments.

Langley

"Looks like the boys are doing pretty well." Nate Gottlieb's Newman-blue eyes tracked back and forth across the tactical data display, noting bomber tracks disappearing along the outer edges of the defensive screen. "The division in Three-Zero Echo splashed four or five. The other four fighters are still headed toward the main body of the enemy," he told Gideon. "Every last one of our functional AIM-54s is airborne right now," the CSO added. "But the Toms should bag a lot of bombers with them. If there was ever a target-rich environment, they're in it."

The men in CDC saw the two Tomcat-Hornet sections close to Sparrow range. "They're going after the bombers," Gottlieb observed. "I doubt they'll get a shot at the targeting birds or fighter escorts out of Mozambique. Thank God the TLAMs wasted the MiG bases on southern Madagascar."

"Yeah, but there's plenty more Backfires behind these," Gideon responded. Satellites had kept him posted on the progress of the Pacific Fleet regiments. "It's gonna be a busy night."

1915 Local
Grid Three-Five Charlie

Circus 210 had already fired its four Phoenixes, but continued toward its targets. Since five bombers had gone off the scope, the two aircrew knew their missiles had to have killed at least one of the Backfires. The F-14 and its F/A-18 partner had gobbled up thirty miles in three minutes.

The Tomcat crew and the Hornet pilot in Rampart 405 had never worked together before. But the three fliers felt reasonably prepared for the task at hand, owing to CAG Ballantine's insistence on mixed-section tactics training. "Predator" Prater the RIO monitored his APG-71 fire-control radar—affording greater coverage than two Hornets working together. In effect, Predator was functioning as a mini-AWACS, directing the missile-engagement plan against the Backfires still inbound in its sector.

Still time to spare, Predator thought to himself. He decided to use the secure but time-consuming scrambler radio in the last few moments available. Engaging the scrambler, he allowed the set to synchronize, then transmitted. "Four-Oh-Five, Two-Ten. I'm painting multiple targets now due north. Approaching Sparrow range . . ." He assigned targeting data to avoid multiple engagement—always a risk with two missile-shooters.

In 405, Hornet pilot "Surf" Surface acknowledged the direction and designated a hostile blip in his sector. *'Bout time,* he thought. *The Tom already got off four shots. Now it's my turn, baby!* He rechecked his switches, confirmed the radar lock and—for the first time in his life—made the call in earnest. "Fox one, fox one."

In moments six AIM-7Ms had blazed away from the two fighters. One went ballistic but the others guided and accelerated, gulping up the thirty miles to the Russian bombers at Mach Four.

Langley

"AIM-7Ms away," the communicator called out. "Tomcats report heavy jamming," the sailor added.

Gideon knew this meant trouble. Every Backfire carried at least as much ECM and ECCM equipment as the electronic-warfare variants of Badger. The F-14s' Phoenixes had homed on the jamming of targeted Tu-26s, destroying them, but this had had no effect on the defensive capability of the remaining bombers, as the Phoenix volley had against the less-capable Badgers. And, unlike AIM-54, Sparrows could not home on their targets' jamming.

"Looks like ten good missiles, sir," the seaman announced.

Again over eighty percent, Gideon calculated. *Amazing.* Early versions of AIM-7 had performed poorly against fighters in 'Nam, but they had been improved, and now were being used against the targets they were designed to engage. At one point the Navy had stopped accepting AIM-54Cs due to low quality. AAMRAM's development had been long and costly. He considered his air wing's success so far with radar-guided missiles a tribute to his maintenance crews.

The admiral watched the air battle data-linked to his scope. He was as remote as if viewing a video game, except that each symbol stood for living men, many of whom were his friends.

1916 Local
Backfires

"Look out!" Rodion Berezhevoy would have gasped had not his adrenaline kicked in. Acting on instinct, he grasped the control column from his copilot and shoved forward—hard. *We're going to collide!*

The regimental commander had never seen a Tu-26 in plan view before. Even as the rapid onset of negative G lifted him slightly off his ejection seat, he marveled at the unusual attitude of his number four bomber. In microseconds the spectre appeared, loomed hugely in his windscreen, then was gone somewhere overhead. The colonel centered his controls, resumed level flight and called for crew status reports. All was normal, except for the radioman who was puking into a glove. High-G maneuvering was unusual for intercontinental bombers.

Despite the scare, Berezhevoy understood the situation. The Phoenix barrage, followed within less than five minutes by Sparrows, had undone his regiment's attack formation. When some of the American missiles burned through his electronic countermeasures, individual pilots acted independently. Obviously, Number Four had made a violent left-hand evasive maneuver without thinking of the potential consequences. The colonel resolved to have a word with the man. *If either of us survives.*

It occurred to him that he had never practiced regimental-scale evasive maneuvering after an initial break in formation. *A serious oversight in the training syllabus.* His plane lurched; he wrestled it into position in the regrouped attack formation. The Tupolev's port aileron hydraulic lines were leaking; he was flying with backup mechanical controls. The colonel's attention returned to the present.

For the moment, Berezhevoy was concerned with the status of his forces. Returning control to his ashen-faced co-pilot, he contacted the other formations by jam-proof radio. Ticking off the reports on his kneepad, he felt a sinking, burning sensation in his stomach. The idiot who almost collided with him was the only other survivor from the thirty-nine Black Sea Fleet aircraft that had left their staging bases in Turkestan that morning. The other two squadrons under his command—both from the Baltic Fleet—had lost three bombers each. Berezhevoy was appalled. His makeshift regiment retained just fifteen of the twenty-six aircraft he had led down the Mozambique Channel after the B-1Bs killed the Baltic Fleet divisional and regimental commanders. He did not know the status of the Northern Fleet regiments behind him, but assumed they were as yet intact.

Over the intercom, Berezhevoy told his copilot, "We can still soften up their defenses for the Northern and Pacific fleets. Together, their four regiments have about ninety Tu-26s. If that doesn't do it, we can rearm and refuel in Mozambique and hit them again tomorrow. Maybe get the Badgers and Fencers in on it, too. The Americans are doomed. It's just a matter of time."

Langley

Gottlieb anxiously studied the screen. When the welter of images resolved into renewed, identifiable formations, he counted fifteen returns in the forward regiment. Referring to his notes, he reported. "If Phoenix accounted for five, then the ten Sparrows that guided must have killed four.

"So, the good news is, we splashed nine Backfires," Gottlieb said, "apparently from the leading regiment. The bad news," the CSO added, pointing to new traces on the scope, "is, the trailing two regiments are intact."

Gideon had hoped the AIM-7Ms might have done better than forty percent of those arriving in the target area and a third of those launched, but decided the Backfires' ECM must have been too effective.

"The Tomcats and Hornets have not broken off, Admiral," Gottlieb said. "The other division is continuing after the trailing two Backfire regiments."

"Very well," he said. "Tell them to continue closing the bombers."

"New contacts, bearing two-eight-one," the radar operator reported. "Initial classification, MiGs!"

"How many?" Gottlieb asked, and returned to surveying the scope.

"Coupla dozen, sir." He called up a count. "Thirty-two, to be exact."

"Yipes," the CSO said. "Most of a regiment, Admiral. Against eight of our fighters, four of which are out of radar missiles. What do we do? Call 'em back? They have time to run away."

Once again, Gideon felt the great weight of responsibility bearing down on him, like pulling a nine-G turn. Soberly, with none of their usual camaraderie, he turned to Ballantine, then asked, "CAG, what's their fuel state?"

"The Circus division, real low," Ballantine replied. "The Gunshot division, good. We've got tankers airborne."

The admiral gazed at the scope, where red and blue fighter symbols converged at over 1,000 knots. "What are the odds for the Circus division?"

"They've got a Prowler up there to help them against the radar-guided missiles. If we vector the other Tomcat-Hornet division toward the fighters instead of the bombers, they could take a lot of 'em out, thanks to Phoenix. But I doubt if very many would come home. The other Hornets can't get there in time. After the radar missile exchange, it'd be a dogfight, a big furball. And we'd simply run outa beebees first."

"What do you think?" Gideon asked.

"The Backfires're our main mission. I'd say let the MiGs

come toward us, but keep on after the bombers. Next time, they'll coordinate their fighters and Backfires better. We won't get another shot like this. The reason we have Tomcats is to defend the carrier. My boys know that."

"But you just said they won't come back."

"That's right. If they press the attack, they'll run outta gas, if they don't get shot down first. We can't operate tankers that close to enemy fighters."

"Nate," Gideon inquired, "your recommendation?"

"Gotta go for it," the CSO replied firmly but without enthusiasm.

"The bombers are already in Kitchen range, assuming high-altitude launch and assuming they know where we are," Gideon pointed out. "Is it worth losing eight or more fighters to kill Backfires after they've launched?"

"They'll be back," Gottlieb said. "And, like CAG says, we may not get another shot at 'em anyway."

"CAG?" the admiral asked, for the record.

"Do it."

"Very well. I concur. CAG, order all airborne fighters to continue on their intercept headings for the Backfires. Have the Hornets hunting Bears break off and form sections and divisions to go after the fighters. If they don't arrive in time to help out the Tomcats and other Hornets, then maybe they can avenge them."

1917 Local
Circus 210

Predator got the word via the Hawkeye. Frisbee 605 came up on the guard channel.

"Continue present vector," the Tomcat's airborne controller ordered.

"They expect us to shoot down Backfires with two 'Winders and a gun?" the pilot asked rhetorically.

"Looks that way," the RIO answered. "Guess CAG wants us to make ace or sumthin'."

"Hell of a nice guy, but who's gonna keep the MiGs off our tail while we worry the poor Backfires to death with twenty mike-mike?"

"Uh, ya got me there. I'll be sure and take that up with CAG next time we hoist brewskis together."

"What a clusterfuck," Predator heard over the intercom, but his pilot accelerated toward their targets. The RIO craned his neck around. Sure enough, Rampart 405 followed suit. Prater knew Surf's Hornet was even lower on fuel than his Tomcat.

Backfires

"Colonel, we are nearing our planned launch point." The weapons officer's voice sounded firm, professional. "Enemy naval group identified by Tu-20 targeting aircraft not yet evident on our radar."

"Well, then, fire decoy missiles on data-linked coordinates, according to plan," Berezhevoy replied, then ordered the other fourteen planes in his regiment to do the same.

The weapons officer confirmed the flight data entered into the autopilot mechanisms of the decoys. He opened the ventral doors of the internal weapons bay and activated switches controlling the countermeasure release mechanisms. Small but highly radar-reflective, lightweight decoy missiles were ejected from the weapons bay, and then the doors closed back up. Both decoys' rocket engines ignited; under remote control of the weapons officer, they climbed to 20,000 meters, where their on-board autopilots began controlling their flight. The crewman informed his pilot that both decoys were good.

"Very well," Berezhevoy responded. "Fire antiship missiles," he ordered unemotionally both over the intercom and secure, plane-to-plane radio.

The weapons officer confirmed that the proper data were programmed into the real missiles' inertial guidance systems, under the control of which they would fly toward the enemy's position. Once in the target area, the passive terminal-homing head of the antiradar variant would turn on and start searching for the signal it was designed to lock on to. Berezhevoy knew his missile would seek out transmissions characteristic of the SPG-62 fire-control radar for the Standard SAM. Other antiradiation variants of the missile known to NATO as AS-4 Kitchen and to its makers as *Burya*— Tempest—would home on other air-search and fire-control radars. The true antiship variants with active seeker heads homed on the reflections off targeted ships of the missiles' own radar transmissions.

The weapons officer released the ARM first, followed ten seconds later by the ASM version. The two thirty-seven-foot-long missiles dropped off the pylons under each large, fixed, inboard section of the Backfire's wings. Both *Buryas'* energetic, liquid-fuel rocket motors ignited. Under aerodynamic control of their stubby, delta-shaped wings and cruciform tail surfaces, the powerful, seven-ton missiles lifted almost straight upward.

As Berezhevoy felt his plane respond to the released weight, his own depressed spirits soared with the *Burya* missiles. From launch altitude of 11,000 meters, he watched with satisfaction as his own Tempest zoomed out of sight. The pilot knew the missile was programmed to streak into the mid-stratosphere before leveling off at 30,000 meters. No air-breathing aircraft could fly where the atmosphere was so thin.

Over the next few minutes, Berezhevoy's bobtailed regiment launched thirty big AS-4s. Only the pilots and copilots had a view—restricted as it was—of the missiles' abrupt climbs. Two dozen functioned as intended, leveling off at the proper height, then shrieking to their cruise speed of three and a half times the velocity of sound at sea level. To the colonel's great pleasure, a similar number of decoys obediently mimicked the real Kitchens' flight path.

While rocket-powered missiles could function at 100,000 feet, the motors of most tactical SAMs would burn out before attaining such an altitude. Therefore, the Russian missiles were relatively safe during their high-altitude cruise. Only when they stooped on their targets did they become vulnerable to the hundreds of SAMs carried by American CVBGs.

Berezhevoy was nervous about remaining in the area much longer—barely 200 miles from the enemy battle group. You never knew when more of the seemingly inexhaustible American fighters would descend on you. But the thought of one-ton warheads smashing into U.S. ships was comforting—revenge for the terrible beating the once-proud Baltic and Black Sea regiments had suffered.

Every plane under his command was low on fuel. Ground control on Madagascar reported repairs still incom-

plete to the Backfires' planned recovery bases attacked by
Tomahawks. Backup bases in central Madagascar and northern Mozambique lacked missile stores and facilities for handling bombers; nor were their runways long enough for fully
loaded Backfires to take off. But that's where Berezhevoy
would have to take his regiment. His diversion bases were
Beira and Nacala, Mozambique. Unless tanked, they lacked
the fuel to make Nacala.

Langley

"Jeezus. Look at that!" It wasn't standard phraseology,
but the twenty-one-year-old radar operator made his point.
He gawked at his scope.

"Raid count!" snapped Ballantine.

The boy returned to business. "About four dozen tracks
inbound, sir. Targeting indications are *Oriskany, Carl* and
Bennington." He took a moment to validate his estimate.
"Make it forty-five inbound, sir."

Bubba calculated, *Assume half are decoys. That means
around twenty-three missiles. Average almost eight ALCMs
per ship. It's gonna be a real busy three minutes.*

He knew what was happening topside, throughout the
battle group. The ForceCAP of Tomcats and Hornets would
be short on fuel, most of them out of missiles. By now the
giant, high-speed AS-4s were past the fighter pickets, with
one of the three known targeting Bears still alive. Once into
the missile engagement zone, the human element was largely
negated. Survival now depended on computer-programmed
deception measures and active defenses.

Secretly, Bubba Ballantine didn't trust his Macintosh
SE, let alone any computer contracted by the United States
government.

"Track extrapolation update tending toward the west,"
the radar operator reported. "Looks like they're all headed
for *Oriskany.*"

1918 Local

"*Roseburg* reports paint by I/J-band radiation," the
ESM console operator reported. "Ten gigahertz. Analysis indicates Big Bulge, sir," he told the TAO.

The tactical action officer informed Gottlieb that the surface-search and targeting radar of a Bear-D had illuminated the battle group's unrep ship. *Roseburg* had already transferred much of its reload ordnance to *Langley* and her escorts, but the AOE—53,600 tons fully laden and second in size only to the carrier—was still valuable to the CVBG.

1919 Local
Backfires

Berezhevoy was about to order the fifteen surviving aircraft to reverse course to head north by northwest when his weapons officer came up on the intercom. "Colonel, we have . . . er, I don't understand," the officer said, his voice lacking all its previous confidence. "We're receiving a valid signal from another targeting aircraft."

The colonel mashed down on the intercom button. "What are you trying to say, boy?" His tone was far from fatherly.

"Sir . . . I just don't understand. We're showing *another* American carrier group far south of the . . . of the force we have fired upon."

"That's not our concern now," the pilot told him. "Probably the Yankee amphibious group. Let ground control or the Northern Fleet boys decide whether to attack it or follow up our strike."

Berezhevoy didn't feel as sanguine as he tried to sound. Everyone on board knew there was a good chance that one or the other of the sightings—possibly even both—were decoys. Being shot down by the Americans was almost preferable to being duped by them, if that was what had happened. He feared the worst, but comforted himself with the thought that it was already too late to send course-change signals to his missiles' inertial guidance systems.

Their job done, he ordered his regiment to execute a 160-degree turn and set course for Beira.

Langley

"Splash another Bear." The CDC officer confirmed Rampart 310's kill on a targeting aircraft north-northwest of the battle group.

Bubba Ballantine was not interested in scorekeeping. "The sucker probably already handed off targeting data to the Backfires," he observed.

Standing behind the watch officer in the yellow-and-red-lit combat information center, the air wing commander kept a tight rein on himself. It was so tempting to become emotionally involved in the "game" displayed on the board. *Gotta keep cool,* Ballantine told himself. *Stay frosty.*

Gideon and Gottlieb joined the CAG. "We bagged the Bear that busted *Roseburg,*" Ballantine reported. "No way to detect a data-link transmission from the Bear to the Backfires," he added, "but odds are he spread the word before we splashed him."

"Damn," Gideon said. "There's still a chance we took in the first Backfire regiment, isn't there?" he asked.

"We'll know in a minute or two," Gottlieb answered.

1920 Local

The radar console operator in CDC raptly monitored the impending doom of the three Aegis ships in the CVBG's outer screen. Each second the red arrows moved closer. "Distance to *Oriskany,* 120 miles," the sailor announced.

"Jernstedt will have to decide right away whether to engage or not," Gottlieb noted. "We still haven't been able to determine for sure if the missiles have a lock on *Oriskany* or not," the CSO explained. "Their course to date could go either way. Plus, they could change course. I think we have to order him to shoot as soon as they come within range."

"Yeah, but then the Russians'll know where the Aegis ships really are," Gideon countered.

"They probably already do, thanks to the goddamn Bear," Ballantine threw in.

"For all they know, those radar returns could be decoys instead of the real McCoy," Gideon observed.

"Can't take that chance," Gottlieb said.

Gideon had just decided to give Captain Eric Jernstedt, *Oriskany's* skipper, permission to fire at will when the radar operator spoke up again. "Reanalysis indicates tracks not guiding on cruisers or destroyer," the seaman concluded. He called up a path extrapolation, then excitedly announced,

"They're gonna miss! Don't know what's wrong, but they're not headed for *Oriskany*."

Beaming with delight, Gideon, Gottlieb and Ballantine exchanged knowing glances. Each man thought *Our decoys!* and permitted himself to hope that the ploy had worked. Hours previously, en route northwest from *Langley*'s early-morning launch point to her present position, the officers had dispatched two Vikings westward. They'd dropped seven floating, radar-reflective decoys in a 200-mile-wide circular pattern northeast of the stricken *Spruance*-class destroyers. The formation of corner reflectors was centered about 500 miles east of *Novorossiysk*, along the path flown by *Langley*'s diversionary strike aircraft in attacking the Russian V/STOL carrier group.

"They've taken the bait!" the operator shouted gleefully. "They fell for it. The decoys suckered the missiles! Dumb mothers."

"So much for smart weapons," Gottlieb interjected.

1921 Local
Backfires

Berezhevoy knew why the MiG pilots didn't shoot; fired from beyond visual range, their big radar-guided missiles posed a greater threat to the Russian bombers than did the Americans' small, heat-seeking AAMs. But still he damned the Viets to eternal hellfire for arriving late.

"Fighters!" the weapons officer sang out. "Four o'clock low. Range under fifteen kilometers."

Closing to the heart of the AIM-9L envelope, Berezhevoy realized. *Taking no chances. Wish to hell I hadn't decided to bring up the regiment's rear*. He knew that the Americans' all-aspect AAMs allowed them to attack from angles other than dead astern, avoiding the Backfires' 23mm tail cannon.

The weapons officer saw the hateful fighters climb and swing into line astern of the Backfire formation. "Six o'clock level!" he called. "Range, ten kilometers."

Berezhevoy knew they would stay out of 23mm range, but ordered the gunner to fire anyway. It might disrupt the enemy pilots' concentration.

Red tracer rounds arced toward the U.S. navy aircraft,

but fell seaward far short of their targets. The systems manager ejected flares, but the Sidewinders' seeker heads were too sophisticated to be suckered.

The four American fighters launched eight AIM-9Ls; seven guided toward the two rearmost bombers. Four found the Backfires' jet exhaust.

Berezhevoy felt the detonations. They seemed too weak to have ruined his hundred-million-dollar aircraft, but the warning lights on his instrument panel left no doubt. Both engines were gone.

Enraged, the colonel shut off fuel to the huge, 50,000-pound thrust Kuznetsov engines. At least the Yankees had not been able to attack the trailing regiments, those still carrying missiles. "Prepare to eject," he ordered.

Berezhevoy saw the Tomcats and Hornets streak past. They pressed on, ready to chop to bits as many more Backfires as their limited supply of 20mm cannon rounds would allow. He imagined that the fighters were using their last reserves of fuel to maneuver for shots on the bombers outside the arc of their 23mm cannon, which outranged their M-61 Gatling guns.

The thought *They'll go for the pilots* suddenly came to Berezhevoy. It was the surest way for fighter pilots armed with not very powerful guns to destroy big, tough aircraft. In the final seconds before punching out, while his wounded beast glided down to a more clement altitude, the colonel felt he had met combat face-to-face. He and his enemy might ride into battle on the most technologically advanced war machines yet devised, but their fight still came down to murder. The American fliers were going to personally shoot highly trained men under Berezhevoy's command. He was glad to be out of this war. "Eject," the colonel ordered.

Langley

In CDC, Ballantine watched the performance of his mixed-section fighters, courtesy of data links from the E-2C, ES-3A and EA-6B. He yearned to be in action with his men, but realized that blood would flow on *Langley* soon enough.

With 'Winders and twenty mike-mike, the four engaged fighters sent more Backfires tumbling toward the warm ocean below. From the Russian first regiment, just four bombers remained to limp to relative safety in Mozambique. But now toothless Tomcats and stingless Hornets faced destruction. As they banked for home, CAG knew his fighters could run but not hide. Sixteen MiG-23 Floggers chased the unarmed U.S. interceptors south; ES-3A intercepts made them Vietnamese. *What's old is new again,* the CAG thought.

Within six minutes, Ballantine witnessed:

The Prowler earn its $120 million price tag, jamming or decoying the Floggers' volley of radar-guided AA-7 missiles, which could not home on jamming . . .

The talker report that the hightailing planes, now on fumes, were "squawking"—emitting IFF recognition codes —as they entered the arc of cruiser *Oriskany*'s Block IV SM-2s, the longest-range variant of Standard SAM . . .

The Floggers close on the Tomcats and Hornets, looking for a shot with AA-8 or AA-11 heat-seekers, the Vietnamese apparently unaware of the Americans' low fuel state . . .

The bugging-out fighters drawing the Floggers within range of Captain Jernstedt's Block IV Standards . . .

Oriskany's skipper waste his precious Block IVs shooting at the enemy fighters rather than waiting for the antiship missiles to come within range . . .

Langley's other two Tomcats launch AIM-54Cs at the trailing two Backfire regiments, already in launch formation . . .

Another four flights of Viet MiGs vector toward these F-14s and their F/A-18 wingmen; the carrier aviators continue streaking toward Sparrow range of the bombers, ignoring the enemy fighters; the Prowler turn its ECM pods against the new threat . . .

The worst possible thing happen—the Americans lose the race to hit the second-echelon bombers before AS-4 launch; 150 Kitchens and decoys glowing red on the blue screen, their extrapolated flight paths indicating that a Bear must have linked them the Americans' real coordinates . . .

The Phoenixes, arriving late, tearing the Backfire formations apart before they turned around . . .

The two homeward-bound sections drop off the scope, out of JP-5; the Hornets far to the north, the Tomcats close enough to *Oriskany* and *Bennington* for their crews to be rescued by the cruisers' Seahawks . . .

Oriskany's Standard SAMs knock about half the Floggers out of the African sky and the surviving MiGs break off their pursuit, scattering like startled chickens . . .

Langley's own ESM console operator receiving the J-band signal of AS-4's active homing head, indicating the end of the antiship missiles' cruise phase . . .

The first barrage of antiship missiles home on *Langley's* active and passive radar decoys, air-dropped hours earlier far to the west; Gideon's glee at the news . . .

The second wave of AS-4s split in two directions, those from one regiment seeming to home on *Oriskany* and *Carl,* while the others headed for *Bennington* . . .

Carl, her magazines depleted, radiating for the more valuable *Oriskany* so the antiradar Kitchens couldn't guide on the cruiser's transmissions . . .

The oncoming missiles diverge toward separate targets; the three escorts' Aegis computers prioritizing threats among them; a number of Kitchen tracks aiming toward *Roseburg,* the group's fast oiler and ammo resupply ship . . .

Oriskany commence firing at the active-homing ASMs and passive ARMs.

Unconsciously, Gideon and Gottlieb moved closer to Ballantine. "This is it," the admiral said. "Wish we had back the sixteen SAMs Jernstedt shot at the Floggers." On the display, the two missile streams continued toward their targets, spreading out like the clawed wings of a bat as it stoops to catch its prey.

1925 Local

Gottlieb was glued to the status panels for the three Aegis ships. The newest cruiser was already firing Standard SAMs at a furious rate. By data-link, her two Mark 41 vertical launcher systems emptied before his eyes. Every three seconds, another Block IV SM-2—the long-range variant of Standard—was subtracted from each VLS inventory total. He visualized the advanced SAMs emerging from their launch cells in a yellow-orange fireball, then within milliseconds leaping straight upward, trailing white exhaust. Keening over, they would arch northward toward the Kitchens still cruising nineteen miles up—a river of missiles over twice as high as the jet stream, flowing more than ten times as fast.

"So you're telling me we've got around seventy AS-4s headed our way," Gideon concluded.

"Probably a few more, sir," the CSO replied. "But they can't reach *Langley*. They were pretty clearly launched against the Aegis ships and maybe *Roseburg*, as I indicated."

"I meant our group, Captain," Gideon said frostily.

"Yes, sir. Sorry," Gottlieb gulped.

The admiral spoke quickly to let his friend off the hook. "What do you think, Nate? Can we handle 'em?"

"Yes, sir. We may take some hits, but the three Aegises theoretically have enough missiles to knock down at least half of the Kitchens, if the system works anywhere near as well as advertised. Unfortunately, we'll waste a lot of the Block IVs and some of the medium-range SAMs on decoys. Point-defense and countermeasure systems should handle most of the leakers, if not all of 'em."

The officers watched the radar scope in silence for a moment. Then Gideon said, "I hope you're right. I'm gonna pray, just the same."

"Couldn't hurt, sir," Gottlieb responded, and held up crossed fingers. "Even a single Kitchen hit on a cruiser could be fatal." Then the CSO observed, "They're within range of *Arthur*'s extended-range Standards now."

"Do you think she should engage?" Gideon asked.

"No. It would give her position away, and probably ours along with it. She couldn't shoot missiles that far fast enough to make it worthwhile. The Aegises can defend themselves. We'll need all *Arthur*'s SAMs to protect us —*Langley*—later. Just thought I should give you the option."

"Well, I concur," the admiral decided. "Have her hold her fire." Gottlieb gave Gideon's order to the data-link signalman.

As the leading Block IV SM-2s neared the first flight of inbound radar returns, senior personnel huddled around the radar console. Its operator crossed himself and kissed his thumb, then rapidly returned his hands to the keyboard.

"Here we go," Gottlieb said, with more tension in his voice than usual. Symbols of both American and Russian missiles disappeared. "Probably a high percentage of decoys in the first wave," the CSO surmised.

"Do you have to tell us that right now?" Bubba objected. No one responded to the comment. The long-range missiles continued to eat into the evening's second and third volleys of AS-4s and decoys.

1927 Local
Battle Group Charlie

Those few officers and men abovedecks were treated to a rare spectacle. And it occurred to more than a few of them that their lives might be the price of admission to the elaborate show. The Aegis ships—*Carl, Oriskany* and *Bennington*—unloaded eighty medium-range Standards in about a minute. White missile plumes rocketed vertically into the sky, where the SAMs were captured by the two *Ticonderoga*-class cruisers' phased-array radars. With continuous mid-course guidance, each command lasting mere microseconds, the big Standards streaked toward the AS-4s. It was a multidimensional problem in spatial geometry—trying to bring one highly supersonic object into contact with another. And it was extremely difficult; sensors showed only forty-one SM-2MR kills, many of which were decoys.

Lookouts were hard-pressed to focus their attention on their respective zones. So much was happening everywhere. Distraction- and seduction-mode chaff was popping from every ship, filling the air around each vessel with clouds of tiny, bright, metallized flakes that shone in the low sun like artificial snow. A few helicopters flew low around the edge of the battle group's screen, dumping passive decoys into the water. Spotters noted a couple of large splashes, instantly followed by dark, smoky explosions. And still eighty-five missiles and decoys came on. *Oriskany*'s computer assessed at least forty-five of them as Kitchens.

1931 Local
Langley

"*Roseburg* reports two hits," the CDC talker announced. "One detonation. Fires aft. Dead in the water. Commo links good."

"Very well," Gideon replied. "Nate," he said, turning to Gottlieb, "damage report."

Gottlieb had just realized that the attack was over; it had seemed to last hours. That no more hostile activity showed on the radar console had taken a moment to sink in. He was sweaty and more tensed up than at any time he could recall in his life. "Uh, wait one, sir," the CSO answered, and hurried to the battle group status board.

"Oriskany reports no damage, but she's down to three SAMs," Gottlieb informed Gideon and Ballantine. *"Bennington's* also unhurt. *Roseburg* and *Carl* both took bad hits. *Carl's* stern is gone. She's dead in the water. Preliminary assessment is that she won't last. She's out of SAMs, anyway." *Mahar's luck finally ran out,* he thought. *But she prolonged* Oriskany's *life. And* Langley's.

The CSO summarized the exchange. "The Kitchens bypassed the cruisers, presumably because *Oriskany* and *Benny* didn't radiate until late in the game and *Roseburg's* radar return was stronger. About a dozen ARMs homed on *Carl,* and some active variants. One passive- and one active-homer hit her. The majority of the active antiship missiles guided on *Roseburg.* The Kitchens or their targeters apparently thought she was the carrier.

"The cruisers and *Carl* expended 114 Standards against the AS-4s—twenty-eight Block IVs and eighty-six Block IIs and IIIs." The CSO sat down in the swivel high chair in front of the board and tried to relax. *"Roseburg* splashed eight leakers with Sparrow, RAM and twenty mike-mike," he noted. "She did well. May help save our ass, if the Russians still think they hit us. By drawing off the active-homing ALCMs, she's already saved the cruisers."

"Jeez, I hope we can do as well as her when it's our turn," the antiair warfare staffer commented.

"I hope to Christ so. We've got three Mark 29s instead of one and an extra Phalanx over her," Gottlieb replied.

Gideon silently toted up the ship casualties in his mind. First, the two *Spruance* destroyers, *Davenport* and *Wheatley.* Now *Carl* and *Roseburg.* Not to mention the Russian vessels and aircraft. He forced himself to guess at the number of lives lost and bodies maimed—perhaps 1,000 American dead and wounded so far—then asked the hardest question. "Casualties?"

"Estimates not complete yet, Admiral. Not on the board yet, anyway. My staff is working on it."

Ballantine stared at the status board and bit his lip. He

turned to the AAW specialist. "How're we fixed to meet the next wave?"

"Shit, Bubba. *Benny*'s essentially the only Aegis with any SAMs left." He checked his console. "Forty-seven. All medium-range. *Oriskany*'s got just three."

"Our goalkeepers, *Arthur* and *Meyring*, are still fully loaded, but they can't shoot fast enough to stop a full-scale attack. We pulled *Meyring*'s Harpoons and reloaded with SAMs, so she has forty SM-1s and *Arthur* has sixty SM-2s. A total of 150 Standards. Missile hits on *Roseburg* blew up her standard reloads. Not that we have time to reload enough missiles to do much good, anyway. Pacific Fleet Backfires should hit before midnight." The man's voice was flat, emotionless. "How about your guys, Bubba?"

The senior CAG reached for a phone. He called his weapons officer and asked one question. Nodding slowly, he turned back to the CDC watch. "No more Phoenix. Less than a dozen each Sparrows and AMRAAMs, with a coupla dozen 'Winders." His words filled CDC with an icy chill. Battle Group Charlie could not survive another air attack.

16

1832 to 2355, Friday, 4 June

1832
East of Babanango Aerodrome, Vryheid, Natal

"We can expect an attack between sundown and moon-rise," Vorster told his platoon leaders. "That means possibly within an hour." The company commander knew that the Viets were equipped with night-vision goggles, so didn't need to wait for moonlight—another of their many advantages.

"Sir, we can't hold here and we can't pull back," Macdonald observed. "What are we going to do?"

Boy must have read my mind, Vorster thought. *He'll make a good soldier, if he survives the night.* Macdonald was right; their bobtailed, makeshift battalion, which was holding an eight-kilometer, north-south front east of Vryheid, couldn't resist another major probe, let alone a single-axis attack. But Dirk Vorster had an answer. "Why, we attack, laddie."

"Sir?"

"Look," Vorster snapped. "The wogs won't just bungle through here; they'll continue probing and patrolling, looking for our weak spot. Then they'll shove everything they have through there. That's doctrine. But if they run into a company five or six kilometers ahead of the expected main line of resistance, they'll be confused." He shrugged in the dark. "Can't do any worse than we are now." He looked around, took in the grim, shadowed faces, and turned back to his red-lit map. He sketched out his attack plan—two platoons to advance, one to continue manning the company's defensive position. He asked for questions, but there were none.

Vorster assembled the two ambush platoons in the middle of the company line, so as not to draw adjoining units' attention to their movement. He ordered the men to cinch up their web gear tight, in order to sneak through their defensive works as stealthily as possible. He didn't tell his men that battalion had not approved this foray. Technically, it was desertion, but the whole company couldn't stop a determined enemy push, so Vorster figured he might as well leave one rifle platoon and the mortar section in the trenches. He would try to do some good with the other two platoons—with or without orders. He had to hope that the companies defending their flanks didn't shoot his patrol in their first few hundred meters. Nor did the captain consider it necessary to mention that an entire Viet motor rifle brigade was headed their way, expected to arrive tomorrow.

"Remember," Vorster added, "anything ahead of us is hostile. All communication by radio—you won't be able to see hand signals until the moon rises. All right, then. Move out." In three-man teams, sixty troopies slithered over the parapets and under the wire, then stood to traverse the mine field. Vorster reflected that the only advantage of holding a long frontage was that it made it much easier to get away with unauthorized raids. Safely past the mines 1,000 meters in front of their lines, the Afrikaners formed up into marching order.

It had gone 1930; an hour to moonrise. No sign of the enemy as yet. Vorster wondered if his assessment of the wogs' battle plans was wrong.

1942 Pretoria; 2042 Local
Frisbee 605

"Mitch, can you see them?" Tony Chimola, visually blind but electronically omniscient in the E-2's tunnel, had the stricken ships on his scope. However, he relied on his pilot and copilot for eyeball reports on the world outside.

At first the CIC officer thought that his query had gone unheard. Seconds later the pilot's voice snapped back over the ICS. "Yeah, I see 'em." From the Hawkeye's left seat, Mitch discerned the sickening yellow glows to the south. The shipboard fires to either side of the E-2, though many miles off and five miles below, grew brighter in the gathering dusk. "How we doing otherwise?"

Chimola heard the fatigue in Mitch's voice. It was to be expected of a crew flying its second four-hour mission of the day. The CICO rolled his shoulders to ease some of the strain, assessing the variety of sensor information uplinked to him. "Well, the outer escorts took it in the shorts. *Roseburg* has a bad fire from an AS-4 hit. They think she'll sink. *Carl* was practically blown out of the water. Not many survivors." *And she's got a steel superstructure,* he thought. *What woulda happened to* Arthur *or* Meyring?

"How about our guys?" The aviator's natural concern was for his carrier and its goalkeeping escorts—the ships he saw around him every day.

"Not a scratch." Chimola exhaled and swallowed hard. "But more Backfires are on the way. Sure as hell."

Mitch absorbed that information. "Yeah. Well, I guess it's a good thing Gideon kept our group apart from the 'phibs. The gomers never hit 'em. We shot down all their AWACSes and bombed their bases. They never found the PhibGru again after busting it, when was it, two days ago?"

"Yeah, I think. But cut the talk about shooting down AWACSes," Chimola replied. "Coulda just as easy been us." He felt the onset of a bad headache—partly from the constant throbbing of the turboprop engines, partly from the job pressure. "I dunno, Mitch. That upgraded AS-4 is one mean mother; it flies too damn high for anything but late-model Standards to reach it. And once it dives it's too fast and too smart for any other SAM to intercept it."

The big turboprop droned onward, the crew sitting in silence.

2000
USS Hornet, *Mozambique Channel*

With a clipboard in one hand, Captain Ken Coxen strode to the front of the briefing compartment of the amphibious assault ship. A green cloth covered an easel with a map of the Natal-Mozambique coast—a map he had only studied within the hour. *One thing about the Corps,* he thought, *it makes you into a good impromptu speaker. And it gives you a chance to shoot a wide variety of people.*

Seated in the room were the thirty-five members of the battalion landing team's reconnaissance platoon. Looking at them, Coxen was struck again by their youthfulness. He estimated the average age at twenty—eight years younger than himself. The overall impression was one of determined chins and sidewall haircuts, looking as salty as only first-cruise marines can look.

The platoon commander, First Lieutenant Chuck Smith, and his senior NCO, Gunnery Sergeant Josh Lindquist, sat up front. Of the platoon members, only Coxen and Lindquist had combat experience, dating from Grenada and Kuwait.

"Gentlemen," Coxen began, "this briefing will acquaint you with the mission you have been assigned by the landing-force commander. I will accompany you ashore for maximum coordination." He didn't say that he wrangled permission from the LFC because he had trained this platoon.

"Our objective is the Mozambican air defense center covering the border region into Natal, South Africa." Coxen lifted the veil off the easel and pointed out the facility. "Battle Group Charlie no longer has Tomahawk Land Attack cruise missiles to take out the center, so we're elected. The purpose of this mission is to cover the arrival of *Langley* aircraft, as well as some of our own, at dispersed fields in Natal."

Satisfied that he had everyone's full attention, Coxen continued. "This is a hurry-up operation. There's only been time for the most basic planning. We still don't know the exact target time, but it will be relayed to us once it's known when the jets are expected ashore. Obviously, they'll be low on fuel, probably out of ordnance and looking for landing fields that don't want to be found. They'll be in no condition to fight their way in.

"Therefore, it's up to us to neutralize the air defense facility. That affords the jets and helos a window of opportunity to land unopposed. We'll fly ashore by CH-53 Echo; it's over 500 miles—three hours' flight time—so you can bag some zees en route. Unless you're one of those poor mothers that can't sleep in noisy, cold, vibrating helos. Ashore, we'll be met by Zulu territorial units and some SADF personnel. We'll refuel and get mission specifics at that time, but I can say this:

"Everything and everybody in that control center is important. That means we don't leave any equipment intact, and we don't leave anyone alive." He paused for emphasis. "Anybody got a problem with that?" He looked around. "Good. Now, here's the preliminary schedule. . . ."

2025
East of Vryheid, Natal

Walking forward through the night in a wide line-abreast, Vorster's two platoons treaded up the gentle slope of the upper White Mfolozi drainage, following the railroad tracks northeast to strike the R69 running east out of town. Two-man scout teams preceded the main advance, listening more than looking. There was very little noise—occasional metallic clinks from equipment, a shuffling footstep, no talking at all. The tension wrapped around the soldiers, twisting tighter with each meter advanced.

Vorster's radioman, never more than six feet away, tapped him on the shoulder. The handset floated out of the dark, as if suspended in space for him to grab. Speaking low, Vorster said, "CO here."

"Captain . . . Picket Three." The scout's Afrikaans voice was hushed, excited. "There are troops ahead of us. Seventy meters or so. Number unknown."

Vorster quickly checked with his other scouts, who had found nothing. A plan formed in his mind. Amplified reports from Picket Three indicated a sizable body of troops—Vietnamese for certain, perhaps a battalion. *In for a penny, in for a pound,* Vorster decided. He chose an enveloping maneuver, trusting surprise, shock and confusion to offset his smaller numbers. He told his exec, "We're going to ambush them, force them back."

"Then what, Dirk? We can't pursue."

"Haven't you heard? Ambush is killing. Killing is fun."

Then things fell apart. The forwardmost scouts on each side stumbled within visual distance of each other, and both reacted identically. Frightened soldiers flopped to the ground, put their selectors on full auto and opened up.

"Bloody hell!" Vorster screamed. He ran forward, fearing he had lost control of the fight before it began. *No plan survives contact with the enemy.* Winking lights and varicolored tracers sliced through the night, giving Vorster an eerie sensation. *Those thousand points of light are muzzle flashes*!

Vorster heard a shouted report that one platoon was flanking from the right. He didn't know about the left. *Must sort it out later.* All he knew for sure was that a close-range firefight was just up ahead, and he intended to participate. Grenades flashed in the darkness. His index finger went from the safe position, curling around the trigger. He ordered the command section forward.

Even in the dark, target selection was not difficult. Vorster and his troopies adopted the pragmatic philosophy that if you saw a muzzle flash, the man behind the weapon was coming from the opposite direction and therefore wore a different uniform. Noise washed over Vorster in waves of semi- and full-automatic fire. He smelled the residue of ball rifle powder, saw ill-defined silhouettes. In a lull he withdrew a spare magazine for his R4 rifle and stuffed the reload in his belt for easy access.

Then he saw two human forms to his left front. They hadn't seen him.

The old South African philosophy took over. *If the other chap has a curved magazine, deck him.* These two carried AKs, now visible in the moonlit atmosphere. Vorster knelt, saw his front sight merge with the right-hand silhouette and pressed the trigger.

Joseph Siphageni flinched at the muzzle blast, only fifteen meters away. His adrenaline surged as his radioman went down beside him. Siphageni swung on the muzzle flash and, firing from the assault position, hosed the area ahead of him. He saw his first tracers strike low, raised his fire a bit and emptied the magazine.

Dirk Vorster saw a blinding light, then felt rounds slash through his body from left kidney to upper right lung. The three impacts were indistinguishable; they struck as a single stunning blow. He was too startled to notice the pain that switched off all other sensation.

The Boer crumpled in a heap. Siphageni flopped to the

ground, reloaded and sat up. His left sleeve had been pierced by one of the dead man's bullets. *That was too damn close!* He decided he was too far forward, especially with a fluid, unclear situation. A runner scrambled up to him. "Comrade Major! The sapper captain has ordered a withdrawal. He says surprise is lost. We must reorganize."

Siphageni cursed bitterly. He outranked the pioneer company commander, but tonight tactical decisions were up to the Vietnamese. "The fool! This ambush means some part of the line is very weak," the African told his battalion chief of staff. *But at least my command will live to fight tomorrow. Maybe we can go back to scouting. And I got to kill fascists,* he reminded himself. "Very well," he said. "Search dead and wounded officers, take some prisoners, then disengage slowly."

2200 Pretoria; 2300 Local
Langley

The mood in flag country was subdued. Chuck Gideon glanced around the table at his battle staff and recognized the looks; they went beyond apprehension. *We're going to lose the rest of the force,* he said to himself.

"Bubba, you have the most recent info. Where do we stand?"

Ballantine looked over the top of his reading glasses at the handwritten figures. "Admiral, without SAMs or enough air-to-air missiles, we can't repel another divisional-strength Backfire attack. It's that simple." *There,* Gideon thought. *It's out in the open.* He nodded and the CAG continued. "We have just two options as I see it, sir. Which really means we have only one. First, we can keep the air wing aboard and just hope we get lucky and survive the next attack. My op-anal guys rate that prospect at no more than fifteen percent."

"We knew that going in," Gideon said. The operational analysts—high-powered mathematicians, mostly—had wargamed this scenario repeatedly. "Okay, what's option number two?" He suspected what was coming.

Ballantine pointedly dropped the paper, removed his glasses and leaned toward Gideon. "Admiral, launch the strike birds and Vikings. Send 'em ashore to the dispersed strips the South Africans have prepared. We can retain some of the remaining Tomcats if you like, to use up the last Sparrows, although the odds of hitting any Kitchens are low. Really takes AIM-54s. Only the helos are needed here." He glanced at Slats Slattery, who nodded. "They'll be useful for search-and-rescue."

Gideon turned to the deputy CAG. "Slats, what do you think?"

"No doubt about it, Admiral." Slattery's tone was decisive. "We're arming the Hornets and Intruders with a generic overland warfare loadout. Rocky's troops are stuffing spares and missiles in the S-3s, and we've already identified critical maintenance people to take those seats with whatever tools they can carry."

"You're saying we should send the attack birds ashore to work with the marines and South Africans?"

"Yes, sir. We can still do some good there. Which, after all, is our primary goal if I understand things correctly." He raised a finger in caution. "But we need to act fast, Admiral."

Slattery decided to expand upon his thoughts. "I'm not saying we can sustain shore-based ops very long. But if the message traffic I've seen over the past couple of days is accurate, we'll have some compatible ordnance and fuel waiting for us." He shrugged. "Otherwise, we're gonna lose the rest of the air wing anyway, sir. Might as well get some extra mileage from it."

Gideon knew it was the only way to stay in the fight, but he wanted to give dissenters a chance to speak. "Anybody disagree?" He waited for a long three-count. Flying off a sinking ship in order to live to fight another day was acceptable, but the admiral knew it galled naval aviators to abandon a carrier that hadn't even been hit. Yet nobody spoke. "Okay," he said, pounding the table with one hand. "I'll arrange for a message to the South Africans and give them a time frame to expect you guys." He looked directly at Ballantine. "CAG, launch 'em."

2309 Pretoria; 2409 Local

In his stateroom, Gideon had failed to nap. Try as he might, the admiral couldn't force himself to relax. Knowledge of the limited time available had made the chore no easier. He'd hoped to bag ninety minutes—a full REM cycle

—but hadn't been able even to reach the first level of sleep. For an hour, he'd tossed and turned, his mind racing the whole time, filled with images of flaming horror. Then the torturous attempt to rest had been interrupted by an alerting tone over the intercom, followed by the voice of the TAO. "Frisbee 602 found 'em, sir," the CDC officer reported. "Backfires."

"I'll be right down," the groggy CO replied. He was tireder than when he first lay down. The nap idea had been a mistake.

2310 Pretoria; 0010 Local 5 June

To Bubba Ballantine it said a great deal about the competitive nature of naval aviators that some conspired how to be the *last* to launch from *Langley*. A bragging point for future Tailhook symposiums or squadron reunions hung in the balance.

But when Ballantine heard an Intruder crew plotting to grab that dubious honor, he put an instant stop to the practice. He picked up the phone in CAG ops, called the air boss and told him in no uncertain terms to shoot every flyable bird off the pointy end—in any order possible.

Bubba had one other squabble to settle. His contingency plan called for at least two Tomcats operating ashore. He wanted their powerful radars as a hedge against E-2 losses. The problem was, both designated F-14s belonged to the Blazers. CAG had directed that Ostrewski and Colley be one of the crews, and they were Felines.

The VF-182 skipper was MIA, so the exec may have been feeling defensive when he casually said, "That damn Ozzie's hijacking one of my birds." Ballantine's sonar ears took in the comment and he jumped in with both feet. Poking the offending commander in the chest, Ballantine snarled, "I will not have that kind of parochialism in my air wing!"

The Blazer exec thought, *Well, what kind will you have, CAG?* But he thought better of voicing it.

Bubba continued his face-to-face "discussion." Still poking, he exclaimed, "Every goddamn airplane on this boat is *mine*. They belong to *me* and I'll goddamn well see that the best goddamn crews fly them."

"Yessir . . . I just . . ."

"Ozzie's the best F-14 driver in this air wing. I'm the high-time Tomcat pilot around here, and I'm taking the other Turkey with the RIO of my choice. Any questions?"

"No sir . . ."

"Good!" Bubba stalked away, leaving hushed voices and raised eyebrows in his wake. Sideways glances and raised eyebrows expressed the tacit message. *CAG's showing the strain. Better keep an eye on him.*

For all Ballantine's concern, the launch already was under way. Plane directors' wands brought aircraft to the catapults in random order: Pine Tree 620, Bronco 410, Fish Hook 704, Rampart 307 and 311, Talent 500. The "shooters" noted that most of the S-3s and E-2s were being held back as essential personnel and spares were loaded aboard. Some aircraft—a mighty few—boasted full ordnance loadouts. Most launched with only partial loads. There just wasn't time.

When he had time, Phil Ray swiveled his captain's chair to watch from the bridge. In the dark, jet engines went to afterburner, cats fired, steam drifted away in the carrier's diminished relative wind. As he looked, each white exhaust accelerated upward—and out of his life.

2320 Pretoria; 0020 Local
Grid Three-Three Echo, Southern End Mozambique
Channel

The Backfire division commander counted himself lucky. Major General of Naval Aviation Yuri Konchalavsky's forty-nine Tu-26s from two Pacific Fleet regiments were supported by defense-suppression Badgers and MiG fighters from Mozambique and the few bases on Madagascar still operational. He spread the specialized ECM aircraft across a wide front. Land-based Su-24 Fencers could also augment defense suppression, if they arrived on time to coordinate with the Backfires.

The general's electronic threat panels told him his formation was painted by airborne as well as surface-ship radar, but it mattered little. The first regiment was armed primarily with antiradiation AS-4s, plus some active, antiship variants in the second squadron. His ground controller on Madagascar had ordered this regiment to launch against the ships targeted by the second wave of the previous strike, most of which aircraft he knew had come from the Northern Fleet. The trailing Pacific Fleet regiment, armed with a higher proportion of active *Buryas*, was to concentrate on more recently detected returns.

The Backfire force CO knew what a muddle the Baltic and Northern Fleet divisions had made of targeting. *Not the strike aircrews' fault,* Konchalavsky allowed. His job would be easier than theirs had been, as the enemy's location and disposition were more reliably known this time. Two Bears had picked up radar returns farther south and east than those attacked by his predecessors. ESM indicated a high probability that these contacts were genuine. The general did not intend to waste his missiles. He wanted to sink a real aircraft carrier so much that he could, as the Amis said, taste it.

So far there had been little opposition—only heavy ship-based jamming that his powerful airborne radars eventually could penetrate. The division commander marveled, *Where are their interceptors?* It amused Konchalavsky that a lack of enemy fighters should worry him.

His weapons officer informed him that it was time to begin the launch sequence. Within minutes, Konchalavsky's first regiment and command flight achieved an exceptional eighty-percent launch rate of missiles and decoys.

Even though the Tupolevs had detected no American fighters, the CO ordered each six- or seven-plane squadron and the three-plane regimental command flight to bank for Mozambique as it fired its missiles. His own divisional command flight, however, would orbit until all six squadrons had launched their *Buryas*.

2325 Pretoria; 0025 Local
Langley

"Frisbee 602 reports the first Backfire wave has launched, sir," the CDC talker announced. At practically the same moment, Gottlieb and Gideon watched dozens of new tracks flash white on the large blue screen of the radar console.

"Very well," Gideon said, almost absentmindedly.

"Regimental-scale attack," Gottlieb assessed. "Formation suggests only two squadrons, though, plus some independent flights."

"Make it eighty new contacts, exactly, sirs," the radar operator said.

"Assuming two missiles and two decoys per Backfire and that these bandits out in front here are unarmed ECM birds, that's a hell of a success rate from twenty-five bombers," Gottlieb observed with professional detachment. "Must've put in a lot of maintenance hours tweaking up those babies."

The operator wanted to yell at the captain, to ask how he could call giant machines programmed to kill everyone on *Langley* "babies," but restrained himself.

"More than we can handle," Gottlieb whispered in Gideon's ear.

"Knew that already, Nate," the admiral replied. The lurid, hideous images from his sleepless nap flashed again briefly across the movie screen on the inside of his skull.

2327 Pretoria; 0027 Local
Pacific Fleet Backfires

Reports from the last squadron indicated that it had completed its mission with nearly the same degree of success as the first. The total for Konchalavsky's two regiments was impressive—forty-nine Backfires had launched seventy-eight ALCMs and eighty-one countermeasures. He felt deeply gratified that all those months of intensive training over the North Pacific had paid off over the Indian Ocean. He was more than a little surprised that the missiles worked so reliably after their long journey.

Much as he wanted to stick around to see the results of his division's attack, the general knew that it was wiser to let the Bears and AWACS planes find out for him. *If the Americans don't strike their bases again. In which case, satellites. Not that our RORSats have done such a splendid job so far.*

Confident that at least Pacific Fleet Naval Aviation had performed its long-range mission with precision, Konchalavsky banked for Beira. The divisional commander expected the African base to be a sweltering tropical shithole—but then, he'd spent most of his life in frigid Siberian or arctic shitholes.

Now Konchalavsky could scarcely believe his good fortune in meeting no fighters. Despite all the Northern, Baltic and Black Sea Backfires lost today, he would be the commander rewarded for destroying the American battle group. Though his bombers had faced no opposition, results alone counted in the Russian military. Back in Vladivostok, another star surely awaited the general.

2328 Pretoria; 0028 Local
Langley

Although the figure flashed on the screen, the radar operator read aloud, "Number of high-speed contacts, 159." He called up additional information. "Altitude, 98,400 feet. Range to leading return, forty-eight miles. To trailing return, 210 miles. Bearing, 343 degrees true to eastern edge of contact stream."

Gottlieb pointed at the symbols on the big blue screen. "Looks as if the trailing missiles are diverging from the main stream," he observed, tracing an extrapolated path on the same southeasterly course. "Seems the second wave of Kitchens is headed straight for us. We been made, somehow. Thought we shot down all their Bears. Satellites, maybe. Or ESM."

"Or Hallion's spacemen," Gideon put in, pleased that he could maintain good spirits.

"*Oriskany* and *Bennington* initiating engagement," the CDC talker reported. Gideon, Gottlieb and Ballantine exchanged glances. The admiral conjured Russian missiles flaming down out of the night, trailing their screams behind them. Soon the stream of ARMs, decoys and ship-killing Kitchens would begin taking a toll of Battle Group Charlie, on Gideon's ships and people.

2329 Pretoria; 0029 Local
USS Oriskany

Bright explosions ripped the night as two of the ship's three remaining SAMs passed within lethal range of Kitchens. Fragments of the AS-4s spewed into the water. On the Aegis cruiser's bridge, a lieutenant absorbed the air defense scene and felt an eerie sense of *deja vu*. He thought, *It's just*

like "Victory at Sea." Only then did it occur to him he might
not be witnessing a victory.

Down in CDC, Captain Jernstedt saw that *Oriskany's*
UYK-44 had assessed thirty-eight of the incoming contacts as
missiles. Sixteen had guided on his cruiser and an equal
number on *Bennington*. Six Kitchens homed on the stricken,
immobile *Carl*—presumably active-seeking variants, since
the destroyer wasn't radiating. With *Oriskany's* VLSes out of
SAMs, fourteen still dived on her. Jernstedt ordered all emitters shut down. No ALCMs went ballistic, but the passive-
homers clearly ceased tracking the maneuvering ship. Still,
the captain knew *Oriskany* might not be able to travel far
enough in the seconds before impact to avoid the missiles,
now memory-guided. He saw that a few active-homing
Kitchens fell for decoys or were jammed. It seemed just possible that his ship might be spared; he allowed himself an
instant of hope.

Robotics took over completely. With ten antiship missiles still homing, at least eight of which had valid lock-ons
amid the chaff and violence, *Oriskany's* Phalanxes picked up
the nearest missiles. Twitching with nervous electronic energy, the white-domed Gatling guns scanned back and forth,
identified and prioritized their targets and opened fire.

A buzz-saw whine was heard throughout much of the
warship, and a pall of smoke sifted briefly in the wind around
both Phalanx stations. Two fireballs exploded less than 1,000
yards out, but others bore down on the cruiser. Jernstedt
knew that his hope had been false. The impact alarm
sounded.

2330 Pretoria; 0030 Local
Langley

For the second time in five hours, Gottlieb watched
data-linked SAM totals run down on the antiair console, as
distant *Bennington's* two VLSes emptied of medium-range
SM-2s and nearby *Arthur* began firing extended-range Standards from her forward-mounted, twin-arm Mark 10
launcher.

The pace at which *Bennington's* aft Mark 41 fired
slowed dramatically. The keyed-up CSO exclaimed, "Damn!"
After slightly bobbing his head for a moment, Gottlieb said,

"Fallback. Gotta be. Missile musta wiped out a coupla launch cells when its motor failed. Damn," he repeated.

The computer determined preliminarily that *Oriskany* and *Bennington* had destroyed some seventeen targets, of which it guessed eleven were actual missiles. Then the data-link from *Oriskany* died.

Shortly after *Bennington*'s last SM-2MR disappeared from the antiair console, her feed also went down. Voice links from the two cruisers remained up. The talker said that *Oriskany* and *Bennington* both reported hits. *Oriskany* added that the previously immobilized *Carl* was also heavily damaged by another active-homing Kitchen.

Gideon nodded to acknowledge the talker. *Outer escorts and unrep ship gone. Deal with that later,* he thought. Neither the admiral nor Gottlieb spoke. Their attention was focused on the radar console, which showed the second wave of missiles and decoys launched by two dozen Backfires. The seventy-six returns in the threat stream appeared headed straight toward *Langley* and her inner escorts, CG *Arthur* and FFG *Meyring*.

"Looks like some of the ARM variants are already homing on *Arthur*'s SPG-62s," Gottlieb assessed. "The others are still in cruise phase, waiting for *Meyring* to light up her Mark 92s and probably our Mark 91s." Neither the frigate nor the carrier had yet turned on the radars of their SAM fire-control systems. *Meyring*'s modified SPG-60 director and Separate Tracking and Illumination Radar allowed her to track four targets at once, but she was under orders not to illuminate any ALCMs until the Kitchens came within range of her SM-1MRs. She was still relying on data-linked surveillance information.

"Over thirty of the contacts have to be AS-4s rather than decoys," Gottlieb continued. "The computer can't prioritize them very reliably until they dive."

He and Gideon watched the missile stream continue toward the carrier and her goalkeeping escorts. The FFG commenced firing her old Standards at about half *Arthur*'s rate. When the CG's single Mark 10 ceased firing, the officers saw that the cruiser had successfully launched fifty-eight SM-2ERs in half a minute, knocking down thirty more incomers. Due to the long range of the engagement, only nine kills were definitely assessed as real Kitchens. Gottlieb shook his head and said, "Not good. Her close-in systems'll be overwhelmed." Gideon remained silent. Both men knew that the old cruiser's job description called for taking hits instead of *Langley*.

Now that frigate *Meyring* was the only escort still shooting area-defense SAMs, *Langley* lit up her own Mark 91 point-defense SAM fire-control system.

2332 Pretoria; 0032 Local

On the bridge, Ray saw them coming. The Kitchens dived practically straight down, their motors burning all the way. Four AS-4s—the captain assumed they were antiradar variants—streaked toward *Arthur*, on the northern horizon. A Standard detonated ahead of the first Kitchen; it went ballistic. The second missed, exploded on the far side of the cruiser and raised a huge geyser. The third hit; Ray cringed, but no detonation followed. Flaming liquid fuel splattered across *Arthur*'s superstructure. The stream of tungsten pouring from a Phalanx tilted back at maximum elevation connected with the fourth, blowing it vividly to bits. Then he saw the active-homing ALCMs stoop on their prey.

USS Arthur

On *Arthur*'s bridge, Captain Roland Siegfried glanced around. Despite the fire, he was beginning to allow himself some optimism. The *Belknap* cruiser had splashed two missiles for sure, and maybe another. "Looks like it might be over, Stu," he said to the officer of the watch.

"Ah, I don't know, sir. There's still—"

"Missile off the port quarter! It's gonna hit!" Nobody could identify the voice, not that it mattered. The AS-4 slashed out of the smoke and haze, its active radar seeker locked on the ship's image with kamikaze determination. Its six-minute, 240-mile flight ended in the ship's engineering spaces.

Langley

From the bridge, Ray saw several Kitchens guide on the slowly settling, ship- and air-delivered chaff clouds, but one hit the cruiser. It blasted a jagged hole in *Arthur*'s midship, momentarily snuffing out the missile-fuel fire raging there. A new conflagration promptly flared up. Horrified, the carrier skipper watched the cruiser's aluminum superstructure start to melt. *It's* Belknap *all over again,* he thought, remembering the 1976 collision involving the first ship of the class. The cruiser ceased firing SAMs. Although still under way, she was out of action.

Ray could not see frigate *Meyring,* but her SAMs were still much in evidence, he noted gladly. The least capable Standard-armed escort was the last area air defense ship left operational. The AS-4s were falling too fast around *Langley* for the FFG's single-armed launcher to make much impact. Neither did the carrier's ECM seem to have any effect; the captain figured that her SLQ-29 ESM system had not gone active, since the active radar variants of Kitchen had displayed the ability to home-on-jam.

Still, the skipper was greatly relieved to see *Langley*'s six SH-60F helos hovering around his ship. Even as he watched, three Seahawks successfully decoyed AS-4s. Glee mounted within him as more ALCMs chased chaff launched by *Langley*'s four Mark 36 SRBOC mortars.

2333 Pretoria; 0033 Local
CDC

"*Arthur*'s hit!" the commo officer reported. "Amidships." Then he stood next to the talker.

"Active variant musta homed on her jam," Gottlieb assessed.

Seconds later, the officer relayed a new message, "Another AS-4 exploded in the forward deckhouse." After a further pause he walked over to his superiors and added, "Just about everybody on the bridge is believed dead."

Gottlieb saw that *Meyring*'s forty SM-1MRs had knocked out eighteen targets, of which at least six were ALCMs. But twenty incoming symbols remained on the scope. The computer determined that most were real missiles, homing on the carrier.

On the consoles, men watched death approach. The radar operator suddenly thought of the first time he'd played Space Invaders as a kid, over a dozen years ago. Now in

lethal earnest on this video screen, his defensive weapons
were wearing away at an enemy onslaught dropping from the
edge of space, eating down his "city's" shields. Every barrier
chipped away contained flesh-and-blood men like him—
battered, burned, blasted, suffocated, scalded, lacerated,
crushed, traumatized, maimed and drowned for real, for
keeps.

Bridge

The carrier's own umbrella now opened against the rain
of ALCMs. With the AS-4s down to less than ten miles, Ray
saw the forward Sea Sparrow box launcher train and elevate;
he assumed the other two did the same. The doors of
the Mark 29 were flung back; within twenty seconds, its six
RIM-7Ms popped out of their cells, rocketed over the flight
deck and climbed to meet the incoming AS-4s. Two SAMs
hit Kitchens, igniting brilliant explosions. Flaming debris described a fiery parabolic arch seaward. Another detonated
close enough to produce a red-orange swath across the sky.

In rapid succession, flashes of light illuminated the
bridge from different angles, telling Ray that Sparrows from
the other two Mark 29s had found their marks. *How many?
Five?* No explosion was close enough to produce burns.
*When are we gonna learn to wear white antiflash gear like
the Brits?* the captain wondered. He comforted himself with
the thought that he had at least banished rolled-up sleeves
from the bridge.

Her point-defense missiles expended, *Langley*'s last-
ditch, close-in weapons took over. Ray saw Rolling Airframe
Missiles accelerate out of the other two cells in the Mark 29.
Within thirty seconds, all ten RAMs shot away, guiding initially on the ASM's active, terminal-homing seeker heads. He
knew they would quickly switch over to heat-seeking.

With all *Langley*'s eighteen Sea Sparrows and thirty
RAMs fired or failed, the captain was sure her antiair officer
in CDC would shut down the MFC sets of the carrier's Mark
91 system. But he also felt positive that a target as long, wide
and unmaneuverable as *Langley* was vulnerable to ARMs
guiding on memory.

Ray witnessed the forward Mark 15 CIWS go into action. As best he could under fire and out of CDC, the skipper

had monitored the reliability and effectiveness of the battle group's defensive systems. Not all of the close-in weapons worked, but realistically, the old salt hadn't thought they would. Some CIWSes malfunctioned immediately; others had gotten a radar lock, then broken tracking. But most filled the air with dense patterns of heavy 20mm slugs—regardless of what was downrange. Within seconds, he saw, heard or felt *Langley*'s three Phalanxes each bag a "leaker." Excitement and delight welled up in Ray's chest, nearly swamping his dread.

Then the captain's spirits fell as rapidly as a plunging Kitchen. Ray saw what he had hoped never to witness but had feared for days. In sickened fascination, he watched the AS-4 dive toward the forward flight deck. Most bridge personnel instinctively ducked; their skipper winced but did not cringe or take cover when the ALCM hit. He felt the impact transmitted speedily through *Langley*'s steel skin. White exhaust blinded her skipper, obscuring what little vision he retained. Abruptly, the cloud was scattered by a massive concussion; fragments of deck plating flew toward the island.

To his astonishment, the mesmerized, stunned captain found himself still standing, weak-kneed. Even on the bridge, he could smell—almost taste—the metallic smoke. Ray called CDC to report that, in case the battle group staff hadn't noticed, one of the biggest, fastest antiship missiles in the world had slammed into the old aircraft carrier. Its metric-ton warhead had detonated to port of the forward elevator and abaft the starboard catapult blast shield. Plating gaped; the elevator was tilted upward at an angle, useless. He did not know to what level the missile had penetrated.

Ray figured it was an ARM that had homed on the two pairs of Mark 91 MFC directors mounted on the island, each with a circular, concave and convex antenna. The ship's movement since the sets had been shut down accounted for the miss.

While on the intercom, the skipper caught the light of another exhaust trail out the port windows and felt through the open wing hatch the shock of the Kitchen's passing. He quickly reported another AS-4 inbound, presumably an ARM memory-guiding on the aft Mark 91. It struck before Ray hung up; he flinched, but no explosion ensued. "Dud," he said, too hopped up to feel relief.

Still more brilliant flame light and noxious fumes assaulted the dazzled, shaken skipper, followed by a rougher rattling than the first impact. In the next instant, a throbbing, long-lasting, hollow roar jarred him. He guessed the *basso profundo* blast had come from the hangar deck. *Very bad.* Hustling to the open hatch, he felt a rush of heat. *Fires already.* He rang up CDC again to report that a third ALCM had crashed through the middle of the flight deck.

2334 Pretoria; 0034 Local

While craning his neck upward from different vantage points, the captain got damage control on the line. After long seconds of scanning the night, Ray realized that that was the last missile. Exhaust haze and fire smoke obscured the stars, debris still rained down from the flame-lit sky, but no more live missiles hunted his wonderful ship. She was wounded, but already damage control—his well-practiced crews—had her healing. *Langley* was still operational. No other vessel but an American carrier could have survived such an attack so nearly intact. Ray was proud—and glad to be among the living.

Yet, functional though *Langley* might be, her battle group was gone. It hadn't taken much time. But then, the CVBG had survived long enough to perform its primary mission.

Hangar Bay Three

The AS-4's 2,200-pound warhead had detonated on the hangar deck with a violence compounded by the steel confines of that space.

Unexpended rocket fuel instantly ignited and spewed burning sheets of flame in 360 degrees. A partially fueled SH-60F parked within thirty feet of the detonation was torn apart, and its flammable liquids also ignited.

Those men in the immediate area never knew it, of course. Their bodies were vaporized, incinerated or shredded, according to their proximity to the explosion. They were the fortunate ones. Though warned of impending attack, some men had ignored the overt risk and worn their ordinary uniforms. Consequently, the jet fuel that misted and ignited doused some men well away from the initial explosion. The results were indescribable.

Indescribable. That was the word in Metalsmith Second Class Jerome Franklin's mind. Already aware of the growing heat, he rushed toward the conflagration to lend a hand with fire-fighting. He saw a small group of men struggling away from the inferno. He stopped, gaping at two sailors holding up a blackened humanoid figure between them. "It's Chief Reicher," croaked one of the whitehats.

Franklin wondered how anybody could tell. He looked hard, seeking a hint of something recognizable. Even above the thick, roiling smoke, the odor of roasted flesh was evident. The shapeless, vaguely human form was draped in ribbons of . . . something. Even its feet were malformed globs. Forcing himself to function, thankful he was wearing gloves, Franklin helped lay the thing on a stretcher for the medics to haul away. He had seldom thought about the U.S. navy's synthetic underwear, polyester uniforms and easily shined plastic shoes. Nor did he know that the immediate area around the fire easily was 900 degrees Fahrenheit, or that nylon melts at 500. But *Make mine cotton* flashed in his mind as he glanced at his sturdy, dark-blue dungarees.

When the superheated flames torched off, automatic sprinkler systems kicked in from the hangar bay overhead— at least, those that weren't destroyed in the explosion. Fire-fighting crews were quickly on the scene, dragging high-pressure hoses from storage at fog-forming foam stations. But the high-order detonation had ripped structural steel like tissue paper in some places, and other frames were buckled or warped. Hoses caught on twisted, blackened metal or wrapped around an incredible amount of debris, all of which hampered fire crews.

Those closest to the flames roaring in the hangar-deck oven had to retreat. The searing heat was overwhelming, and the first teams fought a holding action. Moments later better-equipped crews appeared in naval fire-fighting ensembles— flame-resistant NFEs with visored helmets, instead of the ordinary oxygen breathing apparatus. But some NFE sailors snagged their silvered suits on jagged deck plates. Some slipped in the foam and fell—one gashed an arm on a wicked sliver of deck plate. The others stayed and fought. Frequently they could see no farther than ten or fifteen feet in the smoke. Additional sailors like Jerome Franklin hauled and linked hose sections, each progressively heavier and bulkier than the last. The metalsmith felt his strength waning and wondered how long he could keep going. *I've gotta sit down. Just for a minute. . . .* Somebody handed him another length of hose.

2335 *Pretoria; 0035 Local*
Bridge

The captain stood on the port wing, studying the horizon with big pedestal-mounted binoculars. He had no reports of *Langley* men overboard, but, through smoke drifting past, Ray could make out sailors in the flaming water around *Arthur.* Some floated lifelessly. Choppers from the cruiser, frigate and carrier were picking up those their mates judged in most need.

As he searched the surface, a huge underwater blast bulged the sea; a bubble rose, killing many more men. He knew that others would soon die who now thought themselves perfectly healthy; water shock injured people internally without causing obvious external damage.

The captain leaned over the railing. Down on the battle-damaged flight deck, steel plates were being secured over the gaping holes. He recognized some of the boys at work below, scurrying effectively or leaning into fire hoses. *So young. Baby-faced. The kind of kids no one knew in high school, except other runts. But look at 'em now.*

2345 *Pretoria; 0045 Local*
CDC

Less than thirty minutes after the first Pacific Fleet Backfires launched their missiles, Chuck Gideon was virtually an admiral without a task force. Nathan Gottlieb's reports came to him with appalling frequency.

Nearly a hundred miles to the north, the Aegis ships suffered their final agonies. Despite minor design changes to lessen the top-heaviness of *Ticonderoga*-class cruisers, *Oriskany* had capsized, with heavy loss. "Rolled that puppy right over," said one sailor in CDC, too low for the admiral to hear.

Her sister *Bennington* was still afloat but down by the bow and listing to port, her pumps working at full capacity to keep her wallowing above water. The failure of any one of them would mean she shared a similar fate.

Carl, already dead in the water after the previous onslaught, had disappeared in a rippling, snarling flash. No word on survivors—if any.

Arthur, steaming onto *Langley*'s engaged side and absorbing AS-4s meant for her, was immobile and down by the stern. Struck by two antiship missiles, she was now afire, drifting, her superstructure melting.

Meyring, the lone *Perry*-class frigate, somehow had escaped unscathed.

Finally Gideon asked about the unrep ship, *Roseburg,* mistaken for *Langley* and wounded in the first Backfire attack. Gottlieb checked his clipboard. "She's sunk, sir. Thought I mentioned that." *I know I did. Chuck's tired.*

Gideon nodded, staring blankly. "There were women aboard."

"Ah, yes, sir." *We're an equal-opportunity navy. Girls can drown right alongside the boys.* "No word from *Eureka* since the signal that she got her Tomahawks off." He checked his watch. "About ten hours ago."

The admiral swiveled in his chair. "And how are we doing, Nate?"

"Well, Phil says we're not sinking. But with damage to the cats and two elevators, we can only operate helos."

"They'll finish us at dawn, you know," Gideon said in a low voice. "If not before." He spun in his chair again. "What do you recommend, Nate?"

Gottlieb sat down next to his friend. "Chuck, I don't see that we have much choice. Even if the PhibGru or UnRepGru sends a couple of ships to rescue survivors, we can't pick up everybody. A lot of our guys are going to spend a few days in the water."

The admiral without a fleet rubbed his chin. He needed a shave. "Okay. Make preparations for abandoning ship when it becomes necessary. I doubt if *Meyring* will survive very long, unless Rybakov decides to spare her for rescue work. And we can't count on that, can we?"

"No, sir. I'm afraid we can't."

Gideon affectionately punched Gottlieb's arm. "Go to it, Nate."

2355 Pretoria; 0055 Local
Hangar Bay Three

When it was over, minutes or hours later—the metal-smith had no idea—Franklin wrenched off his OBA. He checked the gauge. *I'm almost out of oxygen.* He looked around the hangar. The flames were beaten down under a blanket of aqueous foam. But immediately he knew the area was uninhabitable, as the dense smoke had only begun to dissipate. He staggered portside, seeking something resembling fresh air along the railing. Coughing, forcing himself to breathe evenly, he slumped to the deck. He tried to move a leg to make himself more comfortable, but decided he was too tired. *I'm going to sleep right here,* he thought.

Somebody tapped him on the shoulder. He looked up to see a maintenance supervisor, equally grimy and spent. "Come on, Franklin," the lieutenant gasped. "Let's get back to work. More fires below and aft."

As the officer turned and walked away, Jerome Franklin struggled to his feet. It took nearly all his strength.

Repair One Bravo

CWO4 Christopher Martin ran Repair One Bravo, the damage-control station on the main deck. As per standing orders, when the inbound missile alarm had sounded, all engineering personnel not on duty mustered at One Bravo. Formerly an instructor at the navy fire-fighting school, Martin was accustomed to spending forty-five minutes describing how to suit up and affix the oxygen breathing apparatus necessary for working in burning spaces. But now he cut his remedial training lecture down to forty-five seconds. As each engineer appeared, he ran through his condensed lecture, had the sailor repeat the instructions and sent him on his way.

Technically, it should not have been necessary. Each carrier sailor is required to attend fire school, but some had graduated months or years before. None had fought a genuine fire at sea.

It seemed that Martin had hardly begun passing out NFEs and OBAs when the first crew returned. "Mr. Martin," pleaded one sailor, "our oxygen canisters are almost empty."

Martin grasped the man's apparatus and looked at the gauge. It registered one-fifth. "What the hell you been doing, sailor?"

The boy shrugged. "Fightin' fires, sir."

Martin nodded. "Okay. I guess when it's for real, you go through oxygen a lot faster than in a drill." He shouted back over his shoulder. "Danny, keep the extra canisters charged up. These guys are using sixty minutes' worth of air in twenty minutes."

Damage Control Central

Commander Pete Clanton needed a third hand to pick up the phones that were his lifeline throughout the ship. His master-control board was a kaleidoscope of flashing lights, showing the location of fires and serious damage. He was just responding to a call from the bridge when he was rocked by a high-order detonation from farther aft. He shouted into the receiver, "Can't talk now, Cap'n," and slammed down the phone. *That'll get me fired,* he thought. Then he relaxed. *Phil knows I'm busy.* He picked up another line and listened hard, shifting his weight as the carrier heeled over in a turn. *Phil's turned crosswind to put the smoke to starboard. Good move.* "Yo, Gerald. Whaddaya got?"

"Jet-fuel fumes ignited in the uptakes, Pete," said the damage-control assistant. "I'd guess the fuel torched when it contacted the heated surfaces of the smokestack. Burning like a son of a bitch." Clanton knew the DCA was probably right. JP-5's flashpoint is 140 degrees Fahrenheit, but the engine room uptakes were several hundred degrees higher.

"Casualties?"

"Ah, we don't know yet, Pete. Several for sure. Maybe half the flying squad. We're getting the survivors topside for helo evacuation to another ship, but it'll take a while."

Damn, nowhere to go. Clanton swallowed hard. "Gere, I doubt there's an undamaged ship left in the battle group." He thought hard. "Okay, listen. Get the seriously injured

topside, but send a responsible petty officer to get your guys
back down there. ASAP. We need everybody. Okay?"

"Yes, sir." There was a slight pause. "Pete, what about
the dead?"

"Move 'em out of the way and scavenge any usable
equipment. Clear?"

"You got it, boss." The line went dead. *No time for sentiment,* Clanton thought. Immediately he turned his attention
to replacing some of the flying-squad casualties. The thirty-
man squad was like the reserve platoon of an infantry company—a quick-reaction force to plug the gap in the confusion
and turmoil of battle. But *Langley* was running out of
reserves.

PART THREE

Amazon Babes in Zululand

17

0001 to 1730, Saturday, 5 June

Almost nothing was recognizable on the hangar deck aft.
Fire hoses snaked across the deck and the residue of aqueous
foam was everywhere. So was blackened, twisted debris and
wreckage where the AS-4 had penetrated the overhead and
detonated near a helicopter. Captain Mel Hyers, the ship's
exec, stood aside to allow the survivors of a fire-fighting crew
to get past. Several of the sailors had removed their helmets
and let the upper portions of their NFEs drape around their
waists. Hyers knew that the fire-retardant material allowed
heat neither in nor out. Consequently, men often fainted
from heat stress. This crew, he supposed, was cycling to the
back of the line to wait twenty minutes before returning to
the fires still burning farther aft. The kids certainly looked
like they needed a rest: sweaty hair; clammy, moist skin; and
sunken, hollow eyes.

Leaning against a fitting, Hyers glanced around again.
He rested his grimy, sweat-darkened back against the bulkhead marked "FFF"—a fog-forming foam station, apparently
damaged in the initial explosion. Casually, he picked at a fist-
sized substance caked to the bulkhead. *What's this?* he won-

dered. He poked at the blackened object, which had the appearance and texture of a burned roast. Then he knew.

0043
Northern Zululand

Burning torches danced in the dark, swaying melodically in time to the ancient chants of Zulu war songs. The *Langley* aircrews could not hear the alto chorus until the last jet engines wound down, but the warmth of the greeting at the isolated airfield was beyond anything they had expected.

Slats Slattery descended the built-in ladder on the Intruder's starboard side, now aware of the strangely beautiful *a cappella* music washing around him. A jeep's hooded headlights flashed briefly, then died, but there was enough ambient light to discern the surroundings. The bouncing, rhythmic dancers closed in on him, cowhide shields and *assegais* visible in the dark. Slattery sensed his pilot at his side and whispered, "Jim, I thought I'd seen some pretty weird gigs in twenty years, but this retires the trophy."

From the jeep emerged a slightly built African wearing khaki fatigues without insignia. He was flanked by two six-foot-seven Zulus, who appeared even taller in their feathered headdresses. The man in the middle stopped, saluted palm-outward and introduced himself. "Brevet Major General Nigel Mkize, commanding the North Natal Irregular Forces." He extended a hand. "Welcome to Free South Africa, gentlemen."

The deputy CAG warmly shook hands. "Commander Patrick Slattery, Carrier Air Wing 18, sir." He introduced the senior officers joining him at the nose of the A-6. "We have about forty aircraft either here, on your adjoining fields or still inbound," he explained. "My senior air wing commander, Captain Ballantine, is with the last batch." Then, at a loss for words, he blurted out, "We're about all that's left of our battle group."

Mkize nodded comprehension of those terrible words. He linked arms with Slattery and pulled him toward the jeep. "We can make good use of your aircraft, Commander. With most of the marine amphibious group coming ashore, and my units now in place, we have a formidable combined-arms force in the enemy rear." Mkize intentionally used the American phraseology to demonstrate his grasp of the basics. The aviator, after all, was a white foreigner who might wonder at the spectacle before him.

Turning with a hand extended toward the dancers, the general explained, "Commander Slattery, we have much to discuss and many plans to coordinate. But first, please take a moment to acknowledge our ceremonial greeting to fellow warriors from the sky."

Slats peered into the darkness. The shimmering light revealed a spectacle right out of *National Geographic*. Chanting and moving in unison, ranks of young women jumped while bent over double, clapped and stamped, then straightened up and executed a series of deep knee bends. In one rhythmically swaying row, unmarried girls were armed with little *assegais*, which they beat on hide shields, only about as long as a forearm. The performers' precision equalled the Rockettes', but the degree of difficulty and the energy required were of an order of magnitude greater than any routine Slattery had ever seen. It looked more like a mating ritual than a war dance or welcome ceremony—a workout video with seminaked rather than scantily clad exercisers. The commander hardly knew what to say; he feared committing a *faux pas*. But the Zulu was bemusedly studying his reaction, so Slats decided to be truthful. "Very impressive, sir," he commented, then searched for suitable words. "Umm, very athletic. I hope they fight half as well as they dance." Mkize beamed, flashing his fine, sturdy white teeth. The American relaxed.

Fifty yards away, an S-3 crew had just exited its aircraft on the parking ramp. The pilot sidled up to VS-23's maintenance overseer, Chief Elwood Bromfield, a husky black NCO from Philadelphia. "Chief," the pilot intoned, "do you see what I see?" Even in the dim light it was apparent many of the female dancers were topless. "Look at those Amazon babes! 'Cept I think Amazons only had one tit."

Elwood Bromfield folded his arms and chuckled aloud. "Lieutenant, if this is TDY, I'm puttin' in for PCS orders as of now." The Viking pilot grinned in the dark. Temporary duty of this sort could indeed breed the desire for a permanent change of station. But the aviator knew things could turn exceedingly unfriendly once the air wing's presence became known.

0044
Richards Bay, Natal

Rawhide Flight approached the coastal airstrip in trail, running lights doused. In the lead Harrier, Rawhide Five, Major Mule Halloran kept his attention outside the cockpit, piercing the African darkness with his night-vision goggles. It had been a fairly short flight from *Hornet,* but the marine was edgy just the same. He didn't know for certain what kind of reception he would receive. And nighttime navigation over unfamiliar terrain always increased the pucker factor. *There . . . something flashing.* Halloran relaxed slightly. The advance tactical-control party was in place, guiding the Harriers to their new operating area.

Rawhide Five began its descent into what was now known as Landing Zone Delta.

0101
Advanced USMC Base, Northern Zululand

Captain Ken Coxen folded the target-area map and tucked it into his camouflage fatigue jacket. Then he handed the SADF aerial recon photos back to the Boer liaison officer and stepped out of the tent. His two fire teams from the battalion recon platoon were lined up, waiting to board the helicopters with their Zulu guides.

Coxen finished applying the last of the two-tone camo face paint, not caring whether some green tinted his close-cropped sandy hair. He rubbed the rest on his hands, then walked up to his senior NCO. "All set, Gunny?"

"All set, Skipper," replied Gunnery Sergeant Josh Lindquist. For a moment the two marines exchanged glances in the dark. Lindquist trusted Coxen's judgment; the captain was a "mustang," a former enlisted man, himself. That counted for a lot. First Lieutenant Chuck Smith, leading the security element, already was boarding his men on the second helo from *Hornet.* The platoon leader's squad would secure the extraction site for a fast getaway.

"Let's man up, Josh." Coxen counted the men as they boarded the two CH-53Es. Among his two thirteen-man squads he mentally ticked off those he would most rely upon: Bunch, his lead radioman; Simpson and Lander, his best

M-60 gunners; Sharp and Bartlemay, his scout-snipers; Scott and Colflodt, his explosives experts; plus McCarty and Janis, with the SMAW rocket-launchers.

In ten minutes the two Super Stallions were turning up, ready to go. Light signals coordinated their movements as they taxied for takeoff, accelerated out of ground-level turbulence and ascended into translational lift. Then, without radio calls or navigation lights, the big Sikorskys climbed out to the north, their eighty-foot rotors thrashing the night sky.

In the rear of Sea Dragon 26, Ken Coxen reviewed the plan. He had conducted a thorough, ninety-minute briefing with everyone involved: aircrews, South Africans and his marines. Like all good planners, he had allowed for contingencies, including the "Oscar Sierra Factor"—no plan ever worked to perfection. But he felt the Front Line States' air defense center should itself serve to reduce the "Oh Shit" possibilities. "The gomers may have outsmarted themselves," Coxen had told his men. "By relying more on camouflage than active defenses, they've made our job easier." He had not said that only poor enemy radio discipline had showed the South Africans where to send their photo-recce drones.

Ken Coxen looked at his watch. Fifteen minutes left. He unsnapped his holster, drew his .45-caliber Gunsite Service Pistol and, with finger outside the trigger guard, racked the action. He thumbed the magazine release, topped off the mag with a loose round, and reloaded. Then he applied the safety, holstered the GSP and nodded to the others. A metallic clatter filled the helo as marines tapped magazines on helmets to seat the cartridges, shoved the mags home and tugged the charging handles. Coxen leaned back and closed his eyes. He knew some officers would be aghast at his men's carrying loaded weapons. *Screw 'em,* he thought. *That's the kind of thinking that got 241 guys killed in Beirut.* Coxen felt that marines who could not be trusted with loaded guns in a combat zone had no business in the Corps—and that neither did their leaders. Ken Coxen trusted his troops.

0140
Over Southern Mozambique

The marines felt Sea Dragon 26 decelerate from its 110-knot cruise speed. Flying nap of the earth with night-vision goggles called for an extraordinary order of skill, but the Sikorsky's crew was experienced in clandestine ops. Coxen knew the first approach to a landing zone would be a touch-and-go—a deception to confuse unexpected observers as to the genuine LZ. Another dry run would be made before the real insertion, with two more on the egress route.

0159
USMC Landing Zone, Maputo Province, Mozambique

Sea Dragon 26 approached the LZ nose-high, ramp extended for immediate unloading. The big helo's 65,000-pound weight had hardly settled before the marines were off-loaded. As the Sikorsky's three GE turboshaft engines spooled up for takeoff, Coxen's team dispersed in a hasty perimeter. He checked his watch. Right on schedule—three and a half hours until dawn.

Coxen looked around in the gloom. He felt alone and terribly vulnerable—literally in deepest, darkest Africa. A form appeared at his side. "This way, sah." Then the Zulu was gone, ghosting his way through the bush.

0329
Air Defense Center, Maputo Province

The green image possessed an eerie quality, not quite real. Ken Coxen adjusted the focus of his AN/PVS-5 night-vision goggles, scanning the air defense center's layout beneath its camouflage netting. He was especially interested in the perimeter defenses. Scoping the area from atop a small rise, he was pleased to note the South African intel was accurate: two roving guards and a fixed checkpoint on the northern side. He timed the rovers' schedule, then crayfished backward, rejoining his team.

"It's just like we figured," the captain explained in a soft voice. "They're overconfident this far behind the lines." Sketching the layout in the sand, he said, "Josh, put the snipers here and here, flanking the checkpoint. Coordinate their fire so the roving guards are out of view when they shoot. Have our flankers shoot the rovers when they hear the snipers. I'll coordinate the SMAWs." A few other terse orders for grenadiers and squad automatic weapons, and the war council broke up.

Sergeant Roger Sharp and Lance Corporal Mick Bartlemay positioned themselves to put the checkpoint in a crossfire. With night scopes attached to their M-40 bolt-action rifles, they had a clear field of fire—almost a ridiculously simple 200-yard shot, slightly downhill. Midway between them was Josh Lindquist, armed with his own NVD and radio. As soon as the roving guards disappeared around the corner of the concrete bunker, the gunny spoke into his handset. "Green light. Go."

Neither sniper had ever fired "for record" before. But they snuggled up to their fourteen-pound rifles, inhaled deeply and expelled their breath. With segmented crosshairs glued to the sentries' chests, the marines took the slack from their triggers. Both Remingtons bucked in recoil. Two-tenths of a second later the .308-caliber bullets struck almost precisely where intended as both marines smoothly cycled their bolts. The M-249 squad automatic weapons on both flanks of the bunker fired simultaneously, hosing tracers into parked vehicles and suspected personnel quarters. M-203 grenade launchers *thunked* in the dark.

Seconds later an armed guard appeared from the right. Bartlemay saw him first, surprised that anyone had survived the SAW machine guns. The sniper tracked him smoothly, allowing a body-width lead. The surprise break came as the trigger sear disengaged, the firing pin snapped forward and the round went. Through the scope Bartlemay saw his target drop, kick once or twice and move an arm. *Heart shot,* thought the sniper. Chambering his third round, he was surprised at how calm he felt. *The only thing I feel when I kill is the recoil of my rifle.* That's what the macho T-shirt said.

0330

Sitting on the ground between the snipers, wearing shooting-range ear protectors, were Corporals McCarty and Janis, the SMAW gunners. Their big Shoulder-mounted Multipurpose Assault Weapons weighed nearly thirty pounds loaded, but were well-balanced. The two gunners sighted their segmented T-shaped reticles on the bunker's double doors and fired tracer spotting rounds from the side-mounted tubes. Both rounds struck slightly below the hinges, so the marines adjusted their aim, fired again and hit what they wanted. They thumbed their selectors to the electro-magnetic setting and pressed the triggers.

Electrical currents fired the nine-and-one-half-pound rockets, which screamed from their tubes at 712 foot-seconds. McCarty and Janis felt a warm flush on the backs of their necks, but not even their earmuffs prevented a near-painful stab as the rockets peaked at an incredible 190 decibels—half again as much as an M-16.

The sensation lacked the concussive effect of heavy mortar or artillery fire, but the sound of the rockets leaving the tubes was the loudest noise that Coxen had ever heard. The projectiles shrieked the 200 yards to their target in one second, striking within inches of their aiming points.

One double-hulled door was wrenched off its upper hinge and the second collapsed inward, nearly torn in two. In thirty seconds the SMAWs were reloaded, ready to provide follow-up shots.

0331

Ken Coxen and his seven-man entry team passed the checkpoint. Lance Corporal Simpson set up his M-60 at the gate while the skipper knelt with his portable radio behind some sandbags. "Josh and Andy, this is Ken."

"Josh here," replied Lindquist from the hillock. Staff Sergeant Anderson checked in with "Andy's up." He was keeping his team with one M-60, the SAWs and M-203s in a U-shaped perimeter facing the bunker, providing withdrawal support.

Coxen keyed his radio. "We're about to enter. Keep me informed. Out." Good as his intel was, he had no more than an educated guess on the bunker's interior layout. Therefore, he had decided on pure force—a *coup de main*. After all, he reasoned, surprise without violence was of no use.

"Remember," Coxen had told his marines at briefing, "everybody in that place is important. That means everybody dies."

The eight marines in the entry team were set: weapons ready, soft earplugs inserted, pulses elevated. Coxen mo-tioned to Lance Corporal Simpson, who joined the CO. "The kid's an artist with a '60," Lindquist had stated. Tonight the twenty-year-old gunner would make his concert debut. The CO pointed at Simpson and said, "You're on."

The lanky machine gunner poked his muzzle through the gap of the doors and hosed a long, scything burst into the darkness. Then Coxen and Simpson rushed inside, closely followed by the others.

Coxen tripped over a mangled body—evidently a guard positioned just inside the door. Nobody else was visible in the anteroom. Reaching a corner, he called "Grenades," pulled the pin and tossed a flashbang. It was intended to stun rather than kill, but a volley of four fragmentation grenades immediately followed. They burst across the room, erupting with orange-white flashes in the darkness. A quick three-count and the marines followed up the explosions, exploiting their advantage.

Most of the bunker's twenty-odd occupants were deaf-ened by the SMAW blasts or the flashbangs. Some were tem-porarily blinded. The frags killed two or three, but the main effect was panic and confusion—which was precisely what Ken Coxen wanted.

To avoid "friendly fire," the marines executed a pivot maneuver in line abreast, sweeping the control room from near to far. Driving Russians, Vietnamese and Africans be-fore them, the killers shot anything that moved. The smoke and confusion worked to their advantage, but even with ear-plugs the gunfire ringing off the thick walls was painful.

Loudest was the M-60. Simpson had an E-2, with short-ened barrel and pistol foregrip for better control. The young machine gunner chopped away at a group of electronic spe-cialists, herding the survivors with short, accurate bursts. Amid the noise and confusion nobody heard him giggle to himself. In thirty seconds nearly every technician still alive was crowded into a corner, screaming shouts of terror and rage in three languages.

Coxen stepped forward two paces, took in the pitiful sight and slung his M-16. *It's gotta be done,* he thought. He called "Rodriguez" and extended a hand. The PFC handed Coxen his M-249, which the skipper braced against his hip. Then he opened fire. Other marines followed his example. In seconds the quivering mass of flesh was shot to ragged, bloody tatters. Trembling slightly, Coxen thumbed on the safety and returned the SAW to Rodriguez. Then he turned around. "Gene! Get to work."

Warrant Officer Scott and Staff Sergeant Colflodt moved from one console to another, affixing suction grenades with delay fuses. Working smoothly, they rigged every installation in a matter of minutes. Then they activated the detonators. It was definitely time to go.

0340

The entry team sprinted through the U-shaped defensive perimeter, which then collapsed backward upon itself. There was sporadic firing from the bunker complex, none of it threatening. Coxen, Lindquist and Anderson briefly consulted behind the hummock north of the bunker. "Everybody accounted for?" the CO asked.

Anderson nodded. "Gibson and Sirrine are dead; I have their tags. Heckart's wounded but ambulatory. Everybody else is okay."

"Bryant caught a ricochet in the bunker, but he'll be all right," Lindquist stated. "Uh, Skipper, we have one extra," the gunny added.

"WHAT?" Coxen's voice was unintentionally loud.

"Spiegel brought along a prisoner."

Coxen pounded his knee with a fist. "Goddamn it, Gunny. We don't have time for POWs. Our orders were kill 'em all and let God sort 'em out." There was no response, so he asked, "Where's Spiegel?"

Private First Class Greg Spiegel called in a loud whisper, "Here, sir." He shoved a small human shape ahead of him. In the red-lens light, Coxen made out a bound-and-gagged Oriental in a green uniform. A Vietnamese colonel's uniform. Some of Coxen's anger abated.

"Why'd you capture him, Private? You knew our orders."

Spiegel's voice was respectful yet defensive. "He surrendered to me, sir. He was unarmed. The rules of land warfare—"

"Shut up," Coxen snapped. *God preserve me from marines who read international law and think for themselves.* Still, the intel weenies would want to talk to the gentleman.

"All right, Spiegel. You caught him, you clean him. He's all yours till we get back. Now, let's move out smartly."

0440
Extraction Site Montezuma, Maputo Province

The Zulus set a fast pace, and the marines marveled at their ability to move so rapidly yet silently through the bush. The extraction zone was three and a half miles from the bunker, and Coxen's force had made it in under an hour.

Approaching the EZ, Coxen motioned to Corporal Bunch, who had not been more than an arm's length away during the hike. The CO picked the handset off the radioman's harness, engaged the scrambler switch and waited. Hearing the tone, he called, "Montezuma, this is Tripoli."

The radio crackled in the still night air. "Roger, Tripoli, I read you. We're all set, Ken." Lieutenant Smith's voice was calm and confident.

"We're on the way." Coxen replaced the handset and grinned at Lindquist. "This is going too easy, Gunny. What do you think?"

Abruptly Lindquist raised a hand and cocked his head. "I think I hear a chopper from the north."

Coxen's insides went cold. The CH-53s would arrive from the southeast.

0445

Coxen's guides made first contact with Smith's perimeter guards. The Zulus crept within fifteen feet before announcing themselves. One of Chuck Smith's men heard an ambiguous voice and turned toward the sound, rifle at the ready. Something tugged on his pants. "Jesus Christ!" The private almost emptied his thirty-round magazine—and his bladder.

The Zulu stood up, six feet of blackness in the dark. A gentle laugh. "No, mon. I haven't seen Him tonight." Waving to some invisible companions, he said, "Come. The command post is thirty meters ahead." The marine watched the raiders file past, wondering, *How the hell did they know that?*

Ken Coxen and Chuck Smith warmly shook hands. "We

got away clean," the captain explained, "but apparently helos are hunting for us."

"Yeah, we've heard 'em fly past us on both sides," the lieutenant said. "My Stinger teams are ready, but I'm for calling in our birds right now."

Smith dropped to the ground, picked up his radio handset and made the call. "Sea Dragon, Sea Dragon. This is Montezuma. Tripoli has joined up and the Echo Zulu is secure." A crisp acknowledgment snapped back. Then Smith added, "Dragon, be advised. Hostile choppers are airborne in this vicinity at the present time." The mike clicked twice in acknowledgment.

Sea Dragon 26

"There's the signal." First Lieutenant Jerry Wahl made out the Morse code signals of the red-lensed flashlight. *Dash dash, dash dash dash, dash dot* . . . "M-O-N, that's our guys."

"Tell Two-Seven we're headed in," ordered the pilot, Major Steve Stuyvesant. The second Stallion would remain in a low hover several hundred yards astern while the first pickup was made. Then Dragon 26 would cover its partner and they both could get the hell out of Dodge.

Through his night goggles, Stuyvesant's vision was restricted to a narrow green arc straight ahead. He could see little inside the cockpit, but that was not important. He was more concerned with unseen objects outside his external vision, and could only trust that the recon team had selected a completely clear area. As he eased the collective down, the seven-bladed rotor's pitch lowered and the big Sikorsky settled into a bumpy landing. The crew chief already had the ramp lowered.

Wahl was on the radio again. "Two-Seven, this is Two-Six. We're down and loading at this time. You are cleared inbound, over."

Coxen's team and part of Smith's scrambled aboard, leaving the Stinger shooters and one fire team as a last-ditch defense against unexpected attack. Then Stuyvesant added power, came up on the collective, pushed the cyclic slightly forward and eased into the air. Stuyvesant, Two-Seven and

Smith were on the same frequency for maximum coordination.

"Dragon, this is Montezuma. We have an unidentified helicopter headed straight for us, distance maybe two miles!" Smith's voice eloquently carried his concern.

"Two-Seven, this is Two-Six," called Stuyvesant. "Wave-off, wave-off. We'll see what happens before you attempt pickup," he intoned.

"Ah, roger, Two-Six. Maintaining position," came the reply.

0446
Extraction Site Montezuma

Chuck Smith stared at the aerodynamic shape through his PVS-5. "Damn, he's seen us," the lieutenant said to no one in particular. He turned to his Stinger team leader. "Wait a bit more, Hank."

"Aye, aye, sir." Sergeant Hank Carmet hefted the thirty-five-pound surface-to-air missile and launcher on his shoulder and began tracking the heat source of the helo's engine. His assistant was a PFC carrying the sensor package linked by electrical umbilical to the launcher itself.

"Goddamn Hip," Smith said, lowering his goggles. The Russian-built Mi-8 altered course slightly to the west, evidently planning to skirt the extraction zone and call in gunships on Dragon 26. Two-Seven still was beyond range of the Mozambican crew's night-vision devices.

"It's your show, Hank." Chuck Smith said.

"Yes, sir." The NCO had a green light, indicating his missile's seeker head was tracking the target. Carmet pressed the trigger and the five-foot-long Stinger blazed off the launcher. Accelerating to nearly twice the speed of sound, it ate up the mile and a half to the Hip in under six seconds.

The enemy aircrew could not help but see the missile launch in the night sky. The pilot immediately turned away, popping flares that illuminated the darkness with a cascade of garish magnesium splotches.

The Stinger's infrared and ultraviolet sensors instantly scanned the heat and light from the flares, as well as the intended target. The missile was not deceived by the closest flares, which its improved logic board told it to ignore, since their flight pattern contrasted noticeably with the helo's.

But the last flare captured the Stinger's interest. The white-hot source was close enough to the target to warrant a slight change in flight path, and the eight-pound warhead detonated on impact with the flare.

Thirty feet from the Hip's tail rotor, fragments spewed in all directions. A handful of splinters slapped the spinning blades, knocking them slightly out of alignment. The Mozambican pilot immediately felt the vibration. Not knowing the extent of damage, he turned westward to safety, broadcasting a call for help to everyone in range.

Chuck Smith slapped Sergeant Carmet on the shoulder. "Good enough, Hank." He looked to his radio operator. "Like the shepherd said, Let's get the flock out of here. Call in the helo. Saddle up, people!"

He checked his watch. *If those jet jockeys are on time, they'll be able to land without interference from these gomers.*

0650
Kuznetsov

Rybakov realized that twenty-four hours had passed since the one-ton bombs had struck *Varyag*. That hideous morning now seemed so remote, irreal, nightmarish. Since arriving onboard his new flagship, he had kept the memories of destruction at bay by burying himself in work, planning retaliation.

His first job had been to organize a new battle group to hunt down *Langley*. To guard against an attack on his rear by *Eisenhower*, the American CVBG in the South Atlantic, he'd had to leave behind some of *Kuznetsov*'s antiair and antisub escorts. But, reinforced by remnants of the *Varyag* group picked up en route, Rybakov felt strong enough to engage *Langley*. He planned to steam at flank speed to the northeast, find and finish off his wounded quarry, then come about, rejoin the assets left behind and face United States Ship carrier *Eisenhower*.

Naval Aviation Theater HQ at Antsiranana, Madagascar, had reported the *Langley* group completely destroyed. No recce assets had actually seen any American ships burning, so

Rybakov considered this claim exaggerated. Yet radar tapes and ESM intercepts indicated there was a good chance that *Langley*'s escorts had in fact been effectively wiped out and the carrier herself badly wounded. The admiral wanted to avenge *Novo* and *Varyag* in kind by mounting an SLCM and sea-based air attack on the presumably stricken carrier. But he hoped that the enemy CV would be found and sunk by land-based air or submarine action before the reformed *Kuznetsov* group could launch such a retaliatory strike. This would allow Rybakov immediately to turn around to fight *Eisenhower*. Alternatively, he could continue northeast to attack the U.S. PhibRon, expected to attempt landings on the Natal coast today or tomorrow.

Langley apparently was still able at least to make steerageway, since RORSat and ElIntSat search of last night's strike area had failed positively to ID the carrier, despite picking up a number of large stationary returns classified as warships. Rybakov feared some of the radar and ESM contacts might be floating decoys. Bear flights were restricted both by the shortage of aircraft and the felt need for fighter escort.

As his group steamed northeast, the admiral's staff had planned combined air, surface and submarine actions, just in case land-based Tupolevs failed to find and finish *Langley* on their own. Although Antsiranana hadn't fully owned up to the problem, Rybakov was sure that few of the six dozen operational naval bombers in-theater could actually be used. The bases on Madagascar were still not functional, despite hours of runway repair. The dispersal bases in Mozambique lacked adequate facilities and weapon stocks. If the Tupolevs could mount a massive, coordinated attack, so much the better, but the admiral expected that land-based air would require more time to reorganize, refit and rearm. At least command and control links were still up. Rybakov knew he would need the bombers to help him take out *Eisenhower* tomorrow, if not *Langley* today. Against a damaged aircraft carrier and a single escort, he figured, a massed Tupolev attack shouldn't be necessary. Better to save the planes and missiles for use on the full-strength American battle group now approaching the west coast of South Africa.

At this point, Rybakov had more faith in his submarines than in the land-based naval air arm. Six nuclear boats from the *Novo, Varyag* and *Kuznetsov* groups—three torpedo and three cruise missile attack subs—were currently hunting *Langley*. He hoped that, wounded, she might be noisier than normal. The Russian SSNs were under orders, upon detecting the carrier, to sneak close enough to fire anticarrier torpedoes without waiting to mount a coordinated strike with cruise missile subs, surface ships or aircraft. The admiral believed in standard Russian combined-arms doctrine—indeed had helped develop it—but felt there were always exceptions. In fact, one of his contributions to doctrine had been to increase flexibility and give unit commanders more freedom than in doctrine for land and air combat.

Most ships in the *Kuznetsov* group had steamed 700 miles since yesterday's American attacks, averaging nearly thirty knots. Passing *Varyag* en route, Rybakov's strike force had picked up two *Sovremenniy*-class destroyers from her group, bringing his total to ten surface warships. Although the *Kuznetsov* group already included two cruisers armed with long-range SS-N-12 and SS-N-19 SLCMs and its own two *Sovremenniys,* the destroyers' extra short-range SS-N-22 antiship missiles could come in handy in case of a surface engagement. Rybakov felt that the damaged cruisers and unhurt antisub destroyers remaining with *Varyag* could adequately protect her for now.

During his daylong chase after the American carrier group, the admiral had tried to sleep. But as soon as he closed his eyes, images of destruction glowed red on the inside of his eyelids, as if waiting there. Still, as he sat in the captain's chair on *Kuznetsov*'s bridge, Rybakov leaned back, folded his hands on his chest and lowered his lids. At that moment, the intercom from CDC rang. The talker announced receipt of a signal from a submarine.

Rybakov took the phone from the sailor. Chief of Staff Smirnov was on the other end of the line. The exec reported that *Nineteenth All-Union Conference of the CPSU,* a torpedo attack sub of the class called Akula by NATO, had picked up screw noises consistent with an American carrier. Originally escorting the *Novo* group, the sub had steamed due east from her previous morning's position at the good acoustic speed of ten knots. The very quiet, 1988-vintage SSN had made the passive contact during its last coasting period.

"Visual?" Rybakov asked, trying to restrain his optimism and excitement.

"No," Smirnov replied, "but screw noises indicate both a carrier and at least one escort. He raised his radioelectronic intercept mast before transmitting the report. ESM analysis supports the acoustic classification. We're running a plot back from last night's *Burya* tracks. I'm looking at it right now. Tends to back up the initial conclusion. Shall I order Madagascar to sortie a Tu-142 to investigate?"

"Yes, by all means," the reinvigorated admiral answered. "I'll be right down."

Rybakov ordered the watch officer to maintain present course and speed, then fairly bounded from the bridge. He would continue to close in for the kill with SLCMs, Rooks and Yaks, but now dared to dream that the *coup de grace* could rapidly be administered to *Langley* without surface or air action. In all the world there was no better instrument for that purpose than the monstrous 650mm Russian anticarrier torpedo.

1200
Northern Zululand

Major General Nigel Mkize stood before the crowded room, looking at the mixture of black and white faces. The uniforms were even more diverse: aviation green, American and South African camouflage patterns, plus a mixture of nondescript quasi-military fatigues. It truly was a combined-arms force, with U.S. naval aviators and U.S. Marine Corps armor, air, artillery and infantry, not to mention Regular and Irregular South African units.

With a meter stick for a pointer, Mkize began his briefing. "Gentlemen, the key Front Line States' position is here" —he tapped the map, tracing the supply route that sustained the enemy drive. "If we cut off their second-echelon formations, the spearheads will run out of fuel and ammunition. That in turn will force a stalemate at least—an allied victory at best. They will not be able to resupply by sea in time to retrieve the situation, since additional American forces are on the way."

Mkize turned back to face the roomful of officers. "Now, we have assembled in this region a smaller force than the enemy, but a more versatile, more capable one. And the enemy is yet unaware of our strength or intentions. Though we have never worked together, we have ensured thorough liaison at every level. Our main problem is aviation assets. Captain Ballantine of USS *Langley* will explain."

Bubba took the floor, making a point of speaking plainly yet confidently. "We have some forty carrier aircraft dispersed at three sites, plus the marine Harriers and helos," he began. "We're strong on attack aircraft and weak in fighters, though the F/A-18s can perform that role. We have two E-2Cs and two EA-6Bs, so we're in good shape for early-warning and electronic countermeasures. But we only have the ordnance we could load before launch, and few of our birds got off with full loads. That, combined with declining aircraft availability, means we have to maximize every plane and crew. We'll only get one or two sorties out of most of our planes. We have to make each of them count." He paused for emphasis.

"Now, there's some good news as well. General Mkize tells me that the South African Air Force has delivered NATO-standard bombs that we can use. That's especially good news, because we have more Vikings than anything else. Our S-3 squadron is pretty good at overland bombing. But we're awfully short of standoff weapons, so defense suppression for our air strikes will involve commando teams and aerial deception." He looked at Mkize. "Sir, I'll turn it back to you."

Mkize had the entire operation in his mind, and reviewed the plan. "Our artillery and armor will do the main execution," he explained. "But in order to get your aircraft at their targets, we need to deprive the Front Line forces of radar direction for their SAMs and fighters. That in turn requires fast Commando strikes against enemy air defense centers well behind their lines. My scouts and the marine landing team already are working out those schemes. But timing is crucial. We shall only have a twenty-to-thirty-minute window to make maximum use of all our assets. Zero hour is 0540, day after tomorrow." With that, Mkize flipped the chart for his audience. Then he told them the plan.

1201
SADF National Command Center

General de Villiers felt better. He remembered the old American slogan: *The marines have landed and the situation is well in hand.* They hadn't actually landed in force yet, he knew, but air and ground elements were ashore.

The bulk of the noon briefing had been as gloomy as any during the now weeklong war. Before 0530 hours that morning, the northern, Cuban prong of advance through the Eastern Cape had hooked up with the Russian paras manning the enemy's perimeter defenses around De Aar. The marines driving up from the coast were less than a day away from the key rail and road junction. When they reached De Aar, the country would be cut in two. News from the other fronts was nearly as bad, with the possible exception of Natal. Moreover, during the night, Russian Backfires had effectively destroyed the American carrier battle group.

Yet the general was more hopeful than at any time in the past seven days. If anything, the horrible casualties the Yankees had sustained—already ten times those from the Gulf War—reassured him of their continuing support. He knew they would start dictating policy right away, but the surviving politicians could worry about that. The U.S. had committed herself to the defense, indeed the salvation, of his country, his people.

De Villiers studied the most highly classified document in the entire command complex—the list of dispersal bases for American naval and marine aircraft in Natal, alternate sites and assignment of types to each. For one wistful moment, he wished that his son had lived long enough to participate in combined ops with the U.S. naval and marine fliers.

Good as he felt, the general would not allow himself to breathe easily until the marines actually came ashore. He had over fifteen hours still to wait.

1230 Local
PLA Nineteenth All-Union Conference

The sub's fire-control officer turned to his commander with an air of satisfaction. "Sir, we have a firing solution to the American carrier group."

Captain First Rank Sergei Ivanov turned from the chart table. "Range to target?" It had been a long haul from the *Novorossiysk* group. Six hours had passed since initial sonar detection of the carrier, during which time both man and machine had plotted contacts to work out the geometry of a firing solution. For five hours, the submariners had quietly, patiently stalked their quarry to maneuver into a good torpedo launch position. Ivanov knew he had the ideal ship for the job; its class had originally been designed to hunt stealthy American *Ohio*-class Trident ballistic missile subs.

"Twenty-six miles, sir. Our targeting data still indicate only one escort near *Langley*. Therefore, I recommend two volleys of Type 65 torpedoes in order to saturate the American defenses."

Ivanov's crew-cut head nodded briskly. "As you recommend, Semyon." The skipper's voice was tight, controlled. He realized that if his torpedoes found their target, he would be hailed as the hero of the submarine service. Nor would his audacity go unrewarded. Avenging *Novorossiysk* would assure him of rapid promotion. He could scarcely fail to achieve command of all Russian sub forces in the future. Ivanov could almost feel the fleet admiral's stars on his shoulders already.

Two hundred feet down into the Indian Ocean—beneath the surface layer—a giant Type 65 was ejected from each of the Akula's two 650mm tubes. The big tubes permitted shorter-ranged, 533mm antisub torpedoes to swim out— a much quieter firing procedure—and allowed the submerged launch of large, land-attack cruise missiles.

On receipt of launch confirmation, Ivanov checked his stopwatch. Even in one of the world's most computerized subs, he liked to rely on his own brain as much as possible. Success this afternoon against a single target would not only secure his place in Russian naval annals, it would immediately launch him into the forefront of the world's historical sub commanders. Even few Japanese, German, American or

British aces had sunk 80,000 tons, and no one ever with four torpedoes. The ticking of the old-fashioned watch tolled the most portentous seconds of his life.

1235 Local

After what seemed a peacetime reloading drill, another pair of the long-range antiship torpedoes followed the first, thirty-one minutes from their targets.

Immediately after the last "Torpedo away" signal, Ivanov ordered his SSN to come to radio mast depth.

1251 Local
Meyring

"Captain! Torpedo alert portside! SQR-19 signal analysis estimates two to four wake-homers inbound. Headed right up *Langley*'s ass. Maybe ten minutes out." The talker in CDC hardly required an electronic circuit to transmit the warning.

Commander Ray Frisella took an instant to absorb the latest bad news in a very bad day. *How'd they get this close?* He turned to his communicator. "Doug, alert *Langley*." Then he picked up a phone. "Exec . . . hello, Frank? Yeah, I know. Look, we've got a little time yet. Get as many nonessential personnel off the ship as you can. Floater nets, rafts, whatever. We're gonna take one, sure as hell." Frisella wanted to say more but there was no time. *We'll never save more than a couple dozen,* he realized.

"Helm, bring us astern of *Langley*. Keep station until I say different."

"Aye, aye, sir." Knowing what the skipper was up to, even as the frigate heeled over in its turn, the helmsman wished he had a less essential job.

1259 Local

"Bridge, CDC. High-speed torpedoes closing in. Estimate two minutes to impact."

"Understood," snapped Frisella. "Weapons department, it's all yours. Launch the 46s and noisemakers."

A tube-launched Mark 46 lightweight torpedo shot

overboard from *Meyring's* port quarter. Sending a torpedo to kill a torpedo was akin to shooting a bullet out of the air with another bullet, but *Meyring* and *Langley* counted on the Mark 46's warhead to provide area coverage. On the bridge, in CDC, in the engineering spaces—all over the tiny escort —men counted and cursed and prayed.

The lookouts knew first, then the sonarmen. A white geyser erupted volcanolike from the water, and seconds later the sound of the explosion reached the frigate's sensors. There were short-lived male barks, shouts of exultation and survival. Then sonar reported, "Single torpedo still coming, Captain. Negative on the decoy."

On the bridge, Frisella braced himself for what he knew was about to happen. The rest of the bridge watch followed his example. In his mind he saw his wife giving birth to their first child. Then the giant torpedo sped twenty-five feet under the keel, and there it detonated.

The twenty-six-inch-diameter weapon contained a 2,200-pound warhead. Water pressure, even at that shallow depth, combined to focus the powerful blast upward into the frigate's hull. The result was beyond anything seamen had known, a rat's sensation of being shaken in a terrier's mouth. High-tensile steel was ripped apart in an earthquake of violence at sea. Those not killed or maimed by the blast were thrown off their feet, striking unyielding bulkheads or falling overboard into a caldron of seething water and overpressure. On *Langley,* lookouts clearly saw daylight between *Meyring's* keel and the ocean. Incredulously, they watched the 3,650-ton escort snap in two and sink from sight in a matter of seconds. Two hundred men had just died. Sailors on the carrier turned to one another with the same thought churning in their minds and visible in their eyes. *We're next.*

1304 Local
Langley

Nobody aboard the carrier ever knew that *Meyring's* deception measures had been fifty percent effective. The first Type 65 of the Akula's second spread locked onto the sunken frigate's "Super Nixie," decoyed by the turbulence-producing device, which duplicated a ship's wake.

The fourth torpedo was not deceived.

Boiling up *Langley*'s wake with a twenty-knot overtake, the homing monster passed beneath the carrier's thirty-seven-foot draft from astern. Just below the huge screws, a metric ton of high explosive detonated with the same force that had snapped *Meyring*'s back.

The violent, jarring explosion was felt everywhere, in all of *Langley*'s hundreds of compartments. But at 80,000 tons, the *Forrestal*-class carrier displaced twenty-two times the *Perry*-class frigate. The specially designed antitorpedo spaces outside her keel were crushed, absorbing some of the immense shock, which still physically shook the ship's vast structure.

On the bridge, Phil Ray regained his balance and picked up the phone connecting him to Damage Control Central. "Pete, how bad are we hurt?"

"Don't know yet, Captain." Commander Clanton, the damage-control officer, was still assessing the information available to him. "We've got flooding in several compartments, and I've sent teams to investigate. It's worst in engineering. No word on casualties yet. I'll get back to you when I know more."

Ray hung up the phone. He ordered a preliminary report sent to flag quarters, appreciative that Chuck Gideon wasn't looking over his shoulder right now. Then the skipper called CDC. "Captain here. We're alone now, so we gotta rely on our helos and *Meyring*'s pair for ASW. Work up a rotation schedule to keep at least three airborne."

"Aye, aye, sir," the watch officer replied. He checked his aircraft status board and saw that HS-24 had five SH-60Fs available, combined with the dead frigate's two B-models. The lieutenant commander turned to his inner-zone defense officer. "I got a bad feeling about this, Chuck. If there's one Russian sub out there, you know there's more."

1305 Local
Nineteenth All-Union Conference

"Type 65 detonations on target bearing, Captain," the sensor operator said. "At least two possible hits."

Ivanov didn't know whether to be pleased or disappointed. Explosions at estimated time of arrival of the torpedoes at the carrier were a good sign, but not conclusive. And this prize was worth every bit of Ivanov's extra effort. He called to his navigator. "Continue closing the target on this course. We're in position to launch more Type 65s or we can fire cruise missiles." He turned to his exec. "Boris, your recommendation?"

"Ah, we have a good fix on the enemy carrier, sir. A cruise missile attack may catch them by surprise after the torpedo barrage."

The captain scratched his chin, concentrating on the problem. "But undoubtedly there are aircraft searching for us, too. A missile launch could give away our position. No, we'll follow up with short-range torpedoes." Ivanov turned back to his navigator. "Burst-transmit the target coordinates to Rybakov, the PLARKs and *Varyag* group's boat— *Seventy-five Years of S.S.R.* Then take us down to seventy-five meters and make turns for ten knots. We'll kill this carrier one way or another."

1306 Local
Langley

The main engine room on the seventh deck was hell at sea. Dark and cavernous with searing heat, even the bulkheads glowed red. Steam filled the space as inrushing seawater evaporated. Gerry Miller, the DC assistant, had run out of supervisory petty officers and was on his second foray into the superheated oven. Looking through his NFE visor, he assessed the situation with his heart in his throat. *The plates here are only three-eighths of an inch,* he thought. *They won't cool anytime soon even if we do beat the fire.* Spontaneous combustion had already ignited flammable materials in adjoining compartments, compounding the crisis.

Guided by the beam of his helmet light, Miller found his way back up one of the ladders to make another report. He nearly tripped over two forms in the smoky gloom. It was obvious that one man was seriously injured. Miller bent over to bear a hand and recognized the casualty as Boilerman Third Class Harry Repogle. The boilerman's partner, Hector Gonzales, and Miller pulled Repogle to his feet and slung him over Gonzales's shoulder in a fireman's carry. "I'll follow you up," Miller shouted. Gonzales nodded and scrambled up the grillwork so fast that Miller hardly could keep up.

Miller undogged the hatch, pushed it open and allowed Gonzales to pass. Following, the DCA secured the hatch, pulled off his helmet and OBA and bent down to examine Repogle. The man's eyes were glazed over. There was no discernible pulse, and Miller noticed a deep gash in the skull. Gonzales looked at Miller with infinite sadness. "A beam or somethin' knocked him down, sir. He gashed his head on the grill." Gonzales wiped his smoke-stained face with a smoky sleeve. "Is he . . ."

Miller grasped the young man's arm. "Yes, son, he's dead. You did all you could." The grip tightened. "Now let's go. We have a ship to save."

1500 Local
Nineteenth All-Union Conference

"Range to target?" Ivanov asked.

"Three miles, sir." The navigator was keeping a track chart.

"Hmmm. I'd like to get closer but I don't think we dare." He mulled over the tactical problem, assessing the risk-benefit tradeoffs as submarine commanders have done for eighty years. *I'd like another periscope view, but this close, no. We've pressed our luck far enough.* "Torpedo officer, we'll fire a spread of Type 53s on target bearing. Three are to run preset and three on acoustic homing. Navigator! As soon as we've fired we'll go deep and come thirty-five degrees starboard. I want to depart away from the carrier's port quarter."

Both officers acknowledged and turned to their stations. The torpedo officer set his twenty-one-inch-diameter fish to run at nearly top speed—forty knots, minimizing the time for enemy countermeasures. Moments later he called out, "Ready to fire, Captain."

Ivanov's voice was eerily calm in the control room. "Fire torpedoes."

Six Type 53s ejaculated from the submarine's bulbous shape and their battery-driven motors kicked in. "At present range, running time is four minutes, thirty-five seconds, Captain," the weapons officer announced.

"Helm, come hard right to 080. Diving officer, take us down fast!"

1501 Local
Sharkfin 611

The aircrewman pressed his hands close against his helmet. *Damn!* "Lieutenant, high-speed noise from the southwest. I make it multiple torpedo tracks."

The pilot immediately called out the threat. "Alpha Bravo, Sharkfin 611. Sub-launched torpedoes about two miles southeast. We're trying to intercept. Out."

The CDC officer acknowledged and directed another Seahawk toward the torpedo track. The geometry was going to be tight. The ready helo on deck began turning up to launch. It would hunt the submarine that had just fired, hoping the airborne birds could decoy or destroy the inbound fish.

Throughout *Langley* the alarm sounded. "Brace for torpedo impact port!"

1502 Local
Nineteenth All-Union Conference

"A lot of activity up there, Captain," the senior sonar *michman* announced. It was no surprise to anyone aboard, as a series of dull *thumps* were transmitted through the water. "Apparently helicopters have dropped homing torpedoes. I believe two of our fish have been destroyed. There are also noisemakers in the water." He pressed his earphones hard against his head. "Can't tell if they have decoyed any torpedoes . . . too much noise."

Ivanov turned to his weapons officer. "Semyon Ilych, time to impact?"

The man checked his stopwatch. "Fifteen seconds, Captain."

In a quarter of a minute their ears told them that Semyon's watch was accurate.

Langley

The port lookouts saw the wakes first. But their warning did little good, as the ship was only capable of six knots. The senior petty officer grasped the railing, leaned back and watched the white wakes disappear under the flight deck overhang. *Two amidships,* he thought.

There was one explosion, and a ringing sensation rose upward through *Langley*'s steel frame, penetrating the soles of men's shoes up to their ankles. Geysering spray descended over the flight deck and part of the bridge, settling like a summer shower. Yellow gear moved on deck, but in several seconds men breathed easier. "One's a dud," exclaimed a plane-handler at the base of the island. His senior chief snarled, "Yeah, and one's stickin' in our hull, just waitin' to go off."

Moments later Phil Ray had a preliminary report. "Blast damage below the waterline around frame fifty-five," Pete Clanton explained. "A couple of compartments destroyed and localized flooding. I think we can handle it, Skipper. The ordies are looking at the dud."

Maybe we'll get out of this yet, Ray thought as he switched to the CDC line. Then the watch officer interrupted. "Captain! *Meyring*'s helo has many torpedos inbound from the south! He's trying to decoy 'em but he says there's too many!"

1503 *Local*
Nineteenth All-Union Conference

"*Seventy-five Years of S.S.R.* has fired eight torpedoes, Captain. He is about twelve miles southwest of us." The exec's report was delivered in an awed voice. *How many fish does it take to kill a damned American carrier? We've shot eight ourselves.*

Ivanov absorbed the information stoically. The *Sierra*-class SSN from Rybakov's group had arrived just in time. Obviously, even with superior numbers and no fixed-wing antisubmarine aircraft left, USS *Langley* remained a tough target. "We'll keep our distance for now," Ivanov said. "In the unlikely event the carrier remains afloat after this attack, I will finish him with a cruise missile." Privately, Ivanov resented sharing the kill with that poacher Popov, but there would be glory enough to go around. *Let's just get it over with.*

1504 Local
Sharkfin 611

The Seahawk ran across the eight torpedo tracks from west to east, dropping SLQ-25 Nixie decoys. But there were too few noisemakers left, and the torpedoes were too fast. The copilot saw one or two tracks divert, taking the false bait, but the other half dozen bored on in.

Nobody who saw the impacts would ever forget it. *Langley*'s 80,000-ton bulk, nearly motionless, lay exposed to the torpedo volley like an elephant staked out for a firing squad. One fish passed close astern, one ahead. The other four struck along an 800-foot length of the carrier's battered hull.

Seen from the air, there was no sound—merely the white wakes churning through the blue-gray sea to end at the black-gray hull. Alabaster geysers, dirty brown at the base, sliced vertically from the waterline. The plumes hung suspended momentarily in midair, then showered down upon the crippled ship. The combined impact was violent enough to snap the mast, which dangled crazily by its wires. Flight deck equipment was thrown overboard as the carrier canted to port, now down by the stern.

The copilot looked at his pilot. There was nothing to say.

1630 Local
Langley

USS *Langley* was sinking. Her fate was now obvious to even the youngest whitehat abandoning ship. Down by the stern, listing more to port, the forty-year-old carrier had perhaps an hour remaining.

Captain Phil Ray looked down from the canting walkway. The abandon-ship drill was proceeding relatively well, but there was still much to do. He had made certain the two high-priority prisoners were moved from the brig, under armed guard. Documents were being shredded or jettisoned in weighted bags. Cryptanalysis equipment was being destroyed. But there was nothing to do about the nukes remaining aboard, other than confirm their ID numbers. *They'll be safe enough at nearly 3,000 fathoms,* Ray thought.

Then, with a start, he noticed an irregular row of shoes

and personal gear accumulating along the flight deck—a carrier sailor's sense of *deja vu*. He thought, *Like* Lexington *at Coral Sea*.

Ray turned inboard to the passageways of the 02 level, inclining slightly to the right as he made his way aft. Accompanied by his marine orderly and a damage-control chief, the skipper intended to follow custom in being the last living man off the ship. The small party had found only a few bodies and no wounded. The medical crews had been thorough.

Turning a corner near flag country, Ray glanced at the heritage board showing *Langley*'s previous captains and Professor Samuel Pierpont Langley, pioneer aeronaut. There were also framed photos of her namesakes—the first American aircraft carrier, CV-1, commissioned in 1922; and CVL-27, an *Independence*-class light carrier launched in 1943 and eventually sold to France. Ray sadly shook his head and muttered, "Two for three."

"Sir?" the chief asked solicitously.

Ray turned to the man, who saw the beginning of tears in the captain's eyes. "I said two for three, Chief." The skipper gestured toward the photos. "The first *Langley* was sunk in 1942, delivering army planes to Java." He shrugged. "We're the second sunk with that name. I guess there'll never be another *Langley* in the U.S. Navy."

"Uh, no sir. Guess not." The chief exchanged glances with the orderly. Taking Ray's arm, the damage-control expert softly said, "C'mon, Skipper. We better get down to the flight deck."

Three sets of footsteps echoed in the empty hallway.

1700 Local
Sharkfin 614

Chuck Gideon looked down from the helo's open doorway. He wished he had time to speak with Phil Ray and CAG staff. But the carrier's exec apparently had things under control. *Good man*, thought Gideon. He barely could pick out Captain Hyers at the base of the island, walkie-talkie in hand, coordinating the efforts of helo lifeboats.

The battle group commander shot another glance at the men in the water. Most were safe in motor whaleboats, rafts or floater nets. But several had improvised flotation devices

—surfboards, inner tubes, and even a large, green swimming-pool dragon somebody had bought for his kids. Gideon smiled to himself. American ingenuity—no end to it.

The admiral slammed shut the door and keyed the mike on his headset. "Let's get to the *Hornet,* son."

"Courtesy of Prosecutor Shuttle Service, Admiral." The pilot accelerated the Seahawk away from *Langley.*

1730 Local
Langley

"She's going, sir!" The petty officer unnecessarily pointed out the spectacle to Captain Phil Ray, who merely nodded. Burning oil still coated the greasy sea. Dancing firelight shadows played on the distorted hull of his ship. Underwater detonations rocked the boat, dooming to slow death many men still floating in the water.

Ray noticed his ship was going down in almost perfect unison with the sun; he convinced himself the effect was not a teary-eyed optical illusion or the figment of an overwrought dramatic imagination. The vivid tropical sunset tinted the smoky scene in lurid colors.

From the motor whaleboat 1,500 yards off her port beam, *Langley* resembled a ghastly, shallow letter V. Her bow and stern slowly rose in an arc toward one another, accompanied by the audible scream of tormented steel. "Her back's broken," stated Pete Clanton with a simplicity unexpected of an engineer. "Those last torpedoes did it."

Everybody knew he was right. The huge 650mm homing torpedo had been bad enough. The first Type 53 hit was survivable, but four more on the same side had proved fatal. Steam escaped from fractured lines, heavy equipment tumbled off the flight deck and more agonized, inanimate wailing followed.

Some men wanted to turn away, trying to remember their ship as they had first seen her—serene, majestic, powerful. Tough, streetwise teenagers; egotistical aviators; grizzled old seadogs; detached professionals—all the essential types required to run a carrier—were transfixed. Nobody did look away. Not until the last few seconds.

Bobbing in their lifeboats or floater nets, or merely riding uneasily in life preservers, *Langley*'s crew watched her die. Phil Ray looked around as the bow portion slid under. Two kids at opposite ends of the whaleboat were crying into their sleeves, one comforted by a chief with more years at sea than the youngster had ashore. The skipper regarded his men with a full heart. Nobody ever fought harder for their ship, Ray thought. For a moment he comforted himself that perhaps this was the way for a man o' war to die—in harness rather than meekly submitting to the cutter's torch. But he'd had enough of life at sea. He thought of his gorgeous red-headed wife in Rancho Santa Fe. *Nellie, I'm coming home.*

Then the stern upended, paused briefly—an abused steel monolith in the South Indian Ocean—and slid vertically out of sight. Ray didn't know what else to do, so he came to attention and saluted. He didn't trust his voice. Not now. Nobody did.

18

6 and 7 June

0110, Sunday, 6 June,
Southwest Indian Ocean

The rocking of the whaleboat was the first thing to stir Li's awareness; without opening his eyes he sensed the moonlight. A slight breeze blew out of the west. He listened for movement in the boat, but heard none.

Slightly opening one eye, the Korean shot a glance at the other occupants. Both sailors were slumped asleep at the stern, with the marine at the bow. Li noted that the overweight American traitor snored no more than four steps away. The other manacled prisoners were dozing similarly. For a moment Li debated whether stealth or speed was required, and decided upon the latter. At this moment nobody was alert enough to stop him.

Li Sung Hwa gathered his legs beneath himself, ignoring the cramps from sitting overnight. Carefully rising, he judged the distance, took three wobbly paces and stretched out his chained hands.

Ira Odum awoke unable to breathe. Something viselike was secured around his pudgy neck, and the pressure was increasing. Saucer-sized, his eyes gawked and his mouth gaped wide, trying to inhale. But the cold, metallic grip on his throat squeezed off that effort. Looming above him was a dark form that he finally recognized as the Mongolian features of the Korean. A croaking groan escaped Odum's mouth.

Sensing one of the other prisoners moving beside him, Li knew he had to hurry. He increased the tension of his manacles around the American's neck and, with superior leverage, forced the man lower to the gunwale. Then, with terrific strength, Li pulled Odum toward him and abruptly reversed the motion, viciously smashing the bald head onto the gunwale.

Ira Odum felt the splintering blow as a ringing, soaring pain at the back of his cranium. But there was something else —disbelief and panic. And in the grip of that panic he died.

Li smashed Odum's broken skull twice more, then unwrapped the manacles from the raw-rubbed neck and sat down in the bottom of the boat. The marine in the bow belatedly drew his pistol, uncertain of what to do. Li knew the Americans probably would not kill him. But even if they did, he had prevented the traitor from telling his secrets.

In the dim light, Li Sung Hwa allowed himself a rare smile.

0130,
Near Mtubatuba, Zululand

"You should find this very interesting reading, Captain Ballantine," said Major Bernard Meterkamp. Late yesterday, the South African Air Force liaison officer had parachuted into the dispersal base and makeshift air wing HQ, bringing candy-stripe-bordered papers in his map case and an intimate knowledge of Front Line State aviation in his head. He handed the American naval aviator a folder marked "Enemy Order of Battle, Northern Natal and Southern Mozambique."

Bubba Ballantine scanned the typewritten forms. He was surprised at the high proportion of FLS units that had been positively identified. But as an aviator, his attention naturally focused on air defense organizations. Meterkamp sensed the big American's interest and ran a finger partway down one page. "This one is of particular interest, I believe." He smiled.

Ballantine read the ID and looked up. The South African saw disbelief and gratitude in his eyes. "You got to be shitting me. Is this confirmed?"

"From two independent sources. You'll understand that we don't identify sources at operational level, but you may regard the information as accurate." Meterkamp enjoyed showing the Yanks—even relatively friendly ones such as this one—that he knew his job. "Apparently the Vietnamese regard this battalion as something of an elite unit," he explained. "It holds battle honors dating at least from 1972. As you see, it's part of the International Friends Air-Defense Division."

The air wing commander said, "Yeah. Battalions named for Robert Mugabe, Fidel Castro, Ramsey Clark . . ."

"Exactly. It's Hanoi's way of honoring old allies. Many communist or socialist nations christen units like this—"

"Show me," Ballantine interjected.

"Excuse me?" Meterkamp was mildly upset at the interruption.

Ballantine turned toward the regional map. "On the chart, Major. Where is this Comrade . . ."

"Oh, yes. Right here." He fingered a road junction near the border.

Bubba Ballantine adjusted his glasses, eyeballing the topography. In his mind, a plan was forming for the best use of the fifteen-plane "squadron" on the N2 freeway at KwaMbonambi. "Get me Slats," he said.

0330
Northern Natal Coast

Operation Evil Hyphen began in darkness and noise, but the memorable thing was the relative lack of confusion. That was what bothered Lieutenant Commander Tyler Amick of Assault Craft Unit Nine. *When things look too good to be true* . . . he thought. From the moment his LSD—landing ship dock—had let seawater into her ballast tanks and lowered her ramp to allow a few feet of the Indian Ocean into her docking well, the operation had gone off without a hitch. An hour ago, his air-cushion landing craft had slid out of the dock landing ship's well right on schedule, followed by three other LCACs. Since then, the hovercraft had maintained course and speed over a calm sea. *Forget it,* Amick told himself. *There's still plenty of time for things to go wrong.* Behind him, the LSD mothership had fallen over the horizon; the dark African shore loomed ahead.

Amick's hovercraft carried a single M-1E1 Abrams and assorted supplies. The four-marine crew of the sixty-ton tank rode in the cargo well. The ride wasn't exactly smooth, but Sergeant Bob Creech, the tank commander, knew he was a lot better off than grunts who had to plunge through the surf in AAVP-7A1 armored amphibious assault vehicles rather than over the waves in LCACs. He pitied the poor "snuffies" in the back of the amtracs, puking their guts into their helmets all the way to shore.

Riding the first LCAC into the beach, Amick noted that the other three craft in his unit were guiding on him reasonably well. Any other time it would have been exhilarating, skimming the ocean at twenty-five knots through the predawn. But now he was too busy with navigation and command-control chores to worry.

The coxswain tapped Amick's shoulder. "Sir, there's our signal."

Amick looked up and saw the blinking red light from the beach, now only a half mile away. He checked his chart and nodded. "We're maybe a quarter mile too far north. Let's ease over to port."

"Aye, aye, sir." The coxswain gently turned a few degrees left and the eighty-eight-foot LCAC lined up for its final run-in to the beach. Amick's thoughts turned back to his original problem. Nocturnal amphibious ops held obvious hazards, but equally obvious advantages. The landing was a compromise among those variables. Departing the task group from twelve miles offshore reduced transit time to the beach, but once the sun rose those ships would be visible from land. However, the CATF—commander of the amphibious task force—felt it more important to get the landing force's heavy equipment ashore rapidly. Amick couldn't fault that logic. And since there had been no enemy response, he assumed the marine raid on the regional defense center had succeeded.

Air-cushion vehicles and helicopters had greatly simplified amphibious operational planning. Both kinds of transport allowed descent on stretches of shore with underwater gradients too steep for old-fashioned, over-the-beach landing

ships or craft and freed planners from the tyranny of tide
schedules. Since this was a now-or-never operation, the marines still couldn't do much about phases of the moon and
weather, but at least they didn't have to move equipment
ashore from LSTs and men in Armored Amphibious Assault
Vehicles—big, 25-ton, waterjet-powered descendants of
World War II amtracs.

According to intelligence reports, the landing area was
marshy with irregular terrain—not the best spot for an amphibious assault. But the area was undefended and an LCAC
was capable of boosting its maximum 200-ton loaded weight
across four-foot obstacles. For those reasons, the opposition
was unlikely to suspect this area as a U.S. landing site. If
need be, it could transit back to the ships at fifty knots
empty. And once the Marine Expeditionary Unit was ashore,
the CATF's job was done. There could be little reinforcement anytime soon. Amick recalled the shipboard briefing:
"Gentlemen, this is an all-or-nothing evolution. If we win, we
win big." The alternative was too obvious for statement,
though Amick knew that contingency plans had been
drafted.

Within a hundred yards of the beach the LCAC had
decelerated, and the high-pitched whine of its four Avco gas
turbines lowered accordingly. Riding a cushion of air, the big
assault craft bore its burden over the marshy flats to the
unloading area. Just to the west was the St. Lucia Game
Reserve, and the U.S. Navy "'gators" vied with crocs and
hippos sliding through the water. *Those are real pros in the
'phib business,* Amick thought, but his flesh crawled at the
thought.

The LCACs startled waterbirds into the air. A flock of
frightened flamingos fluttered into flight at the sound of
high-powered engines. *Hard to be sneaky around here,* the
lieutenant commander reflected. He remembered that the
briefer back on the ship had made a lame joke about the marines' getting to go on safari in one of the world's greatest
wildlife refuges.

Using night-vision goggles, Amick and the other LCAC
commanders followed hand signals from Zulu guides and the
advance party of the task force's tactical control squadron.
Marines began efficiently unloading men and equipment,

and then the LCACs and tracked carriers headed back out to sea.

Amick's craft coasted to a stop and the bow ramp was lowered. Moments later a slightly built man in khaki dungarees tramped up the ramp, accompanied by one of the beachmasters. The latter, a full lieutenant, shouted up to the bridge. "Tyler, that you?"

"Yo! Be right there, Stan." Amick scrambled down the ladder and sought out his friend. Though Amick was one grade senior to Stan Bonham, they were in the same business and the same navy—not merely the United States Navy, but the 'gator navy. They knew and respected one another from long practice at Camp Pendleton and points west.

But the informality soon vanished. Bonham's tone turned official. "General Mkize, may I introduce Lieutenant Commander Amick?" Ritual salutes were exchanged on the LCAC's cargo deck.

"Welcome to Free South Africa, Commander." Amick had been briefed on Mkize but didn't know exactly what to expect. The voice was cultured, British. The handshake was firm, businesslike.

"Thank you, sir. I was told you would meet us here."

"I shan't stay long, but I need to confer with the landing force commander. Is he ashore yet?"

"Ah, no, sir. Colonel Holden is still afloat for better communications. He'll be in with the next wave."

"I see. Apparently I was misinformed, but please tell the colonel we need to confer as soon as possible. We have much to do."

"Aye, aye, sir." More salutes, and the Zulu war chief was gone. *Well, it's a weird, wide world we live in,* Amick reflected. *'Gators subordinate to Zulus, but this war is about them, I guess.* He felt better. *If this is the only glitch tonight, I'll be one happy camper.*

0430
St. Lucia, Northern Natal

Brevet Major General Nigel Mkize exchanged salutes with Colonel Bruce Holden, leader of the still-landing Marine Expeditionary Unit. The two men looked at one another across a span of ten feet and two cultures, and both found reason for confidence in what they saw. Mkize took in a recruiting-poster marine: handsome, well-built and self-confident—which is to say, egotistical. It was said of "Battling Bruce" Holden that he'd had more experience of wine, women and war than any officer in the Corps. It sounded more like a Parris Island drill instructor's boast, but within limits for bird colonels, it was true. Vietnam, *Mayaguez,* Beirut, Grenada and Kuwait—and those were only the ones he could talk about.

In turn, Holden saw less a brother officer than a damned innovative organizer. What he knew about the Northern Natal Light Infantry was limited—that was one reason for this meeting—but his liaison people had startled the big Kentuckian with their accounts of Mkize's success in raising and training 30,000 troops in mere months. Holden had seen enough minority personnel scrape by in the U.S. armed forces to make him skeptical of whether they earned their ranks through ability or affirmative action. But he was also experienced enough to know that gooks, spics and ragheads could kick your butt if you became complacent. And, nominally at least, the Zulu outranked him.

Mkize waited for the American to return his salute, then grasped the outstretched hand. Holden's finger pressure was enormous. *Americans love their juvenile games,* Mkize thought, trying not to wince at the marine's grip. They shook three times, then released. "General, thank you for your help in unloading my people and supplies. We sure appreciate it."

"Well, certainly, Colonel Holden. Allow me to welcome you to Free South Africa. We have much to discuss."

No chitchat. Right to the point. That's good, Holden decided. The roar of an engine behind him prompted a rearward glance, and the small group moved aside. Mkize looked on approvingly as the amtracs clattered by. With difficulty, he restrained his enthusiasm at having so much hardware dropped in his lap. "The maritime prepositioning ships will off-load as soon as the beach is clear," Holden explained. "I'm told that enemy coastal forces are light in this region, so maybe we can get ashore without trouble. My heliborne raiders have neutralized the command center, which ought to buy us some time. The air strikes will also provide us good cover."

"Excellent," Mkize replied. *Nothing goes according to*

plan, my friend. But I'll gladly take whatever I can get. He decided to cut to the chase, as the chain of command had to be established immediately. "Colonel, may I suggest we deal with our command structure straightaway?"

Holden nodded. "General, I like straight talk," he stated, strangling on an attempt to address the former Third World cop as "sir." The experienced American warrior commanded over 2,200 marines—an 867-man rifle battalion, a composite helo and Harrier squadron, heavy weapons units and a service support group—plus 590 navy specialists and frogmen. The Marine Expeditionary Unit included only eight 155mm howitzers, eight TOW antitank missile launchers, twenty Stinger SAMs, five tanks and twelve AAVs, which, though heavy, could be used on land as tracked APCs. But the maritime prepositioning ships carried dozens more armored vehicles, artillery pieces, missile launchers and other heavy or specialist equipment. To the Zulus, this meager materiél constituted great riches.

Mkize risked a fraternal pat on the American's arm. "Then we shall get along marvelously." *God, I hope so.* "It is my understanding from Pretoria that your battalion, with its supporting arms, will fall under my operational control. You will, of course, retain administrative control of your force."

Inhaling, Holden straightened visibly. Mkize held his breath. "That is in accordance with my orders as well." Holden's voice was flat. "But I hope that we'll make operational decisions jointly. My staff has very competent individuals for command-control, artillery, armor and aviation assets."

Mkize breathed easier. "Colonel Holden, I would not have it any other way." *Well, that wasn't much of a lie.* "Between us, we can do a great deal of good here in Natal."

Holden unzipped a smile. "Actually, General, I figure we can do a great deal of *harm!*" Battling Bruce's laugh was a touch too shrill for Mkize's liking. But the Zulu war chief thought, *I don't have to like Holden. I only have to work with him for a week or so. After that, it doesn't matter.* Then he changed his mind. *No, that's wrong. Holden matters, because the future of Zululand matters.* It was going to be a long week.

0525
Over Southern Mozambique

Rampart 300 and 309 hugged the earth, almost merging
with their early-morning shadows in places where the terrain
rose in dunes and hummocks. At 370 knots, or 425 mph, the
two Hornets left seven miles in their jetwash every second.
Navigation over unfamiliar ground, low and fast to minimize
chance of detection, called for an extraordinary order of skill
and experience—exactly the kind of talent required of strike-
fighter pilots.

In the lead Hornet, Lieutenant Commander Grant
Grundmeyer checked his watch. Flying by DR—old-fashioned dead-reckoning computation based on clock and compass—was his specialty. Most aviators relied upon their
inertial navigation systems with constant readout on latitude
and longitude, plus their laser-disk moving-map displays.
"Grunt" Grundmeyer only used them as backups to what
other VFA-183 pilots called the computer between his ears.
He'd been a math major at Annapolis, and used his old slide
rule as fast as some used calculators.

So far, so good, Grunt thought to himself. *Two minutes
to the initial point with Psycho tucked in tight.* Lieutenant
(junior grade) Eric Thaler was the junior pilot in the squadron, a former psychology major with enough experience in
stress response during the past few days to write his doctor's
thesis. Psycho lacked Grunt's capacity for DR navigation but
trusted him implicitly—while maintaining a running tab on
his own inertial navigation system.

As an additional backup, Grundmeyer had selected a
distinctive landmark to positively identify his initial point.
And there it was, within several seconds of his estimated
time. He turned port, put the camel's-hump twin-peaked
kopje on his nose and, clicking his microphone switch twice,
looked over at Thaler. Psycho clicked in acknowledgment,
tossed Grunt a salute and pulled up into a hard left turn,
accelerating to the southeast.

Grundmeyer continued southward for another minute
before banking into a ninety-degree, three-G left turn on his
final approach. He scanned the cockpit, double-checking armament switches and HUD display. His radar warning receiver was quiet so far, but that probably wouldn't last.

Daybreak was a logical time of attack, and the opposition would have its Flap Wheel sets "up."

Grunt's outboard pylons were selected, with the port rail Shrike antiradiation missile on standby. He allowed himself a brief moment of anticipation. "Good morning, Vietnam!"

0528
Vietnamese Antiaircraft Artillery Site, Maputo Province

Comrade Captain Nguyen Ma Bac stepped from his command trailer and stretched his arms behind his back. He worked one shoulder, rubbing the semipermanent crimp, a result of spending the night in his wickedly uncomfortable seat, staring at radar scopes and monitoring several radio frequencies. Technically, a battery commander was not required to perform such mundane tasks, but Nguyen felt obligated. The experience level in his unit was still lower than he preferred, and while most of his men were capable, he kept a close eye on everyone. Sometimes he wished for the 1970s organization his superiors and his aunt often described. Naturally, it would be fine to have girls in his battery, but for professional reasons too. Teenage females had better dexterity and hand-eye coordination than many males; girls seemed inevitably cheerful and anxious to please.

Pushing such thoughts from his mind, Nguyen stepped down from the trailer and walked around the battery. He enjoyed the morning air, warm but not yet hot, and stopped to appreciate the lightening eastern sky. From atop the ridge he had a splendid view of the surrounding landscape, growing golden yellow in the low sun. Nguyen glanced in that direction, not yet needing to shield his eyes against the glare. *If they come this morning,* he thought, *that is the direction.* The imperialist air pirates would come in low, with the sun at their backs. It was doctrine. Therefore, the entire battery of 57mm radar-controlled guns stood to at first light—all five officers and sixty-six men.

The battery commander strolled out to one of the 14.5mm machine-gun positions that were constantly manned during daylight. They provided close defense for the battery's radar station some 300 meters from the S-60 gun sites. Half of the 14.5 crews were Africans, which worried him.

Not that their revolutionary fervor was in doubt, their standard of training inadequate. But communicating with them was a problem. None of them spoke Vietnamese, and only two of his men had learned any Portuguese. What communication existed between the African and Vietnamese comrades was accomplished with a mixture of French and Russian, with a little English and much body language.

Nguyen waved to some of the African gunners—at least a few of them seemed awake—and turned back toward the trailer. Phan, his deputy, was sprinting toward him from nearly a hundred meters away, shouting something about the regimental-level warning radar. Then Nguyen heard the jets, but something was wrong. The noise was from the west.

0529
Grunt Flight

The Hornets ti ied their run-in almost perfectly, Grunt from the west and P sycho from the northwest. The dual-axis attack was calculated for each F/A-18 to strike one flak site while both converged over the third. Thus, the entire battalion would be covered in a matter of seconds, since each battery was within five kilometers of its neighbor.

When Grunt popped up over the western rim of the ridge, he had perhaps ten seconds to spot his target and line up his approach. As he pulled forty degrees nose-high he moved his stick precisely, rolled 180 degrees and stopped inverted. Through the top of his canopy he spotted the distinctive hexagonal shape of the AAA battery and rolled upright with his nose below the horizon, then began reciting the attack pilot's litany.

"Looking for twenty-five degrees nose-low, rad alt to HUD." Deft finger movements ensured that Grunt's radar altimeter data was displayed on his head-up display, which was crucial. Through the HUD he took in the ground before him—"Terrain looks flat"—and began his step-down altitude adjustments. "Fifteen degrees for 1,500; smooth down to 1,000." He monitored his HUD data for altitude and airspeed and slightly retarded the throttles. Now five degrees nose-low at 1,000 feet and 430 knots, Grunt settled his "death dot" on the distribution box in the middle of the six S-60 guns. Then he pressed the button on his control stick.

Flak Site

Nguyen Ma Bac glanced upward, caught a glimpse of the twin-tailed jet with its nose seemingly pointed directly at him, and went pale in the early light. He flung himself to the ground, aware that the 14.5mm machine gunners behind him would only have a fleeting shot. None of the battery's 57mm guns was likely to get off a round.

Nguyen covered his head as heavy machine gun fire erupted around him.

Grunt Flight

Grant Grundmeyer had selected the port outboard station on his underwing pylons. When the release circuits closed, ejector cartridges fired and kicked three of the 488-pound cylinders off their racks, overcoming the aerodynamic forces swirling beneath the wings.

Upon separation from the racks, each of the Mk-20 cluster bomb units was split apart by a linear shaped charge. From each cylinder spewed 247 dual-purpose charges that, detonated 500 feet over the target, covered 51,600 square feet. Statistically, each of the 1.35-pound bomblets burst inside an area of 209 square feet. Those impacting on solid objects, such as weapons or vehicles, exploded instantly. Their shaped charges could penetrate the top armor of most tanks, so thin-skinned vehicles were especially vulnerable.

The vast majority of the total of 741 bomblets struck soft earth, and most of them functioned. Their sensitive fuzes activated small rocket motors that tossed the submunitions back into the air, where they burst into hundreds of fragments.

With overlapping coverage from the three cluster bombs, the battery's entire 85,000 square feet were splattered. The pattern was denser toward the center, but each of the six S-60 guns was sprayed—with their seven-man crews.

0530

Grunt felt the Rockeyes eject from the racks and continued straight ahead, driving for the eastern site three miles away. He knew that Psycho had struck the northern battery and would hit the third site any second.

There! Grundmeyer caught Rampart 3509 crossing diagonally from his left and saw the Rockeyes spew onto the flak site, throwing up dust and smoke. One or two bursts of blue-green tracer fire vainly tried to follow Psycho but fell well behind him.

Twenty-five seconds after hitting his primary, Grunt dropped his remaining CBUs on the easternmost battery. Observation of the results was limited owing to dust, smoke and flames, but as he pulled off the target Grundmeyer glanced back between his Hornet's twin tails and saw secondary explosions—probably from the stacked ready ammunition by each 57mm gun.

Jeez, six Rocks on one AAA battery, Grunt thought. *Slats was right—payback's a real bitch.*

Flak Site

When the world finally stopped shaking, and when his own trembling came more under control, Comrade Captain Nguyen Ma Bac unsteadily got to his feet. A deafening roar persisted in his ears, and he tried to blink the dust and smoke from his eyes. He had been hit by three small slivers of metal but as yet did not notice the pain. Through his dulled senses he realized how lucky he had been. The Hornet had struck while he was still outside the battery's main perimeter. Had he been inside the hundred-meter circle he probably would not have survived.

With dust still settling and sunlight filtering through the smoke, Nguyen stumbled back toward the command trailer. It was ripped apart by hundreds of fragments, and he saw only two men rising to their feet anywhere near the guns. He didn't yet know it, but of the seventy men in his battery, thirty-eight were dead or dying and nineteen more were seriously wounded. All he did know was that his world had been shattered in a way he had never imagined. Looking around, he took in the most obvious sights: the radar van perforated with hundreds of holes and the dish shattered; one gun barrel lopped off at half length; a bloody, shredded uniform containing raw meat a few steps away. Nguyen's world had been reduced to perforated scrap iron and twitching hamburger.

The Comrade Jane Fonda Antiaircraft Battalion had, for practical purposes, ceased to exist.

0540
Circus 204, Over Northern Natal

Low-holding, Ozzie thought. *What a drag.* He turned the VF-182 Tomcat onto another leg of its racetrack circuit at 7,300 feet. *Best stay away from even altitudes in case the gomers catch on to us.* He and Fido would have preferred a higher patrol station, but that would have increased chances of radar detection from farther inside Mozambique. The duty E-2 was positioned well southeast, actually orbiting out to sea. Though the Hawkeye radar was optimized for maritime surveillance, the F-14 crew knew that the Peeping Toms practiced hard at overland intercepts. *If there's any MiGs up today, Chimola will spot 'em.*

"Hey, Oz. It's past target time. Can we go home now?" Fred Colley's voice carried a sense of urgency over the intercom.

"What's the matter?" The pilot sensed his RIO's discomfort.

There was a slight pause. "Ah, my stomach's a little upset. Musta been some of that African food we ate last night."

Ozzie's temper flared. *Damn it, Fred. Why didn't you say so?* Ostrewski choked down his ire. He knew he was getting edgy. Back-to-back battle group defense missions, losses of friends, the frantic launch from *Langley;* now living in a damn tent and almost no sleep. "Okay, stand by."

As the lone F-14 covering the various strike groups, Ozzie felt obliged to remain airborne as long as possible. The Hornets could look out for themselves, but the Vikings would be dog meat for any interceptor. And it was difficult to leave a potential skyful of bogies from which Ozzie Ostrewski could pick and choose. But so far no hostile aircraft had appeared. *Maybe the Prowlers are zappin' 'em. Or maybe they're still blind from the grunts' raid on the command center.*

Something else bothered Ozzie. He knew that a high-maintenance bird like the Tom could fly only one or two more sorties without increasingly degraded systems. Fuel and oxygen used on this flight would have to be replaced, even if no ordnance were expended. If no Mozambicans—or Cubans or Koreans or whatever—intercepted this flight, the sortie was largely wasted. The thought appalled him. He moved the stick to bank southward when Fido chirped, "Contact! Data-link from the Hawkeye. Multiple bogies bearing 350, forty miles."

"How many?"

"Dunno, pardner. It's a pretty strong image. I'd say maybe one flight in welded-wing, painting as a single."

Ozzie flipped Master Arm and snugged up his torso-harness fittings. Then he crossed himself. "Are they a threat?"

"Hang on . . ." Fido's bowels settled down. *Wonderful what adrenaline does.* "They're just trolling the border, west to east. I think they're scouting." Colley tracked the radar return a bit longer. "The Prowler must be givin' 'em fits . . . they're headin' away."

Ozzie briefly pondered the chances of a long-range radar shot. Then CAG Ballantine's orders came to mind: *Bring your missiles home unless you gotta shoot to save yourself or somebody else. We don't have enough to spare for just running up the score.*

Ozzie Ostrewski, CVW-18's top scorer, reluctantly turned for home.

0545
Fish Hook 703, over Zululand

Rocky Petrocelli shook his head in disbelief. Circling after takeoff from a mile-long stretch of the N2 coastal freeway, he watched his "strike Vikings" form up for their first overland bombing mission. After one more orbit Rocky gathered in his other five S-3Bs and set course away from their improvised base near the Hluhluwe Nature Reserve. The VS-23 CO couldn't resist rolling one wing low for a quick look down. He'd been told there were rare white rhinos in these parts, but none of the Miocene leftovers showed themselves.

Petrocelli turned his attention back to business. His

CoTac—copilot and assistant tactics offer—occupied the right seat, more as a lookout than anything else, but they were alone in the aircraft. "No point in taking SensOs and TacCos on a truck-hunting flight," Rocky had said. Lou Tran had practically genuflected, begging to fly the mission, but CAG Ballantine was firm—"We got work for you on the ground, translating Vietnamese radio intercepts."

Had there been time, Rocky would have removed some of the Vikings' ASW equipment as a weight-saving and security measure. As it was, Fish Hook 703 carried four 500-pound bombs under the wings. He was only fifty miles from his target, so drop tanks were unnecessary.

"War Hoover Flight" headed west at low level, navigating by unconventional means. Strapped to the skipper's kneeboard was a carefully folded chart labeled *Suidelike Afrika Padkaart*—a South African road map. His target was a bridge twenty-seven miles east of Vryheid on the R69. General Mkize's intel said a brigade of the Second Vietnamese Motor Rifle Corps was approaching the gorge, and could be "interdicted" by air attack.

Petrocelli shook his head again. Other aviators used to razz the Viking squadron about its practice bombing missions during air wing workups at Fallon. Now Rocky prepared to put that experience to use. *Four nights ago I nuked two subs and now I'm "interdicting" goddamn trucks. I can hardly wait to see what tomorrow brings*! He laughed aloud. The lieutenant CoTac chuckled politely and quickly turned his face to the window.

0550
Over Northern Natal

The six Vikings crossed a branch of the Mkuze River south of Mahlangasi, then picked up the main river westbound. But Rocky was far too smart to follow the river itself. "The dinks'll spot ya that way ev'ry time," he had said. "Stay to one side or th' other, an' keep low to the ridges." So far his flight profile had worked.

Rocky's CoTac nudged him, then pointed. "Skipper, there's our escort."

Petrocelli followed the finger and, looking high and right, saw two dart shapes approaching. "Good eye, kid." He rocked his wings in the join-up signal and, without a radio call, the strike package was formed. Two Hornets led by Lieutenant "Eager" Ed Pell of VFA-183 were on time, on course. Rocky nudged his partner. "I just love it when a plan comes together, don't you?"

0556

"Sir, I make it four minutes to target."

Rocky nodded and checked his armament panel. The 5,300-foot mountain ahead at ten o'clock gave him a cross-reference to his merge with the R69. There was still no op-position, so for the first time in the mission Rocky opened up on his scrambler radio. "Hoover Flight from Lead. We'll at-tack as planned. Lead section goes in first, second section at the end of the column, third holds high. Ramparts, take the flak sites. Everybody copy?"

Confirming calls came from the two section leaders and Eager Ed. With that, Rocky shoved up the power to the two turbofans, pulled the stick back and climbed to attack alti-tude. Running in toward the target from the north side of the road, he crested a ridge—and exclaimed, "Holy smokes!"

The mild oath would have been humorous anytime else. But there, stretched along several miles of paved road, was a motor rifle brigade: several hundred vehicles with, according to the Zulus, some 2,500 Vietnamese and 500 Mozambicans. Rocky wasted no time sightseeing. He had achieved surprise —the Viets never expected land-based aircraft in their rear— but time was precious.

Leading his wingman down from an 8,000-foot perch, Rocky saw the bridge over the gorge. Leading elements of the brigade already were across on the western side. Rocky jockeyed stick and rudder, carefully lining up the span in his crude "bombsight"—the junction of his windscreen wiper and its supporting arm. Angling slightly across the bridge, he waited until he felt he could wait no longer. Then he waited some more. His CoTac was to read off the altitude in 500-foot increments, but the kid was too absorbed with what he saw to say anything.

Fifteen hundred feet over the bridge, Rocky released his Mark 82s. Then he pulled hard and felt the fuzzy gray-ness of five-plus Gs. When he looked back he saw that one

500-pounder had struck, exploding a scaly old BTR-50 at midspan. His wingman in 704 now was down the chute, and though both bombs missed the span, one detonated on a structural beam.

Streaks of blue tracer fire belatedly laced the air from five ZSU-23-4s in the column. Pulling around for a good look, Rocky saw secondaries on the bridge and was startled when an eruption sent visible shock waves outward from the middle of the column. He heard a muffled call, "Three-Oh-Six is off," and realized one of the Hornets' cluster bombs had just erased a flak wagon and nearby ammo trucks.

Rocky's second section already was at work on the end of the column. The leader, a lieutenant commander from Kansas who called himself "Tex," astutely put both his bombs halfway up the steep canyon wall, creating a medium-sized avalanche. His wingman did likewise at the east end of the bridge. Swirling smoke and dust convinced Rocky that the Vietnamese column was stranded, unable to proceed forward or backward. He had hoped to drop the span, but the boulders and debris in the road convinced him the Viets would be a long time clearing a path.

Rocky called in his third section, orbiting east of the action. Armed with Chilean CBUs, Fish Hooks 710 and 712 swung wide and attacked from the southeast, dodging the light flak. Three or four SA-9s streaked upward from the six BRDM armored cars, and instantly drew the fury of the Hornets. Both Vikings dropped in one pass, leaving a crackling, exploding line of trucks and T-55 tanks the length of the column.

It was over in two minutes. Rocky keyed his mike, calling in the clear. "Hoover Flight, looks like a good job. Let's get outta here . . ." He assembled his mini-strike force and called for damage reports.

"Ah, Lead, this is Tex. I've got a big hole in one wing and maybe some damage aft." The concern in his voice was obvious. Rocky took that as a bad sign—Tex was a cool head.

"Ah, rog, 705. Can you make it back?"

The pause gave Rocky his answer before Tex's reply. "Negative, Hoover Lead. I'm . . . ah, I'm headin' for Point Delta. My wingman's with me."

He's going to eject over the safe zone, Rocky realized. "Hoover 706 from Lead. You copy?"

"Affirmative, Lead. I'm with him. See you back on campus."

"Roger. Hoover Lead, out." *Show-off squirt,* Rocky thought. *Tryin' to show how cool he is when I know damn well he's near petrified.*

Minutes later Rocky and all of War Hoover Flight heard a plaintive electronic whipping sound, the emergency beepers of Tex and his CoTac. Hoover 706 reported two good chutes, descending into friendly territory.

The CO expelled a breath of audible relief. *I can't believe we got off that light.* He glanced back at the stretch of detritus-strewn highway. *Lotsa good targets still stuck there,* he thought. *Well, they ain't goin' anywheres.*

0600
National Route R69, Northern Natal

Private Yuri Sverdlov had had enough. Ears ringing, dust in his mouth and nostrils, he levered himself up from the remains of the radio trailer. His damaged hearing could not detect the retreating sound of the American jets, but when he saw a few other TsRB security troops moving outside, he decided it was safe. Checking himself and finding no major wounds, he stumbled to the exit and tripped over a body. *Chernavin,* he gasped.

Tears welled up in Sverdlov's eyes. His lips quivered and he began to cry. Not that the late Vasilii Chernavin was a close friend—Sverdlov had had no close friends since being transferred in disgrace from amphibious assault ship *Ivan Rogov*. But the nineteen-year-old radio technician had seen too much and experienced too much in the past few weeks. Standing in the doorway, it all came back, washing over him like effluvium from a backed-up sewer. The awful experience of the firing squad, the wrath of that swine of a major, the rugged living conditions ashore with these new "comrades." The ghastly things he had seen them do.

Sverdlov wiped his face ineffectively on his jacket sleeve. He glanced left and right. Confusion was still spreading in the wake of the air attack. Without further thought, the radioman picked up a stack of documents, stuffed them in a valise and slid out the door. He scampered under the trailer and four steps later he was half running, half sliding downhill. He did not yet know exactly where he would go, but a plan was forming in his mind.

0800
North Natal

Sverdlov realized he should have taken some food before the air strike. He had been hiking east, keeping to the hillsides along the highway. It took a lot of exertion. The former battle policeman had found some potable water, but now all he could think about was eating. He knew this was bad, since he had to stay alert. There was very little cover in this dry country.

Then he heard renewed bombing to the west, toward a city his stolen map labeled "Frygait" in Russian.

Near the R69, East of Vryheid

"Air attack warning! Take defensive stations!"

At first Siphageni thought it was an unannounced drill. Then he saw the Vietnamese officer pointing overhead, saw the ZSU 23mm guns belatedly tracking the inbound jets and heard SAMs launch. From there his professional instincts took over. He bailed out of the BMP and scrambled into the brush fifty meters away. Most of the Viets, he noticed, were taking cover below or behind their vehicles. *No experience of air attack,* Siphageni thought. He'd learned long ago that when airplanes hunt trucks or tanks, you don't hide under the vehicles. *That's like camping on the bull's-eye.*

From his concealed position, Siphageni had only a fleeting view of the aircraft. He was certain they couldn't be SAAF, as South Africa's air force had gone down fighting over a week ago. Then he glimpsed the ungainly silhouette of an A-6 and he knew. *American carrier aircraft. They must be operating ashore. How did they do that?*

Talent 500, Above the R69

Hanging against their restraints, Crunch Neslie and Slats Slattery had a weird upside-down view of the world as they pulled through before rolling upright in their pop-up attack. Angling down toward the enemy column, the A-6 crew had seconds to juggle the myriad items demanding their attention—time to release, drift angle and position relative to the target.

Crunch's aimpoint was a large fuel truck near the end of the column. With the wings level in a fifty-degree dive, he saw the aiming reticle move in his sight and squeezed the "commit" trigger on his stick. From there the attack computer took over. As long as the pilot held the Intruder straight along the selected axis, the bombs would go where Lieutenant James Neslie and Sir Isaac Newton intended. Crunch mentally counted, *One-potato, two-potato . . .*

He never got to three-potato. The outboard ejector cartridges fired and the cluster bombs left their pylons. Disciplined aviator that he was, Crunch waited one more potato to avoid slewing his bombs. Then he jammed the stick hard over, pulling off his attack heading.

Slats fought the Gs, turning in his seat to assess the damage. Two other Intruders also were pulling away, and a Hornet flak suppressor jinked off-target to the right. "Looks like we done good," Slattery said over the ICS.

Crunch's outlook was broader at that moment. "Long as there's no MiGs waiting for us in the traffic pattern back home."

Slats tensed his back muscles to force down a nervous shiver. *I wish he hadn't said that.*

0803
Near Vryheid

Slowly, cautiously, Joseph Siphageni unearthed himself. He had pulled dirt and wood over his body as minimal protection from bomb fragments, and he emerged unhurt. The jets were gone, but the residual effects of their attack lingered in the air, in men's eyes and throats. And in their minds. Through the dust and smoke, Siphageni heard the familiar dirge—the moaning of the wounded and dying. Armored vehicles and trucks burned the length of the column, while others were slewed crazily on both sides of the road.

Cluster bombs, Siphageni thought. He'd been on the receiving end of South African CBUs and he loathed them. A man stood a chance against conventional bombs, but CBUs were so . . . indiscriminate. However, as a detached professional, he recognized their utility. *Area weapons are appropriate for a lengthy target like this,* he reflected. Looking around, he realized his column was stuck for the present. The route was blocked ahead and behind, both by terrain and by wrecked vehicles.

Siphageni's radio operator loped up to him. The youngster had small cuts and abrasions but seemed otherwise unharmed. "Comrade, I just heard a general alert over the command net. Headquarters says that fascist attacks have closed the mountain passes leading to Vryheid, and that regional air defense is diminished by a Commando raid." The boy smiled.

"What's humorous about that?" Siphageni asked.

"Well, we're to be alert to possible enemy aircraft!" As both men laughed aloud, their Vietnamese comrades muttered quiet curses at the indifference of Africans to a dire situation.

2000
Mtubatuba, Zululand

Inside his command tent, Mkize rose to address his and Colonel Holden's staffs. "As you know, gentlemen, materiel is being unloaded from your prepositioning ships virtually without enemy opposition. For this we have the U.S. Navy and Marine Corps to thank." He nodded toward the marine commander. "The SAAF previously destroyed the chemical-delivery capability of FROG, Scud and Scaleboard missile units on our front. Enemy air bases in southern Mozambique have been knocked out by Tomahawk missiles, and Colonel Holden's Marine Expeditionary Unit has built up effective air defenses in the landing area with remarkable speed.

"If all goes well, we should eventually have enough equipment and supplies to maintain a 16,500-man U.S. Marine Expeditionary Brigade in combat for a month. At our present rate, fighting as guerrillas, it would take my 30,000 Zulus half a year to consume such largesse. But soon we'll be guerrillas no more. Thanks to your arrival, Colonel, we're going on the offensive. Tonight, I'll outline a plan of attack. I want your suggestions now and shall rely on your detailed planning over the next twenty-four hours to ensure its success. I intend to aim for jump-off at 0200 hours on Wednesday, 9 June. I want you to tell me if that's possible."

In the lamplight, Mkize spread his arms over topographical charts of the Vryheid region and the Mozambique-Natal border. "Gentlemen, this plan is based upon actions in two directions simultaneously. Though widely separated from the prime objective, the western phase serves a dual purpose. First, it draws enemy attention away from our move into Mozambique. And secondly, it disrupts enemy lines of communication even if the northern phase fails." Americans and Zulus alike followed the bony finger tracing the snaking red lines—arteries, really—through the tan and brown landscape of northern Natal.

"Three main routes service this entire region," the Zulu war chief explained. "The R66 runs south from Pongola near the Swazi border. It is intersected by the R69 here, about sixty kilometers east-northeast of Vryheid. The R69 runs through very mountainous terrain, and therefore is vulnerable to interdiction.

"Thirty kilometers south a lesser route, 618, also intersects R66. But it does little good because its western terminus is back on R69 near Hlobane Dam." He glanced around the table to make sure his listeners were following him.

"That leaves the R33, generally north-south between Vryheid and Piet Retief, also well up on the border." He tapped the spot with a fingertip.

"The main transport routes I have just described are widespread and almost equally vulnerable," Mkize explained. "With careful timing, I think we can convince the Front Line commanders that our scattered forces in the area are far stronger than they really are. The keys are these mountain passes—one or two each on Routes 66, 69 and 33. If we control them, we control communications to Vryheid and points south."

Colonel Bruce Holden immediately saw the advantage of Mkize's plan—simplicity. "Very well, sir. This phase can be accomplished with minimal personnel and assets. Now, what about the major move northward?"

Mkize gave his guest a professorial look. "Colonel, are you by chance familiar with traditional Zulu military doctrine?"

"Uh, yeah." He gave the Texas hook-'em-horns gesture

and almost a shy smile. "Bulk of forces in the center of body, and flanking forces left and right." Holden knew about the 1879 Zulu War from his professional reading.

"Quite so," Mkize replied. "And the military wisdom of my ancestors still applies. I propose to place your amphibious and special-operations forces in the right horn, heliborne marines in the left and my Zulus, supported by your tanks, in the head." His hands described an enveloping motion on the map. Pointing toward the rear, he explained, "A mixed force of marine air, armor, fire-support troops and Zulus will form the loins. With some of your amphibious vehicles, and using captured enemy transport and our personal vehicles, we will have a mobile reserve. In all, our 'bull' will involve 30,000 Zulus, your 2,800 marines, SEALs and other navy personnel."

"Okay, at first glance it looks promising. But what about enemy defenses in the region? Our intel shows mine fields along the border."

Holden's air liaison officer spoke up. "Sir, I'm coordinating with General Mkize's staff and the *Langley* air wing. We just got word that Israeli fuel-air explosives will be available to detonate the mine fields. And supporting TacAir and artillery will be in place, as you ordered."

Holden took in the scheme. "General, my compliments. If this plan works—and I think it can—the Front Line offensive on this front will run out of steam for lack of supplies." Holden knew that even with Mkize's divisions, the Zulu-marine force probably could not win outright victory in the region. But according to his bible—Manual FMF-1, titled *Warfighting*—that wouldn't be necessary. A smaller force could neutralize a larger one by maneuver, deception and disruption of enemy command-control. His gray eyes met Mkize's brown eyes in the lamplight. "But they can still reinforce by air, and we lack the airpower to interdict them for long."

Mkize nodded. "Just so, Colonel. But we only need control the main landing areas, not the entire airspace over the region. And since we already hold Vryheid, the enemy cannot land there.

"Please correct me if I'm wrong, sir, but Vryheid and vicinity opens the way to the coast. When we laid out this plan, it was with the knowledge that we were only buying time. America is a creature of the air and the sea. The UER and its allies are creatures of the land. With access to our shore, and by breaking the Russian sea-lift, your air power and navy can force a stalemate throughout South Africa. From my viewpoint, that is equal to a victory." *A Zulu political victory,* Mkize thought. *Something this white man probably neither knows nor cares about.*

Holden nodded his understanding. "All right, General. I agree. Now, with my armor and artillery at the jump-off points into Mozambique, I think we can expect some unwelcome attention from the Johannesburg area. It should ease the pressure on your . . . forces for a while." He had almost said "your people," but caught himself. "The question is, will this plan buy enough time for American reinforcements to arrive in-theater?"

Mkize smiled brightly in the gloom. "If it does not, sir, then this is going to be a futile exercise. And I shall probably get killed to no good purpose." His laughter filled the tent with impending joy of battle—and filled Colonel Bruce Holden with a shivering sense of dread.

1700, 6 June EST; 0000 Pretoria, Monday, 7 June
White House

Menaced by boom mikes, assaulted by flashbulbs and klieg lights, the President and Secretary of State sat on the gold brocade couch under the "Scenic America" wallpaper in the oval-shaped, ground-floor Diplomatic Reception Room. Callaway insisted on and got decorum from the White House press corps. He selected reporters to ask questions, but let his two guests, the British and French ambassadors, do most of the talking.

"Thank you, Mr. President," acknowledged the elegant woman from ABC, Laurie Luft. "Ambassador Quirk," she asked, "President Rodinkov has accused Britain of attacking and sinking Russian ships off South Africa, including the aircraft carrier *Varyag,* previously damaged by the U.S. Navy. Do you still deny torpedoing any Russian ships?"

"Her Majesty's government has not declared war on the Union of Eurasian Republics. We have condemned the invasion of South Africa but remain neutral in that conflict. To my knowledge, there are not even any Royal Navy surface vessels within striking distance of South Africa. As for *Varyag*, I believe the Americans left her in a bad way on Friday, wasn't it? I must assume she sank from internal explosions. It's entirely possible she was scuttled."

"A follow-up, Mr. President?" Callaway nodded.

"You mentioned 'surface' ships," Luft said to the British ambassador. "What about subs? This afternoon, the Russians lodged a complaint against you at the UN, charging undersea harassment all over the Atlantic."

"As you may know, Miss Luft," Ambassador Quirk responded, "neither my government nor yours ever comments on submarine operations. I am at liberty, however, to say that we are investigating the Russian complaints. With respect to the *Varyag* incident, I may point out that a sub leaving from Britain a week ago Saturday last could scarcely have reached southern Africa by now, except at top speed for the whole 6,000 miles. And, I might add, it would have had to run the Russian submarine barrier across the equator."

"But you keep nuclear subs around the Falklands, don't you?"

"I'm sorry, Laurie," the President interjected. "You've had your shot." Then, to the large, pugnacious, ill-toupeed CBS veteran, Callaway said, "Don."

"Ambassador LeGros, the French Indian Ocean Squadron—thirteen ships and an unknown number of subs—left your island of Reunion some days ago and rounded the southern end of Madagascar."

"If you say so," the large, muffinlike diplomat replied.

"Now the squadron appears to be cooperating to some extent with the American amphibious force off Natal," the reporter Campbell continued. "It has been suggested that this move replaces our carrier group wiped out by the Russians. There have been suspicious sinkings of Russian freighters all along the East African coast. The Russians blame France. Experts I've talked to tell me that Russian sea-lift operations have virtually been shut down. They all agree that the few American subs believed to be in the area couldn't have sunk all these cargo ships. They say the French Navy wanted to announce its presence in this way without attacking Russian warships."

"Do you have a question, Don?" the President inquired.

"Yes, sir. Mr. Ambassador, does this naval activity mean

your government has finally decided to get into the act in South Africa? And if so, have you told the Russians?"

"That's two questions, Don," Callaway smiled, plainly enjoying his power. "You're big, but you only get the same number as anybody else. Pick the one you want the ambassador to answer."

"I can answer both," LeGros said. "The French Republic is not at war with anybody, so we haven't had to inform anybody of warlike intentions. I do not know that French warships in the Indian Ocean are cooperating with American amphibious operations. Allow me to add that, if our ships are in the same general area, it may be difficult for French officers to distinguish an attack on U.S. naval vessels from an attack on those of my nation. I'm sure that the Union of Eurasian Republics appreciates this fact."

"A quick follow-up, Mr. President," the pushy correspondent bellowed. "With all due respect, sir," Campbell asked before anyone else could be recognized, "just what have you and the ambassadors been talking about? The weather?"

"As a matter of fact, we have," Callaway replied. Without missing a beat, he said, "Ellen," and pointed to the doyen of the White House beat, a wizened wire service crone every bit as combative as any of her younger colleagues.

"Mr. President, I also have two questions. First, when will the Pentagon give us the evidence it supposedly has that the Russian Navy attacked us first? And second, do you intend to send American ground troops into combat to prop up the apartheid regime? After the carnage at sea, do you think the American people will stand for that?"

"I don't want to set a precedent here. I'll answer both questions, or all three, but you forfeit your follow-up," the President responded. "First off, as we've said repeatedly, we can't make all the information on the Russian attack available right now, for security reasons. Second, I can't comment on possible ground operations, for the same reason. Third, yes, I do think the nation would support limited combat ashore, if it were successful and if it led to both peace and freedom in South Africa. Those are the goals of my administration. That's why I moved the carrier and amphibious groups into the area in the first place."

If the landing doesn't succeed, I'm dead meat, Callaway

thought. *And the sacrifice of all those kids may be on my soul.* "Okay, one last question. This was just supposed to be a photo op. Chuck," he said, indicating the gregarious, fat, black reporter for *Stars and Stripes,* "make it quick."

0600 Monday, 7 June
USS Dwight D. Eisenhower, *off Southwest Africa*

Captain Winton Foster felt better now. He was always nervous sitting on deck, guzzling fuel at the rate of 22,000 pounds per hour with his twin F404s in idle. But once airborne with his wheels in the well, he was in his element. He glanced down from Old Salt 300 and took in the spectacle below. As the air wing commander of "Ike," he was flying his accustomed F/A-18C belonging to the Saints of VFA-163, and the rest of Air Wing 16 was climbing to join him. Foster saw Boomer 506—an A-6E of VA-165—launch off Cat Three as part of the heavy strike package.

Eisenhower continued into the wind, her bow wave flashing white in the early-morning sunlight as jet after jet lifted off her deck. "Famous" Foster—so named for his self-styled role as world-famous boy hero—would have preferred a night strike to break into the South African war, but time was desperately short.

With *Eisenhower*'s air wing pulling into range for a shot at the eastward-retreating *Gorshkov* group, Union forces in the theater were increasingly vulnerable to the powerful battle group. Foster knew that *Roosevelt*'s repairs were almost complete, and every other American carrier was headed this way. Before long, there'd be multi-CVBG task forces off South Africa—Kuwait revisited. And now the French and British were threatening to pile on. *Typical. Just like the Frogs,* he thought. *Wait to see which way the wind is blowing before choosing sides. Probably just don't want to miss out on arms sales to South Africa after the war.*

Foster had heard some VF-161 aircrews speculating as to whether there would be enough MiGs to go around, and had put it down to pre-mission jitters. Aviators would always rather die than look bad, but he had reminded the Chargers that this was a shooting war—the first for all hands.

With practiced ease the thirty-five-plane strike was assembled in minutes, without unnecessary radio chatter. Foster turned eastward, leading the base element of Boomers and Saints with VF-162 Hunters flying escort while the Chargers swept ahead on MiGCAP. The target-area escort was free to roam, as hard information was scarce. Foster hoped the Hawkeye, ES-3 and two Prowlers could provide some data en route. Otherwise the air wing would take potluck—bomb, strafe or radiate anything that looked promising along the coast or a few miles inland. Either way, he knew his genuine mission was not destruction, but presence. The violent announcement of the arrival of a new U.S. battle group in the theater was bound to have salutary effects from the Cape to Moscow. And the second strike being readied for launch—fifteen Hornets and Intruders from VFA-164 and VA-166—would reinforce the message.

Foster double-checked his outbound heading. The moving-map image on his multifunction display panel showed the African coast 200 miles ahead.

0700 EST; 1400 Pretoria; 1500 Moscow
White House

"Dr. Epstein would lahk to see ya'll immediately, suh," Mrs. Thornburgh announced over the intercom. "He's chahgin' up from the Situation Room this veruh minuht."

Callaway was enjoying the weak morning light in the Oval Office, reading memos and savoring a few minutes alone. *Never enough time just to think,* he considered yet again. Mildly peeved, he took his feet off the desk, flipped the switch and said, "Okay, send him right in." *This better be good.*

The national security adviser entered, trying to hide some secret glee but beaming nonetheless. Grasping a folder in front of his hips and bouncing on the tip of his toes, Epstein grinned wordlessly. Then, just as the President was about to complain about the delay, he said, "They want to cut a deal."

"Who does? Over what?" the President asked, hoping he knew the answer.

"The Russians do. Over South Africa. At least at sea." Epstein brandished the folder.

The President's eyes brightened. He swiveled smartly

and stood up. "Lemme see," he ordered, and strode across the room.

Epstein slipped a paper out of the folder. "Here's their offer." He handed it to the President. "Looks as if they want to cut their naval losses, sir," he commented. "Maybe they think they're doing well enough on land that they don't need naval air support anymore." He could see that Callaway was engrossed in the document and wasn't listening.

The President held up a hand to let Epstein know he was concentrating. He scanned the single-paged communique once quickly, then went back over it point by point:

"1) UER Task Force not allowed to attack U.S. PhibRon off Natal, in exchange for no strike by *Eisenhower* CVBG against *Gorshkov* group off Cape Province.

"2) UER carriers permitted to fly off air wings; U.S. CVs permitted to support ground war.

"3) Neither side to interfere with rescue and salvage operations at sea.

"4) Lines to be drawn on map to keep fleets separate. U.S. CVBGs not to advance beyond Cape Town; PhibRon, French CVBG not to go past Durban. British subs to withdraw west, leaving remaining UER ships alone."

The President grew visibly excited, but kept his peace. Epstein could see him mulling it all over, like a bull chewing its cud. The process was almost audible.

"Hot damn!" Callaway exclaimed at last. "I can't hardly believe it. Gotta be a trick. I'm inclined to accept it, just as it is." He reread the terms. "Have you pulled Hub outta the Tank?"

"Yes, sir. I've notified the CNO and other relevant Pentagon personnel. We can have a meeting straightaway."

"Good. Knew I could count on you. Unless the JCS see somethin' I missed, looks to me like all we got to talk about is area-of-operation boundaries. Whaddya think?"

"I concur wholeheartedly, Mr. President." For the first time in two weeks—months, in fact—the adviser saw a ray of hope. *Maybe it will turn out okay after all.* Little in life was so wonderful as having made the right choice at a crucial moment.

1702
Kuznetsov

The admiral smashed his fist against the bulkhead in rage and frustration.

The orders from Moscow to stand down stunned Rybakov like a left hook to the jaw. Sinking *Langley* and its escorts had evened the score for the *Varyag* group. Tomorrow, he had intended to send *Hornet* and as many other amphibious ships to the bottom as possible—and Frenchies, too, if they got in his way. Now the politicians had deprived him of the chance to settle accounts for loss of *Novo.*

He crumbled the signal paper. Regardless of whether the outcome of the war left him in favor or disgrace in the Kremlin, he intended to carry on the fight. And to give a shot at long life to some young aviator whose Rook he would appropriate. Like the Crimean War admirals who fought on land after their fleets were destroyed, Rybakov was going ashore.

1830

Colonel of Aviation Nikolai Glinka didn't know whether to feel insulted or honored. Aside from the professional bile he felt at the sinking of his once-beautiful ship, *Varyag*'s air wing commander was unaccustomed to following any other pilot up the ski-slope ramp. But flying number two in the formation to the fleet admiral wasn't really much of a demotion. *At least I have an airplane,* Glinka thought ruefully. Most of *Varyag*'s other jets were long since gone.

Taxiing aft on his adopted flattop, Glinka jockeyed throttle and steering to place his Su-25 before the jet-blast deflector. He recalled the 1989 sea trials—when *Kuznetsov* was still named *Tbilisi*—and the embarrassing moment when Pugachev's Su-27 exhaust melted part of the jet blast deflector. Now American ordnance had accomplished far more destruction on *Varyag,* which had then been *Riga.*

Glinka watched as Rybakov's Sukhoi ran up full power on both engines. The attack jet trembled visibly, as if anxious to be airborne. Then it was accelerating up the ramp. Glinka held his breath. This was the crucial phase of launch.

Rybakov's far out of practice, the wing commander acknowledged. *If he isn't careful about pitch control . . .*

The unarmed Su-25 hung for a moment, nose-high and sustained against gravity by the relative wind now burbling over its wings and 18,000 pounds of turbojet thrust. "Get your nose down, damn it!" Startled at his outburst, Glinka instantly checked his microphone button. Fortunately, it was clear.

As if in response to the unheard command, the Rook's pointed nose dropped thirty degrees. There was a bauble as the pilot overcontrolled, but the jet leveled off and flew straight ahead. With both thrust and lift working for it, Glinka—and everyone else topside—breathed easier.

1831
Above Kuznetsov

So did Pyotr Rybakov. He allowed his pulse to back off a few RPM, then eased into a clearing turn to port. He set up a racetrack orbit overhead the carrier, waiting for his other seven Rooks to launch and join him.

It had been a long, long time since he had personally taken off from a carrier, but Pyotr Rybakov knew he had made the right decision. The sea battle was over. The rest of the campaign would be decided ashore, where he could safely lead his remaining aircraft and pilots. *What conceit they must think I have—an old war-horse back in harness one last time.*

But the doubt fell away as Rybakov looked over his shoulder. Though his helmet knocked against the canopy, there were the other seven Rooks formed up in two flights. Rybakov rocked his wings and turned westward. His chart showed the four possible landing fields—Dundee, Ladysmith, Pietermaritzburg and Durban. Depending upon local conditions, he would land at one of those. Then he would try to coordinate the efforts of his remaining Yak-141 jumpjets, dispersed at their hideouts.

Feeling twenty years younger, Pyotr Rybakov flew toward the African mainland. Ahead of him, the sun began to sink.

19

8 June

Mkize's communications officer didn't bother with niceties. He flipped aside the flap of his commander's tent and swept his flashlight across the cot. "General, I bring exceptional news."

"Important?" the busy general asked. The commo officer nodded. "Very well, then. I'll be along momentarily."

0006

A skeptical Mkize paced into the operations center. Shuttled off in one corner were the commo officer, his staff intelligence officer, and representatives of the SADF and U.S. marines. They were clustered around a very young, frightened-looking Caucasian. The uncertainty was visible in the boy's blue eyes.

"This is our defector?" Mkize asked skeptically.

"Yes, sir," replied the marine liaison officer and his Russian-language expert. "Name's Sverdlov, Private Yuri Sverdlov. His documents appear genuine. He says he's a communications technician with a TsRB unit that was hit in an air attack yesterday. He says he used the confusion to escape, got lost and finally decided to sit tight. But he had no

510

food, only a little water, and thought he had to give up or starve. He bumped into one of your patrols on a main road a couple hours ago."

Mkize looked again at the grimy, disheveled youngster. The boy returned his gaze from the improvised table containing personal documents and a bound folder. *Well, he looks dirty enough and frightened enough,* Mkize thought. *But then he would, wouldn't he?* "Mchunu, you said he has valuable intelligence for us."

"Yes, sir," the intel staffer replied. "The folder contains not only radio frequencies and tactical callsigns, but the schedule for changes in each for the rest of the month."

Mkize nodded. "If he is genuine, obviously he is of much use. But how do we know he isn't here under orders?" Instinctively, Mkize felt the young Russian was on the level. *Nobody can pretend to look that scared.*

The marine interjected. "General, he says he was forced to participate in a firing squad aboard an amphibious landing ship called *Ivan Rogov.* Says it was punishment for a fight between Russian and Vietnamese marines. That, combined with what else he's seen in South Africa—he mentioned some atrocities we've confirmed as genuine—convinced him he wanted out of the TsRB."

"Very well. What is he asking for the documents?"

"He wants to remain with us until there's an armistice or until we leave. After that, he wants to go to America or Canada. Someplace with a Russian community."

Mkize waved a hand. "Yes, yes. That's to be expected. But how can we know we're not being deceived?"

The marine nodded to his NCO linguist. Two or three brief exchanges ensued, ending in a resigned gesture from the Russian. The translator said, "General, Yuri here says he'll do anything you ask him. Repair captured equipment, advise on UER comm procedures, anything. If his information doesn't prove out, he says you can shoot him."

Nigel Mkize thought for a moment. He spoke to the marine but looked directly at Private Sverdlov. "Tell him that I accept his offer."

0148
USS Mount St. Helens

Lieutenant Commander James Rixey was having no luck with the debrief. Even though the most seriously-wounded survivors from the ravaged CVBG had been choppered to the PhibRon, Rixey's ammunition ship and other resupply vessels in the unrep group were stuffed with rescued men—and a few women. All his interviewees had been sailors—until now.

Sitting across from the two waterlogged aviators, the admin officer tried to convince them to open up. But on the other hand, he couldn't blame them for preferring food over conversation. *Poor bastards—almost four days afloat in a raft in the middle of the damn Indian Ocean.*

Brillo Huggins speared another mouthful of medium-rare steak. It was delicious. A corpsman stood by, gauging whether the A-6 crew was in danger of gorging on the unaccustomed feast. Ever since ejecting from Killer 530 after the *Novorossiysk* strike, the pilot and B/N had subsisted on meager survival rations.

Rixey decided to try again. "Look, I know you guys are hungry. But your squadron will want to know about you right away. So will your families."

Sleaze Olsen looked up, his bathrobe's cuff almost dangling on his plate. "You mean we've already been reported MIA?"

The personnel officer shrugged. "Well, I don't know for sure, after all the activity and confusion. But it seems that with . . ."

"Pass the sauce," Brillo asked. A steward shoved the Heinz to him.

". . . the truce at sea, things will get sorted out." Rixey sounded hopeful.

Sleaze laid down his fork. "Look, Commander, what more can we tell you? We hit our target, took battle damage on the egress and punched out. Just say that Huggins and Olsen of VA-186 are still afloat."

Rixey knew when to stop. "Okay, okay." He rose to leave. "Say, if you don't mind me asking . . . what did you guys do for four days in the water?"

Brillo shook more sauce onto his steak. "To tell you the

truth, I thought we'd go crazy out there at first. But toward the end, we broke the code." He looked up. "We figured out the Meaning of Life."

The admin officer gaped at the aviator, uncertain whether Huggins was serious or not. "You solved the mystery of the ages. Right."

Sleaze pointed at his empty plate. "Hit me again," he told the steward.

"No, it's true," Brillo insisted. "Well, actually, Justin here did most of it. He's gonna write a new dogma—the Book of Sleaze."

The corpsman, the steward and the officer all waited expectantly. Sleaze accepted another mini steak and sighed aloud. "The Meaning of Life," he intoned, "is infinite. It is precisely what every human soul chooses to make of it." He plunked a salt shaker back onto the molded plastic tabletop with a sound that rang, high and pure, across the eons.

0156

The ship's sleepy but excited chaplain, tape recorder in hand, paced into the galley, asking for Huggins and Olsen of VA-186.

0230
Ingwavuma

Major General Nigel Mkize stood before the crowded room, looking at the mixture of black and white faces of his tactical commanders. The green, khaki, camouflage and occasional civilian colors blended into an ironic concept in his mind. *My own "rainbow coalition."*

With a meter stick for a pointer, Mkize began his briefing. "Gentlemen, the key enemy positions are here, at Catuane, and here, farther north at Goba and Namaacha, where the roads from Swaziland cross into Mozambique." He tapped the map, then traced the supply routes that sustained the Viet drives into Natal. "If we cut off their logistics and follow-on formations, the spearheads will run out of fuel and ammunition. That in turn will force a stalemate, at least on this front—an allied victory at best. They will not be able to resupply by sea in time to retrieve the situation, since additional American forces are on the way."

Mkize turned back to face the roomful of officers. "Now U.S. navy aircraft ashore and remnants of the SAAF are pounding columns on these roads, the bridges that carry them and fortified border crossing points, plus the air defenses that cover them. The object of our ground offensive is to shatter Front Line State and Vietnamese forces remaining in southern Mozambique and to drive on Maputo. Not only is it the capital, but an important logistics and command center. Seizing or threatening Maputo may force Mozambique out of the enemy coalition.

"Field fortifications on the Natal-Mozambique border are manned by FLS infantry, essentially garrison troops. They're backed up by mobile, armored reserves—mostly Viet in the combat roles. These counterattack forces are estimated to be in divisional strength, with over 300 T-62s and -55s deployed along the frontier in one tank and three motor rifle regiments. American satellites show another 250 T-34s and T-54s dug in along the seventy-kilometer border from the Lebombos to the sea. Our ground observations confirm this. Total opposing strength in Maputo Province is estimated at 50,000, with a high proportion of service support troops. Reinforcement and air support from Gaza Province are possible.

"In the eastern, coastal lowland, the marshy terrain favors the defense, although it also keeps the enemy's trenches agreeably moist. In the west, during the past two days, we have kicked Viet observers off the Lebombo heights and helicoptered in marine 155mm batteries. To avoid telegraphing our intentions, these howitzers have thus far only shelled west over the crest into Swaziland, not the breastworks to the east in Mozambique. The enemy's strongest fortifications are around Catuane, here, opposite Ndumu, and east across the central plateau toward the swampy zone. That is where we shall hit him." Mkize paused to let his listeners react, then settle down.

"Had we more fire-support weapons, I should have attempted breakthroughs in three different places along the line—west, center and east—probing for the weakest spot. Then I should have sent our second echelon through any openings, reinforcing with third-echelon reserves and all our heavy firepower whichever thrust made the best headway toward Maputo. But I command a corps' worth of men with only a brigade's worth of heavy equipment, so I've decided to concentrate our fire and assault troops at a single decisive point—the enemy's strongest. My staff and Colonel Holden's people concur. As you Americans say, we're running at the other man's strength.

"Against top-quality opponents, this approach might well fail, but I rely on the ineptitude of Mozambican commanders and the low mobility, morale and training level of their troops. I also count on flanking attacks by the marines —the horns of our buffalo—to reduce enemy pressure on our main effort—the lunge of the buffalo's head and loins.

"At the same time, eastward to the sea, our older, less well-equipped and well-trained Zulu *impis* will lay down fires and mount local offensives to fix FLS troops there in their defensive positions. While, as I noted, the marshy lowland is ill-suited to maneuver warfare, USMC helos, hovercraft and amtracs may cross it with relative ease." Mkize moved the meterstick to the opposite end of the border. "Other heliborne units will fall on the enemy rear out of the west, from over the Lebombos, having flown north through Swaziland, screened by the mountains. Finally, Colonel Mtetwa's *impi* and a marine company are already engaged in operations to cut off the Viet forces besieging Vryheid. Even should this attack fail, it will divert enemy attention from our main blow.

"Besides our own captured antitank weapons, Marine Cobra helicopters and TOW vehicles will blunt the enemy's counterattack. The Viet mobile reserves will also be reduced by air and artillery attacks in the initial bombardment.

"You small-unit commanders are familiar with the general layout of the enemy's defenses on your attack frontages. We haven't had much time for practice assaults, but we hope that, following the attentions of the U.S. Navy and Marine Corps, the terrain won't look the same in any case. Questions?"

Mkize waited; there were none. "Good," he continued. "As you all know, our main advantage is land-based aviation in the enemy's rear, and Captain Ballantine of USS *Langley* already has explained the air plan in general. He now has more detail."

Bubba took the floor, feeling more confident now that he had met some of his colleagues. "Basically we're reorganizing the air wing into three composite squadrons, each with a Prowler and Hawkeye plus S-3s, A-6s and fighters. We'll be operating out of four main areas along a 140-mile stretch of the N2 coastal freeway," Ballantine explained, "here at Hluhluwe, Mtubatuba, KwaMbonambi"—he stumbled over the alien names—"and Richards Bay for the marines." Embarrassed, Ballantine grinned self-consciously at Mkize. The tension was broken by a Harrier pilot who chimed in, "CAG, how do you expect me to land at a place I can't even pronounce?" Laughter rippled through the crowded room.

Ballantine regained his composure. "Additionally, the Zulus have prepared alternate sites along Route N2. However, the AV-8s and helos probably will be the only birds to use these, in case they're discovered at Richards Bay." He looked at Mkize. "General, that's all for now."

Mkize had been uncertain how much to divulge about his intelligence, but he felt that some indication would encourage his diverse command. He chose his words carefully. "Gentlemen. We have one additional but significant advantage. Our knowledge of enemy forces is far better now than it ever has been heretofore. You may rely upon that. I firmly believe that the detailed knowledge we have lately acquired can make a tremendous difference for us all." He spoke firmly, seeking to inspire confidence. But he dared not tell his troops that his "significant advantage" was a very frightened young man whose primary credentials were the fear and suffering Mkize had seen in his blue eyes.

0510
East of Vryheid

As a junior officer—and a foreigner at that—Captain Ken Coxen was acutely aware of his command relationship with Colonel Mtetwa, leader of combined U.S. and South African forces in the Vryheid area of operations. But the marine was pleased to note that the Zulu not only sought his advice, but actually heeded it. The ambush about to be sprung was a case in point.

Crouched on a narrow ledge perhaps 100 feet above the winding mountain road, Coxen and his liaison team confirmed last-minute details with Mtetwa's people. Placement of the command-detonated mines had been overseen by Coxen's ordnance people at dusk, lest disturbed dirt betray the site in daylight. Heavy machine guns already had been sited by the guerrillas, and Coxen approved the disposition. *Those guns were laid by a man who knows his business.* Lastly, the booby traps were installed. Classic ambush philosophy: give the enemy one place to run, and that's where you put the claymores.

Mtetwa had enforced strict radio silence in the area for hours, but the opposition was typically verbose. Zulu eavesdroppers tracked the armored column's progress via captured radios, affording the ambushers a half-hour notice. When the grinding, clattering sound of tracked vehicles carried through the still night air, Coxen gave the stand-by signal up and down the line. Coordination would be tricky—the front and rear of the ambush were half a mile apart.

When the hooded headlights of the lead vehicle rounded the bend, Coxen tapped Warrant Officer Scott on the shoulder. The heavyset Arizonan twisted the detonator handle, and the road erupted in a mini-volcano of orange-white light, flying debris and clouds of dust. Somewhere in the conflagration the scout car disappeared over the ledge, rolling downhill. Gunfire erupted in a long line midway up the slope, with troops and vehicles trapped in an unobstructed killing zone. The volume of return fire was meager by comparison as most of the armored vehicles buttoned up.

Through the din of machine guns and rocket-propelled grenades, Coxen listened for the detonation upstream. He shouted into Scott's ear, "You hear anything from the rear of the column?" Scott shook his crewcut head. "Nothin', Skipper. I think somethin's gone wrong."

Moments later the radio operator tugged at Coxen's sleeve. "Sir, the observation post around the bend says the command-detonated mine didn't explode." But reading Coxen's mind, he added, "So the Zulus blew up a fuel truck and that's blocking the way."

Coxen exhaled audibly. "Okay, thanks. I guess it doesn't matter."

The others had to agree. Panic-stricken Vietnamese tumbled from trucks and personnel carriers. Rushing for the downhill slope, desperately seeking refuge from the uphill gunfire, they plunged headlong into the row of claymore mines lining the road. More garish splotches erupted in the night, though burning vehicles and scything tracers illuminated most of the column's length.

Then, because mass killing has a momentum all its own, the guerrilla gunfire slackened. Coxen was impressed with the Zulus' fire discipline, but he misinterpreted its meaning. After all, he was a conventionally-trained professional, reared in the western military philosophy. But this was tribal Africa.

Most of the Zulus had slung their rifles, preferring instead to use machetes or knives. At close quarters in the dark, Coxen admitted that it made sense—fewer friendly casualties from indiscriminate semi- and full-auto fire. But now the marine realized the reason was nothing so pragmatic. A great many of Mtetwa's warriors simply relished the satisfaction of hand-to-hand combat with the invaders.

After the initial flurry of explosions and gunfire, the mechanized column wavered. The racket of gunfire nearly died, almost immediately replaced in volume by a frenzied, melodic shouting that sounded a lot like "Boogaloo." Actually it was *Usuthu.* Coxen assumed it was a Zulu war chant. *Is that what the 24th Foot heard at Rorke's Drift?* he wondered. Impelled by a fascination beyond reckoning, he followed the mad surge down to the road.

Sensing they were cut off front and rear, with nowhere to go uphill or down, the Viets began surrendering. Or trying to surrender. But the Zulus were literally on top of them, leaping down from rocky overhangs, swarming over vehicles and dragging terrified soldiers outside.

Coxen looked around. Everywhere he glanced, interesting things were happening. He tripped, recovered his balance and stepped on something neither hard nor soft. He recalled a passage from John Thomason, the marine officer whose writing in the 1930s helped define the image of the Corps. A short story set in the Sino-Japanese affair contained the observation, "this was not, evidently, the sort of war in which either party burdened itself with prisoners." Coxen wiped his bloody boot on a clump of grass and climbed back uphill. His work was done. *I wonder how things are going to the northeast,* he thought.

Behind him the chanting rose in the dark.

0538
Near Ndumu, Border of Mozambique and Natal

Mkize checked his watch. He knew that timing was everything. His first assault echelon had to stay far enough back to avoid casualties from the Zulus' and marines' own preparatory bombardment, but close enough to get into the enemy's fortifications before the opposing troops could recover from the artillery and air strikes.

His attack plan was based on the German offensives of 1917 and '18, using the cream of *Inkatha's* fighters. Well-armed battalions of picked men—all strong, healthy, resourceful, reliable young volunteers—had been specially trained in infiltration tactics. During the night, one platoon in each company had crawled as close to the enemy's forward listening posts as its lieutenant dared. Their object was, immediately after the initial air and heavy artillery strikes, swiftly to overwhelm weak points in the enemy's defenses or to rush through gaps blasted by fire-support weapons.

At the moment the artillery barrage lifted or moved rearward, the advanced platoons—thirty or forty men equipped with light machine guns or automatic rifles and laden with grenades—would rush forward. Covering fire would be laid down by the other two platoons in each company and by battalion-level mortar batteries.

At this stage, the USMC and captured tanks would fire from overwatch positions 1,000 to 3,000 meters south of the main enemy trenches. They were to engage armored vehicles hull-down in the defense line. Company and battalion direct-fire weapons—heavy machine guns, automatic grenade launchers, recoilless rifles and antitank rocket launchers—would simultaneously shoot at bunkers and other strongpoints not handled by the M-1s. Marine engineer vehicles were to support Zulu sappers clearing paths through the fortifications.

At the points attacked with superior force, the stupified and reduced defenders should easily be overrun. Unattacked stretches of the defenses would be bypassed, surrounded and mopped up later by normal infantry units. By infiltration to achieve local superiorities of firepower and mass, Mkize hoped his outnumbered attackers could carry theoretically unassailable fixed positions. Colonel Holden had signed off on the risky venture, laying the reputation of the U.S. Marine Corps on the line.

One advantage the Zulu "Stoss" troops had over the Germans in World War I was tank support, however modest. Mkize believed that assigning even five M-1s or T-55s to each infantry battalion could greatly increase the odds of success. The first, company-strength assault echelon was to find the enemy's weak points or punch through the forward positions, the second would consolidate the Zulus' hold on a stretch of the border, then tanks and other captured or marine armor would carry the third echelon into the depth of the enemy's defenses.

Doubts still haunted Mkize over the use of his few tanks. He knew the Abrams was not intended as an infantry support weapon and that tanks are always best used *en masse*. But the general decided he had no real choice. Even if he concentrated his American and Russian tanks, he'd still have only a battalion's worth. Instead he assigned a large platoon to each assault battalion.

The Catuane defense zone covered ten kilometers, manned by two 3,000-man garrison brigades, immediately backed by 5,000 more troops in fire support units and one tank and one motor rifle regiment of mobile reserves. Desertions were reportedly lower in this area than farther east, in the swamps. Mkize's assault echelon consisted of two 2,000-man *impis*—eighteen companies in six battalions—one attacking east of Catuane and one west, between the town and the mountains. The three follow-on *impis* of the Catuane front contained 8,000 less well-equipped and trained Zulu fighters, plus a modicum of support troops and weapons.

At the same time as the Catuane action, two *impis* with 5,000 soldiers would mount holding actions all along the line east to the sea. Another mobile 2,000-man *impi* waited behind the eastern stretch of front. In the unlikely event of an enemy offensive in that zone, the reserve *impi* would counterattack; if the *Inkatha* operation in the west were successful, the *impi* would cross the border.

Mtetwa led another 3,000 Zulus in the Vryheid AO. That left 8,000 mostly lower-quality troops in support roles, manning defensive positions and as corps reserve.

Mkize knew the German offensives of 1918 ground to a halt for want of mobile reserves. Since he couldn't exploit breakthroughs with large tank formations, the general at least had provided his follow-on echelons with trucks. Given the expected weakness of opposition from FLS forces and limited American air cover, these vulnerable vehicles had a good chance of surviving. Only the Viet mobile forces would have to be destroyed directly.

Though few in number, the marines made Mkize's major offensive possible. He also had assurances that, if the attack was proceeding reasonably well but starting to bog down, the U.S. might fly in its two airborne divisions. The general knew he could not rely on this promise, however, so prayed additional American help wouldn't be needed to sustain the drive on Maputo. It was all a carefully calculated risk.

The Zulu general heard attack jets clear the crest of the Lebombos and dive on the FLS positions around Catuane.

0540

Clear across the northern horizon, the dawn was brightened by the flash of fuel-air explosions. Mkize exultantly shook a clenched fist. He knew that FAEs could be ferociously effective, but there was no guarantee the blast weapons would work. Too many things could go wrong—the F/A-18s delivering the fuel canisters might be shot down or deterred by antiaircraft fire; after release, the containers could fail to open properly or atmospheric conditions could prevent adequate dispersal of the tiny droplets; the precise, airborne timing switches might fail to ignite the fuel-air mixture at the right microsecond.

Clearly, the low-altitude detonations were sufficiently powerful to send a high-pressure shock wave along the enemy's defense line. The blast hit the ground with enough pounds per square inch to set off antipersonnel mines and, in some areas, antitank mines as well. Troops in forward listen-

ing posts and parts of the first main trenchline were suffocated to death or stunned into stupidity; even survivors bled
from the nose and ears.

At the same time, other Harriers, Intruders and Hornets struck regimental, brigade, divisional and corps command posts in southern Maputo Province but out of artillery
range.

No sooner had the naval aircraft departed than the first
volley in the artillery barrage whistled overhead, arching past
Mkize's command post toward key targets in Mozambique.
The limited, whirlwind shelling benefitted from detailed
knowledge of enemy positions. The marines' towed 155mm
howitzers hit forward defenses while their self-propelled
guns struck deep in the rear. Vietnamese counterbatteries,
equipped with Russian 130- and 152mm gun-howitzers plus
multiple rocket launchers, outranged the Americans. But
Harriers, Intruders and Hornets would silence many of the
opposing long-range batteries on their second sorties of the
morning.

Later, surviving USMC Harriers would strike bridges
between Catuane and Maputo or provide on-call, close air
support for attacking infantry.

Near Catuane, Mozambique

A freight-train rumble filled the air. Men still bewil-
dered or terrified by the titanic explosions less than a kilometer to their south now stopped work, or awoke, or merely
glanced skyward. Whatever the strange noise was, it boded
ill.

Then the shells began falling.

Until now, Catuane's laconic garrison had enjoyed an
easy war—a few guerrilla nuisance raids, no more. As a supply depot feeding the stream of Front Line States' logistics
southward, the city had been busy but hardly inconve-
nienced. But the first explosion of a 155mm shell, only thirty
meters from the command center, instantly changed all that.
Steel splinters smashed through thin walls, shattered windows, started fires and ended lives. Those few professional
soldiers in the garrison noted that the barrage was methodi-
cally walking its way across town, south to north. Something

dreadfully unexpected was down there across the border, beyond the Ndumu Wildlife Park.

0550
Inkatha *Command Post*

"Artillery fires shifting to second line of defenses, right on cue, Nigel," reported Conco, Mkize's chief of staff. "Forward assault platoons moving out. Battalion CPs say they're rising up as one man. And I don't think they mean that figuratively."

"Only to be expected," Mkize replied. "The assault troops volunteered for unknown dangerous duty and only one volunteer in three was selected." In fact, he was glad to hear the good news. It was inevitable that, under enemy fire, even some elite troops would fail. A man whose mind wanted to rush into machine gun fire might find his legs unwilling to obey.

0600

"They're already in the first main line of trenches on both sides of Catuane," Conco said, relaying reports from *impi* and battalion chiefs of staff directly observing the operations. "One battalion on each side of the objective has already released its follow-on companies. They're fanning out in the fieldworks."

"Are you positive?" Mkize asked.

"The unit commanders are, sir," Conco answered. He rarely said sir. "The assault troops have even filled up parts of the trenches for the tanks to cross."

According to Mkize's plan, the second echelon would occupy defensible stretches of the front; through these gaps would pour the third echelon, riding on tanks or in APCs. Normal infantry *impis* would follow in trucks or on foot. If the whole front appeared to crumble, then thousands of other *Inkatha* soldiers would join the 12,000 Zulu and 900 Marine ground troops attacking into Mozambique, not counting USMC engineers and specialists, plus USN SEALs and demolition teams. Mkize guessed that late in the morning or that afternoon, the attackers should run into at least two regiments of counterattacking Viet armor and artillery.

The Marine aviators' and gunners' job was to defeat this threat.

"Excellent," the general replied. "Signal the *impi* commanders to release the tank platoons assigned to support those two battalions."

0638
Catuane

In the only remaining operational CP of the Fourth Mozambican Infantry Brigade, a harried major grabbed a succession of phones. Some lines were dead, some simply did not respond. With plaster falling on his bare head and an unceasing din outside, the staff officer fought to gain some concept of what was happening. At that moment he was the senior surviving Mozambican in the vicinity, a fact he would not grasp for some hours. But the news he received was bad enough. With one hand pressed against his free ear, he struggled to understand the frenzied voice in the phone. ". . . of the border! Do you understand? Enemy tanks," . . . something garbled . . . "the road south of . . ." The line went dead.

Enemy tanks, thought the major. *That simply is not possible.*

0629
North of Ndumu, Natal

"Target eleven o'clock! T-62, about 900 meters." Inside his M-1E1 battle tank, Sergeant Bob Creech decided that target selection was easy. Pick out the biggest and work your way down in size. The enemy tank was partially hidden behind a fuel truck recently abandoned by its terrified driver.

Corporal Vincent Benelli laid his sight reticle on the target, double-checking the range. It was like threading a needle to miss the valuable fuel rig and hit the tank. He called "Round out!" and squeezed the trigger. The 120mm gun rocked in recoil and the gunner let out a war whoop as the high-explosive antitank round went home. Creech, Benelli and the driver, Thorn, all saw the explosion on the T-62's motionless turret. Only the loader, Zerba, lacked a view. But he immediately opened the breach, ejecting the spent case, hefted another XM-830 shell onto the tray and slammed it home. "Loaded, Bob."

"I think we got their attention," Creech remarked into the intercom. "Let's take it on down the line a bit." Thorn urged the M-1 forward, toward the blazing fire gushing thick, black smoke. In another circumstance Creech would have felt queasy, driving down a main highway deep in enemy territory with minimal infantry support. But Lieutenant Spanger's platoon had enjoyed clear going so far. Unlike the army version of the Abrams, at least Marine Corps M-1s had phones to talk to the grunts outside. Occasionally a friendly voice, faintly British, hailed Creech, letting him know the path was clear. The tanker had met his "seeing-eye Zulu" only briefly, but so far so good.

Up ahead Spanger's Abrams slowed perceptibly and the turret slewed to the right. "Skipper's onto something," Creech announced. The lead tank's main gun flashed and a half-second later another Mozambican vehicle exploded a half-mile away. The road to Catuane clearly belonged to the visiting team for now. But Bob Creech wondered how long five tanks—even sixty-ton monsters like the Abrams—could keep up their mini-blitzkrieg.

1202
Inkatha *Command Post*

Mkize's intelligence officer strode up to him with a sheaf of paper and a million-dollar smile. "Sir, we have the latest signals intercepts out of Mozambique. They seem to be in total confusion."

The general glanced at the marine liaison officer assigned for communications intelligence. "Captain, what do you make of this?"

"General, I don't speak the language. But since they're transmitting in the clear, they're obviously spooked—uh, disrupted. From reading the transcripts, I'd say the 'Biques' are scared shitless. Keep after them, sir."

"Exactly what I intend to do," Mkize replied. "Especially since their combat units are spread so thin up there. But we have to be prepared for counterbattery fire and frontal aviation attacks. That's where your liaison staff comes in. Please keep me informed constantly of availability of both artillery and air. Communications will be critical on this point, you know."

"Yes, sir. We're making good use of our frequency-agile radios, and we're not transmitting from any observation or command post for more than an hour or so. Whatever else happens, you'll have good comm, sir."

Mkize nodded, staring at the marine's equipment. The captain wore a Beretta M9 pistol on his web belt. Mkize swore silently. *For the millions the Americans squandered on that unnecessary project I could feed and arm my ten divisions for two or three years.* Mkize patted his own Browning High-Power, designed in 1935. He'd used it twice as a sergeant, long ago but not so far away.

Turning to the area map, Mkize gestured to his staff. "We are continuing to launch air strikes against enemy second-line positions, and the Harriers seem to be doing their job. They're expanding the area of conflict, forcing enemy defenses to disperse accordingly."

The marine decided to interrupt with some unwelcome news. "Excuse me, General, but you need to know. One airstrip, Landing Field Delta, has been hit with surface-to-surface rockets. We don't know how the enemy located it—presumably covert means."

Mkize frowned in concern. If the Mozambicans found one airstrip, they could find others. "Extent of damage?"

"Serious, sir. Two jets destroyed, three damaged and the runway unusable for at least two days." The marine checked his clipboard. "Fairly light casualties, but . . . ah, Captain Ballantine was killed taxiing his F-14 out of the way."

Mkize's head shook as if he'd been slapped. *He was a good man.* "All right, what else do you have for me?"

"Ordnance is running short. I expect that the Harriers will be restricted mainly to air-defense missions by tomorrow."

"Then time is more crucial than ever." The warchief tapped both flanks of his frontal assault with a pencil, east along the coast road and west through Swaziland, up the N4 toward Boani. "Assuming we capture Boani, we'll consolidate our forces there. That's almost eighty miles from our start lines, and shortage of fuel or ammunition will probably force a halt. But if not, should enemy resistance fail to materialize, we'll be only twenty miles from Maputo."

"General, do you still intend to take Maputo?" The American's voice carried both hope and concern.

Mkize turned on a smile. Waving his pencil professorially, he said, "Well, if not, at least I'll make them think I'm going to. And in this business, Captain, perception has a way of becoming reality."

20

9 June to 1 November

0453, Wednesday, 9 June
Near Pietermaritzburg, Natal

Dressed for battle, once again feeling the familiar tension of the G-suit around his thighs and abdomen, Pyotr Rybakov was surprised at his inner calm. The goal of the dawn mission—not that it mattered much—was to help spring the remnants of a Vietnamese brigade from encirclement. The surrounded force had been trapped retreating from Vryheid, some 280 kilometers north-northeast of his jump jet squadron's hiding place along the N3 motorway.

The briefing was wrapping up—routine stuff about weather. For the first time in many days Rybakov withdrew his wife's photo from his wallet. She was fifty now, and growing toward plumpish. But the serene gray eyes smiling out of the photo were the same ones he had always known. *Ivana,* he thought. *I left you ashore these many years, and you settled for third place in my life. Behind the sea and the sky.* A twinge of guilt coursed up his spine, causing a shudder. Rybakov admitted to himself that his marriage had lacked passion and commitment. It was—comfortable. He folded the wallet into his flight jacket. *I'll make it up to you, Ivana. I promise.*

The briefing ended and Rybakov stood up. The other officers in the room leapt to their feet as the admiral strode out of the hut. Glancing left and right, he saw two emotions in their faces. *Admiration or disbelief,* he assessed. *But both sides wonder about my sanity. Well, at least there's good precedent.*

In deciding to lead what might be the last combat mission of *Kuznetsov* and *Varyag*'s diminishing air wings, Rybakov was following Russian tradition. He remembered admirals Kornilov and Nakhimov—for whom the cadet academy was named—after victory over a Turkish squadron at Sinop. Nakhimov led the defense of Sevastopol after Kornilov was killed in the Crimean War, fighting ashore after the destruction of their fleet. And in the Great Patriotic War, Soviet sailors had earned an honored reputation as infantry. Rybakov dismissed any thought of suicidal tendencies which he knew were being attributed to him. *I no longer have much of a fleet,* he told himself. *But I can still fly and lead men in the air.*

He hefted his borrowed helmet which, like his borrowed flight gear, belonged to a junior Su-25 pilot Leonid Harshenko. The boy had a baby son whom he had never seen. In part, the childless Pyotr Rybakov wondered if he were trying to compensate somehow for that situation. Then he pushed such thoughts from his mind. He was a military man, and there was still a war to fight. That was reason enough.

0554
Landing Zone Echo, Zululand

Mule Halloran did not like the dispersal plan for his squadron's Harriers, but he recognized the necessity. Since coming ashore on LZ Delta at Richards Bay, the AV-8Bs had been dispersed in pairs to outlying fields. It was a complex situation which compounded the already-difficult logistics, but at least *Hornet*'s helos could operate almost anywhere, and Halloran acknowledged the hard work of the SADF and Zulu personnel in supporting their newfound aviator friends.

But there were hostiles about as well. With a load of South African cluster bombs under his wings, the marine had done his weight-and-balance computations and now, strapped into Rawhide Five, he was ready to roll.

Halloran had conventional flight controls for his jump

jet, with one exception. Just inboard of the throttle was another lever controlling the jet nozzles in his fuselage. In computing his takeoff roll, he calculated that under present field elevation and temperature, he would lift off at ninety-five knots so he moved his "speed bug" to that setting on the airspeed indicator. Then he set his nozzle selector stop at sixty degrees.

Looking over at his wingman, Halloran nodded his head and advanced the throttle with his left hand. The bomb-laden Harrier accelerated down the tarmac and, when his airspeed passed the ninety-five-knot mark, he moved his hand from the throttle to the nozzle selector and pulled it back to the stop. The jet nozzles rotated from their full-aft position to sixty degrees down, and the little bomber responded by bounding into the air. Mule punched the landing-gear button, felt the wheels tuck away, and continued climbing. Still without looking into the cockpit, he advanced the nozzle control forward and felt the transition from vertical to horizontal flight.

0619
Approaching the Pongolo River, Natal

Pyotr Rybakov was no longer an admiral. He was Black Rook 51, leading two flights of Su-25s. The identity pleased him greatly. But he feared he was in over his head. He had been too long out of the cockpit for tactical flying. Things happened so fast, with such complexity! He had embarrassed himself during joinup after takeoff, requiring an extra circuit of the field to assemble his small strike force. But he knew his pilots would forgive the pride of an old airman who chose to risk his life in his first combat flight against the enemy.

Rybakov checked his map again, and the motion jostled his control hand. The Sukhoi bobbled unevenly, then straightened up. Navigation had proven relatively easy, owing to prominent landmarks along the ingress route. Rivers and distinctive mountain peaks had marked his progress. Now, just moments from his scheduled pop-up prior to attack, he reviewed the procedures. *Master armament switch, on. Weapon stations selected. Head-up display set for rocket trajectory. Here we go.*

The lead Rook waggled its wings and two heartbeats

later it pitched into a thirty-degree climb under full power. Clearing the last ridge, Rybakov rolled left and spotted the target. It was much as he had been briefed: an encircled friendly unit with its back to the river. The Zulu-American force had been pounding the pocket for hours. Why anyone was left, Rybakov could only guess. *Probably the enemy is low on artillery ammunition,* he surmised. He immediately sized up the situation and keyed his mike. "Rook 51 Flight, follow me down. Rook 56 Flight, attack enemy positions to the northeast." It was a quick-and-dirty assessment, but there was no time for anything else. If the friendly force could break out to the northeast, it might escape into secure territory.

At the apex of his climb, Rybakov coordinated stick and rudder, pulling through to align his nose with the target. He selected a line of artillery pieces and thumbed the button on his stick. *Not yet, not yet* . . . Flak bursts erupted ahead of him. Stinger missile trails arced upward.

Now! He clamped down on the button and his rocket pods erupted in orange-black violence. He didn't feel the first hit on his airframe, as the rockets were still spewing out. But he definitely felt the second. The jet was slewed off course and Rybakov tried to correct. *Something's wrong. She's not responding.* There was a muted shout in his earphones. His wingman, Antonov in Rook 52, apparently. *Can't understand his call. Better pull the nose up. The ground's getting close.* He pulled on the stick, felt the onset of three Gs, and horsed the Rook upward. Fire-warning lights, falling hydraulic pressure. *Controls will fail. Not much time.* He looked around for something. What? Automatic weapons fire streaking by. High-pitched thunks somewhere aft.

Down there—a camouflaged position of some sort. Rybakov pushed hard on the stick and his body lightened in his seat. He tried to bring the nose into line to fire his last rockets. More shouting in his earphones. *Why don't they shut up?* He thumbed full-forward trim, trying to ease control pressure without much success. The ground was very close now. The angle didn't look good. *Controls won't respond. I'm going to miss* . . .

For a second, Rybakov thought of Anatoly Levchenko, the MiG-23 pilot who dived his crippled Flogger into Mujahadeen positions in Afghanistan back in '86. That act had made the colonel a posthumous Hero of the Soviet Union. Rybakov already had an HSU on his dress uniform. He didn't care about medals. But briefly he did wonder why he had not ejected.

In Black Rook 52, Senior Lieutenant Antonov saw his leader dive into the earth at 480 knots.

0622
Pongolo River

Prostrate on the ground, Siphageni cautiously raised his face from his grimy sleeve. The merciless enemy artillery fire had lifted momentarily and he shook his head to clear away the mild concussion. He still retained enough of his hearing to detect the Russian naval jets pulling off-target. Apparently one of the Sukhois had been shot down—he could see the smoke of its pyre several kilometers away—but the others had forced the fascists to cease fire. *Got to move quickly,* he told himself.

Siphageni stretched himself off the earth, tapped his radioman on one shoulder and shouted, "Come on!" He took three faltering strides before he realized the radio operator had not followed. Looking back, Siphageni realized why. Without another wasted motion, he turned northward to cross the river while there was time. His experience told him that the opportunity created by the air attack would not last long. Nearby, Vietnamese and his own Xhosa scouts still seemed stunned by the barrage. For a heartbeat he pondered whether to assemble some of these troops around him and herd them with him to safety.

To hell with them, he decided. *A large group will only draw fire. I'll travel faster alone.*

Hefting his Kalashnikov, Major Joseph Siphageni turned his back on his erstwhile comrades and began a long, solitary journey to safety. He consoled himself with the knowledge that the loneliness of command sometimes had its benefits.

0630
Landing Zone Echo

Approaching the hacked-out landing zone, Mule Halloran lined up his approach from 1,000 yards out. He lowered his wheels and moved the nozzle selector back through the safety gate for full reverse thrust. Decelerating through 100 knots, he felt the Harrier's wings begin to lose their lift so he compensated with power, increasing the thrust through his nozzles.

As the AV-8 reached zero forward airspeed, Halloran advanced the nozzle lever to the vertical position. His reaction-control system now took over: a series of thrusters in the nose, tail and wingtips. From the pilot's perspective, the control inputs were normal but in fact his conventional controls had ceased working in the alien world of zero airspeed.

Adjusting his descent with throttle, the pilot kept his wings level while watching the landing officer's directions. The Harrier slowly settled onto the turf, blasting up grass and twigs. Halloran felt the mains touch down with the familiar jostling of landing. Then he retarded the throttle and shut down. *Log another point-six in green,* he thought: thirty-six minutes of combat time.

Inside another thirty-six minutes he would be ready to take off again.

1730, Thursday, 10 June
Landing Field Alfa, Zululand

Slats Slattery crawled down the side of Talent 500 and slumped against the Intruder. He was quickly surrounded by curious South Africans and a handful of Air Wing 18 fliers. "How'd it go, sir?" someone asked.

The deputy CAG took off his helmet and dangled it from one hand. "Okay, far as I know. Radio's not working real well anymore. Pulling off-target we lost most reception. Don't know what the problem is." Crunch Neslie rounded the nose and offered his B/N a swig of fruit juice obtained from a teenaged Zulu girl. Slats drained the can in one gulp.

VA-186's ordnance officer elbowed his way through the crowd. "Sir, we have enough bombs left for about six more sorties. After that . . ."

"Yeah, I know, Gunner," Slattery replied. "Trouble is, we only got three birds left here. Unless . . ."

"Usuthu! Usuthu!" The chant filled the air of the remote dispersal strip. Almost immediately the Zulu guards, male and female, launched into a joyous bedlam of dancing

and singing. To a casual observer, the movements would have appeared choreographed.

The Americans looked around, alternately startled and confused. Slattery's gloved hand went to his pilot's shoulder in concern. "What the . . ."

A smiling black face loomed above Slattery. He recognized Captain Mdlalose, the airfield defense officer, who saluted palm-outward. "Sah! Radio relay from General Mkize's headquarters." The smile grew wider, which hardly seemed possible. "Mozambique has sued for a separate peace. Hostilities in this region will cease at 2300 hours."

Slats Slattery and Crunch Neslie stared at one another. Their expressions spoke the same thought. *It can't be.* "I'm sorry, Captain, but that's bound to be a rumor." Slattery's voice carried an edge. Things were bad enough without wild gossip upsetting his troops.

Mdlalose produced the message flimsy. The originating office was SADF Headquarters, Johannesburg. The text was signed by Christiaan de Villiers, Chief of Staff.

Crunch found his voice first. "If that's true, then the whole invasion . . ."

"Will collapse!" Slats exulted.

A conga line of Americans—half unbelieving, half ecstatic—formed up behind the native chorus. And for a little while in the African jungle, naval aviators and Zulu warriors went a little insane.

Inkatha *CP, Ndumu, Natal*

"Why?" The question was asked a dozen times at once.

Nigel Mkize turned from the command set and put down his earphones. His staff thought him uncommonly subdued for the occasion. But a few who knew him better than most understood. *He's thinking of his motherless children.*

"My friends," Mkize began, taking in the marine and SADF liaison teams. "It is official. Maputo has formally requested a cease-fire, and Johannesburg has agreed." He sensed the still-unanswered question. "Apparently our offensive has succeeded. Signals intelligence shows widespread confusion throughout southern Mozambique as a result of our amphibious landings, the heliborne assaults through

Swaziland and especially the armored column through Catuane toward Maputo."

"They still don't realize our strength," a marine whispered aloud.

Mkize smiled at last. "Correct, my friend. Their perception of our reality has worked in our favor."

2331
SADF National Command Center

General Christie de Villiers had received the confirming message from Acting State President Vlok, as befitted the Republic's leading soldier. All was quiet on the Natal front for the past half hour; the enemy was apparently honoring the truce.

Now, ramrod-straight, yet somehow stooped, the general walked up the steps of the command bunker into the darkness. He paced slowly toward a patch of grass overlooking the golf course and sat down heavily. Then, elbows on his knees, balled fists in his eyes, he allowed himself to cry for his dead son, for his nation, and for himself.

U.S.S. Hornet

Rear Admiral Charles Gideon received the flash message in flag country. He read the form twice, initialed it and handed the clipboard back to the communications officer. Looking around the living space, the admiral sought a consensus among the faces there. He spoke for everyone when he said, "I just hope to hell it was worth it."

2330 Pretoria; 1730 EDT
White House

President Vernon Callaway poured a long one into the glass of Admiral Domingo Fernandez. Alone in the office, they knew they would not be interrupted for at least a few minutes. CNO clinked his glass against his commander-in-chief's. "Short war," the admiral toasted.

Callaway took a sip, savoring the Ten High. "How's that, Hub?"

"I was just thinking of an old squadronmate of mine. Callsign Pirate. He used to drink to short wars."

"Well, he got his wish this time."

CNO swished the amber fluid in his glass. " 'Fraid not, sir. He died toward the end of that Israeli-Arabian thing a few years back."

Embarrassed, Callaway changed the subject. "Well, this one was longer than I hoped for but shorter than I feared."

"Yes, sir." Fernandez inhaled another mouthful and felt the rush. "You really think the truce will hold?"

The long face nodded decisively. "I do. The Front Line main supply routes remain cut off in Mozambique. Elsewhere the battle's a stalemate. With more of our forces arriving in-theater, and with the standoff at sea, we have the momentum."

"How long to make it official, Mr. President?"

"Shit, Hub, you don't have to 'Mr. President' me in here." He poured another two fingers in the admiral's glass. "Maybe a month, maybe less. The Russians are real accommodating now that the U.N. has stepped in. Lets 'em off the hook with a modicum of face-saving."

Fernandez set down his empty glass. He was just tight enough to ask a genuine question. "Okay . . . Buddy. Now I'd like to know. Who won?"

Callaway set down his own glass and levelled his gaze at CNO. "Well, Hub, in a way *you* won. Naval aviation won, both afloat and ashore. This stalemate wouldn't have been possible otherwise. I'd imagine there's another big deck or two in your future as a result of this war."

"Mr. . . . ah, hell. Buddy. That doesn't answer me. I don't mean who won the war, I mean who's the big winner? Or is there one? I've got several thousand casualties to account for. I need to know—for myself." He jabbed his chest with a thumb.

"Yeah, I know, Hub. I know." Callaway spoke softly. "I'll tell you who's the big winner. It's nobody in this room, and it for damn sure isn't any of the marines or sailors or aviators out there in Evil Hyphen. You know who's the big winner?" Fernandez shook his head. "I'll tell you. The Zulus."

"Political clout in South Africa." Fernandez slurred the words.

"You got it. They were the decisive force in Natal and

Mozambique. After this war, not even the most radical apartheid mongers or ANC socialists can deny the Zulus a leadership role in the new government. And there *will* be a new government."

"How do you think that'll work?"

Callaway shrugged expansively. "Damn' if I know. Maybe the white man's obsolete in Africa now. Maybe the blacks will have things all their own way. Or . . . maybe the survivors will realize they all need each other."

Domingo Fernandez picked up his empty glass. "Mr. Pres'dent, I'll drink to that."

2100 Pretoria; 1500 EDT, Friday, 11 June
White House

Callaway told his secretary, Mrs. Thornburg, to show his national security adviser into the Oval Office.

"The secretary of state is on her way over, sir," Epstein said. "Ambassador Skolskin has already arrived."

"Good," the president replied. "Sooner we get this over with, the better."

"Skolskin is waiting outside. He wants to go direct from here to New York. Their U.N. ambassador will make the armistice offer as soon as they know your response will be favorable. I think they were afraid you'd turn them down, or at least not let them propose a general cease-fire. I'm sure they appreciate anything you can do to help them save face."

"Ha!" Callaway exclaimed. "When have Russians ever appreciated any goodwill gesture? If so, they sure show it in funny ways."

He never changes, Epstein thought yet again, but this time with some affection. *Well, not trusting them may have paid off, at least in this instance. Depending on the kind of government South Africa and the UER end with, and how you count the cost. And on what happens to this government. I doubt very many of the families of those thousands of dead American kids would consider the result worth the price.* He told the president, "Skolskin says the Front Line States have all agreed to accept a cease-fire."

"Big deal," Callaway responded. "After Mozambique defected, what chance did the Russians have of keeping Madagascar and Zimbabwe in the war? And Zambia,

Tanzania, Angola and the others sure as hell weren't gonna go it alone."

"Well, sir, perhaps if Moscow continued supplying them, they might have kept at it."

"The DIA says their troops have already had it. They're quitting in droves, shooting their officers and commissars."

"Yes, uhm, possibly overrated reports, but definitely suggestive of a trend. But, be that as it may, it seems the UER's greatest concern is getting the ANC to go along with the armistice. Skolskin also wants our help with President Vlok, the French and British. He's afraid that Pretoria wants to continue the war, now that they have the upper hand."

"You think we should bail 'em out?"

"In effect, yes. I believe we should accept Rodinkov's terms, or something like them, and intercede on the Russians' behalf with South Africa and her supporters, our erstwhile allies," Epstein said. Callaway was amused to hear his adviser say "Russians" for once. "The French and British got in late," he continued. "They may want to improve their positions to enhance their post-war leverage, to inflate what Pretoria owes them."

"Okay, I want to hear just what the Russians are offering," the president said. "Wanna feel out Skolskin. But in principle, I agree with you. Britain and France do deserve some consideration, though. Make sure Moscow doesn't spring any surprises on 'em at the U.N. I want them consulted. I'll talk to Vlok myself, after I listen to Skolskin. Anything else?" Epstein shook his head. "Then show the slimy bastard in."

1746, Saturday, 12 June
Goba, on the Swazi-Mozambique Border

Major Joseph Stalin Siphageni knew he was a wanted man. Both the fascists and their *Inkatha* running dogs had put a price on his head. His face was on posters in every post office in Natal and the Eastern Transvaal, under the heading, "Wanted for Mass Murder." From radio reports he knew he'd been denounced as a terrorist by former "comrades" who would do anything to save their own miserable skins— traitorous swine who had surrendered or allowed themselves to be captured. *Should have shot that bourgeois pig Mangope when I had the chance,* he fumed.

The ANC officer checked his dress and kerchief, then hoisted a clay jar onto his head. He estimated that by mingling with a group of refugees, mostly women, he could pass for another displaced person in the dark. He knew that paperwork and inspecting of documents had become exceedingly lax along the border in the past few days, and as long as he drew no attention to himself, he should be able to get across.

Siphageni felt a certain bitterness at having to sneak back into Mozambique disguised as a woman, especially after his high hopes of only a month previously. But he acknowledged that in his business, inherently a high-risk endeavor, a certain failure rate was to be expected. As for the disguise— well, a world-class terrorist could not afford a conventional ego. *My work is my pride,* he thought. *I know how successful I am. And so does Moscow.*

He shifted the weight on his head and began the long, dangerous walk back into Mozambique, toward a dubious freedom.

1730 EDT, Monday, 14 June
White House

The aide announced, "Admiral Gideon, sir."

Buddy Callaway rose from behind the big wooden desk and strode with Texas-sized steps toward the open door. Seeing what was coming, Gideon braced himself and smiled, "Permission to come aboard, sir?"

Callaway grasped Chuck Gideon's right hand in both of his own and initiated a Johnsonian bout of hand-shaking. "Admiral, they taught me at Annapolis that we don't salute under cover, but you deserve a highball if any sailor ever did. Please sit down." The aides closed the door and would hold any calls short of ICBMs inbound to Washington.

Gideon sat on a sofa, laying his uniform hat on the adjoining antique table. Callaway wondered how Gideon would react if he tossed the gold-braided cap onto a longhorn hat rack in the corner.

"Admiral . . . hell, Chuck," Callaway began, pulling

up a chair, "I'm not going to keep you long. I know you're anxious to see your family. Jackie, isn't it?" He knew it was.

"Yes, sir. It's been a long time." *Political memory,* Gideon thought. *Knows the names of wives and children.*

Callaway leaned forward conspiratorially, elbows on knees, hands clasped. "Chuck, it's no secret that members of Congress are howling for your hide. There's talk about an investigation of unauthorized release of nuclear weapons down there in the IO."

Gideon's stomach churned. *Oh, my God.* He collected his thoughts. "Well, sir, I'm guilty. You see, we had no conventional ASW weapons that could . . ."

"Forget it," Callaway snapped, waving a hand. "I'm not interrogating you, Chuck. Matter of fact, I know your reasoning and I completely endorse your actions. Admiral Fernandez has given me a preliminary briefing. Far as I'm concerned, SKINCs are tactical weapons, and that's that. True, some ambitious congressmen could make things rough for us. But I'm leading up to something of a . . . well, a political nature."

Gideon felt the old tingle in his gut. The same feeling just before the ball was snapped on fourth and long.

"Chuck, if your career should end prematurely, I want you to think about working with me—long as I have a job!" He smiled broadly at the implications.

The admiral shrugged. "Doing what, sir?"

Callaway leaned back. "Oh, like being my vice president." He received a disbelieving stare in reply so he elaborated. "Naomi isn't well, Chuck. Truth be known, it's woman problems." He waved a placating hand again. "Oh, don't get me wrong. She's capable enough, a hard worker and all that. But she was laid up for most of the South African affair and she's probably going to step down. So I'll need a new veep before long."

Gideon shook his head. "Mr. President, for Christ's sake. Why me? You've already said as much that I'll be a political liability on the hill."

"Admiral Gideon, you just fought the biggest naval battle in half a century. You were outnumbered and outgunned but you gave better than you got. Presidential careers have been built on less."

He's nuts. "Sir, I also lost my entire battle group. I still don't know exactly how many young Americans died under my command. Between that and the nukes, I figured my career was washed up."

"As I said, maybe your Navy career *is* nearing an end. If not, that's terrific. We can certainly use you, especially with a third star. But aside from the military considerations, you played an extremely important role in a tense period of international relations. You have wider experience than you realize, Admiral."

"How's that, sir?"

Callaway leaned close again. "Chuck, I'll be blunt. You're the black admiral who just broke up a huge seaborne invasion of the Republic of South Africa. You helped save the Pretoria government, which even now is undergoing considerable change." He paused for emphasis. "Don't think for a minute that I don't have some idea of how rough that had to be for you."

Gideon's gaze drifted to the portraits of Washington, Lincoln and Teddy Roosevelt. *Three beautiful carriers*, he thought. He looked into Buddy Callaway's eyes. "Mr. President, hasn't it occurred to you that you're assuming a lot? You don't even know if I'm a Democrat."

Callaway pointed a finger. "Gotcha. You're a registered Independent."

"Affirmative. But do you know why, sir?"

"Well, no. Ya got me there."

"All my life, sir, I've been defined by my appearance rather than by my character or my ability." He saw Callaway start to interrupt. "Please let me continue, Mr. President. When I entered the navy there weren't many black officers, and even fewer aviators. But in aviation, either you can hack it or you can't. Regardless of what anybody in the squadron thinks of you personally, they can't deny your status on the greenie board."

"Greenie board?"

"Yes, sir. In every squadron ready room there's a board showing the grade for each pilot's carrier landings. Green is a good landing, yellow is fair, red is definitely bad. Mine were nearly always green."

"Okay, I get your point, Chuck."

"Excuse me sir, but you don't. You see, whether I was in the navy or outside, I found three kinds of people. Some, but not enough, took me for who and what I was. Some of those were Democrats, some were Republicans, some were just liberal or conservative.

"The second group—well, one way or another, it insulted me. Most of those people didn't care so much whether I could hack the program, they just bent over backwards to accommodate me. And that's goddamn demeaning. It says 'We won't promote you on ability, only on the basis of affirmative action.' So I rejected that philosophy out of self-respect.

"Now we all know about the third group, Mr. President. Those who hate you regardless of how well you do your job. Well, I found Republicans and Democrats alike in that bunch. After all, the Klan is mostly Democratic. So what I'm saying is this: neither major party showed me anything. And that's why I'm an Independent."

"But still, you went to war on the side of Pretoria. And I think I know why. You just said it—self-respect."

"That's close, Mr. President. I did it because of my professionalism. I'm a flag officer in the United States Navy, and I had lawful orders from my commander-in-chief."

The President swished his bourbon and said, "Lemme tell you a story, Admiral." He sipped and began. "Back when I was a backbench congressman, I was watching the battle for Hue on the news. I spied a marine captain. He was directing the fire of a jeep-mounted recoiless rifle across the river into an NVA position guarding a bridge. I recognized the young man. He was from my district, from a dirt-poor farming town hard on the Louziana line. This place was all black, one of the last black agricultural communities in Texas —maybe the country. Later I learned the kid was an Aggie. Back then there weren't many negroes at A&M. He'd worked his way through college, helped by an ROTC scholarship. His dad was dead; the family farm lost, his brother in jail, his mom and sister on welfare. He helped 'em out as much as he could." Callaway took another swig.

"The way he handled himself in Hue was a beautiful thing to see. You could tell that even the most benighted redneck had to respect him. On the third shot, they hit the machine gun nest or whatever it was. Maximum range for a 106, I imagine. The performance brought tears to my eyes.

"Days later, he was killed. Practically the last day of the battle.

"That young captain could've done anything after that, could've been anything. President I have no doubt, if that's what he wanted. But I expect his ambitions were higher." Callaway let Gideon react to the little display of self-effacing humor, then wrapped up. "By actual count, I went to a dozen funerals of East Texas boys killed in that goddamn fiasco, and that was the only one I out-and-out blubbered at."

The man is shameless, Gideon thought. *It's insulting if he thinks tugging on my heartstrings is gonna win me over. But it's working, the bastard.*

"That was the first war we ever fought 100 percent racially integrated. Remember, military desegregation was still underway in Korea. If we'd won in Vietnam, it could've helped us build better relations in this country. Instead it tore the races apart just as surely as it did the generations, classes and regions.

"The war with Iraq came at a time of worsening race relations. I think in some small way it helped bring us together. It didn't really last long enough or produce enough suffering to have a lasting emotional impact, if you know what I mean. Your war lasted even less time, but it sure as hell produced pain clear across the country. And it had racial overtones, undercurrents, whatever you want to call them." He paused to take a drink.

"I see what you're driving at, sir," Gideon replied. "But why run with the guy most directly responsible for all that pain?"

"You're wrong there, Admiral. I'm the guy most responsible. In fact fully. You performed a hopeless task brilliantly."

"But why remind people?" the admiral asked. "Won't it look like an electoral gimmick, tokenism? First you run with a Jewish woman, then a black man. Just like NASA back in its PR heyday."

"Look at it another way. Maybe it's a way of honoring the people you commanded, living and dead, and all the other American fighting men and women who've helped create, preserve and extend human freedom on this planet. Not to mention peace and prosperity.

"Plus, what if I happen to think that, out of the 100

million or so people eligible for the job, you are the best
qualified to take over as President if the booze should finally
catch up with me and I keel over?"

"Do you think that?" Gideon countered, feeling himself
being had but not sure how to handle it. *It must be like this
for girls when they start dating.*

"Well, I want you to know something, Chuck. I'm offering to nominate you because, as you say, you can hack the
program. Now, there's plenty of people who'll vote for you
because your skin is dark. We both know that. And there are
those who'll vote against you for the same reason. Think you
can take that kind of heat?"

Chuck Gideon stared at the carpet for a long time. Then
he stood up. "Mr. President, in the past month I've been
shot at by cruise missiles and torpedoes. I've had my flagship
sunk from under me. I've lost thousands of lives and billions
of dollars in hardware." The admiral looked around the
room. "I don't see how I can do any worse here." He paused,
raising a finger. "But there's one limiting factor."

"My God, what?"

"Jackie, sir. She just hates to entertain."

Buddy Callaway and Chuck Gideon warmly shook
hands.

*Attitude Adjustment Hour, Friday, 10 September
Las Vegas Hilton*

Major Skip Terjeson felt double-damned. It was bad
enough to be thrown into a crowded suite filled with navy
pukes—even hospitable navy pukes in town for the annual
Naval Aviation Symposium. But to be saddled with The Colonel was just too much. In fact, Terjeson couldn't control
that human powerhouse alone. Nobody could. That was why
the Nellis Air Force Base pilot had two huge escorts and a
squadron friend along to ride shotgun.

Terjeson squeezed through the press of bodies into the
corner with a banner proclaiming, "Air Wing 18—Home of
the Professionals." The suite, Terjeson knew, had been reserved by survivors among the *Langley's* aircrews after "that
African thing." The air force pilot introduced himself to the
senior officer, apparently the air wing commander.

"Welcome aboard, Major. I'm Pat Slattery, the new CAG." They shifted drinks to their port hands and shook.

Terjeson looked around. Then, in a loud whisper he said, "I'm here with, ah, our guest," he began, nodding his head toward the bar. "Any problem?"

Slats shook his head. "Negats. We're sort of old shipmates. Besides," he gestured, "he's acquired a seeing-eye commander."

Standing at the bar with a Vietnamese-born officer wearing a "Lou" nametag was Li Sung Hwa, lately colonel of aviation and Hero of the Democratic People's Republic of Korea. A few of the naval aviators and their female companions cast suspicious glances at Li's fading facial scars, evidence of expensive plastic surgery. But in a way he fit into the crowd with his gaudy Hawaiian shirt and celebratory attitude. Nobody wore uniforms, other than the Tailhook Committee's blue polo shirts, and the din of a few dozen conversations was effective ECM against any eavesdroppers.

Terjeson's cover story seemed to have merit. He was to introduce The Colonel—Li's unofficial callsign over the Nellis ranges—as an "exchange pilot" from Korea. *Stretching the truth a bit, but what the hell.* It was either that or endure another of Li's stormy tantrums, after which he shut up like a clam. His stony silences could last for days, until he got the twitch again and had to purge his system with some eight-G maneuvering.

Skip leaned over to his partner, an F-16 instructor called Gringo. "You realize this is all your fault. If you hadn't mentioned this shindig, Li never would have heard about it."

Gringo smiled archly, one arm around a willowy brunette. "Hey, Skip, unwind. Have a drink, enjoy life. The Colonel is." Gringo returned his attention to the brunette, who asked how long he'd been commander of the navy's Topgun fighter school.

Terjeson groaned and looked back to the bar. Li gulped another drink—it looked like vodka this time—and wiped his mouth. Then he launched into an animated discussion of the vertical performance of the MiG-29, complete with flying hands and fractured English. Skip noticed that two fliers paid especially close attention—a Tomcat driver called Ozzie and his RIO, Fido. Both had two rows of red stars inked on their nametags. The small crowd of aviators kept The Colonel's tongue lubricated, soaking up the combat wisdom of the erst-while Tiger of the North.

The guy's amazing, Skip thought. *Gambles by night, flies all day and still hasn't lost an ACM hop.* Early that morning The Colonel had humiliated a couple of hot young NATO pilots during a Red Flag exercise. Tran had told Skip that Li's motivation at cards and air-to-air practice was the same as it had been in real combat—to destroy Yankee pilots to avenge the killing of his family. As an adversary trainer and gambler, the Tiger destroyed American egos rather than bodies, but Lou felt the Korean found the process at least as satisfying.

A Hornet driver called Psycho tried to buy The Colonel another round, without success. Li pulled a wad of fifties from his shirt pocket and, in an expansive mood, announced drinks for the house. He could afford it, and not just out of his substantial U.S. government salary. His formidable powers of concentration made him a killer competitor at draw poker, and one casino already had barred him as a card counter.

Terjeson suspected that Colonel Li would be reined in soon by his spook sponsors. His knowledge was invaluable, but in order to keep him talking and cooperative, the spooks had to let him fly. A lot.

Skip smiled to himself and wondered, *Who's conning whom*? But even The Colonel showed signs of mellowing. Ordinarily a defector wouldn't see daylight for a year after reaching the States, yet here was Li out in the open after just three months. *He must have traded some big-time info for this fling,* Terjeson mused. But he also knew better than to ask.

There was a mild excitement at the doorway, and ex-*Langley* aviators let loose a chorus of cheers and whistles. Terjeson saw a tall hispanic officer—he was obviously an officer despite the civvies—enter the suite. With him was a well-built black officer shaking hands and trading jokes with the carrier fliers. Slattery edged off his stool. " 'Scuse me, there's CNO," he said to his guest. "The other gent's our battle group commander. He's just been named Tailhooker of the Year."

Terjeson was unfamiliar with the title. Sensing the bluesuiter's uncertainty, Slats explained, "With this crowd, that's somewhere between a Navy Cross and the Medal of Honor."

1200, Sunday, 31 October
Sevastopol

Rybakov made the right choice, thought President Rodinkov. *Better a dead hero than a live scapegoat.* The State Council had made sure that the admiral's wife received a generous pension and preferment in housing.

On a windswept bluff west of Balaklava, overlooking Cape Chersonesskiy, Rodinkov shuffled the pages of his ghost-written eulogy. The breeze tugged at the papers, threatening to send the speech sailing off the dais and out over the sea. The President could have let a navy official dedicate the statue honoring Rybakov, but Rodinkov wanted to get out of Moscow. The ceremony gave him an excuse to spend the weekend at his seaside dacha at Sochi, just 510 kilometers east-southeast across the Crimean Peninsula and the Black Sea.

Unfortunately, his absence also gave his enemies a chance to depose him, but Rodinkov hardly cared anymore. He was sure to lose his job one way or another sooner or later—probably sooner.

When, on the plane, the President had first read his speech, he was not surprised to find it stuffed with the usual rubbish about "socialist internationalist duty" and "progressive, peace-loving peoples everywhere." Rodinkov had then decided to take the memorial ceremony seriously. He would deliver some of the formulaic cant, but also add the truth— that Rybakov was a Russian patriot who pioneered techniques and equipment to extend his nation's mastery of the sea and air.

Rodinkov thought about the ANC major he'd decorated last summer, after the South African debacle. The president had told the African that he was lucky his side lost, and meant it.

"Running a country is harder than making a revolution," Rodinkov had said. "I should know. In next year's elections, I'm sure to lose—if they're held. It doesn't matter. I'm set for life. My agent already negotiated a contract with a

French publisher and booked me a lecture tour in the States." Major Siphageni had been shocked into silence.

Thin, polite clapping told the President that it was time for his remarks upon the unveiling of the statue. The wind carried the forced, unfelt applause away, so that it sounded pathetically weak against the forces of nature. *Like socialism,* thought Rodinkov as he rose stiffly. The President shuddered in the gloomy, wet, cold squall off the sea. Rain spat in his face; he cleared his throat and began to read.

1315 Monday, 1 November
Cape Town

"To the National Unity Party," toasted Sergeant Nandi Ndhlovu.

"To the national unity government," corrected State President Nigel Mkize. He wanted to kiss his fiancée but it hardly seemed proper for a newly installed head of state, clad —ridiculously, he felt—in tie, tails and sash of office. "We're a coalition government," he said. "It's rather like marriage, only usually less long-lasting." The engaged couple clinked glasses, smiled at each other, and sipped their champagne.

The post-inauguration reception was going well, Nandi thought, though she kept telling herself that she had no standard of comparison. She gathered that the diplomatic corps had been harrumphing from Pretoria to Helsinki at the procedure Mkize had adopted—circulating in the elegant dining hall rather than standing in a formal receiving line, exchanging pleasantries (i.e., lies) with ambassadors, bureaucrats and office-seekers.

"I thought your speech was splendid," she said. "Everyone has commented on it."

Mkize glanced left and right. "My dear girl, everyone *always* says that about inauguration speeches." He grinned at her. "You'll come to understand these things when we're married next month." Mkize winked broadly and she giggled in appreciation at his confidential tone. Then he pointed with his drinking hand. "Ah, there's a gentleman I want you to meet."

Mkize led Nandi across the floor, weaving through clusters of people in the experienced fashion of an old bush fighter. "General de Villiers! I am so pleased you could attend." *He looks immaculate,* Mkize thought. *And he looks ten years older.*

The Chief of the South African Defense Force drew himself to attention in the manner a Coldstream Guardsman might emulate. "At your service, Mr. President." The pale-blue eyes twinkled for the first time in Mkize's memory. "As always."

"Yes, General. As always." He turned to Nandi. "I wish to present my fiancée, Miss Nandi Ndhlovu. Actually, Sergeant Ndhlovu. We were stationed together when . . . the war began."

De Villiers bowed solemnly and grasped Nandi's extended hand. "My pleasure . . . Sergeant."

De Villiers noticed the traces of scar tissue on Nandi's face—residue of plastic surgery. *So she's the one.* He had heard the stories.

Nandi looked the general up and down. *This one is a soldier,* she decided. She had seen enough imitators to know the genuine article.

The old Boer turned and extended an arm. "Mr. President, Miss Ndhlovu, may I introduce a wartime colleague?"

A husky black officer in a U.S. Navy dress uniform brought his heels together and bowed slightly. "Captain Dexter Jackson," intoned de Villiers. "We, ah, served together much as you did."

"Mr. President," Jackson began. "I am requested to extend the greetings and best wishes of Captain Slattery. His air wing is in training for its next deployment and he is unable to attend."

Mkize shook Jackson's hand. "Why, yes, thank you, Captain. I received a letter from Slats—er, Captain Slattery." Mkize smiled self-consciously. "We owe a great deal to him and to . . . Captain Ballantine. All those fine men." An awkward silence fell upon Mkize.

Jackson leaned close, trying not to appear too familiar, and whispered, "Our young friend Yuri also sends his regards. From Alaska."

De Villiers felt he should interrupt. "Mr. President, may I compliment you on your address? I believe you put many minds at ease today."

"Thank you, General. That was in fact my intent. I felt

all along that the path to lasting peace and unity here lay in a combination of pragmatism and conciliation."

"Sir, I was particularly taken with your examples of Reconstruction after the American Civil War and the Versailles Treaty of 1919." Looking at De Villiers, Nandi almost could imagine that the general had been present at the latter event.

"Well," Mkize replied readily, "history can show us how not to achieve goals as well as how to gain them." He looked around, lest anyone overhear his penchant for plain talk. "In point of fact, I feel I'm ceding little in allowing the ANC to organize as a legitimate political party. Its backing of the insurrection and participation in the invasion have badly depleted its support. We all know that. Conversely, battlefield success and growing white membership have strengthened the *Inkatha* Freedom Party and our coalition with the National Party, Conservatives, PFP and Labour."

Jackson noted the revelation for what it was—a shrewd assessment of the nation's political status. *As somebody said, politics is the art of the possible,* he thought. "Ah, Mr. President, I'm curious. I thought the cadence of your speech, the phraseology, seemed reminiscent of Dr. Martin Luther King, Jr. Am I right?"

Mkize looked knowingly at the American. "Well, certainly. Dr. King was a gifted orator, and our movement has much in common with his." Mkize raised a cautionary finger. "But you'll notice that I was careful to include attribution!" The irony was not lost on Jackson, who glanced at his mirror-finished shoes and chuckled.

"One more question, if I may, Mr. President," the American requested. De Villiers, sensing others pressing for Mkize's attention, started to drag his guest away, but the new South African leader indicated his willingness to respond. "Thank you, sir. What do you make of the fear of widespread white emigration?" Jackson asked. "Myself, I've seen little to support it."

"An extremely important subject, Captain. A top priority of this government—and of my speech—was to reassure whites. In the long run, I actually hope to attract quality people here from elsewhere, much along the American model."

The naval officer considered Mkize's comment further proof of the new president's acumen. Besides a parliament based on one-man, one-vote, Jackson knew that the constitution provided for a senate that effectively gave whites three votes, Asians and coloureds two and blacks one. There were sixty-eight black senators, fifty-four white and twenty-eight from other ethnic groups. The Zulus and other moderate blacks benefitted from this arrangement, since most whites, coloureds and Asians belonged to parties in the *Inkatha*-led coalition. This amounted to majority rule, while safeguarding minority rights.

"Pleased to meet you, Captain. And do remember me to Captain Slattery. Now, if you gentlemen will excuse us . . ." Mkize said. At the same time, the new State President nodded to let the coloured leader of the Labour Party, waving for Mkize's attention, know he was headed toward the new law and order minister's part of the room next.

"Certainly, sir," the general replied. De Villiers extended his pale, blue-veined hand and Mkize gripped it firmly. Jackson saw, in that moment, an end of one epoch in South Africa and, with good will, the beginning of another.

Glossary

This list includes only nonfictional acronyms and other abbreviations found in the book; adding definitions, names, code names and alpha-numeric designations for aircraft, missiles, systems, ranks, titles and organizations would have required too much space.

AAA:	Antiaircraft Artillery
AAM:	Air-to-Air Missile
AAV:	Amphibious Assault Vehicle (AAAV or amtrac also possible)
AAW:	Antiair Warfare
AdCap:	Advanced Capability
AEW:	Airborne Early Warning
AFB:	Air Force Base
AGI:	Auxiliary, Intelligence Gathering (spy ship)
Air BOC:	Air-Launched Blooming Offboard Chaff
AK:	Kalashnikov assault rifle (not same as AK-630 Gatling gun)
AKM:	Modified version of AK-47 assault rifle
ALCM:	Air-Launched Cruise Missile
AMRAAM:	Advanced Medium-Range Air-to-Air Missile
ANC:	African National Congress
AO:	Area of Operations
AOE:	Auxiliary, Oiler and Ammunition Resupply (CV escort ship)
APC:	Armored Personnel Carrier
ARKR:	Russian acronym for CGN

ARM:	Antiradar Missile
ASat:	Antisatellite weapon
ASM:	Air-to-Surface Missile or Antiship Missile
ASPJ:	Airborne Self-Protection Jammer
ASRoc:	Antisubmarine Rocket
ASW:	Antisubmarine Warfare
ATGM:	Antitank Guided Missile (also ATGW)
AWACS:	Airborne Warning and Control System (Aircraft)
BDA:	Bomb Damage Assessment
BMD:	Russian armored airborne fighting vehicle
BMP:	Russian infantry fighting vehicle
B/N:	Bombardier/Navigator
BRDM:	Russian armored scout car
BTR:	Russian APC (BTR-50 tracked; BTR-60 wheeled)
BVR:	Beyond Visual Range
CAG:	Air Wing Commander
CAP:	Combat Air Patrol
CBU:	Cluster Bomb Units
CCD:	Charge-Coupled Device
CDC:	Combat Decision Center
CE:	Cooperative Engagement
CentCom:	Central Command
CEP:	Circular Error Probable
CG:	Guided missile cruiser (CGN nuclear-powered)
CIA:	Central Intelligence Agency
CICO:	Combat Information Center Officer
CinC:	Commander-in-Chief
CIWS:	Close-in Weapon System ("Sea-Whizz")
CNO:	Chief of Naval Operations
CO:	Commanding Officer
ComSat:	Communications Satellite
CoTac:	Copilot/Tactical Coordinator
CP:	Command Post
CPO:	Chief Petty Officer
CPSU:	Communist Party of the Soviet Union
CSO:	Chief Staff Officer (also CoS for Chief of Staff)
CVBG:	Aircraft Carrier Battle Group
CV:	Aircraft Carrier (CVN nuclear-powered)

DCA:	Damage Control Assessment
D-CAG:	Deputy Air Wing Commander
DCI:	Director of Central Intelligence
DD:	Antisub destroyer (DDG guided missile destroyer)
DIA:	Defense Intelligence Agency
DOD:	Department of Defense
DShK:	Russian 12.7mm heavy machine gun
ECM:	Electronic Counter-Measures
ECCM:	Electronic Counter-Counter Measures
ECMO:	Electronic Countermeasures Operator
ELF:	Extremely Low Frequency
ElInt:	Electronic Intelligence
ElIntSat:	ElInt satellite (also "ferret")
EmCon:	Emission Control (electronic silence)
EO:	Electro-Optical
ESM:	Electronic Support Measures
EWO:	Electronic Warfare Officer
EZ:	Extraction Zone
FF:	Antisub frigate (FFG guided missile frigate)
FFF:	Fog-Forming Foam
FLIR:	Forward-Looking Infra-red
FLS:	Front Line State
ForceCAP:	(Task) Force Combat Air Patrol
FROG:	Free Rocket Over Ground (Unguided Russian artillery missile)
GFC:	Gun Fire-Control
GHQ:	General Headquarters
GLONASS:	Russian equivalent of GPS
GPS:	Global Positioning System
GRU:	Soviet Military Intelligence Directorate
HARM:	High-speed Anti-Radiation Missile
HE:	High Explosive
HOJ:	Home-on-Jam
HSU:	Hero of the Soviet Union
HUD:	Head-Up Display
HumInt:	Human Intelligence source
ICS:	Inter-com System
IFF:	Identification Friend or Foe
IFV:	Infantry Fighting Vehicle
IR:	Infrared
IIR:	Imaging IR

ISAR:	Inverse Synthetic Aperture Radar
JCS:	Joint Chiefs of Staff
JBD:	Jet Blast Deflector
JOTS:	Joint Operational Tactical System
KGB:	Soviet State Security Committee
KPV:	Russian 14.5mm heavy machine gun
KT:	Kiloton
KZDF:	KwaZulu Defense Force
LCAC:	Landing Craft, Air Cushion
LGB:	Laser-Guided Bomb
LSO:	Landing Signal Officer
LZ:	Landing Zone
MAD:	Magnetic Anomaly Detector
MFC:	Missile Fire-Control
MG:	Machine gun
MiGCAP:	CAP against any opposing fighters
MPS:	Maritime Prepositioning Ship/Squadron
MRL:	Multiple Rocket Launcher (e.g., U.S. MLRS, Soviet BM-21)
NAS:	Naval Air Station
NATO:	North Atlantic Treaty Organization
NBC:	Nuclear-Biological-Chemical (protective gear)
NCO:	Noncommissioned Officer
NFE:	Naval Fire-fighting Ensemble
NRO:	National Reconnaissance Organization
NSA:	National Security Agency or Adviser (Spec. Asst. for NS Affairs)
NSC:	National Security Council
NTU:	New Threat Upgrade
NVD:	Night Vision Device
OBA:	Oxygen-Breathing Apparatus
OFS:	Orange Free State
OOD:	Officer of the Day or Deck
OTCIXS:	Officer in Tactical Command Information Exchange System
OTH:	Over the Horizon
OTH-T:	OTH-Targeting
PAC:	Pan-Africanist Congress
PFC:	Private First Class
PFP:	Progressive Federal Party
PhibRon:	Amphibious Squadron
PhibGru:	Amphibious Group

PK:	Russian general-purpose machine gun (also Kill Probability)
PLA:	Russian acronym for SSN
PLARK:	Russian acronym for SSGN
RAM:	Rolling Airframe Missile
RDF:	Radio Direction Finding
RF:	Radio Frequency
RHAW:	Radar Homing and Warning
RHIP:	Rank Has Its Privileges
RIO:	Radar Intercept Officer
RORSat:	Radar Ocean Reconnaissance Satellite
RPG:	Rocket-Propelled Grenade, Antitank
RPO:	Russian flame weapon
RPV:	Remotely Piloted Vehicle
RSA:	Republic of South Africa
RTB:	Return to Base
RWR:	Radar Warning Receiver
SAAF:	South African Air Force
SACP:	South African Communist Party (CPSA also possible)
SADF:	South African Defence Force
SAG:	Surface Action Group
SAM:	Surface-to-Air Missile
SAR:	Search and Rescue (usually a helo operation)
SARH:	Semi-Active Radar Homing
SAW:	Squad Automatic Weapon
SEAL:	Sea-Air-Land (USN Special Forces troops)
SensO:	Sensor Operator
SigInt:	Signals Intelligence ("signals" are communications)
SLAM:	Standoff Land Attack Missile
SLBM:	Sub-Launched Ballistic Missile
SLCM:	Sea-Launched Cruise Missile ("Slick-'em")
SMAW:	Shoulder-mounted Multi-purpose Assault Weapon
SoSuS:	Sound Surveillance System
SOSS:	Soviet Ocean Surveillance System
SP:	Self-propelled (usually an armored fire support vehicle)
SPG:	Russian antitank recoilless rifle
SRBM:	Short-Range Ballistic Missile
SRBOC:	Super-Rapid Blooming Offboard Chaff

SSBN:	Nuclear-powered ballistic missile submarine
SSGN:	Nuclear-powered cruise missile sub
SSK:	Diesel-electric attack sub
SSM:	Surface-to-Surface Missile
SSN:	Nuclear-powered attack sub
SSR:	Soviet Socialist (or Sovereign) Republics
STIR:	Separate Target Illumination Radar
SurSat:	Surveillance Satellite
SWIP:	Sensors and Weapons Improvement Program
SWO:	Surface Warfare Officer
TacCo:	Tactical Coordinator
TAO:	Tactical Action Officer
TarCAP:	Target Combat Air Patrol
TARPS:	Tactical Air Reconnaissance Pod System
TASM:	Tomahawk Antiship Missile
TerCom:	Terrain Contour Comparison Mapping (TLAM guidance system)
TLAM:	Tomahawk Land Attack Missile ("Tlam")
TLAM-C:	Conventionally armed TLAM
TLAM-N:	Nuclear-armed TLAM
TOW:	Tube-launched, Optically aimed, Wire-guided antitank missile
TRAM:	Target Recognition Attack Multisensor
UnRep:	Underway Replenishment
UnRepGru:	Underway Replenishment Group
UHF:	Ultra High Frequency
VHF:	Very High Frequency
VLF:	Very Low Frequency
VLS:	Vertical Launch System
V/STOL:	Vertical or Short Takeoff and Landing
WO:	Warrant Officer
XO:	Executive Officer
ZSU:	Russian self-propelled antiaircraft gun system
ZU:	Russian 23mm antiaircraft gun

About the Author

A former managing editor of *The Hook,* the journal of carrier aviation, BARRETT TILLMAN's writing has won awards from the American Aviation Historical Society and the Air Force Historical Foundation. He coauthored *On Yankee Station,* a definitive history of the naval air war over Vietnam, with Cdr. John B. Nichols, USN (Ret.) Mr. Tillman currently lives in Athena, Oregon.

Barrett Tillman's next novel of military action will take you to the Battle of Midway and beyond— from the cockpit of the greatest dive bomber ever built. . . .

DAUNTLESS

Turn the page for an exciting preview of this book, and look for the Bantam hardcover, a June 1992 publication in honor of the 50th anniversary of the most crucial aircraft carrier battle ever fought: Midway!

Saturday, 6 June 1942

Baker Eighteen, 1235

There was no longer any doubt. The mysterious Japanese battleship just didn't exist. Rogers raised his microphone and called his gunner. "Barnes, I'm damned if I see anything down there. How about you?"

"No, sir," the reply shot back. "Just miles and miles of miles and miles." Under clear skies with only a few cloud shadows, the ocean was wide open to search. As a precaution, Barnes had opened his canopy and deployed his guns, but the chances of enemy aircraft appearing clearly were zero. *No pun intended,* Rogers thought. Still, it had to be cold in that open cockpit at 22,500 feet.

Rogers looked forward again, past Shumway up to the scout formation. Wally Short had followed orders, swinging south around the enemy cruiser-destroyer force, and hunted another thirty or so miles beyond those vessels recently pummeled by *Hornet* SBDs. Rogers mused that Burnett and DiBella had called it right. The Bombing Eight searches had almost certainly spotted the same enemy force, but one pilot reported it fifty-two miles from its actual position.

Radio static buzzed in his earphones. "Scarlet Lead from Red Base. Scarlet Lead from Red Base, over." Rogers perked up. He realized *Enterprise* might have some new information.

Lieutenant Short's clipped voice snapped back. "Red Base from Scarlet Lead. This is Wally. Go ahead."

"Scarlet Lead, you are advised to expedite your attack and return. Please acknowledge."

"Roger. Out."

That's telling 'em, Wally. Rogers felt that every pilot who heard the transmission probably held similar sentiments. *The staff sends us clear out here on a wild-goose chase, then tells us to hurry up and attack the original target.*

DiBella had told some VB-3 pilots of a similar situation on Thursday. Evidently unable to stand the torturous waiting, Captain Browning had grabbed the microphone from a staff communicator and exhorted the air group to attack the Japanese carriers. *Enterprise*'s CAG, Lieutenant Commander McClusky, had flippantly replied, "Wilco. As soon as I find the bastards."

Short's division eased into a gentle starboard turn—the mark of a considerate leader. Too tight a turn would have either thrown the trailing sections to the outside of the turn or caused them to stall while pulling too hard to the inside. Shumway brought "VB-63" around in trail, heading back to the northeast as Short began letting down for a fast run-in to the attack.

Numerous radio calls competed for Rogers's attention. Few of the pilots identified themselves, further compounding the potential for confusion. He thought he recognized a fighter pilot who called, "There is a BB over there!"

Short cut through the chatter. "This is Wally. Target is one BB, ahead about forty miles." More calls ensued, including at least one from *Enterprise*. Apparently some pilots were uncertain of their targets. But Short would not be rushed when there was no need. Taking time to assign targets, he also made sure that everyone was in place before attacking.

"Smith from Wally. What the hell are you doing over here?" It was unlike the cheerful VS-5 skipper.

We're all tired, Rogers thought. Four miles below, the victims became more identifiable—at least in size. Rogers eyed the largest. *It could be a battlewagon; then again . . .*

"This is Wally. Pushing over on rear ship now . . ." Something indecipherable as another pilot blocked Short's transmission. Then, "Our objective is the rear ship. Step on it!"

As Shumway nosed over on the rearmost ship, Rogers noticed that the standard, set-piece attack had turned to hash. Two- and three-plane sections, even five-plane divisions, had selected their own run-in headings. *Just as well,* he decided. *It'll split the AA defenses.* He glimpsed Fighting Six's F4Fs slanting down to strafe the two destroyers, suppressing their gunfire. A thought occurred to him.

"Barnes, we won't worry about Zeros. Swing around and call the altitudes for me." The gunner acknowledged, stowed his twin-.30 mount and rotated his seat forward.

The target was a big one all right, but Rogers decided it was not a battleship. Somebody had said something about a *Mogami*-class cruiser, and the rakish silhouette seemed to fit the recognition card. Whatever her identity, she was making fifteen knots to the southwest. And she was in trouble. Aside from the severe oil leak trailing in her wake, her topsides were visibly battered from the *Hornet* strike.

Rogers watched for his interval on Shumway, then tipped over from 15,000 feet.

He began setting up the dive geometry. Running in downwind, bow to stern, was not the preferred method, but there wasn't much ack-ack to distract him. "Twelve thousand, sir." Barnes's attention alternated between his own altimeter and the big ship down below.

Let's see, I have to allow more lead than normal, for I'm diving downwind. That'll push my bomb farther along the fall line. But she's not moving very fast, so . . .

"Ten thousand, sir."

He adjusted his controls, placing the crosshairs between the first and second turrets.

"Eight thousand."

Some light flak coming up, but it's not bad. A few tracers crossed his field of view. He realized that one of the nearby destroyers was still in business. *Forget it. They can't hit you at wide deflection.*

"Six thousand."

Waterspouts geysered around the battlecruiser. He had the impression of cascades drenching the forecastle of the battered gray shape. Shumway was dropping and pulling out.

"Five thousand, sir."

The Dauntless was trimmed up, solid in that steady dive that designer Edward H. Heinemann had given to the aviators of the U.S. Navy. Rogers checked the ball in its arced housing below the crosshairs. *Nailed smack in the middle. This is good, this is very good.*

"Three thousand feet." More tracers, seemingly nearer.

It won't get any better. Is this how DiMaggio feels when he knows he's put one in the bleachers? Pull!

The Mark XIII, released at 2,800 feet and 240 knots, fell clear of the belly rack. The SBD's bomb-displacing fork lofted the half-ton weapon in a downward arc, clearing the propeller and sending the bomb toward its target. The fuse safety wires were stripped from the vanes, which began rotating in the relative wind around the aerodynamic shape.

Six-point-eight seconds later the solid-case weapon hit IJNS Mikuma's C turret, two and a half feet port of the centerline. The Mark 21 nose fuse was crushed backward by the impact, and the Mark 23 tail fuse plunger was impelled forward to initiate detonation.

One-hundredth of a second later, 537 pounds of tri nitrotoluene were ignited. The bomb's 460-pound casing was shattered into thousands of jagged steel splinters, hundreds of which slashed into the cruiser's bridge. Blast and fragments killed many of the personnel there, and Captain Sakiyama was instantly knocked unconscious with head injuries.

Still recovering from his dive, Phil Rogers felt Max Baer connect with a bare-knuckle roundhouse blow that knocked his right foot off the rudder pedal. Rogers's ephemeral confusion was instantly replaced by searing pain as Hideki Tojo inserted a red-hot poker into the pilot's calf. Rogers cried in surprise, pain and fear, and saw the Pacific Ocean filling the view in his windscreen.

USS Yorktown, *1250*

"The captain says let's break for lunch in about ten minutes," Delaney said to Callaway. "Pass the word."

"Aye, aye, sir." Callaway turned to Riker and said, "Chief, I'd like you to round up Newland, Slagle, Moshafsky and Hilden. Soon as you can after chow, let's meet portside amidships to transfer the rest of the portable gear we'll need."

Granville Riker beamed his pleasure. He tugged on his chief petty officer's hat and set about organizing the crew he would need. Working topside in the sunshine offered a pleasant contrast to the semilighted confines of the fourth-deck generator room. But electrical power was being restored with *Hammann* alongside, and somehow that made a sailor feel better. The list was only slowly being corrected, but every degree represented a return to something approaching normalcy.

"Who's for sandwiches and coffee on the flight deck?" Callaway asked the work crew. In fifteen seconds he was the last man through the knee-knocker hatch into the passageway and the ladder leading topside.

Baker Eighteen, 1255

Rogers did not remember recovering from the dive. He was sure he had blacked out from the panic-induced hard pull on the control stick. Since his usual G tolerance was over four and one-half times the force of gravity, he assumed he had pulled five or more Gs.

He checked the magnetic compass suspended from the canopy bow; the Dauntless was headed northeast. He scanned the gauges and found that he had to force himself to focus on them individually. His practiced scan was gone—destroyed by the pain in his right leg and the damage to his confidence.

He remembered the dive, remembered the crossways tracers and his reaction. *They can't hit you at wide deflection.* Famous last words.

The R-1820 was running smoothly at cruise power. *Oh, yes. I did that after Bernie joined up.* He looked off his port wingtip and saw the other SBD less than a wingspan away. Burnett's face was plainly visible in the open cockpit, but somehow the features were slightly blurred. Rogers felt again the warm liquid running down his leg into his sock. *That's why.*

He tried to focus his thoughts, to concentrate on what was important. *Bernie will lead me back to the ship.* The irony struck him. The worst navigator in the squadron leading the best—well, at least the best ensign.

He estimated they were cruising at 6,000 feet—it was too hard to decipher the altimeter just now. *Gotta clear my head.* He reached for his oxygen mask. Then, *No, not yet. Need to stop the bleeding. But how?*

Tourniquet. They don't give us medical kits, but they should. Why didn't somebody in BuAer think of that? He made a mental note to write an indignant letter to the Bureau of Aeronautics, Navy Department, Washington, D.C. *Gentlemen: I'm bleeding to death over the goddamn Pacific Ocean because none of you thought any of your aviators would get shot full of holes in the performance of their duties. Screw you very much. Philip Rogers, Ensign, USNR*

He picked up the microphone and remembered to depress the key. "Barnes, I'm gonna try to put a tourniquet on my leg. Can you hold her steady for a while?"

"Yes, sir! Just one minute."

In the rear cockpit Radioman Bill Barnes leaned down to his left, unclipped the control stick from its bracket and carefully inserted it into the socket in the floor. He moved it side to side and saw the wings rock in response. "I got it, sir."

Rogers let go of the controls. He thanked God that Barnes had been so persistent in badgering him about getting some stick time. Many pilots refused to devote limited training time to showing their gunners how to control the plane. The navy had thoughtfully equipped the SBD-3 type airplane with stick, rudder pedals, throttle and flight instruments in the rear cockpit. There was no way to extend wheels, flaps or tailhook, but that was all right.

Unfastening his seat belt, Rogers reached under his Mae West and fumbled with his jacket zipper. In frustration, he removed his gloves and stuffed them between his parachute and his seat. Once the jacket was unzipped, he unbuckled his cloth flight-suit belt and withdrew it from the loops around his waist. It was surprisingly hard work.

He noticed a slight change in engine pitch and saw the nose climbing above the horizon. But Barnes caught the error and leveled out. *Good boy.* Rogers had impressed upon him that flying perfectly straight and level was one of the most difficult of all aviation skills.

Rogers lifted his right leg, slipped the belt beneath it and fumbled with the buckle again. Once the belt was through the loop, he cinched it—hard—between knee and crotch. First aid instructors said to release a tourniquet every five minutes—or was it fifteen minutes? Rogers decided to leave it tight.

He leaned back for a moment, his helmet against the headrest. He was tempted to close his eyes. *No, better not.* Instead, he reached for his oxygen mask and strapped it on. He turned the regulator to one hundred percent and sucked in the vapors. *Slow and steady; don't hyperventilate.* In a few minutes his light-headedness began to abate a little.

He put his hands back on the controls and waggled the stick in the I've-got-it signal.

"All yours, sir," Barnes said.

Rogers moved the stick again. It was easier than talking.

USS Yorktown, *1336*

Except for the slant of the deck, they might have been picnicking on a cruise ship. The early-afternoon sunshine beamed down through low, broken clouds, providing a balmy atmosphere. Sitting on the deck edge in their respective groups, men were enjoying cold sandwiches and hot coffee, discussing the progress of *Yorktown*'s rejuvenation.

"Commander Delaney says the list's down to twenty-two degrees," Callaway told Chief Riker. "Funny, how only five or six degrees can make so much difference."

Callaway swung his legs into the starboard catwalk. He could look down on *Hammann*'s stern and count the depth charges on their racks. But he was more interested in the portable gear his gang would shortly move aboard the carrier: two submersible pumps and more hose lengths. He noticed lines rigged from the destroyer's bilges to the carrier's starboard tanks, further enhancing the counterflooding effort.

He looked back up the deck and called, "Chief Riker, I'm going over to the *Hammann* to make sure our gear's ready to move. Meet me there with your crew in a few minutes." Riker acknowledged with a wave and Callaway swung himself down to the destroyer's stern.

Automatic weapon fire greeted his arrival. *What the hell's going on?* He sprinted to starboard and looked forward, toward the noise. He saw a 20mm mount unaccountably firing into the water. Then somebody yelled, "Torpedo attack!"

Now he understood. The gunners were trying to detonate a spread of torpedoes racing toward *Hammann*'s vulnerable starboard beam. Callaway saw white geysers several hundred yards out. Though he could not see the torpedo wakes, he knew that's where they were.

Hamman's port engine churned beneath his feet as the skipper ordered full astern in hopes of backing out of danger.

Unnecessarily, general quarters sounded and sailors scrambled around Callaway en route to their stations.

But CJ Callaway had no GQ station on this ship. He looked back up at *Yorktown,* and thought he saw Riker staring down at him from the canted deck. The distance between them was measured in yards. It might as well have been millennia.

Callaway looked back to seaward. Now he saw at least two faint traces in the water, barreling toward him at forty knots. More 20mm bursts splashed across their path, to no effect. He gripped the rail, entranced by the scene, as the scarlet thread of anxiety was double-woven into the tapestry of his consciousness. He heard one last chattering burst from the Oerlikons, then braced himself.

This is it!

The first torpedo—one of four from the Japanese submarine *I-168*—smashed into *Hammann*'s number two fire room. Callaway felt it as an impossibly vicious rending of ship and sea and even sky. The blast overpressure broke one eardrum as it broke the destroyer's back. He was never conscious of the 1,700-ton ship breaking apart beneath him as he was flung in an ungainly arc into the sea.

He had enough presence of mind to gulp in a lungful of air before dropping headfirst into the water. He crawled his way upward, out of darkness and into the light, emerging from the roiling turbulence of the disturbed ocean. Breaking the surface, he had only a faint image of *Hammann*'s remnants sliding under—no longer secured to *Yorktown*'s side.

Then two more Type Ninety-one torpedoes punched into the carrier's vulnerable belly, ripping her innards apart. She reeled terribly, settled back down and began to die.

Callaway and dozens of *Hammann*'s crew floundered in the water, some killed outright by the additional torpedo detonations. Some, like Callaway, were far enough from the impacts to survive with internal injuries from the blast pressure. But Callaway was dully aware of a sailor next to him, spitting water and crying and thrashing in futility to escape what was coming.

"Good Christ! The depth charges aren't safetied!"

Moments later the destroyer's shattered stern reached the preset depth of the weapons intended to crush the hulls of enemy submarines like the one that had just killed *Hammann* and *Yorktown.* But CJ Callaway, son of Jimmie and

Clydia of Jacksonville, Texas; husband of Angela; and father of Vernon, never registered that thought as the charges exploded and crushed the life out of him.

Baker Eighteen, 1349

Rogers heard Burnett make the call. "Red Base, this is Scarlet Flight. Three Baker Eighteen is returning with a wounded pilot. Request you take him aboard immediately."

There was no response and Rogers thought Bernie would have to repeat the call. Then *Enterprise* came back. "Scarlet, please stand by." More silence.

"Mr. Rogers, what do you think's going on?"

"Don't know for sure, Barnes. I guess . . . I guess they're deciding whether to risk a fouled deck with so many planes in the air. They may tell us to ditch."

Barnes absorbed that information, then replied, "Want me to take it for a while, sir?"

Rest while you can. "Okay, thanks. Just keep it on this course. The task force is up ahead. I think Mr. Burnett has the ships in sight."

"Yes, sir." Barnes sounded remarkably calm for a young man who was about to trust his life to a wounded pilot in a deck-landing attempt or a crash-landing in the ocean.

Rogers bit off a moan, even though nobody could hear him. His thigh was almost numb from the tourniquet but his lower leg was now in constant pain. He rubbed his thigh and, for the first time, pulled up the leg of his flight suit. He was astonished at the amount of dried blood on the khaki fabric.

Damn! I can't afford to lose any more. He wasn't sure, but he thought the bleeding had abated, if not stopped. It was a nasty gash, but only an entrance wound appeared on the right side. *Whatever hit me is still in my leg.* This time he did groan. *Damn it to hell—hurts like a son of a bitch.*

"Scarlet Flight from Red Base. We are recovering fighters first. Damaged aircraft will recover last. Over."

Rogers raised the microphone. "This is Baker One-Eight. I'm hit in the leg, bleeding like hell." *Well, I was bleeding like hell. And I damn sure can't get that blood back.* "Over."

Another "Stand by." Then, "Baker Eighteen from Red Base. Your choice—land in the water now or wait for the others to recover. The forward destroyer has been alerted. Estimate ten minutes to complete recovery. Over."

"I'll wait. Over." *Why did I say that?*

He looked down at the surface. It was rippled by a strong breeze, but there appeared little or no wave action. *Good ditching weather.* It occurred to him that he might have more gasoline than blood to spare. He took the controls again.

Burnett led 3-B-18 in a descending racetrack pattern astern of the carrier. He timed it well. As the last Wildcat snagged a wire, Bernie led Rogers into a straight-in approach, driving up the carrier's white wake. Rogers appreciated the setup. *I won't have to make any turns.* GUMP: gas —enough; undercarriage—*thump-thump,* down and locked; mixture—rich; prop—low pitch. Flaps and hook—down. Canopy—locked back. Rogers felt the Dauntless yaw awkwardly as his pained leg protested against the movement of rudder correction.

Barnes's voice came over the intercom again. "Sir, our starboard flap's all shot up. Part of it's gone!"

That explains it. "Barnes, if we go in the drink, get out as soon as we stop moving. Don't wait for me."

"Aye, aye, sir." Rogers didn't honestly think his gunner would leave the aircraft without him. Neither did Barnes.

"Baker Eighteen from Red Base. Be advised, you are approved for one pass at the deck. In event of a wave-off, you are to proceed straight ahead and ditch in front of the destroyer one mile off our port bow. Acknowledge."

"Baker Eighteen. Roger." *Now shut up and let me land.*

Rogers found his senses heightened as he approached the ship. Still sucking oxygen, he thought the colors seemed brighter in the vivid sunlight. The sound of his engine was louder, clearer. Half a mile from the stern, he noticed the signal flags streaming from their halyards and the smoke from the large, rectangular stack. And there were the LSO's paddles.

Get me aboard, Lieutenant. Keep me coming. The colored paddles suddenly canted, right one up, left one down. *Level your wings.* Rogers corrected with a crisp movement of the stick. But the controls felt sloppy. *Looking better, lineup is fine, maybe a little low. Yes, there's the "low" signal. Two corrections on one pass—not so good. A tad of power. Careful, don't overcorrect! Level the nose. C'mon, where's the cut?*

Rogers glimpsed a "high," then something that looked a lot like the cut. *Do it!*

He held slight back-pressure on the stick, chopped the throttle and felt the Dauntless start to settle. Immediately he knew the LSO had given him a gift—a cut instead of a wave-off. Rogers felt the lurch as his hook snagged the wire before his wheels contacted the deck. *Shit—an in-flight engagement!*

The SBD's nose lifted as the arresting wire ran out to its limit. Then, with airspeed and forward motion depleted, the dive bomber dropped eleven feet downward toward the unyielding wood planks. Rogers braced himself in his seat.

It came with more force, more concentrated violence, than anything he could remember. It was worse than any catapult shot. The landing-gear oleos compressed to their limits, hardly damping out the initial impact. Hitting port main-mount first, the SBD's weight blew the left tire, and then the starboard wheel smashed down.

Phil Rogers was pitched forward. Too late, his right hand shot out to brace his body. His face went into the padded end of his sight, which imprinted itself below his right eye. He saw flashes of light and stars in daytime.

The Dauntless rocked tremulously, seemed to shudder, then quivered to a stop. When Rogers's vision cleared, he looked left and saw the bulge in the aluminum skin over the port wing. *Landing gear's busted,* he realized. *Almost came through the top of the wing. Good old Dauntless.*

Then the crash crew was there, unbuckling him and lifting him trembling from the cockpit, and one of them was saying, "We've got you, sir. We've got you."

Novelist Edward Gibson, a *Skylab* astronaut, is also a contributor to the design and planned operations of Space Station *Freedom*. A superb storyteller, he draws on firsthand experience to create these enthralling tales of the twenty-first century.

R EACH

Reach is the story of Commander Jake Ryder and the *Wayfarer 2*, a deep-space probe sent out to determine the fate of its sister ship, turned suddenly and mysteriously silent. It is a heart-stopping account of uncommon courage and resolve in the face of awesome and destructive forces at the limits of human understanding.
❑ 28541-6 $5.99/$6.99 in Canada

I N THE WRONG HANDS

In a near-future where space stations dot the Earth's orbit and where Moonbases dot the lunar landscape, cloning and genetic engineering have been nearly mastered. Astronaut Joe Rebello soon finds himself dealing with not just the plot of a mad yet brilliant scientist, but the challenges of conquering space in order to save humanity from an unnatural blueprint for the future.
❑ 29567-5 $5.99/$6.99 in Canada